Evan Green is a well-known Australian journalist and broadcaster. He is the author of the bestselling *Alice to Nowhere*.

EVAN GREEN

ADAM'S EMPIRE

Futura

A Futura Book

ISBN 0 7088 3274 1

Reproduced, printed and bound in Great Britain by
Hazell Watson & Viney Limited
Member of BPCC plc
Aylesbury Bucks

Futura Publications
A Division of
Macdonald & Co (Publishers) Ltd
Greater London House
Hampstead Road
London NW1 7QX

A member of Maxwell Pergamon Publishing Corporation plc

Contents

INTRODUCTION

1919

The wind grew stronger and spat sand at them. The man pulled the boy closer to him. He tried to moisten his lips but they were as cracked and dry as old parchment, and the tip of his tongue drew blood. He sucked at it. God, he was thirsty.

They would have to move. The wind was changing direction. They had crouched beside the car to avoid the worst of the storm but now the wind was blowing from the south-west, and they were exposed to the onslaught of dust and sand. He saw one violent gust coming towards them, weaving and twisting through the bush as though searching for a target. It swung their way, stirring an angry red-brown cloud that blotted out the trees as it passed. One moment he could see a dead clump of mulga, stark as a piece of wrought iron, and then it would be gone, swallowed, like sticks disappear in a vat of boiling, muddy liquid. He closed his eyes and turned his head. The gust hit them and the boy, stung painfully, cried out. The car rocked. Waves of grit lashed its metal panels.

'Come on.' The man dragged the boy to the front of the car. He kicked the car's jack out of the way and sat on the sandy track, tucking the boy's head into his lap.

The child coughed and the man cursed. Not at his son, but at the wind and the sand, the heat, and at his luck. For more than six days now, they had been stranded in this flat wilderness of sand and clay and dead trees.

The boy looked up, his eyes red from the storm. 'When's he coming, dad?'

'Soon, Adam.' He looked back down the track, and felt despair.

The wind eased and the flies returned, to torment their cracked and bleeding lips. They sat beside the car, enduring the heat. Then the sun went down and the flies went away and the air no longer scorched their nostrils as they breathed. The man stood up and handed his son a can of brown water. The boy sipped and handed the can back. The man did not drink.

'Well Adam, I think we're in trouble,' he said, putting the can on the floor of the car. 'What do you reckon?'

Adam shrugged his shoulders.

'Jesus, you don't talk much, do you?' Tough little bugger, he thought, and started to smile, but the action hurt his lips and he pressed the back of his hand to his mouth to ease the pain. He tasted oil. He was coated with the stuff, from all the hours spent under the car, trying to fix the broken gearbox.

'I'm thirsty,' the boy said. It was not a complaint but a statement of fact.

The father nodded. His throat was so parched he had difficulty talking. And he was becoming weak and dizzy. With an effort, he leaned forward and ruffled his son's hair. Dust rose, ringing the boy's head like a reddish halo.

'We haven't got much water, and we've got to save the stuff, son. We'll have a drink later, when it's cooler. It'll do us more good then. You won't sweat it out. Right?'

Adam Ross, nine years of age, eyes full of grit, lips split from sunburn, and aching with thirst, nodded agreement.

There was nothing to eat. The man's rifle was on the running board of the car ready to be used if they saw a kangaroo or emu or even a hawk. But they had seen nothing.

The flush of colour drained from the sky, as though chasing the departed sun. Shadows merged. Adam walked down the track, drawing patterns in the sand with a stick.

'Keep your eyes open for a lizard,' the man called. There should be a few lizards about, he thought. Not much of a feed, but enough to keep the two of us alive. He took the rifle and laid it across his lap.

'Christ, I'm so weak and dizzy I couldn't hit an elephant, let alone a lizard,' he said softly and then realized, with a start, that the boy had returned and was staring at him. 'Jesus, son, you look filthy.'

'I could shoot something, dad.'

The man nodded. 'Probably could. A real Dead-eyed Dick, aren't you? Did I ever tell you that you were a good kid?'

The boy, surprised, shook his head.

'I should have.' The man lowered his head and slowly put the rifle back. 'Given you a few beltings, though, haven't I?'

The boy scratched at the sand with the stick.

'Well, I'm sorry. I've had problems and things on my mind and ... well, you know.' The boy was studying him intently, concern on his face. 'I've always loved you, son. I've tried to do the right thing by you. I want you to remember that.'

Adam ran the tip of the stick around his boot. 'Isn't anyone going to find us, dad?'

Oh Jesus, thought the man, I've raised me a smart kid. And look what I've done to him. Brought him on this God-forsaken track and put a hole in the gearbox and killed the pair of us.

He gazed at the darkening land beyond the track. The gaunt outlines of dead trees surrounded them. They were ringed by a vast, arid emptiness.

'I think you're man enough to hear the truth, Adam,' he said, his throat rasping with dryness. 'And to tell you the truth, I reckon the answer is no. No, I do not think anyone's going to find us. What do you think of that?'

The boy had been concentrating on scratching a circle around his feet. 'What are we going to do, then. Will we have to walk somewhere?

'I don't know. Maybe we should.' There's no water around here, he thought, and we're running out. The water bag was empty and much of the foul-tasting stuff he had drained from the radiator had gone. He had given most of it to the boy. He himself had not tasted water for two days.

The boy thought more clearly when he moved, and he walked around the stricken car. He jumped the black stain that ran from beneath the belly of the car and spread across the track. He touched the lacquered wooden spokes of the rear wheel, and removed a stone that was wedged in the tread of the tyre. He could remember when the wheel was taller than he was, but that was when the car was new. Tools were scattered in the sand and he hopped through the maze of spanners and screwdrivers and wrenches. He made a game of it, picking a path through the tools. Usually, his father stowed these precious items in a special box which he had made to fit the running board but since he had given up trying to fix the gearbox he had just left them in the sand. The boy returned to the front of the car. He touched one of the brass headlamps.

'Which way?' he said.

'What?' The man had lowered his head, to try to clear the dizziness fogging his brain.

11

'Where would we walk to? Back, looking for Tiger?'

'His name's Mr Miller. Don't be cheeky.'

'Well, back looking for Mr Miller?' The boy could see the faint reflection of his face on the polished brass of the lamp. The image was distorted, so that the jaw was twice the length of his forehead. He raised and lowered his head, and studied each grotesque change. His lips seemed swollen, like a clown's. He touched them. They were swollen.

'I suppose so,' said the man. 'I don't think he can be coming.' God, *I didn't* mean to say that to the boy, he thought. All the time they had been stuck here, he had been telling his son that Tiger Miller would be along soon. And he should have been. He was supposed to be only a couple of hours behind them. Where the hell was he? All his mate had to do was take the truck from their camp into Broken Hill and collect the supplies and then follow them. Maybe Tiger's truck had broken down, although he was good with machinery and boasted that he could fix anything. Maybe he had become stuck in the sand hills near the border. Or he could be stopped just a couple of miles down the track. If they walked back and found him, they would have enough drink and food to last them for a month or more.

Again, he cursed himself for having broken his own golden rule: he had travelled into country as dry as this without extra food or water. They'd eaten the bread for the first day, thinking Tiger would be along. The water in the bag had lasted a couple more. Jesus, what a fool he'd been. Him of all people, who'd roamed this country all his life. But he had been in a hurry to get to the Frome because they had been delayed on the other job and he didn't want to keep old man Lawson waiting. Cranky old bastard might have given the job to someone else. He was like that. Anyhow, Tiger was getting all the stuff and he was supposed to be right behind them. Could he have got lost? Maybe he'd taken another track and was already at the homestead, wondering where he and the boy had got to. Or maybe he had stayed in Broken Hill and got drunk. No, not that, he reasoned. It was seven days since Tiger went into town and besides, the old bloke reckoned he drove better when he was a bit full.

He took a deep breath and a fire raged in his throat.

If they did not move, he and the boy would probably last longer. Maybe an extra day. But if Tiger *were* just down the road, broken down or stuck in the sand, and they sat and waited with

12

the car, they would perish needlessly. No one else would be on this track at this time of the year. It bore no tyre marks but theirs. Ahead of them, only the wind had marked the sand, rippling and layering the track as it would through clay pans and sand dunes and thickets of mulga.

'I think we should stay here a while,' the man said, and wondered how long he could last. He gave the boy water and put the can back in the car. And ached with thirst.

A breeze ruffled their clothes and the first chill of night touched their skin. Every night, they had started a fire, to keep warm and to be seen in case someone was near. The man gathered wood and lit a new fire. The boy cleared stone and thorns from a patch of soft sand near the track, and they lay down.

By midnight, the fire had diminished to glowing coals and they were shivering. The man pressed his lips together, hoping for moisture, but the air was dry and cold. He stood giddy and weak and tormented by thirst and shuffled to a place where the limbs of a long-dead mulga lay rotting on the ground. He dragged them back to the fire. Sparks showered across his legs as he dropped the wood on the coals. He stood there hypnotized by the glow and crackle of fire, until the heat of the new flames forced him to retreat. He stumbled and fell and hurt his hip but he stayed on the ground because he felt too weak to move. He picked at a splinter in his hand.

He slept for a while but woke feeling stiff and cold. He crawled to where his son lay, and drew the boy close to him.

How long was it since he had had a drink? God, he had been thirsty before, but never like this. His tongue was swollen and he had difficulty breathing. He must drink. No point dying and leaving the kid to perish on his own.

The fire was dissolving into splutters and crackles as the last of the wood burned. He should get more wood, but he couldn't do a thing without a drink. He stared at the fire, and saw visions of water. Bushman's water. Small streams, with wide sandy banks and thick gum trees. Dams, muddy and yellow and cool. Steaming water, gushing from bores. Cooling bore drains, with soured pools flanked by brilliant green moss. Towns where water came from taps. Pubs with ice in their drinks. A blackened billy boiling on the fire. His eyes glazed, he stared at the dying fire and imagined paradise.

His throat was on fire, scorching all his senses. Must have some water, he thought. Forgive me, son, but if I don't drink something, I'm not going to be much good to you.

As gently as he could, he pushed the child away from him and tried to stand. For some time, he remained crouched, knees bent and one arm braced against the ground, while he waited for his head to clear. He stood and swayed. He fumbled for his watch and strained to see the hands. Four o'clock.

The moon had risen and the sky blazed with light. The land around them had turned an eerie blue-grey and the trees, dead and forlorn by day, sparkled like freshly painted posts.

He reached the car and grasped the can of water. It was half full. Enough for a few more days if they were careful. He sipped sufficient to moisten his lips and tongue and then, unable to control himself, filled his mouth. He kept the water in his throat as long as he could, savouring the relief it brought. The water had a bitter taste.

He breathed deeply. The air was sweet and cool.

He dragged another dead branch to the embers of the fire, and watched it crackle into flames. Good firewood out here. Feeling better, he scanned the horizon for any signs of lights, or of another fire.

The boy moved.

'You awake, Adam?'

'Yes.' He sat up. 'Isn't it bright?'

'The fire?'

'No. The sky. All the stars and the moon.'

'It's lovely. When your mother was alive, she used to like waking up on moonlit nights like this. She'd sit up in bed for a long time, just gazing out the window until she got cold, and then she'd wake me up and I'd have to put my arms around her to keep her warm.'

'I'm cold.'

The man sat beside his son. 'Here, get in my arms and keep warm. Do you reckon you could count all those stars?'

'No.'

'Have a go. Go on, I've taught you how to count.'

'There are too many, dad.' The boy turned and smiled at his father. The man squeezed him.

'Adam, have you ever been sorry I didn't send you to school?'

The boy shook his head vigorously.

'I suppose I should have sent you. I'm not sure I've done the

14

right thing by you. I just wanted you with me. Remember that.'

'It's been good, dad. I don't want to go to school. I want to help you.'

'And you have, you have. Now count those stars for me.'

The boy laughed. 'There are hundreds of them.'

'Oh no, Adam, there are thousands of them.'

'I can't count that high.'

'Yes you can. You just count to a hundred, and then you count to two hundred and you go on like that until you get to a thousand.'

'When do I get to a thousand?'

'When you get to ten hundreds. You just stack them away, one hundred at a time, until you've got ten, and then you've got a thousand. It's easy for a smart bloke like you.'

'It would take a long time.'

'Ah, that's true. But you've just got to be persistent. Just got to keep trying. Smart blokes aren't necessarily the ones that do well, in this world. It's the ones who are persistent – who keep on trying – who do well.'

'Do you reckon I'll do well, dad? Good as you?'

The man gazed up at the stars, and wiped one of his eyes.

'Do you like this country, Adam?'

'Yes'. The boy had never known any other. He and his father had been wandering the outback for as long as he could remember. His father sunk bores and dug dams and they had roamed the far west of New South Wales and through the north-east of South Australia, working on remote properties – the sort of places where water was needed desperately.

'Yes, it's great country, but never trust it, son. It's beautiful, but it's treacherous. Deadly like a snake. Take it for granted, take risks with it, and it'll turn on you. Kill you.' Just like it's going to kill us, he thought.

'Water's the key. This is good country with water, but deadly without it. You can make a good living if you've got water. But without it, you've got no chance at all. The good places out here are the ones where the owners have developed good water. Bores, dams, that sort of thing. You remember that. Promise?'

Adam promised.

They began to walk after dawn. They scraped a thick arrow in the sand and lined it with rocks, to indicate their direction of travel, and then followed their own car's tracks back towards the east.

'No point going the other way,' the man reasoned. 'It's more than ninety miles to the first homestead and we'd never make it. There's a fair chance that Tiger Miller's somewhere on the track behind us, so we'll dig in the bed of the creek and make ourselves a soak. We'll have a good drink and then you can have a bath. You're a mess.'

'How far, dad?'

'Not far.' He remembered crossing a creek. When was it? Seven days ago? Probably thirty miles back. Just a low line of trees and a slight depression in the track. Still, if they dug a soft part of the creek bed there might be water. Probably only flowed once every couple of years. And there hadn't been any rain out this way since last winter. Almost certain to be dry. Still, it would keep the boy going.

'Where there's a creek, we'll find game,' said the man. 'Probably a few kangaroos. They'll go there for a drink. What's say I shoot one for dinner. How would you like some kangaroo stew?'

'I'd like something to drink,' said the boy, and thought for a while. 'What would you cook it in, dad?'

The man had begun to weave across the track. He staggered and leaned on the rifle for support. 'Tripped on something,' he said, his voice a croaking sound. 'Got to watch where I'm walking. What did you say then? How will I cook it?' He bent over the rifle. 'Yes, I see what you mean. No pot. Well,' he said, starting to walk again, 'I reckon what we'll do is have roast kangaroo instead. Cook it in the coals, like the blacks do. Tastes better that way, anyway. OK?'

The boy nodded. He doubted that his father could cook anything at the moment. He looked dreadful. His lips were swollen to gross proportions and were mottled black, from scabs and flakes of sunburned skin. He could not speak properly. When he did talk, it was more of a rasping mumble than the clear, slow progression of words that normally issued from his father's mouth. And he swayed as he walked. He was now holding the rifle by the barrel and letting the stock trail in the dust. He never did that.

'Can I take the gun?' The boy tugged at his father's shirt.

The man turned awkwardly, as though drunk, and looked back

down the track, searching with unfocused eyes for the person who had spoken.

'Dad!' The boy pulled the shirt again and the man, unbalanced, fell. He went down slowly, folding joint by joint, like a puppet whose strings are slackened. But he held the can of water, and came to rest on his back with the can above his chest.

'Never spilled a drop,' he said, slurring the words so badly that Adam scarcely understood him. The man lay there, breathing heavily. Adam had seen drunks like that, men who had come back to camp so full of whisky or rum or metho that they had fallen on the ground, dribbling and vomiting and wetting their trousers. He hated seeing men he knew and liked reduced to babbling, stinking figures that crawled in the dust and spat profanities at their mates. He would never get drunk. Never. But his father was not drunk.

'Would you like some water?' he said. 'You haven't had much.'

The man shook his head. 'Help me up, lad,' he croaked.

'Want me to take the water, dad? I can carry it.'

'Just do as I tell you.' And with the boy's help, he got to his feet. He took only one step. His knee folded, and he twisted forward, stumbling across the rifle which he was using as a walking stick. He lost his grip on the can. The water splashed on the sand and left a dark stain.

'Christ,' said the man, falling to both knees. He looked at the boy and at the stain and began to sob. Adam cried too. Not because of the lost water, but because he had never seen his father weep.

Another wind storm came that afternoon, bringing with it sand and earth and shreds of vegetation that it had torn from the vast plains south of Lake Frome. Storms were bad that summer, but this was the worst.

The man and the boy had left the track to climb a ridge of rock and spinifex, to look for any sign of Tiger Miller's truck, or for a line of trees that might indicate a creek. They saw neither. There were dunes to the north-east and a huge clay pan, mottled and buckled from years of drought, to the east and the south. Occasional stands of mulga with blackened, leafless branches lacerated the sky. And to the west was the storm.

At first, it was just a blur, a red smudge that danced on the heat vapour rising from the plains. Within minutes, it had grown into a

17

gigantic cloud that blotted the lower half of the sky. The storm had a clear, well-defined front that was folded in vertical corrugations, like the drapes of a curtain, and for some time it looked like a beautiful thing, a moving mountain of red and brown with reflected flashes of sunlight and striped shadows dancing and rolling across its fluted face. Then the moaning of the wind reached them and the earth seemed to tremble. They stumbled from the ridge to seek shelter, as the first strong gusts ruffled the spinifex and sent grains of sand and dust scudding across the clay flats. Then the day became dark. The moan became a howl and the storm enveloped them in a choking, swirling, shrieking fury.

It hurt them and buried them, and then it passed.

The boy regained consciousness. He coughed and was aware of pain and pressure. He was on the ground, lying on his side. Stones were hurting his ribs and hip. There was a heavy weight on his body and legs. He moved his arms, feeling the mass pressing down on him crumble as he lifted his hands. It was sand. He was under sand but his face was covered by something else. His fingers investigated. It was a piece of cloth. Some sort of garment. He could not breathe easily and he pulled the cloth away from his mouth and nose, and filled his lungs with raw, warm air. He coughed again. Dust rose, choking him. In a frenzy to breathe, he broke clear of the mound of sand that rimmed his back and stood, hunched and sore and and spluttering for air.

He examined the garment that had protected his face. It was his father's shirt.

The boy sneezed, firing mud and grit from his nostrils. His ears were clogged with sand and his throat was afire with a dreadful burning. He coughed again, a hacking explosion of air and dirt that sent pain spearing through his chest. He reached for the rag he carried in his trousers and found the pocket full of other things. He reversed the pocket, and sand and seeds and stones cascaded to the ground. He shook the rag and blew his nose and wiped his eyes. His eyes ached.

The sun had set and the sky glowed like burnished copper.

The plain, where the storm had caught and overwhelmed them, had changed. Before the storm, it had been crusted with yellow clay and sprinkled with stones and clumps of circling spinifex. Now it was carpeted with soft red dust. Fresh ridges of sand, rippled into parallel patterns by the wind, rose from the plain like small waves. In the faint monochrome of the evening light, the scene was like an old sepia photograph of a choppy sea.

There were scores of sand ridges, and all reared against some obstruction. Every tin bush, every pincushion of spinifex, every rock was flanked by a buttress of sand. All of these new dunes were shaped the same way – rising from the west, from where the wind had blown, and ending in some object that had formed a barrier to the flying sand.

The boy and his father had tried to reach the shelter of a low stand of mulga, but the storm had overtaken them on the plain. The man was weak and had fallen several times. Eventually, he had thrust his son to the ground and curled his body behind him, to shield him from the wind's lethal sting.

Dazed and sore, and choking with thirst, the boy turned to study the mound of sand that had protected him from the storm. Loose grains trickled into the cavity he had left. The mound was humped and curved, and unlike any other on the plain, and Adam felt a sickness in his throat.

He saw his father's hand.

He scratched at the sand, tenderly, fearful of what he might discover. The sand flowed easily on one arm, a bare shoulder, and the back of the head emerged. The hair stood up. It was always unkempt. Adam could remember his mother telling the man to do his hair and he never did. She always told him and he never did. Just smiled and ruffled it to make it worse. That was one of his earliest memories of his mother. Almost the only one. She parted her hair in the middle. She was dead and so was his father.

He was too dry to cry. He coughed and would have been sick but there was nothing for his stomach to deliver. He scooped a handful of sand and the mound crumbled. An eyebrow, the nose and one gaunt cheek were exposed, revealed like rocks left by a receding wave.

The mouth was open and choked with sand.

Adam brushed around the face, hoping to stroke it back to life. Gently, he removed grains from the eyelashes and plucked sand from the whiskers on his father's cheeks. But he could not touch the mouth. The sand, filling the mouth and the lungs, was death and he could not touch it.

So he walked away until he was near the track. There, he fell down and sobbed and coughed and hurt until, finally, he went to sleep.

*

BOOK ONE

Young Adam

ONE

March, 1929

A special train brought the circus to town. It was a long train, for this was a big circus, touring the country areas of South Australia. There was a carriage at the front, with red and white banners flapping from its sides and people in gaudy costumes waving from the windows. A man with a top hat and a brightly striped coat stood in the doorway of the carriage. He held a whip in his hand and when he cracked it, the train driver blew the steam engine's whistle, and the small crowd waiting in the railway yards cheered. Behind the carriage ran a line of waggons bearing caravans, boxes, machinery, rows of pipes and stacks of chairs, painted panels, rolls of canvas, tents, poles, ropes and clusters of metal pegs that had been mangled by thousands of sledgehammer blows. At the end of the train were cages with placid-looking animals and a box car that disgorged wild-looking people.

There was much clanking and shouting. Seagulls wheeled into the air, screeching in protest. A wind blew from the south-west, sweeping across the gulf and bringing with it the smell of salt and rotting seaweed.

It was a hot day in Port Augusta.

Near the railway yards and not far from the water's edge was the paddock where the circus was to perform all that week. Men with skin blackened by years of dirt worked in the heat all day. They sweated and cursed and flicked at the flies that tormented them. They bolted together sections of pipe, assembled wooden frames, stretched canvas, lifted poles, hammered pegs and strained on ropes. Gradually, the grassy paddock became a place of billowing canvas and striped booths.

People from the town came to watch. Eyes crinkled against the glare, they wandered through the streets, staring at tents with ropes fluttering in the breeze, at crimson caravans, sweating

23

bodies and animals whose coats were thick with dust and flecks of straw. The man in the top hat walked among the crowd. Long threads trailed from the frayed sleeves of his striped coat.

He had a voice that boomed, as though amplified. 'We open tonight, my friends, direct from triumphant performances in Port Wakefield, Port Pirie and all major centres in between.'

'Were you in Burra?' asked an old man, whose face was creased and blotched like antique leather.

'Yes, my friend,' boomed the man in the top hat, tapping the side of his boot with his whip. 'Three magnificent nights. The most exciting times, the good people of Burra said, since the great days of the copper rush.'

'My brother lives there.'

'Ah, I believe he may have come to our first performance. Sat in the front row. I presume, sir, he is a distinguished-looking gentleman, like you?'

The man nodded. 'Taller than me.'

'That's him,' said the man, slapping his whip against his boot. 'Enjoyed the show immensely. And I trust that you, sir, will emulate that contented and happy gentleman by gracing us with your presence on opening night here in Port Augusta.' He prodded the old man in the ribs with the handle of his whip and turned to the crowd. 'Opening night is tonight, ladies and gentlemen. The show starts at eight o'clock but there is a great deal to entertain and delight you before that time. Side-shows, featuring some of the most distinguished performers in the world. A boxing booth, in which local gentlemen with brawn and bravery may challenge champion pugilists in the manly art of self-defence. It pays to be early. Yes sir, the wise come early and see the best shows and get the best seats.'

A camel, tethered by the nostrils, gazed at the crowd through glazed eyes and rolled its jaws. A man leading a small black bear on a chain walked past, carefully dodging the fresh piles of manure. Two elephants, sides streaked with clay, swung their trunks from side to side, like pendulums on a pair of grandfather clocks, and shuffled their feet, as though anxious to be somewhere else. A man in a long cotton coat hand-fed four white horses.

A lion lay in a cage, head up but eyes closed, trying to ignore what went on around it. Its tawny hide was as worn and dusty as an old rug. Some boys threw pebbles at it. The lion flicked its tail.

One boy, growing bolder, picked up a stone and advanced on

24

the cage. He threw the stone, hitting the lion's mane. The animal rose and walked to the far side of the cage. It lay down again. Dust rose from its coat. It closed its eyes.

The boy picked up another stone.

'Hey, drop that!'

All the boys turned. A broad-shouldered youth stood behind them. He was carrying a sack, which he lowered to the ground.

'Don't throw that,' he said gently. 'You'll hurt it. Put the stone down.'

'What's it to you?' said the boy with the stone.

'Yeah, it's not your lion,' said another boy, and some of the others sniggered.

'It's only an animal,' said the first boy.

'And you'll make it angry,' the youth said. 'And if it got angry, I think it could bust out of that cage. The bars don't look too strong to me.'

'The lion doesn't look strong, you mean,' the boy said. 'Who'd be afraid of that thing? It looks like it's got the mange.' With measured insolence, he tossed the stone into the cage.

A puff of dust rose from the lion's hindquarters where the stone had struck. The animal half-turned its head and curled its lip, revealing a few yellowed teeth.

The boy turned to see what reaction his throw had provoked, but he was too slow. The youth had moved with remarkable speed and had seized him around the waist.

He lifted the boy and tucked him under one arm. He walked to the cage.

'Seeing you're not afraid of the lion, we might as well put you in there with him,' he said. The boy began to yell. His friends backed away. Some laughed, others were wide-eyed with fear. One of the boys turned to run and rammed the man in the top hat.

'Here, here,' he boomed, pushing the small boy to one side. He faced the tall youth, who had his victim – violently wriggling and kicking – gripped so tightly that the boy's face was turning red. 'And what might you be doing, young sir?'

'He's going to put me in the lion's cage,' screamed the boy. 'Make him let me go.'

'They were throwing stones at the lion,' said the youth. He had long, fair hair and he tossed his head to clear his eyes.

The man moved closer, studying both the youth and his prisoner. 'Pray tell me,' he said, 'would this person you are clutching with such care be a friend of yours or, perhaps, a younger brother?'

'Never saw him before. He just wouldn't stop throwing stones.'

'Ah,' said the man, prodding at the youth with his whip. 'Well, I am afraid I must remonstrate with you, young sir, because it is not yet time to feed the lion. We are very strict about that.'

The boy, who had been quiet, kicked and screamed.

'Goodness me,' said the man in the top hat, 'the meal is becoming very lively. We must restrain it, before it becomes bruised and unappetizing. Old Leopold likes his meat tender.'

He grabbed the boy's thrashing legs. 'If you would be kind enough to hold the other end, we might search for an appropriate place to lay our burden to rest.'

He winked at the youth and, puffing with the effort of carrying the boy, backed towards a place where the elephants had defecated. 'Shall we say here?' he enquired. 'It gives promise of a soft landing. An appropriate place, I would say, for a young marksman who would have my lion for his target. Now, my friend, on the count of three ...'

After the boy had run away, crying and pursued by his laughing friends, the man turned and studied the youth, who had gone to collect his sack.

'We may have been a little cruel, but such measures are sometimes effective. I believe I should thank you.'

'That's all right. I don't like people hurting animals.'

'Very commendable. You will come to the circus tonight?'

The youth looked at his feet.

'Do I detect a certain enthusiasm for the prospect, but a matching lack of funds?'

The youth looked puzzled.

'You'd like to come, but you have no money?'

'I'd like a job,' said the youth, looking the man in the eye.

'Ah,' breathed the man, injecting a vast amount of sadness into the sound. 'Indeed, a common request in these harsh times. A job indeed. Would that I could comply. But the truth is, lad, I have no job to offer. I can, however, offer you a ticket to tonight's performance, to take your mind from the worries that must be plaguing your thoughts.'

The youth shook his head. 'No thanks.'

'A proud man. Mm. Commendable. Do you live here?'

'No. I only arrived here today.'

26

'Where do you hail from, lad?'

'All over. Up in the north mainly. Came from Broken Hill originally.'

'What's your name?'

'Ross. Adam Ross.'

'And you want to earn some money, that right?'

He nodded. The man studied him for several seconds, as though trying to make up his mind about something. He rested his chin on one hand.

'Can you fight?'

Adam stepped back.

'Dear boy, don't be alarmed, but you're strong and I saw the way you handled that urchin.' He wiped dirt from his coat. 'I'm not proposing that we come to blows. What I mean is, can you box? You know, the manly art of self-defence. With gloves. Can you fight like that?'

Old Tiger Miller had taught Adam Ross two things: how to drill for water, and how to defend himself. Tiger had been an old pug, a bare-knuckle fighter down on the Victorian goldfields in his younger days, and he had gone to great pains to teach the youngster how to look after himself. They used to practise at nights around the campfire; the old man, wasted and wrinkled from too much drink and hard work, with his body crouched and fists up high, and the child, straining to reach the man and flailing away with his fists and being cuffed and chided until he calmed down, kept his guard up and tucked his chin into his shoulder and jabbed and hooked and behaved like a proper fighter should. They would re-enact some of Tiger's best fights, move for move. One of them, fought on a grassy flat beside a creek five miles out of Bendigo, had gone for twenty-eight rounds, each being called when a man was knocked down. They fought in slow motion and with some humour because Adam would lose his temper when Tiger kipped him on the nose and he would swing away, and the old man would pick him up and tickle him and they would roll in the dust, laughing together. But that was a long time ago.

'Yes, I can box a bit,' Adam said.

'Do you mind getting a black eye, or a bleeding nose?'

He shook his head. He had suffered a few of those in his time. 'Why?'

The man stroked his chin. 'Well, we have a boxing troupe here. Do you know what that is? No? Well, it's a group of men,

27

professional pugilists, whom I employ to fight anyone who challenges them. Do you understand? Someone in the crowd – a smart, strong young fellow like you or sometimes a person whose sobriety has been overtaken by enthusiasm – steps forward and challenges one of my champions. And the crowd pays to see the bout. Now, my problem, Adam, is getting people to challenge the better boxers. Any fool will have a go at someone he thinks he can paste all over the ring. And I've got a couple of men who take a hiding every night. But I've got a couple of good fighters and they're the ones the crowd pay to see. Do you understand what I'm getting at?'

'No.'

'Well, I've got one boy in the troupe, a black by the name of Jimmy Kettle. About your size and probably not more than four or five years older than you. He's good. Very fast and hits hard. The trouble is, he's gaining a reputation and it's difficult to find someone to climb into the ring with him. Now, if you really want to earn some money, and you reckon you can handle yourself pretty well, I'm prepared to pay you to challenge Jimmy Kettle.'

'What do I get?'

'Five shillings if you go five rounds. I'll tell you what – two and six if you step into the ring, the rest if you see out the distance.'

Tiger had taught Adam all the tricks he knew, it was one thing to box and pretend with an old man and something else to step into a boxing ring with a professional. And an aboriginal. He'd heard their heads were thicker.

'I've never used gloves,' said Adam.

'Well, you'll have to use them. Tell you what,' said the man, taking such a deep breath that his chest puffed like a pigeon's. 'My fights are all absolutely legitimate. What you would call fair dinkum. Nothing rigged, or anything like that. But I'll have a word with this young fellow and make sure he ... well, you know, I'll make sure he understands our agreement, and that he coasts along a bit.' Again, he prodded Adam with his whip. 'Five shillings. A fair amount of money for fifteen minutes' work. Keep you going for a while, I dare say?'

Adam thought for a moment. 'Could you throw in a feed?'

The man looked at him and smiled. 'Like that, eh? Certainly, my boy. A meal, and five shillings for five rounds.'

As instructed, Adam went to a plain grey tent, and a man who coughed a lot gave him three slices of buttered bread and a plate of stew. He went outside to eat and to look at the elephants, which he had never seen before. A hunchback and a boy carrying two buckets arrived and started to wash the animals. The boy kept bringing buckets full of water which the man threw over the animals. He then scrubbed their hides with a long-handled broom.

Adam moved closer. He watched for a few more minutes.

'What are they called?' he said, soaking up some gravy with a piece of bread.

The hunchback turned. He let his broom rest high on one elephant's back and looked at Adam from under one raised arm. He had a remarkably pointed chin. 'Ginny and Rajah,' he said, in a shrill voice. 'This one's Ginny.'

'No, I mean what are they? What do you call them?'

The man lowered the broom, and leaned on it. 'You playing games with me?'

'No.' Adam wiped the plate clean. 'I never seen such animals before.'

The man started to scrub Ginny's trunk. 'Well, they're not kangaroos and they're not bullocks. These are called elephants. Biggest creature on land. Amiable, too, which is just as well. This little girl could squash you flatter than a piece of toast if she felt like it. Lucky she don't, eh?'

Adam nodded. 'Where did you get them?'

'Oh, I didn't get them. They belong to Mr Carter, the man who owns the circus. The feller with the top hat. But if you mean where did they come from, they come from India.'

'Where's that?'

'Well, it's a long way away,' said the man, and stopped scrubbing to wait for the boy to return with some more water. 'Over the sea. Didn't you learn about India in school?'

'Didn't go to school.'

'I thought all kids were supposed to these days. Where's that boy with the buckets?' He turned awkwardly. 'Come on, Mick, I haven't got all day,' he shouted and then, in a softer voice, spoke to Adam. 'I never went to school either. Do you want to end up like me, washing some big lump of leather like Ginny and cleaning up her dung?'

Adam shrugged.

'Why didn't you go to school?'

'Wasn't anywhere where there was a school. My dad used to sink wells and travel all through the bush and when he died, an old mate of his looked after me. And he sank wells and travelled from one station to another and took me with him and I just never went to school.'

The boy arrived, bearing two heavy buckets and puffing as he struggled with the load.

'He's been to school,' said the man. 'He can recite poems. Long ones. What are you doing here anyhow? You're not working here, are you?'

'No.'

'Well, where'd you get the tucker?'

'The man with the big hat told me to come to the tent and get a feed.'

'In return for what?'

Adam said nothing.

The man handed his broom to Mick. 'Here, you scrub her for a while. I haven't done her back feet. Make sure you clean between the toes.' He walked to Adam, his head bent back at a sharp angle to overcome the severe curve in his spine.

He took Adam by the arm and led him away from the elephants.

'Careful where you step,' he said. 'Those creatures drop dung everywhere when they come to a new place. The train trip makes them nervous.' He pinched Adam's arm. 'You beware of Mr Carter. He's a great man with the words but he's got a mind that's as gentle as a rat trap. In other words, take anything he promised you with more pinches of salt than the cook put in that stew. Has he got you to do something? Come on, lad, tell me.'

'He's going to pay me five bob if I challenge one of the blokes at the boxing tent.'

'Which one?'

'A blackfellow. Some funny name.'

'Jimmy Kettle?'

Adam nodded. The man let go his arm and faced him. 'Go now. Just be grateful you've got a free meal out of Cedric Carter and piss off. Do you live in town?'

'No. Just arrived. I've got no money.'

'Get out anyhow. That bloke'll knock your teeth in. Losing them's not worth five bob.'

'I'm not frightened of him.'

'Oh, for Jesus' sake! If I had a penny for every time I'd heard someone say that, and mean it just like you do, I'd have enough

30

money to own a hundred elephants, and be able to employ twenty people to scrub them twice a day. Look, son, being frightened or not being frightened isn't the question. This Jimmy Kettle is a pro and he's dynamite. He hasn't lost a match and he's hated by every white bloke who fancies himself from Naracoorte to Ceduna. Carter's always finding some bloke who needs money and telling him he'll get that black bastard to go easy on him. And then he tells his man to cut the other bloke to ribbons and that's what he does. Kettle's taken out more teeth than the best dentist in town. I've seen poor bastards on their hands and knees, with their front teeth out and blood in their eyes and a nose as flat as an iron, and trying to get up because their mates are watching them. That's what it's all about, you see. Carter knows that if the locals hate his man Kettle, they'll come back in droves to see him fight again, in the hope that some white bloke will flatten him. To put it to you straight, son, the game ain't fair and you're going to get slaughtered.'

'What's he fight like?' Adam said.

'Like a demon. Haven't you been listening?'

'No, I mean which hand does he hold out in front, and does he have his hands up high or down low? Things like that.'

The man scratched his long chin.

'Don't know that I've ever noticed. Let me think.' He put his own hands out in front of him, left hand leading, then the right. 'This way. With the right hand out.'

'A southpaw,' said Adam. Like the man Tiger had fought near the creek bed five miles from Bendigo. Tiger had won because he reckoned he had worked out a way to beat southpaws. 'And does he hold his hands up high? Like this?' He demonstrated.

'No. Lower down. He holds his hands down in front of his waist. Very fast with them. The other blokes don't see them coming. You talk like you're a boxer. Are you?'

'No.'

'Well, don't waste your time in all this fancy talk, then! Just go back to town and forget about fighting Jimmy Kettle.'

But Adam took his plate back to the grey tent, thanked the man, and then wandered towards the boxing tent. He was thinking of all the nights he had pretended to be the best southpaw in the goldfields, and how Tiger had beaten him every time.

31

TWO

The boxing tent was packed and the striped canvas walls shimmered from the movement and noise of the crowd. The sun had gone down an hour ago. Four light bulbs glowed from leads strung across the roof of the tent. Each bulb wore a crust of frenzied insects, and shone yellow through a fog of dust and tobacco smoke. The air was foul. The sickly-sweet aroma of fresh vomit mingled with the smell of wet sawdust, dried sweat and belched beer fumes. No one seemed to mind. The crowd bubbled with good humour.

A voice boomed out details of the next fight.

'Ladies and gentlemen, the main bout of the evening. Bringing together the Dark Demon, Jimmy Kettle, undefeated in more than one hundred fights throughout the length and breadth of South Australia, and his challenger tonight, the fighting whirlwind from the golden city of Broken Hill, Snowy Ross. Give them a great hand as they enter the ring.'

Someone broke wind loudly and some girls, standing in the front row, giggled and covered their mouths as they looked at each other.

Adam shouldered his way through the crowd.

'Come on, Broken Hill!' one man shouted.

'Give him the name of a good undertaker there,' another man said. People laughed.

Jimmy Kettle, wearing a blue dressing gown, pushed his way to the ring. He kept his head down. A volley of hisses sliced the air.

The referee was waiting in the centre. He was bending over, trying to wipe something from the cuff of his white trousers. He glanced sadly at Adam and began to talk in a flat, mechanical voice that had made the same speech a thousand times.

'Gentlemen, the rules are simple. No gouging. No clinching. No rabbit-punching. Hit only with the fist.' He spoke with his eyes on the ground, as if something on the sawdust fascinated him and he dared not take his eyes from it. He was a small and gnarled man who looked as though he himself had spent a lifetime being gouged, clinched, rabbit-punched and hit with the fist. His ears clung to the sides of his skull like flattened blobs of putty and his nose was a mangled bridge between eyes and mouth. He bent to pick at his cuff, where fresh globules of blood were congealing.

'If there is a knockdown, the other boxer has to step back. I won't start counting until he does. No kicking or punching while a man is down. On one knee is counted as being down.' The referee's eyes flashed at Adam. 'You understand that?'

Adam nodded.

'Just flatten him, Snow,' one man in the crowd yelled. 'I've got a zac on you.'

'The nigger'll knock the tripe out of him,' a voice growled.

'Wanna make it two bob then?'

'You're on.'

The referee was checking the laces on each boxer's gloves. Adam noticed that his gloves seemed bigger than those on the aboriginal's hands. They looked softer, puffier.

The other boxer shuffled his feet in the sawdust and began to skip, letting his arms hang loose and jiggling his gloves so that they danced like leather balls on lengths of rope. He had long arms. Tiger had always said not to watch the other fighter's hands. You had to anticipate, and to do that you had to look in the other man's eyes, to see where he was looking so you knew where he would try to land the next blow. Adam looked at Jimmy Kettle's eyes. The black man was looking at him. Rather, he was looking through him. He showed no signs of seeing anything. His eyes were pink where they should have been white and they seemed strangely lifeless. It was as though no one lived inside.

Outside the tent, someone started banging a drum. A horse whinnied.

The ring was a crude affair. Just a rope lying on the sawdust and marking a square. The crowd stood beyond the rope. They were mainly white men although Adam noticed two aborigines in the second row, smiling constantly and flashing broad, stained teeth. Near them was a dark woman. Her eyes were strangely wide, as though she were frightened.

Adam had never fought with gloves or been in front of a paying crowd before, but he had been in plenty of fights behind shearing sheds or in half-lit streets where people had gathered to watch, and he recognized the look on the faces of this crowd. All flushed and excited, as though they were going to do the fighting, not him. Weak men, anxious to see someone else get hurt. They liked to see a young bloke lose a few teeth and end up with a face as rough as theirs.

33

Adam was not frightened of Jimmy Kettle. He was curious. He wanted to find out how good he was. Being hurt didn't worry him. He had been hurt before. When he was a boy, old Tiger had got drunk a few times and forgotten to pull his punches. Then Tiger would cry and say he was sorry and try to kiss the boy, and that was worse. Adam would rather have taken more punches than see the old man cry. He hated that.

But Jimmy Kettle was a pro, probably better than Tiger had been, and he fought every day of the week. The aboriginal had taken off his gown. He was wearing bright blue silk shorts, splashed with rust-like stains. He bounced up and down, alternately swinging and bending his arms, like a shearer trying to get the circulation going on a frosty morning in the shed before the first merinos came bleating out of the pen. He had thin legs but wide shoulders, and when he bent his arms, the muscles knotted impressively. He would hit hard, but looked a bit fine around the middle. There was not an ounce of fat on him, but he mightn't like a few good whacks to the body.

Jimmy Kettle turned his back on Adam and threw a few punches in the air. The crowd whistled. The boxer's skin was intensely black and peppered with curious scars. They were not cuts – more like burn marks.

'Hello, Jimmy,' someone in the crowd sang, using a high-pitched falsetto. A few men laughed. The aboriginal turned, his eyes wide open, and looked about him nervously.

'Don't forget, Jimmy.' The same unnaturally high voice. A group of men whistled and clapped. 'We're all here,' one shouted. They were near the dark girl. She had covered her face with her hands.

Kettle's nostrils flared like a horse in distress.

'The fight is over five rounds. Each lasts three minutes. When the bell rings, you go back to your corner. You understand that, son?' The referee, his voice still flat and without emotion, glanced at Adam.

'Get on with it,' someone shouted.

'Shake hands and come out fighting,' said the referee. 'Just touch gloves, son. That'll do.'

Adam walked to his corner. The gloves felt strange, and he tried a few jabs with one glove into the open palm of the other. You shouldn't hurt your hands, he thought. He had taken off his shirt and his boots and was wearing just his long pants. He had a length of rope for a belt. He felt half-naked, and a real amateur compared to the aboriginal, with his silk shorts and proper boxing boots.

He had enjoyed the make-believe of the challenge. There was a man with a big drum out the front of the tent and all the fighters from the boxing troupe had lined up on an elevated platform, on one side of the entrance. Jimmy Kettle had been the last fighter introduced, and there had been much booing and hissing. As he had been asked, Adam waited until the crowd was thoroughly stirred before stepping forward.

'And what is your name, sir?'

'Ross.'

'We'll call you Snowy Ross. Goodness knows, young man, you may be another champion fighter like the great Snowy Baker. A big hand for the challenger. And where did you say you came from ...?'

The bell rang, and one of the spectators pushed Adam in the back. He stumbled.

'Jesus, he can't even stand up,' someone said.

'He'll be all right. Go and knock the nigger's block off, Snow.'

Jimmy Kettle was in the middle of the ring, dancing lightly. Adam walked towards him, moving slowly and recalling what Tiger had said about southpaws. The big punch is the left hand, so keep away from it. That means circling to your left, or to the other man's right, to put him off balance. He must think he's fast to carry his hands so low, Adam thought. Adam, by contrast, raised his fists and held them high, where Tiger had taught him. He looked at the other man's eyes. They were alive now. Bright and burning.

Jimmy Kettle hit him on the nose. The punch came so fast Adam didn't see it properly. It wasn't hard. Just enough to sharpen his eyesight and make him sniff. A straight right, flicked from down low. The left will be coming close behind, Adam said to himself, and he rolled his head out of range and felt the glove whistle past his ear.

He circled to his left, and did one skipping lap of the ring. Kettle shuffled after him.

Adam was near the rope. The crowd was spilling over the line, and a man pushed him. Kettle swung a right. Adam, falling from the push, felt it graze his scalp. Jesus, that was hard. He went down on one glove and the black man rammed his knee into his

35

face. Adam came up hard and fast, and rammed his shoulder into the other man's body and heard the gasp of surprise. He straightened and his eyes were within inches of the black man's face. He wrapped his arms around the other man and pulled tight. The man's breath exploded in his face.

'That's for kneeing me in the face,' Adam said, and then winced as a glove hammered his kidneys.

'Enough of that,' hissed the referee and thrust a calloused hand between them.

The right again and again, looping out wide. Adam ducked inside. He pushed his opponent away, stepped back and then skipped in and threw his first punches. A straight left, short and delivered with no backswing, and a right cross. Nothing hard. He wanted to get his timing right. The gloves felt strange. kettle hit him high on the forehead with a left that came skidding off his forearm. Adam jabbed, and hit the other man on the nose.

He danced to the left, stopped to let Kettle catch up, and then skipped away again.

'You're supposed to fight,' the referee said. 'You can do all the dancing you want in town.'

Adam looked at the referee and the aboriginal hit him with two quick rights and a left that landed on his ear. Adam pushed him away. He searched for the other boxer's eyes.

'Get him, Jimmy!' It sounded like a girl's voice.

Kettle threw a left and Adam, expecting it, slipped beneath the glove and rammed his left into the aboriginal's stomach. The eyes blinked. He doesn't like them there, Adam thought, and came in quickly, left foot forward and knee bent slightly. He swung the left arm hard into the body once more. This time, he really put some power into it and then crossed with a right that travelled no more than a foot to the black man's jaw. It didn't land exactly where he wanted it. It was those blasted gloves. But it sent Kettle sideways and the crowd shouted.

The bell rang. The referee thrust his rough hands between them and sent them to their corners.

'Where have you done your fighting?' drawled the man in Adam's corner, as he flicked water across his chest.

'First time I've been in a ring.'

'Yeah? Let's see. Have you got any cuts?' He rubbed both Adam's eyebrows with his thumb. 'You look clean. What's your name? Les Darcy, or something?'

'Ross,' said Adam, and then recoiled at the smell of the sponge the man wiped across his face. He breathed deeply. He felt all right. Kettle was fast and he hit hard but he had already learned a few things about him. First, he didn't like being hit hard in the middle. Second, he threw his best blows from out wide. Not hooks so much as swings. The bell rang and Adam noticed that the man in the top hat had been in Jimmy Kettle's corner and was now slipping back into the crowd.

Kettle rushed him. He threw a flurry of punches, mainly rights but the occasional stinging left. Jesus, he could hit with that hand. Adam skipped away, keeping to the left all the time. I'll make this bloke cranky as hell, he thought and kept circling, bobbing and weaving and catching most of the blows on his arms and gloves. He noticed a pattern in Jimmy Kettle's attack. He would tap his right thigh with his glove three times before launching an attack. Just little taps. An unconscious mannerism, perhaps, but he always did it, and Adam waited.

One, two, three and here it comes. Adam weaved to the left and moved out of range, so that the aboriginal had to spin to his right, off balance and unable to use that lethal left swing. Kettle straightened and Adam circled to the left again, slowly, ready.

One, two, three and the punch was coming again. Adam was already moving, body swaying backwards. Not too far, because he wanted to be in range. The glove grazed his chest. Kettle, nostrils flaring, came after him. A little shuffle of his torn boots, and he was close. His right glove was back down in the firing position, hovering above the thigh.

One, two went the glove, tapping the long thin muscle on the black man's thigh, and Adam fired his left. Kettle had already tapped the third and was lunging forwad, glove sweeping up, when Adam's straight left hit him flush in the mouth. Kettle's eyes bulged and his intended blow changed to an involuntary lifting of the glove, to protect his face. He was surprised, hurt and off balance, and there was all his body, from the hairless chest to the top of his blue trunks, square on to Adam and unprotected. Adam moved. The fist went home like a piston on a steam engine. It sank into Kettle's middle and Adam, still watching the other man's eyes, thought they would explode. The eyes popped, large and unnatural and glazed in distress. Kettle's mouth hissed open, revealing two missing front teeth. Adam swivelled and chopped the mouth with his left. He was close, and rising, and the blow only travelled a few inches.

Kettle fell back on his haunches, arms spread out to hold himself in a seated position, and the crowd screamed. It was a weird sound, full of lust.

Adam looked around and saw the man in the top hat. His expression was not pleasant.

Kettle was on one knee, wiping his mouth and retching. The referee looked confused.

'Foul blow,' called the man in the top hat. 'Ring the bell,' he called, and the bell sounded.

'Back to your corner,' snarled the referee and pushed Adam.

The man in Adam's corner was wiping his glasses. 'Never seen him put down before,' he said, in a soft voice. 'He's won one hundred and five bouts in a row. Did you know that?' He replaced his glasses, pushed Adam on to his stool, and squeezed the sponge over his head. The water, trickling down his face, tasted foul, a mixture of stale water and other men's sweat and blood.

A man near Adam's corner snarled encouragement. 'Knock his balls off, son.'

'Yeah,' piped a high voice, 'knock the knackers off the Kanaka.' Men laughed. The girls in the front row giggled again and looked at each other and covered their mouths to disguise the fact that they understood such *awful* words.

'Hello, Jimmy!' Again the falsetto voice trilled through the tent. 'Got a teeny-weeny guts-ache?' A few men whistled. 'Jesus, it's the Queen of the Fairies again,' a rough voice growled.

'You're in for a bad night,' the high voice warbled. 'And it's going to get worse.' The last word was sung, contralto-fashion, and many laughed. Faces turned to see where the noise had come from.

'This time, Jimmy,' came the sing-song voice, from somewhere behind the aboriginal girl. Her head was bent back, as though someone had hold of her hair.

The bell rang.

They met in the middle of the ring. Kettle, still breathing painfully, backed away. Adam followed. Kettle continued to retreat, but suddenly threw a right that looped around the back of Adam's neck. He pulled the white youth towards him. Their heads clashed.

'Are you one of them?' Kettle whispered, his arm locked around Adam's head.

'Here, no clinching,' said the referee.

'Are you with that mob?' the aboriginal said, with urgency in his voice. His ear, pressed hard into Adam's face, was wet.

'What mob?' Adam hissed. 'What are you talking about?'

They circled each other, prodding with outstretched gloves.

Jimmy Kettle seemed to have regained his breath. He swung a right that thudded on Adam's elbow and followed with two more quick blows. 'You know,' he grunted, and sniped another right that stung Adam's nose. 'You're one of them. OK, you white bugger, I'll do you.'

Adam did not see the left. It came from somewhere down low, glanced off his bent right arm and pounded into his chest. It hurt, far more than it should have, Adam thought, and skipped back out of range.

'I've had enough of you bastards,' the black man was saying, almost shouting, and there was a strange look in his eyes now, part fury, part despair. Adam had seen a mad shepherd look like that once, just before the bloke had cut his throat on a piece of corrugated iron. That man had gone crazy from drinking methylated spirits and thought demons were chasing him. He had sawed his throat through on the jagged edge of a water trough. Adam had seen that when he was thirteen.

The right and left came so fast that Adam had trouble distinguishing which was thrown first. He was dazed, trying to get back on his feet, but had landed in the crowd and was floundering and in a squirming mass of people. He could hear the uproar, but was not sure where it was coming from. The right side of his face had gone dead. A salty taste was spreading in his mouth.

Kettle was above him, feet dancing, eyes blazing. Adam heard a girl scream, saw Kettle turn, and then he lost sight of the other boxer as he rolled on bodies twisting beneath him. He found himself on his hands and knees. He heard someone counting. 'Six … seven …'

'You cut your mouth, mister,' a small boy said, from somewhere close to his face.

Adam lurched to his feet but tripped on a man's outstretched leg and fell again. 'He's had it,' a voice boomed above the bedlam. 'I told you this nigger was too good.'

Adam jumped to his feet. The referee grabbed his gloves and rubbed them against his shirt, to clear the leather of any sawdust. 'Why don't you stay down, son?' he whispered, without looking up. He pulled roughly on Adam's wrists, so that he could easily have fallen. But Adam pulled back. His head was clear. His cheek and one part of his mouth had no feeling but his eyes were working and so was his brain.

'He's got something in his glove,' Adam said. Or tried to say, for his mouth would not work properly, and his words were slurred.

'Fight on,' said the referee, and waved the boxers together.

Jimmy Kettle came at him, eyes blazing, arms thrashing. Adam skipped back and landed awkwardly. His legs were not working as they should. He swayed his body and the rush of air told him how close the left had come. Get the feet moving, bounce back, move to the left, keep away from the crowd and that rope, hold the hands up high, get the eyes back into focus. His feet ploughed through a deep patch of sawdust and he wondered what sort of advantage the aboriginal had by wearing boxing boots. He glanced down at Kettle's boots and was whacked in the ribs. Watch the man's eyes! He could swear it was old Tiger shouting at him. Adam skipped to the left. That was better, The hips, the knees worked smoothly, his muscles were responding as they should. Backwards again, then a dart to the side, under a swing and back again. Kettle, exasperated, dropped his hands even lower and shuffled after him. Adam drove his left out. It was a straight blow, with the fist screwing at the end to give bite to the impact. Flush on the nose. No one likes it there. The other man's eyes blinked. Into the nose again. Harder this time and with a lot a shoulder movement behind it. Kettle's face sprayed water. A pinkish mist stained his upper lip.

Adam hooked a left into Kettle's stomach, saw the distress in his eyes, and did it again. Another left, and Kettle, arms crossed over his middle, backed away. But his body was bent, like a tree about to topple.

Adam tried a right hook. Kettle's mouth flew open and the lips waved like the seam of a flag. Another straight left to the nose. Again and again. The pink beneath the nose had turned to red, and drops of blood hung from the black man's chin like glistening stones in a pendant.

Adam fired his straight left again, getting up high on his toes to snipe above the other man's gloves. Then he bent his knees and, as Kettle raised a glove to wipe his nose, he drove his right into the stomach. Kettle made a noise like a belch, dropped his gloves and bent forward. Adam hit him with a left, a straight corkscrewing spear of a punch, and then hooked with a right to the head. Kettle was already on the way down and the glove bounced off his skull.

'Ring the bell.' It was the man in the top hat, calling from the back of the tent.

'It's not time,' said a deep-voiced man. 'You ring that bloody bell early again and I'll throttle you. Just start counting the nigger out,' the deep voice went on, 'unless you want to leave town on a stretcher.'

Kettle was on the ground, rolling in the sawdust and drawing his knees to his stomach. The crowd began to count: 'One ... two ...' The referee, looking sick, joined in: 'Three ... four ...' then stopped when he noticed Adam standing near him in the middle of the ring. 'Get back, you white-haired bastard,' he shrilled. 'Get back to the ropes or I'll stop the count.'

Adam moved away. 'Five ...' boomed the crowd.

'Five,' echoed the referee, and stood over the fallen boxer. Kettle, his mouth and chin slimy with blood, rolled on his side. He tried to lift himself on one arm but fell back, and was still writhing and grunting and bleeding when the count reached ten.

The referee made no attempt to lift Adam's arm in victory. He hastened from the ring, swinging his hands to hack a path through the crowd. People surged forward, brushing the tent poles and causing the hanging light bulbs to swing in long arcs above their heads. Adam stood where he was. A few men thumped him on the back. But the crowd was more interested in the fallen boxer. Tiger had seen a hanging when he was a young man. The crowd must have been like this, Adam thought. Not interested in the executioner. Just the victim.

The crowd formed a tight circle around Kettle. Adam forced his way through them, suddenly sickened by the whole business.

The aboriginal lay on the ground, squirming like an insect with its wings plucked. Adam squatted beside him. 'Are you all right?' he asked, touching the other man's shoulder with his glove. Those rotten gloves! They were part of this business where you tried to hammer another person into unconsciousness to entertain a mob of mindless oafs. With his teeth, he loosened the laces of his gloves and flung them at the crowd.

Kettle had stopped writhing and now lay on his side, with his arms locked around his knees and his head pressed into the sawdust. His breath whistled through swollen lips.

'Here, I'll help you.' Adam got down on his knees and slid one arm behind Kettle's shoulders. He pulled him into a sitting position. A few people clapped.

'Jesus, that was a good fight,' one man said.

'Bloody nigger went down like a shithouse in a windstorm,' another man said and belched.

'Oh, he was game, Harry. Give him that.'

Jimmy Kettle, sitting and nursing his chin on his knees, looked at Adam with bewilderment in his eyes. He wiped his mouth and examined the bloodstained glove. He took a deep, noisy breath. 'Who are you, mister?'

'I'm the bloke they paid five bob to fight you,' Adam said.

'Who? Who paid you?' He touched his nose and winced.

'The fellow in the top hat.'

Kettle got to one knee. 'You hit hard, mister.'

'So do you,' Adam said and, suddenly remembering how much he had been hurt in that final round, grabbed the aboriginal's left glove. It felt hard.

'What's in there?'

Kettle pulled his hand away. 'Jesus, mate,' he whispered conspiratorially. 'Don't say anything.' He rolled his eyes in distress. The crowd had closed in tight around them again.

'Get back,' Adam roared, jumping up and swinging his arms. 'Go home. It's all over. Go,' and he charged a group, and people started to leave.

Once more, he knelt beside the injured boxer. 'It wasn't my idea,' Kettle said, rubbing the padding of his left glove. 'Where's Mr Carter?'

'The bloke in the top hat? No idea. I saw him at the back of the tent a while ago. Why?'

'I'm going to need help.' He sat down again. 'Can't breathe too good yet.' He stayed like that for a few moments, wheezing and swaying backwards and forwards. Adam wiped the aboriginal's chin and, as tenderly as he could, removed caking blood from around the mouth and nose.

'I think the bleeding's just from the nose,' Adam said. 'You're going to have to breathe through your mouth for a while but it doesn't seem too bad.'

Kettle nodded. 'You're not with that mob, are you?'

'What mob? What was all that about, anyway?'

Kettle shook his head and tried to sniff through his clogged nostrils. 'Doesn't matter. Thought you were someone else, that's all.' Adam helped him to his feet, and steadied him, with an arm around his waist. The crowd was still dispersing. Dozens of people were jammed around the entrance.

'Jimmy.' It was the falsetto voice and a few in the tent laughed. 'Jimmy,' the voice repeated, 'we'll be waiting outside.'

'And we've got the sheila,' a rough voice shouted and someone laughed.

Jimmy Kettle took a deep, awkward breath, and looked in Adam's eyes. 'Do you want to help me?'

'To do what?'

'To get out of here alive.'

THREE

They left by crawling under the canvas at the rear of the tent. A small boy, who had watched in astonishment, crawled after them. 'Get away,' Adam whispered.

'This is the way I come in,' the boy said, grinning. He ran into the darkness.

Adam guided Jimmy Kettle to the blackest area in the shadow of the tent and sat him down. The aboriginal grunted in pain.

'What is it?' Adam said anxiously.

'Stinging nettle.' Kettle moved to one side and sat in some long grass. He still wheezed.

'Sore?' Adam asked.

'Hard to breathe.'

'Sorry.'

'That's all right. I was going to knock your head off.'

Adam laughed quietly.

'No, I mean it. Feel that.' Kettle offered his left hand and Adam, groping in the dark, felt the glove.

'What's in it?' He could feel a hard ridge at the edge of the leather padding.

'Lead. There's a sheet of the stuff inside the glove. It's a special glove. Mr Carter told them to put it in the glove just before that last round. After you flattened me the first time.'

Adam felt the glove again. 'How much lead?'

'Just a thin strip of the stuff. Makes the glove heavy. Your arm gets tired, but it hits hard. The last time I used it was down at Crystal Brook. There was some bloke there who was giving me a hard time. Big bloke, built like a sugar bag. Mr Carter got them to put the lead in the glove and I busted the feller's jaw. You could hear it go crunch.'

'By the Jesus.' Adam touched the glove with awe. 'You could kill a bullock with that.'

'Yeah. Sorry. I wasn't too worried because I thought you was one of them.'

'Who? The mob you keep talking about? Who are they?'

'Just some blokes. Take me gloves off, will you?'

Adam fumbled with the laces. Although in a semi-circle of lighted tents and caravans, he and Jimmy Kettle were in a grassy paddock that was in almost total darkness. A strong but fitful wind began to blow. Electric globes, strung on a line across the front of the boxing tent, swung with each gust, sending shafts of light scything through the night sky. Off to their left was the main circus tent, a great red and white striped marquee that glowed like a lantern. The wind ruffled its gaudy walls. Stencilled images of people – rows of them – moved across the flapping canvas. Adam shivered. It was cold.

The lights in front of the boxing tent went out. A voice from the other side of the tent called out: 'Where the devil is he?' The voice was high-pitched and angry. 'Well, spread out then,' he shouted, as though answering a question. 'You two, get in the tent and make sure he's not hiding. The rest of you search around here. Anyone seen that other cove yet?'

Kettle stood up, grunting with pain. 'Come on.'

'I've got to get my shirt and boots,' Adam said.

Kettle breathed deeply. 'OK. See you again.' He began to walk away, bending low, partly to avoid being seen and partly because his middle was still too painful for him to straighten his body.

'Hang on,' Adam said.

'No fear. They're going to kill me.' He kept moving.

'Oh, come off it. They'll just look around for a while and then go away. I can't leave my clothes.'

The man on the far side of the tent was shouting again. 'Of course I want you to bring the sheila. Hang on to her. I'm going to cut off that nigger's balls and stuff them down her throat.'

44

Adam, horrified, turned to Jimmy Kettle but the black man had gone. 'Where are you?' he hissed. An answer, more a grunt than a word, sent him moving to one side, running so low that his knees bruised his chest. He saw the outline of Kettle against the glow of the main tent.

'You're going the wrong way,' he said, and stopped. His mouth was hurting. He touched it and was surprised to find it wet and sticky. He spat some blood on the ground. 'They'll see you against the light. Come back this way.' And he stood and waited with his hands on his knees, while his tongue played with the torn tissue of a cut within his lip.

'Look, I don't know what this is all about,' Adam said, straightening, as the aboriginal reached him, 'but if you just go off, running around like a rabbit, then those blokes will see you and get you. So let's just slow down and find somewhere to hide. Better than running around.'

Kettle was close to him now. Adam could see the shine of his boxing trunks, reflecting the lights of lanterns hanging from a row of distant caravans. 'Those pants are like wearing a mirror,' Adam said and pulled the other man to the ground. 'Let's just sit down for a while and keep still and see where the others are. Maybe you could tell me what this is all about.'

'Later.' He sucked in a deep breath.

'I've got to get my clothes,' Adam said, more to himself than to Kettle. He suddenly had a thought. 'And five bob. The man in the big hat owes me five shillings.'

Kettle looked at him. He had big eyes. Even in the dark, Adam could see they were smiling. 'Do you reckon you'd get it?' he said. He spoke with the soft, almost hushed voice Adam had noticed with so many aboriginals.

'Why not?' Adam did not finish, for a light flashed near the main tent. The silhouettes of two men appeared against the glowing canvas. Kettle had seen them too. He rolled on his stomach and watched the men search the area beside the tent.

'Because those blokes over there are looking for you as well as me,' he said. 'They must know we're together. You go near Mr Carter and they'll jump you. There'll be a bloke waiting where you left your clothes, too. I know that mob. Harris is a clever bastard.'

'Who's Harris?' Adam said, still watching the two men. One was carrying a long object on his shoulder.

45

'The one with the funny voice. Come on, let's get out of here.'
More men, with torches, had appeared around the side of the
darkened boxing tent and they were much closer. Kettle rose to
his hands and knees and began to move, crab-like, towards the
darkest part of the horizon. 'Hurry up,' Kettle called. 'Follow me.
I know somewhere we can go.'

Adam followed, not understanding why they were being
hunted, but knowing he was in danger.

They half-ran, half-crawled for several minutes, passing the final
line of caravans, hearing the murmuring of animals tethered
nearby, and crossing a road. Kettle led them away from the circus
and across another road until they were in a region of
undulations, covered by gravel and salt bush. Only when they
were on a slight rise did he stand up. He looked back, scanning
the darkness for signs of pursuit.

Adam studied the lights of the town, fanned across the southern
horizon. 'I came to Port Augusta with nothing, hoping to make a
bit of money. I've been here one night, and I'm leaving with less
than I came with. I get talked into fighting you, you do your level
best to knock my head off with a lump of lead in your glove, and
here am I helping you. You might tell me where we're heading,
and just who are those blokes we're running away from. And
Christ!' He thumped one fist into the other hand, having thought
of something. 'I left my bag back there. I've got to go back.' He
started to walk towards the town, then hesitated. 'You wait here,'
he said. 'Have a breather. I'll come back and get you, but I've got
to go back and collect my bag. Everything I own's in it.'

'Big bag?' the aboriginal said.

'No.' Adam grinned, hurting his mouth. 'Another shirt, a
blanket, things like that.'

'Not worth it, mate. I know those blokes. You go near those
clothes and it'd be your balls they'd be stuffing down Nellie's
throat. Have a look at this.' He turned his back to Adam. 'This is
what they did to me last time.'

Adam strained his eyes in the poor light. The side of his face
was losing some of its overall numbness and starting to sting. He
spat more blood on the ground. 'Can't see,' he said. 'What is it?'

'They burned me. Put cigarettes on my back.'

Adam remembered the scars he had seen before the fight. 'Why
did they do that?'

Kettle did not answer for a while. One foot pawed at the ground. From the circus came the booming sound of a brass band. Bursts of laughter followed. One peal ran into the next. It was a hollow, disembodied noise, that rippled through the night like thunder from an unseen storm.

'Those are the clowns,' said Kettle, closing his eyes and imagining the scene. 'Used to get dressed up myself some nights, depending on what sort of fight I'd had. The show will be over in half an hour and people will be everywhere. We'll want to be well away by then.' He looked up at Adam. 'I've got a sheila. Name's Nellie. She was at the fight tonight.'

Adam remembered the young woman with the frightened eyes. 'The one you kept looking at?'

Kettle nodded. He reached for a stick and started scratching at the gravel around his boots. 'They brought her here. She comes from Port Pirie, down the gulf about fifty mile. Met her there a year ago. When we went back to Pirie about six weeks ago, she was waiting for me and we ... we got round to ... you know, we did what a bloke does with a sheila when he likes her.'

Another peal of laughter came rolling from the distant circus.

'Anyhow, she works for Harris. You know what he does?'

'No. Never heard of him. Never been down this way before.'

'He runs a place. Don't know what the proper word for it is. He's got a few of them. One up here. Bigger place at Pirie, though. It's a knock shop. You know, where the blokes go for a root.'

'A brothel?' Adam had seen a few of those, although always from the outside. Once, Tiger had made him wait outside one, saying he was going to see the doctor, and had been embarrassed to come out and find Adam (who was only ten at the time) talking to a couple of the girls who were having a lot of fun supplying him with his first lesson on the facts of life. 'This Nellie works in a brothel?'

'Don't know what you call it but Harris had her working there. Anyhow, none of the girls are allowed to mix with blackfellows. One of his rules.'

'But isn't she ...?' Adam began and stopped, embarrassed.

'She's half-caste,' Kettle said. There was no emotion in his voice; just a matter-of-fact statement. 'Her father was Irish or something.'

'She looks pretty,' Adam said, trying to soothe the hurt he felt he had caused. Kettle, so fierce in the boxing ring, looked

47

curiously vulnerable out here in the dark.

'Harris has a few strong-arm men working for him,' he said. 'You know what I mean? Bouncers. Blokes who throw out the drunks and the troublemakers. Anyone who starts belting one of the girls. Anyhow, one of these bouncers found out about Nellie and me and told Harris. Harris gave Nellie a belting and told her to stay away but she came back and they caught us ... they found us ... you know, together.' He threw the stick away. 'That's when they did this to my back. Hurt a lot.' He touched Adam's arm. He had seen the flash of a torch. 'They're getting closer. Let's get out of here.'

'But what about my things?'

'Get them tomorrow if you want to. Not tonight. Come on, I know somewhere where we can stay.'

'Where?' Adam asked, limping after Kettle but glancing back. He could see the circus clearly. Peals of laughter and the clash of cymbals rolled across the darkened space. 'How far are we going?'

'Not far.' Kettle was walking fast, and Adam had almost lost sight of him. 'To the north-east. There's a blackfellows' camp in a creek bed. We'll go there.'

'Do you know anyone there?'

Kettle stopped to let Adam draw level. 'Got an uncle and some cousins should be there. I come from up this way.'

'Whereabouts?'

'Beltana.'

'Isn't that up north?'

'Yeah. Couple of hundred mile. Come on. That light's getting closer.' He resumed running.

'Why did Harris follow you up here?' Adam asked, straining to keep up.

'After they burned me, Nellie ran away. She told me what Harris done and I went to his place after the show one night and hid outside until he came out. Smoking a long cigar, he was. Anyhow, I thumped him and nearly shoved the cigar down his throat. Gave him a good going over. He tried to pull a gun on me so I kicked him in the balls, although I don't know that he's got any. People reckon he's a bit of a poof. That's why he's got that funny voice.'

Adam, jogging awkwardly because he had cut his foot in the darkness, said: 'And this Harris brought your girlfriend here and he reckons he's going to kick you back. Is that it?'

'He won't be satisfied with a kicking,' Kettle said. 'Nellie told me he's had other people killed. He's a real bad bloke, that feller. He doesn't do the killing himself, though. His blokes do it for him. I'll bet he's got the feller I belted along with him. He did most of the burning. Cruel bloke, that one.' Kettle slowed and turned. 'How's your foot?'

'Not bad.' Adam was glad to stop. He lifted his foot and touched the wound. 'Must have cut it on a big stone.'

Kettle moved again, loping through the dark with an uncanny ability to avoid obstacles. They swerved around bushes, missed large clusters of rock and kept well clear of dark stands of mulga, whose leafless branches reached out for them like blackened strands of barbed wire. Occasionally they stopped, to look back for any sign of pursuit or to feel their way through an eroded gully. They reached a road. Kettle knelt in a clump of salt bush at the edge of the track. Adam bent beside him, and was pressed to the ground. 'What's up?' he whispered.

'Someone coming,' Kettle said, crouching even lower and placing a finger over his companion's mouth. Adam stayed still, conscious of his own heavy breathing, and a minute later heard the crunch of gravel. Two men passed, talking softly.

They waited a long time before moving.

The camp was in soft sand on the edge of a creek bed. The creek itself, powder dry and without a trace of water, was split into three channels by ridges studded by rocks and tall trees. The trees sighed in the night wind and their gnarled white trunks glowed with the soft reflections of a camp fire. It was not a big fire, for aborigines rarely waste wood on a showy bonfire, but the burning sticks hissed and crackled and flashed light on the faces of six men seated around the flames. A group of gins, unmoving and with heads bent low, sat near some trees. Smaller fires that had been used for cooking marked the area of the camp. The embers winked red and white as the breeze ruffled the ashes.

An aroma of cooked meat and burnt hair, from a wallaby that had been the evening meal, drifted from the camp. Some dogs, thin and twitching like worms, ran out, growling. The faces of the men around the main fire turned to study the intruders.

'G'day, Jimmy,' said one man, fatter than the rest. He had a face that glistened like polished black leather. 'Who's the white feller?'

'Friend of mine,' Kettle said, speaking loudly. He turned to Adam. 'What's your name? Is it Snowy or something?'

'Yeah. But my real name's Adam. Adam Ross.'

'Sit down,' said the fat man. He had white hair and would be an old man among aborigines, Adam judged. He found it hard to tell their age. This man might be fifty or sixty.

'Where's your clothes?' said the man, with the hint of a smile. 'You with the white hair, you're dressed like a black feller.' A titter of laughter came from the gins near the trees. Their faces sparkled with shy smiles.

'This is my uncle,' said Jimmy Kettle, indicating the fat man.

'Pleased to meet you,' Adam said and sat down. He had been in blacks' camps before and felt relaxed. He was glad to be off his feet.

The uncle nodded solemnly and waved his hand, as though introducing all his companions by the fire, but said nothing. The old men's faces dipped in greeting. All were smoking pipes.

'Had to leave my clothes back at the circus,' Kettle said. He was sitting cross-legged beside Adam. 'There's someone after us.'

The old man noded. 'How long you in town?'

'Few days.'

One of the men blew smoke from his mouth and issued a mellifluous jumble of words. Adam did not understand the language he spoke. The uncle listened, his head tilted to one side, and then said: 'Why's this feller after you?' He looked at Adam, grabbing him by the knee and feeling his bone and muscle, as though he were judging a beast before cooking it. 'What you done, eh?'

'He's after Jimmy,' Adam said, and the old man looked deep into the fire. Slowly, he turned his head to look at his nephew.

'This bloke, he's a bad man,' Kettle said.

The uncle shook Adam's knee. 'You cold, white feller?' Adam shook his head. 'Will be. Gets cold at nights. Still fighting, Jimmy?'

Kettle nodded.

'Doing good?'

Kettle nodded again and looked sideways at Adam, knowing he would say nothing; he already knew that much about his new friend.

For the first time, Adam noticed wurlies beyond the ring of cooking fires. Some were made in the traditional way, with branches woven into crude, open-fronted shelters that stood no more than waist-high. Others showed the influence of the white man, for they used manufactured materials: jute bags, lengths of pipe and sheets of galvanized iron. And there were more people in the camp than Adam had realized. He could now see some children, playing with bones in front of some of the wurlies, and more adults – the younger ones – among the trees. A twig cracked. He turned to see three young boys walking from the nearest channel of the creek bed. They smiled and their teeth flashed reflections from the flames. Two girls, taller than the boys, emerged from the shadows of the creek. They smiled, and said something to Jimmy Kettle.

'They think your hair's a funny colour for a young feller,' he said. Then he bent towards his uncle. 'Can we stay here the night?'

The old man put a stick on the fire and waited for the tip to burst into flames. 'Not as fancy as the circus,' he said.

'Yeah, well, I can't go back there tonight.'

'You got blood on your nose,' the man said, tapping his own nose to indicate the location.

'The other feller hit hard.'

'Had some tucker?'

Kettle nodded, and glanced at Adam, asking him the same question.

'Yes,' Adam said. 'I had something before the fight.'

The old man pushed the stick deeper into the fire and wrinkled his face as the heat on his fingers became intense. 'You a boxer too?' he said, withdrawing his hand and blowing on it.

'Oh, just tonight,' Adam said. Kettle looked at him, eyes anxious. The old man leaned forward and with a fingernail chipped some drying blood from the side of Adam's chin.

'You got a bleeding mouth,' he said.

'Yeah.' Adam touched his lip. 'Tough business. I don't think I'll try it again.'

'Jimmy's my sister's son. He ain't been beaten in a hundred fights.' The old man slurred his words in a babble of pride.

'He's a great fighter,' Adam said.

'Too right,' said the old man, settling back on his haunches. 'Wouldn't you like some tucker, young feller? We got plenty bread.'

'No thanks.'

Jimmy Kettle sniffed painfully and stared into the fire.

The old aboriginal stood up, holding his back as though his joints ached. He was wearing an old football jumper that had red and black stripes running from his neck to his thighs. His pants were torn above the knees and his bare feet were so deeply calloused that, when he stood on a glowing ember that had popped from the fire, he did not flinch. 'Who's this man chasing you, giving you trouble?' he asked.

'Just a white feller,' said Kettle.

'Feller that hit your nose?'

'No. Someone else.'

The old man bent down and prodded his nephew on the arm. 'Why don't you bash him up?'

'Not just one feller. There are lots of fellers.' Kettle rubbed his arm. He had stopped a few of Adam's blows on the muscle and his arm ached.

'They follow you?' said the old man, looking beyond the creek towards the town.

'No. Haven't seen them since we left the circus.'

The old man kicked some sand on the fire. Some of the other men stood and did the same. There was much sucking of pipes. As though signalled, the gins near the trees stood and walked to their wurlies. 'You sleep up there,' the old man said, indicating the northern end of the creek. 'Long way up. Take your white feller friend with the white hair and sleep up there. Better you go up there now.'

'Really, uncle, no one followed me,' Kettle protested.

'All same, go long way up the creek.' The old man was agitated.

'What's happened?' said Kettle, anxiously. 'There been trouble here?'

One of the men spat into the smoking fire.

'Little bit of trouble,' the uncle said. With one bare foot, he moved an unburnt stick away from the side of the fire.

One of the boys who had come from the creek spoke. 'They came and belted Billy.'

'Who came?' Kettle said.

'Town fellers,' said the old man.

'Billy had been drinking,' said the boy. 'He couldn't stand up. They said he'd been in a fight with someone.'

'Who were these town fellers?' said Kettle.

'Few blokes,' said the uncle who now, with great delicacy,

52

spread his toes and lifted the piece of wood and placed it with some other firewood.

'Mr Mailey brought them,' said the boy. 'He hit Billy over the head with a big piece of wood. This big.' He demonstrated, arching his back to stretch his arms as far as they would go.

'What happened to Billy?' Kettle stood up and faced his uncle.

'He was very crook for a couple of days.' The old man wiped his hands on the end of his jumper.

'Where is he now?' Kettle looked about him, at the shadowy groups scattered along the banks of the creek. 'Is he better?'

'He's dead,' said the boy. 'The copper split his head open. Said he'd bashed up one of his friends in town.'

'What copper?'

'Mr Mailey.'

'Mailey's a policeman? He killed Billy?'

'Very cranky feller,' the uncle said and began to walk from the fire. 'Now better go and sleep. Up along the creek. Past the big dead tree. And you better take this, white feller.' He paused beside a wurlie and threw Adam an old flannel shirt. 'Be cold tonight.' And he looked through the trees at the glowing skyline where the lights of Port Augusta bounced from low clouds. 'That Mr Mailey's a very cranky feller,' he muttered, and the old men looked worried, and shuffled to their sleeping places.

FOUR

The moon rose and only the brightest stars withstood the flood of light. Along the creek, the white trunks of the gum trees glistened like wax. Lordly and cold, they soared above the intense shadows they cast. The wind died. Branches that had creaked and groaned became still. Beyond the creek, the plain that was a hurtful region of stony ridges and needle-pointed grass was transformed into a soft fuzz, as gentle as a velvet cover spread casually across the floor of a candlelit room. A thick silence, pulsing with the faint chirping of insects, settled on the land.

Adam Ross and Jimmy Kettle walked to a place where the creek bed curled to the left. Floods had scalloped a wall along the outer side of the bend, and they chose a site where water had gouged a small cave from the soft earth. It was not the most comfortable of bedrooms, for the floor was uneven and embedded with stones. A tangle of broken timber, debris from a past flood, was wedged in one corner. It was a difficult area to clear but the cave had the benefit of being almost totally dark, whereas the sandy bed of the creek shone in the moonlight and Kettle, who had grown even more agitated since leaving his uncle, insisted on sheltering in the shadows. Even when the cave floor was cleared, he did not sleep but sat, wide-eyed and restless, looking back at the camp. The fires still glowed faintly. Wisps of smoke curled among the trees and flashed, faint as spider webs, when caught by shafts of moonlight.

Adam had carried the flannel shirt. He offered it to the aboriginal. 'Do you want this?' he said. 'It'll help keep your ribs warm.'

'No.' Kettle folded his arms, putting his outstretched fingers against his sides. 'They're too plurry sore. Besides, you white fellers feel the cold more than us niggers.' He smiled. 'I'll be OK.'

Adam put on the shirt. All the buttons were missing. It was too large for him and he wrapped it across his chest, like a double-breasted coat, and tucked the ends in his pants. He rested on one elbow. 'What are you going to do?' he said.

'Don't know,' Kettle said. His nose was swollen and clogged by blood and he was breathing noisily through his mouth. 'Probably go back in the morning.' He sniffed. 'See if Harris and his mob are still around.'

'And if they are?'

'I'll come back here. I often come out here when we're in Port Augusta. Do a bit of hunting.'

'But aren't you supposed to fight tomorrow night?'

'I'll send one of the young fellers with a message to Mr Carter. He can do without me for one night.'

'What about the girl?'

Kettle lowered himself on to his back. 'Don't know,' he said.

'Will she be all right?'

'Probably get a belting,' he said softly. 'She's used to that. Don't suppose another one will hurt her.' He sniffed again.

They came after midnight. Shouts and the screaming of women woke Adam. The creek bed was still bathed in light and he could see people running through the camp. Some had torches. He saw one man swinging something high above his head. There was an awful thud and a scream that turned to a gurgle.

Jimmy Kettle sat up. 'What's up?'

'Something's happening at the camp,' Adam whispered. In the darkness of the cave, he groped for the pile of timber and selected a long, heavy piece. 'I think your uncle needs a hand.'

From the camp came a shriek of great pain. A dog snarled. There was another thud, and a dreadful yelping. Adam was about to leave the cave when a cracking of wood sounded above and behind him. A man, short and thickset, slithered down the bank just to his left. Adam pressed himself to the floor of the cave.

'It's OK,' the man said, puffing for breath, and talking to someone still on top of the creek bank. 'Just watch your step.'

'All right. Well, you watch the creek in case any of them come running down this way.' The voice was curiously high, almost feminine. Another figure, then two more, stumbled down the slope, showering dust and sand as they moved towards the creek. They stopped, backs to Adam, but so close he could have touched them with the stick he held in his hand. One was a woman. She fell in the sand and was dragged to her feet, struggling and cursing.

'Give the bitch another uppercut if she doesn't shut up,' the man with the high voice said. He was the smallest of the group. He patted his hair into place. 'Come on. Let's get there before they go mad and kill the lot. I want someone left I can talk to. And don't let anyone get away. I'm going to nail this bastard.'

'That's Harris,' Kettle said, so loudly Adam thought they would hear. But the group began walking down the creek bed, picking their way through islands of scrub and rotting driftwood. 'They've got Nellie,' Kettle breathed, and tried to rush from the cave. Adam restrained him, locking his hand around the aboriginal's mouth.

'For God's sake be quiet!' he whispered and waited until the men were out of earshot. 'You won't do any good bolting out there. Let's just find out what's going on. We can follow them, but let's do it quietly. OK?'

Kettle nodded and Adam took his hand away. Kettle touched his nose. The bleeding had started again. 'Oh Jesus,' he groaned, eyes fixed on the backs of the men. 'Harris and his mob. How did they follow us?'

'Maybe they didn't,' Adam said. 'You said you often came to the camp. Maybe they found that out, and came here to check. If they don't see you around, they'll probably go away.'

At the camp, someone screamed. There was a flurry of running and shouting. A wurlie collapsed and someone cried out, amid a clanging of iron. A black man fell in the remains of a fire and sparks showered across the sand. Someone laughed.

'Everyone stay where you are,' a voice commanded. A woman was wailing. Two children were running through the trees, with a white man in pursuit.

'No shooting,' the man in charge ordered.

'I won't need my gun,' a man answered, his voice a breathless, mirthless laugh.

A child shrieked. There was a thud, like metal sinking into soft wood, and a curious little squeal. 'That's one of the buggers,' the man laughed and the wailing of the woman in the creek bed became louder.

'OK, boss,' called the man.

The other voice, that of the man in charge, answered: 'Well, just get back here and don't let anyone else get away. Now, where's the chief of you mob of thieves? Where are you, Uldari?'

Adam, following the group walking towards the camp site, could see the old men of the tribe. They had been shepherded together, near the remains of the main fire. Near them, another man writhed on the ground. Beside him was the body of a woman.

A white man, carrying an axe, used the handle to shove one of the old men forward. It was Jimmy Kettle's uncle. A man wearing a khaki uniform walked from the shadows.

'You still here, Uldari? Thought you'd have enough sense to piss off after the other night.' He was carrying a small wooden club, strapped to his wrist by a leather thong. He stepped forward and hit the old man across the face. Uldari sprawled on the sand.

'All right,' the man in khaki said. 'Where's that nephew of yours, that Jimmy Kettle? A friend of mine wants to talk to him.'

'Don't know, boss,' the old man mumbled. He was face down in the sand and had his hand over his mouth. The man in khaki stepped forward and kicked him in the side.

'Take your hand away from your mouth when you speak to me,' he roared.

'Sorry, boss. Don't know where he is.'

The man kicked him again and then used the toe of his shoe to roll the black man on to his back. 'How's Billy?' he said.

'He's dead, boss.'

'Oh, what a shame. I might grab me one of your young blokes and charge him with murder.' The man's toecap toyed with Uldari's ribs. 'Matter of fact, I've got me a witness who says he saw your son hit Billy over the head with a lump of wood. We'd have to hang him for that. Put him on the end of a rope and hang him until his eyeballs popped out.'

'No, boss.'

'Oh, yes, boss. We'd hang him all right. Now, if you don't want that to happen, just tell me where Jimmy Kettle is.'

'Not here, boss.' The old man raised himself on one elbow. 'Why you want him, boss?'

The man hit him again with the club. Not as hard as he had before, but enough to make Uldari wince with pain.

'You just stay down on the ground until I tell you to get up. We want him because he stole a lot of money. Bad boy that nephew of yours. Took it from the circus. He's a thief. Going to be thrown into gaol.'

'No, boss. Jimmy didn't take no money.'

The man in khaki knelt down. 'Now, how do you know that, eh, you old maggot-ridden bastard? Saw him tonight, did you? Where is he? Just tell me, and I'll go away.'

'Don't know, boss.'

The man stood up. 'Don't know boss, eh? All right. You.' And he pointed to a young woman, standing wide-eyed near a collapsed wurlie. The woman did not move. A man carrying a rifle grabbed her by the arm and propelled her towards the man in khaki.

'You do what Mr Mailey tells you, you black slut,' he said.

Mailey stood in front of her. 'Now, you tell me where Jimmy Kettle is.' The woman rolled her eyes. 'Not going to talk?' Mailey said, pleasantly. 'Hey, Hec!'

One of the white men stepped forward. He was a huge man. He stood with his head forward and mouth open.

'Hec,' said Mailey, 'you still got that donkey in the back yard?' The huge man nodded, grinning.

'Does it still like rooting abos?' The man nodded and grinned even more broadly. 'Good. Well take this black lady home and give her to the donkey. See if that makes her talk.'

Hec, giggling, grabbed the woman by the wrist. Mailey walked

57

back to Uldari and rammed his club into the back of the old man's head, burying his face in the sand. 'How about that? I'm going to hang your son and let a donkey have one of your women and all because you won't tell me where Jimmy Kettle is.'

Adam paused behind a tree. The group he had been following had reached the edge of the camp. There, they stopped and then split up. One man stayed with the woman while Harris and the thickset man entered the camp. Harris called out: 'Mailey! Nothing up this end. Any sign of him?'

Mailey shook his head. 'I'll bet he's been here. It's the most likely place for him to run off to.'

'What about the white fellow?' Harris said, in his piping voice.

'You see a white feller?' Mailey asked, prodding the back of Uldari's head. He stepped back a pace. 'What did he look like, Mr Harris?'

'Snowy hair. Broad shoulders. Tall. Probably cut about a bit.'

'You see him, old man?' Mailey tapped each word with his club on Uldari's shoulder.

'No, boss.' The old man spat sand from his bleeding lips.

'You lying old bag of filth,' Mailey said and hammered the aboriginal across the shoulder-blades.

Adam was trying to count the number of white men at the camp. There was the man called Mailey. He had a club, and a revolver in a holster strapped to his belt. There was a man with a large axe, another with a rifle and Hec, who now had hold of the gin around her waist. She was struggling but Hec had lifted her so that her feet were running in the air. Adam could not see whether he was armed or not. On the edge of the camp area, having emerged from a clump of bushes, was another man with a long-handled axe. He was leaning on the axe, as though short of breath. And there were the people Adam had followed, all still with their backs to him. There was Harris, who appeared to have no weapon. Beside him was the barrel-like man – the one who had given Adam such a fright when he had slithered down the bank – and the man guarding the half-caste woman, Nellie. Eight men. At least one revolver, one rifle and two axes.

Where was Jimmy Kettle? Adam had lost sight of him on the way down the creek. He turned and saw the boxer, his silk shorts glinting in the cold light, creeping towards him. He reached Adam and his eyes were blazing. He was carrying a large rock in each hand. 'He killed those two piccaninnies,' he said, spitting the

58

words through his swollen lips. 'I been over there and I seen them. He chopped them up.'

'Well, get down,' Adam said softly. 'There are eight of them and they've got guns.'

'Don't care,' Kettle said, shuffling his feet in the sand. He reminded Adam of a scrub bull about to charge.

'Kettle's worth one hundred pounds, sergeant,' Harris called out.

'Is he?' Kettle said and began to run, charging at Harris. Oh, my God, thought Adam, and began to run too, heading for the man with Nellie. Kettle had forgotten about him, and was going straight for Harris.

The man with Nellie jumped with surprise as the black figure raced past him. He released the young woman and began to draw a pistol from inside his shirt. The weapon was just clear of his body when Adam reached him and swung the stick he had been carrying. The wood splintered on the back of the man's head. He staggered and turned, and stared open-mouthed at Adam. Adam hit him hard on the jaw and the man fell on his back in the sand. He had not uttered a sound. The woman jumped back, alarmed. Adam lunged for her arm. 'Come on. I'm with Jimmy,' he said, the words clattering from his mouth as he dragged her back towards the tree where he had been hiding. 'Get in there,' he ordered, shoving her under a bush. 'Don't come out until I come back for you. And don't make a sound.' She was pretty, Adam thought, catching a glimpse of a shocked face with high cheekbones and unusually large eyes. He turned back to the camp. Once again, people were shouting and screaming.

A cloud scudded across the sky, blotting out the moon. The creek bed darkened and the gum trees turned to stark black columns supporting the night.

The man in khaki, Mailey, had resumed beating Uldari when he became aware of the flurry of movement at the northern end of the camp. 'What's up?' he shouted, and his uncertainty seemed to trigger movement throughout the area. The big man, Hec, let go the gin and she ran away with him lumbering in pursuit. Some of the older men, who had been sitting, cowed, watching Uldari being humiliated, got up and ran for the trees on the far side of the creek. Others followed. The woman who had been wailing ran to some bushes and came back immediately, tearing at her hair and screaming.

'Stop them,' Mailey shouted. 'Don't let anyone get away.'

Mailey was charging through the camp, stumbling in the dark and bumping into the slippery bodies of a couple of young boys who were running across the creek. 'Stop them,' he shouted, not seeing where they had gone. He drew his hand-gun from its holster.

Hec, chasing the gin up the creek bank, fell in a hole. The clear snap of a breaking bone was followed by his roar of pain. Two young men, who had been hiding in the trees, fell on him with rocks and his cries became louder.

'Jesus,' said Mailey. 'You all right, Hec?' There was no answer. The mother of the young boys who had been axed in the bushes ran up to Mailey, wailing and screaming, and clawed his face. He clubbed her to the ground. 'Shoot the bastards,' he called out, wiping his cheek and swearing when he felt blood. 'We're being attacked. Shoot to kill.'

The man with the long-handled axe limped from a thicket to the right of Mailey. 'I've been speared, sergeant,' he said. 'They got me in the leg.'

'Well, use your gun,' Mailey roared, still wiping his cheek, but the man had collapsed. A long spear projected from his thigh. 'Shit, what's happening?' Mailey said and turned towards Harris.

Harris was back on his feet, facing the advancing policeman. Jimmy Kettle was behind him, one arm around Harris's neck, the other twisting the white man's right arm in a hammer lock.

'Put your gun down,' Kettle said. His face was partly hidden by Harris.

'Like hell,' Mailey growled. 'Let that man go, nigger, or I'll blast you into dog's meat.' He raised the gun.

Kettle tightened the arm lock and Harris screamed, an ugly, high-pitched sound, more like the shrieking of a parrot than a human cry.

'You can do what you like, but I'm still going to blast you,' Mailey said. He moved closer, until he could see both men clearly. He aimed at their heads.

Harris was weeping. 'Jesus, sergeant,' he wheezed, 'put that thing down.'

'Is that Jimmy Kettle?'

'Yes,' Harris said, and then stiffened as the aborignal applied more pressure to his throat. 'You're choking me,' he protested and squirmed in Kettle's hold, his feet kicking and dancing like a puppet's. Mailey stepped closer.

'Get back,' Kettle said.

'Why should I, son? What will you do if I don't? Hit me over the head with Mr Harris?' Mailey moved forward another step.

Kettle retreated, dragging the threshing Harris with him.

Mailey looked about him, his brow suddenly knotted. 'Gus, Dave,' he bellowed. 'Where the hell are you?'

Having hidden Nellie beneath the bush, Adam climbed a ridge and followed a sandy channel that ran parallel with the camp site. As he reached a fallen tree, the long cloud obscuring the moon broke into fragments and silvery light dappled the creek bed. He crouched low for fear of being seen. The scene was astonishing. Near him, just below a small embankment tufted by grass, was a white man who seemed to be biting and scratching his own leg, much like a dog worrying a flea. Only after a few seconds did Adam notice the quivering shaft of a spear projecting from the man's thigh. Pain had brought the man to the edge of madness. He had attempted to pull out the spear and now, with his trousers drenched in blood, he was alternately trying to wrench the weapon clear, then rolling on the sand in agony, pummelling the leg or beating his head. To the left, Old Uldari was trying to rise from his hands and knees. A gin had crept to his side. Nearby were two bodies, a man across a woman. The man's legs twitched but the woman, dressed in a frock saturated with blood, seemed lifeless. On the far bank was the big white man known as Hec. He was slumped on his face, with one leg bent at an unnatural angle. The woman who had lost two children to the axeman was sitting on the sand, holding her head and moaning. The hollow echoed with sounds: the piteous lament of the woman, the groans of the injured, the sudden swish of feet on sand as the two old aboriginal men ran away, and the choked gurglings of Harris, who was dangling in Jimmy Kettle's arms. And the voice of Mailey, now low and calm, as he advanced on Kettle.

'What's happening, sarge?' the man with the rifle said. He flashed the torch at Harris.

'Just move around that way, Gus,' Mailey said, using his hand-gun to point a path to his right. 'Just get over there and move close to our black friend so we can teach him a lesson.'

'Keep back, or I'll kill Harris,' Kettle shouted. His frenzy had cooled and he was frightened. He stumbled as he retreated, releasing his grip on the man's neck and then reapplying the hold with such force that Harris kicked wildly.

'You'll kill him, will you?' Mailey said amiably, moving forward a step as he spoke. 'Now I'd argue with you about that, son, because I don't think you could. You could break his arm, I suppose.' He took another step. 'But that wouldn't kill him. Hurt him, of course, and just make all of us angrier. And you might as well take your arm away from around his neck. Do you know how long it takes to strangle a man? I do, lad. I've done it.' He advanced one more pace. 'Takes a long time. I'd be on you, blasting holes through that black hide of yours, long before you could throttle Mr Harris.'

Jimmy Kettle backed against a tree.

Mailey lowered his gun. When he spoke, his voice was soft and low. 'They tell me you're a bit of a boxer. Let's see how good you are, and how well you fight with a bullet in your belly. Come on, Gus,' he said, not looking at his friend, 'let's get him.' And snarling like a wild animal, he sprang forward.

Gus did not join the attack. Before he could move, Adam came charging from the ridge, vaulting the man with the spear in his leg, and ramming his shoulder into the small of the other man's back. The impact sent Gus cartwheeling into a bush. The rifle hit Adam on the head. He fell to his knees, stunned.

Jimmy Kettle tried to fend off Mailey's bull-like charge by thrusting Harris at him. But Harris, fearful of being hurt, kicked violently and wriggled to one side so that Kettle, unbalanced, fell and landed beside his prisoner. Kettle grabbed Harris and hauled him, still struggling violently, across his body, but when he looked up Mailey was standing over him and smiling.

'I've got a clear shot at your belly,' Mailey said. 'A good place to put a bullet in someone who's caused a lot of trouble.' He spread his feet and took aim. 'It'll be a simple story, son. We came here to arrest you for stealing from the circus. Your Mr Carter will vouch for that. It's all arranged between him and Mr Harris. And then I'll just say that while we were here, we were attacked and had to shoot a few of the blacks in self-defence. Very simple, really.'

'What about the kids?' Kettle spat out. 'Your bloke butchered them with an axe.'

'Very simple. One grave will solve the problem. No one will know. No one will tell. Certainly not you, Mr Jimmy Kettle.'

Mailey did not see the black woman rise behind him. But he heard her screaming like a banshee and felt her clawing at his head.

He half-turned, and her fingers gouged his ear. The gun went off.

Kettle felt the sudden kick as Harris's backbone thudded into his chest. Then the brothel keeper from Port Pirie twitched once and went limp.

The woman, still screaming and clawing, wrestled Mailey to the ground. He dropped the gun. She jumped on his back, pulling his hair as he groped in the sand for the weapon. Near them, Jimmy Kettle pushed the body of Harris away from him, and sat up.

Mailey, having regained the gun, struggled to his knees with his left arm locked around the woman's head in a cruel hold. He saw Harris. 'Jesus Christ,' he gasped, struggling to hold the woman who had twisted on to her back with her legs bicycling in the air.

The bullet had burned a neat hole where the second button on Harris's shirt had been. A stain, charcoal-coloured in the moonlight, was spreading across the material. Mailey, aiming his gun at Kettle, tried to stand but the woman kicked so fiercely that he lost his balance and fell. He landed with her head beneath him and she shrieked, this time with pain more than anger. He applied even more pressure to the head lock. Her cries were muffled as he manoeuvred his armpit over her nose and mouth. 'Stop kicking, you crazy bitch,' he growled, shaking her like a cat with a mouse in its jaws. 'Gus,' he shouted, 'Where the hell are you?'

'Right here,' a voice answered from behind Mailey. He turned, shuffling on his knees in the soft sand to see Adam.

'Who are you? And where in the name of ...' but he had no chance to finish the question, for Kettle picked up a stone and hit Mailey behind the ear. Mailey slumped forward, locked in a kneeling position with his head touching the sand. He groaned loudly. The aboriginal woman, released from the hold, began to beat his back.

In horror, Adam stared at the body of Harris, who was lying on his back with his mouth open and teeth bared in a snarl. 'What happened?' Adam said. 'Is he dead?'

Kettle nodded. 'The sergeant shot him. Meant to shoot me.'

Wearily, Kettle moved to the woman. She was still beating Mailey's bent back, although no longer with a flurry of blows. Now, near exhaustion, she was thumping the policeman with slow, measured blows, like a drummer beating time for a slow march. She was sobbing hysterically.

Kettle pulled her to her feet and she stared at him, uncomprehendingly. 'You must go,' he said tenderly. 'Go to my uncle. Take him away. You must all go away.' He pushed her, gently, towards the place where his uncle was now sitting. Kettle began to follow her but Adam restrained him.

'We've got to get away from this place, too,' he said. 'Quickly. That policeman's going to be on his feet any minute and there's another bloke over there that I hit. He's only winded, I think, so let's go now. Otherwise there'll be more killing.'

But Kettle kept walking, moving erratically, eyes searching the camp. Adam ran after him and grabbed his arm. Kettle turned, his face fierce. 'Those kids were chopped up,' he said. 'Ever seen a little boy with his arm and leg cut off?' Shaking himself free of Adam's grip, he pointed towards a clump of bushes. 'It's over there, white feller. Go and have a look for yourself. It's like a bloody butcher's shop.'

He stopped near his uncle, and began to weep. The old man nodded, and tried to stand. The gin and the woman who had attacked Mailey were helping him. Kettle looked around, searching.

'The girl's safe,' Adam said.

'Nellie?' Kettle turned, his face wrinkled with concern. Another cloud swept across the moon. Adam moved closer, more anxious than ever to be moving from the camp in the sudden dark.

'I hid her under some bushes back there. She's all right.' Adam could see only Jimmy Kettle's eyes. They were blinking rapidly. The rest of him – face, body, even the glossy trunks – had merged into the slate-grey shadow engulfing them. The eyes blinked again. 'Truly,' Adam said, reaching out and touching the other man. 'She's OK. She's frightened, but she's safe. I'll take you to her.'

The eyes closed, and Adam could see nothing of him. 'You get her,' Kettle said, from somewhere in the dark. 'I've got to make sure my uncle gets away. You take her to the cave up the creek. I'll meet you there.' And he was gone.

FIVE

Adam retreated, moving north along the creek's edge and trying to recognize the shapes of trees outlined against the sky. He groped for familiar objects: the trunk of a sapling growing at a grotesque angle and then a boulder projecting from the base of a grassy knoll. He had passed those in his pursuit of Jimmy Kettle. He had run then. Now it was a slow, blind man's progress back, feeling his way and keeping to the left of the camp so that he could avoid Mailey. He could hear the policeman, still grunting with pain and muttering. There was a track behind the tree. On hands and knees, he felt for the stones that marked the path. The bush where he had hidden the woman was somewhere near. He reached out, and touched the spiky leaves of a plant.

'Nellie?' he whispered, and shivered with cold and fright as he waited for a response. Nothing. She's gone, he thought. Or she's too frightened to answer. He crawled a little further along the stone-strewn path. 'Nellie,' he tried again, a little louder. 'It's me. Jimmy's friend.'

From somewhere close behind, Mailey groaned loudly and when, at the same moment, fingers touched his ankle, Adam's stomach wrenched with shock.

'Here.' She was still under the bush. Adam, shaking, crawled back. 'What's been happening?' she breathed.

'I'm not sure,' Adam said, fighting to control his voice. 'There are bodies everywhere.'

'Jimmy?'

'He's all right. He'll be with us in a moment. We've got to get out of here quickly.' He took her hand.

From the far side of the camp, a shout rang out. 'Hey, sergeant, where is everyone?'

There was no answer. Adam, who had risen to his feet, stood still. He forced the girl to do likewise by the strength of his grip. It's the eighth man, he thought, the one with the other axe.

'Can't see a bloody thing,' came the voice, sounding good-humoured. 'What was all the noise about? Who'd you shoot?' There was a sudden cracking of timber, and the sound of someone falling. 'Shit. Just fell down a hole. Have I come to the right place? Are you there, sergeant?' More timber snapped. 'I stopped one of them. Had to chase the bugger for half a mile but I got him. That's one abo that won't have any use for a barber again.' A grunt of pain followed as the man stumbled. 'Hey, sergeant?' Now there was anxiety in the voice.

Adam shook the woman's hand to suggest they should move and with him leading they crept along the creek bed, away from the noise of the newcomer. They had left the region of rocks and were in soft sand when the man at the camp began to shout again. Alarm sharpened his voice now, the sort of edge that a frightened child has when crying from a darkened room.

'Sergeant? Where the hell are you? I just found Hec. I think he's dead. There's a hole in the middle of his back. Sergeant! Sergeant Mailey?'

The moon reappeared, edged by a grey border of cloud. Adam dropped to the sand, pulling the woman with him. He looked back. No one. Just trees and bushes, either ghostly, glinting grey or black with shadow. No humanity on the horizon, only the curving silhouette of vegetation, iced with sparkling leaves.

Adam tugged the woman to her feet and made for the cave in the high, water-ravaged bank on the outside of the bend. When it rains, he thought, the water must really race down this creek bed. And he was comforted. Natural disasters he could understand, not the sort of wild slaughter he had seen that night.

They trudged through deep sand, climbed to the cave, and settled in the shadows. Noises drifted to them. From somewhere far away, a dog barked. The drone of insects lapped their ears on waves of faint sound. And then a violent shout, shocking in its volume. And a second voice, deep and slurred, the words difficult to distinguish. A third voice joined them. Torches flashed.

The dog barked again. It was a lonely sound, from another world.

'Where's Jimmy?' Nellie whispered, her voice brittle with fear.

The torches went out. Adam put his hand over her mouth. Her cheeks were moist and he was conscious of the roughness of his hand on her skin. From the camp came a hideous screaming. Adam felt Nellie's head jerk backwards, away from his hand. 'Was that Jimmy?' she said.

Another scream. The mutter of voices.

'No, not Jimmy,' Adam said, pressing himself against the floor of the cave and peering towards the camp. The screams gave way to a deep sobbing. Several men were talking at once, as though comforting someone. 'My guess is they've pulled the spear out of that man's leg,' Adam said.

She said nothing for a long time. They heard more sobbing, and men talking.

'How long do we have to wait here?' she said eventually, touching his back. Her fingers were cool. A woman had never touched him like that before.

'Until Jimmy gets here,' he snapped. Or, he thought, until the other men come looking for us and we have to move. A stick cracked. He strained to see any movement. The sound had seemed close – someone moving slowly across the ground. 'Where are you?' It came from somewhere above them. It was Kettle.

'Here.' Adam crawled to the edge of the cave and looked up. 'Where are you?'

'Up here. On the bank. Have you got Nellie?'

'Yes. She's all right.'

'Get up here. There's a path just to the left. Hurry up. They've started to follow your tracks up the creek. Be quiet. They're getting close.'

They left the cave, sliding on their bellies. At the place where Harris and his party had blundered down the bank, they climbed, inching their way to the top, and keeping low to avoid being seen in the bold wash of moonlight. It was a brilliant night, the sort that inspires people to dream of times before and beyond them.

An awful sound, part scream and part call for help, ripped from the camp. 'Oh, for God's sake,' growled a man's voice, so close that Adam's skin tightened with fright. Someone was near them, in the creek bed. 'We should have throttled him,' the man said. 'I know they're close but they'll hear that and bolt before we can catch them.'

Adam pressed his face into the roughened dirt. A hand grabbed his wrist.

'Quick,' Jimmy Kettle said, voice hushed but so close to Adam his breath played on his ear. 'They're just down there. They'll pick up your tracks in that deep sand in a moment and then they'll be on to you.'

Crawling, they followed Kettle beyond the rim of the creek's bank to a row of scrub. On the far side of a clump of acacia, Kettle stood. He was naked. He reached for a bundle he had left on the ground.

'We get away from here,' he said, ignoring the woman, who was staring at him. 'They'll be up here soon.' Bundle under one arm, he began to spring through the scrub. The pale soles of his feet flashed as he ran. Adam had difficulty keeping up. His foot ached and he felt dizzy from the rifle blow. The woman lagged behind. Kettle stopped, took her roughly by the hand, and ran on. She stumbled many times but he did not slacken his pace.

67

They came to a gibber plain. That night, the polished ironstones could have been waves on a vast lake, reflecting moonlight from a wind-ruffled surface. It was beautiful and deadly, for anyone walking across the plain would have been seen like sails billowing from a yacht. So they kept to its edge, moving at Kettle's steady run, and staying in the shadow of the scrub.

At last, Kettle stopped. The woman fell to the ground, gasping for breath. As Adam limped to join them, Kettle undid the bundle he had been carrying. Clothing and footwear spilled on the ground. He brushed sand from his buttocks, and pulled on a pair of trousers. 'Bit big,' he said, wheezing for air. 'But better than walking round in those fancy bloomers. Here, try these on.' And he tossed a pair of boots at Adam.

'Where did you get these?' Adam said, sitting down.

'From someone who won't want them.' Kettle threw a shirt at him. 'Try this, too. Better than the one you've got. This one has buttons.'

Adam cleaned his cut foot and tried on the boots. Then he put on the shirt. He stood up. 'Good fit,' he said. 'You were busy back there.'

'Flat out as a lizard up a drainpipe,' Kettle said, and flashed a smile. He cupped his hands around his swollen lips, as though the smile had hurt. 'Had to get out of that boxing rig,' he said. 'The copper'll be looking for us. Have to. He can't just hush up the whole business. Not with white fellers killed. Be all right if it was just a couple of blacks. No one gives a stuff about us. The copper'll probably say I shot Harris. Don't know how. Didn't have no gun. But he'll say it, just the same. So I couldn't go round in shorts and boots. See me a mile off.'

'What did you do with your things?' Adam said.

'Buried them under a rock.' He walked to Adam's side, and bent to pick up Adam's discarded shirt. 'Don't leave nothing lying around. That copper'll find them, and then he'll find us.' Kettle handed the shirt to Nellie. 'You haven't got much on,' he said. 'Use this. It'll keep you warm.' It was the first time he had spoken to her that night.

He sat down and tried on a pair of boots. 'Too big,' he said, wriggling his toes and feeling where they touched the leather. 'Still, better than nothing.' He stood up. His new pants crinkled around the knees. He shuffled forward, feet splayed wide. 'If I had a stick and a hat, I could be Charlie Chaplin,' he said.

'Who's he?' Adam said.

Kettle looked at Adam in surprise. 'Never heard of Charlie Chaplin?'

'No.'

'You're a funny one for a white feller. Haven't you been to the movies?'

'To a picture theatre? No. But I saw one at Broken Hill. Had all lights across the front.'

'Never been inside one? You fair dinkum?'

Adam nodded. He tucked his new shirt into his trousers.

'Where you been all your life?'

'All over the place. Mostly in the bush.'

'How old are you?'

'Nineteen. At least I think so. My father died when I was about nine and that was ten years ago. What about yourself?'

'Twenty-four.' Kettle sat down and began untying his boots. 'Or maybe twenty-five. My mum used to tell me I was born on the day they were celebrating King Edward's birthday but I'm not sure what year. You younger than me?'

'Suppose so.'

'Never been beaten by a younger bloke before. You got a boy's face but a man's body.' He tried on another pair of boots.

Adam laughed. 'Where'd you get all the shoes?'

'Three white fellers flat on their backs. Not walking anywhere.'

'But there was that policeman back there, and some other white men. You must have been under their noses.'

'All running round like chooks with their heads off. Easy for a simple blackfellow like me to pinch.'

'How's your uncle?'

'They all got away.'

'Was he all right?'

Kettle stood and put weight on his new footwear. 'You white fellers have got funny-shaped feet,' he said, taking a few tentative steps. 'Yes, he's good. Been beaten by the police before. You get used to it.' He sniffed a few times, and touched his nose and swollen lips.

'How's your face?'

'All right.' He sniffed again, as though proving his nose worked. 'Let's get moving. That copper'll be looking for us so he can butcher a couple more blackfellows. And one white bloke who saw what happened back there.'

*

69

They kept moving, not following a set course but heading away from the creek and seeking whatever shelter was available. They moved through thick scrub that snaked along the line of a depression in the land. That led them to another watercourse, edged by tall trees. They walked in single file along the row of trees but, when the trees ceased, they were forced into open country. They made for a low range of hills that seemed no more than deeper shadows on a grey landscape. The moon, high in the sky for the last hours before dawn, wore a ring of mist. The clouds had gone. It was cold. And damp, for moisture sucked from the ground during the baking heat of the day was settling back to earth, and they were chilled.

They reached the hills. Sprouting tussocks of spinifex hid jagged outcrops of rock, and they had difficulty climbing to the top of a ridge. From a vantage point on a crumbling buttress of rock, they looked back to the lights of Port Augusta. The town fanned around the head of Spencer Gulf. The lights of a ship, coming up the gulf, twinkled on the placid waters. The horizon glowed with the lights of another town further south, but between themselves and Port Augusta there was no light. Just a wide stretch of land, striped and blotched with the deep greys and blacks of the bush at night.

'No sign of them,' Adam said, but Jimmy Kettle watched and listened for another ten minutes before he agreed, and then they slept.

Dawn was close, and the sky had flushed and grown pale, as though embarrassed that the sun might find it with the moon and the stars.

A light wind had risen, and there was dust in the air.

The sun came out of the Flinders Ranges. It boiled on the rim of the mountains like the white-hot spill from a smelter, bubbling and distorting in shape as it blazed through the layers of mist that lingered on the peaks. In the first moments of dawn, long, cool shadows raced to the far horizon and then, as the sun took shape and rose higher, came racing back again, to retreat into pockets of blue that dappled the western flank of the ranges.

The sun bleached the sky. Where the moon had shone, an eagle circled, lazily stroking the rising currents of air. It spiralled above a high rock outcrop, where three persons slept.

Adam was first to wake. The right side of his face was still

70

numb around the cheek and the inside of his mouth was swollen and lacerated. His tongue traced the jagged path of the cut from the base of a tooth to the inner edge of his lip. He ached in many places. His foot was sore and his body was sore, either from the fight or from having slept on the stony rise. He sat up. He was thirsty.

He began to stand. Then, remembering the flight of the previous night, he lay on his stomach and wriggled his way to the edge of a rock shelf. They were surrounded by a dry landscape. The Flinders Ranges, folded ribbons of blue and red and misty violet, were far to the east. To the north was the glint of a salt lake. To the south was the tongue of water that was the tip of Spencer Gulf, and around it, in a pathetic huddle of buildings, was Port Augusta. The town was less easy to distinguish in daylight than it had been at night. It sparkled at night. Now it was just a collection of lumps and shadows, gathered on a pinch of shoreline that was surrounded by an immensity of land.

There were more lumps and shadows to the west, but they were the marks of wide plains coated with stones and salt bush, and pimpled by occasional low hills. The view that way was an unbroken vista of aridity. Adam could see occasional dark ripples, which would be lines of low trees following the path of some watercourse, but he knew, from a lifetime of living in dry country, that those creeks would be dry.

He touched his lips, and was more conscious of his thirst. He wondered where they would find water. Not in these hills.

Adam had once met a man from the east, who had spoken of rivers that always had water in them. Even small rivers and creeks. He himself had seen the Darling once, when Tiger had taken him to Menindee. Otherwise, the waterways he knew had beds of powdery sand and polished rock. They flowed only in the hours that followed a heavy storm, and that was rare. To Adam, water was something you drilled for, dug for, and used sparingly, not something that lapped the banks of a gentle stream.

Jimmy Kettle coughed and sat up. One eye was closed, his nostrils were caked with blood and his mouth was swollen. 'I'm thirsty,' he croaked.

'Not much water about,' Adam said, looking about him. 'No matter which way we go, we've got a long, dry walk. Any ideas?'

Kettle crawled to join Adam on the edge of the rock. 'About what?'

71

'Which way to go.'

'Any way except back towards town.' He nodded at the distant smoke curls of Port Augusta. 'How you feeling?'

'Sore. Bit thirsty.' Adam shifted on his elbows. 'Can't see any sign of anybody.'

'Reckon they've gone back to Port Augusta. The copper'll expect us to head for town ... sometime. He's probably back there now, thinking up his excuses for what happened.' Kettle edged back from the ledge. 'All the same, let's keep down low. Never know who's watching or looking for us.'

Adam noticed a trail of dust, moving through the salt bush plain to the west. 'How would those people have got to your uncle's camp last night? Would they have walked?' He asked the question without turning his head. His eyes were following the dust trail.

'Don't think so. Knowing white fellers, they'd have had a couple of cars somewhere.'

'Well, there's a car over there.'

Kettle slithered back into place beside Adam. They watched the dust corkscrewing across the plain.

'He's going fast,' Adam said. 'Twenty, maybe thirty miles an hour.'

'Yeah. Must be the main road.'

'Where's it go?'

'Alice Springs, I suppose. That car's going north.' They watched until the car had disappeared and the dust had spread to a thin cloud which drifted across the salt bush. 'Wasn't the copper,' Kettle said, and crawled from the ledge. He stopped beside Nellie, who was still sleeping.

'Is she all right?' Adam asked.

'Those blokes knocked her around a bit,' Kettle said, shifting on to his haunches and studying the woman.

Adam joined him. Nellie had the flannel shirt across her shoulders. There were bruises on her face. One cheek was swollen. She had high cheekbones and her skin – where it was not purpling with bruises – was a lovely dusky brown shade. Adam felt a stirring of memory. She reminded him of someone, somewhere, from some other time. 'What are you going to do with her?' he asked, thinking, as he spoke, that he sounded like some station owner discussing a mare.

'Don't know.'

'How will you get her back to her home?'

Jimmy Kettle glanced at Adam and smiled, with the indulgent look of an adult who has heard a child say something foolish but amusing. 'She'd be as dead as you or me if she went back to Pirie.' He paused. 'What's your name again?'

'Adam.'

'Adam. She can't go back, Adam. She can't go to Pirie. She can't go to Port Augusta. She can't go anywhere she's likely to run into that copper or the men who were at the blackfellows' camp.'

'Were they all policemen there with Mailey?'

'Jesus, no.' Kettle breathed deeply, and held his ribs. 'That was just a killing party. A hunting party, out for sport. Just a private mob. That bastard Harris paid for that. Some of his men, Mailey, a few blokes from town.'

Adam thought for a moment. 'Was all that because of the young lady?'

'And me,' Kettle said, and smiled again.

'What are you laughing at?'

'You. You called her a young lady. Long time since anybody called Nellie that.'

'If you're not going to take her back to Port Pirie, where are you going to take her?'

'With me, I suppose.'

'For how long?'

Kettle shrugged. 'Long as I feel like it.'

'You mean you'll live with her. You'll marry her?'

'Maybe. Hey, Adam,' he said, touching his swollen eye. 'You know one good thing about being a blackfellow? You can't get a black eye.'

'Looks blue to me.'

'You white fellers get black eyes. We black fellers get blue eyes. Not blue eyes like you got here,' he pointed at his eyeball, 'but blue eyes out here, where it gets all puffed up.' He cast his one good eye at Nellie. 'I reckon we just get as far away from here as we can. Away from the copper Mailey. What you going to do, Adam?'

Adam ran his fingers through his hair. 'I hadn't thought. Go back to Broken Hill, I suppose.'

'You got family there?'

'No. I've got no family.'

'Well, why do you want to go back there?'

'Where else could I go?'

'Anywhere else. I remember when you walked up last night and said you was going to fight me, Mr Carter said you come from Broken Hill. That copper will be looking for you pretty hard. You're a white bloke, see, and that makes you very dangerous to him. No one's going to believe me but they might believe what you said. Follow?'

Adam nodded.

'You can bet that Mailey'll be good mates with one of the policemen in Broken Hill. And he'll have him looking for you. So you can't go to Broken Hill. You got to go somewhere else.' Kettle touched his nostril and checked for signs of blood on his fingertip. 'You got a good wallop,' he said, and grinned, revealing a gap, two teeth wide, at the front of his upper jaw.

'How'd you lose the teeth?' Adam said. 'Boxing?'

The other man lowered his head and shook it. 'Tribal business,' he said. He looked up, and tapped his closed mouth. 'Part of becoming a man,' he said, in a mocking tone. 'Makes me look beautiful.'

'How did you become a boxer?'

'Because of a white feller out at the copper mine near Beltana. He taught me. Saw me fighting once, just as a little kid. Gave me few lessons. Trained me. Just like you train a dog. He used to take me to the pubs. Put money on me and I used to fight other young fellers. Anyhow, I started flattening a few bigger blokes and the circus came up that way and I got a job with Mr Carter.' He shook the sleeping girl by the ankle. 'Hey, wake up. We lie here all day, we're going to die of thirst.'

Nellie stirred, and Adam crawled to another part of the rocky outcrop. He studied the country to the west. 'I've only seen one car use that road,' he called back to Kettle. 'It looks good and quiet. There's a homestead just beyond the road. I can see the windmill and a few roofs. Water's what we need, so I reckon we should head that way. In any case, that's about the only direction we can go. South is the town, east is too close to the creek where we were last night, and Mailey's sure to have some people out there looking for us.' He pivoted towards the north. 'And the country's too dry up there. No point perishing of thirst.'

He returned to the others. Nellie was staring at him. She had long eyelashes. Adam looked away. 'What say we move?' he said.

'It'll be like an oven up on these rocks before long.'

They left the hills and walked towards the road. The journey took longer than they estimated because of the spinifex, which infested much of the plain and forced them into winding detours to clear the clusters of needle-like spikes. In places, they had to force their way between plants, and their legs and arms were scratched and punctured. The air became hot, and every breath seared their throats. After three hours of painful walking they reached the road.

Adam breathed in the thin, scorching air. 'Can't see the windmill any more from down here,' he said, and no one answered. He had been the leader that morning and they were reduced to following. 'We'll have a breather, and then head that way.' He nodded to the west. Neither Kettle nor the woman objected. Both were used to hardship, and being told what to do.

'I stayed at a place once that had a bathroom with running water inside the homestead,' Adam said, picking a stalk of grass, brushing dust from it, and sucking it. 'Just turned on the tap and water came out.'

'Where was that?' Kettle asked, in the manner of one who does not really care about the answer. The woman stared at Adam.

'Broken Hill. Just out of the town, by about twenty miles.'

Kettle massaged one arm, to ease the soreness. He smoothed the skin around some spinifex scratches. 'Ever been to the city?' he asked, still examining his arm.

'Been to Broken Hill a few times.'

'I mean somewhere bigger. Like Adelaide.'

'No.' Adam threw away the stalk. It was too dry and fibrous. He put a pebble in his mouth and rolled it across his tongue, trying to promote the flow of saliva. 'Don't think I'd like a big city,' he said. 'People who've been there don't seem to like it too much. They all want to come back out here.'

'I went to Gawler once,' Kettle said. 'You could see Adelaide if you climbed a hill.'

'Did you go to Adelaide?'

Kettle shook his head.

'Why not?'

'Not good country for blackfellows.' He stood up and raised his hand, commanding silence. After a moment, he said: 'There's someone down the road.'

Adam turned to look. 'Is there a car coming?'

'It's not moving.'

'Well, what do you hear?'

'Hammering.'

Adam listened but heard nothing. 'You've got sharp ears, mate,' he said. 'You're as good as a cattle dog, the way you hear things.'

'Better,' Kettle said, and grinned. 'If I was a dog, I'd only bark and you wouldn't know if it's been a cat that had got me nervous. Seeing I'm not a dog, I can tell you it's people, not a cat. They're down the road, about half a mile.'

'Let's have a look,' Adam said, standing and adjusting his trousers around his waist. Picturing a car with a waterbag slung across the front, he began to walk.

It was a bus. Not that that was clear from the first sighting. The end of the road disappeared in the shimmering mirages of a heat haze and the vehicle materialized out of the vapours like reflections in a hall of mirrors: playful images, that spread wide and then high, and danced upside down.

Adam walked closer, until the image had stabilized. It was a small bus, bulbous in shape, and looking like a cicada with its big square radiator, headlamps on stalks, and a fat, rounded tail. Four people were beside it. Adam stepped to the side of the road, among some bushes. The others followed. 'What do you make of it?' he asked.

'Not Mailey,' Kettle said.

'Looks like they're changing a wheel,' Adam said. The other man nodded his agreement and sat down, looking distressed. Adam crouched beside him. 'What's up?' he said.

'Eye's sore,' Kettle said, touching the side of his face. 'Nose's sore. Mouth's sore. Rib's sore. Now my feet are sore in these flaming boots.'

Adam ruffled his hair. 'What say I go and have a word with them? You and Nellie wait here and have a bit of a breather. If it's clear, I'll wave for you to come on down.'

'You're a good bloke for a white feller,' Kettle said, and tried to smile.

Adam moved towards the bus, walking along a rut furrowed deep in dust near the edge of the road. He could see only four persons at the bus, and his eyes searched the bush for others. No, just four. One was kneeling and hammering something. The sound

76

reaching him was strange, as though made by a hollow, rubbery drum. People were talking. It was not the bubble of normal conversation that reached him but the drone of despair. There was something vaguely unsettling about the scene, and Adam felt he was walking into an old dream. The immobilized vehicle, the scattering of tools through the dust, the scrawny-looking trees edging the road, the waterless country around them, and the feeling of gloom – all were images that jangled at his memory.

A tall man with greying hair was working over a wheel that lay on its side in the dust near the bus. He was hammering the bead of the tyre, trying to force it over the rim. A woman, also grey and tall, was watching. Two children were near her. There was a girl, maybe ten years of age, and a boy, taller and maybe fourteen or fifteen. He was holding a tyre pump, ready to go to work when the tyre was in place on the rim. They had their backs to Adam.

'Can I help?' he said, and the woman jumped with fright.

'Where in the name of the Lord did you come from?' she gasped, clutching the girl with both hands and pulling the child in front of her. The woman began to laugh. 'Oh, you gave me such a start.'

The man stood upright, hammer in hand. He looked up and down the road. 'I don't see a motor car or a horse, so I gather you came on foot,' he said, in a voice that was heavily accented. 'Which means that you are doing better than we are. We have the luxury of a motor omnibus but we are not moving. You are on foot but you *are* moving.' He wiped his forehead. 'I am not used to this. We have had a puncture which Josef and I have repaired adequately but now, unhappily, I cannot persuade this tyre to go back over this wheel.' He raised his shoulders in a gesture of hopelessness. 'It just will not go.'

Adam stepped forward and took the hammer. 'You could do with a bigger hammer,' he said. 'Even so, you've got to be careful not to damage the bead.' He examined the tyre. 'And you've been hitting it the wrong way.'

Gently, he pushed the man out of the way. Part of the tyre was in place in the well of the wheel and Adam, using his feet, forced the tyre deeper into the well. Then he moved to the side where the tyre was stretched tight across the rim, stood on the wall of the tyre and carefully beat the edge of the rubber, back towards his feet. He worked from one end, gradually easing the rubber over the rim. With a loud clonking sound, the tyre slipped into place.

'What a clever young man,' said the woman. Her voice was accented too, but not as heavily as her husband's. 'How did you do that?'

'I've done it before,' Adam said.

'You must show my husband sometime.'

'Could I have a drink of water?' Adam said.

The man rushed to the front of the bus and unhooked a canvas water bag. 'Of course, of course,' he said, offering the bag to Adam. 'Have as much as you like. We have plenty. There are several drums of water inside.'

Adam drank. When he had finished, he said: 'Where are the rest of the passengers?'

The man laughed. 'This is not a passenger bus, young man. It used to be, but I bought it and it is now our home.'

'Where are you going?' said Adam and drank more water.

'To a place called Coober Pedy.' The man nodded with satisfaction as Adam drank, as though he were slaking his own thirst.

The woman interrupted: 'My husband, who is a fine wine-maker, has decided we will make our fortunes by finding precious gems called opals.'

'We didn't want to leave,' said the girl. 'They made us.'

'Hush,' said the woman, patting the child's shoulders.

'I've seen opals,' said Adam.

The man bowed, as though acknowledging a statement of immense significance.

Adam scraped at the dust with one boot. 'My name's Adam Ross,' he said.

The man bowed again. 'My name is Hoffman. Hans Hoffman. This is my wife, my daughter Anemone whom we call Annie, and my son, Josef.' The boy regarded Adam with intense blue eyes.

'I have two friends with me,' Adam said. 'They're up the road. They're very thirsty. May I wave to them, so they can come and have a drink?'

'Goodness me,' said the woman, her voice drenched with concern. 'Bring them down straight away. Are they all right? Have you been walking far?' She searched the road for a sign of the others.

'They're aboriginal,' Adam said.

The man looked at him. 'You make that sound like a crime.'

'No, they're my friends. It's just that some people ...'

'These friends of yours could be Zulus or Eskimos and what would it matter?' the man said. 'I am German. I have had many people treat me as though I were the devil himself and do you know something, young man? Not one of those who have behaved with malice towards me has been an aboriginal. Get them to join us quickly, so they may have water to drink. It is very hot out here.'

Adam walked to the middle of the road and waved.

'Come, come, Josef,' said the tall German to his son, who had followed Adam. 'Start to pump the tyre. It will not run without air, you know. And we have a long way to go to get to Coober Pedy.'

BOOK TWO

Coober Pedy

ONE

May, 1929

Adam was dreaming again. It was a wild dream, filled with contrasting images. One moment, he was in dark places, where lights flickered on walls and the smell of damp clay sweetened the air. The next, he was on a plain that was hot and drenched with sunlight, and the smell was of dust. He was walking, always walking, but never getting anywhere. His mother was there. Just in front of him but moving at such a pace that he never caught her. One instant she was a shadow, flitting past those faint lights on the wet clay walls of some cavern, and then she was walking in the sun, regally and slowly, but too fast for him to catch, and casting a shadow on the plain.

He rolled on his side and coughed as a thin cloud of dust rose and tickled his throat.

Adam opened his eyes and it was dark. Not just dark – black. So black that he felt he had no body and his eyes were burning in a head that had been separated from everything else – his body, the world, everything. He closed and re-opened his eyes, to make sure they really were open and he was awake.

He sat up. The dream had gone and, with it, the confusion. He stood and walked towards the place where the curtain should be, his hands outstretched for the first rough touch of hessian. It must be like this when you're blind, he thought, and yawned. He stumbled on a boot and kicked it to one side. The smell of damp clay was strong.

The tips of his fingers touched the coarse vertical seam where he had sewn two opened sugar bags together. He drew the curtain to one side, pulling it gently to avoid jamming the rings on the crude bough rail he had constructed, and stepped into the next room. It was nearly dawn and a pale greyness, as faint as mist, hovered in an open doorway. The walls, carved from clay and rock and curving upwards into a dome of shadows, glistened in the fragile light.

'You up already?' The voice came from the darkest corner of the room.

Adam nodded. 'Going to be warm,' he said, moving to the doorway and leaning against a timber upright. Outside, the world seemed split in two. The sky was awash with colour but the land was dark and stained with the dregs of night. The horizon, a jumble of low mounds and intensely black, sliced the bottom off the heavens with the precision of a razor slash.

'I'm hungry,' Josef Hoffman rose from his bed and joined Adam.

'You always are.' Adam studied the boy. He had changed a lot in the last two months. No longer the thin and pale-looking youngster Adam had seen beside the bus stranded near Port Augusta, he had become a little taller, more muscled and deeply tanned. In the faint light of pre-dawn, he seemed skinned in brown leather. Adam put his hand on the boy's shoulder, realizing, with something of a start, that his friend would grow to be a powerful man, probably bigger and stronger than he. 'You'll just have to wait,' Adam said, stepping into the open and gazing up at the sky. No cloud was in sight. It would be another hot day above ground.

He turned to the boy. 'There's no food inside and your parents won't be up yet.'

Josef scratched his stomach and carefully removed an insect that was wading through the fuzz of hair that rose to his navel.

'Any water?' He flicked the insect at a wooden beam.

'There's some in the can. Go easy with it. We'll have to try to get some more today.' Adam walked further from the doorway, touching the flanks of earth that formed the channel-like entrance and turned to study his new home. It was just a hole in the side of a hill. The boy remained, still scratching himself.

'Have a drink. Go on, there's enough for that.' Adam smiled. Josef would starve to death if he told him. 'And after you've had some, will you bring me a little? Just a little.'

The boy disappeared. The black hole remained, a rectangle of shadow that represented two weeks of hard work. Two weeks and two rooms. Not bad, he thought. And the home – his home, his *first* home – should be perfect when the summer came to sear the gibber plains that ran from these low hills. It never got hot in an underground house, the others had told him. Didn't get cold, either. The earth acted as a perfect means of insulation.

The hill was a mound, rounded like a pudding. In the full light of day it was ugly, all dust and scratchy bushes and shattered rocks the colour of sour milk, but now, in the few minutes before the sun rose, it seemed beautiful in a cool, eerie way. The first wash of light was turning its eastern face a deep red, as though someone were blowing gently on the black ashes of a fire and bringing forth a glow. A few wisps of grass, as dry as straw, clawed at the sky. There was not a tree in sight. Not on his hill. Not anywhere.

He breathed deeply. It was cooler out here.

'Here's your water.'

The boy offered him a tin can. Its outer edge was rounded and ribbed and blackened by fire. It had once held peaches, but Josef had laboriously curled the top to make it into a drinking vessel. It was half-filled with water.

'That enough?' Josef asked anxiously, as Adam raised the can to his lips.

'More than enough.' Adam let each gulp of water linger in his mouth before swallowing. It tasted of mud and olives, for the container in which they stored their drinking water had once held olive oil and, no matter how they tried to clean its surface, the aroma remained.

'Much left?' Adam asked, burping slightly.

Josef demonstrated with thumb and forefinger. 'About four inches. Just enough for a bath.'

Adam studied the sky. 'And pigs should fly today.'

Josef grinned. The only water they had for washing was in a shallow metal basin. There was just enough water in the basin to cover the first joint of his little finger. The water had not been changed for three days. They would wash in it again today.

Coober Pedy had opals, but no water.

A rough wall, crusted with stones and exuding the smell of freshly disturbed earth, ran from the side of the hill. It was made from the rocks and soil Adam had removed in scooping out his home. He had shaped it into a windbreak, to stop dust and sand blowing through the open doorway. Near the wall's end, it turned at right angles to give the effect of a half-completed courtyard.

Stepping cautiously on bare feet, Adam walked beyond the turn in the wall. A lizard scampered in front of him.

The Hoffmans' bus was parked on the other side of the wall. A canvas awning stretched to one side. The bus chassis was supported on rocks to level the floor. Long fingers of drift sand tapered from the rocks and from the bus wheels. Already the vehicle was looking derelict.

At first the Hoffmans had slept under the awning. But now the nights were growing chilly, and they had moved inside. The interior of the bus had been modified to be like a caravan, with beds, a table, some seats and an ice chest. There was no ice, of course, so the chest was being used to store some of their provisions, to protect them from the ants that had decided to share the site.

In a mining settlement where most people lived under the ground, the Hoffmans were living in the bus because Mrs Hoffman was terrified by the thought of entombment. Living within the earth was like being in a grave, and she feared death. Which was strange, Adam reasoned, because she coped with life so well.

Adam, the most bush-wise of the group, had chosen the place where the bus was stationed. It was on the eastern side of the hill to get afternoon shade, and a nearby knoll was perfectly placed to cast a long shadow when the sun swung to its higher summer orbit. But even with the blessing of the benevolent hill, the bus would be an oven for most of the day all through summer. The Hoffmans would have to move or perish.

The bus squeaked.

'I think your parents are awake, Joe,' Adam said, returning to the doorway. 'Someone's moving in there.'

Josef had put on his trousers and was struggling to tie the belt. The buckle had broken and he was trying to knot a piece of rope he had added to the leather. 'Might be mother,' he grunted, concentrating on the knot. 'I'll go and see if she wants a hand to get breakfast.'

'Better see if it tastes all right before the rest of us try it, just in case,' Adam said and Josef, grinning, ran to the bus.'

Sunrise was close now and the sky had changed from apricot to the blue of limpid watercolours. The hill was losing its magic and was starting to look rough and ugly. Adam went inside. He lit a candle. Shadows lapped the walls.

For a moment, it was a fairytale cave. Soft and glistening and mysterious. The candle beam flickered and the room seemed to sway. The light surged one way, then the other, and the grooves cut by his pick became long ribbons, twisting in a gentle breeze.

It was a rough job. He looked at the pick marks again and saw not twisting ribbons but the marks of a novice digger. Some of the miners he had met in this place dug shafts with exquisite care, leaving flat walls with herringbone patterns that were as good as you'd find on a fine suit. He had been tempted to square off the walls and ceiling and make it look more like a conventional room, but old Horrie Smith had told him to leave it like it was.

'Cut the corners out and make it look pretty and you'll have the whole thing collapsing around your ears,' the old fellow had said, so Adam had left it like it was, with the walls ribbed by rough grooves and the whole cavern shaped like the inside of an egg. Except for the floor. That was flat. He could not imagine the floor falling around his ears, so he had chipped the earth and rock to be so level that he was thinking of topping it with floorboards.

It was small. The first room, the main one, where Josef slept and all their things were stored, could be crossed in four paces. It was a little wider but, to the right, the headroom was restricted because Adam had encountered great shelves of rock that forced him to keep the roof low and to raise the floor. Where the bottom slab of rock tapered away, he had cut a deep shelf in the wall. On that shelf they stored some of their most precious possessions – the olive-oil tin with their drinking water, spare candles, matches, rope and tools. When they got food, they would put it there too. Adam intended to cut the shelf even deeper. It was cool and dry back there, and things would keep for a long time.

The room had its dry places, like that shelf, and some damp spots. Some of the dry places were too dry, and that worried him. They seemed likely to crumble. He did not share Mrs Hoffman's fixation about being buried alive but he was aware that caverns could cave in. If he jumped on the floor, he could start a trickle of gritty earth falling from the ceiling. It came from a seam that was so dry he could gouge out dirt with his fingers.

He jumped, and a fall of sand sparkled in the candlelight. A moment later another trickle of grit cascaded from the domed roof, and Adam held his breath. The fall ceased.

Part of the wall was oozing moisture. He could measure its progress by the movement of the thin, wet line that meandered down the wall, curling around projecting knobs of stone and bobbling through the maze of cuts left by the tools he had used to hack out this chamber. With a thumbnail, he scratched a groove beneath the tip of the moisture trail, and saw the new mark turn dark as the dampness spread. There was water back there somewhere.

Adam's own room was smaller. It was to the left, through an opening that was more a hole than a doorway. A rising outcrop of rock made a natural step and the opening was arched, again because Adam had been forced to follow the line of some rock that formed part of the ceiling. To give himself privacy, he had made a curtain out of sugar bags. The main room was one that anyone could use: Josef, Jimmy, anyone. But this room was his domain, a place of his own. He wanted that – somewhere, no matter how small or crude, that he could regard as his own territory. One day he would amount to something and he would have his own property, just like the rich land-owners he had done jobs for, but for now this dark little hole, off to one side of an underground chamber in the flank of a rocky hill in the arid wilderness of northern South Australia, would have to do.

His bed was a mattress made of bags he had sewn together and stuffed with straw. He sat on it and pulled on his boots. Then he lay back, legs crossed, and thought about the last few weeks.

TWO

There never seemed to be any question whether Adam, Jimmy Kettle and Nellie would accompany the Hoffmans to Coober Pedy. Mrs Hoffman insisted. It was as simple as that. Meeting the German family was a godsend, of course, a chance for the three of them to get well clear of Port Augusta. Adam, however, had said nothing to suggest he would like a lift in the bus; he was proud and he would have worn the soles from his feet before asking help from anyone. Jimmy Kettle, who had a deep-rooted mistrust of most white people, had seemed inclined to keep walking once they had slaked their thirst.

No, it was Mrs Hoffman. She was a curious woman who made a great show of being an obedient wife yet actually made most of the important decisions for the family.

She knew immediately that some violence had taken place because all three of the newcomers were bruised and cut. Anyone could have deduced that, of course, but she seemed to feel, from some deep instinct, that something awful had taken place. And so Adam and Jimmy had told her about the violence at the camp, about the killings and about their flight.

It was as though Mrs Hoffman knew. That was the strange thing. She didn't seem shocked or even surprised by what they said.

'They'll blame me for what happened,' Jimmy said, and Mrs Hoffman nodded, acknowledging the wisdom of his remark.

'The police will be after us,' Adam said.

'After me,' Jimmy said. 'They know my name. It was me they were looking for. They said I'd stolen something.'

'And had you?' Mr Hoffman asked.

'No!' Jimmy shouted, and Mrs Hoffman looked accusingly at her husband.

'That sergeant will be out to get Jimmy and me too, I suppose,' Adam said. 'We're the only ones alive who know the truth. At least, the only ones who are likely to talk. None of Jimmy's people back there at the camp are going to say anything and that sergeant knows that.'

'We're not going to talk,' Jimmy said. 'No one'd believe us. Least they wouldn't believe me. I'm only an abo and as soon as they got me in a cell, that would be it. I'd be found swinging from a rafter with a belt around my neck and they'd say I'd hanged myself.'

Hans Hoffman was deeply shocked. 'It cannot be true. You say policemen did this murder?'

'A police sergeant was there,' Adam said. 'He seemed to be the leader. He was the one who shot Mr Harris. I don't think he meant to, but he killed him all the same.'

'You should go back into town,' Hoffman said, shaking his head as though he did not believe his own words. 'Go to the authorities and have this police sergeant charged.'

'You are a fool, Hans,' his wife said gently. 'The "authorities" are the men who did the killing. Do you remember what happened when you went to the authorities, after those people set fire to the shed? They said it was just an accident. That you should go away and not pester them. They laughed at you.'

'That was diferent.'

'I fear the reaction will be the same. Maybe worse. Oh Hans, don't you *see*?' She took her husband's hand. 'If the man in charge of the police was the person who did those terrible things, what chance have our young friends got? They might well be murdered themselves. That police sergeant couldn't let them talk and send him to the gallows.'

'I believe in law and order. I believe in justice.' The tall German's eyes were closed, as though he dared not look at his wife.

'I don't know why you should. The principle is fine but the practice is very shaky. Those words have no meaning to some people. Did they mean anything to those creatures who burned our shed? Did those heroic young men who slashed our vines have a sense of justice? Those brave young people who sneaked in at night and poured kerosene into the vats, were they inspired by a sense of law and order? No, they just hated us because we were Germans.'

'But these people are not Germans,' Hoffman said miserably.

'No, but two of them are black, and that's worse. This young black man, with such a sore face' – she reached across and touched Jimmy on the cheek – 'this young man saw his friends and family killed last night for no reason other than they were black. Is that right?' She looked at Jimmy, taking her hand from his face and pointing at his eyes. 'Did your people start the fight? Did they try to kill the policeman?'

'No.' Jimmy was overwhelmed by the woman's fervour.

'No,' she repeated. 'They were just slaughtered because there are some men who think the aboriginal is no more important than some wild animal. Those men did not feel concern at killing mere blacks. Just as the good people who were our neighbours for all those years did not think it worth while making any fuss, getting into any trouble, when all those dreadful things happened to us, just because we were Germans. After all, their country had fought the Germans in the war, and some of them had had sons killed by Germans, and therefore we, who had lived peacefully among them for many years, were not worth worrying about when those ruffians, those bigoted oafs, who thought we were becoming too sucessful and posing some sort of threat to the "real" Australians, just came in and destroyed ... destroyed ... destroyed.'

'What happened?' Adam said.

The woman did not answer. The man spoke. 'We were growing

grapes just outside Adelaide. Some young people, sons of some of our neighbours, did various things to try to drive us away.'

'And they succeeded,' the woman said bitterly. 'And so Hans Hoffman, master wine-maker, is going to dig for opals.'

'I hear there are fortunes being made,' Hoffman said.

Mrs Hoffman turned to Adam. 'You will come with us,' she said abruptly. She began to smile. She had decided. 'You cannot stay here. You cannot go back to Port Augusta or your lives would be at risk. That is certain. And besides, we need someone who can help us change tyres. And maybe show us how to dig a hole in the ground. Can you dig?'

'I've sunk a few bores, dug a few dams.'

'Excellent,' she said. 'So please, all of you, travel with us even if it's just for a little while. We have food and we have water and we have room. Could you ask for more? And we, I am sure, will need you. I have a feeling more tyres will go bang before we reach our destination.'

The bus had suffered twenty-three punctures on its long journey to the opal fields. It had also been bogged in sand fifteen times, and required much digging and pushing to extricate. For a couple of days, they had followed the transcontinental railway line. At Kingoonya, after camping for two nights to regain their strength and replenish supplies, they had branched north and followed a track that speared across red gravel plains, rose and dipped through ridges of orange sand, crossed occasional creek beds of deep, powdery sand and rambled over flat lands surfaced with a fine grey dust that billowed behind them and entered every crevice in the vehicle. On the eighth day they reached their destination. The Hoffmans had travelled more than six hundred miles to reach Coober Pedy, and there was no longer any doubt that Adam, Jimmy and Nellie would stay with them and dig for opals.

Adam was growing a beard. He had only begun shaving in the last eighteen months and then only spasmodically, so abandoning the practice was an easy decision to make in a settlement that suffered a chronic shortage of water. In the privacy of his underground chamber, he stood before a fragment of mirror propped on the shelf and studied the reflection. The beard was still short and so fair that Adam rubbed the ends to make sure he had found the limits of growth. His skin reacted in a pleasant way. No wonder dogs liked being patted, he thought, and rubbed the bristling growth on his throat, stroking the hair towards the point of his chin. He studied himself in the glass. It did not look much of a beard. Most of the other men had great black or grizzly grey affairs that sometimes hung to their chests. Still, it took time to grow hair and a blond beard would surely be noticeable when it became longer.

Jimmy Kettle stepped through the opening into his room. That man could move more silently than anyone Adam knew and he turned, embarrassed.

'How's Father Christmas?' Jimmy said.

Adam made a show of fingering a scab on his throat, as though he had been examining it in the mirror. 'Good,' he said. 'How's Nellie?'

'She's good.' Jimmy sat on Adam's bed. 'You're looking more like Bror Danielsson every day.'

'Who?' Adam turned, smoothing the hair on his chin.

'A big Swede I knew in Port Pirie. He had a beard that was so pale it looked like he'd tied a white handkerchief around his throat. Big strong bugger.'

'What did you call him?'

Jimmy looked up in surprise. 'Bugger. Are you offended or something?'

'No, not that. You said he was a big something or other.'

'Swede.'

'Yeah. You mean like a carrot or turnip?'

The aboriginal laughed. 'No. Swede. He came from there.'

'Where?'

Jimmy lowered himself until he was lying on the bed. He looked at Adam, whose chin was bristling with a golden glow in the backlighting of the candle. 'You haven't been around much, have you? Don't know much about the world.'

Without waiting for an answer, he bounced to his feet and touched Adam on the chin, grinning as the beard tickled his fingers. Adam pulled his head back and Jimmy shaped to cuff him with his right hand. 'You're getting slow,' he said and skipped back, tripping on the mattress and flopping down on it. 'Swede. That's a type of man. You're probably a Swede, with all that snowy hair. Was your father a Swede?'

'I don't know. What is it?'

Jimmy reclined on the mattress once more, cupping his hands

92

behind his head and crossing one knee over the other. 'Sweden's a place.'

'You mean like Port Pirie?'

'No. It's a country.'

'Like Germany?'

'Yeah. Well, I don't know whether it's like Germany or not, but it's overseas somewhere. It's certainly not in Australia. All I know about it is that the blokes have funny names and they've got the whitest hair you've ever seen. There are a few of them working in the steel mills at Pirie. Big buggers. All slow, like you.' His right hand shot out and he flicked Adam on the ankle. Too late, Adam moved back. Jimmy put his hand behind his head again and closed his eyes.

Adam rubbed his ankle. The flick had stung. 'I hope you're comfortable on my bed.'

Jimmy nodded.

'Why don't you move in here with me? You and Nellie. There's plenty of room.'

'I'll have this bed.'

'No. This is mine. You can sleep in the other room. It's bigger, anyhow.'

'No. This bed or nothing.'

'All right, you can have my bed.'

Jimmy opened his eyes. 'No, thanks.'

'Come on. No joking. You can't stay where you are. Move in here with me. I built it for all of us.'

'Yeah, I know.' Jimmy uncrossed his legs and twisted his body, so that his feet rested on the wall.

Josef came in. 'Hello, Jimmy.'

'Good day, kid.' His eyes were closed, but the lids fluttered a greeting.

'What's a Swede?' Adam said.

The boy looked puzzled. 'You mean the thing you eat?'

Jimmy laughed and took his feet off the wall. He sat up. 'This kid has a mind that thinks of only one thing. What'd you have for breakfast, Joe? A horse and cart, or just the horse?'

Josef smiled. A piece of damper stuck to his chin. 'Do you mean a Swede? A person?'

The other men nodded.

'Well, a Swede is someone who comes from Sweden and speaks Swedish.'

'Clever bugger, isn't he?' Jimmy said.

'Where is it?' Adam asked.

'Sweden? North of Germany, across the sea. Next to Norway. Across some more water to places like Estonia, Lithuania, Latvia and Finland.'

'You're a walking encyclopaedia,' Jimmy said, enunciating each syllable. But then, cat-like, he jumped to his feet and threw a right-handed punch that stopped inches short of Josef's face. 'But don't show off.'

The boy did not move. He was used to Jimmy's mock attacks. 'Wasn't showing off,' he said, discovering the crumb and pushing it into his mouth. 'Adam asked me where it was and I told him.'

'I bet he learned a lot from what you told him.'

'I did,' Adam protested. 'Now I know what it is and where it is.'

'But you've never heard of those other places. Do you know where Thinland is?'

'Finland,' Josef corrected, and Jimmy rained more blows on his stomach.

'Finland,' Adam said. 'Know it well. It's just across the water from where Swedes come from. Near Stonia.'

'Estonia.'

'That's what I said. Joe, I've been trying to get Jimmy to stay with us, instead of sleeping out there in that kennel he's built himself. You try and convince him.'

'Yes, Jimmy,' Josef said. 'Please. How many times have we got to ask you?'

'Couple of million.'

'No, seriously.' The boy's eyes were pleading.

Jimmy tapped him lightly on the nose. 'Look, professor, you're only a kid and things are different when you're a kid, but if I moved in here and lived in the same place as you and Adam, no one would talk to you. Except the other blacks and you wouldn't want that because they stink. Look, Joe, the blacks live where I live and you live where you live.'

'Balls,' said Josef.

Adam turned on him. 'Don't use that sort of language.'

'Jimmy said bugger.'

'I don't care. You don't use that kind of language.'

'I can because I'm only a nigger,' Jimmy said and laughed so much the others joined him.

'Christ,' said Adam, 'You know what I mean. My dad never let me swear or be disrespectful and I don't think you should.'

'Adam's right,' Jimmy said, hitting Josef in the stomach with a slow-motion blow that he delivered like an exclamation mark. 'You don't want to be foul-mouthed. The people who get respect in this world are those who can speak proper.'

'Properly.'

'You young bugger.' He delivered another exclamation mark.

'But balls is all right. They're something you kick.'

'You know what you mean and I'll kick yours if you're not careful,' Jimmy said. 'Your mother would faint if she heard you talk like that.'

'She wouldn't know what I meant,' the boy said wickedly.

'And neither should you.'

'Well, if I don't use such words, will you come and stay in here with us? Please, Jimmy.'

'No.'

'Oh, but no one's going to say anything.'

'Aren't they? Anyhow, I couldn't live in a rabbit burrow like this. I'd go crackers. Got to be out in the open.'

'Well, it's up to you,' Adam said, leading them into the other room. 'I built this. It's not much but I want you to share it. There's plenty of room for you and Nellie. And there's no door, so you can see the sky outside. Joe wants you here. I want you here. It's only you that's saying no, not those blokes out there.'

'Yeah, I know,' Jimmy said. 'And so do you. Within a week, the storekeeper wouldn't sell you provisions. Then someone would throw their garbage in here and a few days later there'd be a stick of gelignite tossed in here while we were out working the claim. You know that. You know the system.'

Adam said nothing, but Josef, shuffling his feet nervously, said: 'They wouldn't do anything like that.'

Jimmy looked at him, his eyes sad but his mouth lifted in a smile. 'What happened to your dad, kid, when he tried to grow grapes? And he was just a Kraut, not even a black.'

As far as anyone knew, no aborigines had ever lived at Coober Pedy before the mines. There was nothing there for them. There was no water, no trees and so little game that a hunter would have perished seeking food in a region of dry salt lakes, withered creek beds and gibber plains. In summer, the heat reflected from the shattered rock coating the land was as searing as the lick of an open furnace. In winter, the nights brought near-freezing temperatures and, between seasons or whenever nature felt cantankerous, strong winds blew that could suck the moisture from a body or blast the skin with sand and grit.

John McDougall Stuart had explored the area in 1858. Opals were discovered in 1915. Soon after the first miners camped there, some aborigines drifted in. They were used to harsh living and found existence on the fringes of a mining camp preferable to the live-or-die business of hunting. Besides, there was liquor and the white man in outlying places was more inclined to break the law and hand out the occasional bottle of booze for some favour. Say, the loan of a wife or a young daughter for a few nights ...

The Stuart Range ran through the area, but 'range' was a grandiloquent title for a string of low, anthill-like mounds that disturbed the burning peace of the plains. Folded and buckled and trailing eruptions of stone and sand, they were pimples on the face of the earth.

Low scrub grew in pitiful clusters of vegetation, but not one tree disturbed the purity of the horizon's curve. It was the lack of suitable timber, as much as the fierce climate, that forced the opal gougers to live underground. With no timber there were no huts, and the plentiful hillocks in the vicinity of the first strikes, together with the nature of the soil, made burrowing a reasonable alternative.

Having no traditional name for a place for which they had no use, the aborigines called the site Coober Pedy, or 'white fellow's hole in the ground'.

The miners at the opal fields came in three colours. The whites, who were in the majority, lived in a scattering of underground dwellings, tents and vehicles, and because the country was so overwhelming in its sense of spaciousness and frightful emptiness, they tended to live close to each other. It was more comforting that way, and a town was developing. The Chinese, traditional miners of Australia's riches, were also there, although in smaller numbers. They too stuck together, but lived on one side of the settlement, close to the leases they operated. And there were the blacks.

About twenty aborigines lived at Coober Pedy. They kept apart from the others, having erected their crude wurlies on a gravelly plain that bore a scab of dead blue bush. The wurlies were flimsy structures, no more than hip-high and built on the lean-to principle, with a couple of sticks supporting a lattice of branches torn from the dead bushes.

In all of Coober Pedy, only one couple lived in isolation: Jimmy Kettle and Nellie.

Every night on the journey north to the opal fields, Jimmy and the girl had slept near Adam and the Hoffmans. Once they had reached their destination, however, he had taken Nellie and set up camp so far from the others that it took him fifteen minutes to walk to the hill where Adam lived. He had constructed a shelter out of a wagon wheel, bags, and cardboard. The wheel had lost its spokes and Jimmy had lowered the wooden rim, still bound by a rusting metal tyre, into a narrow trench that he had dug in the rock-hard soil. Then, with one third of the wheel buried and supported by a foundation of small stones and compressed earth, he had wired bags to the rim and stretched them to the ground, where he had secured them with rocks. Sheets of cardboard lined the inside of the structure and made a rough floor. With its part-circular entrance and tapering sides, it looked like a cone cut down the middle. But it was distinctive, and Jimmy took pride in that – even if there was not enough room for the pair of them to lie with their legs stretched out.

He had built his shelter beyond the blacks' camp. They were very different from him, coming from tribes who had hunted far to the north and speaking dialects he did not understand. They were more primitive than his people, and he despised them for it. Even the crudest of the men he knew from Beltana were superior to these people. No longer able hunters but spongers who had been thrown off remote cattle stations, they were lost souls drifting between cultures. They possessed a few grunting words of English. They were filthy and had eyes that had become matted with disease, and he could arouse no feeling of kinship with them. But he camped nearer to them than to the whites or the Chinese because they were black and he was black, they had broad noses and so did he, and he knew he should live near them.

There was one other reason why he had chosen such a remote location for his dwelling, and it was to do with survival.

Jimmy was certain that Sergeant Mailey would still be searching for him. If he came here, or sent a policeman looking for him, the first place that person would check would be in the main settlement, where Adam had dug his home. The word would quickly spread that a policeman was in town. It would spread to the blacks, who would tell him and, because he was farther from the settlement than anyone else, he would have just that much more of a start. And if Mailey or one of his men came looking for him at night, he would hear him coming across the gibber plain.

Jimmy had also changed his name. Kettle was too distinctive to retain, so, with a touch of humour, he had called himself Black. Not that surnames seemed to matter up here. In a tiny settlement that was more than three hundred miles from the nearest police station and where there was little communication with the rest of the world, he was just another aboriginal who had drifted in to the opal diggings. He had let it be known that he had stolen the girl from her tribe and was on the run from her family. Many young blacks did that and white people, generally, were sympathetic. They did not approve of the tribal system of a young girl being betrothed to an old man. Better a healthy young fellow with the guts to take the woman he wanted than some old flea-ridden elder, they said, and winked at Jimmy. He even saw envy in the eyes of some of the men and, if anyone called him anything, it was simply Jimmy.

THREE

Old Horrie was still complaining about the Chinese. 'Those bloody chows have been at it again,' he thundered as he approached Adam's lease. Adam straightened. He had been working on the windlass and welcomed the rest.

'What's up?' he said.

Horrie limped closer. His left leg had been broken in a mine accident near Coolgardie in 1897 and it had set in a bow, so that he swung his leg wide and dipped his hip with every other step.

'Thieving bastards.' He reached the younger man and spat on the heap of soil that lay piled beside the windlass. 'They've been down there again. Heaven only knows what they've taken.'

'You sure?' Adam wiped dirt from his hands. Horrie was

always complaining about something.

'Bloody sure. I'd say two of them had been down there by the marks I found. Took out maybe a dozen buckets. God knows what they got in them. I'm in the richest lode you ever seen and those yellow thieves have been sneaking down there while I've been sleeping. I tell you, young fellow, I'll do 'em in. Jesus, that's the worst thing a man can do up here, rob another bloke's lease.'

Horatio Smith had come from Western Australia in 1920, bringing with him a lifetime of mining and prospecting experience and a pathological hatred of the Chinese. He had worked on the goldfields at Coolgardie and Kalgoorlie and then gone south to the Norseman district. Thousands of Chinese had been in those places. They were poor, industrious, patient and different, four qualities guaranteed to stir discontent among others.

The Chinese were regarded as a threat. If there were jobs around, the men with funny hats and pigtails were inclined to work for less money. If someone found gold in a remote area, the Chinese would be among the first wave of followers, lugging impossible loads through spinifex and salt bush and across the brutal quartz ridges. When others abandoned a site, the Chinese moved in. Patient scavengers, they sifted through dumps, finding the gold the original diggers had overlooked. Old Horrie reckoned you couldn't admire a man for that. It was un-Australian to profit from the labours and oversights of another person.

However, his hatred stemmed from a single incident. After some years in the mines, he had gone prospecting and worked the country to the north and north-east of Kalgoorlie. It was semi-desert and tough country in which to survive, let alone find gold. He planned a journey to the Warburton Range, more than three hundred miles east of Laverton, and bought supplies from a Chinese merchant in that town. He had two horses, one to ride (because his bad leg made walking long distances impossible) and one to carry his supplies. The Chinese merchant was a fat man who always smiled. Horrie did not trust people who smiled a lot but he had no choice but to do business with him, and bought oats to sustain the animals through the worst stages of the journey. On the first night that he fed them the oats, the horses were sick. On the second night, they died. The journey back to Laverton was a nightmare, but when he reached town he found that someone had used a shotgun to blow off the merchant's head. There had been some argument over money.

Horrie felt cheated. He had wanted to kill that man himself. He loved those horses.

Adam had heard of a Western Australian weed that killed animals like that. He had once suggested that Horrie's horses might have eaten the weed, but the old man growled that the oats were poisoned and they had never talked about it again.

A hawk was circling overhead, its wings twitching as it stroked the rising currents of hot air.

Adam picked up a shovel and leaned on it. 'How do you know it was the Chinese who've been down your mine?' he said.

'That's the way they work. All smiling and bobbing their heads, but as soon as a man's back is turned, in they sneak to rob you blind. Haven't you seen the way they're always noodling around the mullock heaps?'

Adam nodded. He could see nothing illegal about fossicking through old dumps. 'It seems to me they go to a lot of trouble for very little return,' he said mildly.

'They're spying on you, that's what they're doing,' Horrie said. 'I had to chase a couple of them off the other day. Watching me, they were, and pretending to be picking up things and looking under stones. I had to tell them to piss off.'

'They were on your lease?'

'Right next to mine. I'll bet they're the ones.'

Adam felt uncomfortable. He had found the Chinese friendly. 'What are you going to do?'

'Something. We had ways in the west. Believe me, if they try anything again they'll wish their mother had never met their father.'

Adam smiled. Horrie was more than seventy and, apart from having a bowed leg, his back was bent and his hands were starting to curl from arthritis. 'Just don't break too many jaws,' Adam said, and Horrie sniffed.

'Where's your mate?'

'Down in the drive,' Adam said.

'Well, get him up, and I'll take you over to my place. I want to show you something.'

Adam bent over the shaft. 'Hey, Jimmy. Come on up for a few minutes.'

'What's up?' a voice boomed.

'Just want to nick over to Horrie's for a while.'

'I'll stay down here. It's cooler. Besides, if I get too much sun I'll turn red.'

100

'Funny bastard,' Horrie said. 'He's not a bad bloke, that abo of yours.'

'He's not mine,' Adam said. 'We're working together.'

Horrie nodded and scratched his bent knee.

'What do you reckon?' Adam asked. 'Should Jimmy come up?'

Horrie, who had been his guide to safe mining practices, shrugged. 'It's all right if he just takes a breather down there, but don't let him keep on working while no one's on top.'

Adam nodded. Horrie worked on his own but he had fifty years' experience at the game. With new chums, it was important to have at least two working as a team, and for the man at the face to have someone up top as a safety cover. Not that anyone enforced any safety practices at Coober Pedy. It was a free-and-easy town.

Jimmy was working only eighteen feet underground. Together, he and Adam had sunk a shaft to the level where opal should be found and they were digging a drive to the north-east, towards the far boundary of their lease. The tunnel was just high enough for them to negotiate on hands and knees. They took it in turns. One dug in the cool of the mine while the other winched the buckets to the top and sweltered in the sun. They only worked in the mornings. It was too hot later in the day for the man on top to keep on working, hauling up the buckets and sifting through the loads.

'Just take it easy and I'll be back soon,' Adam shouted.

'No hurry,' Jimmy answered, and Adam saw the flash of his teeth as he smiled from the bottom of the shaft.

They went to Horrie's lease, skirting the mullock heaps that surrounded some abandoned diggings.

'Take care,' the old man called as he hobbled across a ridge formed by adjoining dumps of earth. The dark rectangle of a shaft yawned on either side. Each crumbled at the edges. Weeds sprouted from the softer earth. 'Treacherous, across here. There was a bloke killed here last January,' he said, stopping briefly to rub his knee. He could have slipped and gone arse over head down the hole. In any case, he broke his back and cut himself pretty bad. Wouldn't have died straight away.' Horrie coughed and spat noisily.

'Why don't they cover them up?' Adam said, following slowly and staring in fascination at the way the other man kept his balance, despite his bad leg.

'The old mines?' Horrie spat again. 'What would they cover them with? There's no timber to spare. Oh, a few of the blokes – the ones who make all the noise in town – keep on saying that something should be done, but who's going to do it? You? Me? No bloody fear. It's just a matter of common sense. You know there are holes in the ground, so you keep clear, or take care. Anyhow, you can't mother men all their lives. There comes a time when they've got to look out for themselves. Be careful here, son.'

He moved around a low bush which partly obscured a shaft. Adam followed.

'In any case,' he said, 'most of the blokes who walk away from these diggings are broke anyway so they're not going to spend any money or time in covering up a hole in the ground.' He stopped and turned, leaning on his leg. 'Never expect anyone else to do anything for you and you won't go wrong in this world, son. Then if they do, it's a nice surprise and, if you're lucky, you'll get one or two nice surprises in your life. Only a few.' He spat and wiped his lips. 'When it comes down to it, most people are bastards anyway. Come on, I can't stand here talking all day.'

It was early afternoon and mirages were dancing on the edges of the earth.

They went down Horrie's mine, the old man going first with one foot in the bucket and Adam working the winch. Horrie grinned as he went down, for he was happier under the ground than above. His bad leg stuck out, as though he were a rider about to mount a horse. He wore pants that had once belonged to an expensive suit, a waistcoat, and a bowler hat which he chose for style but justified by saying it was the only hat strong enough to deflect falling rocks.

Adam followed, lowering himself down the rope. It was a narrow shaft, no more than three feet wide, and he had to take care, as he worked his way down, not to jag his back on the rough wall. It was a short journey, past distinctive layers of clay, then quartzite, and then a wedge of worn pebbles that looked as though they had once rolled on the bed of a river. He reached the seam of iron sandstone in which opals might be found and his feet touched ground.

Horrie had worked this claim for a year and had driven three tunnels from the shaft. He was lighting a kerosene lantern. 'This way,' he said, getting on one knee and dragging his bent leg after him.

The air was cool and, the deeper into the mine they crawled, the more did the walls breathe a hint of moisture. At first, the tunnel ran straight but then it wormed through a series of twists and dips, where Horrie had pursued promising leads. The air reeked of burned kerosene. Oily smoke stains coated the roof. In places, the walls had deep pockets gouged from them and the recesses flashed colour.

Turning, Horrie saw Adam had noticed. 'Yeah,' he nodded. 'I've found a bit. A lot of potch but some good stuff mixed up with it. Those all ran out. Just little pockets. Wait till you see what's up ahead.'

For a moment, Adam was in darkness as Horrie turned a corner but when he, too, had squeezed around the bend he found himself in a broad chamber where it was possible to stand. Some digging tools leaned against a wall. Scraps of food and a few crumpled sheets of paper were in one corner.

'Now,' said the old man, breathing heavily and pointing back the way they had come, 'I found marks on the floor made by other men's boots. I leave a very special trail and at least two men with two good legs apiece have been in here. That's point number one.' He stroked his bent leg and pointed at the wall, where a clean, vertical cut of sandstone shone in the lantern light. 'See this? When I left yesterday, there was a bulge here.' He hobbled across, and defined the former line of the wall with his hands. 'There was colour in there, too. Just a slice, thin as a knife blade, but I reckon it was going to open up into something really good. Now, it's gone. They've taken off a couple of feet of the face. Neat though, you've got to give them that. You wouldn't know they'd been here.'

He went to the other side of the chamber where he selected a prospector's pick from a pile of implements.

'Those bastards weren't clever enough, though. When I work, I cut this way. Swing like this. Got to, because of the leg.' He demonstrated, chipping at some loose flakes with a low, left-handed swing. 'It's not comfortable for me to swing the normal way, yet all these marks here were made by someone who stroked with the pick the other way. That's how I know it wasn't me who did this, just in case you're thinking I'm an old fool who can't remember what he does from one day to the next. The old memory's not too good, I know, and my mates are always ribbing me about forgetting things, but I couldn't have done that work. It's fresh, too, as you can see.'

Adam touched the wall.

'See,' said the old man, seizing his arm to make sure he did not leave. 'Fresh marks. Edges still clean-cut. Hasn't been time for them to turn powdery. Now, what's all that tell you, young feller?'

'You've been robbed.'

'Indeed I have. And last night. What else?'

Adam looked about him, as though seeking the answer in the shadows of the chamber. 'Nothing,' he said. 'I don't know who did it.'

'Oh, I do. The chows. No risk. But I don't mean that. Don't you see, they're going to come back? That's why they were so neat. They didn't want to make it obvious that someone had been down here so they went to a lot of trouble to clean up. The floor's even been swept, for God's sake. Look, you can see the marks.' Again, he grabbed Adam's arm and steered him to the place. 'They must have brought a little broom with them. Look at the pattern on the floor. I never done that. Not a footmark, though. It's only in the tunnel that you can pick up the marks they made. Too hard to sweep, I suppose. By Christ, I'd like to get hold of their pigtails and wrap them around their throats.'

He flung the tool to the ground. A shower of grit fell from the roof.

Adam looked about him. The chamber covered a greater area than the main room in his dwelling. Several small drives ran from it, radiating like spokes from a hub. 'You've been doing a lot of work,' he said.

'Yes, I have.' He spent several seconds examining the roof. 'Lot of work. Reckon I've dug enough dirt in my life to fill Sydney Harbour.'

'Ever been there?' Adam followed the other man and sat on the floor. The lantern was between them, and their shadows divided the cavern into quarters.

'Sydney? No.'

'Wonder what it's like?'

'Dunno.'

They sat in silence. Horrie chewed at a broken fingernail. 'I'm going to get those yellow bastards,' he said eventually.

'You sure it was the Chinese?'

He nodded without looking at Adam. 'Not one little doubt. 'Don't you say anything about this. I don't want anyone to know. That'd only frighten them off. I want them to come back, because when they do, I'll be ready for them.'

'Do you want a hand?'

He smiled. 'No, mate. That's good of you, but I'm not crippled yet and I know how to handle these bastards.'

'Why don't you get Fred and Bernie to come along?' They lived near Horrie and were the only other people on the diggings the old man trusted.

'No, mate. I can do this myself.'

'Take care.'

Horrie muttered something and fell silent again. It was cool on the floor.

'This is better than gold-mining,' Horrie said suddenly, as though they had been discussing that subject.

'How?' Adam picked up a fragment of rock and examined it.

'Not as hot. The last claim I worked in the west was dry. Not a scrap of water. I know it's just as dry in this God-forsaken place but at least a man can get underground, where it's cool. This is paradise down here.' He turned awkwardly. 'What you got there?'

Adam tossed him the rock and the old man turned it over in his hand. 'Rubbish,' he said, and put it in his pocket.

'I had to dry blow on the claim I had out from Leonora. Know what that is?'

'No.' Adam picked up another stone and Horrie slapped his knee.

'Never pick up things in another man's mine, son. Makes the owner nervous.'

Adam dropped the stone.

'Dry blowing is what you have to do when you're working on the surface and there's no water. Specially if you're a bit short of gear.' He reached across and picked up the stone Adam had discarded. 'Without water, you can't sluice the dirt away from the granules of gold. So you get two dishes.' He paused while he examined the stone. He threw it away. 'You fill one dish with dirt, pulverize it, and then, holding it as high as you can, let the dirt fall down into the dish below.'

He stood up, and held an imaginary dish out from his chin.

'The wind blows the light stuff away.' He puffed, imitating a desert breeze. 'When the top dish is empty, you pick up the one on the ground, which might be half-full, and go through the whole process again. You do that a few times.'

He sat down. He paused, as though thinking of something else.

'In the end, you've got just a little bit left in one dish. You pick out the stones and gravel and chuck them away, and then you blow what's left across the bottom of the dish.' Eyes closed, he breathed gently on an imaginary mix of grit and gold dust. The tips of his tea-strainer moustache fluttered.

'Makes a man very dry,' he said, and let his chin rest on his chest. He breathed deeply several times.

Adam thought he might be asleep. 'I'd better be going back,' he said softly.

Horrie opened his eyes. 'How's your mate? Working out all right?'

'Jimmy? Yes, we're getting on well.'

'Found any more opal?'

'Not since that first strike. Still, that gave us enough to buy a few things.'

'How's that woman of his?'

'Nellie? Don't see much of her.'

Horrie arched an eyebrow. 'You must be the only bloke she don't see a lot of.'

'What do you mean?'

'Nothing. It's just that she's been moving around a bit, having a word or two with a few people. I don't think she likes it here. Wouldn't mind heading south, and not too fussy who she travels with, if you know what I mean.'

'She can't go back to her tribe,' Adam said, remembering Jimmy's story about stealing Nellie from an old husband-to-be.

'Never seen an abo woman who looked less like a tribal gin in my life,' Horrie said and stood up, wincing with the effort. 'Got some work to do. See you later.'

'Yeah,' said Adam, and left.

Josef was at school. The classroom was the bus and the teacher was his mother. Every night after dinner, Mrs Hoffman saw that he studied for two hours. When Adam entered the bus, they were studying German.

He laughed. 'That's not school work,' he said, rubbing Josef's hair so that it stood up, like the comb on a cockatoo. 'You *are* German. That's like me studying Australian.'

'I'm studying the German language,' Josef said. 'There's no such thing as an Australian language.'

'You better not tell Jimmy.'

'Oh, I don't mean aboriginal,' the boy said. 'That's not a real language. Australians speak English, just like Americans or New Zealanders or South Africans.'

'But why are you learning German when you know it already?'

Mrs Hoffman spoke. She was also trying to mend a shirt. 'We are studying German because it is important that Josef knows how to speak it properly, and write it correctly. It will help him in his studies. He may wish to become a scientist, and German is the language of science, and he should not forget it.' She put down the shirt. 'Why don't you let me help you with English? It is important that you learn to read and write.'

Adam turned and pretended to adjust a curtain on a window.

'I know how you feel and I understand,' she said. 'You are a very bright person, but you will be dreadfully handicapped if you don't learn to read and write.'

'I can sign my name.'

'And that's good,' she said. 'But how will you know what you are signing if you can't read? And you will miss out on so much. Hans is a great reader and gets so much enjoyment from his books and magazines.'

Hoffman had been reading in a corner of the bus. Anemone was sprawled across his lap, asleep. 'Look what I have discovered this very night,' he said softly, holding a magazine in the air. 'I have been reading an article about opals. I may soon be the most knowledgeable man on this earth when it comes to opals. It is just that I can't find any.' He laughed and the girl stirred.

Hoffman and his son were working on a lease next to Adam's. They had found nothing, and the hard work and disappointment had etched fresh lines on his face. The lines crinkled into a smile. 'I thought, for instance, that opal was an amorphous hydrated silica. See what a clever fellow reading has made of me?'

'Hans, don't tease,' Mrs Hoffman said, concentrating on a stitch.

'I'm not teasing. That's what I thought.'

'What?' she said, looking up and biting through a thread.

'That opal was amorphous. In other words, that it had no crystal form of any kind. Now here is some fellow writing that he believes it contains microscopically small crystals of a type of silica known as crystobalite.'

'So,' she said. 'What do those big words mean?'

'That we didn't know as much about opals as we thought.'

'Is that important?' Adam asked. 'I mean, what that fellow wrote?'

'No,' Hoffman said. 'Not as important as who is prime minister or how much a loaf of bread costs. What it might explain, however, is why opals give off such marvellous colours. It could be those tiny crystals dispersing rays of light in different ways, depending on how you hold the opal.'

Adam had found an opal that flashed colours as subtle as those cast by a sunbeam through a soap bubble. He had spent hours studying it and holding it to the light, and sold it for twenty pounds. He could appreciate the beauty of the stone but had no idea what caused it to flash so dramatically.

'I wish I could understand those sort of things,' he said.

'If you learned to read, you could,' Mrs Hoffman said. 'Why don't we have, say, thirty minutes every day, and I'll teach you. You're so smart I'm sure you'd learn very quickly.'

'Maybe,' Adam said.

'Good,' she said. 'We'll start tomorrow.'

Hoffman shuffled his magazine. 'You do not have to be able to read to realize that my wife is a very determined woman who does not necessarily listen to what men say.'

Adam stayed a little longer. Often, he listened to the lessons while mending something, or glancing through the pictures in one of Mr Hoffman's magazines, but he found the German lesson incomprehensible. He decided to go to bed, and excused himself.

It was cool outside. The sun had set an hour ago but only the brightest stars glowed in a sky that was still tinged with the blue of daylight. He was wearing shorts and a faint breeze tickled his legs. The air was thick with smells and sounds. Smoke from cooking fires lapped the rim of the hills. The aroma of a dozen meals drifted past. He heard a woman's raucous call to a child. A dog barked. Two men were arguing. A clatter of laughter, sharp as jangling crystal, burst from the Chinese camp. The Hoffmans' lesson droned on.

Mrs Hoffman was asking a question in the tone that teachers always seemed to use, no matter what the language.

'*Funfhundert*,' Josef said, laughing, and Adam was swamped by a sense of shame. He loved that pair and yet he had no idea what they were talking about. He might as well be the family dog – loved, but never their equal. It was strange: Josef depended on him and regarded Adam as his natural superior, but if Adam did not learn things then it would be the young German who would

108

become a boss and it would be Adam who would work for him.

Mrs Hoffman could read and write in four languages. He would try to learn one. He might even learn some German.

'*Schnell*,' demanded Mrs Hoffman, her voice muffled.

'*Vierundzwanzig*,' answered Josef, his voice bright and certain of the answer. Adam smiled. There was no doubt about it, young Joe was a smart kid.

FOUR

A lizard scurried for shelter as Adam neared the entrance to his underground home. He paused, conscious of something or someone near him. He turned but there was no one in sight.

'Anyone inside?' he called and entered the burrow. He groped for the candle. The familiar scent of wet clay mingled with another, faint and pleasant, that he remembered from somewhere, some other dark night. He turned.

'Don't light the candle.' It was Nellie's voice.

'Where are you?' His heart was pounding. 'You gave me a hell of a fright.'

'I'm over here.' The voice came from the direction of his room.

'Where's Jimmy?'

'I don't know.'

His eyes were growing accustomed to the dark. Her body was a shadow sloping across the entrance to his room.

'Would you like some water?' he said. 'I got a fresh lot today.'

'I had some.'

'Oh.'

She retreated to his room and he could no longer see her. 'What are you doing here?' he said, following her.

'Aren't I welcome?'

'Of course you are. Oh,' he said, suddenly relaxing, 'are you and Jimmy going to move in?'

'Not Jimmy. He's too nervous to leave that rabbit hutch he's built out in the middle of nowhere. But I'm ready to move in with you.'

'Well, I don't know.'

'Why don't you light a candle now?' she said. 'I can't see you.'

Adam touched the shelf and fumbled with a match. The light flared. She was close to him, leaning against the wall with her hands behind her hips. His shadow flickered across her body.

'Are you on your own?' she said.

'Yes. Joe's doing school with his mother. They're learning German, would you believe. Nellie, what are you doing?'

She had begun to take off her dress. She paused with her face half-covered. Her legs were exposed. Her skin seemed dark and shining against the raw rock.

'I'm tired,' she said. 'I want to go to bed.'

'But that's my bed. I'll have to make up one for you outside. Young Joe sleeps out there too.'

She dropped her dress on his mattress.

'I thought you were supposed to wear things under that,' he said. His voice was husky and he coughed.

She placed cool fingers on his chest. 'Not always,' she said.

Adam had never seen a naked woman before. Not a young one. Nellie had a beautiful body, and a tremble of excitement shook his belly.

'Someone will see you,' he said.

'You're seeing me.'

He spun away from her. 'Nellie, get dressed. Or get under the blanket. Do something.'

She put her arms around him. Her breasts burned into his back. 'How's this?' she said. 'You're very big. And strong. Lovely muscles.'

One hand stroked his shoulder.

He shook clear of her touch and turned. 'Stop it,' he whispered. 'Someone will come in and see you.'

She took his hand and placed it on her left breast. 'Don't you like me?'

He pulled his hand away. 'Christ, what are you trying to do?'

'Why are you so shy?' she said, laughter on the fringe of her voice.

'Someone might see you. See us.'

'Oh, if that's all you're worried about.' She slipped past him and blew out the candle. 'Now, no one can see me. Or you.'

She touched his waist.

'Nellie,' he hissed, backing away. 'Light the candle again. Get dressed.'

She giggled. 'Haven't you had a woman before?'

'What do you mean?'

'Oh, Adam, where have you been?'

He had backed against the wall. Her silhouette swayed in the faint light from the doorway. She advanced.

'Do you like me?' She was close, but he could no longer see her.

'Yes. Of course.'

'My father was white.' A hand slipped inside his shirt.

'Was he?' Adam heard his voice and was surprised. It sounded like someone else speaking.

'He was a ship's officer. He was very tall. He came from Finland.'

'That's near where the Swedes come from.' Adam's leg muscles were tensing uncontrollably.

'Is it?' she purred. Her hand toyed with his belt.

'Please, Nellie!'

'Does that mean please do or please don't? Oh, aren't you big!'

Adam's first impulse was to hit her. No one had ever touched him there before. He had been kicked there but never caressed, and her touch was so gentle. He put one arm around her, and held her roughly. His body was quivering.

'Here,' she said, using her free hand to unbutton his shirt, 'let me help you.'

Horrie Smith was prepared to wait all night. He had settled into a hollow near an abandoned shaft and covered himself with a sheet of canvas. There was no moon, and he reckoned someone would have to step on him to see him. He had a flask of rum and took an occasional sip. He hated the cold.

They came at one-thirty in the morning.

Horrie had just dozed and, shaking himself awake, saw a shadow move. The shadow divided into two forms. Two men, bent low, were heading towards his lease. One had a torch which he held almost at ground level. He knew where he was heading and unerringly followed a path between dumps and mine shafts until he reached Horrie's lease. The leading man kneeled and fiddled with a bag he had been carrying.

'Keep going, you yellow bastards,' Horrie mouthed. He licked his lips.

The light went out. The two men, lying on the ground now,

glanced around to make sure they had not been seen. They did not speak.

Horrie kept his face pressed against the earth. 'No one's watching you, you thieving pair of chows,' he said to himself. 'Just go down the mine and see what I've got for you.'

The two men did not move for more than a minute. From somewhere, a colony of insects throbbed with a sound so faint that it was felt rather than heard. The stars blazed in icy silence.

There was a slight squeak and the hiss of rope and one man disappeared. The windlass worked in near silence, and so it should have, for Horrie had spent some time that afternoon oiling and adjusting it.

The other man followed.

Horrie had a drink. He was so stiff that standing was difficult. Painfully, he limped towards the shaft. He needed no light. He knew every inch of this piece of land and he did not want to risk being seen. And he was in no hurry. He wanted to be certain the intruders were well into the drive before he went down. He reached the top of the shaft. He could hear no sound, nor see any light. He waited.

Eventually, the sound he anticipated reached him. It was a steady chipping noise.

With great care, Horrie winched the bucket to the surface. The chipping continued. He lowered himself. Once, the windlass creaked and he stopped, fearful of discovery. Chip, chip, chip. The ring of metal against rock continued.

At the bottom of the shaft, he stepped awkwardly but quietly from the bucket. He crawled into the tunnel. The sound was louder now and ringed by faint echoes. A light, pale as a gas flame, hovered on a wall where the tunnel turned.

Hands lifted to touch the roof, Horrie searched for the first fuse. His fingers found it, still in the groove he had cut. He pulled it down and crawled along the passageway, feeling for the second one.

The digging stopped.

The old man waited, not daring to breathe. There was a clicking sound, as though someone had dropped something. No one spoke. The chipping resumed.

Horrie found the second fuse, pulled it clear of its hiding place and touched the explosive, to make sure the charge was in place. He needed to strike a match and timed it to coincide with the regular stroke of the pick. He lit the end of the fuse, shuffled back down the tunnel, and lit the other one. He started counting. At twenty, he was able to stand in the bottom of the shaft. It took him another five to get in the bucket and ten more to haul himself a few feet from the floor. There, he waited.

The explosions almost coincided and he smiled with pride. A blast of air rushed from the drive and he coughed as layers of dust shuffled up the shaft. He waited for the air to clear and lowered himself. He only needed a few seconds to confirm that the tunnel was blocked.

He hauled himself to the top, lowered the bucket again, took a long swig of rum and began the slow journey back to his dwelling. His leg hurt, but he felt good.

FIVE

'I love your beard,' she said, stroking the fuzz on his chin.

He wriggled away from her and put his hand on her lips.

'Shh. Joe will hear you,' Adam said.

Nellie giggled and locked her ankles around his leg.

'He's asleep. I can hear him snoring.' She took his hand and lowered it to her bare breast. Adam wrenched his hand clear and listened for any sound from the other room. The rasp of heavy breathing filtered through the rough curtain separating the two underground chambers.

'He's not snoring,' Adam said weakly.

'He's asleep though.' She touched his chin once more, and he let his head drop back on to the mattress.

'It tickles,' she whispered, and blew gently in his ear. 'And it's lovely and white.'

'You'll have to go,' he said. 'It'll be dawn soon.'

She let a cool fingertip trickle down the side of his face.

'Where will I go?'

'Back to Jimmy.'

'Not out there. Not in that rat's nest.'

'But you're his girl.'

'I thought I was your girl.'

He turned his head. God, what had he done? He sat up, and she entwined her arms around his waist.

'You must go,' he said. 'Joe will be awake soon and he'll come in this time. Besides, Jimmy will be looking for you.'

'No, he won't. Not here, anyhow.'

'Get dressed.'

She squeezed harder. 'He might look in the Chinamen's camp but he won't come here. Let's do it again.'

'Why would he look for you with the Chinese?'

'Because that's where I've been.' She rubbed her chest against his.

'Stop doing that.'

'I thought you liked it.'

He sighed. 'Be quiet. You'll wake Joe.' And then, after a pause, he added: 'When were you in the Chinamen's camp?'

'The last few nights.'

'What for?'

'They pay good money.' She released her hold and ran her fingers through her hair. 'I've got to get out of this place and if no one'll take me, I'll have to buy a ride with someone.'

Adam stood up, confused. 'You've been doing this? With the Chinese?'

'You're all the same when the lights are out.'

He groped for her frock and, finding it near the shelf, threw it at her. Even in the dark, he could see the flash of her eyes.

'I've been doing it with the Greeks and Dagos too,' she said, so loudly that he turned, certain that Joe would hear. 'So what? Everyone does it. Everyone likes it. Why not get paid for it?'

'I haven't got much money,' he said bitterly and began to put on his trousers.

'You don't have to pay,' she said, slipping the frock over her arms. 'It was fun. Never had such a big man who'd never done it before. You can pay next time.'

'There won't be a next time,' he said, and led her through the other room and out into the night.

'I think I'll go and find myself a Chinaman,' she whispered, and walked away.

Adam watched her leave, her hips swaying in an exaggerated roll, and felt the heat rising in him again. He felt confused and ashamed, and sat on a rock and waited for the sunrise.

*

A camel train reached town soon after ten o'clock. There were sixteen animals in the line. They were tethered nose to tail and laden with crates and sacks and drums that they had carried from the railway at William Creek. The camels had travelled through Anna Creek cattle station and then spent four days winding through the sand ridges and salt pans to the south of Lake Cadibarrawirracanna. A windstorm greeted their arrival and their swaying loads bobbed above the fury of dust like flotsam on a brown torrent.

One man rode astride the leading camel. His face was wrapped in white cloth and his body, hunched against the storm, was shrouded in a loose blue garment which flapped in the wind. Another man, smaller and younger and dressed more conventionally in shirt and trousers, walked alongside the animals, flicking a long stick and occasionally bursting into a run to whack the hide of some beast which had aroused his displeasure.

A gust of wind, more violent than the rest, lashed the procession. The rider bent his covered head, the young man on foot turned his back to the wind and the camels, moving with the precision of a squad of trained dancers, raised their legs in sequence as the sting of sand touched their knobbly knees.

They passed the underground water tank, which was the only source of water in the town. The tank had been constructed seven years earlier and could hold half a million gallons of rainwater but, as Coober Pedy had more dust storms than rainstorms, the tank was mainly filled with dirt. Two men sheltering behind a dray, near the tank's hand-pump, waved a greeting. The man on the camel responded with a thin hand which emerged briefly from the blue shroud and then clutched at the billowing garment to wrap it tightly across his body.

The camel train snaked its way towards the store. The building was a small, oblong structure with walls of corrugated iron nailed horizontally to uprights which were no more than roughly trimmed tree trunks. A row of drums, dented and sandblasted, stood at one corner. At the back of the building lay a scattering of wooden crates and a small pyramid of empty bottles.

In the doorway was a man. He leaned against one post and had his thumb tucked into the front pockets of his waistcoat.

'Lovely bloody weather,' he said when the rider of the leading camel had drawn level. 'And don't give me that bloody Afghan

115

bullshit about it being the will of Allah.'

'Yet it is the will of Allah,' said the rider from within the folds of his headdress. He pressed a whip against his mount's shoulder, and the camel folded its legs and see-sawed to the ground.

The rider dismounted. The wind plucked at his clothing. The other camels shuffled to a halt, their jaws rolling and their eyes weepy and wreathed in sadness.

The Afghan unravelled the cloth that covered his lower face, revealing a long nose that curved toward a lean brown jaw. Stained teeth glistened in a smile.

'Truly, only a man as inspired by greed as you would choose to isolate himself in this substitute for hell,' he said, and touched his forehead. 'And how are you, my friend?'

'Bloody awful,' said the man in the waistcoat, and shook the camel-driver's hand. 'Got everything?'

'Everything,' he said and raised his other arm, as though offering thanks to the Almighty for allowing such a miracle to happen.

'Potatoes?'

'Of course. The finest I have ever seen.'

'Bullshit. How's your nephew making out?' The man straightened in the doorway and glanced down the road at the young man with the stick who was beating a camel which refused to kneel.

The other man sighed. 'He is as much comfort to me in my old age as a vest of thorns. But he enjoys the work.'

A gust of wind rattled the iron walls of the store. The storekeeper blew his nose and spent a few seconds studying the fresh stain on his handkerchief.

'What was the trip like this time?' he said, looking up at the other man. 'Any better?'

'The track around the lake with the impossible name becomes more difficult with every journey. In truth, it is so bad I do not know why I subject myself to so much misery by coming to this accursed place.'

'You come here because you enjoy robbing me.'

'You have a cruel mind, to say something that causes me so much pain.'

'And you, Saleem Benn, are a thieving arsehole. Come inside and get out of this bloody wind. Don't suppose I could tempt you to have a drink?'

The Afghan smiled. 'Your generosity overwhelms me but your desire to turn me from the true path continues to sadden me. You know ...'

'Yes, I know. The will of Allah or something. You don't think he'd see you in here, do you? After all, it was you who reckoned this place was like hell. Surely this Allah of yours wouldn't be in hell?' The storekeeper smiled and waited, taunting the other man to respond.

'He is everywhere,' the Afghan said with great patience, and walked back to the track. There, he signalled his nephew that he was about to enter the store. The young man waved his understanding, and began beating the camel nearest him.

'He gets great pleasure from hitting the animals,' the Afghan said softly when he rejoined the storekeeper. 'But he does not hit hard. To him it is a game, and I think in truth he is still frightened of such imposing beasts.' He sighed. 'It is often the case with people who have a lack of confidence in themselves that when they feel something – fear, love, even respect – they will go to great lengths to appear to feel something else. Is that not so, my friend?' He had eyes of an intensely dark brown and he fixed them on the other man. The storekeeper squirmed.

'You talk a lot of bullshit,' he said, and led the Afghan into the building.

It was dark in the store. There were no lights and the shutters had been closed against the storm. The iron walls drummed to the beat of the flying sand.

Saleem Benn lowered his head and gently wiped grit from his closed eyelids. When he had finished, he looked up to see a young black woman sitting quietly in a corner of the store. It was Nellie. She had made herself a seat among some sacks.

'Get off that stuff,' the storekeeper growled and turned to the Afghan. 'She's been here for a couple of hours. Wants a lift to the railway. Reckons she's got money.'

Saleem Benn pulled the cloth flowing from his headdress across his mouth. His eyes said 'No.'

'Might help pass the nights,' the storekeeper suggested, his eyes widening to make sure the inference was understood.

'It is not possible,' the Afghan hissed.

The man shrugged. He walked to Nellie.

'He won't take you,' he said. 'Nick off.'

'I've got money,' Nellie pleaded.

117

'I told him that. Do you want to buy anything? Lollies, tobacco or something?'

'No.'

'Well, piss off.' He grabbed her arm and pulled her away from the sacks. 'Come on, you make the place look untidy.'

'It looks like a brothel anyhow,' she said.

He tried to slap her, but she jumped clear. She faced him for a few seconds until, sure he would not strike again, she relaxed and tucked some loose hair into place.

'In fact,' she said, 'it's worse than a brothel.'

'Yeah, and I bet you'd know,' he said. He raised his hand. 'Now get out before I give you a belting.'

She did not move. He picked up a broom. She backed away. To leave the store, Nellie had to negotiate a narrow corridor between a shelf stacked with clothing and some wooden crates against which leaned a row of shovels. She brushed against the robe of the Afghan. 'Thanks very much,' she said softly.

'Cheeky young bitch,' the storekeeper said, and lunged at her. She scampered through the open doorway. The wind shredded her hair and moulded her frock to her body. The Afghan watched.

'Ought to take the lot of them out in the bush and shoot them,' the storekeeper said. He put the broom against the counter.

'You are too harsh,' Saleem Benn said. Nellie had begun to walk away.

'Who's harsh? You're the bastard who wouldn't take her.'

'That was an act of kindness.'

'Bullshit. You just like to stuff camels – rather have a black camel than a black woman.'

The Afghan took a deep breath. 'Truly, my friend, I find your words distressing.'

'Too right, because they're true.' He lifted his waistcoat and scratched his stomach. 'She'd have been all right for a couple of days, at least till you could have put her on the train at William Creek. Better-looking than most of them. Most of the blacks, I mean, not camels.' He roared with laughter.

The Afghan went to the doorway. The leading camel returned his stare.

'Can a man not love his animals without vile things being suggested?' he asked. 'And can a man not reject a plea for assistance when to give that help would cause suffering?' He turned and his robe shuffled as he folded his arms. 'It would have been cruel to have taken that young lady where we have to go. Can you imagine the suffering one has to endure near the lake with the impossible name when the winds blow and dust fills the air?'

'No worse than here,' said the storekeeper.

'Oh, it is different,' Saleem Benn said and gazed down the road, where the string of resting camels faded in the murk of dust. His young assistant was now sitting beside one of the animals. He had his head between his knees. Nellie had gone from sight, but an old man was hobbling towards the store.

'Someone is braving the wind to do business with you,' Saleem Benn said and the storekeeper joined him in the doorway.

'Horrie Smith,' he said. 'He won't spend much.'

The Afghan touched his forehead. 'I will go to tend my camels and to speak to my nephew. It would seem he has done so much whipping he has exhausted himself.' He left and the wind turned his clothing into sails.

The storekeeper waited for Horrie. 'What brings you out in this weather?' he asked when the old man had reached the building.

'Just want to get out of this wind,' he said.

'Not working this morning?'

Horrie shook his head. He limped through the store, looking around him as though searching for something, and then sat on the sacks where Nellie had rested.

'You all right?' the other man asked.

Horrie nodded. 'Had anyone in this morning?'

'A few people.'

'Any Chinese?'

The storekeeper shook his head. 'Why?'

'Nothing. Just heard there'd been some trouble down in the Chinese camp.' Horrie stared intently at the other man.

'Never heard a thing. What sort of trouble?'

'Couple of blokes missing. Something like that.' His fingers tapped a rapid march on his knees to hurry the pace of the response.

'What do you mean, missing? You all right, Horrie?'

The old miner stood up. 'Good as gold,' he said. 'So you haven't heard anything about a couple of Chinese being missing?'

'Not until now. Why? Is there some sort of noise over their way?'

'Place is quiet as a church. Can't work it out,' Horrie muttered.

The storekeeper scratched his head. 'Well, I don't know what you're talking about, but I haven't heard anything about any Chinese, missing or present.'

Horrie sniffed. 'I need some metho for the stove. Got any in?'

The storekeeper wrapped a bottle of methylated spirits in newspaper and handed it to him. Horrie scratched in his pocket for the money.

'Want anything else?' the storekeeper asked.

Horrie examined a crowbar. He looked up. 'Bloody strange, isn't it?'

'What?'

'Doesn't matter,' he mumbled. 'When are you getting some spuds in?'

'Just arrived. Should have them unloaded in an hour or two.'

'Well, keep some for me, will you?'

The storekeeper opened a notebook. 'How many do you want?'

Horrie moved to a sack where bags of nails were kept. 'You sure none of the Chinese have been in this morning?'

'Absolutely. Now, how many do you want?'

'How many what?'

'Oh, for Christ's sake, Horrie! How many spuds?'

'I don't know. Whatever you reckon.'

The man closed the book. 'Would you like me to peel them and mash them as well, and bring them down to your place when you feel like eating?'

Horrie looked up. 'Have you seen Fred or Bernie about?'

'Not for a couple of days.'

'I might go and have a word with them. It's bloody strange.'

'You're bloody strange,' the man said to himself as Horrie limped from the store.

Outside, the old man watched the two Afghans begin the task of unpacking the camels. He stayed there for some time, looking but not seeing, for his mind was on other things. He had buried two Chinese during the night, but this morning the Chinese camp seemed normal. No one was wailing in distress. No one was searching for missing friends. In fact, no one seemed to be missing.

SIX

The candle had burned low and the flame was spluttering in melted wax. Adam stopped digging to light a new one. He was glad of the rest. It was hard work in the small drive he had started and his skin oozed sweat. He stank. The smell had nowhere to go in such a confined space and every breath he took was filled with a reminder of his exertions. His back ached from the constant bending and his arms were weary from wielding his small pick.

He concentrated on lighting the new candle. The wick flared. He let a few drops of molten wax splash on the sloping shelf where he had been working, rammed the base of the candle into the wax and held it steady until he was sure the joint had set. The kopi, or claystone, in which Adam had been digging was a light honeycomb colour and, with the candle erect, the flame burned in a tiny arched gallery of intense brightness.

Some of the miners worked in the dark to save the cost of candles. They dug by touch and sound, recognizing the abrasive scratch of opal-bearing ground and being able to discover and work around a find in the dark without damaging any of the precious stones. But they were experienced men who had mined for years. They were also broke, so they developed their peculiar skills through necessity. Adam needed light. He had only found opal on one occasion and was not sure what sound his pick should make when it struck a promising seam. Finding opal by candlelight was difficult enough. Trying to do it in the dark, with the possibility of missing good opal or, worse still, destroying it with a casual blow of the pick, was a risk he would not take. Besides, he preferred the comfort of the light. He liked being underground because it was so quiet and cool, but he found the utter blackness of an unlit tunnel overwhelming.

He resumed digging. He had cut a deep slot in the wall, following a level, because he knew that opal might be found at the end of this descending crack in the claystone. In ages past, water rich in silica may have flowed down such a line and come to rest in a pocket of rock, there to harden into the glass-like substance called opal. The colours were purely a matter of refracted light. That much he had learned from Mr Hoffman. He could not understand why but accepted that opal had no colour of its own. Its magic was in being able to bend white light into rays of gorgeous colours. Something to do with those crystals that Mr Hoffman had been talking about, and the way certain crystals turned light in certain ways.

Adam thought about Nellie and swung hard with the hand pick. He didn't want to think about her. He made himself think about opals.

Some people claimed the stones were unlucky, but the Hoffmans reckoned that was just because European opals, mined in Hungary hundreds of years before, were inclined to crack or craze. They said those opals were mainly volcanic and had a high water content, so that when they dried they broke up and became worthless. The opals here were different. What was the word? Sedimentary. That meant all this land had been under water. Hard to imagine.

He levered loose a large slab of claystone and shuffled back as it fell near his knees. Even here at Coober Pedy some opals contained a large proportion of water and, once exposed to the air, they tended to dry and crack. Strange, that, he thought. A stone that had taken millions of years to develop and then had been buried out of the sunlight for a few more million years could craze and become worthless within months, once exposed to light and air. Like butterflies. Adam prepared to make another stroke with his pick. Butterflies spent months hidden in cocoons and then suddenly they turned into beautiful, floating creatures that perished in a day or two. It was as though nature intended its most spectacular creations to be fragile to emphasize the rarity of a truly beautiful thing.

The tip of his pick bounced from the surface. It made a scratching noise. It was different from the dull thunk it had been making as he chipped away at the kopi. This was a harsher sound and the hairs on the back of his neck tingled. He shifted the candle, moving it closer to the rock face. The level had widened into a seam of red. Within that seam, tiny patches of a whitish substance glistened in the candlelight. He brushed away some grains of dirt and touched the white spots. They were hard. He tried to lever one out of the surrounding earth but it seemed to be deeply embedded. Gently, he used the blade of an old screwdriver to scrape flakes of claystone from the new area. Again he brushed dirt away and saw a wedge of pale white. He chipped more earth away and a much larger slab of white was revealed. Potch. Opal all right, but worthless. It had no colour.

Adam settled himself on his haunches and shook his head. His hair sprayed dust. Still using the old screwdriver, he dug around the exposed potch. He could not afford many tools, and the screwdriver was good for fine work. He had found it on the ground at Crowder's Gully, where the initial opal strikes had been made about fourteen years earlier. That area was sprinkled with the relics of failed enterprises.

A spot of perspiration hovered on his eyebrow and he wiped it clear. He ground the blade into the seam of red grit and winced. His father would have thrashed him for using a screwdriver for digging. His father had been meticulous about using implements for their proper purpose. He smiled at the memory. A little boy, hacking away at an old iron bar he had found and ruining his father's rasp, and running away to elude his father until he had to go back to the camp to eat ...

No one was going to give him a belting for mistreating this screwdriver. It had been years since the tool had touched a screw. Even when Adam had found it the metal was grey with age and the blade rounded from gouging. He wondered who had owned it. Had he made his fortune like a few men who had come to Coober Pedy, or had he trudged down south, penniless? That's the way most of the miners left. Some managed to sell what they had, like Darkie Robinson who ran out of cash and credit and sold his dugout, all his mining and camping equipment, and an old Ford truck for ten pounds. He left owning only the clothes he wore but at least he had a few quid in his pocket. That was more than most of the new arrivals had been bringing with them in the last few weeks. They were all talking about something called the Depression, and about how tough life had become. They did not impress Adam. Things had always been tough.

The potch thinned and ran out. The red seam, however, continued. It was as bright as jam in a sponge cake and its course began to descend.

Adam followed it, working at a furious pace, first with the large pick and then, as he narrowed the depth of the drive, with the small hand pick. The claystone was flaky and he made rapid progress.

He was working on his own. It was the first time he had been down the mine without Jimmy to help him, but Jimmy had not arrived at the mine site and Adam, embarrassed at the happenings of the previous night, had not gone looking for him.

Adam kept digging. He spread the loose rock on the tunnel floor behind him and hacked and wormed his way deeper underground, following the tantalizing thread of red grains that marked some prehistoric division in the earth. The level continued to descend. The red line grew thicker. Adam became excited. Because it was running downhill, water could have trickled down the same path millions of years ago, and if there was silica in the water it could have set into opal. All it needed was some hollow in the rock to act as a cup and let the silica begin to gel and harden into stone.

He wanted to keep going. He knew he should clear the fallen rock and leave an unimpeded space behind him, but he decided to keep digging at least while he still had room to swing the small pick.

He first realized he was in trouble when his foot became jammed. He had cut a long, tapering wedge into the claystone and had squirmed, lizard-like, into it. As he dug he passed loose rock and dirt along his body and used his feet to push it back down the tunnel. Then, as he made a hefty push, rocks from the roof of the tunnel fell on his left foot and it took him several seconds to free it.

He looked back but could see little in the massive shadow cast by his upper body. He took the candle from its latest perch near the seam and, twisting in the narrow tunnel, held the light near his knees.

What he saw horrified him. His feet rested against a wall of cut rock and partly compressed dirt – a solid mass, strong as a dam wall, that he had been kicking and stamping into place. There was a shallow opening at the top, so he was still getting air. Of course he could dig himself out, just like he had dug his way in. But to do that he would have to turn, to get his head and hands next to the wall, and he was so tightly squeezed into the drive that turning was imposible.

He had sealed himself in the mine.

A post office is among the most imposing buildings in a town: all tall columns and wide steps. Or, if the settlement is too small to deserve such magnificence, it may have wide, impressive walls of dull brick, sliced into oblongs of trusty respectability by a noughts-and-crosses pattern of neatly scored white mortar. The post office is a measure of a town's substance.

The Coober Pedy post office was a dugout. It was set in the side of a hill. The hill had the patchy pancake colour of weathered and bleached claystone, and its base sloped gently so that the entrance to the dugout was through a tapering trench. There was a red 'Post Office' sign embedded in the earth to identify the establishment, and a sheet of corrugated iron jutting above the door to prevent small stones rumbling down the hill and hitting customers on the head.

The post office had been there since 1920. The mail was carried by a contractor who drove his truck once a week from the east—west railway at Kingoonya.

The postmaster, Benjamin Moore, was sweeping the floor, trying to get rid of some of the dust, when Horrie Smith walked in. The old miner ducked his head to avoid hitting his bowler hat on the corrugated iron awning, and then, having negotiated the hazard, rapped his hat against his leg to shake the dust from it.

The postmaster waited for him to finish and then swept the fresh dust from the floor.

'You're a funny old coot,' Horrie said, replacing the hat at the appropriate angle.

'If I let the dust stay where it fell, there'd be no room for me inside a week,' Moore said. He was wearing braces and pants and a white, collarless shirt. 'What can I do for you?'

'Just wanted to get out of the wind. Crook, isn't it?'

'Real bastard.'

Horrie removed his hat, examined it for a few moments, and then put it back on his head.

'Any of the Chinese been in today?' he asked casually.

Moore put the broom against an earthen wall. 'One came in this morning. Han Ling. The old bloke with the crook foot. Why?'

'Just wondering. Heard there'd been some trouble over in their camp.'

'Did you? Han Ling didn't say anything.'

'You sure?' Horrie took his hat off again.

'Absolutely.'

'Nothing about anyone being missing?'

The postmaster shook his head. 'What's up with your hat?'

'Nothing.' Horrie put it back on again. 'Seen Bernie about?'

'No.'

'Or Fred?'

125

'His mate? No. Why?'

'Just looking for them.'

'Probably out of the wind if they've got any sense.'

Horrie tapped his bad leg. 'Anything else happening?'

'Don't know about anything *else*. I don't think *anything's* happening. Might in a day or two, though, when the policeman gets here.'

'A copper? What's he coming for?'

Moore took the broom again and mustered a scattering of gravel that had been blown through the doorway. 'A bloke called Travers reckons he's been robbed. He wrote to the police.'

'Who's Travers?'

He had assembled the gravel into a small pile and swept it out through the door. 'A new bloke in town.'

'Don't know him. Don't like some of these newcomers. They're stirrers.' Horrie spat on the floor and then, conscious of Moore's look of distaste, covered the spot with his boot. 'What'd he lose, anyhow?'

'Opal. What else?'

Horrie grunted and ground his boot over the spittle. 'Never prove that,' he said. 'It's one man's word against another's. No point calling the police. You take care of things yourself.'

'Well, he's new,' Moore said, replacing the broom once more and examining the floor with suspicion, in case more dirt had gusted in while he was talking. He walked behind the counter.

'The place is changing, Horrie,' he said. 'Not like the old days. It's this Depression. Strange lot of drifters coming up these days.'

'When's the copper due?' Horrie took his hat off again and spun the crown on one finger.

'Tomorrow. Day after, maybe.'

Horrie stood up. 'Those Chinese are a queer bunch, aren't they?'

Moore looked puzzled. 'How do you mean?'

'Did one of them send for the police?'

'No. I told you. It was a bloke called Travers. He's a pommie, I think.'

'Do the Chinese have much to do with the police?' Horrie limped to the door and spat again. 'You know,' he said, turning and wiping his mouth, 'do they go to the police when there's trouble or do they keep to themselves?'

'I wouldn't have a clue. What's this with the Chinese, anyhow?'

126

'Probably keep to themselves,' Horrie said, ignoring the question, and stepping out into the dust.

The postmaster began to walk after him. 'The storm's still blowing,' he called, but the old miner had gone.

Adam had been thinking of Tiger.

The old man had been a good teacher. 'When you're in trouble,' he had said, 'slow down and take the time to work out what you should do. Don't rush or you'll turn a small problem into a disaster.'

Adam remembered the advice because Tiger had given it to him so many times, so he spent a few minutes just lying in the trap he had made for himself, thinking about what he should do.

At first he was frightened. It was a strange fear, new to him, of being hemmed in. For a few minutes he imagined he could not breathe, but it was just the fear and he forced himself to take slow, deep breaths. There was air, and he felt better.

He had so little room he could only just roll on his side, but he did that and gazed at the candle burning brightly near his face, and at the streak of red in the rock wall that had tempted him so far into this ridiculous, worm-like position. He forced himself to think of the things that were in his favour. He closed his eyes, taking comfort from the yellow glow of the candle. The flame was so close that he could feel the heat on his forehead and eyelids, but the rest of him was cool. That was good. It would be unbearable to be trapped down here in great heat. What else? Well, he was tired and at least he could rest for a while. A rest might do him good, for he would need strength to burrow his way out.

So it was cool, and he could rest where he was. He thought about those two advantages and decided that they were heavily outweighed by the fact that he was trapped in a confined space at the bottom of a mine.

He wished Jimmy were up top. He would come looking for him and dig him out. He wondered where Jimmy was. Maybe he was sick. No. Jimmy never got sick. Maybe he had gone looking for Nellie, or had found her and taken her away. That was what she wanted – to get away from this place and go south, where there were trees and houses above the ground and people.

He couldn't blame her. This was no place for a woman. Even a black woman.

He squirmed and brushed his shoulder against a rocky wall.

Why had he thought that? About Nellie being black, because he hadn't thought about her being an aboriginal. About being different. She was simply a woman to him, neither black nor white, just a woman and a good-looking one at that.

Not that Nellie behaved like most aboriginal women he had known. I'll bet she wishes she were white, Adam thought, and stared at the candle. He breathed deeply, and the flame flickered towards him.

He thought about Nellie, and his night with her. A wave of guilt washed over his body and receded, leaving him shivering. He felt angry and jealous, as well as guilty. How could she do that with someone else?

Some dirt fell in his eye and, with difficulty, he moved one arm to his head and brushed the dirt away.

She was desperate. She would go with anyone. She hadn't done those things with him because she loved him or even liked him, but because there was just a chance he might help her leave town. He was as important to her as a train ticket. Nothing more.

But how could she have done it? Held him like she did, and curled into his body, and been so soft and warm and gentle?

Adam thought of the first night he had met her, back in the creek near Port Augusta. He remembered the way she had reached out and touched him. He was used to people who felt rough when they shook hands, but her fingers had been cool and soft and there had been the suggestion of something else …

He thought of Jimmy and felt ashamed. He tried to reason why. He had certainly enjoyed the sensations. Should you be ashamed because you enjoyed something so much? Was it because they weren't married? He couldn't see the sense in that, although he knew that some people felt strongly about it. Why should something be proper if you were married and wrong if you weren't? How could a physical act, one that happened with such a gush of emotion that it seemed to be the most natural thing in the world, be good if some minister or priest had said a few words, and bad if he hadn't?

He still felt bad.

He tried to think of something evil or disgusting or unnatural that he and Nellie had done, and couldn't. It had been surprising. There had been strange smells and little animal-like grunts but he couldn't think of anything wicked about them. He supposed what he and Nellie had had was called sex and he had heard some people say that sex was dirty. Generally, they were people he didn't like. Hypocrites who would talk about God one minute and then not pay you all the money they owed you for a job. What was it Tiger had said? 'If your neighbour goes to church, get up early and brand your cattle?' Tiger hadn't gone to church. Not that Tiger was a particularly good man, but at least he didn't pretend to be something he wasn't.

Adam didn't like pretence. So what was he going to tell Jimmy? Nothing. He was glad his friend wasn't at the mine. He couldn't face him.

Had Nellie really been having sex with other miners? It had seemed so personal. She had touched him and he had touched her and, as his skin rode on hers, his body had twitched as though jolted by a trickle of electricity.

He mustn't see her again. But he wanted to. He ached for her.

He moved, and the flame wavered in the disturbed air. There was little left of the candle. He would have to do something before he lost the light.

He tried to kick a path through the wall of rubble at his feet but the action merely compressed the material into a more solid barrier. A shower of dirt fell from the roof. He stayed motionless for a few seconds and the fall ceased.

The candle flickered again and Adam stared at it, seeking inspiration.

He would have to dig his way out. To do that, he had to turn. That meant he had to scratch out a chamber, just big enough for him to move his body to one side so that he could then tuck his legs beneath his body and perform a slow somersault. Then he would be facing the other way, and he could start hacking at the mullock that blocked the tunnel.

What a lot of extra work because of his foolishness! It was because of last night. He was not thinking clearly.

He began chipping away at the seam.

The rock to the side was harder and Adam had cut only a few inches from the wall when the candle flared and spat wax and went out. The dark was absolute.

He waited a minute, sniffing the acrid smell left by the departed light.

He tried to see something and his eyes throbbed from the effort, but there was nothing. He whistled, and a dozen canaries

129

answered him, and he smiled and whistled again, mimicking bush birds, and his hole in the ground rang with their noisy responses.

He let the sounds die and lay there, gasping. There isn't much air in here, he thought, and was pleased that he was no longer frightened. Keep digging, the mind behind his eyes said. It was somewhere in the middle of his head, burning hot, commanding him to move.

His fingers groped for the place where he had been working. He touched the remains of the candle. A little beyond that were a few loose slabs of claystone and a dribbling of the red dirt that formed the seam. He scooped them clear, brushing them past his body. He chipped at the rock. He worked tentatively, for he was frightened of hitting his face in the dark. Pushing rather than swinging the tool, he chipped at the wall and felt some flakes break away.

The tip of the pick became wedged in some unseen recess. He pulled hard but could not free it. He exerted pressure on the handle and heard the crack of rock breaking. A large slab fell against his hip, hurting him. He rubbed himself and tried to push the slab past his body but it was too big, and he left it where it was.

Still smarting from the pain in his hip, he resumed chipping. There was a harsh sound. He scratched at the surface with a finger. He touched something smooth.

The wind had dropped. Having stripped the land of every loose grain and gathered them into howling hordes of red dust, the storm faded. Gusts that had lashed at everything in spiteful frenzy became gentle puffs. Trickles of wind cast ripples in the sand. Dust was returned to the earth and a red softness coated the town.

Nellie sat near a cluster of empty drums. She had sheltered there since leaving the store. The wind had whipped her hair to straw. She was caked in dust and her eyes, damp from weeping, trailed stains of bright red.

She heard someone approaching and, not wanting to be seen, crawled into a space between the drums. There were blankets on the ground, for she had been sleeping there. Dust covered the blankets and she looked at them in distaste, because she hated the dirt. A few of her possessions were stacked in a gap between two drums. She selected a comb and began to untangle the knots in her hair.

The footsteps came closer. Someone was walking slowly, with an uneven, shuffling gait.

She crouched low to avoid being seen. Horrie was limping past. He stopped, and drank from a bottle. He was muttering to himself. Nellie saw his face clearly, and his eyes had the look of madness.

SEVEN

Adam heard the sound of falling stones and the creak of the winch rope.

'You down here?' It was Jimmy Kettle.

'Too right,' Adam called, and his voice was deafening. He felt like laughing with relief.

'Where the devil are you?'

'At the end of the drive. I've blocked myself in.'

'Hang on. I'll get a light.'

Adam relaxed and listened to the noises that meant rescue. A shower of pebbles rattled down a wall. He heard the scratch of a match and the shuffling sound of trousered knees crawling along the tunnel floor.

'Where are you?' Jimmy called, his voice near but muffled by the barrier of rock fragments. Adam could see a flicker of light. Suddenly, he felt hot and exhausted. His hip ached.

'I'm here,' he said flatly.

There was no movement from the other side of the barrier and when Jimmy spoke he sounded baffled. 'Where? I'm at the end of the drive. Have you turned into a snake and gone underground?'

'Just dig me out. I'm on the other side of all that fresh stone.'

'How long have you been there?' Jimmy asked, and Adam heard the scraping of rocks and the sound of dirt trickling into freshly exposed hollows.

'Don't know. Couple of hours maybe.' He was bent at an awkward angle and he spoke with difficulty.

'You all right? Not hurt or anything?'

'No.'

'What happened?' A rock was wrenched clear and smaller

stones fell in its place. 'Did the roof fall in?'

'No. I just got lazy and ended up sealing myself in.'

'Can you breathe?'

'Just. I've been working like an ant for the last hour or so trying to get out and it's become as hot as hell in here, but I can breathe.'

'Are you caught under rocks or something?'

'No.'

'Well, why aren't you digging from that side?'

'Because I can't turn.'

'Jesus! What were you doing to get stuck like that?'

'Working.' Adam wriggled his body to clear the stone that was still near his hip. 'Working on my own.'

There was no answer.

'You still there?' Adam called. He saw the light grow brighter. Jimmy was holding the candle at the other end of the shallow opening near the roof.

'Have you got a light?' Jimmy said, his voice booming through the gap.

'No. Went out a long time ago.'

'Just as well I came looking for you.'

'Where were you?'

The light grew faint. Adam heard Jimmy grunting.

A rock clattered to the floor.

'I was busy,' Jimmy said, puffing. 'You shouldn't work on your own.'

'Yeah. Well, I did.' Dust was filling the tunnel and Adam coughed. 'Take it easy!' he called. 'I can't breathe.'

'Do you want to get out or not?' Jimmy said.

Adam coughed again. There was the noise of stones falling and bouncing against each other.

'Been a big storm,' Jimmy said, still digging with his hands. 'Dust everywhere. Half the country's blown away.'

'Was that why you didn't come earlier?' Adam said. Each breath he took was now clogged with dust and Adam could feel the fear of confinement rising in him again. 'Take it easy, mate,' he called. 'I'm getting more dirt than air.'

Jimmy paused. 'There's not much room,' he said. 'I'm on my belly, and it's hard work with your hands. Have you got all the tools?'

Adam spat to clear his throat.

'They're somewhere here. I can't see without a light.'

132

'Well, it's slow work like this.' Some stone fragments rattled down the tunnel and Jimmy flung them clear.

'There was a reason I didn't come this morning,' Jimmy said, his hands as busy as a dog burying a bone. 'I wasn't bludging on you, Adam.'

'That's all right, Jimmy,' he answered and thought, please be quick and try and keep the dust down, or otherwise, I'm going to faint. He felt sick.

'I was looking for Nellie.'

Oh Christ, Adam said to himself. 'Why?' he called lamely.

'Because I didn't know where she was.' The digging had stopped.

'Where was she?' Adam said.

'Don't know. I couldn't find her.'

Adam said nothing.

'She's been trying to nick off.' The digging resumed.

Adam coughed. He spoke quickly. 'Is there much more dirt to move?'

'Don't know. All I can see is my end of it. You've been shifting a lot of rock if this is all stuff you've moved today.'

'Yes, I've been busy.'

'Nellie been sleeping with you?' Jimmy said. He asked the question casually and continued working. Adam could hear the rattle of stones.

'Jesus Christ, Jimmy,' he said, and pressed one hand to the top of his head as though to hold the truth back. Don't let him say any more, he thought.

'Oh, I don't mind,' Jimmy said. 'I kicked her out a couple of weeks ago.'

Adam wriggled to a new position. 'What do you mean?'

'Kicked her out. Gave her the arse. She'd been doing nothing but complaining. Hang on a second, I think I'm near the end of this stuff. Can you see the candle?'

The light was brighter.

'I'll try and clear the hole out, so's you can breathe better,' Jimmy continued. There was more scraping. 'She's been trying to get someone to take her back down south. Half the blokes in town tell me she's been sidling up to them.'

'And doing what?' Adam didn't want an answer.

'Oh, doing what she does best. She's had more roots than a wombat.'

'Jesus, Jimmy, she's your girl.'

'Not any more. Hasn't she had a go at you? I reckon she likes you.'

'You almost through?'

Jimmy did not answer. Adam heard him grunting with the effort of moving stones.

'You're a funny bugger, Adam,' he said. 'What are you, shy or something? Never had a root with a sheila before?'

'I thought she was your girl,' Adam said softly.

'She's not my girl. She's not your girl. She's not anyone's girl. She'd get in the cot with any bloke to get out of this place. She's had more pricks in her than a blackfellow's foot.'

Small stones rolled against Adam's feet.

'I think I'm nearly through,' Jimmy said.

Adam's tiny cavern was sudenly bathed in light. Jimmy began to laugh.

'I can see you now,' he said. 'You look like a rabbit waiting for the ferret to bite it on the ass.'

Adam squirmed into place. 'You clear?' he said and pushed hard with his boots.

'Good on you,' said Jimmy.

Adam felt strong hands grip his ankle and he was dragged, feet first, from the trap. He saw the candle and Jimmy's teeth exposed in a smile, and he vomited.

'Jesus, that's a nice way to greet a feller! I brought some water. Want a drink?'

Adam nodded his thanks. He rested on his elbow, gasping for breath and conscious of the bitter taste in his throat. 'It's good to be out,' he said. 'Thanks.'

Jimmy patted him on the ankle. 'You'd better not do that again, had you?'

Adam took some water and shook his head. The water swallowed, he rolled on his back and looked at Jimmy.

'You don't mind about Nellie?'

'How many times has she been to bed with you? Ever since she left me?'

'I thought you said you kicked her out?' Adam sipped more water and stared at his friend. Jimmy's face, brightly illuminated by the candle, was beaded with perspiration.

'Bit of each,' he grinned. 'I decided to kick her out about the same time she decided to leave. You haven't told me how many times.'

134

'Just last night.' Adam wiped his face. 'I've been feeling bad about it ever since.'

'You *are* a funny bugger. No need to worry. She's only a sheila.'

Adam turned away.

Jimmy tugged at Adam's trouser leg, like a dog seeking attention. 'Don't tell me you like her?' There was amusement in his voice.

'I thought I'd done the wrong thing by you. I didn't mean to. I didn't want to.'

'No worries,' Jimmy said. 'She's not the first sheila I've had and she won't be the last. And if you think you're keen on her, forget it. She's not worth it.'

Adam handed him the water.

Jimmy drank. 'Besides,' he said, wiping his lips, 'you don't want to go messing around with a gin. It's not good for you. She's black and you're white.'

'So what?'

'So it means nothing to you but it means something to everyone else. A black man with a black woman is one thing but a white man with a black woman is dirt, and he's treated like it. All right out here, but you go back south and see how people behave. You're not keen on her, are you?'

Adam shrugged.

'Was it your first time?' Jimmy was smiling and he might have been Adam's father, asking him how he enjoyed his first taste of golden syrup or some other delicacy. It was a kind, soft look.

'Yes.'

'Did you think you were going to blow yourself in half?'

Adam grinned. 'Something like that.'

'I was thirteen the first time I tried.'

'Oh, cut it out!'

'Dinkum. The girl was about sixteen or seventeen and she treated me like I was a little pet dog. Christ, when I came, though, I suddenly turned into an Alsatian.' They both laughed. Adam felt so good.

'Have you done it many times?'

'A few hundred, I suppose.'

'Oh, Jimmy!'

'No. True. Fair dinkum, I've had more than a hundred girls. They used to wait outside the tent.'

'You're pulling my leg.'

Jimmy pulled his leg. 'Let's get out of here. You're covered in dirt and you've got scratches all over you. You ought to get cleaned up. You look like a blackfellow, and a rough one at that.'

'Let me have the candle first.'

Jimmy passed it to him, and watched in astonishment as Adam crawled back into the hole.

'What the hell are you doing?'

'Just looking at something,' Adam said, his voice megaphoning from the end of the drive. He came squirming back. He had retrieved the small pick and handed the candle to the other man. 'You know how some of the miners work in the dark and reckon they can tell what they've found by the sound and the feel of things?' He waited for Jimmy to nod, and enjoyed his puzzled look. 'Well, when I was trying to get out, I struck something that made a different noise, and felt different, once I'd cleared around it. Go and have a look.'

Candle in hand, Jimmy crawled into the opening.

'It's on the right,' Adam called. 'At the end of the level, where the seam dips down a bit.'

Adam could hear Jimmy brushing the wall with his fingers. Suddenly, his friend exploded into profanities and started to laugh. He reversed out of the hole, his legs pumping like pistons in his haste to get back.

His eyes were wide.

'It's all pink and colours like that and it's as big as my hand!' he said, his voice racing. He grabbed Adam by the shirt. 'It's not the stuff they call potch, is it?'

'No,' said Adam laughing. 'It's not potch. That's got no colour. That stuff in there is flashing like a rainbow. I think we've found ourselves a big opal!'

When the storm died Saleem Benn unloaded his camels, working with his nephew and two men whom the storekeeper engaged for the job. It was tiring work, for each camel carried about eight hundredweight of goods. The load was arranged on a rig which spread the weight on either side of the beast, and this had to be removed evenly or the camel could be injured by the sudden unbalancing of its huge burden. Eight hundredweight between four men was difficult work. Then the rigs had to be unloaded and the goods carried to the store and stacked in their appropriate places. By the time the work was finished, the two casual labourers had, indeed, laboured for their two shillings.

The Afghan was anxious to leave. He had to water his camels within a few days and there was a well just to the east of Lake Cadibarrawirracanna, on the track to Anna Creek. Coober Pedy had water from the partly silted underground tank, but it had to be paid for and Saleem Benn was not prepared to layout five shillings for the quantity his animals would consume. Better to have his nephew toil for half a day lifting buckets from the deep well. Thus, as soon as the work was finished and Saleem Benn had been paid, the camels rose like puppets on tightening strings and the train of animals lurched out of town.

It did not go far. Less than an hour's journey to the east was a sandy creek bed and there the robed Afghan camped. The camels were now one hour nearer the well and he silenced the protests of his nephew with that fact. But the truth was that Saleem Benn loathed towns.

Ten minutes after sunset, he knelt facing Mecca and prayed for the fourth time that day. Then he rose, gazed at the shadowed wilderness surrounding him and felt content.

But then a meteorite traced a white line across the sky. It shone brightly despite the paleness of the evening, and Saleem Benn shivered, for he knew something dreadful was going to happen. The meteorite, he noted, pointed towards the town.

Adam burst into the Hoffmans' bus. The slab of opal in his bag bounced against his thigh. Had he not been breathless from running, the words would have flowed uncontrollably from his open mouth.

Two men were sitting in the bus, drinking tea. Mrs Hoffman was wiping her eyes.

'You're late today,' Josef said, looking anxiously at his friend.

'You're scratched,' Anemone said. She was eating a crust of bread.

'Are you all right?' her father asked.

Adam nodded, still unable to speak. He had run all the way. He looked anxiously at Mrs Hoffman.

'Oh, it's all right,' Hoffman said. 'My wife has just heard a sad story. By the way, I should introduce you to these gentlemen. You may have met the postmaster, Mr Moore?'

Adam and the postmaster nodded at each other.

'And this is Mr Thomas, an opal buyer from Ceylon. He is looking for good specimens.'

Thomas had skin the colour of lead. He wore a suit, with waistcoat, tie and shirt of intense white with a rounded collar. He began to rise.

'My hands are too dirty to shake,' Adam gasped, his chest still heaving. He offered one hand as proof, and the man sat down.

'You should sit down too,' said Hoffman. 'You look as though you're about to have a heart attack.'

'Don't say that!' Mrs Hoffman sobbed.

'What's wrong?' Adam said, as he sat.

'He was only your age,' she said, and touched his shoulder.

'Who?'

'The poor boy Mr Moore was telling us about. The one who found the opals.'

'Who's found opals?' said Adam, suddenly feeling cheated. 'Someone my age?'

Moore smiled. 'I was just telling Mr Thomas and Mr and Mrs Hoffman about Willie Hutchinson. He was the one who found opals here in the first place. He was drowned when he was about your age.'

'Please continue,' said Thomas.

'Well, the men went out looking for water and young Willie stayed in the camp, or he was supposed to.' He glared at Josef. 'Like a fool, he wandered off and when his father and the others came back that evening, Willie was nowhere to be seen.'

'What happened?' Adam said.

'He drowned,' Anemone said.

'No, he didn't,' her mother said. 'Don't interrupt, Annie.'

'But the man said he did. He told us Willie drowned and you started crying.'

Moore coughed, a light discreet cough. 'No, my dear. He drowned some years later. When he was only fourteen, he found opal.'

'Just in one day?' Anemone asked.

'Yes, my dear. He just wandered a few miles from the camp and came to those low hills, and found several pieces of precious opal.'

'How did he dig down and find all that opal in one day?' Anemone had begun to twist the crust in her fingers. 'We've been here for months and haven't found any.'

'He found them on the ground,' Thomas said and beamed.

'Then why don't we look on the ground instead of digging down so far?' Anemone said.

Thomas stood up. 'Because, young lady, all the opals above the ground have already been picked up. Now you have to dig for them. If you will excuse me, I must be going. I have to meet some people who want me to buy things from them.' He shook Hoffman's hand. 'You have been too kind.'

'How could you find opals on top of the ground?' the girl asked Adam.

'I don't know,' he said and, acting on impulse, stood up too.

'They weren't much good,' Josef said. 'They were all cracked from being out in the sun.'

'You have bright children,' Thomas said and left the bus.

'They talk too much,' Hoffman said ominously.

'Willie's father was going to belt him until he saw the opals,' Josef said and eyed his father.

'I'll be back in a minute,' Adam said, and followed the man out of the bus. He ran after him.

'Mr Thomas,' he called.

The dark man in the suit turned. He was not smiling.

'You buy opals?'

'Yes. That's why I came here.'

Adam opened his bag. He withdrew the slab of stone and its colours shone like a soft sunrise. 'How much would this be worth?'

Thomas sucked in his breath.

'Whose is this?'

'Mine.'

'Where did you find it?'

'On my lease. This afternoon.'

'May I look at it more closely?'

He took the stone and rolled it in his hands. He looked at Adam.

'Did you find it on your own?'

'I run the mine with a mate. Jimmy Kettle.'

'What a strange name!'

Adam lowered his head. He was so excited he had forgotten. 'I mean Black. Jimmy Black. The other's just a nickname.'

'Very amusing,' Thomas said, examining the stone.

'Is it worth much?'

139

'It's hard to say. There are several opals here. You'll have to cut them. I'd have to weigh them. I'd like to examine them in better light. I'm using the post office as my base. Could you come around there?'

Adam nodded. 'The colours are good, aren't they?' He sounded uncertain.

'Young man, they are magnificent. I cannot give you a definite figure now, but I would say this sample is worth ... well, many hundreds of pounds ... maybe a thousand ... possibly more.' He stroked his nose and was silent for several seconds. 'Have you told anyone about this?' he said softly.

'No.'

'Don't! My experience in places like this is that you should tell no one. Not even your closest friends. Do you live in the bus with the Germans?'

'No. I live right here.' Adam pointed to his dugout.

Thomas smiled his parson's smile. 'I have to go. You come and see me tomorrow at the post office. I will be there from nine o'clock.'

Dazed, Adam returned to the bus. One thousand pounds! He tried to imagine such an amount in cash. It would have to be in notes, he thought, although the money he had earned had almost always been paid to him in coins, and not many coins at that. To him, a two-shilling piece was a prize – to look at when someone gave you one, and to hold in your pocket until it became as warm as your fingers. And now, here was this man with the grey-coloured skin talking about one thousand *pounds*. There were ten two-shilling pieces for every pound. He had learned to count so he knew that. Tiger had said it didn't matter if you could read or not, but if you couldn't count people would rob you ... Ten two-shilling pieces to a pound meant ... what was it? ... ten thousand two shillings in a thousand pounds. He tried to imagine so many coins, but he could not. They would certainly overflow his bag, and pour out.

What he did know was that with one thousand pounds he could buy his own property. He had heard people saying that the prices of properties were tumbling. Things were so bad that some people were walking off the land. A man with money could get himself a real bargain. It might not be a big place, but it would be his own.

His eyes were wet and he wiped them.

At the bus, the postmaster was leaving. He had one leg on the ground and the other, bent at ninety degrees, was high up on a step. Moore was portly, and in this pose he reminded Adam of a teapot.

Mr Hoffman was in the bus. 'When does he arrive?' Hoffman said.

'Tomorrow. Maybe the day after.' Moore removed his leg from the step and breathed deeply with the effort. 'It's a silly business. I can't imagine why he's wasting his time coming.'

'It's a shame he's not staying. We could do with a policeman here all the time.'

'We've got by without one for long enough, Hans. We can look after things ourselves. Don't need other people telling us what to do. Coming to the bonfire tonight?' The postmaster had begun to walk away and asked the question without turning.

'I suppose so,' Hoffman said. 'It's getting very hard to find wood these days, and there are four of us.'

'Send the kids out,' Moore said, still walking. 'You only need one piece each to go there. See you later.' He passed Adam and nodded.

Hoffman studied Adam so intently that Adam thought he had guessed his secret. He had run to the bus to tell the family of his find, but Thomas had said he shouldn't tell anyone and now he was confused.

'I don't think,' said Hoffman, speaking slowly, 'that I have ever seen you look so dirty.'

Adam smiled. 'I got stuck in the mine,' he said, and at that moment resolved to say nothing about the opal. He would see Thomas tomorrow and find out how much the opal was worth, and then tell his friends.

'Was there a fall?' Hoffman asked, looking concerned.

'No. I was just digging in a narrow drive. I got stuck a bit.'

'How stuck?'

'Oh, for a couple of hours.'

Hoffman's eyes rounded in alarm. 'You were pinned?'

Adam laughed. 'No. Nothing like that. I just had trouble getting out of a hole I'd dug myself into.'

'You must be careful.' He put his arm on Adam's shoulder. 'It's dangerous down there. I worry every time Josef is working.'

'How did you go today?' Adam asked, shifting his bag to the other hand, so that it would not bump against the other man.

'We did not work much. When the wind started to blow we

141

came back. It was too unpleasant up top. It was all right for Josef, of course, but far too uncomfortable for an old wine-grower like me up on top and being whipped by the dust.'

Adam nodded. Hoffman rarely went down the shaft because he found climbing difficult. Young Joe did most of the digging, but Hoffman, who was strong, lifted the bucket and spent hours sifting through the mullock. He had found a few chips that way. They were not worth much but at least they indicated the presence of opal, and their discovery served to rekindle the family's enthusiasm. The Hoffmans had been thinking of moving to another lease. The Coober Pedy diggings now stretched for forty miles and Mr Hoffman had contemplated giving up his present mine and trying his luck at 'the Jungle' – so called because a stunted tree grew on a ridge there. At 'the Jungle', opal had been found in shallow ground, and Hoffman was tempted by the thought of finding precious stone without having to burrow for it.

'You're going to keep trying, aren't you?' Adam said. 'I mean you've done so much work where you are, and there's still a lot of ground on your lease you haven't explored.'

'I suppose so,' Hoffman said.

'I heard of a bloke who found opal on an abandoned lease. He just dug fifteen feet deeper than the first man on the lease and struck it rich.'

'It's a very risky business. And very unfair in many ways. Tell me,' Hoffman said, his tone changing, 'why were you in such a hurry to get here? I don't think I've ever seen you so out of breath.'

Adam looked at his boots. 'Nothing,' he said. 'Just felt like running.'

'What it is to be young!' Hoffman too gazed at his feet and a visitor might have assumed both men were searching for something on the ground. Hoffman was merely looking for the correct words. 'I think, my young friend,' he said eventually, 'that it was not an experience you enjoyed, being caught underground like that today. I know, had something like that happened to me, I would have been very frightened and, having got out, I would have run from that place as fast as I could.' He looked at Adam but there was no response. 'There is nothing wrong in being frightened by such an experience.'

'I wasn't frightened,' said Adam, looking up. 'Well, I was when

I was down there, but once I got out I was all right. It was just something that happened. There was no danger.'

'Then why did you run here? You must have been running very fast to be so out of breath.'

Adam felt the weight of the opal in his bag. He wanted to tell this man, but he thought of Thomas's words. If he told Hoffman, the man would tell his wife and she would tell Anemone and young Annie would tell everyone. Specially at the bonfire tonight. The whole camp would know.

'I just felt like running,' Adam said. 'I guess it was good to be up on top again.'

Hoffman nodded.

'Do you have water in your dugout? Good. Then go home, and clean up your scratches and wash yourself. You are as dear to me as a son, Adam, but frankly at the moment you stink.'

Adam grinned.

'It's true. I have a very highly developed nose and if you were a wine I would pour you down the drain. Go back, clean yourself up and have a rest. Are you going to join us tonight?'

'I don't have any wood,' Adam said.

Once a week the miners had a community camp fire, to which each participant was required to bring one piece of timber.

'I will make sure Annie brings two,' Hoffman said, and Adam left, feeling stronger for having said nothing about the opal.

EIGHT

Drunkenness was rarely a problem at Coober Pedy in the late autumn of 1929 because few of the miners could afford to buy liquor. Few of them smoked, either. Again it was not through abstemiousness. There was just no cash for anything other than necessities. Most had come to the field to earn 'tucker money', to make enough to eat. Sharing adversity and poverty, they had become good-humoured about their lot. Contrast fuels the blistering flames of envy and unhappiness, but at the community fire that night there was no one to envy. Everyone was short of something that mattered and all knew the pinch of not having enough water or food. They were isolated and, being together in isolation and deprivation, they were happy. And sober. Which is why Horrie Smith made such an impact when he arrived at the fire. He was drunk, and so drunk that he rolled rather than walked and trod on people's outstretched legs, and spoke to no one because he seemed to be beyond speech. He was carrying an old and twisted piece of wood, and used it as a walking stick.

'Jesus, where'd you get the grog, Horrie?' one man in his path taunted, but Horrie trod on him and the crowd laughed. The old miner headed for a clear space on the far side of the fire and there, fell down. The crowd cheered.

Adam, who had been sitting with the Hoffmans, walked across to make sure Horrie was not hurt.

'He's all right, Snow,' the man nearest Horrie's prone form said. Darkie Halliday had come up from Tarcoola, when work on the transcontinental railway had been completed in 1917. He was a fettler on that job and had undertaken the long journey to the opal fields with six of his mates. He was the only one still there. People said Darkie had made a big find five years ago, but he had never shown any signs of having money.

His beard wagged as he spoke. 'The silly coot's been on the metho by the smell of him. Saw him like this a few years ago. Thought he'd given it up.' He leaned on one elbow and stared at the fire.

Adam bent to touch Horrie.

'Just leave him,' Halliday said without taking his eyes from the fire.

The man next to Halliday leaned across. 'If he's been on methylated spirits, you shouldn't touch him. It's a poison and I've seen men become violent when they drink it. He's breathing, so leave him alone.'

The man behind Adam spoke.

'Get his bit of wood and stick it on the fire, son,' he said. 'This is a real blackfellow's fire we've got tonight. I'm cold. Chuck it on and give us some more heat.'

So Adam put the fallen piece of wood on the fire and went back to the Hoffmans.

Dexter Paradine stood up. He had been at Coober Pedy two years. His father had been a copper miner near Wallaroo.

'Time for community singing,' he said. 'You all know "I'll Take You Home Again, Kathleen"?'

'Oh shit, Dexter, that's too high,' someone grumbled.

Paradine's nose wrinkled. 'We have a lady present, Sam. Apologize!'

'Sorry.' Sam, who was sitting on a rock, swung his head as he spoke, casting the word wide so that a fragment might touch the offended person.

'Go on, Dexter, you sing it,' a man on the other side of the fire called and a few men laughed. This was a weekly ritual. There were a number of songs Paradine liked to sing, to show off his rich tenor. This was one.

He took a deep breath, closed his eyes, and tucked his hands into the fob pockets of his waistcoat.

"I'll take you home again, Kathleen ..."

A few voices joined in, suitably muted. A stick exploded in the fire. A dog barked and was silenced by a human growl.

' ... to where your heart has ever been ...'

'He sings nicely,' Mrs Hoffman confided to Adam. 'Why don't you sing?'

'I don't know it.'

'I'll take you home again, Kathleen ...' she whispered, as though the prompting would revive a lapsed memory.

'Kathleen was my mother's name.'

'Oh.' Mrs Hoffman looked sad. She touched Adam's hand and he was embarrassed. He did not want to be treated like a boy. 'It's a lovely name,' she said, voice wreathed in sympathy.

The tenor finished. As always, those who had joined him fell silent for the closing bars and he was able to end on a sustained high note unsullied by lesser voices.

'How about "Mademoiselle from Armentières"?' a man called, his arm raised like a student seeking his teacher's attention.

'Later, later,' Paradine said, strutting to another place where there was no smoke. 'I thought we might sing "Beautiful Dreamer".'

'Shit, Dexter,' Sam, complained and, without pausing, flung the word "sorry" into the cold night air. 'We know you've got a good voice. We've heard it every Friday night for nearly two years. How about giving us a go?'

Paradine smiled. An insult veiled with a compliment was acceptable. He breathed deeply and tilted his head, preparing to issue the first rich notes.

"Mademoiselle from Armentières ..." a voice began, with the

rhythm of a steam train click-clacking over loose joints on the line.

Paradine looked distressed. He lowered his head.

"*Parlez-vous!*" thundered a dozen voices.

"*Mademoiselle from Armentières ...*" and everyone was singing. Even Paradine joined in, quietly and with a strained smile, at the end.

'That was good, Dexter,' Sam said from his rock. 'I feel warm now. Bloody warm.'

'Sam!' Paradine's distress had knotted his brow like rope.

'Sorry, lady.' Sam stood up. 'Where are you, love?'

Mrs Hoffman shyly waved her hand.

Sam bowed. 'Please excuse me. I'm always bloody well saying shit and bloody. No offence meant.'

'It's all right,' Mrs Hoffman said, more to Adam than to the others. 'I am used to swearing.'

'I don't swear,' Adam said, imagining Mrs Hoffman had been accusing him.

'I know, and I think that's a very good thing. I admire a person who can control his tongue.'

'And I don't swear,' Hans Hoffman said, 'so who do you hear using bad language all the time?'

Dexter Paradine had begun 'Beautiful Dreamer'. Someone made a noise like a hen clucking.

'It's Annie,' Josef said, leaning towards Adam to make sure he was heard. 'She said "bugger" the other day.'

The girl pulled her mother's dress. 'I did not!'

'You did,' Josef said, turning on his sister. 'You called me a bugger.'

'I did not.'

'The man is singing,' Mrs Hoffman hissed. She was a woman who was greatly concerned about good manners. She smiled fixedly at Paradine, who had opened his eyes to look her way. A crease of reproach lined his face.

'*Beautiful dreamer, awake unto me ...*'

'She called me a bugger,' Josef said.

His father hit him, slapping him low on the back. 'Be quiet!' he said.

'He's always hitting me,' Josef said to Adam. The boy's face had turned white.

'Oh, he is not,' Mrs Hoffman said, still smiling at the tenor.

'You wouldn't know. He only hits me when you're not around.'
Mrs Hoffman looked at her husband.

'No more than my father hit me,' Hoffman said, the palms of his hands upraised. She blinked rapidly.

'Why did I get hit when I wasn't the one who was swearing?' Josef said angrily.

'Be quiet,' his mother whispered, the words escaping through compressed lips. Paradine finished. 'That was lovely, Mr Paradine,' she called out. 'Please sing another song for us all.'

'Yes, give us a solo,' Sam said. 'Make it so low no one can hear it.' His laugh saturated the crowd.

'Do we all know "Love's Old Refrain"?' Paradine asked.

'I know one refrain,' the man who had started singing 'Mademoiselle from Armentières' shouted. 'I saw it printed on a railway carriage once. It was the "Refrain from Spitting".'

He laughed and most joined him. Paradine sought comfort from the glow of the fire.

'Aren't some people crude?' Mrs Hoffman said.

'I didn't swear,' Anemone said, tugging at the dress again.

'I know, dear.'

'How do you know?' Josef said. 'She said "bugger". I heard her.'

Hoffman hit him again. Josef got up. 'I'm going to bed,' he shouted, and ran towards the dugout he shared with Adam.

'Let him go,' Hoffman said.

'Have you been hitting him?' Mrs Hoffman asked.

'What is this?' Hoffman said, hands raised and an expression of surprise wrinkling his forehead. 'Do you suddenly think I am a person who beats his children?'

'But you hit him then. Twice,' she said.

'He was swearing.'

'Not really. He was just saying what Annie said.'

'I didn't say it,' the girl protested.

The crowd was singing 'The Camp Town Races' and Dexter Paradine was pushing a half-burned stick back into the fire. He looked sad.

'I'll see if Horrie is all right,' Adam said, and stood, rubbing his hip. Some men were singing '*doo-dah, doo-dah, day*' in the wrong place, and the song was becoming a jumble of noise. The dog barked again, and no one cared.

Horrie was still lying face down. Adam bent down and rolled him on his side.

'I wouldn't touch him,' Darkie Halliday said. 'He's rotten with metho. I can smell it from here.'

'He's my friend,' Adam said.

'Doesn't matter. If he wakes up, he won't know his best friend from his worst enemy.'

Horrie opened one eye, grunted, and rolled on his back.

'Don't touch him, Snow,' Halliday said. 'Just leave him where he is.'

The storekeeper arrived at the fire. He was carrying a box in one hand and a sack in the other. He paused near Darkie Halliday. 'I've got your medicine here, Darkie,' he said, winking and tilting his head towards the box. Halliday stood, moving slowly and painfully.

'Arthritis still bad?' the storekeeper asked.

'Real crook. Where's the stuff?' He looked in the box.

'In the corner. In the red wrapping.' He noticed Horrie. 'What's up with the old feller?'

'Full as a boot. Been on the metho.'

'Wonder where he got that?'

'Wouldn't have a clue. This mine?'

'*Doo-dah, doo-dah, day,*' the miners sang. '*Hey!*' The last word was shouted. Halliday removed a package shaped like a small bottle. He examined it closely.

'Not a drop missing,' the storekeeper said. 'That old Afghan is getting better. Never broke a bottle this trip.'

'How much?' Halliday began to remove the wrapping.

'Four bob.'

'Strewth! It gets dearer every time.'

'Gets dearer to bring it here. Just stick the money in my right-hand pocket, will you, Darkie?'

The man behind Adam laughed. 'Are you sure he's got any lining in his pockets, Darkie?' he said and looked around swiftly, to harvest the crop of smiles his joke had raised. He had a red beard and stroked it sensuously. The storekeeper ignored him. He was in this town only to make money and he did not care what people said about him. He had culled Saleem Benn's load for the goods his customers wanted urgently – not to keep faith but because he knew he could charge more if he delivered certain items tonight. He searched the ring of faces for his next customer, struggling to balance his load.

'Where's Ben King?' he enquired.

148

'Over here,' a voice answered. The storekeeper shuffled away.

'Hey, while you're there will you shove another piece of wood on the fire?' the man with the red beard said. 'I'm cold again.'

The storekeeper smiled pleasantly. 'My hands are a bit full, mate, or I'd gladly do it for you. Shame you haven't got an axe, or you could stick the handle up my arse and I'd chop some firewood for you.'

Sam stood up. 'I know I didn't say it, love, but sorr-ee!' The men laughed and looked at Mrs Hoffman. She lowered her face.

Dexter Paradine raised his hands. 'While the grocer is delivering his wares, we might sing another song. An appropriate one,' he said, eyeing the storekeeper who was delivering another wrapped parcel to Ben King, 'might be "Little Brown Jug".'

'Beauty, Dexter!' Sam said and began bellowing the words in such a low key that Paradine could not join in.

'Ha ha ha, you and me, little brown jug how I love thee,' he croaked, more bullfrog than man, and slapped his thigh to keep time. The others followed, generally keeping within a word or two of his lead.

Adam sat on his haunches. He enjoyed these nights. For the first time in his life he felt he belonged to an adult group. And tonight he felt better than ever, for he might now be a wealthy man. Well, not rich like some of the men he knew who operated the big stations, but rich enough to make a start. He wasn't going to spend his life working for other men, condemned to an existence of dependency and subservience like his father and old Tiger had been. He was going to have his own property. He was going to be someone. With a big house and sheds and lots of land where he could walk or ride his horses, and travel a day and never leave his own land.

A hand touched his shoulder. Jimmy had glided into place behind him.

'They make a lot of noise,' he said.

Adam stood. 'I met an opal buyer,' he said, speaking as quietly as possible. 'I'm going to see him tomorrow. Nine o'clock at the post office. Coming?'

'No. You see him. Seen Nellie?'

'No.' Adam looked around.

'Little brown jug, oh, I love thee ...'

Jimmy grimaced. 'Can't stand this kind of music. What's up with old Horrie?'

149

'Drunk.'

Jimmy nodded sagely. 'That's the trouble with some white fellers. Can't hold their grog.' And he retreated to the shadows.

The miners began to sing the song again. *'My wife and I live all alone, in a little brown house we call our own ...'*

Adam stared into the fire. He hummed the tune. He wished he could sing. Not that he would dare sing in front of other people, but he liked singing. Maybe he would have a piano in the big house he would own one day. He would learn to play it. Then he would sing. Softly, and only to himself.

How much was the opal worth? Enough for a deposit on his own place? Almost certainly. He felt good. With money, he could do anything, be anyone. And that money, or the lump of rock that meant cash, was back in his place. It was safe. He had scooped a hole in the base of one wall and buried it.

The opal was his future, or the start of it.

The stars were bright. He started to count them and thought of another time, long ago ...

Some more men arrived. They came as a group and Adam turned to look. They were Chinese. They stayed behind the main ring of miners, choosing to sit on a slight rise so that their bodies were speckled with the shadows of those closer to the fire. They were smiling and, like Adam, nodding to the music.

Horrie stirred. He opened his eyes one at a time. Adam leaned above his face.

'You all right, Horrie?'

The old man blinked. He mumbled words that had no meaning. Adam shuffled back, his head reeling from the dreadful stench that had issued from Horrie's mouth. How could he drink that stuff? He had known that vile smell before, when he had stumbled upon some pathetic wretch lying on the outskirts of a camp, vomiting and trembling and saying crazy things. Always, those men had been on their own and in the last crumbling stages of life. No one wanted to know a metho drinker.

'Ha ha ha, hee hee hee ...' the miners chanted.

'Horrie.' Adam moved close again, holding his breath and touching the old man's shoulder. Horrie sat up, so suddenly that Adam jumped back in fright. He stared at Adam. His eyes were wide open but glazed. Dry spittle rimmed his lips.

'Bastards!' he screamed, lunging at Adam. He fell, and started to cry.

Darkie Halliday sat up. 'Jesus, Snow, I told you to let him be!' he said, his voice alarmed.

'Come on, Horrie, I'll take you home,' Adam said.

Horrie pushed himself to his knees. 'I didn't know it was them,' he said.

'It's all right,' Adam said. 'Give me your arm and I'll help you up.'

'Don't touch me,' he said, his voice shrill. He looked beyond Adam. 'How the hell was I to know?'

'Come on,' Adam said, soothing him.

Halliday edged away. 'You're gamer than Ned Kelly,' he said. 'The old bloke's got a big knife on his hip so take care, Snow. He's as mad as a meat axe.'

'I didn't!' Horrie said. 'I swear to God I didn't know.' He fell against Adam's legs and wrapped his arms around his knees. Even his chin was moist from the tears streaming down his face.

'Come on, mate,' Adam said, conscious of the looks from the men nearest him. Everyone was smiling. Why did people laugh at drunks? 'Come on, I'll get you to bed.'

Horrie stood, his body curved like a question mark. He straightened and his breath exploded on Adam's face in sickening bursts. 'I thought it was those rotten Chinks,' he said, rolling his head in anguish.

'Yeah,' said Adam, turning his head.

'Smells like a shithouse, doesn't he?' Halliday said, grinning and then devoting his attention to the far side of the fire, where Dexter Paradine was singing 'Danny Boy'.

'I did!' Horrie insisted, and gripped Adam with great strength. Adam, holding his breath, looked Horrie in the eye and nodded agreement, until the other man relaxed his hold. They began to walk away from the fire.

'I've been looking for them all day,' Horrie said, sounding more reasonable.

'Who?' Adam asked.

'My two mates.' Horrie slipped and Adam prevented him falling. 'Bastards. Why did they do it?'

'I don't know. Let me get you home. Can you walk?'

Horrie pushed him away. 'Do you think I'm drunk or something?'

'No, mate.'

The old man confronted Adam, his body rocking up and down,

like a fighting cock waiting to strike its first lethal blow. 'Young bastard,' he said. 'I could still whip you.'

'Come on, Horrie.'

'Let's see how good you are,' the old man said and raised his fists, then fell. Adam stood above him. Horrie pushed himself to his knees and elbows. 'Just let me get my wind back,' he said. 'Then I'll flatten you.'

Horrie's coat had parted at the back and Adam saw the knife. It was a long one. He had never seen his friend carrying it. Horrie stayed like that, not moving, for another minute. Adam heard him sob, then sniff, then spit. Finally, he rolled on his back and wiped his face. He groaned. He looked up at Adam and his eyes seemed clearer.

'That you, Adam?' he said, bewildered. 'What are you doing here?'

'Just thought I'd walk with you, back to your place.'

'Oh, that's good of you. Help me up. I must have fallen over.'

Adam helped him to his feet.

'What's going on?' The voice was slurred but the eyes showed recognition.

'They're having a sing-song,' Adam said, and took the man's elbow.

'I'm all right,' he said and pulled his arm clear. He began to walk. They circled the crowd at the fire, heading towards the rise on which the Chinese were sitting.

'Do you know something, Adam?' he said in a small, almost childlike voice. 'I've done a dreadful thing.'

'Have you, Horrie?' Adam was glad the old man was moving.

'Yes, I have.' He began to weep again and stopped. Adam was embarrassed. They were near the Chinese, who turned to look at them.

'I've killed my mates,' Horrie said.

'Who?'

'Bernie and Fred.'

'No, you haven't, Horrie. You've just had a lot to drink.'

'I killed them.' His eyes poured grief.

'Horrie, stop it! Come on. Keep walking. You haven't killed anyone. You're just imagining it. You know, like a dream. You'll be all right in the morning.'

'I thought it was those bloody Chinese,' Horrie said, eyes fixed on Adam. 'You remember, don't you? I took you down to show you.'

152

'You mean down the mine?' Adam tugged at Horrie's arm but the old man shook him loose.

'I thought it was some of those bloody pigtailed thieves and I set myself a little trap for them and I got them. By God, I got them.' He jabbed a finger at Adam. 'Two of them came. I saw them. Sneaking up like a pair of dingoes.'

'*But come ye back* ...' The voice of Dexter Paradine soared on the night air. He had one hand on his chest, as if to hold in the heart that threatened to burst with emotion. A murmur of voices trailed after his high notes.

To one side Adam saw Jimmy. He was sitting halfway up a ridge, on the fringe of the light cast by the fire. He was grinning.

'They knew where to go. They were the ones all right. Straight down the shaft. Straight to where the opal was.'

'What are you talking about?' Adam said.

'I set a trap for those thieving Chinese,' Horrie said, grinding out the words. 'But the clever bastards didn't come.'

'But you said you saw them. Who did come?'

Horrie said nothing. He turned away.

'My God, Horrie! Was it Bernie and Fred?'

The back of Horrie's head dropped in a nod.

'And what happened?'

'I sealed them in.' He half turned his head, so Adam could see one watery eye. 'I set off a couple of sticks of explosive. They're still down there. Bastards. They were robbing me. My own mates.'

'And you ...'

'I thought it was just the Chinese.'

'Horrie, do you know what you've done?'

'I killed the wrong men, that's what I done.' He sniffed loudly. 'They're awful bastards,' he said, turning to reveal eyes that were glazed once more. 'I lost a couple of horses because of them. They poisoned them.'

'Bernie and Fred didn't do that.'

'And you can't trust them. They're always spying on me, and just waiting for the chance to rob me. They've been sneaking down the mine for a couple of nights now.'

'Horrie, you're not making sense.' Adam moved towards him.

'Keep away,' he snapped. He stepped backwards and, reaching behind him, produced the knife. 'Are you one of them?' he screamed, and the Chinese on the rise turned at the sound. 'One step, young feller, and I'll give you a second mouth.'

The knife carved the air.

'Jesus, Horrie, put it down!'

Horrie looked at him closely. 'You're not Chinese,' he accused. 'What are you doing here? You weren't stealing from me.' He backed away. 'No, you can't fool me. You think I'm too old to know what's been going on. But it wasn't you. It was the bloody Chinks. Bastards.'

He swung the knife wildly, and the movement spun him around. He faced the Chinese and, for the first time, saw them. One of them, no more than six paces away, stood up, fear showing on his face.

'There he is,' Horrie growled, pointing with his free hand. 'Look at his face. You can tell.'

Now, several Chinese stood. Horrie advanced on them, walking slowly and wiping the knife-blade on his knee as he went. The Chinese began to back away. One trod on another and fell. With a shout, Horrie charged.

Adam chased him but Horrie, moving with surprising speed, had reached the fallen man. The knife-blade slashed and blood squirted in Horrie's face. He screamed in triumph.

'Please, back there!' Dexter Paradine called from the fire, his eyes straining to see beyond the flames. 'This is a social gathering. Let's have some quiet so's we can get on with the next song.'

The knife flashed again.

'How about the lovely new tune that starts "I'll be loving you, always"?'

A Chinese miner, rock in hand, came out of the shadows and launched himself at Horrie. Adam, about to grapple with his friend, rammed the Chinese with his shoulder and the man fell. Adam saw Horrie's arm raised and grabbed the wrist. He bent the arm behind the old man's back and Horrie cried out, more in frustration than pain. He was snarling, lips flecked with foam and face spotted with the fallen man's blood. Adam hooked his other arm around Horrie's chest and throat and wrenched him away from his victim.

Horrie's first violent slash had removed the man's left thumb. Blood was pumping from the wound. The man's side was also stained red but he was conscious and, with his attacker wrapped in Adam's iron embrace, the Chinese crawled away.

'When the things you've planned, need a helping hand ...'

Hands in his fob pockets, eyes closed, Dexter Paradine was

singing the way he liked it: with no one else joining in. The attention of all those with their eyes opened was on the disturbance at the back of the crowd.

Horrie struggled violently, his eyes bulging from the pressure of the arm across his throat. Adam pulled him backwards and both of them rolled on the ground.

'It's me!' Adam shouted, but Horrie was beyond hearing or understanding. The knife had fallen but now he was trying to claw Adam.

The Chinese whom Adam had pushed rose to his knees and picked up a rock. He wiped his mouth, saw blood and charged, throwing the rock as he ran. Adam wrenched Horrie to one side and the rock shattered on the ground. The Chinese bent to pick up a smaller stone. Before he could rise, a dark figure jumped between him and Adam.

The Chinese straightened, and Jimmy Kettle hit him with a left that split his cheek. He fell unconscious.

The fallen man's companions loomed out of the darkness. The leader carried a spade. He ran at Jimmy, swinging the spade as he advanced. Jimmy swayed to one side and, as the man stumbled from the effect of the wild swipe, sank his left fist into the man's stomach.

Adam heard someone cheer.

'Go back,' he called to the Chinese, for there were more of them edging towards Jimmy. 'This old man's drunk, that's all.' But they were not listening and three of the men, faces contorted in anger, were closing on the aboriginal. The one on Jimmy's right had a pick in his hands and he rushed from the side.

There may have been six blows. Afterwards no one was sure. Certainly, two were needed to put the man with the pick on his knees where he stayed, dribbling blood and trying to put a tooth back through his lip. It was the other blows people could not count. There was a rush of fists, the blur of a black man attacking his assailants, and the other two Chinese were on their backs.

Adam hauled Horrie to his feet. 'That's enough!' he called, shaking the old man like a rag doll. 'Look, this is the bloke who started it. He's drunk. We don't want to fight you. Go away.'

More Chinese had gathered. Their faces blurred in the faint light, they stood around the man with the knife wounds.

Jimmy faced them, his fists resting on his thighs, his feet skipping lightly on the dusty surface.

'It's all over,' Adam said. 'Go home. No need for anyone else to get hurt.'

'*Not for just an hour, not for just a day ...*'

Dexter Paradine, eyes blissfully shut, was singing to a deserted fire.

'Shit,' said Sam, from the group who had gathered near the ridge, 'did you see that? How many did he flatten. Four?'

'Five. Never seen anything like it,' said another man and a few in the crowd started to clap.

Paradine bowed, opened his eyes, and turned, confused. His face darted from the empty rows beside the fire to the backs of the men on the rise. The postmaster, who had been standing at the rear of the group, returned to the fire.

'What happened?' Paradine said. A wisp of smoke drifted across his face and he rubbed his eyes.

'There was a fight with the Chinese,' Moore said. 'I think old Horrie Smith started it.'

'Was it a bad one?' He had moved but the smoke followed him.

'Bad? It was real good.' Moore jabbed the air with a broad fist. 'He flattened five blokes.'

Paradine, eyes streaming, looked astonished. 'Old Horrie?'

'No, of course not. He was too full to know what he was doing. That nigger hit them. The one who works with young Adam Ross.'

Thomas, the opal buyer, joined Moore. He had been standing on his own, away from the glow of the fire. 'Anyone hurt?' he asked casually.

'There was a lot of blood,' Moore said, nodding greetings. 'This fellow will know.' He beckoned to Sam, who was walking back to the fire with a number of men following him.

Sam had heard the conversation. 'One of the chows lost his thumb,' he called, his face animated with excitement.

'How dreadful,' Paradine said, wiping an eye.

'In a fist fight?' Thomas asked, arching an eyebrow.

'No, there was a knife,' Sam said, looking at Thomas, with an expression that said 'I don't know you, do I?', then another that confirmed he did not, before both were extinguished by the joy of having seen a good fight. His eyes turned to Moore. 'Shit, Ben, you should have seen that abo fight! They had shovels and things and he just flattened them. I never seen anyone so quick.'

'He's got to be a pro,' one of the other men said.

'A professional boxer?' Paradine said.

'It was the way he carried his fists and moved.' The man demonstrated.

Sam, watching, grinned. 'You look like a flea that won a Great Dane in the lottery,' he said.

'By the Jesus, Sam,' the man protested, 'only a professional moves like that bloke does. He's been in the ring.'

'I seen a fighter like him down south,' another man said. 'He was in a boxing troupe. You know, with one of those circuses. This bloke looked just like him.'

He turned and they all turned, but Jimmy was obscured by a wall of miners' backs.

'That feller in the circus was the best fighter I ever seen. Can't think of his name.' The man was wearing a soldier's slouch hat and removed it to scratch his head, as though the action would sharpen his memory.

'What's the name of this bloke, anyhow?' Moore asked, nodding towards the ridge.

'Jimmy,' one of the men said.

Thomas touched his nose. 'If it is the partner of young Mr Ross, then that aboriginal has a very unusual name. Something like pot. Jimmy Pot? No.' He touched his hands, placing them in front of his chest as though in prayer. 'Kettle. Jimmy Kettle. Mind you, it is merely a nickname. His real name is Black.'

Moore looked surprised, and Thomas smiled. 'I was talking to young Ross earlier this evening,' he explained.

The man with the soldier's hat scratched his head again. His face was twisted with the effort of thought. 'That was *his* name,' he said, and smiled at the group, relieved that his memory had been restored. 'I saw him box in Port Pirie. He flattened a big bloke. Fastest left I ever seen. He's a southpaw, isn't he?'

Someone nodded.

'That's him. That's the bloke all right. Kettle. Jimmy Kettle.'

'Curious name,' Thomas said quietly.

NINE

Soon after the fight finished, Horrie passed out and lay curled on the ground, sleeping noisily while the arguments and explanations raged above him.

'I saw one of the Chinese with a spade in his hands,' one man said, standing in front of the others to make sure he was seen as well as heard.

'Was that why old Horrie drew his knife?' a man chewing a pipe said.

'Probably self-defence.'

'Jesus! The old bloke taught the chow a lesson.'

The Chinese miners, drawn into a sullen group around their wounded, stared back. The fire had diminished and their faces were masks of aged parchment.

'Didn't Horrie start it?' a small voice asked.

'Apparently not,' the man beside him said. 'Someone had a go at him with a spade.'

'What was the abo doing, then?'

'Just keeping them off Horrie. They were like wild men.'

They turned to study Jimmy once more, but he had gone.

Stan Scanlon arrived, breathless from running. An opal miner, he doubled as the town's first-aid man and carried a medicine chest he had fetched from his dugout. The Chinese withdrew a few paces as he approached, leaving the man who had been knifed lying on the ground. The man held his injured hand against his stomach. He looked at Scanlon through unfocused eyes.

'Soon fix you up, mate,' Scanlon said, kneeling and lifting the man's arm. Blood as dark as treacle formed a glutinous seal to the side of the hand. Scanlon sucked in his breath and heard similar sounds from the miners who had followed and now stood behind him, watching.

'Nice and clean,' he said, his voice husky, and felt someone's knees touch his back. 'Just give me room,' he said softly and the pressure eased. Voices murmured and there was much shuffling of feet. 'This dust isn't going to help,' he said but the movement continued.

Scanlon opened the chest. It contained brandy, castor oil,

Epsom salts, iodine, aspirin and a few rolls of bandages. There were surprisingly few injuries on the field. Most of those who sought aid only needed the brandy.

The injured Chinese was trying to pull his arm free.

'Just let me have a look for a minute, mate,' Scanlon said, gripping the man's wrist tightly and examining the wound. The knife had cut from the top of the palm, alongside the first finger, to the wrist. A piece of jagged bone projected from the opening. Blood trickled over Scanlon's fingers.

'Won't be playing much cricket for a while,' he said in a soothing voice and the Chinese looked at him uncomprehendingly. 'Weren't an opening batsman, were you?' he chatted on, selecting a bandage.

The man fainted.

Adam, left on his own, decided it was a good time to leave. It was also a good time to take Horrie away before he woke and started talking about the men he had buried. He picked up the old man, who hung limp in his grip, and slung him across his shoulder. He carried him to his home. Horrie had dirtied his pants and a sickening stench of excrement mingled with the sweet fumes of methylated spirits. Adam dumped him on the cot, made sure he was breathing, and wiped his hands on a rough earthen wall. He stepped outside and breathed deeply of the cold air. The stars were bright, their intensity diminished only by a low haze of smoke from the fire. He began to walk to his own home. He moved stiffly, for his muscles had grown cold and he ached in several places from the bruising he had received down the mine.

Approaching the fire, he paused. A babble of strange words floated towards him and he saw the Chinese carrying the unconscious form of their companion. The man's hand and lower chest were swathed in bandages. One of the other Chinese turned and, in the faint light, part of his face seemed to be painted purple. Iodine. He must have been one of the men Jimmy felled.

On the ridge, Stan Scanlon was on his knees, repacking the medicine chest. Behind him, a man was taking a swig from a small bottle. He grunted with satisfaction and handed the bottle to Scanlon, who put it in the chest.

A few of the miners had returned to the fire. They were in small groups and stood close to the flames which were dying as the wood supply ran out.

Staying clear of the others, Adam walked beyond the fire. His hip ached and he let his leg drag in a limp. He rounded the small hill into which he had dug his home and stopped, surprised. Lights flashed on the horizon. It must be a car, he thought, and watched for a few minutes as the lights scythed the sky. Traffic on the road was rare, even in daylight, but he had never seen a car coming into town so late at night.

Adam waited for another flash of light. Nothing happened. He was just standing there, stiff and sore and staring at a horizon that was so black his eyes ached from the effort of looking for something in an immensity of darkness. Had he imagined those lights? No. He began to move on, concentrating on finding his way. There was a car out there all right, travelling slowly on the rough track and bumping and pitching and flashing its lights into the sky or stabbing the depths of some dry channel. It must be in a depression, or following some twist in the track that pointed its headlamps in another direction. Whatever it was doing, it was a long way from town.

He reached the entrance to his home and breathed deeply. His head was a swirling thunderstorm of thoughts. Horrie and the men he had killed. The fight with the Chinese. The opal he had found. His forthcoming meeting with Mr Thomas at the post office.

Tomorrow, he would know his future. A rich man, able to buy his own place? There could be more opals. He hadn't thought of that. Another deep breath. The horizon was still dark. Maybe the car had stopped or broken down. He remembered lonely nights beside another car, many years ago.

Feeling cold, he went inside.

Josef was awake. He was burning with anger at the humiliation of being struck by his father in public. Adam let him talk for a while, and then told him of Horrie's attack on the Chinese and of the subsequent fight. Josef asked Adam to repeat the story and his eyes glowed, for he was at the age when tales of violence seem exciting rather than shocking. And, in this story, his friend Jimmy was the hero.

'Do you think he'd teach me to box?' Josef asked.

'I'll teach you, if you like.'

Josef grinned, as though Adam had told a joke. 'No, seriously, do you think he would?'

'Who do you want to fight?'

'My father.' Josef unleashed a flurry of blows into the air above his bed. 'Pow, pow, pow!' he exploded, as his fists struck their imaginary target.

'You're hitting him a lot harder than he hit you,' Adam said, trying not to smile.

'He's bigger than me, so I've got to hit harder. Pow!' He swung a knock-out blow and almost rolled from the mattress. He lay on his side, breathing heavily. 'Did you hate your father, Adam?'

Adam shook his head.

'I wish mine had died when I was young.'

'Don't say that.'

'But I do. He's always beating me and treating me like a baby. Don't do this. Don't do that.'

Adam sat at Josef's feet. A candle was burning on the shelf and Adam's movement cast a shadow across the boy. 'Your father's got a lot of things on his mind,' he said.

'Like what?' Josef pulled at a loose thread on his shirt.

'Like not having any money. Things are very hard for your father. He had to give up the vineyard and now he's been here a few months and hasn't found any opal. He must be worried sick.'

'Well, you haven't found any opal and you're not worried.'

'I haven't got to feed a son who eats like a horse,' he said, and dodged Josef's kick. 'And who said I haven't found opal?'

Josef sat up. 'Have you?'

Adam nodded. 'Today.'

'How big?' He was on his feet.

'Can you keep a secret?'

'Sure. How big?'

'Big. But you mustn't tell anyone. Promise?'

Josef bobbed his head in agreement. 'Let me see.'

'Not so fast. You've got to promise you won't tell anyone. Only Jimmy and myself know about it so far. And Mr Thomas.'

'That funny-looking man who was in our bus? He gave me the creeps. Why did you tell him?'

'Because he buys opals. I'm going to see him again in the morning. Nine o'clock at the post office.'

'If I found a big opal, I wouldn't sell it. Not the first one. I'd have it made into a ring and wear it all the time.'

'You can't eat a ring for breakfast,' Adam said.

Josef skipped on the spot. 'Show me,' he said.

'Promise to keep quiet.'

161

'I won't tell anyone.'

'Not until I've sold it?'

'Not until you've sold it.'

'Well, you stay here.' Adam lit another candle and went to his room. Even as he pulled the bed curtain to one side he was aware of someone's presence.

She was on the bed, her eyes wide in the sudden light.

Startled, Adam pulled the curtain back into place.

'Have you got it hidden in there?' Josef called.

Nellie sat up. She was filthy. Her face was streaked by runnels of mud.

'Never you mind,' Adam said loudly, not taking his eyes from her. 'You just wait till I get it.'

She began to stand. Gently, Adam pushed her back. His expression implored her to be silent.

'How big is the opal?' Josef called, and Adam could hear the boy's feet shuffling in the dirt as he waited impatiently for an answer.

The candlelight flashed in Nellie's eyes.

'As big as my thumbnail?' Josef prompted from the other side of the curtain. 'I've seen one that big. Or is it bigger? Come on, Adam, tell me, please!'

Their eyes met. Her lips curled in the slightest of smiles and she turned, to lie face down on the bed.

Adam swung towards the curtain. 'You'll see in a minute,' he snapped. Now, because of young Joe, Nellie knew about the opal.

What should he do? He thought of leaving the room and pretending there had been no opal, that he had been playing a joke. No – Josef would not believe him and even if he did, he would discover the truth tomorrow and then he would feel betrayed. He could walk out and say he had changed his mind and tell young Joe to wait until tomorrow. That would hurt too much. That would be treating him like a child.

Adam turned, picking nervously at a fingernail.

Josef wouldn't sleep if he didn't see the opal tonight. And then, what would happen to the girl? He couldn't keep her hidden in his room with Joe wide awake and chattering like a monkey all night. What would he do with her? He felt angry. Why had she come back? As if he didn't have enough things on his mind without her hiding in his room. Mr Thomas had said to tell no one, and now there were four other people who knew. He looked down at her

162

again, seething with confusion.

She was face down on the bed, lying still, as though indifferent. Her shoulders were slender.

Oh, God, what am I thinking, he said to himself, and knew the answer. He was thinking how pleased he was she had come back.

'Adam. What are you doing?' Josef's voice was a quiet whine of protest.

Adam knelt at the wall opposite the bed. He had buried the precious piece of rock in a recess there.

'You call out once more,' he said, feeling for the soft patch that marked the place where he had hidden it, 'and I won't show it to you.' He located the spot and quickly scooped dirt from the cavity. What the hell. She knew about it; she might as well see it. He stood, grasping the rock in one hand and turning it, to admire the colour changes as he held it near the candle.

Nellie was not looking. He waited, expecting her to move. She did not. He stepped towards her and touched her shoulder. She turned, looked briefly at the rock in his hand, looked hard into his eyes for several seconds and then rolled on her side, away from him.

'Adam, please!' The plea from the other room was little more than a whisper, delivered quietly so as not to offend, but filled with a bursting curiosity.

Adam stepped into the other room.

The rock he carried was as large as a loaf of bread, and tapered to a wedge shape. He handed it to his young friend, whose jaw dropped in astonishment. For several seconds Josef examined it without speaking. He rolled it in his hands, occasionally blinking as he discovered some new and startling flash of brilliance. Finally, and with reverence, he passed it back to Adam.

'What do you think?' Adam said.

Josef lifted his gaze from the opal to Adam's face. 'Bit big for a ring,' he drawled, and they both laughed.

'Oh, Adam,' he said, suddenly looking serious, 'you'll be a millionaire. You'll be wearing a fancy suit and smoking a big cigar and telling the time from a gold watch on a chain and you'll have a big fat stomach.' He prodded Adam in the belly.

'Cut it out,' Adam said, and held the rock close to him.

'How much money will you get?'

Adam hesitated.

'Enough to buy your own property? That's what you want,

isn't it?' Josef brought the candle close to the opal.

'Maybe enough to put a deposit on a small place.' Adam gazed down on the rock. It was beautiful, like a fire burning in ice, in impossible colours.

'Can I come and work with you?' Josef touched the opal and ran a finger softly along the surface.

'What about your parents?'

'Oh, they're talking about going back somewhere near Adelaide and trying to grow grapes again.'

'When?'

'I don't know. Soon, I think. Unless we find something.' He looked at Adam with mournful eyes.

'Wouldn't you rather grow grapes in some place where there's grass and trees and lots of people your age than live up here in country like this?'

'You like it.'

'I'm used to it. I've always lived in this sort of country.'

'I'd rather live where you lived. I'd rather be with you.'

Adam looked down, embarrassed.

'Would Jimmy work with you?' Josef asked, still touching the rock, his head angled in wonder.

'Half this is his. He can do what he likes. We might share a place. I don't know.'

'You're the only man I know who treats an aboriginal like an ordinary person,' Josef said. 'All the other grown-ups talk about them as though they were – I don't know – just different.'

'Jimmy's my friend.'

'I know that, Adam, but it's not just that. You're ... well, you're fair. Some other people are nice to them but they still treat them like they were pet dogs or something. You treat everyone the same.'

'Why not?' Adam said. One part of the rock, where it tapered to its narrowest width, shone with an intense blue.

'Can I stay with you? If you buy your own property?'

'I'll tell you what. If the opal's worth any money, and if Mr Thomas gives me a lot for it, and if that's enough for me to get my own place, and if your parents don't mind, I'd like you to come and work with me. You're just about my best friend.'

Josef took the rock from Adam and weighed it again in his hands. He kept his head down. 'You could be the richest man in Australia,' he said. 'Like an emperor.'

'What's an emperor?' Adam took back the rock.

'Someone who rules over an empire.'

Adam looked puzzled. 'What's that?'

'An empire? Well, Australia's part of the British Empire. Germany used to be an empire. It's like a kingdom only bigger, I suppose.'

'And you reckon I could get my own empire with this?' Adam said disbelievingly. 'You better get back in bed. You're dreaming standing up.'

'At least you could get a place that would be your own. That's almost the same thing. You could do what you liked and there'd be no one to boss you around. Wouldn't that be great?'

Adam nodded. He was thinking of Nellie in the next room. 'Why don't you go back to bed? You've got to work tomorrow. You never know, it might be your turn to find opal.'

Josef fell on the bed and let his legs swing high and rest on the wall. 'Fat chance,' he said bitterly. 'Everyone else'll find opals and we'll just dig up bucket after bucket of that rotten kopi.'

'Do you want to make a bet?'

'What's that?' Josef lowered his legs and propped himself on one elbow.

'That you end up making more money than me.'

'Here at Coober Pedy?'

'I mean later on, when you've grown up. You're a smart bloke, Joe. Smarter than me.'

Josef slumped back on the mattress. He yawned and looked as though he might go to sleep before answering. He could fall asleep faster than anyone Adam had ever met. 'You sound like my mother,' he said, examining Adam through heavy eyelids. 'Whenever she wants me to study, she talks like that.'

'You mean she tells you you're smarter than I am?'

Josef had closed his eyes. His mouth twitched in a smile. 'Of course not. She tells me I'm smarter than she is. People always say things like that when they want something.'

'I want you to go to sleep.'

'You still sound like my mother.' His voice was slurred.

'Your mother's a nice woman,' Adam said softly. Josef did not answer. He rolled on his side. Adam waited.

A dog howled. The sound came from a long way, and rolled eerily into the room.

'Goodnight, Joe,' Adam whispered. There was no answer. The

boy's breathing grew slower and deeper.

Adam realized he was trembling. It was not the cold. Nor the bruises that burned in his muscles. Nor the excitement of the day nor the shock of what Horrie had said or done. It was the knowledge that Nellie was in the next room, waiting for him. He moved to the candle on the shelf and blew out the flame. The remaining candle was in his hand, and it shook, so that his own shadow became a monstrous thing whose edges raced and receded across the walls and ceiling of the underground chamber.

He had to wait, to calm down, before returning to his own room. He moved to the open doorway and went outside. Sounds drifted towards him. The faint voice of Anemone Hoffman, plaintive in the manner of a child who is half-asleep, was calling for something. From a greater distance, some men laughed. They were probably still at the fire, waiting for the last embers to die. An engine hummed and was silent, as though switched off. An insect chirped. A door slammed, a thudding, metallic sound. And deep silence, creeping in like a tide, overwhelmed everything.

Adam went inside. He paused to make sure Josef was covered and stepped into his room.

Nellie was still on the bed. 'Is he asleep?' she whispered, her face buried in the rough mattress.

'Just,' Adam said. He put the candle on a narrow shelf of rock that projected from the wall near the curtain.

She rose to her knees and sat with her hands looped in front of her. She moved with the grace of a cat.

'Can I see it?' she said, so softly Adam had difficulty understanding her. He gave her the opal and smiled as she almost dropped the rock on the bed.

'It's heavy,' he said.

She put it on the floor. 'Is it really worth a lot of money?'

He shrugged his shoulders.

'Will you be rich?'

Adam picked up the rock and put it back in the hole at the base of the far wall. 'Do you mean rich enough to buy you a ticket out of town?' he said, pushing the seal of loose dirt back into place. He worked with his back to her, so she could not see. When she did not answer, he turned. Her head was lowered and she was brushing dirt from the back of one hand.

He sat beside her on the bed.

'How did you get so dirty?' he said. 'You're covered in dust.'

Her eyes were huge. 'There was a dust storm,' she said.

He moistened a finger and rubbed it across her cheek. 'Where were you? Out in the middle of it?'

'Just about.' She returned Adam's grin, but quickly turned her face. 'I came to say I'm sorry.'

Adam straightened his back. 'What for?'

'Last night.' She stared at their shadows on the wall.

'What about it?'

'The things I said. I didn't mean them.'

Adam stood and walked to the curtain. He opened it slightly, to make sure Josef still slept. When he turned his head was near the candle and one half of his face glowed brightly, and his blond beard sparkled like frost.

'I haven't been sleeping with the Chinese,' she said.

'Doesn't matter. All men are the same, aren't they?'

Her eyes seemed to grow even larger.

'I hear you've been sleeping with anyone who'll have you,' he said, and immediately regretted it when he saw the look of hurt that touched her face.

She nursed her forehead in both hands for some time, but when she looked up it was a harder young woman who confronted him. 'That's men for you,' she said, and her voice was harsh. 'All they want from you is one thing. A fuck.'

'Nellie!'

'It's true. If they don't get it, they make up stories about you.'

'You shouldn't talk like that.' He walked to another wall and leaned against the raw earth, his face enshrouded in its own shadow. 'You sound dreadful when you swear like that,' he said.

'Not ladylike?'

He could sense the smile taunting him. 'No,' he said and turned. She was smiling. 'God, you're filthy,' he said.

'Shouldn't say God.'

'It's better than what you said.'

'Fuck?'

'Oh, Nellie, please.' He faced the wall again. He scratched at some soft claystone. 'I thought you meant what you said the other night.'

'About sleeping with all those men? About going out and getting myself a Chinese?'

Adam's nod was almost imperceptible.

'I was just saying that. I get angry easily.'

He moved along the wall, not looking at her. 'What about all the men you've been talking to?'

'I just want to get away from this place, that's all, and I can't do it on my own. I haven't been … I haven't slept with anyone. Not since I left Jimmy, anyhow.'

'Everyone reckons you have.' He turned and her eyes bored into his, challenging him to believe her. He moved closer. 'Why do you say such terrible things?'

'I told you. I get angry. All men look at me the same way and I know what they're thinking. You can see it in their eyes, the way they lick their lips. It's disgusting. And if they can't have it, they reckon other men must be getting it. A bit of smoked log – that's what they call it with a black woman. Did you know that? No, you probably didn't. You're too innocent.'

He walked away, touching the wall in places and picking at some dirt under a fingernail. She watched him, an amused smile on her face.

'You're like a dog on a chain,' she said. 'Come and sit down again. You'll wake Joe.'

He stopped in the middle of the room. 'Where have you been staying?'

Her eyes blazed. 'You don't believe me, do you? You think I'm covered in dirt because I've been tossed from one filthy chow to the next, don't you?'

'No, I don't.'

'Yes, you do! You're like the others. No one ever believes me.'

'I just asked where you'd been staying.'

She stood and a fine cloud of dust spread from her dress. 'On my own,' she said.

'And out in the open, by the look of it. You could do with a wash,' he said gently.

'It was the storm.'

'Have you had any water?'

'No.'

'There's a little here in the can.' He offered her a jam tin that was half-full of water. She drank it so rapidly he became concerned.

'How long since you had a drink?' he said.

'A fair while.' She looked at him anxiously. 'Have you got any more?'

'Outside in the other room. Have you had anything to eat?'

168

She shook her head.

'Since when?' He touched her face, to make her look at him.

'A few days.' She looked away.

Adam frowned. He had thought at first she was merely drawn and dirty. In fact, she was half-starved and so parched her thirst must have been almost unbearable. And she had endured the dust storm like that.

'You could have died out there today,' he said, his brows furrowed in concern.

'I didn't,' she said, looking straight at him. 'Could I have more water, please?'

'Yes, of course.' He began to leave, but she touched his arm.

'Is there enough for a wash? I know everyone's short of water but if I don't clean myself, I'll die. I can imagine what a mess I must look.'

She's half-dead from thirst and she wants to use water to make herself look better, Adam thought. He had known tough bushmen who hadn't washed for three months or more. They stank but they didn't care. He grinned. He mightn't understand women, but he liked them.

'There's a basin in the corner,' he said, pointing to a dish he had hand-beaten from a sheet of tin. 'I'll get the drum of water.'

He stepped beyond the curtain and groped in the dark for the water he had collected from the town's underground tank. He placed the drum on the floor, and moved past Josef to find a can of meat. Josef stirred. He mumbled a few words and Adam stopped, not daring to move. He could hear faint sounds coming from his room. Metal clanked on wood as Nellie replaced the tin can on the shelf. Clothing rustled. Bare feet shuffled on the dirt floor.

A sliver of light marked the edge of the curtain. A shadow crossed it.

Josef's breathing became slow and rhythmic. Adam waited a little longer, then collected the meat and the drum and returned to his room.

She opened the curtain. She was naked.

He stepped inside, put down the drum and can, and turned his back. He flicked the curtain in place. He was breathing rapidly.

'You've got to stop doing that,' he whispered.

'And saying "fuck"?' she said.

'Nellie!'

She did not speak and he glanced back. She was standing near him, her hands on her hips. Her head, arms and legs were coated with dust but her body was sleek and brown. She was a Venus, with dirty extremities.

She moved, tilting her shoulders and hips at opposing angles. Her breasts bounced slightly.

'Would you mind pouring me some water?' she said. 'I can't lift the drum.'

He tried to keep his eyes from her. 'Why do you give me such a hard time?' he said, as he unscrewed the cap on the drum. 'Bring the basin over here.'

'Because you're so funny,' she said, putting the dish in place. 'I can't wash my body without taking my clothes off. If you find me ugly, you can wait outside.'

'You're not ugly,' he said, starting to pour. 'Just grubby.'

'Have you got a sister?' she said, scooping the first of the water in her hands and drinking it.

'No.'

'How much water can you spare?'

'I can buy some more tomorrow.'

'Can I have a whole basin full?'

'Sure. That's not much.'

'It's heaven,' she said, lowering herself to her knees and putting her hair under the jet of pouring water. 'That explains it.'

'Explains what?'

'Why you stare at me like you do.' She lifted her head and let water run down her face and chest.

'I don't stare at you.'

'You are now.'

He turned his head.

'It's all right. I don't mind. I had four brothers and we all used to get bathed together.' She shook her head.

Adam winced as the spray hit him.

'Why don't you get undressed and have a wash too?' she said, and immersed her hair in the basin. Her back fanned in an arch of glistening skin. Bent like that, with her head out of sight beneath a tumble of hair and her limbs folded into the body, she resembled a lovely brown tortoise shell Adam had once seen.

'I washed before the camp fire tonight,' he said.

She rose from the basin, and her hair was plastered to her head. The longer strands trailed across her shoulders. 'Would you like

170

to wash me?' she said, resting on her buttocks with her hands on her bent knees.

He shook his head.

'Am I the first woman you've ever seen like this?'

He nodded.

'Truly?'

'I've seen a few old gins in blackfellows' camps. But they were different.'

'You've seen tits then.'

'Nellie, please don't speak like that.'

'What's wrong with tits? Are they ugly or something?' She took a deep breath and thrust out her chest. Her damp breasts glistened. 'I've heard men say they were lovely.'

My God, they were beautiful. He felt himself rising. 'No, of course not,' he said. 'It's just the word. The way it's said. It's the way you say it that sounds unpleasant.' He cleared his throat.

'Did you know that most women have one tit bigger than the other?' She cupped her hand beneath one breast, then the other. 'Mine are the same, I think, don't you?'

Adam looked away. She splashed him.

'Don't get shy,' she said and began washing her neck and shoulders. 'Do you have any soap?'

Glad of the chance to move, he went to the shelf and returned with a fragment of sand soap.

'Do you have anything softer?' She stood up and, when he shook his head, turned. 'Scrub my back, will you?'

He hesitated.

'Go on. I can't reach it.' She swung back towards him, and thrust her chest at him. 'Would you rather scrub my front?'

He did not move.

'I think you would,' she said and moved towards him, until her body pressed against his.

TEN

Saleem Benn recognized the sound even in his sleep, and struggled to wake quickly and get to his feet. He heard the pounding of hooves, the snap of salt bush and the weird half-gurgle, half-grunt of a wild bull camel charging into the camp. The fire had burned down to a few cold sticks and the rogue came straight through, scattering ash and trailing flecks of foam from its mouth.

Saleem Benn's nephew rose from his blanket and stood, numb from cold and fear, directly in the animal's path. The camel, its eyes fixed on the string of females tethered on the far side of the Afghan's camp, ran into the boy, sending him cartwheeling like a dead bush tumbling in the wind.

The camel hit the rope, snapped it, and in an instant the females were loose. Crazed with lust, the bull mounted one, driving it on to its front knees. The rest scattered.

Saleem Benn bent for his rifle, rammed a cartridge home, and fired one shot. The rogue bull's head snapped to one side. It made the noise of a balloon losing air, and fell dead.

The Afghan ran to the misshapen lump of cloth and flesh that was his nephew. Teeth bared in anger at what he saw, he turned his rifle towards the night, ready for any more feral camels that had roamed down from the empty deserts to the north and had picked up the scent of his beloved pack animals.

It was a grey morning. Clouds dappled the sky and the threat of rain hung in the air.

At five to nine, Adam reached the post office dugout and stood outside the entrance, unsure whether to go in or not. Over his shoulder was his bag, its canvas bottom distorted by the opal-bearing rock. He had washed, using the remains of the muddy water in the basin. His hair was still wet, and neatly parted.

A murmur of voices came from the post office. Adam moved to the doorway, ducking his head to avoid the iron awning above the entrance. Two men were talking. Their shapes were dark and indistinct in the half-light. One turned. It was Ben Moore, the postmaster. He nodded greetings.

'Is Mr Thomas here?' Adam asked.

'He'll be back in a few minutes, son,' Moore said.

The other man was a bulky shadow in the corner, but Adam sensed the man was studying him with interest.

'Looks like rain,' Moore said.

Adam agreed. 'I'll wait outside,' he said.

'Good idea. He should be along any moment.'

Adam walked well clear of the entrance. He felt strangely nervous. He turned in a slow circle like a dog sniffing for danger before settling for the night.

A cool wind lazed from the west where layers of cloud were gathering to muster strength for their journey across the plains surrounding the town. The breeze was laden with information: the soft promise of rain and the pungent aromas of the morning's fires.

Stan Scanlon approached, heading towards his own dugout and carrying the medicine chest. 'Looks like rain,' he said and stopped to transfer the chest to his other hand. 'Could do with it.'

Adam nodded. 'Have you seen Mr Thomas?'

'That dark gentleman? No. Not this morning. I've just been over to see that Chinese bloke. The one that Horrie got stuck into.'

'How is he?'

'Not too good.' Scanlon wiped his forehead. 'His mates are looking after him. Christ, they've got some weird ideas. Still, there are enough Chinese in this world for some of their ideas to be all right, I suppose.' He tested the weight of the chest. 'No, the bloke's pretty crook, I'd say. Got a fever. Not surprising seeing as how he lost a thumb and had a slice taken out of his ribs.'

Moore appeared at the post office doorway. He waved to Scanlon. 'Got a minute, Stan?'

'OK,' Scanlon shouted and then said to Adam: 'The others are all right. A few teeth missing. Cup lips. That sort of thing. That abo mate of yours can certainly hit. See you later.'

He lumped the chest to the post office and disappeared in the black slot that was its doorway. Like a parcel going into a post box, Adam thought, and walked a little way around the hill, hoping to meet Thomas.

A car was parked on the far side of a cluster of rocks. It looked as though it had been driven a great distance. The radiator and part of the hinged engine cover were streaked with the rusty overflow of a boiled cooling system, while the rest of the car, from its canvas roof to the ribbed metal running boards, was caked with dust and an occasional splash of oil. Leather straps held two spare tyres in racks at the rear of each front mudguard. Two petrol cans were mounted on the tool box which projected from the tail of the car.

Adam walked closer. It was a Dodge. He could not read the

173

name but he recognized the symbols and he knew the model. He was good with cars. He had not seen this one in town before.

'Mr Ross!'

Thomas was beckoning him. The opal buyer was dressed in a dark blue suit and wore a hat whose brim had rolled edges. Adam had not seen such a hat before. It looked expensive. Thomas seemed agitated.

'You have the sample?'

Adam swung the bag off his shoulder.

'No, no,' Thomas said, 'don't take it out yet. In fact, better give me the bag. Come,' he said, when Adam seemed reluctant. He took the bag and began to walk rapidly towards the post office. He looked over his shoulder. Adam, restricted by his sore hip, had trouble in keeping up. 'Hurry up,' Thomas urged. 'I don't have much time. I have to leave town today. I'm a very busy man.'

He reached the entrance to the post ofice. 'You go inside first,' he said, avoiding Adam's eyes.

'There's someone in there with Mr Moore,' Adam said.

'That's all right, young man. Just go in. I have all my things in there. After you. Please. I'm in a hurry.'

It was dark in the dugout. Moore had moved behind the counter and was shuffling some weights on a scale. The other man had gone from the corner. There was no sign of Scanlon.

'Over here, son,' Moore said, not looking up.

Adam advanced to the counter, and was conscious of movement close behind him. He turned slowly. A figure, not tall but broad and powerful-looking, was blocking the doorway. Thomas was outside in the sunlight. He seemed distressed, and clutched Adam's bag with both hands.

'Your name Ross?' the figure in the doorway said. He growled the question. Adam strained to see his face but the light behind was too bright. An arm detached itself from the bulky silhouette and placed a hand against a door post. It was not the casual action of someone leaning for support. It was a deliberate move to block the opening.

Adam glanced around him. Moore coughed and looked embarrassed. 'Better answer, son,' he said.

'Yes it is,' Adam said and backed against the counter.

'How's Jimmy Kettle?' The shape did not move.

Adam turned to Moore. 'I came to see Mr Thomas,' he said. 'He asked me last night to come and see him.'

174

The postmaster, deep in shadow and guilt, fiddled with a brass weight.

'I know all that,' the man said. 'That's why I'm here. I asked you how Jimmy Kettle was.'

'Jimmy Black?' Adam said weakly.

'Jimmy Kettle,' the man said, lowering his arm and spreading his legs wider. 'Mr Thomas told me you said his name was Kettle. How is he these days?'

'I don't know,' Adam said. 'I haven't seen him.'

'Got in a fight last night, I believe.' The man stepped forward a pace. 'Good fighter, is he?' A finger came from the shadow and prodded Adam's chest.

Adam lifted his arms, and moved along the counter. 'What's going on? I came to see Mr Thomas.'

'Where is he?'

'Who?'

'Kettle. Don't play games with me, son.'

'Why do you want to know?'

'Just tell me where he is.'

Moore coughed. 'Better answer the sergeant, son.'

Adam peered at the shadow. 'You're a policeman?' he said, and turned to Moore for confirmation.

'Got here late last night,' Moore said.

'Is it about the Chinese?' Adam asked and, almost immediately, knew it was not, for the sergeant had moved to one side and light played upon his face. He had seen this man before, in a creek bed near Port Augusta.

At first Jimmy had no intention of going near Post Office Hill. He knew Adam would see Thomas, and Thomas would quote him a price for their opal. He knew what would happen then. Adam would come looking for him and tell him the price they would get. He trusted Adam absolutely. But he knew Adam would be excited and boyish, and Jimmy Kettle wanted to give a different impression. He was the calm one in the team. He would take the news quietly. Maybe even talk about something else. He would not smile. He could slip on the same poker face he had used in the boxing ring, and for an hour that morning he practised not smiling. He imagined Adam running across the plain, waving a hand to attract his attention and arriving too breathless to tell him the news he had striven so desperately to bring. Jimmy would

175

quieten him down, chat about the likelihood of rain, and enjoy the frustration that would build up on Adam's face.

Before nine o'clock, however, Jimmy grew restless. He began glancing nervously for the first sign of a running figure. He did not have a clock but he knew it was too early for Adam to be coming; yet he looked. And at a time he judged to be around nine, he began to walk to town.

He had bruised a knuckle on his left hand in the fight and he sucked it as he walked. It helped him think. He and Adam could be wealthy after today. He wondered what he would do with the money. He might give his mother some clothes, or buy her some blankets because she used to complain of the cold. Then there were his brothers and sisters and a few cousins and uncles and aunts. He would help them all because that was the way it was. He belonged to a people who shared. He thought about the uncle he had last seen bloodied and bruised near Port Augusta. He would like to give him something because the old man had suffered to protect his nephew.

It was the coldest morning he had known since coming to Coober Pedy. He wouldn't mind leaving the place. He wasn't a plains man. He liked the range country around Beltana.

He was walking across a gibber plain but imagining he was among the river gums of the creek where he spent much of his childhood. Those old eucalypts had been there for hundreds of years. They were huge trees that were at once both majestic and grotesque. Their trunks, scarred by the struggle to survive droughts and floods and fires, had bulged and split and set like giant fossilized sausages. Yet they were beautiful in the way they fitted the land so perfectly. They were as natural as the blue sky or the outcrops of shattered rock on the crest of hills, and they softened the harshness of a scorching summer's day with broad strokes of shade.

Jimmy's eyes were open but he was seeing another place. He was in a mood to dream, both of the past and the future. As a result, Josef was within shouting distance before Jimmy noticed him. The boy was desperately short of breath.

'Adam's in trouble!' he gasped when Jimmy reached him. 'Mr Thomas sent me.'

Jimmy caught the boy by the arm.

'What happened?'

'I'm not sure. Mr Thomas talks so funny it's hard to

understand him and he was so excited he wasn't making much sense.'

'Who's Thomas?' Jimmy asked and then remembered, clicking his tongue to mark the answer. 'The opal buyer. Has someone taken the opal?'

Josef shook his head. 'A man's grabbed Adam.'

'What?' Jimmy let go and began to run. He stopped. 'Where is he?'

Josef took a deep breath. 'He's in the post office. Don't you go.'

Jimmy had begun to move again. 'Why?'

'Mr Thomas said so. He told me to tell you to keep away.'

'Like hell I will,' he said, bouncing on his feet as anger rose in him like fire. 'No greasy bastard in a suit's going to tell me ...'

He did not finish. He was away, knees lifting high as he ran, jumping rocks and small bushes in his path.

'Jimmy!' Josef called after him, hands on his sides to hold the stitch burning his body. 'It's not like that! He was trying to warn you.'

But Jimmy was well on his way to town, running across the plain as an animal runs for its life: fast and strong, but without reason to temper its pace.

Josef, still burning from his run, watched in anguish, for the opal buyer had been clear about one thing when he came bursting into the Hoffman's bus. Jimmy Kettle had to keep away. The man had brought Adam's bag and told them to hide it. He had blurted out something about Adam being attacked. And he said Jimmy must be warned to keep away. There was some terrible danger.

Weeping with frustration, Josef began to walk back to town. In the distance, he could see the figure of Jimmy leaping bushes and running at undiminished pace.

A few people stood outside the post office. They were twitching with anticipation; insects hovering near a body that is not quite dead.

Jimmy saw them and paused.

'Inside,' called a man whose eyes were unnaturally large. 'He's got your mate.'

He heard Mrs Hoffman calling to him in a voice charged with fear but he was beyond caution. He dashed into the blackness of the dugout.

There was someone on the floor, a figure lying face down with his hands behind his back and manacles on his wrists. There was a man against the wall, a stout man with a collarless shirt, and his mouth open in shock.

'Sergeant Mailey, please, there's no need for such violence.' The voice sounded thin and more like a child's than a grown man's.

Jimmy felt the blow but it did not hurt at first. It hit him across the shoulders and the base of the neck and numbed him and he felt himself falling. And then came the burning and the sweeping wave of sickness.

'Sergeant!' The voice was trembling.

'Dangerous villains,' another voice said from somewhere above him and Jimmy felt a foot pressed against his shoulder-blades. The pain was intense. His mouth tasted dirt.

'I told you, they killed a lot of men,' the voice said, and the pressure on his shoulders increased and a wave of blackness engulfed him.

ELEVEN

Flies were buzzing and the air was foul with human smells.

They were in a small hut. The walls were made of dried mud and stone. Shafts of light bright with floating dust striped the air. A man was relieving himself against the wall. He turned, buttoning his trousers, and looked at Adam.

'You're awake,' he said, and tucked his shirt in his trousers.

Adam blinked a few times. His head ached.

'I've been looking for you two for a long time,' the man said. He pressed a thumb against one nostril and cleared the other.

'The name's Mailey, Sergeant Mailey,' he said and wiped the tip of his nose.

Adam sat up. He was on a dirt floor. For the first time, he was aware that Jimmy was lying near him.

'What did you do to him?' Adam asked and was surprised at the sound of his own voice. It was dry and gravelly.

'Same as to you,' the sergeant said reasonably. 'Gave him a whack behind the ear with a length of four by two.' He sniffed, to test that his nose was clear. 'He'll be all right. Abos have got thick skulls.'

178

'Where are we?' Adam asked.

'In the old police hut. Hasn't been used for half a dozen years or so. It'll do for the purpose though.'

Adam's arms ached. They were behind his back and his wrists rubbed on metal.

'There's a pair of handcuffs on you,' the sergeant said. 'Turn around and I'll take them off.'

Adam turned, not knowing what to expect. He heard the rustle of keys, felt his arms gripped by powerful hands, heard a click and felt the pressure on his wrists relieved.

The sergeant laughed. 'You're as tense as a length of railway line. Did you reckon I was going to hit you on the head again?'

Adam turned slowly.

'It's not you I'm really interested in. It's that black bastard on the floor. He could cause me a lot of trouble.' He eyed Adam. 'You were there, weren't you?'

Adam said nothing.

'Yeah, well, I know you were and that's just too bad for you.'

'Have you been looking for us?' Adam said. His voice still sounded gravelly.

'I told you I had. Don't you listen, or are you just not too bright? Only fifteen bob in the pound. Is that your trouble?'

'I don't follow you.'

'Stupid. Are you a bit short of sense?' The sergeant spat. 'Reckon you must be. No white man in his senses would go running around the countryside with an abo. What's the attraction? Does he let you stuff his girls? Is that it? You've got a taste for smoked log?' He saw the look in Adam's eyes and laughed. 'Don't like that, do you? All right to do it but don't like being found out? Well, I haven't much time for the blacks but some of them are better than white rubbish like you.'

The sergeant had a hand-gun in a holster on his belt. He took it out as he walked to where Jimmy lay unconscious on the floor of the hut. He used the top of a boot to prod him in the ribs.

'Still asleep,' he said, and moved the gun from one hand to the other.

Adam rubbed his wrists, to restore circulation to his hands.

'Is that the same gun you used to shoot that bloke in the creek bed?' Adam asked.

Mailey's eyes became slits. They smoked menace. 'Not a wise thing for you to say, son,' he said eventually. 'I know what happened, you know what happened, and this black bastard knows what happened, but the rest of the world believes that a small-time fighter by the name of Jimmy Kettle shot and killed that upstanding pillar of society, Mr Brothel Keeper Harris. Now, no one's going to take much notice of a nigger, specially if he says a policeman shot a white man. But if someone else backs up the blackfellow, a white man like you, then it's a different matter. Do you get what I'm driving at?'

Adam said nothing. The man held the gun loosely in his left hand.

'If you two turn up in town and start telling a different story, I'm in trouble. There are a few troublemakers and queers around who would love to accuse a white policeman of being nasty to the poor blackman. Get my drift now? No?' he said when Adam refused to speak. 'What I'm saying is I can't afford either of you getting back to town and talking. So, sonny, what I'm going to do is this. I'm going to take you and this Jimmy Kettle character out of town somewhere down south where there's no one around and even the dingoes have pissed off, I'm going to lead you two away from the track and I'm going to put a bullet in each of you, and tell the people in Port Augusta that the two of you escaped.'

He leaned forward. 'Now, that would hurt me because I'm proud of my work, and I'm a bloody good policeman. I don't let prisoners escape. Still, in the long run it wouldn't be a bad thing. But there is an alternative.'

He was so close that Adam could smell the stench of onions on the man's breath.

'Weren't you the character who flattened this abo in the ring?' He saw a flicker in Adam's eyes and went on. 'Good fighter, are you?'

Very gently he punched Adam on the jaw, delivering the blow as a child would in a game. His teeth showed in a mocking smile. Adam, surprised rather than hurt, let his back touch the wall. Mailey had his right fist poised. The left hand still held the gun.

'Now you hit me.'

The man was still smiling. He had a face that looked as though it had been hit many times. The nose was broad and bent. His skin was ruddy and freckled and ridged with scars. This was a man who could take a hard blow, and smile through the trickle of blood. This was a man who would allow himself to be hurt so that he might create greater damage. A cunning man who would provoke action so that he could justify his own brutality.

The smile persisted but there was no humour on that hard face. Just a mocking challenge. He moved his face closer.

Adam thought of hitting him. He could certainly get home a good blow at this range. But his arms were still stiff and aching and his muscles would react slowly. The man knew this. He wanted Adam to try, to land one ineffectual blow that might leave a bruise or blacken an eye. Some mark that would justify the reaction he planed.

'You'd like to shoot me now, wouldn't you?' Adam said and the man swayed back, moving out of range like a snake that has decided not to strike. He studied Adam for a few moments and then strode to the door of the hut. He shoved the gun in its holster.

'Maybe you're not so dumb after all,' he said, and opened the door. It creaked on its set of stout hinges. 'I'll be back,' he said, and went out. A bolt rattled. A lock clicked.

Within the hut, clouds of dust swirled through the shafts of light.

Mailey returned in the afternoon. Jimmy was now awake and sitting against a wall with his arms awkwardly bent behind his body. Both he and Adam were streaked with sweat, for the sun had been beating on the western wall of the hut and the air inside had become stifling.

The sergeant tossed a key at Adam, who was lying on the earthen floor.

'Undo him,' Mailey commanded. He was carrying a baton in one hand and, as Adam rose to work on Jimmy's hands, Mailey prodded him on the shoulder.

'Where's the opal you stole?' he said.

Adam looked at him. 'I didn't steal any opal.'

'Where is it?' the sergeant roared and raised the baton. Adam crawled to the wall and stood up, his hands sliding up the rough surface as he rose.

The sergeant unclipped the strap over the holster. He smiled, the same provocative parting of the lips that had taunted Adam earlier in the day.

'Where is it?' he whispered.

'I didn't steal any opal,' Adam repeated.

Mailey used a foot to roll Jimmy on to his side. 'You haven't undone the cuffs,' he said, pulling out the gun. 'Get back down there and do what you're told.'

He waited for Adam to kneel beside Jimmy.

'I didn't come all the way up here just to look for you two,' he said. 'That was in the back of my mind, of course. I've been around half the state in the last couple of months. Most people thought you'd just disappeared, but I'm a very thorough bloke and I've been moving around, just keeping my eyes open. Even so, I need a reason to travel. A police sergeant can only go where duty calls him. Follow?'

Adam had finished unlocking the handcuffs and the sergeant jabbed him with the baton.

'Throw the key and the cuffs over here,' he said, retreating towards the door. He waited for his order to be carried out.

'I came up here,' he went on, 'because we had a complaint that some opals had been stolen. Some bloke was fool enough to lodge a complaint. Probably get his throat cut when I leave town.' He grinned. 'I know what these places are like. The scum of the earth come here. Trash like you. It's dog eat dog, and who cares?' He cleared one nostril noisily. 'I'm full of dust,' he said, wiping his nose. 'I've swallowed more dust than breakfasts in the last three months looking for you blokes. The inspector thinks I'm checking on things in some of the outposts. You know, studying the law and order scene in places where there are no police. He thinks the sun shines out of my arse. I'll probably get a promotion.'

His chest heaved with the suggestion of a laugh. His eyes moved from Jimmy to Adam.

'So the official reason I'm here is because someone stole some opal. I'll have to make a report. Now you, Ross, I believe you turned up yesterday with some opal. You told that oily black bloke in a suit that you had some opal to sell. Right?'

Adam looked at Jimmy.

'I suppose you found it in the ground,' Mailey said, his voice mocking Adam. 'Yes, of course you did. Who saw you find it?'

'I did,' Jimmy said.

'Of course you did. Who else?'

'We were the only ones down the mine,' Adam said.

'Of course you were. And I don't suppose anyone else saw it when you brought it to the top.'

'I showed it to Mr Thomas.'

'When you got to the top of the mine?'

'No,' Adam said, feeling uneasy. 'Later.'

'Where is it now?'

182

Adam had to think. He had left the rock in the bag with Thomas.

'I don't know,' he said.

'Of course not,' Mailey said. He walked to a side wall and, with his back to the others, began to urinate. 'I'm busting,' he said, turning his face across his shoulder and smiling benignly. 'Had too much to drink. How are you getting on? All right without any water?' He shook himself. 'Don't worry. In another day or so it won't matter whether you've got water or not.'

He moved towards them and suddenly slapped Jimmy across the side of the head with his baton. It was not a hard blow, and Jimmy who saw it coming rolled his neck to lessen the impact.

'Where's the opal you stole?'

'We didn't steal no opal,' Jimmy said.

'Well, where's the opal you found?' He held the baton aloft. Jimmy looked as though he might strike and Mailey smiled.

'Go on,' he said. 'Have a go. See how good you are.'

'Don't, Jimmy,' Adam said softly.

'Don't, Jimmy,' Mailey mimicked. 'No, don't, Jimmy or I'll blow your bloody head off.' He lashed out with the baton, swinging it high above their heads and grinned again as they ducked low to avoid the blow.

'You're not going to tell me, are you?' he said to Adam, studying him with eyes that were deep set in layers of wrinkled skin. Adam looked into those eyes and felt his hair prickle. He had seen such eyes on lizards.

'I'd like to know where you put the opal,' Mailey said quietly.

'Let us out and we'll get it for you,' Adam said.

The eyes flashed.

He turned his back on them and slowly restored his gun to its holster. 'I'll be back in the morning,' he said without looking at them. 'We'll see what a night without water does for you. And don't try anything. My car's out the front and I'll be sleeping in it.'

Mailey went out. He rattled the bolt into place on the door and stood back to examine the lock-up. It was a stout little box of a building that would be an oven in the daytime and an ice chest at night.

He turned and saw a group of men waiting for him just beyond his car. They were nervous, for they held their hats in their hands and shuffled their feet in the dust. He recognized the postmaster, who was trying to submerge himself in the crowd.

183

Dexter Paradine stepped forward. He had his hat in front of him, and passed the brim through his fingers so rapidly that it spun ceaselessly like a felt top spinning on his chest.

'We've had a meeting,' Paradine began.

'And you've decided what?' Mailey said rudely, still walking so that the group had to turn and follow.

'Well, we wanted to make some points,' Paradine said. The sergeant was walking so quickly Paradine had to run several steps to keep up.

'Go ahead.'

'Well, we're concerned about the violence displayed when you apprehended those men.'

'Good for you.'

Paradine ran, to get ahead. 'We felt it was unnecessary,' he said.

Mailey stopped and Paradine almost fell.

'Now listen to me, gentlemen,' Mailey said, growling at the group. 'May I suggest that you stick to your job of digging holes in the ground and I stick to my business of arresting dangerous men.'

No one answered. Mailey started to walk. Paradine skipped after him.

'Are those two men all right?' he called and a murmur of sound agreed with his question.

The sergeant stopped again. He jabbed Dexter Paradine in the chest.

'Those men killed a dozen people. Men, women and children.' He emphasized each category with a jab in the chest and Paradine looked distressed. 'Slaughtered them without mercy. What would you like me to have done? Gone down on my knees and begged them to put on the handcuffs?'

Moore spoke from deep in the group. 'But you hit them bloody hard with a great lump of wood,' he said.

'Yeah, and from the back,' another man said.

'Don't give me that sugar-coated bullshit,' Mailey said, searching the crowd for the man who had spoken. 'These men are going to hang. An extra headache now isn't going to matter much.' He started to walk again.

Paradine pulled at his shirt. 'But they seemed nice young men.'

'So did Ned Kelly,' Mailey said, and spun to a stop again. 'Who was the one who complained about his opal being stolen? Is he with you? Come on. Is he here?'

A hand rose from the back of the group. 'Well, you, sir, are the reason I'm here. Someone stole from you. That's a crime, right?'

A few heads nodded.

'Well, gentlemen, from my investigations it seems that those two "nice" young men stole opal from your mate. They're thieves. Nice fellows, eh? They killed in Port Augusta and they robbed in Coober Pedy.'

Mailey turned and strode away.

'Jesus, I find that hard to believe,' one of the men said. The policeman stopped and turned slowly. He was breathing heavily and each breath steamed with rising anger. His eyes settled on Paradine.

'Did you say that?' he demanded.

Paradine shook his head vigorously and stepped back. Mailey stalked him and as Paradine retreated, the sergeant prodded his shoulder repeatedly.

'Were you the one that just called me a liar?' he said, pushing harder with each word.

Paradine tripped and fell to one knee. His eyes were wide.

'I didn't say a thing,' he said.

Mailey grabbed his ear and pulled him to his feet. 'Don't,' he said. 'I buried the last man who called me a liar.'

Paradine held his ear. Moore stepped forward. 'No one called you a liar,' he said.

The glaze of fury left Mailey's eyes. He scratched his forehead. 'Of course not,' he said, with irony in his voice. 'No one said anything. I was just hearing things.'

A man coughed.

Mailey brushed dirt from Paradine's knee.

'You ought to watch where you're going,' he said. 'The ground's rough. You could get hurt.'

The man coughed again. 'Are you going to give those two fellers anything to eat?' he said.

Mailey rested one hand on his holster. 'Those prisoners are my responsibility, and I'll decide when they get fed, and when they don't. Let me warn you, gentlemen. If anyone goes near that lock-up without my permission, I will treat that person as an accomplice of those prisoners. Do you understand me?'

No one spoke.

'Let me make it clearer then. I will assume that person is

185

attempting to help the prisoners escape and I will take appropriate action.' He turned to leave.

'What do you mean?' Paradine asked. He was still holding his ear.

'I mean, sir,' Mailey said, 'That I will blow your bloody head off.'

TWELVE

In the old Coober Pedy lock-up, the heat grew worse during the late afternoon and the two men's thirst became intense. Then the sun went down and the rough walls cooled and the air inside the hut gradually chilled. The perspiration that had coated their bodies with warm rivers of liquid now dried and cooled and set them shivering. Their throats ached with a crackly cold dryness.

The western wall of the lock-up had only one window, a small opening located above eye level. Through it floated the faint aromas of smoke and food, but, as the night grew darker and quieter, the smells disappeared and only the cold drifted in. Jimmy dozed. Adam, feeling the cold more than his friend, sat against the far wall in a position where he could look out the window. Through the opening winked a star. It faded as a cloud whispered past and reappeared bright and pure, framed in the oblong slit on the mud and stone wall.

He was aware of pain. The back of his head ached. So did his hip. Normally, he could ignore pain or work around it. His life had been hard, with pain a frequent companion. But now he hurt and a lethargy was seeping into his brain. He knew he should be trying to get out, or at least thinking of some way to escape when Mailey came back, but he just sat against the wall looking at the window. Maybe it was the blow on the head. He touched the back of his skull, and ran his fingers tenderly over the lump. Someone with thinner bones would be dead, he thought. He had been told many times he had a thick skull. Usually by teachers who endured his presence for a few days and then had old Tiger take him away again. He had been a nuisance to others for most of his life. No one had ever suggested liking him. Except his father. Maybe old

Tiger; he hadn't said anything, of course. And Nellie.

He thought of Nellie. He stared out the window and saw her big eyes, her fine features with those high cheekbones that gave her an almost cat-like look.

Something flashed through the opening and tinkled against the back wall. Adam stood up. Had he imagined it? He moved closer. He did not see the second missile but heard it hit the wall near his head and thud to the floor.

'Who's there?' he whispered.

'Adam?' It was Josef's voice.

'Where are you?' Adam called and immediately realized the question was ridiculous. The boy was on the other side of the wall, just beneath the window. He was so close to the wall, in fact, that when he spoke the sound was muffled as though he had his cheek pressed against the stone.

'Are you all right? I've got some water. Stand under the window and I'll lower it to you.'

Adam heard the clunk of heavy metal on the window-ledge. There was a scraping sound and his upraised hands felt a flask being lowered on string.

Jimmy was awake. 'Who is it?' he asked, joining Adam near the window.

'Joe,' Adam said, handing him the flask. 'Have some water.'

'Stay away from the door,' Josef called, his voice soft and muffled but charged with the vibrato of out-of-control excitement.

'What are you going to do?' Adam said, his thirst rising as he eyed the shadow that was Jimmy drinking from the flask.

'Just stand back. You might get hurt. Is Jimmy all right?'

'We're both OK.'

'Get ready to run.'

'What are you going to do? Joe, be careful! Mailey's out the front,' Adam said, but Josef had moved. Adam could hear shoes crackling on gravel.

'You had any water yet, mate?' Jimmy said and passed the flask when Adam shook his head.

The door rattled.

'The silly young bugger will get himself shot,' Jimmy said. He had begun to skip on the spot, anticipating action.

Adam pressed himself to the door. 'Joe, the policeman's out there in the car. He'll shoot you if he sees you.'

But Josef had gone.

187

'Any water left?' Jimmy asked. He took the flask and drank noisily. He touched Adam's shoulder. 'I'd keep away from the door. He might have put a stick of dynamite on the other side.'

Adam stepped back. He heard a noise. It was the clinking of a chain. He tried to measure the distance. Twenty, thirty paces away? He could hear two people speaking. Their voices were hushed but urgent, as though arguing. The voices stopped. A series of mechanical noises followed. First, a winding and clanking that was so loud Adam winced. There was a wheezing sound and a backfire as muffled as a discreet cough. More cranking. Then the splutter of a car engine being coaxed into life.

'That's got to be Mailey's car,' Jimmy said. 'Jesus, what's he up to?'

The engine roared.

'And where's Mailey?' Adam said, eyes wide in fearful anticipation. He braced himself for the sound of a shot.

The beat of the car's engine grew faster. The door of the hut twanged and began to shake. The bolt and hinges groaned. There was the furious sound of tyres spinning on dirt. The hut vibrated.

'Jesus, the roof's going to fall in,' Jimmy said and bent low, covering his head.

'He must have put a tow rope on the lock,' Adam said, trying to imagine the scene outside. The engine note rose to a howl. The door buzzed with the strain of the pull.

'The young bugger,' Jimmy said, head covered by his arms but lips parted in a smile of admiration.

'He'll burn out the clutch,' Adam said anxiously, measuring the time the engine had been racing.

There was a snap like a rifle shot and the building ceased to tremble. The door rattled and then sagged on its hinges. 'Broke the rope,' Adam said. So that was it. The effort to free them had failed.

Jimmy stood up. 'I hope he can run fast, because Mailey'll be after him. Poor little bugger.'

The car's engine was still racing. Gears crunched and the engine noise grew louder. The car was accelerating towards them.

As one, Adam and Jimmy leaped for the far wall. An instant later, the tail of Mailey's car rammed the door. Timber shattered. The bottom hinge burst and the splintered door swung high into the room, trailing bolts and pieces of stone. One corner of the car followed. The door fell back, wedging its broken ends around the mangled metal tool box. Petrol gushed from a split fuel can. A twisted door hinge scraped against metal. With a sound like the rush of thunder, the car and the ground beneath it erupted into flames.

The doorway was blocked by the deformed rear end of the car, the hanging door and the sheet of flames. Petrol was trickling into the jail and running along one wall. They had to get out quickly. The car's engine was still running and roaring with the weight of someone's foot on the accelerator pedal.

'For Christ's sake get the car out of here!' Adam shouted to the driver. 'Move it forward. We can't get out.'

To his astonishment a woman answered, her voice shrill with fear. 'I can't find the right gear,' she cried.

'It's to the left and down,' he called.

The engine roared and the car strained to move back, ramming itself into the flaming mess of the doorway.

'That's reverse!' Adam screamed. 'First is to the left and down.'

There was a hideous crunch of metal teeth. The car shuddered, jerked forward a few feet, and stalled.

'Out!' Adam yelled, pushing Jimmy ahead of him. The other man baulked. He would fight any man and face most dangers but he was terrified of fire and the door was carpeted in flame. Worse, the fire had pursued the car and the back of the vehicle was now hissing flames where the blaze had risen to the fractured fuel can.

'Get out! Quick!' Adam said, but Jimmy's legs had begun to shake.

Jimmy shook his head in distress. 'Can't do it,' he said.

Smoke and exhaust gas was filling the hut. Jimmy fell to his knees, gasping for air. Adam knelt beside him.

'Can you get on my back?' he shouted. He had to shout for the hut was a fury of noise with the beat of the car's motor providing a frantic underscore to the crackle of flames. There was a whoosh, and the back of the car boiled yellow.

One opening remained, a low, fiery corner of the doorway. Adam grabbed the other man's arms and put them around his own neck. 'Now your legs,' he said. 'Come on. I'll give you a piggy-back.'

Jimmy got on. He began to laugh but his eyes were closed and tears streamed down his cheeks.

'Hold on,' Adam said, and aimed at the corner. 'Take a deep breath and don't let go,' he yelled. He began to crawl.

'What are you doing?' Jimmy screamed, stiffening his body and locking his arms around Adam's neck.

'Don't choke me. Just shut up and don't breathe.'

On hands and knees, and with Jimmy Kettle's legs trailing in the dirt, he charged the flames. He felt the scorch of heat on his face and then a heat so intense he cried out. But his legs kept driving him on and he thrust his head and shoulders beyond the flames, somersaulting Jimmy over his back.

They came to rest in a tumble of limbs and blisters and scorched hair. A searing pain rose in Adam's legs. He kicked hard and skidded across the ground. Adam felt Jimmy being pulled clear and heard Josef's voice, grunting with exertion: 'Come on, Jimmy, get up! We've got to get away.'

Adam touched his skull and clumps of burned hair broke off in his fingers. Cool hands touched his. They locked around his wrists and dragged him away from the fire.

He lifted his eyes and saw Nellie. He stood up. His trousers were smouldering and his knees stung. He held his burned palms under his armpits.

'Where did you come from?' he said, speaking painfully through blistered lips.

'I was driving the car,' she said.

'I didn't know you could drive,' he said and tried to smile.

'I can't. Joe told me what to do.'

'He can't drive either,' Adam said.

She nodded towards the burning car. 'I didn't mean to hit the building, I just couldn't stop it. I tried to put my foot on the brake but I must have touched the wrong pedal. It seemed to go so fast.' She smiled and touched his lips. 'You're burned,' she said.

He nodded. 'I thought you were going to burn out the clutch.'

'I don't think it matters much now,' she said.

Flames were leaping above the roof of the car.

'Where's Mailey?' Adam asked. He spoke to Josef, who was helping Jimmy to his feet.

'Old Horrie led him away,' Josef said. 'But he'll be back soon. I'll tell you about it later. Come on, let's go.'

'Where?'

'Just follow me. I've got it worked out. By the way, here's your bag. The opal's still inside.' Josef was carrying two bags. He offered one to Adam. Its buttom bulged from the weight of the rock.

'Slip it over my shoulder, will you?' Adam said, displaying his upturned palms as a reason for not grabing the bag. 'Where did you get it?'

Josef had begun to run. 'From Mr Thomas,' he said, turning but still jogging backwards as he spoke. 'He brought it. He was the one who told me you were in trouble. Come on, please hurry! That policeman will be here in a minute. He's only up at the post office with Horrie. He must have heard the noise.'

Behind them an explosion rocked Mailey's car, jolting the tail high above the ground. A spare tyre looped through the air and landed near them. Shreds of burning canvas sparkled like fireflies in the night.

From the shadows on their left, a man shouted. Other voices rumbled in the distance. Josef had resumed running and was heading east towards a low hill that shone dull yellow in the light from the burning car.

'After him,' Adam said to Jimmy, who had been staring at the blaze. 'You all right, mate?'

Jimmy nodded and, without looking at Adam, began to run after the boy.

Nellie was beside Adam. He put one scorched finger on her cheek. 'Thanks,' he said simply.

'Don't make it sound like goodbye,' she said. 'I'm coming with you.'

'You can't,' he said but she was already running after the others. Adam limped after her. She turned.

'What's wrong?' she said and ran back to help him.
'My knees don't want to work and my hip's not too good.'

She put an arm around his waist. 'That's nice, but it doesn't help,' he said, shaking himself free. 'I'll be all right. Just don't lose sight of Josef.'

From somewhere behind them came an enraged roar. Adam, turning briefly, could see Mailey nearing the car.

'I see you,' Mailey shouted. 'Stop or I'll shoot.'

'What do we do?' Nellie said, grabbing Adam's arm and making him wince with pain.

'Run!' he said, and despite the pain in his burned knees and the stiffness in his hip, he ran – an awkward, rolling, high-speed limp that took him quickly across the ground. Nellie ran alongside. A bullet sang its way between them. There was another shot but the sound was different and Adam risked a glance backwards.

What he saw made him pause. Mailey was struggling with someone. The man was old and frail and no match for the policeman. Horrie Smith.

Adam saw him smashed to the ground and saw Mailey turn and take aim.

Nellie tugged at Adam's shirt. They ran again. Behind them Mailey fell, unbalanced by a pair of old hands that had gripped his ankles. Another shot sounded, an ugly muffled explosion, and Mailey arose shaking. But his quarry was gone. Nellie was still pulling Adam along as they rounded the hill and were hidden in its shadow.

The ground was strewn with stones and, in the sudden dark, Adam stumbled and fell. Jimmy was there, more sensed than seen. He reached down to take Adam's arm.

'What's up with your legs?' he gasped, still short of breath from the rush from the gaol.

Nellie answered, 'He's burnt his knees.' She glanced behind her, expecting pursuit.

'They're not bad,' Adam said, allowing himself to be hauled to his feet.

Josef, who had been scouting the track east of the hill, returned to the group. 'We've got to hurry,' he said urgently. 'They'll be here any moment.'

'Adam can't run,' Nellie said.

'Yes, I can,' Adam said, standing erect. He touched one knee and cried out.

'What's wrong?' Nellie said anxiously, for Adam had jumped back not just from pain but in surprise.

'My pants are on fire!'

'They're smouldering,' Josef corrected. 'No wonder your knees are sore.'

Jimmy began to rip away the trouser legs, converting them in to shorts. 'I'll soon fix it. You'll be able to move much better without having burning cloth rubbing on your knees.'

'His knees are all blistered and raw,' Nellie said as Jimmy ripped the smoking material away.

Josef was wriggling in agitation. 'We have to keep moving. If you can ...' He looked at Adam, pleading for movement.

'I can,' Adam began, but the rest of his words were muffled by a loud blast from the far side of the hill. Another explosion, a deep

192

'crump' that shook the eardrums, sounded almost immediately.

A large object rocketed into the sky, cascading sparkes and emitting a sound like a distant steam engine rushing into a tunnel. They watched it tumble through the sky.

'What was that?' Nellie said, allowing her nails to cut into Adam's shoulder in fright.

'Something in Mailey's car,' Adam replied. 'He probably had another can of petrol in the back.'

'He won't be driving back to Port Augusta,' Jimmy said.

Adam gently prised Nellie's fingers from his shoulder. 'No. He'll be coming after us, though,' he said. 'Come on, Joe, show us where to go.'

'How would he know anyhow?' Jimmy said, turning to Adam. His voice was anxious.

'He was here today,' Nellie said.

'I've got it all worked out,' Josef said, leading the group away from the hill. 'Just follow me. I know where to go.'

'Where are we going?' Adam asked, limping at the rear of the line.

'There's a track,' Josef said. 'It goes just south of the hills and joins up with a dry creek.'

'You came here today?' Adam said, trying to ignore the pain from his burns.

'I walked along this track for a couple of miles this afternoon. There are a couple of places where we could hide.' He stopped. 'Take care here. There's a big washout.' Josef waited for the others to cross. He shifted the bag he was carrying from one shoulder to the other.

'What's in the bag?' Adam said.

'Food. I've got enough here for a couple of days.'

Jimmy delivered a mock punch to the boy's jaw. 'You should do this for a living, kid. You could make a fortune busting people out of gaol.'

Nellie helped Adam across the washout. 'He had it all worked out within an hour of you two being locked up in that little building. He was terrific.'

'It was Nellie's idea to get old Horrie to help,' Josef said.

'What did Horrie do?' Adam asked. They followed a weaving path through the bushes.

'He got the policeman to leave his car. Horrie told him some amazing story about two men being buried down the bottom of a mine. Gee, he can spin a good tale! Anyhow, the policeman went with him. We counted ten minutes and then Nellie and I sneaked up to the lock-up. You haven't got the water with you, have you?'

'The flask? No. It's back in the fire, I'm afraid.'

They were clear of the bushes now and Josef increased the pace, taking them across a gravelly plain. 'Can't be helped,' he said. 'There's a little water in the bag, but not much. I filled one of mother's jars. It was all I could find.'

'Your mother will be worried sick,' Adam said. 'How far are you going to take us before you head back?'

Josef stopped. 'What do you mean?'

'Well, the longer you're away, the more she'll be worried. She must have heard all the explosions and the shouting.'

'I'm not going back,' Josef said. 'I'm staying with you.'

Mailey had carried two five-gallon drums in the back of his car. They were laden with petrol for the journey north but he had poured the fuel into the main tank and, that night, the drums contained nothing but vapour – volatile, explosive petrol vapour. When the fire reached them, the first drum erupted and split itself into a tangle of rolled steel. The second, launched by the initial blast, blew out its bottom and shot one hundred and fifty feet into the air.

Mailey was running towards the hill when the drums exploded. The twin blasts flattened him. A shower of glass scythed the air. He pushed himself to his knees and turned. His car had lost its canvas roof. The windscreen and side-curtains were gone. One back door was open and twisted on its hinges. All the wheels were ablaze.

The miners, too, had been blown off their feet. They rose slowly, minus their hats and with hair singed. Some of them began to laugh, not at Mailey's discomfort, but from the sheer surprise of still being alive.

Mailey misunderstood. 'You can laugh,' he roared and the miners were silent, as shocked by the menace in his voice as by the preceding explosions. Mailey got to his feet, swaying and holding his head, for his ears hurt. 'You can laugh,' he repeated, his voice softer but no less threatening, 'but when I catch Jimmy Kettle and his friends, I'm going to blow their heads off. And then I'm going to come back here and do the same to a few of you.'

Dexter Paradine, face pink from the blast, raised one hand as though seeking permission to speak.

'You don't act like a policeman,' he said, his voice squeaky from shock.

Mailey laughed. 'Oh, I'm a policeman all right. I'm the law.'

'You're a bloody madman,' one of the miners said.

The hint of a smile scarred Mailey's face. 'I've noted your face,' he said, waving a finger at him. His hand jerked and he pointed at Paradine. 'And yours too. You've both been obstructing justice. I'll be looking for you two when I get back.'

Horrie Smith had been lying on his back nearer the blazing car than the others. His face was drenched with blood. He lifted his head and gazed at the inferno that had been Mailey's Dodge.

'Burn, you bastard,' he shrieked and fell back laughing insanely.

Mailey shook his gun at the old man. 'He'll be the first,' he said, his voice that of a preacher addressing his flock. 'He is an accomplice, and he will pay.'

'But you've already beaten him half to death,' Paradine said.

'If my car is still burning when I get back,' Mailey said, his voice still booming, 'I will personally pick up that lying, stinking old heap of rubbish and put it on the fire and watch it roast.'

Mailey strode forward and wrenched a lantern from the hands of one miner. 'I'll take that,' he said. 'Now, is anyone coming with me?'

No one moved.

'I'll remember that,' Mailey said. 'You'll all be sorry for this. By God, you'll regret this!'

He strode a few paces from them but turned, as a thought struck him. 'Who's got a car?'

No one spoke.

'Not assisting the police is an offence in itself. Consider yourselves all under arrest. No one is to leave town until I get back. You!' He gestured to the storekeeper. 'You've got a car. Bring it here. Immediately! I am commandeering it.'

The storekeeper spluttered a protest.

'I can arrest you for obstructing justice,' Mailey said, moving closer. The storekeeper edged away from the group, his eyes sweeping his companions for signs of support. No one looked at him.

'Get it,' Mailey thundered, and the man began to walk. 'Run!' the policeman shouted, and the storekeeper broke into an awkward jog. 'And be back here in three minutes!'

The man began to run and his form, hobbling and tripping as he covered the rough terrain, faded from the glow of the fire and disappeared in the night.

'Three minutes!' Mailey yelled when he could no longer see the man. Then he turned towards the hill, searching for any sign of his quarry and chafing to begin the pursuit. Ignoring the men behind him, he began to reload his gun.

Josef was counting. He was up to one hundred and thirty-four. Twenty-six more paces before he would reach the next marker. Then they should keep to the right of something – was it a bush? – and then follow a track down into a gully. One hundred and fifty-five. Almost there. He slowed and looked back. The others were strung behind him, shadows in the black night. One hundred and sixty. Where was it? Two extra steps. He peered into the darkness ahead of him. Five steps. Six. He stumbled. It was a bush and he had almost walked into it. Jimmy bumped into him.

'Where to now, kid?' he said, his quiet voice sounding amused, as though this were a game.

'To the right,' Josef whispered. There was probably no need to speak so softly but the night, screaming silence beyond the pitch of normal hearing, forced whispers from human throats.

A spot on the horizon glowed where the car still burned.

Adam reached the bush. He leaned on Nellie's shoulder. 'Are we still on course?' he asked.

'Yes. We have to follow a track to the right. It gets a bit rough.'

Jimmy completed a slow scan of the horizon. 'And you remember all this from one trip out here this afternoon?' he said.

'Yes.'

'You've been counting your steps?'

'Yes.'

'Jesus! You're wasted as a white man, kid. You'd have made a sensational blackfeller.'

'I just worked out where we wanted to go and then remembered things,' Josef said.

'Where are we going?' Adam said.

'William Creek.'

'How far's that?' The doubt in Adam's voice lifted the words an octave above normal.

'It's the nearest town and there's a railway line there,' Josef parried.

'Yes, but how far?'

'I'm not sure. I think it's about a hundred miles.'

'Jesus!' Jimmy said. 'I think I might go back to the lock-up.'

'What do you mean?' Josef said.

'I mean we'd be better off back there. We've got one hundred miles to go on foot, Adam can hardly walk, the country's as dry as a bone, there are four of us, and you're not carrying enough water for us to clean our teeth. I don't fancy dying of thirst.'

'I had more water but it's back there in that building,' Josef said, his tone defensive.

'It's not your fault, Joe. You've been terrific,' Adam said and turned towards the shadow that was Jimmy Kettle.

'Do you reckon we could find water out there?'

'Probably not,' Jimmy said and sniffed.

'We could dig.'

'With your hands?'

Adam, who had been standing with his hands outstretched like butterfly wings, folded his arms. Nellie moved in front of him.

'I can dig,' she said angrily.

'So can I,' Joe said.

'Yeah, but there's got to be water. No point just digging graves for ourselves.' Jimmy stamped the ground.

'One thing's certain,' Adam said, his arms still folded. 'We can't go back. I wonder if there are any creeks out this way?'

'We're heading towards a creek,' Josef offered. 'There's all sand in it, but it's a creek.'

'We might be able to dig a soak there,' Adam said.

'There's a lake somewhere out here,' Nellie said quietly and the others turned towards her. 'I was in the store yesterday when that Arab with the camels reached town. He came from William Creek and he was talking about a lake he had passed.'

'Probably salt,' Jimmy said.

'How do you know?' She spat the words at him.

'Because they all are. And how would you know? You're only a sheila and you're not even black.'

'What am I then?' Nellie was on her toes.

Adam waved a blistered hand between them. 'Cut it out!' he said. 'Let's keep walking.'

'This way,' Josef said, moving to the right.

Nellie was near Jimmy. 'What am I, if I'm not black?' she whispered, but though her voice was soft the tone was hard.

'You're nothing,' he said, moving after Josef.

'What do you mean?' She hurried to keep up with him.

'Nellie!' Adam called after her. 'Stop it. Don't argue.'

'Me argue?' she said, turning and almost falling. 'He's the one who started it.' She checked her balance and ran after Jimmy.

'What do you mean, nothing?'

Jimmy was smiling. 'Well you're the one who's always boasting that you've got a white father.'

'Well, so I have, but that's not my fault.'

'You make it sound like that makes you better than me.'

She said nothing.

'He was probably just some drunken sailor who nailed your mother in the lavatory behind the pub,' Jimmy said, increasing his pace to keep ahead of her.

'He was not,' she shouted. 'He was an officer on a ship ...'

'For heaven's sake, stop it!' Adam hissed. 'We'll be heard a mile away.'

Nellie turned on him. 'That's it. You take his side.'

'I'm not taking anyone's side,' Adam said. 'We just can't afford to make any noise.'

'You think I'm black and he thinks I'm white,' she said.

Josef had stopped and they stood on the track, shadows confronting shadows.

'I don't think you're anything,' Adam said reasonably.

'That's lovely,' she said. 'So you think I'm nothing.'

'I didn't mean that.'

'Well, that's what you said.'

'No, it isn't. I meant I don't think of you as black or white.'

'No, just a sort of dirty grey,' Jimmy said maliciously.

She struck at him. Even in the dark, Jimmy recognized the movement and deflected the blow with an upraised arm. She cried out in pain.

'You're all the same,' she sobbed and moved to one side. Adam followed her.

'You keep away,' she said rubbing her arm. 'If you'd taken me away from town when I asked you none of this would've happened.'

Jimmy sat on his haunches. 'And if you hadn't slept with all the Chinese in town, you wouldn't be covered in so much crap,' he said.

'I'm dirty because I got dirty helping Joe rescue you from that gaol.' She ground the words out.

198

'I can see a light,' Josef said.

Adam spun around. 'Where?'

'Behind us, but a bit to the right.'

'I did not sleep with the Chinese,' Nellie said, her head down and her voice loud.

'For God's sake be quiet!' Adam said. He put the bag with the opal on the ground. 'Joe, how long is it since you saw the light?'

'Only a few seconds. It was just a flash. There!' He jumped in excitement. A beam of light swept the land to their right.

'That's a car,' Jimmy said, in a matter-of-fact voice. 'Is there a road up there?'

'I don't know,' Josef said.

'Well, you were out here this afternoon.'

'I didn't go up there. It was all I could do to find this track, and remember where all the turns were.'

'I hope he finds you,' Nellie said, shouting the last words.

'Will you shut up?' Adam snapped. 'If he finds us, he'll shoot the lot of us.'

'You're all the same,' she said.

'Nellie, please be quiet. Those lights are getting closer.'

She laughed.

'She gets nutty like this,' Jimmy said.

The lights bounced roughly.

'He's not on the road,' Adam said. 'He's driving across country. It must be Mailey.'

'But he hasn't got a car anymore,' Josef said.

'He must have got someone else's,' Adam reasoned.

'It mightn't be Mailey,' Nellie said. 'It might be someone else driving south.'

'This is to the east,' Adam said.

'And he's not on the road, Nellie,' Josef said earnestly.

'Her white father probably had the pox and was mad,' Jimmy said. 'That's where she got it from.'

'I hate you!' she said. 'If that's someone going south I'm going to get a lift and leave you all here.'

'You do that,' Jimmy said.

'I got you out of that prison,' she said.

'You bloody well nearly burnt us to death.'

She began to wave, trying to attract the driver of the car.

'Nellie, what are you doing?' Adam said. 'That's almost certainly Mailey!'

199

'So what? He didn't see me. He's not after me. I'm going back to town.'

'Nellie, he's mad! He kills people. And if he sees you, he'll find us.'

'Yeah, sit down, you stupid bitch!' Jimmy said.

She waved vigorously. The car had been zigzagging slowly across the plain, sending its lights sweeping in a wide arc. It had been travelling parallel to them but now it began to curve towards their position.

Adam limped towards Nellie. 'Will you get down,' he whispered. 'The lights will be on you in a moment.'

'Good,' she said. 'I want him to see me.'

A bush near them suddenly flickered into shape as the car's lights swept across it.

Nellie continued to wave. Adam reached her. Because of his burns he could not touch her with his hands, so he looped one arm across her neck.

'Get down, please!'

She turned and scratched him. He locked his arm around her and dragged her to the ground. He pinned her beneath his body, and barred her mouth with a forearm. The car's lights passed over them. She kicked hard.

'You're hurting me,' she grunted.

'Well, stop kicking. And if I let you go, will you promise to stay down?'

She kicked again and Adam pressed down on her. He felt moisture touch his arm.

'My lip's bleeding.' Her muffled voice was shocked.

Adam got off, and she crawled clear. 'Oh, I hate you!' she said.

'I don't know what's got into you,' Adam said, crouching on his elbows and watching the car. It was describing a wide circle on the plain.

'Nothing's got into me. You're the one who's been picking on me.'

'Oh, for God's sake, Nellie!'

'And now you've made my lip bleed. Big strong man! Chokes a girl and then cuts her lip.'

'Just shut up for a minute,' Adam got to his feet. The car was heading slowly away from them. 'You there, Joe?'

The boy answered from somewhere on Adam's left.

'How far to this creek?'

200

'Not far,' Josef answered. 'We'd be there in a few minutes.'

'Is it soft sand?'

'I think so. There's a bit of a bank on this side. We could hide there.'

'What's after the creek?'

'I don't know. That's as far as I went today. It swings around and heads the way we want to go. I thought we could follow it.'

Adam nodded. 'At least the car can't drive in soft sand.'

'The car's coming back,' Jimmy warned. The headlights had flashed into view again. The driver was making another lazy circle across the plain, only this time he was closer to them.

'Down!' Adam said, and heard Josef and Jimmy thud to the ground near him. He looked for Nellie. He could not see her. The lights swung towards them, flashed bright in their faces for one instant, and continued their search of the land.

'Let's get moving while he's pointing the other way,' he said. 'Next time he makes a sweep, he'll be so close he can't miss seeing us. Do you think you can find that creek?'

'Of course,' Josef said. He was already moving.

'Where's my bag?' Adam muttered, more to himself than anyone else. 'I put it down just here somewhere.'

'I've got the bag,' Josef said.

'With the opal?' Adam asked.

'Oh no. I've got the food. Where did you put the other bag?'

'Just around here.' He limped back down the track.

Jimmy walked with him. 'Not here, mate,' he said.

Josef joined them. 'Where's Nellie?'

'Nellie!' Adam called, as loudly as he dared. 'Are you all right?'

The rumble of the car was the only sound on the plain.

'Nellie!' Adam tried again.

Jimmy had been scouting around. 'No sign of the bag,' he said. 'and no sign of the sheila. You know what's happened, don't you?'

Adam stared at shadows, not comprehending.

'She's run off and taken the opal with her.'

201

THIRTEEN

The car was returning. As a hawk drifts across the sky in lazy spirals and dives with a terrifying suddenness when it has chosen its prey, so the car turned and came straight at them. It was still a long way away but the menace was unmistakable. With its motor roaring and its body booming from the pounding and leaping and rebounding of its wheels, it raced towards them, a mechanical bird plummeting and fluttering on its way to the kill.

The car drew closer and reared through a succession of bumps. Its lights became bobbing dashes of yellow that splashed the stony plain. Adam stared, mesmerized. Confused and distressed, he had been searching the plain for Nellie when the car turned and, immediately, he had known the driver *knew* where he was. The turn, the break with the slow-motion sweep of the plain, had been so positive, the direction so precise, that Mailey must have known where to head. But he could not have seen him. Not at that distance. Something else had happened.

The noise grew louder, the light brighter. Adam was conscious of a call from Josef to join them in hiding, but he did not move. He raised a hand to shield his eyes from the glare and searched for what he hoped not to find.

It took several seconds for him to see her. She was just to one side of the car, a figure briefly illuminated as Mailey raced past. Adam saw Nellie clearly for only an instant. She was standing tall, not frightened to be seen. One hand was raised to support something slung over her shoulder. The other was outstretched towards the car.

'Nellie,' Adam cried, feeling betrayed.

The farthest rays of the headlights touched him. Josef was shouting to him to hide. He felt naked. His body glowed as the lights grew brighter. Adam turned. He saw Josef's head lifted above his hiding place, his anguished face gold in the overflow of light.

'You and Jimmy stay down,' he called. 'He hasn't seen you yet.'

A dark hand rose beside Josef's face and pushed the boy out of sight.

'See you later!' Adam shouted and began hobbling away from his friends, towards a shadow staining the edge of the plain. It was no more than fifty paces beyond the track they had been following. The shadow might be a deep gutter, a washaway, or a bank edging a creek. Whatever it was, it held the vague promise of shelter and of barring the progress of the car.

The roaring and pounding and clattering was close. His shadow split into several images. The car must be about to run him down.

Adam saw the trench. Ten steps and he could reach it. It was a knee-deep groove in the plain, a relic of past storms where water had scoured a channel with abrupt sides that were studded with stones like a pudding bursting with nuts and fruit.

He ran. He knew his life depended on getting to that ditch before the car reached him. There was the howl of the car's motor, the scrabble of spinning tyres, the thud of stones, the whine of gears and, beneath it all like the rhythm section of some nightmarish band, the rasping of his breath and the bass drumbeat of his heart.

He fell. Without stopping he crawled up a large mound, spidering his way over the top. He rolled through grass and as he rolled his eyes stared into one dazzling headlamp. Then the light reared high in the air. Sand and small stones showered through its beam.

The car had hit the mound. The engine stalled. There was a hiss of steam, a squeak of metal springs and a violent oath from the man behind the wheel.

Adam kept rolling. He tumbled over and over and fell into the ditch. He was lying on his back in the dark shadow. Dust, bright as fog in the glare of the lights, rolled above him.

Mailey was out of the car, bellowing obscenities. His shadow was a black ray, splitting the white clouds of dust.

As Adam's neck ached in anticipation of the bullet he knew would surely find him, he heard a thud, a grunt of pain and the sound of a large mass crumpling to the ground. It was so close he shivered, thinking he had been hit. The bank above him shook. He looked up. The clouds of dust brightened into a solid mist of white. Mailey's shadow had gone.

He dared lift his head. The car's headlamps shone directly into his eyes. Seeing nothing in the blaze of light, he thought he had been tricked and clenched his teeth, waiting for the crack of a gun, the crunch of a blow, for some violence to erupt from the glare.

Nothing happened. He blinked. Near him the ground moved. Slowly, and with a deep moan, a head rose.

It was a silhouette, sharply defined and so close that Adam recoiled. The outline was of Mailey, but a Mailey befuddled by shock and only semi-conscious. He was groaning. His breath still stank. The shadow gained in bulk as he pushed himself to his hands and knees. His head hung from the twin peaks of his shoulders.

A figure flashed through the blaze of headlights. It was Jimmy. He leaped into the ditch.

'Quick,' he said. 'Get up.'

Adam, shocked by the nearness of Mailey, had pushed himself against the far bank. 'Can't,' he gasped. 'My legs won't work.'

'Get on my back, then.' Jimmy bent down and hauled Adam upright.

'What the hell happened?' Adam said, as he allowed his body to fold across Jimmy's shoulders.

Mailey moaned. He lifted one arm.

'Hang on, he'll be on his feet in a moment,' Jimmy said, locking an arm around one of Adam's legs, and gripping a wrist with the other. 'I threw a rock. Got him fair on the back of his ugly head.'

'Where's Joe?' Adam's question shook from his lips as Jimmy broke into a loping run.

'Up ahead. He's OK. Christ, you're heavy!'

Jimmy carried Adam beyond the fan of light and slowed to a walk as he tried to follow the path of the watercourse. Behind them, like a figure spotlighted on a stage, Mailey stood and staggered several paces. He covered one ear with his hand. Adam could see him clearly, for their paths had taken them almost side-on to the car. Mailey dropped to one knee. His free hand groped in the sand. When he stood again, he was carrying the gun.

Jimmy stopped and lowered Adam roughly to the ground.

'Why are we stopping?'

'I'm buggered,' Jimmy whispered. 'Besides, I can't see where I'm going.'

'Well get down. If we keep quiet, he might head off in another direction.'

Mailey walked to the ditch, searched for footprints, and once more looked in their direction. He cupped one hand to his ear, and listened. Adam and Jimmy held their breaths.

'If he starts to walk, we'll lose him,' Jimmy said in his softest voice.

Mailey hesitated.

'Why don't you try throwing another rock?' Adam whispered.

'I couldn't hit him from here.' Jimmy sounded surprised.

'You don't have to hit him again. Just make a noise somewhere else.'

Jimmy felt for a stone. He found one the size of an egg, half-embedded in the bank, and broke it loose. He threw hard, grunting with the effort. The stone landed behind the car.

Mailey spun around. He dashed to the side of the car and, leaving the glare of the lights, became one shadow among others. They heard him moving and then saw the reddish glow of his body as he stepped near the tail-lamp. Again they lost sight of him. They could hear his feet scratching on stones. He stumbled and muffled a curse.

'Let's go while we can,' Jimmy said.

'I think I can walk. You might have to give me a hand.'

Adam put his arm around Jimmy's shoulders, and they continued slowly along the course of the washaway. It would have been simpler to have walked on the plain, but the winding watercourse promised them shelter if they had to hide.

They walked, stooping low and glancing back. The sandy path they were following split into two and they kept to the right, feeling their way along a broader channel where raised strands of gravel and dead bushes had tangled to form low islands.

They heard a rattling of metal and stopped. Mailey was at the front of the car, winding the crank handle.

'Bastard!' Jimmy spat. 'That means he's going to use the car to hunt us down. It'll be harder for us with those lights.'

The engine coughed. Mailey wound harder. The exhaust popped and spat dark explosions and the motor spluttered into life. Mailey flashed from burning bright to shadow as he ran from the front to jump in the car. The engine snarled in a series of bursts and, keeping time, the lights burned brighter.

'Let's hide,' Adam said, dropping to his elbows and crawling to a small island formed by a tangle of flood debris. Jimmy followed. They lay side by side, sprawled on the sand, watching the man in the car only fifty paces from them and feeling vulnerable.

The lights reached them. Their shelter of rotted vegetation

glowed softly. Cheeks pressed into the cool sand, they faced each other, eyes wide in fright, not breathing for fear of any movement betraying them.

The lights moved and stopped on low bushes to their right. They breathed and smiled.

'Where's Joe?' Adam whispered.

'Should be close by.' Jimmy lifted his head to look around.

'Any sign of Nellie?' Adam asked hopefully.

Jimmy turned and Adam could feel the scorn in his look. 'She's gone, mate. Taken our opal and pissed off.'

Adam sat up and used the back of his hand to brush sand from his face. 'I saw her out there, near Mailey.'

'When?'

'When the car first came at us. I think she must have called out to him.'

From the car came the rumble of a higher exhaust note. Its lights swung through another arc and blazed across an expanse of ravaged gravel. Its tail-light glared at them.

Casually, Jimmy slapped sand from his shoulders. 'That'd be right. She'd do that.'

'But why?'

'Mate, she planned all this. She got us out just so she could pinch the rock. Simple as that.' He stood, emboldened by the darkness. 'You stay here. I'm going to find young Joe. Keep your head down.'

'You too. Take care.'

Within seconds, Jimmy had disappeared.

The car horn blew.

'All right, Ross,' Mailey called out. Adam could not see him but his voice, as thin and cold as the night air, reached him with surprising clarity. 'I know you can hear me. We can do a deal.'

The voice grew louder. Mailey must have turned and was facing him.

'It's not you I'm after. It's that black bastard. He's the one I want. You tell me where he is and you can go free.'

Adam lay on his back. The stars signalled a thousand warnings.

'I know you must have hurt yourself. You can hardly walk. You're not going to get far.'

The voice was fainter. He had turned. He certainly did not know where Adam had gone, and was broadcasting his message to the whole plain.

'Tell me where Kettle is, and I'll drive you back to town.'

Adam wondered if Nellie were with him. Hiding in the car maybe. Clutching the bag with the opal. He closed his eyes.

'I'll give you one minute,' Mailey shouted.

Or you'll do what? Adam thought. He sat up. Mailey was crossing the zone of light in front of the car. His face, normally full and ruddy, was as bright as a full moon. He was not standing in one place but moving constantly. He was too wily to offer himself as a target again. He still had one hand clasped to the side of his face. Jimmy must have hurt him. Even injured, and even at this distance – he was perhaps two hundred paces away – Mailey projected an image of great strength and aggression. He would be a formidable opponent. Adam wondered what sort of fighter he would be.

Probably dirty and bull-like. He would rush, content to take a punch so that he could come to grips with his man. Then he would wrestle, not box, and use his knees and elbows, and choke and crush. He was broad and fat around the neck and middle but it was the sort of fatness you saw on men who were extremely powerful. He would bear down on you with all his weight and then start breaking bones.

'If you can't walk easily, just call out and I'll come and get you,' Mailey shouted.

Adam could not see him now. He had moved. There was only the car, a lonely silhouette against its own lights.

'No point hanging for something an abo did.'

Adam stretched out on the sand. They should be moving. He felt chilled. He became aware once more of the pain in his hands. His knees and legs had ached so much during the run that he had forgotten his burnt hands.

'Thirty seconds, son. Just call out. You'll be right. It's not you I want.'

For one absurd moment Adam was tempted to call out: 'Then why did you belt me over the head with a lump of wood?' but he stayed silent. He tried clenching his fists. He was in for some miserable days … if he survived this one. He had been burned many times but only on small areas of his skin.

Adam lay looking at the stars. He found the saucepan, clean and distinct among the stars. What had his father called it? Orion? That was a long time ago. The voice startled him.

'I thought you might have shot through, and gone to get a lift.' Jimmy had returned, as silent as the breeze.

'Had a lot to say, didn't he?' Adam whispered, trying to sound calm.

'Cunning bloke, that one,' Jimmy said.

Adam could just make him out. He was crouching and using his hands to feel the way.

'He must think I'm a fool,' Adam said. 'Where's Joe?'

'Here,' the boy answered and a paler face appeared beside Jimmy. 'You all right?'

'Fine.'

'Did Nellie come back?'

Jimmy answered. 'If she comes back, then Mailey's Santa Claus.'

Josef moved to Adam's side. He dropped to his knees. 'Do you think she meant to steal your bag? She might have just picked it up.'

Jimmy laughed. It was a soft but cruel sound.

'She might,' Joe protested. 'It was dark. Wasn't it, Adam?'

'Certainly was.' Adam's voice was flat. He was looking for Mailey who had disappeared in the shadows.

'She might just have picked it up to help Adam and then got lost.'

Jimmy sniffed. 'I'd keep your eye on the copper if I was you, kid. I think he might be growing a long white beard.'

Adam saw the hurt in the boy's eyes. Josef's face was close to his.

'She'll come back,' Josef said, comforting Adam and reassuring himself. 'I think she likes you, Adam. Do the burns hurt?'

Adam nodded.

Josef pulled his shirt from his trousers and began to tear off a strip of material.

Jimmy gripped his shoulder. 'Shh. Mailey could hear that half a mile away.'

'I've got to bandage the burns,' he said. 'If they get infected it'll be terrible.'

'You out there, Ross?' It was Mailey, back in the lights and using his loudest voice. He was looking their way.

'Jesus!' Jimmy whispered. 'I wish you'd leave playing nurse until we're clear of that copper.'

'I heard you,' the policeman shouted through cupped hands. 'Are you coming in?'

Josef touched Adam. 'What are we going to do?' he whispered.

'Get down and don't move,' Adam answered. 'And don't look up. Your face is shining like a mirror.'

Mailey was back in the car and swinging it through a U-turn.

'We could run.'

The three squirmed into the sand behind the small island. The boy was close to Adam. He was shivering.

'That's what he wants us to do,' Adam said, putting one arm across Josef's shoulders. 'Just stay still. He won't see us.'

'What if he does?'

'Then we all run in different directions. And keep on the other side of this washout. He can't drive the car across.'

'You can't run.'

'Be quiet. He's coming.'

The lights flicked over their hiding place as the car bounced on a patch of gibbers. Mailey did not come straight at them. He followed a line that took him to the edge of the watercourse a few yards from where the three were hiding.

If he turned the car so that the lights swung their way he must surely see them, for they were spread out on the sand, slaughtered sheep waiting to be skinned.

The car rocked as Mailey engaged gear. He was a rough man on cars, Adam thought, and concentrated on the shadows on Josef's back. They grew darker and blended with each other. Mailey had turned the other way.

Cautiously, Jimmy lifted his head.

'Do you know what I'm going to do?'

Josef looked at him anxiously.

'I'm going to piss off. Anyone coming?'

FOURTEEN

They were walking downhill. The slope was so slight as to be almost imperceptible but rain had gouged its way down the hill and cut a deep and sometimes narrow channel. Along this treacherous path they walked, feeling their way in the dark and stumbling on an occasional tangle of roots sprouting from the banks. They ate a little of the food Josef had brought, and talked as they walked.

The slope, slight though it was, persisted and they followed the channel through a series of snaking bends, where the ground rose and fell in a soft swell, an ocean of stones restless before a storm. Then the slope ceased and the land was flat. Little ridges of sand stitched together by gnarled bush knotted its surface.

The channel spread in confusion.

They kept to the north-east following the stars. They trudged along one reach of sand, the overspill of the watercourse, and then, when the sand thinned and disappeared, their feet crunched on a crust of small stones embedded in clay.

They came to a region of thick bush and slept there, feeling secure in its cover until the rim of the sky glowed with the bright warning of a new day.

Adam lay on the ground, cold and sore, and did not move for several minutes. He thought of Nellie. He had been thinking of her a lot. Something, a deep and irrational glow within him, tried to convince him that Josef was right; that Nellie had just become separated from them in the dark; that Mailey had seen her by chance; that she would come back and find them. Strangely, he was not so concerned about the opal. It was Nellie he wanted back.

A fly touched his nostril. He brushed it and winced with the pain caused by the sudden movement. And with the pain, his mind surrendered to cynicism. Jimmy was right. She had stolen the opal. She had shown Mailey where they were hiding. She had betrayed them, and he would never see her again.

He shivered with cold. Jimmy, conscious of the movement, opened his eyes and stood up as though one action triggered the next.

'No sign of Mailey,' he said, brushing away some flies.

Josef woke and scratched himself and tore strips from his shirt to bandage Adam's burns. Jimmy scouted the bush. He returned grinning.

'Come and see what I've found,' he said and led them to a camel. It was two hundred yards away. A young female with a creamy coat, it trailed a rope from its nose. The rope had become entangled in the roots of a bush.

'It's been there a day or so,' Jimmy said. 'Look how it's worn a path around the bush. The more it tried to get free, the more it got tangled. Another day of walking in circles and it'd be on its knees.'

The rope was wound around the base of the bush and was so

210

tight the camel could only just stand with its head erect. It tried to back away from them but though its hindquarters moved, the nose remained anchored to the bush. It rocked in distress and made snuffling sounds, like a child sobbing noisily.

Adam, his hands clumsy in the crude bandages, limped forward, muttering reassuring sounds. The camel shuffled its legs and ceased its painful game of tug-of-war.

Adam stood near it, one hand raised above his head, and repeated the strange sounds.

'What are you doing?' Josef said.

'He's having a conversation in camel language,' Jimmy laughed.

Adam moved to the camel and touched its head. The animal blinked. 'I spent a few weeks helping an old bloke with camels once,' he said. 'That's what he used to say to them. I don't know what it means but it calms them down.'

'Where did you work with camels?' Jimmy said, his voice a mixture of doubt and surprise.

'Near Frome Downs, on an outstation.' He stroked the camel's neck. 'They were drilling a bore.'

'Who? The camels?' Jimmy turned to Josef, waiting for his laugh.

'No, you dill! The blokes with the camels. The head man was an Afghan. Nice bloke. Very quiet.' He was coaxing the camel to move forward, to take the strain off the rope.

'I wonder where this one came from. It's not wild. It's a working camel.'

Josef moved closer. 'There was an Afghan in town the other day. He had a lot of camels.'

'He just wouldn't turn one loose. These things are too valuable.'

'Probably broke away,' Jimmy said, not so much concerned about the animal's past ownership as its future. 'Can you ride one of these things?'

'Me?' said Adam. 'Of course. We used to have races on Sundays.'

'Good,' Jimmy said. 'You ride this one then. The speed you'd be walking at an ant would overtake us, let alone that copper. You get on the camel and me and Joe'll walk and we'll make four times the pace.'

They spent half an hour trying to free the animal. The sun rose. While it improved their vision, the extra light seemed to stir the camel into greater resistance and, tormented by squadrons of flies, it stamped and snorted and pulled.

The rope had become tightly knotted by the camel's earlier turning and tugging and, despite Adam's coaxing, the beast kept jerking and reversing as they worked to free it. At one stage, Jimmy became exasperated and walked away, threatening to turn the animal into steak. The camel, as though understanding, became calmer. It gurgled and grunted and rolled its jaws, but it stayed in the one spot and was soon free.

Using the rope, Adam hauled the camel to its knees and, with difficulty, climbed on its back. The animal see-sawed to its feet. Adam yelped with pain.

'I'll have to ride like a lady,' he said, swinging one leg over the camel's shoulders and sitting side-saddle. 'Hurts the knees too much the other way.'

'Can you ride it like that?' Jimmy asked.

'So long as you don't run too fast.'

'Fat chance of me running! What can you see from up there?'

Adam spent a few seconds surveying the land. They were on the side of a low rise and the extra elevation gave him a clear view across the scrub. The land behind them was cobbled with gibbers. They looked almost beautiful in the soft light. A lustrous purple, spilled paint, spreading in long fingers across a base of ochre-coloured clay. A low range of hills framed the horizon to the south-west. Their flanks glowed orange. To the south-east were a few hills, splotches of washed-out drabness, ground down by countless ages of wind and heat. They would have been the hills they glimpsed during the night in the faintest reaches of Mailey's lights.

He pivoted on the camel, moving awkwardly as he used his hands to lever his body into place. Out to the east, ghostly in the low rays of the rising sun, was a dust trail.

'I can see Mailey,' Adam announced.

'Shit.' Jimmy stamped the ground and the camel reared its head. 'Where is he?'

'Few miles away to the east. Coming this way.'

'Could he see us?' Josef asked anxiously.

'No. We're too far away and we're safe here on the side of the hill. He might spot us if we were on the ridge, though.' Adam swung around to see which way along the hill offered the best shelter.

'We go this way.' He pointed along a line that would take them through scrub for another half-mile without climbing to the top of the ridge. 'He's cunning, that Mailey.'

'Why?' Josef was standing on tiptoe, trying to see over a stand of acacia.

'Well, I reckon he went as far to the east as he reckoned we could cover, and then a bit more, and stopped out there for a couple of hours.' He stroked the camel's neck to stop it tossing its head. 'When the sun came up, he could see anything out there. Easily. All brightly shining in the sunlight, and no one could see him for a while because of the glare.'

'Yeah, he's a clever bastard.' Jimmy spat. 'Why's he coming this way?'

'To get to the hills, I suppose,' Adam said.' If we're not out there on the plain, we must be over here. From the hills he'll get a better view of all the country.'

'What are we going to do?' Josef asked.

'Head for the roughest country we can find. Go somewhere where a camel can walk but a car can't drive.'

They drank a little water from the jar and followed the line of scrub to the end of the ridge. There they turned left, away from Mailey, and using the ridge as a shelter crossed a series of low sand dunes. Jimmy set the course and then followed the others, using an uprooted bush to sweep their tracks from the deeper sand. They intersected the course of a creek, its bed a jumble of stones and striated sand, and followed it to the north.

After an hour, the creek swung to the left and entered a region where there was some grass. A few scrawny trees dotted the banks. The creek broadened to a wide reach of sand where water lingered in a soak dug beneath a low cliff spiked with tall grass, and there they came upon the camp of Saleem Benn.

'No,' the Afghan said. He continued strapping a bag to the side of his riding camel. The other animals were strung together, ready for departure. They were lightly laden, with wooden frames and ropes and leather straps. Being saddled and roped nose to tail, they were anxious to move. They swayed in line, each taking its cue from the beast in front to shuffle its legs or move to one side. They rocked and bobbed, ships of the desert, tied together and riding the slow swell of impatience.

The ashes of Saleem Benn's morning fire were fading to grey.

'But why not?' Josef pleaded and the man's eyes flashed anger that a boy should speak to him in such a way. Like a girl, whining for some useless trinket.

'You yourselves gave the reason,' he said coldly. 'There is a policeman chasing you.'

'He's out to kill us,' Jimmy said.

'I cannot believe that.' Saleem Benn turned his back and put all his weight into tightening the strap. 'Thank you for returning the camel. In truth, I had given that one up for lost. I am grateful for that and forever in your debt, but I cannot give refuge to people who are fugitives. You ask too much of me.'

'We just want to go with you to William Creek,' Josef said, and Adam touched his arm to stop him saying more.

'The man hunting us may be a policeman but he is not *good*,' Adam said, remembering the way the Afghan with the camels at Frome Downs used to speak. 'He murdered a lot of people back in Port Augusta, and now he is blaming us. He is the devil himself.' The old man with the camels had said that a lot. Anyone who displeased him was 'the devil himself'. A funny old fellow. He prostrated himself in prayer even when others were watching, and spoke in a strange way, but he had been kind to Adam.

'Why should he blame you?' Saleem Benn said, turning to stare intently at Adam.

'We were there. We saw the killings.'

'Who did he kill?' His voice cracked, flawed with doubt. He had endured some desperately sad hours: the death of his brother's son and the loss of his camels, then the burial of the boy in these remote folds of the earth, and the long and tiring search for his missing animals. This had not been a good journey. Becoming involved in some escapade with people fleeing from the law was a complication he had no desire to embrace. Yet he was curious.

'Who were these people you say he killed? You.' He pointed to Jimmy. 'Let the black man tell me.'

Jimmy acknowledged the question with a smile that bore no suggestion of amusement. 'No one important,' he said. 'Just some of my people. One of his men cut up two of my nephews with an axe. He bashed my uncle. Then he shot a white man. He didn't mean to. He meant to kill me but he shot this other bloke by mistake.'

Saleem Benn stroked his beard.

214

'I know something about camels,' Adam said. 'You're going to need help. I would work for you if you let us ride with you. You have many camels ... one more now than you might have.'

The Afghan studied him as a man might examine a horse at an auction. 'You do not look as though you could perform hard work for many days.'

'Try me,' Adam said.

'We can work, too,' Josef said.

Saleem Benn ignored the boy. 'How did you burn yourself?'

Adam shrugged. 'There was a fire.'

'The policeman locked them up in the old gaol,' Josef said. 'Nellie and I tried to pull the door down with the policeman's car but it didn't work and we ended up driving the car into the door.'

'Very enterprising,' said the Afghan. 'Who is Nellie?'

'She's a sheila,' Jimmy said. 'Came with us at the start but then nicked off with some opals we were carrying.'

'She stole these from you?'

'Too right.'

Saleem Benn turned to Adam. 'But where was the fire that caused you such burns?'

'The car burst into flames,' Adam said. 'It rammed the gaol door going backwards and the petrol tank split.'

'They are the invention of the devil himself,' the Afghan growled.

'When the tank blew up, the whole doorway started to burn,' Josef said. 'They had to run through the flames. That's how Adam got burned.'

'It was different to that,' Jimmy said, and Josef looked at him in surprise. Jimmy rubbed his hands. 'I'm frightened of fire, see. Always have been. My mother must have swallowed a burning cigarette.' He breathed deeply. 'When the car exploded in our faces, I just couldn't move. Not one inch. Adam carried me out. That's how he got burned. He took me out on his hands and knees and copped all the flames.'

Saleem Benn lifted his head and used his long nose like a gunsight, aiming it at Adam's eyes.

'You did that for your black friend?'

Adam shrugged.

The Afghan turned. 'You say this policeman, the man who is the devil himself, is close to you and you do not have much time?' Not waiting for an answer, he strode along the row of camels,

215

shouting orders and touching animals as he went.

'Can you all ride a camel?' Again he did not pause for an answer. 'No, I suppose not. Never mind. We will learn and my poor creatures will suffer as you struggle to master the art. You may find it painful.' He turned, and the first suggestion of a smile crinkled the edges of his eyes. 'But believe me, my new helpers, you will find the aches and torments of riding so unconventional a beast infinitely more pleasant than having that man who pursues you drain the brains from your skull with a skilfully placed bullet. You say he is in a car?'

'Yes. Over that way.' Adam indicated the direction.

'Well, we will go a way where he may not follow. It may be longer but it will be safer. Now get on quickly. I will show you which animals. We must hurry.'

FIFTEEN

Mailey caught Nellie late in the afternoon. He found her by accident. His car was almost out of petrol and he was returning to Coober Pedy, following the wheel tracks of the supply road from William Creek. She was crossing the road.

Nellie had cut her foot on a stone and was limping. She had been crying a lot in the past twelve hours and her face was a mottle of shiny skin and dust. When she saw the car she made an attempt to run away, but was too tired. She put the bag with the opal under a bush and waited for the policeman.

At the last moment, she had an idea. She lifted her thumb in the classic pose of a hitchhiker. After all, she reasoned, if Mailey thought she was just a black woman trying to get a lift he might not stop. She shielded her face with her other hand.

He stopped.

'Can you give me a lift?' she said hopefully, but keeping her head low.

There was a long silence, punctuated by the buzz of flies. She looked up. Mailey's face, sagging from lack of sleep, was a ruin of lines and shaded hollows. He opened his door. One foot slid to the running board.

'Didn't I see you last night?' he asked. 'Aren't you that tart that's been hanging around with that Jimmy Kettle character?'

Mailey's second leg followed the first. Having pivoted in his seat he allowed his body to follow his legs out of the car. He reached the ground so abruptly his stomach bounced. Nellie took a step backwards.

'I just want a lift, mister.'

He brushed dirt from his clothes and moved towards her. He stank of sweat. 'Don't give me that crap,' he said softly, picking a grass seed from the knee of his trousers. 'Where are they?'

'Who? I just want a lift into town.' She licked her lips and took another step away from him.

'What were you doing out there?' he asked, his voice oily with forced good humour. 'You were the one I almost ran over, weren't you?'

She tried to look puzzled. 'Have you had too much sun?' she said. 'I don't know what you're talking about. I just want a lift into town.'

'Where are they heading for?'

'Don't bother. I'll walk.' She started to move away. He grabbed her arm.

'Did they give you the arse or something? Did the blackfellow get tired of you? Tell you to piss off? What happened? What were you doing out there on your own?'

She said nothing. Her eyes rolled in distress for his grip hurt, and while she squirmed, she thought. It was her temper that had got her into trouble. She was always acting impetuously and being sorry later.

Mailey was talking, but more to himself than to her. 'I just caught a glimpse of someone moving. A young woman. Black. Long hair. High cheekbones. Bare feet.' His eyes roved over her, checking off each feature. 'It *was* you, wasn't it? Running around like a rooster with its head off, panicking. Then I saw the young white bloke with the snowy hair. Were you with him?' He tightened his grip on her arm. 'Were you at the lock-up? Were you one of them that set fire to my car?'

'What are you talking about, mister? You're in your car now. How could I have set fire to it?'

She lifted her sore foot and stroked the cut.

'You listen to me,' he said, his voice rising. 'The young white feller's hurt, isn't he? How bad is he? What's up with him? It's not you I'm after,' he said, reaching out and taking her wrist. 'Just tell me where the others are. Did they come back this way?'

She avoided his eyes.

'No,' he said, glancing back to the east. 'I found their tracks too far in the other direction. They're still out there somewhere. Where are they making for?'

She bent under the pressure on her arm.

'I'll just buy me some petrol, get a few supplies, and go back out and find them. Some of the men in town will know where they're likely to be heading. There aren't many places they can go. I'll find them.'

He applied more pressure and she fell to one knee.

'What are you doing out here anyway?'

She said nothing.

'Tough little bitch, aren't you?'

He let go. She remained on one knee.

'You're from Port Pirie, aren't you? You were a whore down there. Worked for that slimy bastard Harris. What have you been doing up here? Working the mines?'

She wiped her eyes.

Mailey walked around her, adjusting his trouser belt as he moved. 'You're not a bad-looking sheila, you know that? Not all nigger, are you?' He put his boot against her back and pushed. 'Half-caste? Quarter-caste? What are you?'

'I'm an abo.'

'Oh no, you're not. Not all. There's some white blood in there somewhere. The white blood gives you the looks. The black blood makes you a whore.'

Her eyes spat anger.

'Get up,' he said. When she did not move, he undid his belt and withdrew it from the loops on his trousers.

'Ever had a belting?' he asked, wrapping the end of the belt around his fist. 'I mean a good one. The sort that takes your skin off in lumps.' He struck viciously with the belt. She screamed in pain and straightened.

'Did you burn my car, you bloody whore?' he shouted and hit her again.

She fell. He stood over her, belt raised to strike. 'Now, slut, you're going to tell me where your friends are heading.'

*

218

The camel train took three days to reach William Creek. Initially Saleem Benn had headed north, threading his animals through a chain of sand dunes and choosing ground that a wheeled vehicle would find impossible to traverse. Then the Afghan turned towards the east and the party rode along the northern shores of a vast salt lake. The going was slow. There were detours to make around tributaries that snaked on bellies of grey mud. There was much sand, and for hours on the second day they ploughed through ridges that ran as regular as fishbones from the spine of the lake.

They came to a region of mud flats. There the surface had dried into a crust that rested on a thick ooze. The dried mud crazed into plates that buckled under the weight of the camels and the flats pulsed to the beat of their progress, but they crossed and the Afghan knew no car could follow.

On the second night rain fell. At first, the drops were few and fat and they hit the tents with the thud of seed pods. After half an hour of desultory spitting and pattering, a storm erupted. Rain drummed on the canvas and hit the ground so hard and rebounded so high that the land seemed to spout jets of water. The deluge lasted only a few minutes. The camels groaned and wheezed and their hides stank but Saleem Benn was pleased. The rain had obliterated their tracks.

The Afghan was more than a contractor who hauled goods to customers in remote places and carried their produce, like wool, back to market. He was also a merchant. He was prepared to sell items to any stranger he met, and was not a man likely to miss an opportunity. Therefore, on one camel he carried a selection of simple medicines and first-aid items, of the sort prized by people who lived in the outback: castor oil and cod liver oil, tincture of iodine, friar's balsam, Conde's crystals, camphor, molasses, and creams and balms for sprains, bites, burns and scalds.

He treated Adam's burns and much of the pain was eased. He also cut his hair, trimming the unburned locks to match the length of those tufts shortened by the fire. Adam's appearance was transformed, his hair now close-cropped and his beard, having been singed in an erratic pattern, removed with a few strokes of the Afghan's cut-throat razor.

It was only on the third day, after Saleem Benn announced they were within a few miles of William Creek, that the thought occurred to Adam.

219

'What if Mailey isn't following us?' he asked the Afghan. They were walking together, each leading his camel, and the old man turned.

'You said he *was* following you.'

'Yes, but what if he's got ahead of us?'

Saleem Benn stopped and his camel took the opportunity to rest its curved neck on his shoulder.

Adam continued. 'What if he stopped to work out where we might be heading? Say he saw the camel tracks somewhere, but couldn't follow? Where would he go then?'

'Would he not return to Coober Pedy?'

'Only to get petrol and some tucker.' Adam's camel began tossing its head and he pulled hard on the lead to steady it. 'Is there a road between Coober Pedy and William Creek?'

'Of sorts.'

'Good enough for a car?'

'With an experienced driver, I suppose. There are lorries that have made the journey.' The Afghan gazed at the ridge that concealed William Creek. 'The railway line to Oodnadatta is to the left. The track from Coober Pedy comes in on our right. There are, indeed, many ways into such a small settlement.' He scratched the neck of his camel. 'You may be right, Adam Ross. There could well be someone waiting for you. You and your friends stay here. I will leave you your camels, but keep them and yourselves out of sight.'

He pointed to a line of trees whose outline boiled in the heat haze.

'I suggest you wait there, where the animals will not be seen from a distance. I will take the rest of the camels into William Creek, tell them of the sad loss of my brother's son and then come back for you. If there is no one there, I will return within three hours. If I am longer, you will know your suspicions were correct. In either case, I will come back for you. Wait for me in the trees.'

Saleem Benn returned after sunset. Adam walked from the trees to meet him. The camels in the train shuffled their legs and gurgled noisily.

'You are rested?' the Afghan asked.

Adam noticed he usually began a conversation, no matter how urgent the situation, with a polite enquiry.

'Good,' he continued, his bearded head nodding in satisfaction.

'I have had a journey of such complexity that my camels are confused. First in one direction, then another, and now here, over terrain they crossed earlier today. Truly, they think they are going back to that vile place where men live under the ground, and they are not pleased.'

Adam, who had spent hours worrying about the old man's return, was anxious for news.

'He's there?'

'Yes, as you thought. A most unpleasant man.'

'What happened?'

'I saw his car. It was hidden among some peppercorn trees at the back of the hotel, but I approached the building from that side and watered my animals and tied them near there, so I knew he was there long before I saw him.'

Jimmy and Josef joined Adam.

'Where was he?' Jimmy asked. 'In the bar?'

'No. Outside the hotel somewhere. I did not see him until he followed me into the building.'

'He was hiding?' Adam said.

'Probably. I did not see him and my eyes are still good.'

'He's a cunning bastard,' Jimmy said.

'And then ...?' Adam prompted. As he spoke, he peered into the blackness behind the lurching shadows of Saleem Benn's camels.

'Relax, my young friend. He has not followed,' the Afghan said and Adam saw the pale flash of a smile. 'I have taken enough turns to plait a rope. The policeman is still back at the hotel, waiting for you.'

'He knew we were heading this way?' Jimmy said.

'Apparently.'

'Nellie,' Jimmy said. 'That bitch. She told him.'

'You don't know that,' Josef said.

'Grow up, kid,' Jimmy said.

Adam held a bandaged hand aloft to silence the others.

'What happened at William Creek?' he said.

'Well, I went in to the building through the kitchen. I know the people there well and I normally approach from the back. Besides, I thought the policeman would be in the bar. I was surprised when he followed me into the room.' He spat. 'I am very dry. May I have some water?'

Josef brought a flask.

'He is a very large man,' Saleem Benn continued when he had drunk. He wiped his lips with dainty precision. 'Not tall, but wide and thick. He looks extremely powerful. You are wise to be fleeing from him.'

Jimmy sniffed, managing to put defiance in the sound. 'What did he do?' he said.

'Very little. He asked if I had come from Coober Pedy. I said "yes". He asked if I had seen anyone. I said "no". He asked me when I had left and I told him. He asked me why my journey had taken so long and I told him about the loss of my nephew and how that misfortune had hampered my progress. Then the publican, who had come into the room, asked me about the boy, for he had known him most of his life, and the policeman asked no more questions.'

'What did Mailey do then?' Adam asked.

Saleem Benn thought for a moment. 'He said no more. He stood there in the room for some time, listening to my friend and me. Then he went out.'

'Back to his hiding place?'

'I suppose so. He went out of the building.'

'I hope a snake bites him,' Jimmy said. 'I hope he has a crap and a snake sinks its teeth into his arse.'

Saleem Benn looked at Jimmy. His face was grave. 'Your sentiments are uncouth,' he pronounced, 'but contain much merit. I must confess I did not like that man. I was told he had been there more than a day. He had been enquiring about you.'

'And you think he's still in William Creek?' Adam said, again searching the darkness for any sign of movement.

'He will wait there several days and then, when you do not appear, he will drive along the railway line towards Oodnadatta, checking at the stations on the way.'

'How do you know that?' Adam said.

'The publican told me. The policeman told him. He said he believed you would head north, rather than south. He said you had been travelling north since committing your crime.'

'We didn't commit no crime,' Jimmy said.

The Afghan touched his forehead. 'That I believe. I am merely repeating another man's words. Because you have travelled north since that, ah, incident, the policeman believes you will continue to favour that direction.'

'So where do we go?' Jimmy said.

'I am going the other way, towards Hergott Springs, or Marree as they now call it. You may travel with me as far as that town.'

'Do we go along the railway line?' Adam asked.

'I think not. We would all be seen – by railway workers, by passengers in a train, by someone. It is better if we travel a slightly longer but infinitely more private route.'

He moved back towards his camels.

'I know a place north of here that is visited by no one else. There is water there from a spring. It is some distance from here but the going is flat. We should travel there before stopping for the night but once there we will be safe.'

They left the shelter of the trees and headed north. The camels seemed nervous and agitated. They tossed their heads and jerked on the ropes and stumbled. Saleem Benn tried cajoling them and cursing them but nothing eased their distress. Whereas the string of animals normally flowed across the land with the fluency of water over a river bed, they now chopped and curled, like a stream diverted into different channels by a jumble of rocks.

It was a rough ride, and Adam suffered, for the jolting rekindled the fierceness of the pain in his burns. The only cure was to stop but this he refused to suggest. He felt as nervous as the camels. There was something about their resting place in the trees which had filled him with dread and he was glad to leave and to keep moving. The farther they moved the happier he would be, so he said nothing and suffered.

They crossed a rough road and the leading camel tried to turn right and made evil gurgling noises when the Afghan pulled him straight again. They clambered over the raised metal on the railway line to Alice Springs. One of the camels slipped and sprawled, all legs and knees, on the loose metal. The others snapped to a halt until the beast had see-sawed its way to its feet once more.

For a while, a solitary yellow light glowed in the distance. It was the William Creek Hotel, as forlorn as a lighthouse on a lonely reef. Then the light faded and they were alone in the night.

An hour later, Mailey reached the trees. He came on foot, moving slowly and examining the ground by the light of a shaded torch. He discovered the place where they had rested. He searched for tracks beyond the trees, and found the marks left by the departing camels. He followed the trail for a few minutes and then, satisfied he knew the course they had taken, went back to the place where he had hidden the car.

The moon rose and it became easier to see the way. The land was still flat, but some hills, glowing like ice carvings, edged the world to the west.

The camels were now less nervous but they had become disgruntled with fatigue and made loud snuffing noises. Even so, their fluency of movement had returned and the ride became smoother.

Saleem Benn eased his camel alongside Adam's.

'You are more comfortable now?' he enquired. In the moonlight he was a swirl of cloth for a breeze was blowing and his loose garments fluttered about his body. He cleared a space in front of his face, so he could see Adam.

'You have found this ride trying?'

Adam nodded. 'Just a little.'

'We will be there soon. It is a place where we can get water.'

'Good.' Adam's voice could not disguise his pain.

The Afghan straightened his legs so that his body was clear of the saddle. He pointed ahead. 'Can you see a line of trees just to the east of those hills?'

Adam could distinguish a dark blur on the horizon.

'Just to the right is a spring, which pours forth sweet water from a raised mound. It is truly a remarkable sight. I know of no one else who has seen it. We will be safe there. We may even rest a day and let the camels regain their composure, and drink their fill, so they may then tackle the long journey down to Marree. We will go south of Lake Eyre, that way.' He gestured to the right. 'It's very dry country. There are two lakes. We will go between them at a point where I know a crossing that has been used by few men, white or black, and then we will travel south along the Frome River until we reach the town.'

'Is there water in the Frome?' Adam said.

'Only in an ocasional pool. There is one I know where we may water the camels and bathe ourselves. It is a place where there are many birds.'

'You know the country very well. How long have you been here?'

'In this part of the world? Twenty-eight years. I came to Hergott Springs, the place they now call Marree, in nineteen hundred and one. But I have been in Australia longer. I first came to Melbourne with my uncle and two of my brothers and one cousin in eighteen ninety-three. We came to tend some camels that had been purchased for a circus. But when we arrived in that town, the man could not pay. He took possession of the camels first, of course, and we were made to look like villains.' He smiled. 'The world is full of rogues. Unhappily, there are places where a man is judged by the colour of his skin or the hook in his nose. This is one such place, although I must grant that things are not as bad now as they were in the old days.'

'Why did you come up here?'

'There was little demand for people like us in Melbourne. We moved to Adelaide, as we heard camels were being used in South Australia. We spent the last of our money to buy tickets on the train. We then walked to Hawker, more than two hundred and fifty miles to the north.'

'That's a long walk.'

'We had no money but we did have time. Later we moved even further north to Hergott Springs because by that time we had accumulated some money and bought ourselves some young camels. We started carrying goods to the most remote places.'

'You never thought of going home?'

'Of course. But time not only heals, it changes your perspective. We came to regard this as our home. In any case, my young friend, there was little reason to return. I was married before I left Peshawar and had two sons, but my wife died from an illness and I left my sons in the care of a sister, but they too died from an illness. I heard the news while I was still in Melbourne, so why would a man return?'

'What about the others? Your brothers. Were they married?'

'My elder brother's wife was dead. She was stoned to death.'

He let the flap of his head-covering flow across his face so that only his eyes were revealed.

Adam was shocked. 'You mean murdered? Who killed her like that?'

'Oh, it was not murder,' he said, his voice soft and half-amused at the innocence of Adam's question. 'She, a married woman, had looked at another man. That, of course, is forbidden. So she was put to death.'

Adam twisted in his saddle. 'By stoning?'

'Of course. It is the way.'

225

'How old was she?'

'She had been married two years. She was aware of the law. She was not a good wife. They had had no children.'

'And she just looked at another man?'

'It is forbidden. He saw her face.'

'What happened to him? Nothing, I suppose.'

'Oh no. The guilt is the woman's but he was put to death too.'

'Why, if he wasn't guilty?'

'In case he was tempted again. Better death than that.'

Adam was silent for a few moments.

'You believe all that?' he said.

The Afghan breathed deeply. 'You mean in the correctness of such things? Of course. The ways of other people may seem strange to your Christian eyes and I am aware that few people in your country believe as I do. Remember that if you were in Kabul or Peshawar, you would be the strange one, with the odd beliefs.' He turned his camel to one side to avoid outcrops of rock that rose from the ground like a bunch of dark grapes.

'So I believe what I believe to be true. I do not know that what I believe *is* true. No one truly knows if what he believes is the one and only truth, and anyone who says he is certain is a fool. There are many religions in this world and they cannot all be true. We say there is one God and his prophet is Mohammed. You say there is one God and his prophet is his son Jesus. I find that idiotic, but still ... The Jews believe in the same God but do not believe in Jesus. The Hindus believe in more strange gods than one would find in a zoo. Buddhists believe in no god at all. Their holy men shave their skulls. The Sikhs believe in some deity who requires them to grow their hair and bandage their heads. A friend of mine is a Sikh. Strange man. We are forced together by the singularity of our beliefs. We are regarded by your people as being odd and, therefore, we have become friends. United against you Christians, a Sikh and a Moslem who have as much in common as a cobra and a mongoose! Think about that, young Adam Ross. We are united because of our devotion to teachings that you regard as queer. But your practices seem equally strange to us. Are you a Catholic?'

Adam shook his head.

'Catholics expect their most holy women to cut off their hair and abstain from sex and dress in garments that make them look like magpies. Can you see the sense in that? The one truth, my friend, is that we should be tolerant of each other because we do not know who is right and who is wrong, and if your neighbour is right and you are wrong it would be better to have him as a friend and not an enemy in the next life. Do you understand? As a friend, he could put in a good word for us to the one and only true God, the one we did not believe in.'

Adam's camel had fallen behind, and he kicked his heels in its flanks to force it to travel faster. 'But what if it had been your wife who'd been stoned to death for looking at another man and then you died – say twenty years later – and found out that your God didn't exist and that none of the things you believed in were true. In other words, she'd been put to death needlessly. What would you say to her?'

'If we met in heaven?'

'Yes.'

He laughed. 'I think I see in you the mind of a holy man. That is the sort of impossible question they think of. I would apologize to her.'

'A bit late!'

'Not at all. If there is a heaven then there is everlasting life, and what do a few lost years on earth matter? Then I think I would give her a beating.'

'Why?'

'Because she looked at another man. She would have known the law of our people and she would have transgressed. Therefore, she should have been punished.'

'But she was already! She was stoned to death.'

Saleem Benn took a noisy breath. 'My wife was not put to death. She died of illness. It was my brother's miserable wife who committed the crime.'

'I only meant, supposing it was your wife.'

'My wife was a good woman.'

'I'm sure she was. I'm sorry.' But the Afghan did not answer.

They rode through a gully. The camels chose each step with great care, moving as cats do when treading precarious ground. Adam, sensing that Saleem Benn had been offended, started another conversation.

'You seem to know a lot,' he said. 'Can you read and write?'

The other man did not turn. 'Of course,' he said.

'I can't.'

Saleem Benn twisted in his saddle. The leather squeaked. It was a noise Adam liked. Good leather creaking and groaning was the sound of substance, a noise he had grown with, like the clop of horses' hooves, the straining of ropes and the beat and hiss of steam engines.

'A man who cannot read shuts himself off from the rest of the world,' the Afghan said. 'It is not necessary to read if you are always in the company of wise men, but who is? And there are many wise men and they live in many lands and no one man can be the companion of them all. Therefore, to spread their wisdom they must write; to gain that wisdom, one must read. And of course there were wise men who lived before us. How can one learn about them and understand the greatness of their thoughts if one cannot read their writings? Did you go to school?'

'No.'

'Nor did I. But my uncle was a learned man who taught me many things. I read well in your language. Books are my comfort.' He arched his back. 'I ache from so much riding but we are almost there.'

Shadows became trees and the leaves sparkled in the moonlight.

They hobbled the camels and made their camp near the mound spring. Insects chirped. There was an occasional splash of whispering proportions as one tiny insect died and a larger creature gained its nightly meal.

They slept. They did not hear Mailey arrive.

SIXTEEN

Adam slept soundly for a few hours and then woke, troubled by the pain in his hands and knees. It was not yet dawn. Water still rustled in the mound spring but the insects had ceased chirping. Clouds swept across the moon. It was cold and intensely dark. Saleem Benn was snoring. A camel moved and a chain tinkled.

Adam felt thirsty. He stood, taking care not to disturb the others or the animals, and moved cautiously towards the sound of the water. The spring fed a large pool. He had seen it in the moonlight as they made camp. The pool was raised slightly and contained by a natural rim. It was a curious structure, partly covered by a clump of low trees and supporting a ringed garden of reeds and rushes. The water was good; not full of the soda of much of the outback's underground water but sweet and tangy with just a taste of some of Earth's elements. The camels loved it, Saleem Benn had said.

He found the pool and, reaching its border of rushes, groped to find a place where he could drink. He moved around the spring until he was at a place where thick grass grew, long but as soft as moss. There he sat, using the grassy bank to support his back and, cupping one bandaged hand, tasted the water. It had the musky flavour of decaying weed. He reached a little farther into the pool and drank again. It was good.

He was more comfortable leaning against the grass than he had been on the ground so he stayed. Saleem Benn was still snoring. He said the sound calmed the camels. Adam smiled. He was glad to be so far away. He closed his eyes and thought of Nellie and slept once more.

There were noises. A voice shouting and others mumbling responses. Camels rising, wheezing as they moved and clanking their chains. A bunch of cockatoos shrieking and drumming the air with the beat of a hundred wings.

Adam woke flushed with guilt. He had overslept. He sat up and was confused. The sky was pale but the sun had not risen and would not for some time and he could not see the others. Of course, he had gone to get water and was lying on the far side of the pool, hidden from them. Sodden with sleep, he was about to stand.

'Because I'm telling you to,' the voice shouted. It was Mailey. Adam pressed his face back into the grass.

'Put the chain through his belt.' A pause. 'Now put them on his wrists. By Christ, kid, I'll blow your bloody head off! Now do it.'

An ant crawled on Adam's face. He crushed it against his cheek and felt its last desperate sting. He lifted his head a little. Through the rushes he could see Mailey standing, with the other three on the ground. Josef was kneeling beside Jimmy, putting something on his wrists. Saleem Benn was sitting on his heels and alternately glancing at Mailey and at his camels which were trying to bolt in fright and were stumbling over their hobbled legs.

'Now tie the Arab up,' Mailey said, throwing Josef a rope. The

229

boy looked around the camp-site.

'What have you done to Adam?' he said.

The policeman had a gun in his hand. He turned suddenly and examined the area. With his back to the others, he said: 'You mean the snowy-headed bloke? Is he still with you?'

'You know!' Josef screamed. 'What did you do with him?'

Jimmy, handcuffed to his own belt, elbowed the boy on the knee. He glanced to the left where the camels were panicking but saw no sign of Adam. 'Yeah, copper,' he said, risking a look in the other direction, 'what did you do to him after you caught him back there?'

Josef was going to speak but the look in Jimmy's eyes froze the words in his throat.

Mailey lowered his eyebrows. He wanted more.

'When you ran him down with the car,' Jimmy added. 'Just out of Coober Pedy.'

'We saw you,' Josef chipped in, his eyes smiling. 'We were a long way away but we saw you.'

Jimmy tried not to grin.

'You hit him with the car,' Josef added. 'Did you run over him and kill him?'

Jesus, kid, Jimmy thought, don't go too far.

'No, I didn't,' Mailey said quietly and let his eyes roam slowly around him. Through the place where the camels were stamping and blotting themselves with dust. Through the trees where the cockatoos were settling. To the mound spring where the circle of tall rushes nodded to the breeze. Back to the Afghan, the aboriginal and the German boy.

He studied Josef. 'Who are you?' he said, scratching his head. 'I know who the nigger is and I know the Arab, but who the hell are you?'

Josef did not speak.

'Doesn't much matter,' Mailey said. 'You'll end up with the others. That's your bad luck. Now tie up the old man like I told you.'

He waved the gun like a wagging finger.

'This is foolishness,' Saleem Benn said, trying to stand.

'Get back on the ground,' Mailey said.

'This is not your territory,' the Afghan said.

'What are you talking about?'

'All this district, from William Creek to the border, comes

under the authority of the constable at Oodnadatta. He is a good policeman.'

'So am I.' Mailey bristled.

'He is a good man.'

'Oh, and I'm a bad man.' He smiled. 'And it was bad luck for you that I found you with Jimmy Kettle.' He wagged the gun again. 'Boy, take the rope around his waist a few times and then get out of the way.'

When Josef had finished, Mailey pushed him away and knotted the rope behind the Afghan's back.

'What are you arresting me for?' the old man asked, his eyes wide with fear.

'I'm not arresting you.' He pushed Saleem Benn on his side and ran the rope around his ankles, tightening it so that the Afghan was bowed backwards.

'This is a painful position for an old man,' he protested.

'It won't be for long.'

'What's the charge?'

'No charge.'

'What are you going to do?'

'Shoot you. Then bury you.'

The Afghan struggled.

'You can kick all you like. But if you don't stop I'll tie a loop around your neck and then you'll choke yourself. It's up to you.'

'You are murdering us all?'

'All.'

'Even the boy?'

'Why not?'

'You are the devil!'

'You'll wish I was. Do you have a shovel?'

'No.'

'Yes, you do. Boy,' Mailey said, pointing the gun at Josef, 'go and get a shovel.'

Josef looked at Jimmy, seeking guidance.

Jimmy shrugged his shoulders. 'Might as well,' he said.

'Indeed,' Mailey said. 'Make the best of every precious minute, eh?'

Josef brought the shovel. 'What do you want it for?' he asked.

'To dig a hole. For *you* to dig a hole. A big one.'

'Do not bury me with them,' the Afghan said.

Josef was horrified. 'Am I going to dig a grave?'

231

'You're not digging a vegetable garden, son.' He pointed the gun at the old man. 'You might be quick on the uptake but if you want a separate grave, Arab, you'll have to dig it yourself.'

'I cannot dig like this, bound hand and foot.'

Mailey laughed. 'You must think I was born yesterday. Let you go so you can dig? Let you loose so you can make a run for one of those camels? You stay tied up.'

'Are you going to kill us?' Josef said, disbelief in his voice.

'Right,' said the policeman, slapping Josef's shoulder. 'You're a smart boy, son. You'll go far. Now, over there, where the ground's soft, near the rushes. Start digging.'

'How big?' Josef said, confused.

'Well, let's see – there's you, and the old man and him.' He pointed at Jimmy who seemed to be enjoying the conversation. 'Just big enough so you'll all be comfortable and deep enough so no one'll disturb you.'

Jimmy moved his legs, to be more at ease. 'Did the sheila tell you where we were heading?' he said.

'The gin? Yeah, eventually.'

'Nellie?' Josef said. He was nearing the rushes.

'You don't talk, son,' Mailey called after him. 'You dig. If you say one more word, I'll give you a belting with this.' He tapped the buckle on his trouser belt. 'Just like I did to the gin.'

'Nellie? You gave her a belting?' Jimmy said. His lips curled in a smile.

'A beauty. She still won't be able to walk.'

'Why?' Josef shouted. He held the shovel in both hands as though it was something he did not want to touch but dared not let go.

'I warned you, son. Shut up and don't talk. Now start digging.'

From the far side of the pool, Adam kept low, trying to stay out of sight but anxious to see what was happening. He parted some stalks. Above the far line of rushes he could see the back of Josef's head and the tip of the shovel handle.

'Here?' Josef called.

'Oh, Jesus, son, all you've got to do is dig a hole,' Mailey grumbled and walked over. He pulled the shovel from the boy and rapped its blade against the ground in a few places.

'That's fine,' he said, his voice booming for the others to hear and then, in a much softer voice added: 'Just dig the hole, son, and don't worry. I'm not going to hurt anyone. I just want to

232

frighten them, so they'll do what I tell them.'

Adam could not see Josef's face.

'Don't say anything to the others,' Mailey continued. 'Just a little joke between you and me. All right? But you've got to dig that hole. Follow?'

Adam saw the nod. Mailey returned to the others.

'Why did you give Nellie a belting?' he heard Jimmy ask.

Mailey moved close to him and rested a foot on his back. 'You stay down on the ground like the Arab,' he said and rammed Jimmy off balance. Jimmy landed on his face.

'That's better,' Mailey said. 'Eat some dirt. Enjoy your last breakfast.'

'Do not bury me with them,' Saleem Benn pleaded. 'I am a Moslem and they are not.'

'I'll point you towards Mecca,' Mailey sneered. 'Don't give me that crap about being holier than a white man or a black man. I've seen the way you people gather your harems of gins and half-castes and then rent them out to the town drunks.'

The Afghan's nose quivered. 'You insult me and my faith,' he said.

'I'm going to do worse than that.' Mailey turned his back on him. 'How are you going, son?'

Josef stopped digging. 'The ground's real soft,' he called out. He sounded cheerful.

'Good. You'll be finished sooner.'

Mailey turned to find Jimmy pushing himself to his knees. A boot flattened him again. 'Just stay down like a good nigger,' he said. 'You were asking me why I gave the gin a belting. Because she wouldn't talk. You got any tobacco here? I left mine back in the car.'

The Afghan glared at him.

'You're out of it too, are you?' He laughed. 'Never mind, I'll get some later. Do you want to know what I'm going to do with your camels?'

Saleem Benn lifted his head.

'Yes. I thought that might interest you. I might poison them. Or shoot them. Lie on your face, Arab! Go on! Roll over! I'm sick of looking at you.'

'You are vile,' Saleem Benn muttered, but turned on his face.

'That's the way,' Mailey said. 'I'll tell you what. You just lie like that and cause me no trouble and I mightn't even harm your camels. I might just turn them loose. Be a better life than you give them, I'll bet. Riding them all day and riding them all night.'

'You are filth,' the Afghan said and Mailey laughed.

The sun rose and shadows wrinkled the ground. Adam watched, not knowing what to do.

He had no doubt Mailey meant to kill them all. He had said so already, back at the lock-up. The fact that there were two other men, the old Afghan and the boy, would not worry him. Mailey meant to get rid of the witnesses to the slaughter at Port Augusta, and if others had to die, so be it. What was essential was that Adam somehow got closer to Josef, and to the pit he was digging so enthusiastically. Josef, the only one not bound, would be the first person Mailey would kill. Of that, Adam was certain. The policeman would let him do the work, then put a bullet in the back of his head. Adam had to be close at hand, to try to stop him. The sun rose higher and its warmth played upon his back. Flies tormented him. Some ants climbed his leg and he crushed them, conscious of their sickly-sweet smell.

Josef kept digging. Adam looked around for a weapon. There was nothing. No rusting metal bar. No stout piece of timber. A fist-sized stone was a few body lengths away but it was out in the open and he would be seen if he tried to reach it. In any case, he could not grip it. His hands were too tender.

He could get to the other side through the water. He could hold his breath and cross beneath the surface. He was a reasonable swimmer. He had no idea what he would do when he got to the other side but he would think about that when he got there.

He could hear Mailey and Jimmy talking. He could not distinguish the words but Jimmy seemed surprised. Adam lifted his head. Josef was out of sight, bending to his work. Mailey had his back to him. He was waving his arms. Jimmy had a look of disbelief on his face.

Adam moved. Using his elbows he wriggled up the side of the bank between a gap in the rushes. A bird, close by but unseen in a patch of heavy growth, took off in fright and the noise seemed to explode in Adam's ear. Shocked into stillness he stayed, exposed on the rim of the pool.

Josef kept digging. Mailey did not turn.

Jimmy saw him.

Adam caught a glint of recognition, saw a trace of a smile.

Jimmy turned his head to the policeman, said something, and Mailey laughed.

'Run? She couldn't move an inch when I finished with her,' he said loudly. He dropped his voice and Adam caught only fragments of words. He slid into the water. It was cold. He moved as gently as he could but a ring of water spread across the pool. He looked back. There were clear marks where his feet had dug grooves in the bank.

'How deep do you want it?' Josef yelled and Adam thought, 'Oh please, don't bring him over now while I'm here on the edge of the water!'

'More,' Mailey shouted, and Adam kicked for the other side. He glided beneath the water and entered a world of green with rings of light extending above him. The bed of the pool was rocky and covered in slime. It was colder near the bottom. He pulled himself forward, moving from rock to rock. His lungs started to ache.

The pool became shallow and his head and the back of his shoulders broke the surface. He was near the edge where a dense clump of reeds hung, heads bowed from the bank. Feeling numb from cold, he dragged himself towards their shelter.

'I've struck rock,' Josef called, so close Adam shivered with fright. He moved carefully, hauling his legs to the edge of the pool so that his body lay along the water line. Someone would have to stand at the spring and look over the reeds to see him.

'Let's see, son. How far down are you?' Mailey was persisting with the act. For a moment Adam had doubts. Mailey didn't sound like a man planning mass murder.

'That's not bad,' he said when he had reached Josef. 'You're a quick worker. Deep enough for three.' He chuckled and Adam imagined the wink. 'Deep enough to fool the others, eh? Just make it a bit wider. Where it's soft over on the other side.'

Adam heard footsteps drawing closer to him, heard the crunch of stones and saw the rushes above him waver. The earth next to his head shook. Mailey had sat on the bank.

'That's right. Nice clean strokes. Make it look good. Got any rubbish or other stuff you want buried?'

'Not that I know of,' Josef answered, puzzled.

'Shame to waste such a good hole.' The man laughed. 'Good water here, isn't there?'

'Yes. Saleem Benn knew about it.'

'Did he? Must know the country well.'

235

'He reckons no one else ever comes here.'

'Really?' Mailey cleared his nose. 'How long since you've seen your friend? The one with the mop of snowy hair.'

The shovel stopped scraping earth. 'Adam? A couple of days.'

'Keep on digging. Where was that?'

Josef hesitated before speaking. 'Near Coober Pedy. I thought you'd run him over.'

'No. I haven't seen him.'

Adam wondered if he could stand, reach over the rushes and grab Mailey. He was trying to measure the distance in his imagination when Mailey stood again.

'Didn't he catch up to you, son?' he said.

'I thought you caught him. We haven't seen him.'

'He seemed to be injured.'

'He was burned.'

'Badly?'

'Real bad. He could hardly use his hands or legs.'

'That so? Poor bloke's probably perished out there.'

Josef said nothing.

'I think he was strong enough to hit me on the head with a rock. See? I've still got the cut. Go on. Have a look.'

There was a long pause. Adam wiped his eyes. They were still blurred from swimming under water.

'You didn't do it, did you, son?'

'What?'

'Hit me with a rock. You wouldn't do a thing like that?'

There was no answer.

'You didn't set fire to my car, did you?' Mailey asked the question quietly.

'What car?'

'Oh, it doesn't matter, son. That'll do. Get out of the hole and give me the shovel.'

Adam drew his knees under his body and pushed himself up. Mailey was a few steps away from him. His gun was in its holster. Josef was climbing from the hole he had dug. He passed the shovel to Mailey.

'Now son, I want you to go over to the others and undo the rope around the Arab. Are you right?'

Josef was brushing dirt from his knees. Mailey gripped the shovel handle as a baseballer holds a bat. Josef turned and prepared to leap over the pit. Mailey lifted the shovel behind his back and began a long swing that would have crushed the back of the boy's head.

Adam jumped to his feet. 'Joe!' he shouted.

Josef turned, saw the swinging shovel blade, saw Adam, saw the venom in Mailey's face and tripped, half falling into the hole. The shovel whistled over his head.

Mailey, swung off balance, turned as Adam charged. Hoping for one good blow, Adam ran down the bank his right fist already aimed at the man's head, but he caught a toe in a root and pitched forward and slammed Mailey in the stomach. He cried out with pain. His hands were useless.

Mailey grunted, stepped back and raised the shovel. 'Well, well,' he said, eyes darting to the bandages on Adam's hands and knees. 'The young man with the burns. Couldn't hurt a pussy cat, I'd say.'

He poked at Adam with the blade. 'Like to try again? I could shoot you easily enough but I think I'd rather carve you up with this. Come on. Have a go.'

Adam stepped back.

Having climbed from the hole, Josef flung himself at Mailey's knees. The policeman's legs buckled. Adam charged again. He heard Mailey shout as Josef bit him but then came the sickening crack of a shin bone against a face, and Josef groaned and let go. Adam had one arm around Mailey's neck. The man twisted, wild as an enraged bull, and bent forward, lifting Adam off his feet. He danced around the edge of the pit trying to shake loose the arm gripping his neck. Adam hung on. He realized to his astonishment that he had locked hands and was yelling with pain but the pain seemed to pour power into his arms and he felt his muscles tightening with a strength he had never known.

Mailey tripped and they fell, a bull with a terrier on its back. The policeman tried to burrow his chin into the arm, tried to lever the elbow up and across his face, tried to bore his fingertips into the arm muscles, but Adam held on. Mailey stood again, an extraordinary feat of strength, and raised Adam off the ground. Then he fell backwards, slowly and deliberately, and the hold was broken.

On hands and knees, Mailey went for the shovel as Adam lay gasping on the ground.

Adam heard Jimmy shouting at him to move. Not seeing the attack, he rolled to one side as the shovel cut into the earth. Small

237

stones sprayed across his body. Mailey tried to lift the shovel again and Adam dived at him, locking his right arm around the man's throat.

Mailey roared, an animal cry of rage and pain, but the roar became a wheeze as Adam tightened the grip. He could no longer grasp hands because the pain was too intense, but he could lock his right arm in the crook of the other and apply the free left forearm as a bar across the back of Mailey's head. With one arm he was choking the man and with the other bending the neck. It was a cruel hold.

Adam closed his eyes and heard again the cries of the children in the creek bed and the thud of axes. He saw Jimmy's uncle being beaten and humiliated. He saw black bodies twitching in the last painful moments of life. He thought of Coober Pedy and felt again the thud of timber hitting the back of his head. And he thought of Nellie being whipped by this man.

He heard a growling. It was him, out to cause as much pain as he could.

They rolled in the dirt. Then Mailey sat up and Adam's arms almost lost their hold. Mailey, twisting, managed a quarter-turn and wrapped his arms around Adam's chest. The arms were massive. The hands did not meet but the arms squeezed and Adam thought his ribs would break. Once more able to suck in air and hissing with exertion, Mailey wriggled and twisted in a desperate effort to clasp his hands. The scarlet face, ugly, sweat-stained, with skin swollen to bursting point, was pressed against Adam's, ear to ear.

If Mailey joined hands, Adam was dead. He knew that. The man was stronger than he was. He felt puny in his arms. His ribs would go, then his lungs, then his life.

For a moment, Adam relaxed his grip on the throat and Mailey, suddenly able to breathe easily, lifted his head to gulp in air. His chin was raised and Adam thrust his shoulder into the gap. He rammed the bone and bunched muscle hard into the man's windpipe and tightened the grip once more.

Mailey, realizing the mistake he had made, kicked savagely and staggered to the edge of the spring, dragging Adam with him.

Adam put all his body behind the shoulder and felt the chin move back. His left hand clawed at the man's nose. He blocked the nostrils and forced the head even further back and to one side. His right arm, aching with fatigue and from Mailey's pummelling of the muscles, remained locked around the neck.

Adam had seen men wrestle steers to the ground and twist their heads to impossible angles. He twisted the head in his arms, applying pressure in a series of surging power thrusts.

Mailey dropped to his knees.

Adam spread his legs against the raised bank of the spring and pushed hard. The chin went back a fraction more. Mailey tried to crawl but the move dissolved into an uncontrolled spasm of legs that would not work, and he arched backwards towards his heels. Slowly, arms still locked around Adam's chest, he toppled backwards. Adam thrust again, jerking hard with his right arm as he forced his shoulder into the throat.

The snap sounded like a branch breaking from a dead tree.

Mailey went limp. Adam unhooked his arms and the grotesque head lolled back, its hair slick with perspiration and nearly touching the shoulder blades. The eyes stared at an upside-down horizon. The arms remained locked around his killer.

Josef had been lying nearby, dazed and with hands cupped over a bleeding nose. He got to his knees. 'Are you all right, Adam?' he mumbled, his mouth thick with blood.

'Come and help me, please.'

Josef stood. His eyes widened with horror. 'What happened?'

'I've killed him.'

'Bloody hell!' Josef said.

'Don't swear,' Adam said and began shaking.

Josef spent several minutes trying to unclench Mailey's hands. The boy was still groggy, his nose dripped blood and his eyes were puffing from Mailey's blow. The sheer horror of having to touch a dead person, particularly one who had meant to kill him, made it difficult for him to control his fingers. Adam could not help. He was on the ground with the dead man. His right arm was numb and his hands were raw again. His knees were bleeding.

Jimmy Kettle walked across, his hands close to his belt and the chain linking the cuffs jangling as he moved.

'Is he dead?' he said softly.

'Adam broke his neck,' Josef said.

Adam stared up at Jimmy. He was still wrapped in Mailey's arms and he could not remove his right arm from around the dead man's neck. 'I've got cramp in the arm,' he said simply. 'Hurts like hell.'

'Just as well you didn't get it a minute ago,' Jimmy said. 'How are you, Joe? You look like you've gone ten rounds with Jack Johnson.'

'He kicked me.'

'What are you trying to do?' he asked gently, observing the boy's fumbling attempts to break Mailey's death grip. Josef wiped blood from his nose with a hand that trembled badly.

'Tell you what,' Jimmy said, touching the boy's shoulder. 'You look in his pocket for the keys to these handcuffs and give me the key and let me take care of Mailey.'

Josef found the keys.

Jimmy started to unlock one cuff. 'You go over and help Saleem Benn. The poor old bloke's in a lot of pain from the way the copper tied him up. I'll look after things here.'

When his wrists were free, Jimmy bent down and wrenched Mailey's fingers apart. 'Bastard,' he said, flinging the big hands away from Adam. He helped his friend to his feet. 'I thought he was going to kill you.'

'So did I. I can still hardly breathe.'

Jimmy looked at Mailey's discoloured head. 'Well,' he said slowly, 'all I can say is that I'm glad you're on my side. That bastard's got a neck as thick as a bull.'

He touched the head with his foot. It settled at an improbable angle.

'You know what?' he said, looking away.

'What?'

'I wish my uncle was here. And the little kids.' Jimmy Kettle wept and Adam stood beside him, not knowing what else to do but to stand there, and be near.

Dramatic or tragic moments affect people in strange ways. The group at the springs became ravenously hungry and, once Josef's face had been bathed, they ate an enormous breakfast. Josef had difficulty eating because he could not breathe through his clogged and swollen nose but the disability merely slowed him down – it did not affect his appetite. For all of them, it was as though something as basic and necessary as eating blotted out the nightmare of the dawn.

Mailey's body stayed where it had fallen near the grave-pit. Jimmy was the first to finish eating and announced his intention of burying Mailey in the pit. Adam stopped him and, while Saleem

Benn re-dressed his hands and knees, explained why.

The policeman would be missed and, while no body was found, a search would continue. If police kept on searching for a missing sergeant they would become more and more interested in the two men he was tracking, Jimmy Kettle and Adam Ross.

'Officially, he didn't go to Coober Pedy looking for us, so no one knows about us down south,' Adam said. 'But if he's missing for a while, they'll send someone up here and then we'll spend the rest of our lives running away.'

'Well, what are we going to do?' Jimmy said. 'Bring him back to life? If they find him with his neck broken, they're not going to think it was suicide. We've got to bury him.'

'We'd be on the run all our lives, Jimmy.' Adam examined the fresh bandage on his left hand and offered Saleem Benn the other arm. 'It might be better if I just went to the police and told them what happened. It was self-defence, or whatever they call it. He was going to kill Joe.'

'Do you think they'd believe us?' Jimmy said mockingly. 'An abo, an Afghan, a Kraut kid and a young drifter from the bush who just happened to break a policeman's neck? They'd hang the lot of us.'

'Your friend is right,' Saleem Benn said to Adam. 'They do not like people who kill policemen. They would demand blood.'

'Maybe not,' Adam said.

Josef dug at the ground with his fingers. 'The police didn't help us when some hooligans broke all my father's machinery and wine-presses, and we're white.'

'Only just,' Jimmy laughed and Josef flicked dirt at him.

'I have a solution,' the Afghan said, not looking up from his task of spreading ointment on Adam's hand. 'We will not bury him. Adam Ross is very correct. You would be hunted men if no body were found. In any case, I could not see such a fine watering place polluted by the presence of so evil a body. Better for us to do this.' And Saleem Benn, while continuing to dress Adam's hand, outlined his plan.

He would take the body to another place where there were many ants and where dingoes roamed. Two of his camels would tow the car to the same place. The boy could sit behind the wheel and steer. Josef smiled at that. At the selected site (and Saleem Benn had such a place in mind) he would arrange the car to suggest it had been stalled in sand and he would take Mailey's body a mile away, and spread it in the tortured posture of a man who had died of thirst.

'What about his broken neck?' Jimmy asked and the Afghan nodded, anticipating the question.

In his packs, he had honey and sugar. These he would smear over the skin to attract ants. Within a week it would be almost impossible to identify the body. Within two weeks, there would be little flesh left. And the neck? The dingoes would come and remove some items like hands, feet and, almost certainly, the head. They had done so to the explorer Wills when he had perished at Cooper's Creek, the Afghan explained with some enthusiasm, and the wild dogs at this place were just as hungry.

'What if they don't take the head?' Jimmy asked and the Afghan slapped his thigh, ready to play his trump card.

He, Saleem Benn, would find the body on his next journey to Coober Pedy. If the head had not been removed, he would remove it. He would carry what pieces he could find of the body to William Creek, where no one would be too surprised at such a happening, and there report the tragic death of some poor soul who had fallen victim to a harsh country.

'What if someone else finds him?' Jimmy asked.

'No one will. I will choose a place where no one travels.'

'Yes, but what if they do?'

'You have a fine streak of cynicism in you! It is healthy in an individual although tedious for his companions.' There was an air of admiration in the Afghan's voice. 'But tell me, what would you do if you found a body in the desert?'

'Nothing. I'd keep on walking.'

'You see? Your type does not want to get involved. Other people might be more concerned and spend time burying the body. That would not matter. Sergeant Mailey's disappearance would be explained and the body would rot nicely in a shallow grave. No, my friends, I do not see any problem with this plan. I will chance upon this poor felow when he is nicely decomposed and disjointed and I will take the few, sad remains to the nearest outpost of civilization so that the redoubtable Sergeant Mailey can get a good Christian burial. And so that you, my friends, need never worry about him again.'

And so, after two days' slow travel, they left the car and body in a wilderness of sand ridges to the west of Lake Eyre South. They camped nearby that night, and were badly troubled by ants.

BOOK THREE

Adam's Wife

ONE

Nyngan is an aboriginal word that means 'a chain of waterholes'. The name was given by Major Thomas Mitchell, Surveyor-General of New South Wales, when he was exploring the western plains of the fledgling colony. In an era when most Australian explorers and pioneering settlers were homesick Britons, Mitchell stood out as a man who insisted on aboriginal names being used for new discoveries. Before him, rivers were named after governors in Sydney Town or powdered and petty officials back 'home' in London.

Hills that were worn ghosts of ancient peaks, and whose hollows rang to the thud of kangaroos, were named after misty slopes in Ireland. A muddy waterhole, shrinking by the day in the heat of an Australian summer, could inspire its discoverer to give it the name of a brook in the Scottish Highlands. Tiny settlements consisting of rude huts cut from bark and slabs of iron-hard eucalyptus, were given the names of quaint English towns with thatched roofs and geraniums trailing from window boxes. The bark huts may have baked on a plain that seemed as endless and cruel as the Sahara while the thatched cottages nestled in country as soft and gentle as childhood memories, but no matter. The first whites, alienated in a harsh land, found comfort in familiar names.

Mitchell changed that, and Nyngan was one of the first aboriginal names he wrote on the map. The waterholes in question were on the Bogan river, which the major reached in 1828.

In times of flood, the Bogan (an aboriginal word for 'birthplace of a great leader') is a noble stream by the perverted standards of Australia's inland rivers. It becomes a brown, sprawling sea, slow-moving and confused in direction because it has a choice of so many baffling and vast dead ends to explore. But floods are rare, and an old man may talk of one or two in his lifetime. In dry times, which are so common as to be unremarkable, the river loafs within its banks and slows to a sluggish flow, then stops altogether. The land around it withers and cracks. Long reaches of water shrink to pools of slime and buzz with insects. Trees lean above powdered sand, majestic trunks buttressed by exposed roots that are as tangled as a nest of lizards.

At Nyngan, the holes are deep and the water permanent. White people settled there. Roads ran from there to far-off towns and remote sheep stations. First the bullock wagons, then the coaches and then the railway came to the town. Never big, Nyngan was still the most important junction west of Dubbo. Bourke, on the Darling River, was one hundred and twenty-six miles to the north-west. Both rail and road ran dead straight for almost all that distance, for there was no need for turns in country with no hills to avoid or towns to visit.

In 1934, Nyngan was a busy rail centre. The most important and influential position in town was that of stationmaster, and that man was Hector Maguire. He had a daughter who was slim and blonde with a fair and delicate complexion that was as rare as cool rain on a summer's day.

In December of that year, when the Depression had reduced proud men to tramping the bush looking for work, and when daily dust storms swirled through town and turned the giant locomotives and trucks in the railway yards to shadowy phantoms, Adam Ross came to Nyngan and met Heather Maguire, and fell in love.

Nyngan was the biggest town Adam had seen in more than five years. He came to town to collect a truck that he had bought a few months earlier. It was a strange deal, but typical of the bush. The man who owned the truck was a bore sinking contractor whom Adam had met north of the border near Thargomindah. The old fellow had broken his leg and decided to sell out. He offered the truck and plant to Adam but he wanted to do a few things before parting with the vehicle. He had a daughter in Charleville and wanted to visit her, and then drive south to Nyngan where he lived. The truck needed a valve grind and he would do that. Then Adam could take the truck and the boring plant, and he would be in business. The man wanted to finalize the deal in December.

Adam reached town on the seventh and walked into Nyngan

carrying a rifle and a swag. He had arranged to meet Jimmy and Josef there. They had been working on the railway near Byrock, getting temporary work when part of the line had to be relaid. It was a loose arrangement in which each said he would try to be in Nyngan by Christmas.

For five years the three friends had travelled the inland, seeking work in the remote regions and avoiding the larger towns. They had been through corner country – the north-eastern corner of South Australia, the south-western corner of Queensland and, now, the north-western corner of New South Wales. They had worked with camels and horses, droved cattle and sheep, cut timber and built fences, dug dams and drilled bores. They had done the hardest work and been paid the lowest wages. Sometimes, only one would get work. When that happened he supported the others. But they stayed together.

The business of Mailey's death had gone as Saleem Benn predicted. Two weeks after reaching Marree in the winter of 1929, the Afghan had taken another load of supplies to Coober Pedy and, on his way back, had 'discovered' the policeman's car and, subsequently, his body. He took the body to William Creek where he and his friend the publican buried it, reading some Christian words from a bible that belonged to the publican's wife. When he returned to Marree, Saleem Benn told the story in elaborate detail. The policeman had obviously died of thirst, the old Afghan recounted with great feeling, and people nodded wisely. Yes, they had all heard of men doing crazy things when they were lost and out of water. Unhappily, Saleem Benn had continued, the body had been molested by dingoes. Dingoes and ants. At this point in his story (and he told it many times) the old man had difficulty in continuing. People waited, reflecting the anguish such a hideous discovery would have caused. The ants, which were in plague proportions in that place, had stripped flesh from the bones. The eyes had gone. And dingoes, vile creatures that they were, had taken parts of the body. Even the skull. He had found it some distance away.

A policeman came from the south to investigate. He dug up the remains of Mailey's body and took them back to Snowtown, where Mailey had been born, for a proper burial. The investigating officer found difficulty in piecing together a coherent story because Mailey's actions had been strange and he had left no report of any sort. He had gone to Coober Pedy to investigate an alleged theft of opals, but a later police check at the mining town could find no one who knew anything about such a theft. Mailey, somehow, had lost his official car in a fire. During his brief stay there he had acted violently, threatening several people, and after his own vehicle had been destroyed he had taken another car against the wishes of the owner. It was also reported that Sergeant Mailey had got into some sort of fight that developed when he was trying to take the car and had shot and wounded an old bystander by the name of Horatio Smith. Smith had said he had intended to press charges but had graciously dropped them when he heard of the sergeant's sad death.

It was all very confusing, the investigating officer admitted. Since Mailey's death there had been suggestions of brutal conduct against various aborigines around the Port Augusta area, so the dead man's erratic behaviour at Coober Pedy and William Creek might have been the result of some long-standing problem. Some form of mental illness that resulted in an occasional outburst of violence. All very sad. No one deserved a fate like Mailey's, people agreed. And then people forgot. Mailey was just another stranger who had perished.

Adam, Jimmy and Josef had stayed at Marree for a few weeks with the family of Saleem Benn's oldest nephew. His wife, a graceful woman with skin like oiled silk, had cared for Adam's burns, which had become infected. The three of them stayed in the Afghan part of town, keeping out of sight as much as they could. Not that anyone cared. So many people were roaming the outback, looking for work or just trying to survive where bush tucker was easy to find, that no one took notice of three young men who had drifted into town. A blacks' camp had been set up on the fringe of the dry country to the east of the town and Jimmy became friendly with a couple of young aboriginal men from down Beltana way, where he was born.

Josef crossed the railway line into the white part of town several times and struck up a friendship with the man who ran the store, a building made of iron and roughly hewn poles, with an open front which he covered at night with an awning made of bags. The man offered him occasional work, giving him two shillings and a few groceries whenever he needed a hand unloading stores from a train.

At Adam's insistence, Josef wrote to his mother. He explained what had happened, only leaving out the true version of how

Mailey had died, but did not give his address. He was frightened his father would find him and take him back to Coober Pedy. He gave the letter to a man who was going south, to post somewhere along the way.

Adam's burns had taken a couple of weeks to heal. He was better by the time Saleem Benn returned and so was able to accept the Afghan's offer to go with him on a journey north to Innamincka and Cordillo Downs. Saleem had to take sixty camels on that job, hauling supplies on the way up and bringing back bales of wool from some of the stations. The old man and Adam became good friends. He taught Adam to sign his name more fluently. He would have liked to have given him lessons in reading and writing, but there was little time in the evenings for such things. However, they talked a great deal and Saleem Benn taught him much about his country and India and the other places in the world he had read about. He even taught Adam some words and simple phrases in his native Pushtu.

The round trip took fifteen weeks. On the way back they stopped at Murnpeowie station, in the northernmost part of the Flinders Ranges, and learned that the manager needed a couple of deep wells cleared. He could not pay much, of course, but there was an old Essex on the property that had been left there years ago by a shearer who had since died and they could have the car as half payment for the work. So Adam, Jimmy and Josef had finished the job with Saleem Benn in Marree and then gone back to Murnpeowie.

From there, they drove to a few of the stations in the ranges, clearing troughs, digging some new wells, and making dams. One manager recommended them to another, and they worked as far south as the old Curnamona property. Always they stayed away from populated centres and never once went near the north-south railway line or a main road. After nine months in the Flinders, they headed north and eventually entered Queensland, to work on the properties along the Barcoo and Thompson rivers.

Adam had developed into a resourceful bush mechanic, partly from natural aptitude but mainly from necessity. He had plenty of practice in fixing cars because of the Essex's voracious appetite for wheel bearings and other mechanical parts, but on a property west of Windorah, where they had built a stockyard and an outriders' hut, they exchanged the car for a bay gelding and, with their pooled savings, bought two other horses.

By the time they returned they were fair horsemen. Jimmy was the best. He had a natural flair for riding and an affinity with the animal which made him a joy to watch. Josef had no great natural balance and often seemed to be heading in a different direction from his horse, but at least he developed to the stage where he could chase a couple of steers that had broken away from the mob and bring them back and not fall off. Adam did not ride with the gifted fluency of Jimmy, but he was safe and kind on the horse and the boss of the drive was pleased with him. More than the others, he observed what was going on and learned from it because he was determined to have his own property one day, and he had worked out that the people who made money were not necessarily the best horsemen or the best bushmen but the best managers.

So Adam entered Nyngan on 7 December 1934 to start work as a bore-sinking contractor. He was twenty-four and about to become boss of his own business. He felt good, though footsore and hungry. He went to a café run by a Greek family and spent two and sixpence on a big meal of steak and eggs and chips and then went down to the waterholes on the Bogan river and camped. The next day he went to the address of the man who was selling his business and found that he would be away for another four days. The man had gone to Dubbo to see a doctor about his leg.

Adam went to the railway station to see if anyone knew when trains would be coming from Dubbo. He also wanted to enquire about the repairs to the line being carried out at Byrock, where Jimmy and Josef were working. As soon as the job was finished, they would head south to join him. And then, as from 1 January 1935, they would go out and drill more bores, sink more wells, and make more dams than anyone in the state. He was smiling at the prospect when he bumped into Heather Maguire.

She was taking her father his lunch. It was packed inside a metal biscuit tin with a picture of a parrot on the lid. The impact jolted the tin out of her hands. Adam caught it.

'What are you grinning at?' she said, flushing angrily. She grabbed the tin.

'Nothing,' Adam said. 'I was thinking about something else.'

'Obviously.' She walked towards the stationmaster's office.

'Sorry,' Adam called after her but she did not turn. There was no one else on the platform. He saw a man in the railway yards and headed towards him. The man walked past a row of flat-top trucks and went into a shed. He closed the door.

Adam knocked on the door. Nothing happened. He knocked again.

'What do you want?' The voice was muffled, as though the man was far away.

'I want to ask you a question,' Adam said.

'I'm having lunch.'

'But you just went in.'

'I've just started.'

Must be the world's fastest eater, Adam thought and tried again. 'Where could I get some information, please?'

'Hard of hearing, are you, mate? I said I was on me lunch break.'

'I don't want to bother you. I just want to know where to go.'

There was no answer.

'Hello?' Adam called out.

'For crying out loud!' came a voice, much closer to the other side of the door. 'Go and see the stationmaster.'

'Thank you.'

'No worries. But don't bother him for half an hour. He's having lunch too.'

'Isn't there anyone working now?'

'Jesus Christ!' The words came in a low grumble. 'A man can't even get a rest when it's time to have some tucker. Go and see the stationmaster. He's paid to answer questions. Just piss off and leave me alone.'

Adam was beginning to wish he was back in the bush. He walked back to the station platform and climbed the sloping ramp at the end. It was extremely hot. He took off his hat and wiped his forehead. The girl who had been carrying the biscuit tin came out of the stationmaster's office.

'You shouldn't be down there,' she said.

'Where?' He replaced his hat. He looked at her intently, and blinked. She was the most beautiful girl he had seen. Not just in the last five years, but ever. She shook her head and ran slender fingers through her hair. It was long and blonde.

'Down there. Where all the shunting goes on. It's dangerous. More important, it's illegal. You can be fined five pounds.'

He grinned. 'I'll keep my eye out for the police.'

'Don't be cheeky. This is railway property. And what are you doing with that gun?'

251

'I own it,' he said and ambled towards her. Adam had grown since leaving Coober Pedy and was six foot one. He was broader than most on the shoulders but lean around the hips. He had spent enough time in the saddle to develop the rolling walk of a horseman. He put his swag and the Winchester on a long seat that was freshly painted in a bright green. 'How old are you?' he said.

She looked shocked. 'A man does not ask a lady her age,' she said. 'A gentleman doesn't, anyhow.'

Adam ignored the barb. 'It's just that you look young but you talk like an old woman,' he said, and sat down beside his belongings. 'Do you know if anyone works around here?'

'Not you,' she said.

'I've just arrived in town. I'm trying to get some information and I can't find anyone.'

'My father's the stationmaster,' she said, seeming to pass such news with reluctance.

Adam stood again. 'Would I find him inside?'

'Don't you disturb him now,' she said.

'I know. He's having lunch.'

'He almost didn't get any.'

Adam looked puzzled.

'That was his lunch you tried to knock out of my hands.'

'Oh. I'm sorry about that.'

Her eyes crinkled in the faintest hint of a smile. 'That's all right. Mother always says I rush about too much and bump into things. What do you want to know? Maybe I can help.'

'Well, I want to know when the trains come from Dubbo. I was supposed to do some business with a man who's gone down there for a few days. I'd like to meet him.'

'There's a train every day. Two on Tuesdays and Thursdays. There's a timetable on the wall. You could have found out for yourself.'

'Oh.' Adam was not going to tell this young woman that he could not read.

'But I suppose you find them hard to follow. Most people do.' There was a real smile on her face now.

'Yes. I'm not used to them.'

'Oh, I've been living with them all my life. They're as familiar to me as the bible. The train comes in at three forty-three every afternoon. At ten past nine, Tuesdays and Thursdays. Who do you want to meet?'

252

'George Curran,' Adam said. 'I've bought his plant.'

'He's retiring from that dreadful life?' she said. 'His wife will be pleased. She's always complaining that he's never home. I heard he had a bad accident or something.'

'Broke his leg.'

'Oh well, that's not too bad. He can still work around the garden. The Currans' place is a disgrace, so that'll be good.' She began to walk away, but stopped. 'You say you've bought all his equipment?'

'Yes.'

'You'll be away a lot then too.'

Adam shrugged.

'Won't your wife object?'

He laughed. 'That'll be the day!'

'You won't listen to her objections?'

'I don't have a wife.'

'Oh. Well, good luck with the new business anyway.'

Adam took off his hat. His hair, bleached to a near-whiteness by years of sun, tumbled around his face.

'There was one more question, but I don't think you'd know the answer.'

She stopped, challenged. 'You'll never know until you ask. My father sometimes asks me things about his job. He says I have a better memory than him. What is it?'

'Well, I have two friends working on the line up at Byrock. There's some railway line relaying going on up there.'

'Yes, I know. A bridge had to be rebuilt because the timbers became rotten and they are putting in new sleepers for three miles to the south and seven miles to the north. There are twenty-five men working on the job.'

'Well, my mates are among them,' was all he could say. He was impressed.

'Don't you think that's a dreadful word?' she said, arching one eyebrow in a way he didn't think possible. She spoke rapidly.

'What?'

'Mate. It sounds common. Particularly the way people around here say it. They make it sound like an insect. Mite. I can't stand ain't, either. Do you say ain't?'

'Ain't sure,' he said.

She paused, then laughed. 'You have a sense of humour. What was it you wanted to know about your friends?'

'When the job's likely to be finished. They're coming down here. They're going to help me with the new business.'

'I don't know,' she said, looking along the line towards the blistering distance, as though the information might be on its way. 'I hear the job's behind schedule.'

'We were hoping to meet here before Christmas,' he said.

'I don't think that's likely.'

'Well,' said Adam, 'that's not good news.'

'You see,' she said. 'You said "that is not". You didn't say "that ain't". I think you are a bit of a tease. What's your name?'

'Adam Ross.'

'I'm Heather Maguire. Goodbye.' And she left.

Adam waited for the train from Dubbo, just in case George Curran had changed his plans and come home early. The train was forty minutes late, but Curran was not on board. Adam bought some meat at a butcher's shop and went back to the Bogan and camped again. It was cool under the trees but, beyond the river, the sky was white and spirals of dust played on the horizon. He looked at the distant town, spitting and fizzing in a mirage of molten walls and silver roofs, and thought of Heather Maguire.

Adam went to the railway station again the next day to meet the train from Dubbo. Curran was not on it. The following day Adam went earlier, about lunchtime, and met Heather Maguire once more. He went early again the next day, and walked with her to her home. It was nearby and had a big garden which one of the railway men used to tend, carting water in dry times from the tanks at the station.

Curran reached Nyngan the next day. Adam helped him fit the new head gasket and paid him the balance of the money owing on the deal. He now had to wait for Jimmy and Josef to arrive, and needed somewhere to stay while he waited. He also had to start thinking about their first contracts. Curran already had enquiries about sinking bores in the Hungerford district and wrote a letter to the man concerned, pointing out that he had sold the business but that the new owner, Adam Ross, would be able to handle the job. There was a spare bed on the Currans' back verandah, so, after eight days of camping on the Bogan, Adam moved in at an agreed rental of twenty-five shillings a week for bed, breakfast and laundry. Adam bought some new clothes, and saw Heather every day.

On 18 December, he got word from Josef that the job at Byrock would not finish until early in the new year. He told Heather and a few days later he was invited to join her family for Christmas dinner.

TWO

Christmas dinner was at lunchtime and it was the biggest meal Adam had ever seen. The Maguires had two roast chickens, a leg of pork, cold ham, baked potatoes, pumpkin, cauliflower in a white sauce and peas. Mrs Maguire had made an enormous pudding and served it with custard and raspberry jelly and a hard sauce that reeked of brandy. Heather was an only child.

'You don't drink, I hear,' Hector Maguire said and grunted when Adam shook his head. 'Good. I like a man with the strength to say no to temptation. Have you ever been a drinker?'

'No.' Adam remembered the wretches he had seen, stinking of methylated spirits, and could never recall a time when he had been tempted to drink alcohol.

'Good.' The stationmaster accepted a second helping of pudding. He was a thin man despite his gargantuan appetite. 'I don't trust reformed drunks, do you?'

'I don't know that I've ever met any.'

'Adam has a sense of humour,' Heather said, and Mrs Maguire laughed.

'I like a young man with a sense of humour,' she said. 'It shows he is well equipped for the hardships and disappointments of life.'

'What religion are you?' Maguire asked.

Adam looked at Heather. She was obviously interested in his answer. 'I don't know,' he said. 'My mother died soon after I was born and my father worked in the bush. There were never any churches.'

'Not Roman Catholic, are you?' Maguire asked casually, his concentration seemingly reserved for the task of pouring more custard on his pudding.

'You mean with priests and things? No.'

'You're Protestant then, but just not sure which one. Great

255

shame, boy. A person should be proud of his religion. Our forefathers went through struggles and much persecution in the cause of their beliefs. We should not forget that.'

Not being sure what to say, Adam said nothing.

'We are Methodists,' Mrs Maguire said, as though Adam's silence were a question he was too polite to ask.

'Not Roman Catholics as the name might have suggested to you,' Maguire added. 'We are Protestant Maguires. Not a lot of us around.'

He had more jelly.

'What do you do for a living?'

Heather leaned forward. 'Adam is starting up his own business. He has bought Mr Curran's truck and all his strange-looking equipment and he's employing two men he knows very well, and he's going to be a contractor.'

'Good for you,' said Mrs Maguire. 'Would you like more pudding? There's plenty there.'

'No thank you.' After years of eating damper and tinned meat, and an occasional galah or kangaroo, Adam was feeling a little sick.

The stationmaster toyed with his spoon. He had not finished eating. He was troubled.

'Working for yourself is fine, provided you're in the right business with a good future and plenty of security. Something like a solicitor or a doctor or maybe a good tradesman. Good honest work. But half the people who say they are self-employed these days are really unemployed. A man with his own business is at great risk. Did you read how many American businessmen committed suicide during the early years of this great Depression? Thousands of them. Wall Street wasn't safe to walk on, there were so many bodies coming out of the windows. They were people who had their own businesses. When things get tough as they are now and will be for many years, if I'm any judge, it's the little man who goes to the wall first.'

'Just have a little more jelly and custard,' Mrs Maguire said and, ignoring Adam's upraised hand, filled his plate.

'You don't eat like this when you're out of work,' Maguire said. 'It's one thing to be your own master, I suppose, but nothing gives you security like a good job.'

'A government job,' Mrs Maguire said. 'There must be thousands of people out there who are starving this Christmas.

256

It's tragic, absolutely tragic.'

'Oh, it's their own fault in many cases,' Maguire said. 'People came back from the war with all sorts of crazy expectations. Just wanted to live it up. Weren't prepared to work hard. War changes people.'

'Hector couldn't go to the war,' Mrs Maguire said. 'Varicose veins.'

'It wasn't that, mother.' He looked annoyed.

'Well, no, but you did have them. Hector was in the railways and that's an essential job, of course. You must have the trains, war or no war.'

'We've been here since 1931,' Heather said, trying to turn the conversation.

'It's a very important position,' Mrs Maguire said, 'particularly with the Depression and the drought and everything. Is there something wrong with the jelly?'

Adam had been toying with a spoonful, holding it above his plate and rolling it like a flabby red bird in flight.

'Is it the raspberry?' she enquired. 'I have some lime jelly in the ice chest that I was saving for Boxing Day. I can quickly get some. Heather, go and fetch it, there's a pet.'

'Please,' Adam said, touching Heather's hand as she started to rise. 'This is fine. I was just listening to what Mr Maguire was saying.'

He ate a mouthful and noticed with pleasure that Heather left her hand in his.

'I've never seen flowers like that before,' Adam said.

Heather had taken him into the garden and they were admiring a wall of blue hydrangeas which were sheltered from the worst of the sun by a row of gum trees. They flourished because of the attentions of Maguire's gardener, the assistant yardman at the railway station. He watered them twice a day, when he started work and when he finished.

'Father's very proud of the garden,' she said, walking ahead of Adam. He followed her past several shrubs, and a Christmas bush dripping flowers. 'He'd like to get a nice garden going over at the station but there's not enough shade or shelter from the wind. He's got a little pig-face growing and a few geraniums but nothing like this. This is nicer. Much more private too, which makes it even better. Father says that if you had a garden like this where everyone could see it you'd soon have it full of cigarette butts and beer bottles.'

'This is lovely. What are those flowers?' He had rounded a corner of the house and faced a dense bank of pink and white blooms.

'Azaleas. They're past their best. You should have seen them a few weeks ago.'

'And what were the ones we saw a few minutes ago? The blue ones.'

'Hydrangeas.'

'Why do flowers in gardens have such fancy names?'

'What do you mean?' She turned towards him and her eyes, blue as the evening sky, dazzled him.

'Well, out in the bush things have simpler names.'

'Like what?'

Adam kicked at the dirt. He had on the new shirt and the pants he had bought, and an old pair of riding boots that he had spent half an hour polishing. Mrs Curran had given him a haircut and the back of his neck still prickled. He scratched it.

'Well, things like Sturt's desert pea or Patterson's curse.'

'They sound dreadful.' She laughed as she said it.

'They're lovely.'

'Even – what did you call it? Patterson's curse?'

'I've seen hills covered in it. It turns them blue. The Flinders Ranges are full of it, although some people over there call it Salvation Jane.'

'How can Patterson's curse become Salvation Jane? You're teasing me again, Adam Ross.' She backed away from him and leaned against the white trunk of a gnarled gum.

'No, I'm not. There's a lot of it around. Haven't you seen it?'

'I rarely go out of town.'

'Really?'

'Well, why would I?'

'But there's so much to see out there.'

'Like dust and flat plains and gum trees?' She hid behind the tree but kept talking. 'We have some friends down at Nevertire and we play tennis there some nights. They have lights on their court. But that's about all.' She reappeared. 'We go down one afternoon on the train. Father reserves a first-class compartment, of course, and then we come back on the train next day. I can see the country from the carriage. It looks boring. I never go anywhere else but down to our friends' place.'

'But you've lived here almost four years.'

'No, I havent.'

'You've been here since 1931.'

'My parents have. I was at school for the first couple of years.'

'Where?'

She left the tree and walked in front of Adam once more.

'Moss Vale. Do you know where that is?'

'No. It sounds nice.'

'It is. It's not far from Sydney, but up in the hills with lovely trees all round, and lots of wealthy folk living in big estates. Some of them have huge gardens. Much bigger than this.'

'I've never seen a garden bigger than this.'

'Really?' She skipped a little, playing a game with shadows on the path.

'What do you do here in Nyngan?'

She stopped skipping and began walking, throwing her hips in an exaggerated sway. 'What do you mean?'

'Well, what work do you do?'

'Young ladies don't work! Do you think I should swing a pick and go out and repair the railroad, like your men friends?'

'Of course not.'

'I just help mother. We keep very busy. Talking of your friends, have you heard any more from them?'

'No. As far as I know they'll be here in the new year.'

'What are their names?'

'Jimmy and Josef.'

She laughed. 'They sound like a pair of blackfellows.'

'One of them is.'

She turned. 'You are a terrible tease, Adam! Have you heard from that man at Hungerford about your first contract?'

'George Curran got a letter the other day. The job's on.'

'That's good, I suppose. How long will you be away?'

'Maybe six weeks.'

'Will you miss me?' She turned away and picked a flower from a bush, then waited for his answer.

Adam shrugged his shoulders.

'What a shy man.' She placed the flower behind his ear. 'That's something to remember me by. Keep it in your diary. Will you write to me?'

Adam hesitated.

259

She brushed a speck from his collar. 'Do you want me to write to you?' she said.

'Heather, there's something I should tell you.'

'That there's no post office? That you won't have time because you'll be too busy? That you don't want to write to me?'

'None of those things.'

She darted away, a butterfly in her own garden.

'Please stay still. I want to tell you something and I don't find it easy to say.'

She came back. 'Oh, such a serious man! What is it? Has your pen been devoured by the Patterson's curse? Is that why you won't write to me?'

'Heather, I never went to school.'

She hovered near a rose bush. 'What do you mean?'

'Just that. I have spent all my life roaming the bush. I just didn't have time to go to school.'

'Not ever? I mean, not even for a few years?'

He shook his head.

'Are you trying to tell me you can't read or write?'

'No.'

'No what? No I can, or no I can't? Oh, Adam, are you teasing me again? Truly I've never met anyone like you. You say the most terrible things with such a serious look on your face as though it were all true. If you're going to be too busy to write to me it's all right. If you don't want to write to me, that's all right too. Just don't turn everything into a joke. I don't like being mocked.'

She moved away again. Adam stood where he was, racked by embarrassment but determined to tell the truth.

'Heather, I am not teasing you.'

'You're serious, then?'

'Very. I did not go to school. No one has ever taught me to read or write.'

'I don't believe you.'

'I can ride a horse, I can fix a car, I can sink wells, I can build a house, I can survive out there as good as the blackfellows ...'

'As well as,' she corrected, but did not look at him.

'I'm as good as any man in doing things, but I cannot read or write.'

'You were never taught?'

'Never.'

She covered her eyes. 'You must be so ashamed.'

'Sometimes. Josef's mother was going to teach me. She was a very cultured woman. She was German.'

'And she was going to teach you English?'

'She was a nice lady.'

'But a German can't teach you English. They have such funny accents. There was a German girl at school and she was a pig.'

Adam found himself searching for faults in Mrs Hoffman, but he could only think of good things. She had been kind to him. Heather held a finger aloft.

'I will teach you to read and write. How about that?'

'That would be fine. But when would we do it?'

'When father is at work. He must not know.'

'Why? Would he get upset?'

'It's not that. I don't want anyone to know that you're illiterate. It's just too, too shameful.'

The thought of spending a couple of hours a day with Heather appealed to Adam. 'What about your mother?'

'Oh, she's a goose. I can tell her anything and she'd believe it. I'll tell her I'm teaching you French. She'd love that.' She stopped transfixed by a sudden thought. 'You don't speak any other language, do you? Mother would like it even more if she thought I was being taught and was advancing my classical education.'

'I can speak a few words of Pushtu,' he said.

'What on earth is that?'

'The language they speak in Afghanistan.'

'Who in the world would want to speak that?' she said.

'Someone who lived there,' he said seriously. 'I'm told there are more Afghans than there are Australians.'

She burst into laughter. 'You say the most outrageous things. In any case, as father says, we should never forget that we are essentially English, and tomorrow I shall start to teach you the King's English.'

Her finger touched her forehead, trapping a thought. 'We should also learn a little French, just to speak when mother is around. Maybe how to count to a hundred.'

'I can count in Pushtu,' Adam said.

'And in Patterson's curse too, I'm sure! The trouble is, I never know when to take you seriously.'

Adam had only cared for one young woman, and she had loved

261

him and robbed him and disappeared. He thought about Nellie a lot in the next few weeks. In fact, the more he saw of Heather Maguire, the more he remembered his first love. He *had* loved her, he decided, because the ache of losing her remained for so long. He had thought about Nellie for a couple of years and searched for her in a hopeless, half-hearted way whenever he saw a few black faces in a group of strangers. In his more cynical moments, he decided she had probably gone south again, to spend the money she got from selling his opal. Or else she had gone back to work in a brothel. That thought really hurt and, in the years after Coober Pedy, he spent many a tormented night tossing on his blanket and listening to the sounds of the hobbled horses grazing, and thinking of Nellie in the embrace of some fat drunkard.

He didn't even know her other name. Nellie. That was all. He could no longer find her even if he wanted to, because to find someone you had to know their surname. He was Ross, not Adam. And she was blank, not Nellie. He couldn't go up to someone in some new town and say 'Excuse me, but do you know Nellie?' They'd think he was talking about someone's pet horse. It was ridiculous and he should forget her.

But in those early years, he couldn't. He remembered the nights in his dugout: the gloss on her skin and the big eyes and high cheekbones, and the jutting breasts, and the way her hips would tilt at a provocative angle. And he remembered other things, like the game way she had walked all night after they had rescued her from the creek-bed near Port Augusta, even though she must have been hurting like hell from the beating she'd been given, and the way she and Joe had broken them out of jail. And even at the end, she hadn't betrayed them. Mailey had had to beat her to get her to talk. He wondered if she were still alive, and decided she was. Nellie was a survivor.

He just couldn't make her out. She did so many bad things and so many good things.

In the last couple of years, the early longing for Nellie had eased. She had been stacked into his file of memories. An important person, like his mother, father and old Tiger, but like them, someone from the past. Someone who had helped shape his life, for better or worse, and then gone her way, never to be seen again.

Adam had hardly seen a woman in five years. There were the occasional wives of station-owners in lonely places but they were almost all middle-aged women, and most looked worn and older than they really were, for outback life is a merciless accelerator of the ageing process. He saw many station blacks but the women were unattractive; just dark shadows who stood as unappealing and unmoving as burnt stumps. Remote women with cheap cotton dresses, fat bodies and thin legs.

Heather Maguire was an outstanding-looking woman in any company. She was the belle of Nyngan and knew it, and Adam, overwhelmed by the thought of such a person showing interest in him and as innocent as only a bush person can be, fell helplessly and hopelessly in love.

If the flame of love is rekindled, there is usually enough light to reveal reflections of the past. And in longing for Heather – blonde, white, cool Heather – Adam saw frequent images of Nellie – dusty, black, hot-blooded Nellie. His days were filled with contrasts. Of how elegant and accomplished was the stationmaster's daughter; of how correct her language, how precise her dress, and how cool and serene her demeanour. He would see her, sheltering in a darkened room while a windstorm raged outside, with not a hair out of place, and she would continue their lessons with not a care in the world. And, while concentrating over the way to print some new letter (first in capitals, then in lower case, then running writing) his mind would recall Nellie, hair tangled, eyes rimmed with dust, constantly dirty and inclined to let the odd foul word slip out.

There was no comparison. Yet he did compare, for Nellie kept hovering in the background. He would see her as she had been, hair matted from the wind and body mottled with dust, and wonder how he could ever have felt the way he did about her. He recalled a hundred stories about white men who had taken black women, and felt ashamed that he had – if only for a few days – been one of them. He must have been ... what was the word Heather would use – depraved? Then, as he laboured over his writing, he would picture himself as he had been after a day down the mine. Hair full of grit, body plastered with dust and mud, and stinking to high heaven. Nellie had been dirty, everyone had been dirty. That was the way it was at that place.

He tried to imagine Heather at Coober Pedy and could not. He could picture her at the bottom of the shaft, cool and with her hair glowing in the half-light, but his mind refused to transfer her above ground to the desolation of the gibber plain and the ruthless blast of a dust storm.

Heather was a soft creature, or so he imagined. She was beautiful and clever and worldly beyond his experience in the way she talked about other people and knew things almost as if by instinct, but she was feminine and vulnerable, as he had always imagined women should be. Good women, that was. Women like his mother, or like the dream creature that floated through his mind when he was not quite awake. Heather reminded him of his mother in many ways. When he thought about it, he realized this was a slightly nonsensical thing for him to say, even to himself, but it felt so true. Heather was the sort of woman his mother had been. He was sure of that.

He loved the lessons she gave him in the garden. He learned the alphabet quickly and soon mastered a couple of 'First Readers' that Heather found in a large trunk of relics from her schooldays. He even managed to speak a few words of French, and would chant *'très bien'* and *'merci beaucoup'* whenever Mrs Maguire fluttered into sight. Heather had been right. The mother was no trouble. The daughter bamboozled her and told syrupy lies and sent her off to do something else.

Adam found the lessons amusing and vaguely comforting. He was much stronger than she was and he had no doubt she would fall into his arms if danger threatened, but she treated him like a boy. He liked that. It reduced an embarrassing thing like learning the alphabet at twenty-four to a game. She seemed to enter into the spirit of the game with enthusiasm, pretending to be stern and even slapping him gently with a ruler on a couple of occasions.

He liked being bullied by someone so pretty. This was probably what people called flirting. Yes, Adam thought, sitting in the garden, near the massed wall of blue hydrangeas, he liked life with Heather Maguire.

Adam spent more time with her than he might have hoped, having lessons all through January. The job at Byrock had been delayed again and Jimmy and Josef were not due to finish until the first week of February. By then Adam had decided to ask Heather to marry him.

He said nothing to her. He needed money to support such a proposal but he had decided. He would get the business started, make a little money and then ask her.

Early in February, Adam drove north to pick up his friends at Byrock. He couldn't wait for them to come south by train as the man at Hungerford was becoming impatient to have the job started. Before he left, Heather gave Adam a couple of letters. They were from him to her.

'Copy these out and send them to me,' she said. 'I don't want people thinking you don't care about me, or that you can't write.' And she kissed him.

The drilling was on a property just south of Hungerford and therefore still in New South Wales. They had to camp on the site eighteen miles from the man's homestead. The heat was intense. There were a lot of hawks in the area and they surrounded the camp, waiting for scraps. Early in the morning and late in the afternoon when the temperature was more bearable, the birds flew out looking for mice and other delicacies and packs of them would wheel in the sky like burning leaves spiralling from a bonfire. But in the middle of the day when heat thinned the air and sent it rising in simmering layers, the hawks found the combination of heat exhaustion and thin air too much. The strong ones tried hard to fly, flapping the air feebly and occasionally stumbling a few steps along the gravelly ground, trying to muster the necessary speed for take-off. None flew. So in the awful midday heat, the hawks spread their limp and liftless wings and used them as props to stop themselves falling on their sides. Adam's camp was ringed by hundreds of birds, hunched like feathered tents.

The men, too, rested in the middle of the day but started work before dawn and usually kept working at night for a few hours by lantern light. Adam had Josef drive into the homestead for regular supplies of fresh meat and twice sent with him the letters to Heather. On a third occasion, he sent another. It was short, and it used phrases from the other two, but it was his own creation.

The property owner was pleased with the way they worked and told Adam of a friend on a nearby station (ninety-three miles to the west, but close by his measure of distance) who wanted a couple of dams cleared and had an old well that needed rebuilding. The well had been shored with timber which had partially collapsed. Adam had done similar jobs many times so he sent Heather a fourth letter, which Josef helped him write, and headed off to the other station.

The man at that property knew of a friend west of Wanaaring who needed a bore sunk near his new homestead, and by the time Adam returned to Nyngan he had written seven letters and been away five months.

Adam came back as an established contractor, with a list of satisfied clients and a record of carrying out some difficult jobs, and a couple of hundred pounds in the bank. He went to see Heather, filled with pride at his success and at having written so many letters.

Heather took Adam into the garden. 'I must say I don't know why you bothered to come back,' she said, walking ahead of him. 'There must be something about your new business that you find intensely attractive. After all, not many people would choose to stay back-of-Bourke, which is precisely where you were, in the heat of this awful summer, chasing from one sheep station to the next and putting lots of little holes in the ground when you could have just done what you said you were going to do' — she paused long enough to fire a backwards glance at him — 'and then come back here. I was expecting you. I had even arranged for us to go to the Stevens' place at Nevertire and play night tennis. We had to miss that.'

'I don't play tennis,' Adam said. If a man had spoken to him like that he would have been angry, but Heather made him feel guilty. And disappointed. He hadn't even thought she would feel this way. He had been excited to get extra work and make such a good start to his business and he had assumed she would share that feeling.

'No, of course you don't play tennis,' she said. 'And you don't go to church and you didn't go to school. You don't do anything normal people do.'

'I work hard,' Adam said. 'Those jobs weren't easy.'

'Do you think you're the only one who's been busy? I wrote ten letters about that tennis weekend. Five to see if we could arrange it on the date I thought you would be back and to the people I wanted to come, and then five more cancelling everything when you didn't turn up. I've never been so embarrassed in my life.'

She had moved ahead of Adam and he followed in silence for a while. The azaleas were a mass of green leaves, and he wondered when they would bloom again.

'I wrote letters too,' he said, seeking a warm response. He was proud of those letters. They were the first he had ever written.

'Good for you. There were two nice ones I had written, and a couple of others that were very short. Hardly worth reading.'

Adam stopped. A couple of parrots that had been feeding in the top branches of a tree broke away, and twigs fell to the ground.

'You're right,' he said. 'I don't know why I bothered to come back.'

Heather skipped behind the tree. 'Did you meet another girl?' Her voice asked softly.

The question stunned him. 'A girl? Where?'

'On one of those homesteads. I'm told there are some very big stations up there and some of the people who run them are millionaires. Men with rich little daughters who'd love a big, fair-headed boy with muscles.'

Adam stared up into the branches above him. One of the parrots had returned. My God, she's jealous, Adam thought, and the thought astonished him. It was such a new situation for him. To start with, he had never considered that he might be seen as being attractive to women. He had, of course, hoped that Heather liked him, but it had never occurred to him that other women might like him too. It had occurred to her, obviously.

'Well,' she continued, allowing half her face to appear around the trunk. 'Was it some little tart, fat as a cow where men like women to be fat, and with a rich daddy who intends leaving a million acres to her one day? Was it that sort of dull, boorish girl? I believe the bush is full of them.'

'There aren't too many people out there at the moment making any money at all, let alone millionaires,' Adam said, bending to pick up a fallen stick. He began to break it into small pieces. 'I haven't met any rich daughters. I didn't meet any poor daughters. I have spent the last few months working in the sun by day and sleeping under a sheet of canvas by night. I haven't played tennis or thought about parties, I haven't had anyone bringing me lunch in a little tin every day. I've dreamed of your mother's chicken and plum pudding and eaten mutton and damper. I've been trying to make money, to get my business going ...'

She had turned away but he reached out and grabbed her wrist. She kept her face away from him. He shook her. 'I asked you once before and you didn't tell me. How old are you?'

She was shocked by the strength of his grip. 'Twenty.'

He nodded and pulled her closer. 'Good. That's old enough. Do you know what I've done more than anything else while I've been away?'

Her eyes were wide and even bluer than he had remembered.

'I've thought about you. I stayed out there, working in heat I

267

wouldn't expect a dog to sleep in, so I could get enough money to come back here and ask your father if I could marry you.'

Her eyes blinked. Nothing else.

'Why would you ask him?' she said.

'Isn't that the proper thing to do?' He released her wrist. She turned with a swing of the hips that sent her skirt cascading around his knees.

'I would have thought it better to have asked me first,' she said.

'I wanted to do it the right way. Like gentlemen do.'

'The right way is to ask the woman first. The other is terribly old-fashioned.'

'Well, will you?'

'Will I what?'

'Oh, for heaven's sake, Heather! Marry me.'

She walked past a bush and broke off a dry branch.

'Wilson says this plant is dying.'

'Don't tease me.'

'But he does.'

'Who's Wilson?'

'The man who looks after the garden. He works for father. He's the most awful drip. But he says the roses will be good. He waters them with dish water. Can you imagine that?' She turned, to see if Adam could picture such a thing. He looked confused.

'Have I ever told you that you are very tall, very strong, very good-looking and very sweet?'

He blushed. 'No.'

'What else do you have to offer me? I mean, a girl can't just give her life to the first good-looking man who asks for her hand. Specially one who hasn't been to church, to school or to tennis and who has none of the social graces. I have the feeling you'd be most out of place in the best company. Oh,' she added, noticing Adam's crestfallen look, 'now I've hurt you.'

'You pick me up one moment and dump me the next. I can't keep up with you. I missed you so much while I was away.'

'I missed you too. That's why I was so disappointed that you stayed away for such a long time.'

'I was trying to get a start. To build a future. For us.'

'You think I'd like to be married to a … what do you call yourself … a hole-driller?'

'I'm a contractor. I drill bores, make wells, dig dams. Anything to do with water. Whether you understand it or not, it is a most

268

important job.'

She was plucking petals from a flower. 'But that's just it. It's only a job and it takes you way out in the Never Never and it's not really a job because you don't even work for anyone. Father says anyone who works for himself these days is a fool. He says things are never going to be the same as they were before this Depression started. One of the girls at school had to leave with only one year to go because her father went broke. Can you imagine the shame? The poor thing. She just couldn't face any of us.'

'A lot of cruel things are happening,' Adam said. 'There are some good men out there who are close to starving. But you know, this Depression isn't going to last forever and one man's misfortune can be another man's good luck. There are going to be some good properties available for very low prices.' He selected another stick and began breaking pieces off. 'If someone had money in a year or so, there could be some real bargains around.'

She faced him and he threw away the stick.

'You mean you want to buy a cattle station or a sheep station or something?'

He nodded, his face serious. 'I intend to have my own place one day. I will become very rich.'

'What, and live out the back of nowhere with a mob of blackfellows and kangaroos as your nearest neighbours?'

'They can be very good neighbours. So long as they're nice kangaroos.'

Her eyes sought inspiration in the branches of a tall eucalypt. 'I never know when to take you seriously. Have you been teasing me? Were you serious?'

'About the kangaroos?' He grinned and she threw a twig at him. It fluttered off course.

'There. You see what I mean.'

His face switched from fun to serious in an instant.

'About wanting my own property? Yes.'

'And what about the other?'

'About marrying you? Yes, although I hadn't meant to ask you yet.'

'I don't understand.'

'I meant to wait a bit longer. You just got me all wound up.'

She found some weeds beneath a shrub and bent to wrench them from the earth. She did it with a deft grace. Adam had never

269

seen anyone do things so well and yet in such a gentle, feminine way. 'Honestly,' she said, 'that Wilson just spends time over here to avoid having to work in the heat of the railway yard. I'm always finding things he's missed. If it weren't for me this garden would be an absolute shambles.'

She stood up and brushed dirt from her fingers. 'Why were you going to wait?'

He waved a fly from his face. 'To have more money. Get a few more customers. Build my reputation. Let you get to know me better.'

'I think I know you well,' she said, and her eyes dazzled him. 'You can't ask me now ... not officially – because it's too soon. People are so stuffy and they would think I'd rushed in. We must be proper. Say later in the year.'

Adam was confused. 'Are you saying yes?'

'Not now. Later in the year.'

'You mean you will marry me, but you're not going to tell me for a few months?'

'Honestly, Adam, sometimes you're just as big a goose as mother! We will be engaged later, when people think we've known each other a decent time, and when you have enough money to buy a ring.' She went on before he could say anything. 'We won't get a ring in this town of course, but I heard there is a jeweller in Dubbo who sells the most exquisite things. We might go down there. Oh, I can hardly wait to tell Pam!'

'Who's Pam?'

'Pam Stevens. Her parents own the tennis court. The lovely one with lights. She has just got engaged to the Rawlinson boy from Warren. He is such a lean, miserable-looking thing with an Adam's apple that sticks out like he swallowed the kettle. Oh, when she sees you, she will be just insane with jealousy!'

THREE

It was on the next job that Jimmy had the accident. They were working on a site between Hermidale and Girilambone and not more than two hours' drive from Nyngan.

The job involved clearing an old well that had stones around the top and timber in the shaft. The owner wanted it cleaned out and rebuilt. It was not a good job because the man did not have a lot of money to pay for the work and because the remaining stonework was fragile and the timber was rotting. In short it was a poorly paid and dangerous job, but Adam took it because it was close to town and he could see Heather every other day. He told Jimmy and Josef he had taken the job because he wanted to build a reputation in the Nyngan district.

He had been to town to get a few supplies they did not really need yet, so that he could see Heather. The well was not far from an outstation on the property. The building had once been the main homestead in the days before much of the land had been cleared for grazing. Even before he reached the site he knew something was wrong. For one thing, there were no parrots in the trees. Usually they were there at this time of the day, squawking and clattering and splashing colour on branches that jutted from the trunks, all white and broken like shattered old bones, but the trees were quiet. He drove his truck along the track that wound through the noiseless trees and followed the twin ruts that were as pure white as shining ribbons, and he knew something was wrong. It wasn't just the absent birds or anything he could see, or not see. He just knew.

They had rigged a triangular structure of water pipe above the well and had a small petrol motor driving the winch. Josef was kneeling beside the shaft and he turned and stood as the truck approached. He started to run towards Adam, then turned and went back to the shaft. Josef was tall now, well over six feet and just starting to thicken, but there were times when he still behaved like a boy. He was acting like a boy now, a frightened boy who is facing some dreadful emergency and doesn't know what to do. He called out long before Adam could hear him.

The truck was noisy and it was only when Adam had turned off the engine and vaulted from the driver's seat that he could understand what Josef was saying.

'He's stuck!' he was shouting. Adam ran to him.

'What do you mean, struck?'

'Stuck! For God's sake, he's stuck down there!' Josef was shouting, needlessly, for Adam was beside him now.

'Jimmy!' Adam called, not loudly but with the soft anxiety of someone who is frightened of what a reply might bring. There was

271

no answer. Part of the old stonework around the edge was missing and dirt was trickling into the hole.

'What happened?'

'There was a rumble, like water running, and then something gave way. Part of the side of the shaft, I think. The whole thing shook and then some stones fell in and then a lot of soil. I've been trying to stop the whole thing from collapsing.'

Adam was kneeling. Josef stood behind him. Behind them, the petrol engine was idling roughly, pop, pop, bang, pop, pop, bang.

'Turn the Lister off,' Adam yelled and when there was silence, he listened. The shaft whispered the sounds of menace. A squeak of timber. A run of gravel. The soft splash of water.

No sound of a man.

Adam called out and his voice bounced around the hollows. He turned to Josef and he felt sick with fear and guilt. He should have been here.

'How long ago did this happen?'

'I don't know. Ten, fifteen minutes.' Josef knelt beside him. He was calmer now, happy to have someone else share the responsibility. Rivulets of dry earth flowed around his knees and disappeared into the shaft.

'Let's get back a little. Both of us,' Adam said. Then, as they shuffled away from the edge, 'Did Jimmy make any noise? Did he call out?'

'He said "shit".'

'Anything else?'

'Nothing. He must have seen it coming. We were talking while you were gone about the rain the other night because we heard water trickling from the sides.'

'You heard it? Water running?'

'Just a little. Jimmy thought there might have been some underground stream down there, and it was coming out part of the way up the shaft.'

'Why did he go down?'

'To see where the water was coming from.'

'Oh, for Christ's sake!' Adam stood up and took a few steps back from the well. He'd known this was a dangerous job, he was the only one of the three who truly understood the work, and he'd gone into town to see his girlfriend.

'Is the cable firm?'

'Hasn't budged.'

272

'Have you tried to move it?'

'Just a little. I didn't put any pressure on it.'

'Good. That was good, Joe. Was Jimmy in the bucket?'

'Yes. I was just lowering him so's he could have a look. He wasn't more than halfway down when everything fell in.'

'OK. I'll tell you what we have to do. We may need help but first I'm going down to have a look. You stay up here and do *exactly* what I tell you. First, get two ropes.'

Josef got the ropes while Adam put a torch and a hooked metal bar in his belt. He tied one rope into a cradle of two loops and fitted it around his hips. They ran the other end through a pully on the triangular rig and Josef began to lower Adam down the shaft.

'Take it very gently,' Adam said, his head level with Josef's ankles. 'We don't want to set off another fall.'

The shaft was wide enough for Adam to be able to reach out and touch the wall. The timbers were splintery and, in places, so rotten he could have gouged a handful of soft wood from a beam. When they had first started the job, the shaft smelled of dry rotten wood and dust. Now it had a damp smell. He could hear water running. It was only a faint sound echoing gurgles and splashes from a distance.

He was following the cable down, fending it off with one hand and using the other to shine the torch about him. He came to the place where the water was flowing. There must have been a burst of water from some long-dry subterranean stream, and it had taken with it a couple of lengths of timber. A dark hole yawned at him. Water was trickling over a lip of ravaged mud.

The cable was not hanging vertically, but was angled to one side of the shaft, indicating that the metal bucket in which Jimmy had been riding was wedged against a wall. He began to spiral on the end of the rope and grasped the cable to steady himself. He shone the torch down.

It was hard to see clearly because his legs and feet got in the way, but there seemed to be a mess of timber and rock about fifteen feet below him.

The rope stopped moving.

'Just a minute. I'm changing my grip.' Josef's voice sounded a long way away. 'Can you see anything?'

'Not clearly. The shaft's blocked. I'll have to get closer. Take it slowly.'

There was a jerk and he started descending once more. He

273

heard water rushing somewhere. The noise grew louder and then broke into a hissing sound. He just had time to lift one arm above his head before he was drenched by a sheet of water. Some mud and small stones hit his body.

'What's wrong?' Josef called. Adam took a moment to answer.

'I just got hit by water. It came through a hole in the side. I think there must have been a big flow while Jimmy was down here. A few pieces of wood have broken away.'

'You're all right?'

'Just a bit wet. I'm all right. Keep lowering me.'

He could see the rubble more clearly now. A few lengths of timber had jammed themselves across the shaft and on one side of the hole they supported a large quantity of mud and earth and rock. It was the side of the shaft where the cable ran to the wall. The bucket was beneath. The bucket and Jimmy and whatever was down there was stopping the debris from falling any further.

A few seconds later, as he dropped even closer, he saw Jimmy's hand, or what was left of it. It was against the wall, fingers bent at such unnatural angles that they must be broken, and raw bone showing.

'Jimmy,' Adam called and watched the hand for a response.

His friend's hand always had been two-coloured: the black of the back of the hand and a creamy pink on the inside of the palm and fingers. Now the pink seemed almost white, almost as pale as the exposed bone.

The hand did not move and a wave of fear shook Adam's body. I won't do anyone any good if I start shaking, he told himself, but he still shook.

'Can you see him?' Josef called.

'Yes. Another five feet.' A shower of dirt fell on him and he thought, I'll have to be careful. Too much noise or any violent action and I'll have the whole lot on top of me. He moved gently, guiding himself along the wire cable towards the hand.

'Is he all right? What can you see?'

'I can't see much and he's not all right. He's buried.'

Adam's feet touched the first piece of timber. One end was embedded in mud and rock near the hand and it was pointing down at a forty-five degree angle.

'Stop,' he said, softly but strongly and he swung at the end of the rope, the sole of one boot touching the wood and the torch beam scanning the awful jumble blocking the shaft. There was no sign of Jimmy other than the hand. It was not bleeding. There was blood in the thin red lines where he could see exposed bone but there was no bleeding. He felt sick, not from the sight but from the expectation of what he might find.

'Throw me the other rope.'

It came snaking down and stopped just short of him. Josef had been measuring the length. He was a clever fellow. You didn't have to tell him anything twice, except personal things like writing to his parents (which he did rarely) or not swearing (which he did often). Now the second rope came down foot by foot. Adam grabbed it and looped a few turns around his arm.

'OK, stop for a minute,' he called and tied the end to the first piece of timber. 'Now, can you lift that?'

The rope shivered under the strain. Jimmy's hand moved, but only because the timber was twisting.

'Hang on. Lower me another two feet and then pull again on the other rope.'

Adam was now almost level with Jimmy's hand. Using the metal bar he dug around the hand, scraping away mud and small stones. The wrist was revealed but the piece of timber with a large rock half resting on it pinned the arm against the wall. Where was Jimmy's head and body? Adam looked at the large rock and grew more fearful.

'Are you ready?' Josef called. A shower of grit hit Adam. He looked up and saw Josef's head framed on the edge of the opening.

'Get away. The whole lot will fall down.'

And when Josef had withdrawn and another stream of gravel had fallen down the shaft and Adam had taken a few deep breaths to steady himself, he added, 'Try again. The rope is on one end of a piece of timber and I'm lifting the other. We have to get it off to get to Jimmy. Be as careful as you can. If anything else falls down here, we'll never get him out. Or me. OK? Now lift.'

Adam could hear Josef swearing. He often swore when he tried to do something that required a burst of strength. He said it made him stronger. The timber groaned and the stone moved and Adam tried to pull the bottom end up and away from Jimmy's arm. It was as heavy as a railway sleeper and Adam, with his feet braced against the wall, could hear his own rope squeaking under the greater load.

The timber moved and the stone rolled. The hand fell forward.

275

Three fingers were broken. Not the thumb or the first finger but the others. Jimmy must have raised his arm to protect himself. Adam hooked the end of the bar under the lower edge of the wood and wrenched the beam clear. The other end swung up.

'I've got the bloody thing,' Josef roared in triumph.

'Well, pull it up,' Adam said and steadied himself, for he had begun spinning on the end of the rope. He watched the long length of wood rising, turning as it went, and prayed his knot would hold. Josef got it to the top and swung the wood clear of the shaft.

When the wood was pulled clear, a large opening was revealed on the far side of the shaft. Adam pushed himself to the other side and had Josef lower him a few feet. By hanging from the rope, Adam was able to see beneath the main barrier and, in the torchlight, he saw the bucket. It was a big device, four-sided and tapering towards the bottom and wide enough to hold two men. There was no sign of Jimmy. That meant he must be in or on top of the bucket. It was nearly deep enough to hold a crouched man. That was good news, he told himself, and tried to believe it. He had been frightened that his friend might have been leaning across the metal lip of the bucket and had been cut in half.

With great difficulty, he climbed back into the harness.

'Adam, we've got help.'

'What?' Adam was near exhaustion.

'Joe Cooper has turned up.' He owned the property. He often came out to see how they were getting on with the work.

'Do you want me to go for help, Mr Ross?' a new voice shouted. He was a funny old bloke, Cooper. Always called another man 'mister'. Very formal. He had been a soldier at Gallipoli and still carried a piece of shrapnel in his leg.

'No,' Adam managed to shout. He felt disorientated and sick in the stomach. 'Just give Joe a hand. We've got two more pieces of wood to lift and I think I can get to him.'

'Is he alive?' Cooper shouted.

Adam hesitated. How could he say it? He was swinging on a rope, catching glimpses of things from a torch whose beam was growing fainter and all he had seen of Jimmy was a mangled hand. The bucket supported a heap of wood and mud and rocks and somewhere in there, broken by stones or choked by mud or speared by a length of timber or God knows what, was his friend.

'I don't know.'

He heard the distant rush of water and steadied himself against the cable. The noise became a roar and he heard the jet of water hit the wall above him. Stones and earth came rattling down the shaft. The water hit him and he bent under the pressure.

'Bloody hell, what happened?' Josef called.

Adam was quiet for a moment. He had been hurt.

'Are you all right, Mr Ross? Jesus Christ, son, let's get him up. We don't want two dead men down there.'

Adam felt himself jerked a few inches up the shaft.

'Stop,' he called weakly. 'Don't move me. I'm all right.' He held the torch in his teeth and began tying the second rope to another piece of timber. This was a short length with one splintered end projecting from the rubble. If he could free that he might be able to clear the rest by hand.

'OK. Pull away.' He put one foot against the knot and pushed hard to force the timber away from the bucket. Nothing happened.

'Come on, pull,' he shouted and a shower of gravel rained on his head and shoulders.

'We'll have to get help, Mr Ross. We can't move it.' Cooper sounded breathless.

There was a crunching sound and a sudden scattering of stones and the beam pulled loose. It swung wildly towards Adam. Another piece of timber kicked high and, with the release of pressure, began to fall. A group of stones followed it. The bucket shuddered and, bearing a load of raised mud and stones and one long piece of timber, swung free.

Adam was still holding the beam. It lifted abruptly, and he was wrenched up with it.

'She coming,' he heard Josef roar, and realized with horror that his legs had slipped from the loops of the rope. He was swinging free, held only by his grip on the wood.

The roped beam swung into one wall, slamming his back against the timbers. The torch fell from his mouth. The heavy wooden beam swung the other way and Adam, legs thrashing in the blackness, went with it. The rope and the swinging wire cable caught and the beam spun.

Adam was shaken loose.

He fell a few feet, turning in a wild somersault, and hit the timber projecting from the bucket. He landed on his chest, clawing for something to hold. The wood lifted at the other end, see-sawing under his weight, and when the end was high enough began to slide off the bucket. Adam's fingers felt a metal edge and grabbed it. The beam went clattering down the shaft and Adam was left swinging by one hand. He was on the bucket and it was spinning and tipping madly under the impact of his fall and the sudden unbalancing weight. The metal edge was rounded and slippery with mud, but he knew what it was and where it was, just as he knew he was dead if he let go.

He found an edge with his other hand and the bucket tilted and swayed. He bumped a wall and swung back with the bucket spinning slowly and the blackness beneath him ringing to the thuds and splashes of falling objects.

'What's happened?' Josef yelled. He could feel the loose rope that had supported Adam. 'Adam!' He was frantic.

'I'm OK.' The bucket was swinging out again but not so violently. 'Lower the rope. My rope.'

'What happened?'

'Just lower the rope. For God's sake do it quickly!' The metal edge was slimy and hard to hold.

'How far?'

'Until it reaches me.' He was finding it hard to talk. 'I've lost the torch. Can't see a thing.'

'For heaven's sake come on up!' Cooper shouted. 'It's too dangerous down there.'

Come on up, Adam thought. What's he think I am? A bird? He laughed. No one else would have heard him for almost no noise emerged. He had no breath to spare. Please, he said to himself, just give me the rope. I can't hang on much longer.

The rope touched his leg and then curled away.

'Stop!' Adam yelled and spent several moments gathering his strength. The rope was somewhere nearby. He let go with one hand and groped in the dark. Nothing. He grabbed the bucket again and hauled his shoulder across the edge, and felt warm skin beneath him.

'Jimmy?' he whispered. There was mud with the skin and nothing seemed to move.

The rope touched his leg again and he bent his knee around it. More secure now, he reached out with one hand and pulled the rope to him. He felt the twin loops, worked his legs into them and pulled the rope up to his hips.

'Jimmy?' He was able to feel now, not needing his arms to support him, and he wrenched away stones and shattered pieces

278

of timber. He touched the side of Jimmy's face. It had not been buried by mud as he had feared, for it had been protected by the broken wood. Jimmy's arm, once pinned to the wall, had fallen beside him. Adam ran his hands along the arm, felt the mangled bone, and groped for the ribs. He felt a faint movement, a rise and fall. Jimmy was breathing.

'What now?' Cooper yelled, and a torrent of stones fell on them.

'Keep away from the edge!' Adam screamed. When he was calmer, he said: 'Jimmy's alive, I think, but you'll have to lift me first. Bring me up gradually. I don't want any more stones.'

It was a hard lift, and the two at the top took nearly five minutes to bring Adam to the surface. He was covered in mud and bleeding from several cuts.

He could not stand, but had to stay there on his hands and knees, wildly disoriented and near total exhaustion. Josef started the petrol motor and the bucket rose slowly to the surface.

The parrots had come back, and were chattering in the trees.

Cooper gave Adam water and bathed his face and hands and washed dirt from a deep cut on his shin. After a few minutes Adam stood and was on his feet when the bucket reached the surface.

The first sight was shocking, all mud and blood with pieces of Jimmy projecting from the mess. But after they had swung the bucket to one side and scooped away some of the small stones and earth and mud, it was apparent that the worst injury, at least in appearance, was to the left arm. It was broken with the bone sticking out below the elbow. The rest of the arm was folded back, looking absurdly neat except for the mangled hand and porcupine fingers.

Jimmy had ducked low just before the fall hit him and had bent his legs beneath him and turned his body to one side. His skin had been ripped in a few places and there were some deep puncture wounds and large areas of bruises. He appeared intact and, as they lifted him from the steel bucket, everything seemed in place. No other bones projected from torn skin, and he was breathing.

Cooper had driven to the well in his car. It had no canvas top and no side curtains and the upholstery had split from too much sun, but it was big and had the high clearance that a bush car needed. They put Jimmy on the back seat, lying him on his back with his knees bent and his head resting on Adam's lap. Josef held the broken arm, using a sheet of cardboard from a soapbox to support the bones and prevent any further damage. Adam had a cloth and a can of water between his knees. He continually mopped his friend's brow and occasionally let drops of water trickle from his fingers on to the lips.

The day was burning slowly to its end. When the road was powdery, dust swirled around the windscreen and stung them, and Adam shielded Jimmy's face with his hat. A tyre punctured on the way and the journey to the little hospital at Nyngan took them three hours. There was no doctor there and the sister in charge immediately rang the base hospital at Dubbo to send an ambulance. She was a thin woman, worn from too much work. She spent a long time with Jimmy, removing dirt and stones and bone fragments from the wounds.

Cooper went to a friend's home. He was shaking from shock and his leg was hurting. Adam and Josef waited in the corridor and drank water from a tap in the patients' bathroom and were stared at by an old woman who roamed the hospital in her nightgown, befuddled by age and too shy to ask questions.

After an hour, the sister emerged. 'The ambulance won't be here until mid-morning,' she said, which they already knew. She looked at the walls, the floor, the ceiling. Every place but into their eyes. 'I think your friend will live. I don't know. Have you had anything to eat?'

'No,' Josef said.

'You should eat. No point getting weak. You won't help your friend that way.'

'What's wrong with him?' Adam said. 'Is he busted inside?'

She looked at Adam's leg. 'You're the one who went down after him, aren't you? You'll need stitches in that leg. I'll do that for you and clean you up. You're a mess. Come on. Into this room.'

She pointed to another, smaller room. The old woman in the nightgown appeared at the end of the corridor.

'Back to bed, Amy. I'll bring you your tea in a few minutes.'

'Could I have some iced vo-vos?' Amy said.

'Yes, Amy. I'll bring you two. Just go back to bed.' She helped Adam to his feet. 'Come on. I'll fix you up.'

'What about his arm?'

The sister risked a glance at Adam's face. He saw a flash of intense sadness before she turned away.

'I think he'll lose that,' she said, and busied herself chasing a stray wisp of hair. 'People expect miracles from us but we're only human. He's lucky to be alive. Now come on, before you put blood everywhere. I've got more to do around here than clean up the floors.'

Adam and Josef stayed at the hospital that night. About ten, the Nyngan doctor arrived. He had been out of town all day, and looked grey with fatigue. He spent twenty minutes with Jimmy. He came out drying his hands and said, 'We can't do any more till we get him to a bigger hospital,' and went home to have dinner. In the morning the ambulance came and took Jimmy away. He was still unconscious. Adam walked around to the place where Joe Cooper had gone and arranged to return with him to the property next day to collect his truck and all the gear. Then he went to the Currans' home and had a cold shower and a sleep. Late in the afternoon, he went to see Heather.

She was shocked by Adam's appearance. He was badly bruised in many places and the stitches in his legs stood out like the spikes on a prickly brush. He told her what had happened.

'I had no idea this work of yours was so dangerous,' she said, speaking softly and holding his hand. 'It was very brave of you to try and help your friend. I hope he appreciates what you did for him.'

'I just hope he lives.'

'Of course.'

'He may lose the arm.'

'Was it his right arm?'

'No.'

'Well, that's not so bad.' She patted his hand.

'He was left-handed.'

She sat for a while, still holding his hand and fascinated by a bruise on his forehead.

'You must have a terrible headache.'

Adam touched his forehead. 'No.'

'Could he learn to write and do things with his right hand?'

'He doesn't exactly earn his living by writing.'

She looked down and licked her lips. It was a delicate action. 'I suppose your friend can't write either.'

'No. At least I don't think so. I've never seen him do it and I've never asked him.'

'You're worried about how he's going to earn a living?'

'If he lives.'

'He'll live.' She squeezed his hand.

'He's going to have an awful battle. There aren't many jobs around for a one-armed blackfellow.'

'What do you mean?'

'Well, he can't go back to the sort of work we've been doing and who else is going to give him work?'

'I don't mean that. You said he was a blackfellow. An aboriginal?'

Adam was touching the stitches through the material of his trousers. He nodded.

'You didn't tell me.'

'Yes, I did, but you didn't believe me.'

She stood and walked a few steps away from him. 'You're always teasing me. I never know what to believe. He is really an aboriginal?'

'Yes.'

'Is he really a friend or does he just work for you?'

'He's a friend.'

She studied him. Then she turned away before speaking. He didn't like it when she did that, because it usually meant she was annoyed.

'I've never known anyone with an aboriginal for a friend. I think that's very noble of you.'

Adam was surprised.

'There's nothing so unusual about it. He's just a good mate.'

'I wish you'd say friend, not mate. How long have you known him?'

'Five, six years.'

'How on earth did you meet him?'

'We had a fight.'

She turned, doubt twisting her face.

'Truly,' he said. 'He was in a boxing troupe and we had a match.'

'You tried to hurt each other and you became friends?'

Adam had covered his eyes with his hands.

'I think that's just so typically male. You fight, you punch each other, then you put your arms around each other's shoulders and go off to the hotel to drink. Why are you sitting like that? Are you ashamed or something?'

Adam looked up and his eyes were wet. 'I was just thinking

about Jimmy. Losing your arm would be bad enough for most people but for him it would be awful. It'd mean the end of him.'

She sat beside him. 'You're upset. Why, Adam, I've never seen you like this and I'm touched. I think you must be a very special man to have an aboriginal for a friend and I think he's very lucky to have you for a friend because you're so concerned about him, and I think it's good for a man to cry. In private, like this. It shows a very warm heart.'

'It's not my heart. I'm no different to anyone else. I was just thinking about yesterday and about him being stuck down that hole. Oh Heather, you should have seen his arm when we got him out.'

She touched his lips. 'Don't tell me.' She let her fingers stray up to wipe his cheeks.

'Losing his arm would be just the worst thing that could happen to him. When I met him, he was a professional fighter. A great fighter, and that means a lot to a man. It made Jimmy different. He felt very special.'

'And he could punch hard with his left hand?'

'Very hard. He had a terrific left hand.'

She touched his lips, drying a corner. 'Frankly, if he only used his left hand to punch people it doesn't sound like a great loss. It would have been different if he had been a great artist or a writer or a great musician or something like that, but not a boxer.'

'He was a great boxer.'

'There is no such thing. People who fight are uncouth.'

'That sounds like something a woman would say. Only I don't know what it means.' Adam tried to smile.

'Uncouth? Uncivilized. Rough. Not nice. Father had a man sacked for fighting once.'

'There's a difference between brawling and being a boxer.' He looked into Heather's eyes. They were bright blue and wide and lovely but he saw no sign of understanding. 'It might be hard for a woman, particularly someone like you, to know or understand how men think, but Heather, there are a lot of men who respect a good boxer. Not ruffians, but good men who think of boxing as a sport. It might be rough, but it *is* a sport and it requires skill.' He was speaking slowly, trying to find the right words. 'Jimmy had a lot of skill. He was a marvel, and because he was so good in such a tough sport, he got a lot of respect.'

She was looking down.

'Heather, he's an aboriginal. He comes from a tribe who live in a creek bed and get spat on and beaten by white men and no one says anything because they think that's normal. Black people get no respect. Some people treat them worse than dogs.' Adam stood up and wiped his face roughly. 'Jimmy was *respected* by white men.'

'Because he could hurt people?' She was still looking down.

'Oh, Heather, there's so much you don't know! Life can be very tough for a lot of people but it's toughest of all for aborigines. I've known a lot of them. I've lived with them, eaten with them. I used to play with black kids when I was a kid. I've known some fine blacks, but most of them never get a chance. Sometimes, there's nothing they can do but fight. That's what Jimmy did.'

'He could have got a job.'

'Where?'

'Wherever it is that black people work.'

'On the railways? Would your father give a bloke like Jimmy a job?'

'I've never met Jimmy. I wouldn't know.' She was studying her fingernails.

'Would your father give a blackfellow a job?'

She looked up and smiled. 'Oh, Adam, don't be so serious.'

'Would he?'

'You really are very strange sometimes. But let me see. Would my father give an aboriginal a job? No, I don't think he would, but it's not because they're black or anything like that. It's just because they're so filthy. You know, their noses are always running and they're covered in dirt.'

'I wonder how your father would look if he had no money, he had no handkerchief, and he had to live in a dry creek bed.'

'Oh Adam, what a ridiculous thought! My father would simply not live in a creek bed. Can you imagine what mother would say?' She considered that thought and smiled, but it was a private smile, nourished by intimate knowledge of the way her parents behaved, and not to be shared outside the family. 'Really, that's just too ridiculous, Adam!'

She brushed a thread from the front of his shirt. 'Now, I'm not going to take any notice of this silly conversation because I know you're still tired and upset after all that's happened. And you're hurt. You should be lying down. You're still in shock. I know all about first aid because my father taught me. Shock is what you get after an accident, and you don't even know you've got it. It can be very dangerous. Now, I think you should have some tea and some of mother's scones and then go back to your place and have a good lie down.'

Adam went to the hospital the next morning. He was told Jimmy had regained consciousness in Dubbo Base Hospital, and was in a serious but stable condition and was expected to recover. He had severe concussion, three broken ribs, a broken kneecap, several deep cuts and massive bruising to the body. His left arm had been amputated above the elbow.

FOUR

Adam saw Jimmy a week later, when he and Josef drove down in the truck. They left on Saturday and drove back on Sunday but it was a miserable trip that accomplished little. Jimmy was still heavily drugged and slept all the time they were there. They sat by his bed, feeling a little sick because of the strange ether-like smells, and they looked at each other and they looked at Jimmy and the great lumpy bandage that was where his lower left arm should have been and, in the end, were glad that he did not wake because they wouldn't have known what to say.

On the way back to Nyngan, the truck hit a kangaroo and broke a headlight.

The drought and the Depression were getting worse and work was scarce. They got a few jobs – some through sympathy, for the news of the disaster and rescue at Joe Cooper's place had spread through the district – but the jobs were small and the pay trifling. The only job of any consequence took them out of town for four days. When they returned, Josef found a letter waiting for him. It was from his mother. It was the first letter he had received since leaving Coober Pedy, and the first since he had grown into a man. He was now twenty years of age and tall and wiry. He was also that strange mix of man and boy that some twenty-year-olds are, with a body that had outdistanced his mind.

'I gave her your address,' he told Adam. 'I hope you don't mind.'

Josef was living at the Currans' too. He and Adam had beds on the back verandah. Josef walked down one wooden step and stood poised above the expanse of dust that masqueraded as the Currans' back yard.

'They've given up opal-mining and gone back to Adelaide. My last letter took five weeks to reach them.'

'How are they?'

Josef didn't answer for a while. 'They've had a rotten life,' he said eventually.

'Is something wrong?'

'Anemone.'

'What about her?' Adam, who had been on his bed, stood up. 'What is it? Is she sick or something?'

'She died. Two years ago.'

'Oh, Joe, I'm sorry.'

'My sister's been dead for two years and I didn't know. All this time and I didn't know.'

'It's awful news.'

'I don't feel anything.'

'It's such a shock.'

'No. It's not that. I just don't feel anything. I haven't seen her for so long. I don't feel sad. I don't feel happy. I just feel nothing.'

Adam could remember the little girl on her father's lap. 'What happened?'

'She got sick. They don't know what it was. She got a fever of some sort and died. Just like that.'

'I don't know what to say, Joe. She was nice.'

'No, she wasn't. I didn't like her.'

'Don't say that.'

'It's true. She was always telling on me and trying to get me into trouble.'

'All brothers and sisters do that.'

'How would you know? You haven't got any brothers and sisters.'

Josef sat on the step and covered his head.

'Do you want to go home and see your parents?' Adam said, touching him on the shoulder. Josef brushed the hand clear.

'For Christ's sake, it happened two years ago. They've got over it.'

Adam was going to speak but then said nothing. When Josef had an outburst, it was wiser to keep quiet and let him get over it.

286

His eyes scanned the back yard where Curran's fox terrier was burrowing near the far fence, but his mind was back in South Australia. Why did the worst things happen to the best people? When he thought it was time to speak, he said, 'You haven't seen them for a long time.'

'Tough luck.'

Adam sidestepped Josef and walked towards the dog. He threw a small stick at it. Curran would belt the dog if he saw it digging in his yard.

'What are your parents doing in Adelaide?' Adam said softly, not turning.

'Father's gone back to the old business, wine,' Josef said, and suddenly wanted to talk. 'They're not really in Adelaide. They're at Nurioopta. It's out of the city. Our old place was about twenty miles away. That's the place we had to leave. Father had his own winery but we were forced to quite. You know the story. We were Germans. Huns. Krauts.' A stick flicked past Adam and he turned to see that Josef had also taken a pot shot at the dog, which had resumed its digging. The stick missed and the dog kept digging. Josef searched for something more substantial. He found a lump of earth and threw it but missed. He was not good at throwing things. 'They lost everything at bloody Coober Pedy,' he said, searching for another missile. 'Their money, their bus, and their little girl. Do you know she died on her birthday?'

Adam shook his head. 'What will you do?'

'I won't go home.'

'Will you write?'

'Probably. I don't know what to say.'

'I'd like to write too. Would you help me with a letter?'

'Sure. You tell me what I should say, I'll help you write.'

'Why won't you go home?'

Josef picked up another lump of earth and flung it at the dog. The dirt exploded against the fence and the dog scurried to safety. 'Stupid mongrel,' he said. 'George will catch him at it one day and nail his hide to the palings.' He dusted his hands. 'I don't want to go home until I've done something. Something important. Can you understand that?'

'Of course. What do you want to do?'

'I don't know. Maybe have my own place.'

'Like a station?'

'Something. It needn't be a sheep station. I just want to own

287

something. To be someone. Like you.' He threw another piece of earth, not at the dog for the dog had gone, but just to throw something.

Adam laughed. 'I'm not anyone.'

'Yes, you are. You've got your own business. People think a lot of you. I don't want to go back home until I've done something. There's no point in going back and saying: "Well, here I am, folks. I've been away all these years and I've wandered the outback and I've grown older and I'm taller but I haven't *done* anything!" There's no point to that.'

'They'd like to see you.'

'And I'd like to see them. But I'm not going back. Not until I've accomplished something. Not until I can say, "Here I am. Look what I've done." '

'That could take a long time. You've just got to look around you to see how tough things are at the moment.'

'I know. I'm still not going back.'

'Parents don't live forever.'

Josef glanced at him. He returned to the step. 'Father wants me to join him in the winery. He says there's a job there if I want it.'

'Do you know anything about making wine?'

'I used to help father. But what's the point? People don't drink wine in this country. Not enough of it, anyway, to make it worth while. My father used to make excellent wines and people used to call it plonk. They think wine's some sort of cheap and nasty drink you have when you want to get drunk and can't afford beer or whisky.'

'I've never tried it.'

'You've never drunk, have you?'

'I saw too many drunks when I was young. Besides, I promised my dad.'

'But that was years ago, and you were only a kid.'

'Doesn't matter. A promise is a promise.' The dog came back and trotted a wary semi-circle to keep clear of them. Its face was split by the nervous smile of fox terriers and its tongue dripped, and when Adam moved to scratch himself the dog darted to one side.

'Well, I haven't made any promises to my parents,' Josef said. 'Only to myself, and that's to *do* something with my life.'

'I'd like my own property one day.'

'I know. Maybe we could share a place.'

'Why not?'

'I'm serious, Adam.'

'So am I.'

'Really?' Josef's foot was resting on the dirt and he drew a circle with his toe, as though defining the boundaries of their lands. 'I haven't got much money.'

'Neither have I.'

'But if you sold your business you'd probably have enough for a deposit. Then you could borrow and pay it off from the profits.'

'What profits?'

'We'd make money. We'd the run the best station in the country. Only I don't have any money, so what am I talking about?'

'You could have a share and pay for it as we went.'

Josef carefully erased the circle he had scribed in the dust. 'There's good land going in the west. I've been reading the ads in *Country Life*. Some of it's very cheap.'

'Where?' Adam was thinking of land he'd seen west of Nyngan. He didn't know any was for sale.

'I saw one block of over a hundred thousand acres that could be bought for a deposit of a thousand pounds.'

'Where?'

'Somewhere called Cobargo.'

'Where's that?'

'I'm not sure exactly. Somewhere near Perth.'

'You mean Western Australia? Jesus, Joe that's on the other side of the country.'

'It's good land, though.'

'I think I'd better make a bit more money before we talk about such things.'

'But you did mean what you said? About sharing a property?'

'Sure.'

'I'd only want a small share. That would be fair. Just a little, so's I could feel I owned something.'

'Would you go back and see your parents then?'

Josef nodded. 'I suppose so. I'm still a bit frightened of my father. That's silly, isn't it? I bet I'm stronger than he is now, and I really don't care what he says about things any more, but I'm still frightened of him. He always preferred Anemone to me, you know.' He bent his head in thought. 'You know, I still can't believe it. I mean, I can't believe that she's dead, but because she died so long ago it's as though she never lived at all.'

As he had been talking, the fox terrier trotted towards him and Josef, absent-mindedly, extended his hand so the dog could see there was nothing within the palm. It came close. He scratched it behind the ear and it stayed, but then he lifted it and hugged it and held it so firmly to his chest that the animal struggled to get free.

One thing Tiger Miller had taught Adam was that disasters usually came in threes. Jimmy had lost his arm, Josef had learned of the death of his sister, and Adam wondered what the third item on this sorry list might be. He found out a few weeks later when he went to visit Heather.

She was in tears. He had never seen her cry before and at first he was frightened he had done something wrong. He was still in awe of her and conscious of her better education and easy grasp of social ways and it seemed he was often saying something – or not doing something – that marked the distinction between them and emphasized his vulgarity. But this was different. She took him into the garden, weeping and wiping her eyes in a useless attempt to stop the flow and told him her father was dying. He had been to see a specialist in Sydney and had returned yesterday and told his family.

Adam took her in his arms. She was shaking and he felt a little ashamed because he liked the feeling of holding her and comforting her and of being the strong one; it was normally she who was in control. He waited for the sobbing to ease.

'What's wrong with him?' he asked.

She put her head against his chest. 'It's too awful to say.'

Adam had known men to die of awful things, from cut throats to venereal disease. He knew Hector Maguire hadn't slashed his throat and could not imagine such a man with VD.

'Is it some sort of illness?' he said, and felt her withdraw a little.

'Of course it is. Oh Adam, sometimes you say the most inane things! If someone's dying, he has to be dying of something. People don't just get told by their doctor that they've got only a few months to live if there's nothing wrong with them.' She turned from him.

'I didn't mean that,' he said, not knowing what he had meant. 'I mean, is it something like TB or cancer or is it something else? I knew a fellow in the bush who died because he'd been gassed in the war.'

'My father didn't go to the war and he would never get something like TB. The doctors say he has cancer.' She whispered the word.

Adam pulled her back to him. He knew about cancer. Old Tiger had died of it.

'I'm sorry. How long does he have?'

'Maybe six months. Oh, Adam, why is life so unfair? Why him? Why does he have to die? Why couldn't it have happened to someone else?'

'I don't know. It always seems to happen to the wrong people. I told you about Josef's young sister?'

Her head bobbed against his breast. 'That was different. She was young and she lived in that God-forsaken place. A lot of children die in the bush. This is ... well, this is just the most awful news I've had in my whole life.'

'Is it cancer of the throat?'

Her back was arched and she looked up at him. 'No. Why?'

'I knew a man who had cancer of the throat.'

'You've known a lot of people who've died.'

'Yes.'

'I'm sorry. That sounded shallow of me.'

'It's all right. I *have* known a lot of people who've died. How is your mother?'

'Distraught. She is totally dependent on father. Goodness knows what she'll do. She may have to go to Parramatta and stay with her sister.'

Adam was alarmed. 'Why?'

'Well, she can't stay here.'

'But it's your home.'

She turned her back and pressed her shoulder-blades against him. 'We don't own this place. It belongs to the railways.'

'I thought it was yours.'

'No. We'll have to move as soon as ... They will want it for the new stationmaster. I hope he looks after the garden. It was my father's greatest joy.'

'It's beautiful.'

'Everything's dead.'

'They'll come back. They'll be lovely in the spring.'

'Why is it plants come back to life and humans don't? Why is life so unfair?'

The trees exuded a strong aroma of eucalyptus and peppermint.

Clouds of insects hovered in the branches. They stirred, fine as drifting vapour, as Adam took Heather by the elbow and began to walk through the garden.

'I don't know anyone who can explain it. The real problem is to live with it. I knew an Afghan camel driver who couldn't explain it but who could accept it better than anyone else I've ever known. His young nephew was killed by a wild camel and that really shook him up but he just got on with life. His wife had died and then his two young sons, all of separate illnesses. He said it was the will of Allah.'

'He sounds disgusting.'

'He was the most knowledgeable man I've ever met.'

'My, that is saying something!' She pursed her lips. 'Out of all the men of great intellect that you've met, you would rank him as the greatest? What did you say he was? A camel driver?'

'He was a remarkable man.'

'And more knowledgeable than anyone you've met, including my father.'

Oh, what have I said? Adam thought, and kept quiet.

'Honestly, Adam, I don't know why I'm so fond of you when you try to be so cruel to me. You know how intelligent my father is. You know how I feel about him. You know the dreadful news, and yet you could say something as hurtful and mean as that.'

Adam held back a branch so they could pass a bush.

'I wasn't comparing Saleem Benn with your father. I meant of all the men I've worked with. I spent months with him a few years ago. He was kind and very wise. That's all.'

She slowed so she walked a pace behind him.

'You should be more careful what you say. You're always saying strange things that embarrass or upset me. But I know you didn't mean it so I forgive you. When we are married you will have to pay a lot of attention to those things. Good conversation is the mark of a gentleman. I shall teach you.'

'Are we still going to get married? You said something about going to Parramatta.'

'I said mother might go there to stay with her sister.' She paused and Adam, recognizing her expression (which said, I have more to tell you) waited for her to continue.

'Mother and I discussed it last night. We were very upset, of course, but one has to be practical. The living must look after themselves. Isn't that right?'

292

'There's no one else to do it.' A cloud of insects flew from a bush and Adam shielded her face.

'Quite right,' she said, looking into his eyes. 'So mother thought it better that you and I get married soon.'

'You've told her we want to get engaged?'

'Yes. Oh, Adam, it's all right. She'll do what I want. But last night mother was very practical. She said a number of things that made a good deal of sense and while some of them might sound ... well, a little indelicate at the moment, they have to be said.' She clasped her hands in front of her hips and looked at them as she walked. 'First is the question of money. We have very little and it will be hard for two of us to live on the little father will leave. It would be simpler if we were supported by ... well, someone else. Oh, Adam, does this sound all too horrible?'

'No, it sounds sensible.'

Her head nodded in agreement. 'Then there's the question of accommodation. Mother does not get on well with her sister but there is a room for her in that house. But it's only a room for one. She could stay there, but I could not.'

'Where would you stay?'

'Oh, you are exasperating! With you, of course. We would be married. And we should be married soon, while father is ... well, while he's well and able to come to the wedding, because mother says he would want to see his daughter married before he goes.'

'What does he say?'

'Well, I'm sure he would want that, so we would have to get married soon. And it would have to be in Dubbo because I would just die if we had to use that tiny little church here. Besides, the minister's such a bore, and father won't be up to travelling soon, so we will have to have the wedding within three months.'

'I haven't saved a lot of money yet,' he said, worried by the pace of developments. 'You wanted a good engagement ring from some fancy jeweller.'

'Something simple will do. Mother got a better ring after they'd been married a long time. It was such a sweet thing for father to do. We could do the same.'

'Where would we live?'

She took his hand but looked at her feet. 'Do you know the Mulrays' place, the one with the lovely big verandah? Well, they're leaving and it will be vacant.'

'I couldn't afford to buy that.'

'You don't have to buy it, silly! The Mulrays rent it. It will be available for thirty-five shillings a week.'

Adam had seen the house. It was on the edge of town and had a stand of gum trees in the front yard.

'It's big,' he said, trying to imagine whether there would be room for his truck and equipment out the back.

'That's just it,' she said. 'It's very spacious. It has four bedrooms and a lovely big living-room where you could give parties. I was there when Rhonda Mulray turned twenty-one. The Mulrays are tedious bores but the house is big. No, it's huge, and it would be just perfect. There'd be room for us and for mother and space left over for any friends we wanted to visit us. Just think, Adam. We'd have a big home and mother wouldn't have to leave town and live with Aunt Violet who is an absolute drip and Uncle Cecil who smokes cigars that *stink*.'

'It's all a bit of a rush.'

She stopped and her eyes seemed to grow larger and more intense. 'You do want to marry me?'

'Of course.'

She smiled and linked her arms gently around his neck and kissed him.

Josef was bursting with enthusiasm. He had been reading a newspaper and seen again the advertisement for the property in Western Australia. It was just what they wanted, he said. It was somewhere north of Perth. The advertisement showed a line drawing of the state, with Perth at the bottom with big buildings sketched in, and the property at the top with hills and a river and plenty of sheep. It was all drawn cartoon-style, and made the city and the property look like near neighbours.

'It sounds marvellous,' he said. 'There's a homestead and sheds and fenced paddocks and everything like that, and there's plenty of water. There's a river running through the station. A river! Can you imagine that?'

'I think I'm getting married, Joe.'

'You mean to Heather Maguire? I know that. You told me.'

'I mean soon.'

'How soon?'

'Real soon. Maybe in a few months.'

'What have you been up to?' Josef said, trying to look serious but losing the expression to a grin.

294

Adam blushed. 'It's not like that at all. Her father's sick. Very sick. In fact they don't think he's going to live much longer.'

The grin vanished.

'So the family thinks we should bring the wedding forward while Mr Maguire is still well enough to attend.'

Josef frowned. 'I didn't know you'd got around to talking about wedding dates.'

'Well, we hadn't really. This just sort of changed things.'

Josef shrugged. 'Take Heather to the west with you.'

'She wants to stay here. It's because of her mother. She'd have nowhere to live after Mr Maguire passes on, and Heather wants her to stay with us.'

Josef studied the advertisement again. He closed the newspaper. 'Where would you live?'

'She thinks we could get the Mulrays' house. They're moving and it's going to be available.'

'But that's just a house, a place in town. I thought we were going to have a property somewhere?'

'One day, yes.'

'But if you buy that now you'd never be able to afford anything else. You can't make money from a house in town. You can't *do* anything there.'

'I wouldn't buy it. I'd rent it.'

'That's worse! That's just giving someone else your money.'

'Well, it's what Heather wants.'

Josef walked a few paces. He spoke without looking at Adam. 'I don't know if I like the sound of this Heather of yours.'

'Why? Because she wants to live here in town?'

'Not just that. She seems to be changing you. Turning you into a real domestic cat.'

Adam laughed.

'No, it's true, Adam. You're changing. You're doing things *she* wants to do, not things you want to do.'

'That's all right. I like the things she wants to do.'

'Yeah, but you'll end up a real hen-pecked husband, I reckon. She'll tell you what to do and you'll jump.'

'You've never even met her.'

'I know, and I know you say she's beautiful and all that, but she's always telling you what you do wrong. She's not going to change.'

'That's just because she's so different to me. I'm as rough as

295

bags and she's gentle and refined. Joe, you must meet her. You'll like her.'

Josef still did not look at Adam. 'Yeah, I probably will. I just don't like the way she's changing you.'

'I think I *should* change. She's been helping me to read and write. She's so well educated and knows so much about people and the way to behave. She's so much more worldly than I am.'

'Bullshit. I'll bet she's like some of those little stuck-up tarts I used to know in Barossa Valley. Went to an expensive school and thought they knew everything. Had their noses so high in the air birds used to fly up their nostrils. But they didn't know anything about the world. Put them in the bush and they'd be dead in a week. You're the worldly one, Adam. You're a terrific bloke. Everyone says so. I don't want to see some stuck-up sheila changing you, and ruining you.'

'Don't call her a sheila. And she's not stuck up.'

'What is she, then?'

'She's refined.'

Josef grunted, not arguing the point but not accepting, either. 'Why does she want her mother to live with you?'

'She'd have nowhere else to live.'

'Jesus, Adam, I don't like the sound of that. Most men I've seen have trouble getting on with their wives let alone having to put up with the wife's mother, too.'

'Mrs Maguire would have nowhere else to live, except with a sister at Parramatta. They're going to lose the house when Mr Maguire dies.'

Josef looked puzzled.

'Well, let Heather's mother go to live with her sister.'

Adam shook his head.

'She doesn't want to. More important, I don't think Heather would marry me if her mother went away. I think she'd go too, to be close to her mother.'

'A woman's place is with her husband.'

Adam had been finding the conversation embarrassing because he had felt he was breaking an undertaking to Josef, but now he smiled. It was a genuine smile, not the twitch of the mouth that guilt orders to hide its presence.

'What are you laughing at?' Josef said.

'You. The expert on marriage.'

'You don't have to be married to know what's right and what's

296

wrong. And stop mocking me because I'm younger than you.'

'I'm not mocking you. You just sounded funny.'

'I don't know why. My mother used to say that. That's why she went to the opal fields. She didn't want to go. She tried to persuade father to stay down south. But when he decided to go, she went with him and didn't argue again or ever say "I told you so" when things went wrong because she said a woman should stick by her husband. She also said a man should never have to live with his wife's parents.'

Adam looked at him in surprise.

'Now why would you ever discuss anything like that? Don't tell me you were thinking of getting married when you were fourteen?'

'Don't be ridiculous! It's just that we used to talk about all sorts of things. Mother was trying to help us avoid problems, I suppose. When we were at the winery, we knew some people whose son got married and went to live with his wife's parents and mother told us what a mistake that would be. She said it never worked. She said young couples should be left on their own. She said mother-in-laws just couldn't stop interfering. She said if I ever got married, I should keep as far away from the bride's parents as possible.'

'A bit rough on the bride.'

'That's all part of marrying a man, I suppose. A woman has to suffer a bit. Anyhow, a man should let a woman know that he's in charge and that she has to do what he wants her to. No marriage ever works if the woman is too bossy.'

'Who said that? Your mother or you?'

Josef thought for a few moments. 'I'm not sure. It's what I think, anyhow.'

'Who was in charge at your place? Your father or your mother?'

'My father. I just told you.'

'Yes, but it seemed to me that your mother was good at getting her own way, and then making your father think the idea was his in the first place.'

'You mean she manipulated him?'

'I don't know if that's what I mean or not. What does that word mean?'

'Manipulate? To twist around your fingers, to make someone do what you want them to do. Do you really think mother did that?' He seemed genuinely surprised.

'Only in a nice way. Tell me, what happened to the man you knew in South Australia? Did his marriage work out?'

'I don't know. I hope not. He was one of the young men who threw rocks at our place. I hope his mother-in-law gives him hell.' Josef shuffled a few steps away from Adam and paused, deep in thought. He turned suddenly.

'Why don't we go to the west and you bring Heather and let her mother stay somewhere else?'

'I couldn't do that.'

Josef had been carrying the paper. He threw it down.

'Your lovely Heather wouldn't like it,' he shouted.

'Neither would I.'

'She wouldn't let you! That's what you mean.'

'I wouldn't want to.' Adam was shouting too, matching Josef's volume.

'Why? For Christ's sake, why? I thought we had an agreement. I thought we were going to buy a place together.'

'We will.' Adam felt wretched, and all the noise had gone. 'We will, Joe. Only not straight away.'

'But when?'

'When I've got some money. When the time's right.'

'You mean when Heather lets you. When she wants you to go. She never will, you know. She sounds like a real town girl.'

'You don't know her, Joe.'

He neither answered nor looked at Adam.

'I know how much this means to you,' Adam said, picking up the paper and looking at the advertisement. He tried to form sounds from some of the simpler words.

Josef snatched the paper.

'Don't go on like that. You sound demented. If you want to learn to read, do it in private.' Josef, blinking from emotion, took a deep breath. It was the point at which friendships are sustained or broken; when a harsh word, longing to escape through lips loosened by anger, can cause irreparable damage. 'You don't know just how ...' he started to say and then halted, stopped by the shock on Adam's face. He sat on the verandah floor, crossed his knees and covered his head.

'Don't look like that,' he mumbled. 'I was only joking. You just looked funny.'

Adam sat on the step. 'It didn't sound like a joke.'

'Well, it was. I'm just not good at telling jokes.'

They sat there, each hurting.

'I didn't know Mr Maguire was going to get sick,' Adam said eventually.

'No.'

There.'

There was another long silence.

'Do you think we'll get a place one day?' Josef said.

Adam nodded.

'She won't let you. I'll bet she won't let you.'

FIVE

It was a brilliant night. The moon was high and, although not full, so bright that its radiance washed the heavens clear of faint stars. Adam walked towards the river, finding his way easily across the moonlit landscape and feeling cold, not because the night was cold but because it looked cold. The moon was a lump of ice, glowing and overpowering in its intense whiteness, and the sky around it was a frosty blue, giving it a strange mist-like quality, all soft and soupy and full of glowing colour, and it reached all the way from beyond the limits of his imagination to the ground he walked on. He stopped frequently and looked up and marvelled.

Normally the night sky had an inky blackness that suggested a limit, as though there were a curtain up there and the stars were merely tiny holes that let the light through. But tonight only the brightest stars were visible and then only as pale ghosts of themselves. The rest had vanished, bleached by the unnatural brilliance.

He looked at the moon and understood why some old-timers wouldn't stare at it. They said it drove men mad. Made them raving lunatics. He couldn't understand that. The moon was so bright and hypnotic that it compelled you to stare at it, just like a lantern draws insects to its glass and keeps them fluttering near its flame until they perish. He looked away.

Adam reached some trees near the Bogan and sat on a soft patch of grass and gazed at the sky once more, avoiding the moon but searching for familiar stars, just as he used to do when he was a small boy and his father was alive and the two of them spent a lot of time together camped in lonely places. Where were the twelve little stars, the ones clustered together like sheep on a distant hill? He could always see twelve, even on the hazy nights when his father could only count seven or eight no matter how he tried and how much he peered through wrinkled eyes or even closed one eye because his right eye was stronger than his left. But tonight Adam couldn't see any of the twelve.

It was as though the past had disappeared.

The scorpion was visible but faint. Some of its tail was missing. He searched for Orion, but it was difficult to see because it was near the moon, right at the top of the sky. He loved Orion. His father used to show it to him and always point out the same things because the stars had been Adam's story books and he used to love to hear the same stories. The constellation was named after a legendary hunter and had two rows of stars arranged in straight lines. They were easy to distinguish in the heaven's jumble of lights and that was another reason Adam had loved Orion. He could always find those two distinctive rows of stars. One was supposed to represent the hunter's belt and the other his sword. As a youngster he had tried to imagine what Orion himself might have looked like but that was difficult because the figure was upside down with his head on the bottom, and because there were just odd stars to suggest the rest of the outline. His father had explained it to him, tracing a finger across the sky to fill the gaps in the line of stars and in Adam's imagination.

Many times in the last sixteen years he had wished his father were still alive. He had felt most strongly about it when he was young, of course, because then he had been lonely and frightened. Since then he had become used to fending for himself, but tonight he felt young again. He felt lonely and vulnerable and in need of advice from some older and wiser person.

He looked for the Southern Cross. Four stars like a kite with the fifth one hard to distinguish on such a bright night. The kite was lying on its side, with the two pointers below it. Draw a line from the top to the bottom of the kite and then draw another line through the pointers, and where the two lines meet is south. His eyes drew the lines. Curious that they should meet in such a deserted patch of sky. All the stars rolled around that point. He'd often spend nights watching sheep or cattle while the heavens slowly revolved around that point, as though the sky was on an axle and that was where the axle was set on a system of heavenly bearings. He didn't know why the stars did that but they did. They all spun around that point. In a few hours the Southern Cross would be higher and the moon and Orion would be lower, much closer to the western horizon, and by the dawn the moon and Orion would have gone and the Southern Cross would be over the other side of the sky and the kite would be pointing south from the other direction. If he could read, he would get a book that explained why that happened. Saleem Benn didn't know. He'd said it was the way Allah had ordained things but he always said that when he couldn't explain something.

He thought about Josef. Tall, gangling, serious, profane, dependent, dependable Josef. He thought about their argument earlier that evening and the memory stung. They'd had arguments before, particularly when Josef was just a boy and they'd been roaming the outback. Most of those arguments had been because Josef was like a younger brother. No, more like a son with Adam like the father, and there had been disputes when he had tried to guide the boy. Most of the time Josef had been content to follow, happy to imitate Adam, but there'd been occasions when he had rebelled and then they'd argued. Adam had always felt he had been right. He might have been bumbling in what he tried to say or do and he had not always been successful (like trying to stop Josef imitating others and using coarse language, but he had done that because he thought it made him sound older than he was), but always Adam had been sincere and convinced that what he was saying was correct, and convinced that his own motives were sound. Tonight had been different. Adam felt he had been wrong.

He wasn't sure why. Certainly, there was the fact that he had disappointed Josef about he property but that wasn't really going back on a promise. He still intended to have his own place one day and he would like Josef to be involved with him. He could understand why Josef thought renting a house in Nyngan would delay things; maybe it would, but a few more years of business experience and making money would mean they could buy a better place. Unless prices went up. Was that what was worrying him? Why he felt guilty? Because he should be acting now, while prices were at rock bottom? No. There was no guarantee values wouldn't plunge even more. But it wasn't that. It wasn't timing or price or even disappointing Joe. It was what he had said about Heather. And about him.

301

Maybe she *was* changing him, turning him into ... what was it Joe called it ... a pet cat?

That was what hurt. The accusation. And the feeling that it might be true.

He was proud of his strength and his ability to show others he was stronger than them and tougher than them. Not silly about it, but just keen to prove he was a man. His father had been like that. He would carry two cement bags rather than one, if lifting one bag was all that the average man could handle. A fellow was still judged by what he could do in a physical way rather than by what he could avoid doing. So he was strong, and proud of it, and he was resourceful. He could do almost any job and if he didn't know how, he would work it out for himself. He was a natural leader, too. Even older men looked to him for orders and did what he said. And he was used to responsibility. That didn't worry him like it did some men. With work, or when mixing with men, he had little trouble in deciding what was best and what he should do.

With Heather, it was different. With her, he felt crude and conscious of his poor education – of his total lack of formal learning – and so he let her talk and did the things she wanted to do. He liked the things she did, and liked the way she did them. He was entranced by her. She was the most beautiful, the most delicate, the most refined creature he had ever met, and if she suggested what he should do then that was fine. He took pleasure in pleasing her by doing what she preferred him to do. That made her happy and it made him feel good. It also made him feel strong because, being more powerful than she in a physical sense, he gained a feeling of strength by submitting to her. It gave him a sense of ... well, he didn't know what the word was but he felt like some great and powerful horse that has a child on its back and behaves gently and responds to the reins, giving the child great pleasure and a feeling of power, when all the time the horse was the one truly in control. That's how he felt. He enjoyed submitting because he wanted to please Heather.

He felt certain she understood and, deep down, respected him for it. What worried him was that other people, like Joe, perceived his behaviour as weakness or, at least, changed character. He didn't want that. What he did with Heather was private. A game, if you like, between two lovers in which both know it's a game and enjoy the pretence but, deep down, know how things truly are and love the other person all the more for knowing and understanding

302

and yet still pretending.

And yet Josef had put doubt in his mind, particularly about the wedding. He'd heard about girls whose only desire seemed to be to get engaged and get married, as though those were the main goals in a female's life. He knew that was silly, having seen too many women who had endured the harsh realities of married life – living in squalid huts, having more children than they could handle or afford, and growing worn and lined from years of hard, unending labour – to have any glamorous misconceptions. Marriage was living and laughing and suffering together. A wedding was just a pleasant way to start it off, not the prime objective of a woman's life.

Yet some women felt that way. He was sure Heather was different. She was too well educated, too poised, too worldly-wise to be deluded like that.

Orion had moved. Had he slept for a while?

The sky didn't seem so bright now, although it was still filled with that mist-like phosphorence. He could see a few more stars. Maybe his eyes were becoming accustomed to the night.

Heather's eyes were incredible. Sometimes they glowed with that same misty, unfathomable blue that filled the sky on this miraculous night. He loved her eyes. They inspired him to do things and yet melted him to a contented placidity. They were extraordinary eyes, full of flashing fire one moment and deep and mysterious the next, and at other times as misty and innocent as a tiny child's, begging him to protect her and inspiring him to please her.

He laughed at himself. You sound lovesick, he thought. It was a pleasant sickness, very different from the way he had felt about Nellie. If that had been love, it was very much because she had been his first woman and everything had been so new, so startling, so exciting.

He was now a grown man. He was different. He was more in control of himself.

Even so he was not comfortable with women. He had known so few that he was not sure how to behave in their presence. The average bushman he had met seemed to have two attitudes to women. They put some on pedestals. If a man was out droving and away from civilization for months at a time he would talk about his mother or sister or maybe his wife as though she were

303

some sort of saint, someone you treated very specially, someone you never swore in front of or were impolite to. Then there were the other women, the ones they met on the way at some remote station or pub. The men treated them badly, specially if they were black or had a touch of colour. He'd known men who would read the bible and talk in whispered awe about their mother and say quite seriously that they would shoot any man who touched their sister (even if they hadn't seen their sister in years), who would then give a half-bottle of rum to an old black man in exchange for a few nights with his gin or his daughter or both. Such men thought that was normal. There were two standards: one you applied to the women who weren't there and who represented all that was supposed to be good, and another to the women who were there and available.

Well, he didn't have two standards. He had never got drunk and traded rum for a black woman. He would never make love to a woman he didn't have some feeling for. In fact, he hadn't been with another woman since Nellie, and surprisingly, he hadn't suffered much from it. That was probably because he worked so hard, and when you're worn out at the end of a day you haven't got the energy for other things.

He and Heather had never touched each other, except on the hands or face, although she sometimes stroked his chest – over his shirt, of course – and did it in a way that excited him. He wondered what she would be like when they were married. How would she make love? Wildly and wantonly like Nellie? No, probably not, although he'd heard men say you could never tell with women. Heather would be soft and gentle and warm.

There were some clouds in the sky, down low to the east.

Many times he had thought about Nellie. He would close his eyes and imagine her arms around him with his head bent into the fold in her neck and her body drawing him into her. She had been slim and electrifying to touch, and impossible to resist when she was wet and naked. Brazen, of course, but lovely, like some lithe animal.

Those had been the only difficult nights in the last five years or so, when he had thought of Nellie like that. He used to feel ashamed because he'd heard that to think like that was sinful. Even so, he thought like that. When he worried about it, he tried to rationalize it by reminding himself that she had been his first and only companion in love-making. He knew, of course, that

Nellie could not be typical of all women ... certainly not of refined young ladies. She was practised in the art. He still found that difficult to think about; that she had once worked in a brothel and earned her living doing something like that with any man who had the money.

Think of Heather! So he thought of her and tried to think pure thoughts, but he kept imagining her without clothes, and pictured himself washing her, slowly and lovingly, with water from a hand basin. She had a lovely body, very white with slender arm and legs and soft shoulders and ...

He should be going back to town and get to bed. He and Joe had a job laying pipe and they'd have to leave early. He walked back slowly relishing the night. Orion was heading for the western horizon, upside down as always.

'You understand I would have preferred Heather to have waited a few more years?'

Adam nodded. 'Of course, Mrs Maguire.'

'And that both Mr Maguire and I would have preferred her choice of young man to have been ... well, shall we say a little more established in his position, to ensure that he could give our daughter the things a person of her position has a right to expect.'

Heather, sitting beside her mother, leaned forward to grasp Mrs Maguire's outstretched hand.

'However, Adam, we all adore you. I want you to understand that.'

'Thank you.'

'Not at all, dear boy. It's just that this dreadful news concerning my poor husband has forced us to re-examine our whole future. It does change everything.' She reached for her handkerchief and covered her face.

'There, mother,' Heather said. 'Father's being very brave. You must be too.'

'I was thinking about the house,' Mrs Maguire said, her voice muffled by the handkerchief. 'We'll have to leave this beautiful place. Life can be so cruel. The finest garden in the district and we're being thrown out.'

She removed the handkerchief and hid it in the folds of her sleeve.

'You have been very gallant, Adam. Offering to look after me, when others would throw me out, is the act of a true gentleman.

Heather told me of your kind offer. The Mulray house won't be the same as this, will it?' She looked at the ceiling as though expecting a comforting answer. 'But beggars can't be choosers and you have done a very noble thing. Thank you.'

Adam nodded. He didn't know what to say. He was embarrassed to see Mrs Maguire cry and left the house as soon as he could.

Josef was on the back verandah at Curran's. He had been out.

'Guess what?' he said. 'I was talking to some of the fellers in the café and they reckon the Maguires owe money left, right and centre.'

'What do you mean?'

'Old Maguire's stone broke. He gets the house for next to nothing, he has one of his men do the yard, and yet still hasn't got a zac to bless himself with. He owes for the groceries, has a big bill at the hardware store, and most of the letters he gets are from people wanting their money. Particularly people who've sent fancy clothes COD to that lah-dee-dah wife of his. And for Heather.'

'Is that what they're saying?'

'Yes. Everyone reckons it's true.'

Adam sat on his bed and removed his boots.

'The poor bloke's not even dead yet and people are trying to tear him apart. Dreadful, isn't it?'

Adam and Heather were married ten weeks later. She looked lovely in a gown whose train spread wider than the aisle, and Adam stood erect but uncomfortable in a rented suit. Mr Maguire had to be helped into the church. His face was gaunt and as grey as the tie he wore and he breathed heavily and noisily all through the service. Jimmy Kettle was there too, having been discharged from hospital a month before the wedding. Adam, who had asked Josef to be his best man, wanted Jimmy to sit in the front row of the church, but Jimmy had taken his place in a corner at the back, well out of the way. Even so, people stared at him. He was thin and wore a borrowed coat with the left sleeve tucked into the pocket.

SIX

Adam and Heather went to Sydney for their honeymoon. The journey had an awkward start. The train did not leave until the morning after the wedding and so they stopped in a hotel in Dubbo. Mr and Mrs Maguire were in the next room. Mr Maguire was sick for much of the night so Heather spent most of the time in his room, talking to him and giving him medicine and comforting her mother. Adam could hear them. He could not sleep and, in the end sat on the hotel's wide verandah and saw the milkmen and the street sweepers scurrying before dawn.

They travelled to Sydney with Heather's aunt and uncle who had been guests at the wedding and stayed with them that night in their home at Parramatta. It was a large house, made of sombre brick and roofed with red tiles and with paths and gardens edged with concrete painted white. It was on a hill near a cemetery. That day it rained and Adam, carrying the bags from the train to the taxi and from the taxi to the house, was soaked to the skin. He had to carry everyone's bags because Heather's uncle had been told by his doctor that he should not lift weights, and he had to pay for the taxi too, because everyone else had run into the house. Even the uncle, who seemed to move remarkably well.

There was only one spare bedroom in the house and that had only one small bed in it, so Heather slept in it and Adam was put to rest on an old and musty couch in the junk room. The aunt's Persian cat slept on his feet. By now Adam had a small cold and a large dose of frustration. He had hoped to be alone with his wife but when the cat jumped on the bed he laughed and made so much noise that the aunt came to see if he was all right. She stroked the cat and made a fuss of it and then put it back on Adam's feet.

She whispered goodnight and asked him to be quiet because her husband was a light sleeper and went back to her room.

Adam stroked the cat for a while. He had not seen a Persian before. It pressed its head hard against his body.

He waited, listening for the sound of slippered feet creeping to his room. He could not go to Heather because she was next to the main bedroom and his arrival and any subsequent activity would

307

wake the others. So he tried to stay awake and gazed longingly and expectantly for a shadow to appear in the doorway.

She did not come and eventually he tired and fell asleep.

The next day, Heather telephoned a girlfriend who had been to the same school and she visited them for morning tea. She had prominent teeth but wealthy parents, for she was driven there and collected two hours later. The car was a big black La Salle. Adam would have liked to examine it more closely but the car left immediately and it soon became obvious that the examination was intended for him. The girl with the prominent teeth kept looking at him. Sometimes her stares were open, sometimes they were furtive, but she always looked at him even when she seemed to be engaged in deep conversation with Heather. He felt uncomfortable, like a stud bull when a potential buyer arrives. The girl drank some tea and ate a lot of scones and left in the black La Salle.

Because he had neither money nor time to spare for a long honeymoon, Adam had booked them into a hotel at Manly for five nights. He had never been to Sydney, never seen surf and, of course, never slept with Heather. The combination of so many unknown attractions appealed to him.

They travelled by taxi to the Parramatta railway station, by train to Central, by tram to Circular Quay, and by ferry to Manly. ('Seven miles from Sydney and a thousand miles from care,' as the sign on the ferry said.)

Adam had never seen so many people or so many houses, so many of which looked so much alike. He had never seen such tall buildings as he found in Sydney itself, nor travelled in a tram or a ferry.

He had only once seen ships, and that was in the narrowing waters of Port Augusta. Never had he seen such big ships, from glistening ocean liners to dank coastal freighters, as he saw from the ferry. He had seen old paddle steamers rotting on the Darling but he had never seen anything like the yachts that heeled behind straining sails or the cruisers and small powered boats that bobbed in the wake of the ferry. The new Sydney Harbour Bridge, grey and arched and massive, stunned him. It was so many times bigger than anything he had seen, (absolutely dwarfing the long rail bridge over the Bogan at Nyngan) that he just looked at Heather and grinned.

308

'I wish Jimmy and Josef could see this!' Adam said and Heather smiled. She had been to the city before. She would like to live in Sydney one day. Strathfield was nice. Not Parramatta where her aunt lived. That was too hot. Nor around the harbour. That would be beautiful, of course, but property was very expensive and there seemed to be a great number of Jews living there. One of her school friends came from Strathfield and her parents had a big brick house in a garden full of English trees. There were other big houses all around. It would be a good place to live. A nice address. Conservative, with the proper sort of neighbours, and good gardens. She liked a good garden.

The weather was fine and they were sitting outside, on a long varnished wooden seat that followed the sweep of the hull. They were on the lower deck, near the entrance way where a length of rope, thicker than any Adam had seen, was coiled neatly on the scrubbed timbers. They had not gone up to the top deck, where the view promised to be even better, because of their bags. They were near the water, which creamed and hissed below their elbows. The sun sparkled on the waves and the wind touched their faces, bearing an occasional fleck of foam, and from somewhere deep within the hull the ferry's big engines thumped and sent shivers of power through the deck.

The ferry steamed past a small stone fortress on an island. Two men and a boy were fishing from one of its sandstone parapets. The boy waved.

'Fort Denison,' a man said. He was sitting near Adam. He was an old man with bulging goldfish eyes. He was wearing a hat and a suit with waistcoat, but with no collar on his shirt.

Adam smiled his acknowledgement.

'Used to be known as Pinchgut,' the man said. 'That's because the old convicts who used to be kept there got so little to eat. You from the bush?'

Adam nodded and Heather looked the other way.

'Thought so. Whereabouts?'

'Nyngan.'

'Things crook out there?'

'Pretty crook.'

'Yeah. Crook here too. Crook everywhere. Still, it's a nice day. I come from Lismore.'

'Oh.' There was no recognition in the response.

'It's up north. Dairy farms. Down for long?'

'About a week.'

The old man looked at Heather's billowy hair and at Adam's tanned and innocent face, and smiled.

Adam turned back towards the fort. One of the men had caught a fish.

'Why did they build a place like that in the middle of the harbour?'

'The fort? To defend Sydney against the Russians.' The old man laughed and his eyes bulged a little more. 'Been all right if they'd only sent small ships, eh?'

'I suppose so.'

'You in sheep?'

'No.'

'I hear things are crook with wool.'

Heather pulled Adam's arm. 'Look at the lovely houses,' she whispered as though the message were too important to be overheard by others. Tall houses, some white and some red brick and all with lawns sweeping down to the rocks that edged the harbour, were drifting by.

'The harbour's better on a Saturday,' the old man said.

'Oh, can you imagine what it would be like living there,' Heather said, still softly so that only Adam could hear.

'Expensive,' Adam said and she squeezed his arm.

'They have a lot of races,' the old man said.

'What of?' Adam said, without looking at him.

'Sailing boats. The sails are very colourful.'

'Don't speak to him,' she whispered.

'There are hundreds of them. It's a marvellous sight.'

'Look at that one with the turrets on the roof,' she said.

Adam nodded. It seemed to satisfy everyone. He had heard music, imagining it came from a gramophone, but suddenly the sound swelled and three men stepped on to the deck. The first was playing a violin, the second had an accordion and the third carried a large wooden box with a slot in the top. The first two were playing 'Ain't She Sweet' and the third was keeping time by shaking the box.

They headed towards them. Adam was delighted. He turned to Heather, his face beaming and his hair dishevelled by a gust of wind.

'I didn't know we got music on the trip, too.'

'There are always musicians,' she said, trying to push his hair back into place with one hand and holding her own with the other.

'Isn't this wonderful?'

'Well, it's only the Manly ferry,' she said.

'I've never done anything like this before.'

'Don't speak so loudly. People will stare.'

The musicians had stopped in front of the old man. The man with the wooden box ceased shaking it and offered it to him. The old man put two pennies in the slot.

They moved on and the man with the violin beamed at Heather and launched into another chorus of the song. The man with the accordion stayed back, leaving room for his companion with the box to slip in front of Adam. He tilted the box so that the slot was more apparent.

'Give him some money,' Heather said, managing to speak without breaking the polite smile she was giving the violinist.

How much? Adam wondered. The old man had given two pennies but Adam could not find the comforting size of a penny in his pocket. All he had was a shilling.

The man with the box beamed as the shilling went in and the musicians went on.

Heather looked at a large house on a headland. 'Why did you give him so much?' she whispered.

'Because I'm a rich grazier.'

She turned. He was smiling ruefully.

'I didn't have anything else,' he said.

'You should have asked for change. Better still, ignored them.'

The old man heard. He smiled sympathetically at Adam.

The ferry rocked as it encountered the ocean swell rolling through the Heads, then eased to a gentle glide as it entered the smoother waters near Manly. The master let the ferry drift in to the wharf, then slowed in a flurry of water whipped by the forward propeller. Ropes snaked between the vessel and the wharf, boarding ramps rattled into place and Adam and Heather prepared to disembark.

The old man stayed where he was. 'I'm going back,' he explained. 'It costs just as much for one trip as for a dozen so I ride the ferry all day. Cheapest entertainment in Sydney.' He winked. 'Have a good honeymoon.'

Adam was worried about his supply of money. Already, everything seemed much more expensive than he had anticipated. He had budgeted for train fares and meals and the hotel but not

311

for taxis, trams, ferries and strolling musicians. He had come to Sydney thinking there would be one railway station, not dozens, and that everything they needed or wanted to see would be within easy distance. He knew Sydney was big but his imagination had created a picture of ten Nyngans. It seemed impossible that one town could be so big, or that so many people could live so close together. Already, he was not sure he liked it. He was fascinated by the harbour and its colour, by the noise of the place, and by the sight of masses of buildings and hundreds of people, but it unsettled him. He was not used to crowds, or to the furious pace at which people moved. And the cost! Why would people expect to be paid if they were just strolling around a ferry playing songs?

He felt bad about giving too much money. There were rules for behaviour in this place – what to do here, how much to pay there – and he didn't know them. They had to get to the hotel and he dreaded the thought of another tram ride or taxi fare. First, he had to learn where the hotel was located. Some men were fishing from the wharf near a sign that forbade fishing and one of them told him the hotel was only five minutes away. The man had a thin and bent cigarette in his mouth and it was stuck to his lower lip and bobbed as he talked. He did not look at Adam and seemed surprised that not everyone knew where the hotel was, but he seemed friendly enough.

Adam carried their two bags. They passed an enormous swimming pool with a wide boardwalk topping the pool's shark-proof fence and paused to watch some boys slide down a long slippery dip and splash into the water.

They entered the Corso, the short main street which linked Manly's harbour frontage with its ocean beach. They walked past cake shops and a jewellers, where Heather stopped to admire a tray of rings in the window. They passed a church and a milk bar and more shops and came to a road junction. On the far side a row of pine trees curved in a gentle crescent and beyond them was a path and a low stone wall and beyond that, the beach.

Although their hotel was to the left (they could see the sign) they crossed the road because Adam had never seen surf. They walked to the edge of the stone wall and gazed down on the beach.

It was much bigger than Adam had expected. He had seen beaches on rivers and had thought that an ocean beach would be something like the spits of sand that poked long tongues into the inner bend of a placid river. This was so long. It ran almost as far as he could see, from a headland a couple of hundred yards to his right near where some flags were fluttering and people were lying on the sand, to a headland far to the north, maybe a mile or more away. It was hard to tell because there was so much mist and spray hovering above the surf. The waves were breaking a long way from the beach. He could count three rows of breakers all the way around the curving beach. Four in some places.

'It's much noisier than I thought,' he said.

'We'll come back and look after we've checked in to the hotel,' Heather said.

'I thought we might rest for a while.' Adam looked at her expectantly.

'No. I feel like walking. I want to look at the shops first and then we can come back here.'

'I'm tired.'

'A walk will do you good. Make you wake up and feel better.'

They booked into their room. Adam had another shock when the porter who had insisted on carrying the bags hovered at the door, waiting for a tip. Having no coins, Adam shook the man's hand.

'That was a simply awful thing to do,' Heather said when Adam had closed the door, but her frown soon dissolved into a smile. 'Even so, it was very clever of you.' She moved forward and kissed him lightly on the cheek. 'You confused the wretch and that was much better than standing there and being embarrassed, as I would have been.'

She had moved away. Adam drew her back to him, and kissed her on the lips.

'What are you doing?' she said, pushing him away but not looking displeased.

'Kissing you.'

'I can see that. I mean why now?'

'Why not? There's been so little kissing I thought you might not remember what it's like.'

She raised her hands to keep him away. 'You must get some more change. It is very humiliating not having the right money.'

'It's very expensive when you do have it,' Adam said. 'This is the most expensive place I've ever been to.'

'This hotel?'

'Sydney. Everywhere you go it costs you money.'

'It's just the way things are down here. You'd soon get used to it. Don't you think it's exciting?'

'Maybe, but I don't think I could stand it for long.'

She moved to a window. They had a view across a row of red roofs. On the right, and partly obscured by a brick wall with a painted sign advertising Dr Morse's Indian Root Pills, was the row of pine trees that lined the beach.

'Isn't it lovely? Look at those trees, and can't you smell the sea? Oh Adam, it's so ... so exotic.'

'You're lovely.'

'Now be sensible. Wouldn't you like to live here?' She turned and placed her outstretched fingers on his chest. 'I mean one day.'

Adam pressed her hand more firmly against his body.

'I've hardly been alone with you since the wedding.'

'Nonsense,' she said lightly. 'We've been together all the time.'

'I mean like this, in our own room. On our own. The first night your father was sick and I hardly saw you and the second night I was in a room full of junk with your aunt's cat sleeping with me.'

'Well, we have plenty of time.' She pulled her hand away. 'Let's go and look at the shops.'

'I thought you might have come to see me.'

'What do you mean?'

'That night at your aunt's. I waited for you for such a long time. All I had was that blessed cat.'

'You expected me to creep through the house? Whatever for?'

'To be with me.'

'But I was with you all day. I have been with you all the time ever since.'

'You know what I mean.'

She pursed her lips. 'I'm not sure that I do.'

'Heather, don't you know what husbands and wives are supposed to do?'

'A husband is supposed to support his wife and honour her, and behave like a gentleman.' She kissed him on the cheek. 'Oh, you look so sad. Come on, let's go down the street. There were some lovely things in that shop on the corner near the church. I want to have another look at them.'

'I can't afford any more rings.'

'Silly. I don't want to buy one now. I just want to look.'

Adam sat on the bed. 'I don't want to look at rings or anything else. Not now. We've got the rest of the week to do those sort of

314

things. I just want to be with you.'

'I'm not sure I understand what you mean. But if you mean what I think you mean, I'm very disappointed in you.'

'What the hell does that mean?'

'There's no need to swear.'

'I wasn't swearing.' He stood and she retreated to the door, grasping the knob as though ready to make an escape. 'Oh, for heaven's sake, Heather, let's not get into one of your silly discussions about words.'

'Hell is not a polite word.'

'And what are you doing over there? You look as though you're frightened of me.'

'I think I am. When you're like you are, you terrify me.'

'Heather, I love you.'

She released her grip on the door knob.

'And I love you, which is why I married you.'

'Is it?'

'What does that mean?'

'Well, since we've been married you seem to have been doing your level best to keep away from me. Are you frightened of men or something?'

'That is a disgusting thing to say.'

'Well, you won't even kiss me.'

'Yes, I will. I have, many times. See, I'll do it again.' She darted past him kissing his forehead. She stopped at the window. 'It's getting cold. Oh please, let's go. There's time for this later.'

'When I said kiss, I meant a proper kiss.' Adam walked to the window and put his arms around her.

'Please. Someone will see.'

'I don't care.' He kissed her on the lips. He felt her pulling away and pressed harder.

'You're hurting me,' she gasped. 'Please, you're very strong. Let me go.'

'Kiss me back.'

'I have.'

'Properly.'

'You are being ridiculous!'

He increased the power of his embrace and she stepped back, stumbled and fell, dragging him with her. She fell across the bed. He landed on top of her, but retained his hold.

'Adam, stop it!' she gasped.

'Are you hurt?'

'No.'

'Then kiss me.'

She began to kick and Adam scissored her legs with his. She wriggled desperately and then tried to beat him with her fists. He was surprised at her strength but had no difficulty in restraining her. Eventually she stopped struggling and lay on the bed limp with her face turned away from his.

'I know what the word is for what you're trying to do,' she said, breathing with difficulty for Adam was still lying on top of her.

'I just want to love you.'

'It's called rape.'

'What's called rape?'

'What you want to do to me.'

He released her and sat on the edge of the bed.

'I'm sorry. I didn't mean to hurt you.'

'You were like an animal.' She crawled to the end of the bed and buried her face in a pillow. 'Men are vile. They are like animals sometimes. I know that, but I'm not ready to submit yet. I want our marriage to be pure and … and *nice* for as long as it can.'

Adam put his head in his hands.

'What are you talking about? How can it be vile if I love you?'

'That's not love. I've seen animals doing what you were trying to do. Dogs in the street and cattle in the stockyards at the railway station. That's not love. That's degrading and ugly.'

'I'm not a dog.'

'You were behaving like one.'

He turned to her. 'Heather, people do make love. It's a very natural thing. How do you think children are born? How do you think you came into this world?'

'Don't you dare bring my parents into this.'

'Every person on earth is here because some man and some woman made love. It's a very natural thing.'

'That's different. What you want to do is have … have sex, and that's dirty.'

'For God's sake, who said that?'

'Everyone, and don't take the Lord's name in vain.'

'Who's everyone?'

Her head was still in the pillow. She punched it a few times, to make it more comfortable. 'Mother warned me you might be like this. She said it was something women have had to put up with for ages. She said if it happened, I should just grit my teeth and wait till you'd finished and then go and have a good hot bath.'

'Your mother said that?' Adam walked to the window. He wondered what Dr Morse's Indian Root Pills were for.

'She did say even nice men can change. There's something in them that makes them behave like animals every now and then. But she said strong men can control themselves and behave properly. Some men take vows of chastity. I think that's very noble and ... well, pure. Men like priests.' She lifted her head and seeing him at the window, sat up. 'Although I'm not so sure about priests. Some of the girls at school told me they'd heard that priests were the worst of the lot. They said they had tunnels out of their monasteries or wherever it is they live, and these connect up with the convents where the nuns live. One of the girls had even heard of a special hospital where the nuns went to have their babies. Don't you think that's disgusting?'

'I've met a couple of priests. They seemed like good blokes to me.'

'That's with men.'

'So?' He was still staring out the window.

'Well, it's different with men. Apart from which you'd all stick together. Mother says men will always defend each other when it comes to something like this. I just think it's disgusting that men who claim to be servants of God can behave like that.'

'You don't know what they do.'

'Everyone says so.'

'Heather, that's just your silly friends. They wouldn't know.'

'They are not silly. Elizabeth Morrison's father is a bank manager and she was one of them who told me.'

'How could a bank manager know? Was he at the convent when the priests came running out of the tunnel?'

'You're being ridiculous.'

'So are you. Why do you always run down people you don't know?'

'I wouldn't want to know people like that.'

She made Adam feel foolish for having asked such a question and he could not think of a response. He was tired anyway. All the emotion had left him, drained by the pin-pricks of the discussion.

'Why don't we go for that walk?' he said. 'There are a few

clouds now. You might need a jumper.'

'We should have gone earlier.' She went to her bag and selected a cardigan. She had brought many more clothes than Adam. 'Tell me,' she said, adjusting her hair so that it fell freely over the cardigan's collar, 'have you ever kissed anyone else?'

'Yes. Have you?'

'Of course. A lot of boys have wanted to kiss me. Are you ready to go?'

'Yes.'

'Tell me, Adam,' and she turned her back on him while she buttoned the front of the garment, 'have you ever made love to any other girl?'

He hesitated and she turned. 'Some little squatter's daughter on some lonely outback station perhaps? Or the lonely young wife of some drover who'd gone off and left the poor thing on her own? Have you?'

'What sort of question is that?'

'One that requires an answer.'

Adam scratched his forehead. 'Only one,' he said.

'Who?' The question was a spurt of venom.

'A black woman. She was naked and I washed her and then we made love.'

'Where was this?'

'In a hole in the ground.'

She stamped her foot. 'You are infuriating, Adam Ross! You will never take me seriously.'

'Well, have you ever made love to anyone?'

'That is an insulting question.'

'Well, it's the same question you asked me!'

'That was different.'

'Why?'

'You know why.'

Adam did not. There were so many things he was supposed to understand. Most of them seemed to be related to people and cities and he was starting to feel that he would be happier in the bush and away from the crowds. But he felt Heather's answer was more a measure of her uncertainty than his and so he said nothing, seeing no point in pushing the conversation any further. He wondered if he would have mentioned Nellie's name if she had pressed him. No. Definitely not. Telling her name seemed like a betrayal.

They went walking, and it was pleasant. They looked at shops that had shoes and clothes in the windows and Heather spent at least ten minutes looking at the offerings in the jeweller's shop. She found a ring she would like to have one day and laughed and squeezed Adam's hand and said she was sorry for the way she had behaved, and he said he was sorry for being so rough. She hinted that things would be different that night, and Adam enjoyed the rest of the walk. She kept squeezing his hand and occasionally, as they stopped to look at something, pressing her body against his.

That night, Heather went down the corridor to the ladies' bathroom to get undressed and returned well wrapped in a dressing gown that hung to her ankles. It emphasized her hair and lovely face because there was nothing else to see. He had begun to undress but she asked that he change in the men's bathroom and he returned to the room tingling with anticipation.

She was in bed. She was lying on her side and close to the edge of the mattress with her back turned to the centre of the bed. She was, apparently, already asleep.

Adam took off his dressing gown and bent down to kiss her. He expected a smile of delight, and maybe one tempting eye to open and flash an unspoken invitation. She did not move. He got into bed and reached across to put his arm around her waist. Her chest rose and fell with deep, slow breathing. He whispered her name but she did not answer. He stayed with his arm around her, wondering if this were some sort of feminine game. She took a deep breath and turned on to her face, so that his hand rested on her back.

'Heather, this is our first night together.'

He shook her. Her hips rolled in a sensuous way. He let his hand drift down.

'What is it?' she murmured. She removed the hand.

'Please don't go to sleep.'

'You were too long.'

'I was only a minute.'

'I waited but then I fell asleep. Let me go back to sleep. I'm very tired.'

'Heather, please. Just turn around.'

'Tomorrow.'

She burrowed her head in her pillow. The deep breathing resumed.

SEVEN

The next night, Heather let Adam put his arm around her as she lay in bed. Lying on her side with her back to him, she grasped his hand firmly and held it just below her ribs. When he tried to wriggle closer she moved away.

'Please move back,' she told him. 'I'm about to fall out of the bed.'

He moved but she stayed where she was.

'Well, come back,' he said.

'No. I'm comfortable where I am.'

'But you said you were going to fall out of the bed.'

'That's because you were pushing me.'

'Well, this time I won't push,' he said and moved towards her. With a speed that surprised him she got out of bed and stood up. It was the first time he had seen her standing in her nightdress. It had a high frilly collar, was pink, and it hung in such a way that it disguised much of her body. What he saw, or imagined, he liked. He blinked.

'Adam, what is wrong with you? As soon as we go to bed, you seem to turn into some sort of monster with a dozen arms.'

'I just want to hold you.'

'You want to maul me. How can I sleep when you're grabbing at me all the time?'

Adam sat up. 'I thought maybe we wouldn't go to sleep for a while.'

'And do what?' Her face was angry but the rest of her was lovely. He was swelling with desire. He looped his arms around his raised knees.

'Kiss and cuddle? Is that what you mean?'

He had been looking at her breasts and she folded her arms. 'And stop looking at me like that. Really, you make me feel so degraded when you do that.'

'You are my wife and I want to hold you and kiss you and make love to you. Is that so wrong?'

'Holding and kissing *is* making love.'

Adam rested his chin on his knees. Maybe she was just teasing him and would get back into bed as suddenly as she had left. She

320

had seemed so affectionate all day, holding his hand, letting her body brush against his, even kissing his ear when he was not looking.

'Please get back into bed,' he said.

'Will you leave me alone?'

'No.'

'Well, I won't get back.'

'I'll make you,' he said smiling.

'Don't you dare!'

Did he see a hint of a laugh, a taunting 'come-and-get-me' look? He slid his legs from the bedclothes and stood up. Horrified, she backed away.

'What's wrong now?' he said slowly.

She stared at him. 'You. What's wrong with you? You're … you're bulging.'

Flushing with embarrassment, he turned and covered himself with his hands.

'Are you sick or something? You're … you're like a horse!'

Adam sat on the edge of the bed. He started to laugh.

'What's wrong with you now?' she demanded. 'Oh, this is all too unbelievable!'

'Heather, please sit down.' And when she backed away, he added, 'Not next to me if that worries you, but on the other side of the bed. You just look so attractive standing up like that that I can't help myself.'

'What do you mean?'

'Your body. I can see it like that and, well, it excites me.'

She sat down so quickly the bed rocked.

'Heather, haven't you ever seen a man before?'

'Of course.' She was not looking at him.

'I mean without clothes. Naked.'

'How dare you even suggest it!'

'Not even a little boy?'

'I don't have a brother. And I am not in the habit of going around and looking at small, naked boys.'

'What about your father? Surely you've seen him undressed at some time?'

'I've seen him without his tie, and I've seen him just wearing a singlet.'

'But with his pants off?'

She stood up and walked to the far wall, where there was a jug

321

of water and glasses. She poured herself some water.

'My father would never expose himself to me and I would die of shame if he ever walked around the house without his trousers.'

'Doesn't he ever have a bath?'

'Of course, but he does it decently.'

'So you've never seen a man?'

She sipped some water.

'And you don't know what a man looks like? I'll show you.' He stood.

'Don't you dare!'

'It's all right. I've calmed down.'

She frowned. 'I don't know what you mean. Don't you dare take your pyjamas off.'

Adam's hand was on the pyjama cord.

'If you take your pants off, I will never speak to you again.'

'I wasn't going to take them off, but you'll have to see me sometime.'

'Why? Do we have to be vulgar and degrade ourselves just because we're married?'

Adam moved towards her but she raised the glass, prepared to throw. He stopped, palms spread in a gesture of pleading.

'Heather, I am just a normal man. You are my wife. I love you, I want to hold you, to kiss you, to see you.'

'You are seeing me.'

'I mean all of you.'

'Just because we're married you expect me to behave like a slut?'

'I expect you to love me.'

'I do, I do.' She lowered the glass. 'I will cook for you. I am a very good cook. I will wash and iron your clothes. I don't like ironing but I will do it. We will go to church on Sundays and have parties on Saturday nights. I will continue to teach you to read and write. I will even show you how to play tennis.'

'And what will I do?'

'You will care for me.'

'I do care for you. That's why I want to hold you and make love to you.'

'Not that sort of caring. I mean provide. You will make money so we can live properly and have a decent life.'

'What about children?'

'What about them?' She looked him square in the eye. 'I know where they come from if that's what you mean. I know that what you want to do gives babies to women. I also know that what's driving you on to behave in this ghastly way is a lust that's built into you. It's probably something you can't help. It makes you just like an animal.'

Adam had visions of some of the stallions he had seen. My God, if I was like that she'd have something to worry about, he thought.

'We are animals,' he said. 'At least that's what I've heard. We've all got strong instincts. Women are supposed to want to have children. Is that true? How about you? Do you want children?'

'One day.'

'Well, how the hell are you going to have them?'

'I've asked you not to use that word.'

'How are we going to have children if we never make love?'

'I don't call what you were doing making love.'

'All I did was put my arm around you.'

'You were pressing your body against me.'

'Well, you were doing that to me today.'

'I was not.' Her blue eyes blazed.

'You were. I could feel your chest. You kept pressing it against me while we were looking at the shops.'

'That is a lie. That is a vile thing to say.'

He sat on the bed again. 'Heather, I can't understand you. You seem so nice to me during the day, so loving and everything, but as soon as we're alone like this, you either pretend I'm not here or you go on as though I was some sort of wild animal.'

'You are.'

'Do you think I'm different to other men?'

'I don't know. Maybe yes, maybe no.'

'I don't think I am. I think any man would want to make love to his wife. For heaven's sake, we've been married for four days and you haven't let me touch you.'

'You see? You're not consistent. You just said we were touching when we were walking today and now you say we never touch. You've caught yourself out.'

'I mean we never touch when we're alone in our own bedroom.'

'The trouble is, Adam, you change at night. You seem nice and sweet in the daytime but as soon as it's time to go to bed, a time when decent people are thinking about sleep, you become some

323

sort of monster. I think you should know I don't like it.'

He forced a laugh. 'Oh I'm very much aware of that.'

She filled the glass again and drank some more water. 'Now, if you don't mind, I think I'd like to go to sleep.'

She walked to the bed without looking at him. Some of her hair had fallen across her chest. She swept it behind her shoulder.

'Good night, Adam.'

'So you're going to go to sleep. Just like that. What am I going to do?'

'If you could read, I would suggest that you read a book. But seeing you cannot read, I suggest you try to go to sleep.' She pulled the blanket around her chin. 'But not in this bed. I do not trust you when you're like you are.'

'And where the hell am I going to sleep?'

'I can always tell when you're in one of your crazy moods. You use that word a lot. It must be appropriate. The devil must be inside you.'

'Where am I supposed to sleep? On the floor?'

'If you like. It might help calm you down.'

Adam began to dress. He had put on his shirt and trousers and was tying a shoe lace when Heather turned.

'What are you doing?'

'I'm going out.'

'Don't be ridiculous.'

'I'm not being ridiculous.' He stood up and tucked a corner of his shirt into his trousers.

'Someone might see you leave.'

But he was on his way out the door.

EIGHT

The carpet was flawed with worn patches and the walls were covered with ornate paper that trailed fibrous tendrils at every seam. The aroma of cigarette smoke and unemptied ashtrays drifted up the staircase. There was a hint of disinfectant and of generations of furniture polish.

Adam bounded down the stairs, conscious for the first time of the stale and offensive smells and the seediness of the surroundings. It was as though his senses had just awakened. He needed to get out. To breathe. To think.

'Going out, sir?' He had not seen the man, who had been behind a desk. He was rising, folding a newspaper as he stood and peering at Adam with a look that suggested he doubted he was a guest but was too polite to make such a thought public.

'Just for a while,' Adam said, temporarily confused and looking for the way out.

'Doors are locked at midnight.'

Adam nodded. He saw the doors. One was already bolted in place. He pushed the other. It did not move.

'You have to pull,' the man said.

'Thanks.' Adam heard the newspaper rustle. He opened the door and stepped outside.

The air was cold and fresh and sharp with salty smells. He wished he had put on a jumper, but shoved his hands in his pockets and crossed the road. A few cars were parked under the pines, their noses facing the beach and neatly in line. There was a Chev and a black baby Austin and a Ford and a red car he didn't recognize.

He walked towards it. A-U-B-U-R-N. He tried to pronounce the word but it didn't make sense. It was a fine-looking car with big silver pipes running from the engine cover. He walked alongside the car and peered inside. He stopped, startled. Two people were lying across the front seat. A man sat up, his eyes wide with fright. Adam turned away, feeling a fool, and walked quickly to the stone parapet that bordered the beach.

There were lights all along the wall. They shone across the sand and whitened the first dim row of breakers, but beyond that the sea rumbled and groaned in darkness. Two dogs played on the sand, chasing each other in turn, wheeling and jumping. In the distance, a man walked near the water line. He was barefooted with his pants rolled up to his knees, and he swung a pair of leashes in one hand. Adam walked along the concrete path, measuring his steps to the beat of the surf. One, two, three, four steps and boom, in came the loudest roll of a breaker. There were other noises, rumbles and splashes and echoes, but there was one solid boom where the first big waves broke somewhere beyond the light. One, two, three, four, boom. It was surprisingly regular, like a mechanical thing.

He passed a couple sitting on the beach. He was going to nod and say 'good day' but he remembered that people didn't greet strangers in the city. Not unless they wanted something.

What was wrong? Was it Heather or was it him? Surely what he felt was natural? Didn't all husbands want to make love with their wives, specially when they were just married? And he felt so *tender* towards her, not rough. That was the thing that made it seem so unfair. If he was behaving like some of the men he'd known who just paid for and took a woman whenever they felt like it, it would be different. But it was not like that. This was love. This was good. At least that's what he felt.

Mind you, he'd never been good at expressing his feelings. Maybe she'd just misunderstood him. He thought he had touched her gently but everyone said he didn't know his own strength and maybe he had frightened her without meaning to. She was a decent girl and very innocent and probably didn't know what to expect. He wasn't too sure himself, come to that; it would be very different with Heather. But whereas he was anxious to find out what it was like, she was nervous.

He turned and walked along the Corso. A milk bar was open and he went in. A man with black hair and a cadaverous face was wiping the tables. He walked behind the counter, wiping his hands. Adam ordered a chocolate milk shake.

'Nice night,' the man said.

'Yes.'

'Down for a holiday?'

'Yes.'

'On your own?'

Adam hesitated. 'Yes,' he said.

A girl sitting at a table in the corner stood up. Adam had not noticed her. She walked to the door. She was still there when Adam left. She had a cigarette between her fingers.

'Have you got a match?' she said, smiling but looking a little shy.

'Sorry. I don't smoke.'

She put the cigarette in her handbag. 'I shouldn't either.'

'He might have one,' Adam said, inclining his head towards the man behind the counter who was looking at them and half-smiling.

'No, it's all right. I won't bother.' She was pretty with brown hair cut short and curled towards her chin to emphasize her waif-like face.

He walked away, shoulders hunched against the cold.

Across the street, a window rattled open and the rich notes of a saxophone poured out. A piano tinkled in the background. Someone laughed and others joined in. High voices. Women's voices. A row of windows flickered with the shadows of passing dancers. The window was slammed shut. Adam felt lonely. He longed to be back in the bush camped by a waterhole. That was being on your own, not being lonely.

The centre of the road had coloured lights above a series of gardens with flower beds and rockeries and squat date palms whose branches moved lazily in the breeze. There were benches and he thought of sitting down but he saw a man sleeping on one and kept walking.

He went as far as the wharf and watched an old man fish for a while and saw a ferry arrive. It was magical: all lights and noise and foam around its bows, but when the people got off it became quiet and all the lights were turned off. A man in a uniform walked past Adam.

'Is that going to Sydney?' Adam asked.

'Not till the morning, mate. That was the last boat for the night.' He hurried away.

Adam walked along the harbour front. Two speedboats were moored to a stairway descending from the main wharf, and small sailing boats were beached on the sand. A bus pulled away from the kerb, leaving the row of bus stops deserted and the air reeking with the pungent smell of diesel fumes. Feeling cold near the water, Adam turned away from the harbour and walked down a street lined with trees.

Some of the buildings bore brass plates which glowed dimly in the light like old medals worn with modesty.

He came to another intersection and turned left again. The Corso was ahead of him once more, with the church on the right. It was a big church, bigger than the one he'd been married in.

He should go back. The hotel would be locked soon and he wasn't achieving a thing by walking around. Except feeling lonely.

He reached the Corso. The jeweller's was on the left. The window was dark but he looked in, not seeing things but thinking of the time he'd spent there with Heather. She was funny about rings. He supposed all women were like that.

Another figure was reflected in the window. It was the girl he'd seen in the milk bar.

'You're out late,' she said. 'I thought you'd gone home.'

327

'I don't live here,' he said.

'Just holidaying?'

'Yes.'

'They're lovely, aren't they?' She moved next to him but looked in the window. 'I often come here and look in. Never be able to afford one, but.'

Heather would never have put 'but' at the end like that. He grinned.

'What are you smiling at?' She was small, not much more than five feet tall. She was wearing a cardigan that looked old and thin and her shoulders were bent against the cold.

'I was just thinking of something. Cold, isn't it?'

She made a shivering noise.

'I thought it would be warm down here in Manly,' Adam said, looking at her reflection in the glass.

'It's not summer,' she said, turning a little so that her shoulder brushed against him. 'When that wind blows it's like the South Pole, isn't it?'

'Yes.' And when she didn't say anything, he added, 'I suppose it is.'

'Where are you from?' She looked up at him. Adam kept his eyes on the window. He could see her clearly. She was probably no more than eighteen or nineteen.

'All over the place,' he said.

'World traveller.'

He laughed. 'Not me. I'm living at Nyngan at the moment.'

'Where's that?'

'Out west.'

'How far?' Her shoulder touched him again.

'Oh, a long way. Not far from Bourke.'

'I've heard of that. Are you from the back of Bourke, then?'

'No. I'm on the other side. This side.'

She leaned against him. 'I'm freezing. Do you mind?'

Adam felt uncomfortable. 'No. Go ahead.'

'Ta. I've been to the Blue Mountains. Katoomba. Ever been there?'

'I think we stopped there on the way down.'

'Probably did. Nice place, isn't it?'

'I only saw the railway station.'

She put an arm around his waist and Adam held his breath.

'Where are you staying?'

'I'm at a hotel.'

'Is it far?'

'On the beach.'

'Oh, that's nice.'

'Yes.'

'How long are you down for?'

'Till the weekend.'

'I hope the weather gets warmer for you.'

'Yes.'

'Still, it'll be warmer in the summer.'

'I won't be here then.'

'No. Would you like to come to my place?'

'I don't think so. I should be going back.'

'Just for a cup of tea. Or beer. I've got beer if you like beer.'

'I don't drink beer.'

'Do you drink tea?'

'Yes.'

'We'll have tea then. It's not far. I've got a nice flat.'

'I should be going back.'

'It's in Darley Road.'

Adam didn't know what to say, so he said: 'Where's that?'

'Right here. We're on the corner. It's just up the hill towards the hospital.'

'No, I don't think I should.' He put his hand on hers, to release her grip on his waist but she held his hand instead.

'You feel strong,' she said.

'I'm married.'

'Well, that's all right. A lot of men are married.' She still held his hand.

'But my wife's at the hotel.'

She moved away from him and then started to giggle.

'I don't mean to laugh but what are you doing here if she's back at the pub?'

Adam shrugged.

'Had an argument?'

'Not really. Oh, in a way I suppose we have.'

'She been looking at other men, has she?'

'No.'

'Over money?'

'No.'

The girl looked at him suspiciously. 'You been beating her?'

329

'No! Of course not.'

'Well, what then?'

Adam shrugged. He shuffled nervously, wanting to move, but tempted to stay.

'I should be getting back,' he said. 'Do you know what time it is?'

'I don't have a watch.' She laughed. 'If I can't afford matches, I can't afford a watch.'

'It's unusual to see a woman smoke.'

'It might be in the bush, not here. It's very modern to smoke. Just expensive.'

'Yes, I suppose it is.'

'You don't smoke?'

'No.'

'That's unusual for a man.'

'Yes.' He smiled.

'Well, let's go and get that cup of tea.' She moved towards him and Adam backed away. She stopped.

'You don't have to be frightened of me. I'm not going to bite you. Promise.'

'I must go. They close up at midnight.'

'It's not midnight yet. Oh, I'm so cold.' She folded her arms and squeezed a shiver from her body. 'Do you mind if I just get close again? You know, use you as a windbreak.'

She was already close.

'Well, I don't know.'

Her arm was around his waist again.

'Am I too cold for you?'

'No,' he said, his body rigid with nervousness. 'But I wish you wouldn't.'

'Why? Am I hurting?'

'No, of course not.'

'Well, no harm done. Come on, it's up here.'

Adam did not move.

'I had a dog like you once,' she said.

'What do you mean?'

'Whenever I wanted to take it for a walk, it wouldn't budge an inch.'

'Jesus,' Adam said, relaxing a little, 'that's the second time tonight I've been called a dog.'

The girl looked at him quizzically. 'By your wife?'

He nodded and took a step, because she had been pulling him gently.

'Did she want to take you for a walk?'

'No. She wanted to go to sleep.'

The girl, still with her arm around his body, comforted him. 'Oh, it was like that. Is she one of those women who always have headaches?'

'Headaches?'

'You know. Never want to do it when you do. Always got a headache or too tired. I've heard about girls like that.'

Some people were walking on the other side of the Corso. Adam twisted to look at them. There were two couples with arms entwined. One of the men was singing.

'Make a lot of noise, some people,' the girl said. 'Still, that's normal. Being noisy and singing when you're happy. Nothing wrong with that, is there? Must be awful to be frigid like your wife, though. Must be hard for a man to take. You seem so gentle, too. Must be awful for you, to be married to someone who's a bit odd like that.'

Adam was surprised. He had concluded most women were like Heather and he was the odd one.

'I came on a bit strong, I suppose,' he said softly, wondering what she would say.

'Most men do,' she said and made it sound as though she knew. 'It's natural. Most women love it. Poor thing, that wife of yours, she must be a block of ice. I mean doing it to you.' She tugged and he started to walk. 'Let's face it ... what's your name?'

'Adam.'

'I'm Erica. Let's face it, Adam. You're a good-looking man, not fat like some of them, and you're real polite. She must be mad to pull the old headache trick.'

'She didn't say she had a headache. She was sleepy.'

'Same thing. And you've got the bad luck to be married to one. How long have you been married?'

'Not long.'

'Not on your honeymoon, are you?'

Adam looked down.

'Oh, you poor thing! Did you give her a hard time on the first night?'

'We've never been together.'

'You're joking?'

331

'True.'

They walked without speaking for a while. She tried to match his steps but kept getting out of time.

'You've got long legs.'

'Sorry.'

'Don't be sorry. My legs are too short. My father used to say I wore them down running a lot when I was a kid.'

Adam slowed. 'Is your father ... Do you live with your parents?'

'No way. Haven't seen him for years. I live on my own. My flat's just up here.'

Adam stopped. 'I shouldn't.'

She walked away from him and turned, looking him in the eye.

'You think I'm one of them, don't you? A streetwalker.'

They were near a streetlight and Adam could see her clearly. She had nice legs.

'Yes. I suppose I do.'

'You're right.' She kept on looking at him, not blinking, challenging him to say or do something. He shrugged his shoulders.

'I charge ten bob. Do you want to sleep with me?'

Adam's throat had gone dry. 'No.'

'Good. Well, come and have that cup of tea.'

And she turned and continued to walk up the street. Not so quickly that her link with Adam might be broken but firmly, as though she were certain he would follow.

He followed. She slowed to allow him to catch up.

'What do you do back in Bourke?'

'Nyngan. Different things. Mostly I dig holes.'

Her eyes darted towards his. 'You're not a gravedigger?'

'Would you give me a cup of tea if I was?'

'You, yes. I knew a gravedigger once and he smelled awful.'

'What of? Dead bodies?'

She laughed. She seemed like a young girl when she laughed.

'Goodness me, no! Garlic. He used to eat garlic sandwiches. What sort of holes do you dig, Adam?'

'Big ones. Usually dams or wells. Things like that. I've got a job next week to drill a bore.'

'Isn't that a pig?'

'Wrong bore. It's just a hole that reaches underground water.'

'Hard work?'

'Pretty hard.'

'Who do you work for?'

'Myself.'

Her face brightened with admiration. 'You're a boss! I'd love to have people working for me. I'd be the world's toughest boss.'

'Why?'

'To get my own back. No one ever did nothing for me. I'd have them working from dawn to dusk and I'd ride around in a fancy car while they all rode bicycles.' She stopped, her face bright with malice and opened a metal gate. 'Here we are. Follow me. There's not much room.'

The building was a three-storeyed structure of red brick. It was severe in style, a box turned on end. The entrance was at the side. A rose garden along the fence had grown out of control, forcing them to walk close to the wall, and then a sprouting of pipes, clinging to the wall and flaked with peeling paint, sent them brushing against the fence.

'Got to know your way around here,' she said, leading him to the entrance way and disappearing in the darkness. 'Mind the steps. There are two of them.'

Her hand touched his. 'I'm over here. To the left. That's it. Now just wait a minute while I find the key. I've got a secret hiding place.'

'Is that why you don't turn on the light?'

'That's right,' she said and Adam heard the key scratching in the lock. 'It isn't because the landlord is too lousy to buy a new globe. There we are.'

Adam heard the door open but saw nothing.

'Well, come on,' she said. 'In you come.'

'Where?'

She giggled. Her fingers touched his shirt and worked their way to his arm. She guided him into the room. He stumbled on a ruffled floor mat.

'You stay here and I'll turn the light on. The man who built this place obviously never meant to live here himself because he put the cord over on the other side of the room.'

On came the light. She was standing on the far side of a small room. The cord still twitched from the ceiling. It had broken at some time and she had knotted a piece of string to its end.

'Well, this is my place. What do you think?'

She reminded him of a schoolgirl, so full of hope and innocence that a cruel word would have destroyed her.

'It's nice,' he said.

'There's another room out there with a gas stove and a sink in it.' She nodded towards an open doorway. 'They call it a kitchen but it's so small that you have to step outside if you want to change your mind. Then there's a bedroom and a bathroom with a tub in it that must have been new when Captain Cook was a boy. Do you want to use the bathroom?'

'No.'

'Well, sit down. I'll get you some tea. Hope you don't take milk 'cause I haven't got any.'

'You've got sugar?'

'In the cupboard.'

'That's fine.'

'I'll put the water on. Sure you don't want to wash your hands or something?' She disappeared through a doorway.

'No. I'm right, thanks.'

'I found my matches,' she called and laughed. 'Now I can light two things with the one match.'

He heard the rustle of paper and the scrape of a match. Gas flared. A tap squeaked and water rushed into a kettle. She reappeared smoking a cigarette.

'It seems funny,' she said, tossing her head to help the first puff of smoke pour down her throat. 'Me with the cigarette and you just sitting there, all prim and proper. Never smoked, haven't you?'

He shook his head. He felt uncomfortable, as though by sitting down he had committed himself to something shameful.

'Would you like something to eat?'

'No thanks.'

'I could make some toast.'

Adam rose. He looked miserable.

'You're not going to run away now, are you?' she said as she re-entered the other room. He heard water running and the noise of cups being washed. 'I'm not going to do you any harm,' she called. 'Just a simple cup of tea. And I would like someone to talk to.'

'Don't you have friends?'

'Sure. Lots of them.' She reappeared in the doorway. 'If I thought hard, I could probably name two of them.'

'Two?'

'If I was lucky, that is. I don't know anyone. Just a little girl on her own in the big smoke.'

She put two cups on the table. They had no saucers. 'The water should be ready in a minute.'

'I should be going,' Adam said.

'I thought we'd gone through all that,' she said smiling. Despite the smile, she looked worried. 'I think you want to go all the time because you don't like me, do you?'

'Yes, I do.'

'You look as though you're ready to bolt.'

'It's just that ... well, I don't know. I feel sort of edgy.'

'You're guilty, that's what's wrong with you.'

Adam sniffed.

'That's what it is, all right,' she said. 'I've seen it dozens of times. A man goes out with another woman and then behaves as though he'd just robbed a bank or something.'

'I'm not guilty.'

'Well, there must be something wrong with me. It's got to be one thing or the other. If you like me, why don't you sit down?'

Adam sat on the leather couch. She sat near him, carefully putting a cushion between them.

'That's just so's you won't be nervous. Now tell me, what's your wife's name?'

'Heather.'

'What's she look like?'

'Tall. Fair. Got nice blue eyes.'

'She sounds disgusting.'

Adam picked at a fingernail. 'She's cleverer than me. I never went to school.'

'I did. Hated it. Couldn't wait to leave.'

'Where was that? Here in Manly?'

'No. Nowra. I come from the south coast. Been here two years.'

'And you've got two friends.'

'On a good day.'

'Why did you come to the city?'

'Why not?'

'I don't like the city. Everyone seems in too much of a hurry.'

'I don't like the country. Everything seems too slow. I had a job for a while in a produce store but I couldn't stand it. I was starting to smell like a horse. When I came up here I got a job as a

335

waitress and that was all right but I got the sack because I wouldn't go to bed with the boss. 'Scuse me, the water's boiling.'

'Is that true?' Adam called after her.

'Absolutely fair dinkum. If it wasn't so serious it would have been funny. He was a big fat slug with a big fat wife and five big fat kids and he went on as if he was Rudolph Valentino or John Barrymore or someone. Used to try and pin me down in the kitchen. I hit him over the head with the frying pan once. He said he was going to have the police arrest me.'

She came from the other room carrying a kettle. 'And I told him I'd tell his wife. Oh, he was frightened of her. If you thought he was ugly, you should have seen her. He could have made a fortune renting her out to haunt houses. Anyhow, he gave me the sack instead. Didn't even pay me the money he owed me. How do you want your tea? Without milk or without lemon? I haven't got either.'

'I've never heard of lemon in tea.'

'It's nice. You want sugar, don't you?'

'Please.'

'I'll get it,' she said as Adam started to move towards the cupboard. 'Just let me check that the mice haven't been in.'

Adam laughed.

'You're in luck,' she said. 'Sit down. Would you like to stay here the night?'

Adam's cup rattled on the table.

'You could sleep out here,' she added quickly. 'You'd be comfortable – and safe.'

'No, I've got to get back.'

'You think I'm trying to get you into bed, don't you?'

'No. I just think I should go.'

'To see that wife of yours. What's her name?'

'Heather.'

'Poor old cold Heather. Do you want to go back to the hotel to be with her? Do you reckon she'll be different? Warmed up a bit or something?'

'I don't know.'

'Well, I do. She won't. She'll just tear a strip off you for being out and then roll over and go to sleep.'

'I've still got to go.'

'Will you come back if you can't get in the hotel? You might have trouble getting in.'

Adam drained his cup. 'Why?'

She pointed to a clock on a shelf above the sink. midnight. Seven past.'

'Jesus!' He jumped up.

She rushed to him. 'Please stay. It's cold out.'

'I've got to go.'

'You're too good for that Heather.'

'You've never met her.'

'Don't have to. I've met you. Would you like more tea? There's some still in the pot.'

'No. You've been good. Thanks, Erica.'

She blushed. 'Well, if you want a bed, there's one here. I mean the couch. You're welcome to that. You're sure you wouldn't like some toast? I've got some bread.'

'And butter?'

'Yes.'

'Anything else?'

'What do you mean?'

'Any other food?'

She pulled away from him. 'Not at the moment. You've caught me a bit short of food, I'm afraid.'

'How long since you've had a good meal? Mutton or beef. Something like that.'

'I'm all right.'

'You're very thin.'

'Well, thanks very much!' She folded her arms across her chest. 'You mightn't think I'm good enough to go to bed with but you don't have to insult me.'

'You know what I mean. You're not eating enough.'

'How do you know?'

'Because I can tell. There's nothing in the kitchen. Besides, when you've worked with sheep and cattle as much as I have you can tell when a beast's not properly fed, and you look half-starved.'

She put her hands on her hips. 'Well, thank you very much! So now I look like a half-starved cow.' After a moment she said, resignedly, 'You want to leave now, I suppose? Go back to that ice queen of yours?'

'I'd better.'

He joined her in the doorway.

'I put ten bob on the table. Get yourself some food.'

She looked up. 'Why the money? I didn't do anything.'

'Yes, you did,' he said and bent to kiss her on the forehead.

'You'd better get doing.' She wiped the side of her nose. 'Or I'll belt you over the head and drag you into the bedroom. Go on. Nick off.'

'See you.'

'Yeah, see you.'

Adam walked up the path, bumped into the stack of pipes running down the wall, recoiled into the rose bushes and reached the gate. Without looking back, he turned left on the road and walked down the hill.

NINE

Adam had trouble getting into the hotel. The doors were locked and although he knocked several times, no one came. He walked around the side and found a door but it, too, was locked. There was an alley at the back and he entered that, feeling his way in the dark past a row of barrels and garbage cans until he came to a high wooden fence with a rickety wooden gate. The gate was locked. When Adam pushed it, a chain and padlock jingled on the opposite side. He heard a dog rush at the noise and automatically stepped back. The dog hit the fence and the weight of its onslaught made the palings shake. The dog snarled but did not bark. It jumped against the fence a few more times. Adam retreated.

He walked back to the hotel's front entrance. On either side of the wooden doors were glass panels and through the glass he could see a light. A figure moved across the light. He knocked and saw the figure straighten and then walk away. He knocked more loudly. The person returned.

'We're closed,' a man's voice said.

'Could you let me in, please?'

'We're shut for the night. Come back in the morning.'

'I'm a guest.'

He saw the man scratch his head, then move to the door. A bolt rattled.

'What's your name?'

'Ross.'

'What room are you in?'

'Twelve.'

More noise. The door scraped open.

'You should have been back before twelve,' the man said.

'Sorry.'

'The rules are straightforward enough. These doors are locked at twelve. I shouldn't have opened them.'

'Well, I'm glad you have.' Adam headed for the stairs.

'Was that you out the back disturbing the dog?'

'I went round there, yes.'

'Shit. Don't do that. He'll take your throat out. That's what woke me up.'

'I'm sorry. I just wanted to get in.'

'I won't open up next time. If you can't follow the rules, you can sleep on the beach.'

Adam stopped. He gripped the banister tightly. It seemed that all he'd heard in recent times was people telling him what to do.

'What did you say?' he said, turning on the stairs. He spoke softly but he could feel the anger rising in him.

The man was middle-aged, heavily built and with grey close-cropped hair. He had been smoking and he threw the cigarette on the floor and ground it with his heel.

'I said the next time you're late you can stay outside.'

'Do you always speak to guests like this?'

'Don't give me that crap, son. If I kept this place open all night no one'd get any sleep. If you want to go out shagging at night that's fine by me, but get back by twelve. And if you want breakfast, don't be bloody late.'

And he walked away.

Adam, befuddled by anger, could say nothing for a few moments. Then he managed to shout: 'What are you running? A prison or something?'

But the man had gone.

Adam thought of all the things he should have said. 'I thought I was the one paying the good money to stay here. I thought you were supposed to give the guests service. I help keep you in a job.' Things like that. But it was too late.

Adam climbed the stairs. He ran his hand along the wallpaper and plucked a loose thread. It ran up the wall, fraying the seam in

339

the paper as he pulled. Good, he thought, and pulled hard once more. He enjoyed the sensation of doing harm to this place; but then the sensation passed and he felt bad. What the hell was wrong with him? He didn't go around spoiling people's walls. But then he wasn't used to people locking him out of buildings and shouting at him. He wasn't used to walking the streets of a big town at night. And he wasn't used to being married.

He reached the top of the stairs and paused. From somewhere on the floor below a door slammed. A faint glow from a light behind the reception desk filtered up the staircase. The place still reeked of yesterday's stale smells.

He didn't like the city. He let that thought circulate through the dark and decided, as his temper cooled, that it wasn't quite fair. What he didn't like most of all was what had been happening to him in recent months. He had been changing. Josef was right. He had become a pet cat. Well, no more. He'd had enough of trying to do what other people expected him to do. He was going to be what he was, not what some people expected him to be.

He knew he meant Heather, not some people. Oh God, why wasn't she as he had dreamed she would be?

There were no lights in the hallway and he stood at the top of the stairs letting his eyes grow accustomed to the dark. He had to turn left and find the third room on the right. He walked to the wall, touched it, and turned left. Almost immediately his feet brushed some empty bottles. One fell, skittling the others. He bent and put the bottles back in place and continued. He passed the first door and brushed against a tall metal ashtray. It wobbled. He caught it but some butts spilled over his fingers. He wiped his hand on his trousers and walked past the second door. Then he stopped, remembering that a bathroom was on this wall too. Which door was the door to the bathroom? Was it two down from his room or three? He went back to the second door and felt for the raised letters on the wooden panel. He had seen the word. It had four letters. He could feel nothing. He walked to the first door and hit the ashtray again. He caught the base but the tray itself fell to the floor. He reached the door and ran his hand across its surface. There they were. One, two, three, four letters. B.A.T.H. He opened the door and turned on the light. He washed his hands, avoiding the partly dissolved cake of soap that lay rotting in a pool of yellow water in a recess beside the tap. He moved to the toilet bowl and urinated and washed his hands again. There was no towel. You were supposed to bring a towel from your room. More rules you were supposed to know. Be a stranger in this place and you could end up locked out or with wet hands. He went out and switched off the light. He tried to close the door gently but it slammed.

Another door opened further along the corridor. Light poured over the carpet.

'Is that you, Adam?' Heather's voice called, discreet yet urgent.

'Yes.'

'Shh. Don't make so much noise.'

It was easier walking with the lighted doorway as a goal. Cigarette butts were spilled across the carpet. He stepped past them.

'Where have you been? I've been so worried.'

She was standing back from the doorway, so as not to be seen from the corridor.

'Just walking.' He closed the door.

'Did anyone see you?' She retreated to the bed.

'I suppose so. There were people about.'

'I thought I heard voices a few minutes ago. Was that you?'

He sat on the other side of the bed and began to remove his shoes. 'Probably. There's a man downstairs. He had to let me in.'

'Did he know who you were?'

'I had to give him my name and room number before he'd let me in. The door was locked.'

She covered her eyes. 'Oh, how humiliating!'

Adam hesitated, a half-undone shoelace in his fingers.

'Why?'

'Well, now he knows, of course,' she said, her face flushed. 'You've been out, like some tramp or drunk, and you come sneaking back in the middle of the night and someone from the hotel has to unlock the door for you. And you tell him your name.'

'So what?' He stood up.

'Have you thought about me?' she said, looking away from him. 'Back here on my own, worrying. And now someone from the hotel knows you've been out all night on your own. He must have a simply dreadful opinion of you. And, of course, all the staff will know that you were out on your own until all hours and I was here, in the room, by myself. Can you imagine how they are going to gossip?'

341

'Why should they?'

His voice shook a little. That was the only sign of the anger he was trying to suppress.

'Because they will. Oh, you wouldn't know! You wouldn't care. You wouldn't even think of it, would you?' She glanced at him and the look was venomous. 'No, not big, strong, stupid Adam! God help me, why did I marry you?'

He walked to her side of the bed and she leaned back, turning away from him.

'Yes, why did you?' he said.

'I must have been mad.'

'You seemed keen on the idea.' He grabbed her shoulder. 'Look at me when you say things like that.'

'I can't bear to look at you. And I wasn't keen. How dare you say something like that? You make me sound like some grubby little common girl.'

'And that wouldn't do, would it?'

She looked at him, not understanding the irony in his voice. Her brow crinkled, but only briefly. She raced on. 'You know why we got married when we did. It was because of father.'

'But why, if you find me so stupid and boring?'

'I don't know.' She shook herself to remove his hand.

'Nothing to do with money, is it?'

She looked at him, her face shocked. 'What do you mean?'

'People tell me your father's got money troubles.'

'What people?'

'There's talk all around town.'

She said nothing. A pair of moths hovered near the bedside lamp. Their wings fluttered madly, and that was all that moved in the room.

'I've said I don't believe it.'

'But you do, don't you?'

'Should I?'

'You oaf,' she said. 'You dull, boring, bad-mannered, uneducated oaf! How dare you even say such things?'

'Is it true?'

'You'd like it to be, wouldn't you? That would make you feel so smug, so very superior. My father is twice the man you'll ever be.'

'Maybe he is, but ...'

'There's no "maybe" to it. He's a man everyone respects. He's the most important man in town.'

'And he owes money.'

'That's a foul thing to say! He does things you could never do. He goes to church. He's a leading member of our congregation. You've only been to church once, and that was to get married. You'll never be the man he is. You can't even read or write properly.'

'Well, why did you marry me?' He shouted the words.

'Don't make so much noise! People will hear.' She glanced back, as though expecting a tap on the shoulder.

'It can't be for love,' Adam said slowly. 'You don't want to make love with me.'

'Not what you call love.'

Adam stared at the light and the moths, but saw again the big house in Nyngan with Heather's mother smiling and whispering to her daughter.

'Was it your mother's idea that we get married?'

'What are you talking about?'

'Or was it yours? You told me once your mother would go along with anything you suggested. Did you think I might be a way out of the family problems? Is that why you married me?'

Her eyes were wide.

'So I could pay the bills?'

She stood and tried to slap him. He deflected the blow.

'Better to be married to a big, strong oaf,' he said, 'than face the disgrace of not being able to pay your bills. Of having people talk. Can't have that, can we?'

She tried to hit him again. He held her and she struggled. She kicked him and he shook her so hard her knees buckled.

'Why the hell are you more concerned about what people say than what you think? Or what I think?'

She bit his wrist. He pushed her away. Gasping for breath, she hit the wall.

'I don't care what you think,' she said, her voice a rush of defiance.

'That's very obvious.'

'Oh, you're so smug! My father's dying, and you're smug!'

A small bag was on the floor. She picked it up and threw it at him. He caught it easily.

'I suppose you're going to beat me now.'

'No.'

'Oh, I see,' she said and tried to laugh. 'We're back to that, are we? Of course. How slow of me.'

'What are you talking about?'

She backed against the wall.

'You are an uncouth, violent man both in what you do and what you say, but I'm not going to give you the satisfaction of fighting. You are too strong for me, and I am not going to allow you the morbid delight of bruising me and clawing me, and making me bleed. Oh no, you'd like that but I'm not going to give you that satisfaction.'

With trembling fingers, she began unbuttoning her nightgown.

'What are you doing?' Adam said. He felt weary.

'I would have thought it was obvious. I am undressing.'

'Heather, please don't.'

'So you can have the pleasure, the animal gratification, of tearing my clothes from me? There is no way I will let you have that ... that victory. I know why you've come back like you have, making that man shout at you and knocking things over in the hall. You're out of control.'

'You're mad!'

'It's not me who's mad. I know why you've been saying those dreadful things and making up all those lies. It's just to make me react. Well, I won't. I'm not going to fight you. Oh, you'd like that, wouldn't you?'

The first button was undone but she was having trouble with the second. Frustrated, she tore it loose.

'If you are beyond controlling yourself, if you are so full of foul lust, then you may take me. But I want you to know I hate you and think you are the most violent and despicable person I've ever known.'

Moving suddenly, she pulled the nightgown over her head and stood, back to the wall with her head turned, eyes closed and teeth biting into her lower lip. One hand was pressed against the wallpaper. The other held the trailing nightgown. Adam had never seen her naked, and he was shocked. The sight itself was inspiring enough. She had a slim and graceful body with pale skin that was already puckering from the cold, and long and truly beautiful legs that met in a delicate triangle of ginger hair. It was the way she stood that shocked him. Her muscles were rigid with fear and she quivered like an insect impaled on a pin.

He said nothing. She stood, pressing herself against the wall, eyes still closed and trembling. Adam sat on the bed.

'Would you like me to go and turn on a hot bath for you?' he said gently.

She opened her eyes. 'Bath?'

'Wasn't that what your mother said? After I do whatever I'm supposed to do you, you're to hop in a hot bath.'

She relaxed, and now she was truly beautiful, her body a mixture of tilts and curves.

'Are you mocking me?' she said, and there was no beauty in the voice.

Adam had decided he could not understand her, and it was pointless for him to try. Instead, he laughed. Just a murmur of sound, but a laugh nonetheless.

'You bastard!' she said, and his smile widened. It was the smile that lit the fuse. She ran to the bedside table and, with that movement, the image was changed: a nude figure, as soft and languid as an image stroked in oils, became a long-legged and rather lean young woman, caught without her clothes on and running across the room. She grabbed the lamp, wrenching the cord from the socket and plunging the room into darkness.

'You callous bastard!' she grunted and hit him with the lamp. It struck him on the chest and fell in pieces to the carpet.

He seized her and lifted her from the floor.

She kicked him. 'Let me go!'

'Well, stop hitting me. I might hurt you.'

'You are hurting me.'

He put her down. She slapped him, her open palm striking his neck.

He stepped back, raising his hands to ward of any more blows.

'So now you're going to punch me,' she said. 'Brute! Go ahead.'

The only light to reach the room was a splattering of beams from a nearby streetlamp. The lamp was faulty and flickered off and on, and what entered the room was filtered by a lace curtain. Thus she stood there, one moment a shadow among shadows and the next a pale figure with skin as ghostly and crazed as marble in the moonlight.

Adam backed away. 'I'm not going to hit you. You're the one doing all the hitting.'

'Bastard!' She was breathless.

'Don't you know any other bad words?'

She tried to hit him again. He caught her wrist and pushed her away. She stumbled and sprawled on the floor. He threw her the

345

nightgown.

'It's cold. Put this on.'

Her hair spilled over her shoulders and touched the floor.

'What are you going to do?' she gasped.

'I'm going to bed.'

He awoke at four, tossing from a wild but vague dream. He felt guilty but could not remember enough of the dream to understand why he should feel that way. He checked the time. He stretched.

Heather sniffed.

'Are you awake?' he whispered.

'Yes.' The word was angled upwards, with a sharp end to cut him for the hurt she was suffering.

Well, he thought, that doesn't sound like an invitation to a conversation, so he stayed silent. He crossed his hands on the pillow behind his head. The streetlight was still flickering, projecting the pattern of the lace curtain upon the far wall.

The pattern was distorted, a bizarre spider web of shadows and little out-of-parallel squares of light. The pattern flashed softly across the wall, then disappeared, then returned. Adam counted. It was regular, like a magic lantern show.

He heard a familiar sound. A horse and cart was coming down the road with the animal's steel shoes clinking on the bitumen surface. Nice sound. It reminded him of the bush. Probably a Clydesdale. He imagined a regal animal, chestnut with a mane flopping over an arched neck. Its hooves would be thick with hair, just like grass sprouting around stumps.

The horse stopped outside the building. He heard voices, and the clink of empty bottles.

'What are you going to do about the lamp?' Heather said, a tone of accusation in her voice.

'I hadn't thought about it.' More bottles rattled.

'Well, you should. You can't just leave it on the floor.'

'I didn't break it,' Adam said gently.

'That's right. Blame me.'

'I'll tell them I did it.'

'Couldn't you fix it?'

'I don't know.'

'You could get some glue.' The statement was a question.

'People must break things. I'll just say I knocked it over. There'll be no trouble.'

346

'They'll talk. They're already talking about you.'

'Let them.'

Questions settled in her breath but she said nothing and after a while Adam thought she had fallen asleep once more. Outside, more bottles touched. The horse moved again. Adam listened until the sound of its hooves and the grind of the cartwheels had grown faint. And with the silence he felt homesick.

He recognized the feeling but realized the absurdity of it. He had no home. Nyngan was where he lived, in a house he had just rented to share with a wife he loved but couldn't understand. He and Heather would be living there in a week, and when Mr Maguire died the mother would move in too. Well, it wasn't the house he was homesick for. He missed the bush. The space. The sense of marvellous isolation. The lack of crowding and the feeling of freedom. And, as his ears strained for the fading sound of the horse, he thought of other things. Subtle things, that went unnoticed at the time but now stirred his senses. The smell of gum trees. Dust in the air when the wind blew and gibbers that crunched under your boots. Waterholes with pelicans and swans. Lone eagles, soaring above the plain or skimming the crags of worn hills. The flash of colour as a squadron of cockatoos turned in the sun. The squawk of galahs. The smell of sheep after rain. The murmur of cattle at night. The squeak of a leather saddle. The sound of a horse pulling a cart.

His home was where those things were.

That was where he felt comfortable, and where his real friends were. He thought about Josef and Jimmy. He missed them. Strange. He hadn't thought about them much in the last few days but now, with a suddenness that made him ache, he wished they were here. Specially Jimmy. He might be crude and rough at times but he was the most honest man he knew. Jimmy might be able to tell him what to do.

'Are they really talking about us?' Heather asked the question softly, but the words jolted Adam back to wakefulness.

'Who?'

'The people at Nyngan. Are they talking about my father? Are they saying those things you said? About money?'

'Apparently.'

'What's that mean?' Her voice was different now. Not caustic or sharp but worried.

'Heather, I don't want to argue about this. All I know is that people have been saying these things to my friends and they told me. That's all.'

Adam mumbled the words, as though by mumbling he could blunt the response. It was the money discussion that had caused Heather to flare last time and he didn't want any more shouting and fighting. All he wanted for the moment was to be left alone. Not to think, but just to remain in silence. Later on, when he was less tired, he would think about the situation. About the things Heather had said and the way she had said them. About why she had married him. About their future. Maybe they would argue then. But not now. He just wanted to lie quietly and think of nothing and maybe drift back to sleep.

'What are they saying?'

He hesitated.

'Are you still awake?' she said, lifting herself on one elbow. Her hair was backlit by the stuttering light.

'Yes.' He breathed deeply, reluctant to start but knowing he must. 'What they're saying is that your father's in debt. They say it's because of bills for clothes and things. They say he can't pay his accounts at the grocer's and butcher's and some of the other shops in town.'

She was silent for a long time, then lowered herself to the pillow.

'What did *you* say?' she said.

'I said I thought it was shameful the way people gossiped about someone who was sick.'

'Did you say that?'

'Yes. Please go back to sleep, Heather.'

'Did they really say father was in financial trouble because of debts to do with clothing?'

'Yes.'

'Whose clothing?'

'Your mother's. Yours too, I suppose.'

She rolled towards him, her body curled, her hand to her face with the thumb pressed to the lips. She breathed deeply several times. He could see her body rise and fall.

'I hate that place, don't you?' she said.

'Which place?'

'Nyngan. I think we should move.'

'We've just rented a house,' he said.

Her foot touched his leg. Gently, her toes stroked his skin, running so lightly across the fine hairs that his whole body tingled.

'What does that matter?' she said. 'We could stop renting it. We could go somewhere else.'

He put his arm around her, straining to be gentle. She touched his chest and her fingertips played with his hair, curling it in slow spirals.

'It's no disgrace to owe money,' he said, holding her more firmly and feeling her stiffen as he spoke. 'A lot of people owe money these days. That's normal.'

'It's the gossip. That's what upsets me.'

'I know. Forget it. Some people just like to see others in trouble. Particularly important people like you father.'

He felt her relax. Her hand moved from his chest to his lips.

'We're not in trouble,' she whispered.

'Good.' He breathed the word through her fingers.

'We don't owe money.'

'Well, ignore the gossip. Who cares what those sort of people say anyhow?'

'I couldn't live there. Not with people like that. Can we go somewhere else?'

'You really want that?' He could not disguise the hope in his voice.

'Of course. You've always wanted a station of your own?'

'You know I have.'

'Well, why don't we get one?'

'Are you serious?'

She kissed him.

'You don't believe what they're saying about my family, do you?'

'I don't believe any gossip.' Both his arms were around her. My God, she feels beautiful, he thought and kissed her neck and followed his lips to her ear. He nibbled the lobe. 'You'd really like to live on a property?'

'With you, yes.'

He turned his face towards her shoulder. 'What about your mother? What will she do?'

'We'll see,' she said and he felt her mouth, open and moist, touch his neck. 'You will take me away from there, won't you?'

'We'll have the biggest and best property you ever saw. We'll have a big house with a verandah all around it and lots of water and plenty of green grass.'

'Can we have a tennis court?'

'You know I can't play.'

'I'll teach you. Will it have lights?'

'Why not?'

'Oh Adam, I love you. You will take me away from those awful people, won't you? And quickly. I don't want to stay there any longer than I have to.'

'I've heard of a place that sounds good.'

'Get it then.'

'It's out west.'

'Doesn't matter,' she rushed on. 'Promise me you'll take me away.'

Just before dawn they made love. It happened suddenly. Heather had been lying with her back to him but with his hands clasped in hers and drawn around her body. Without speaking she turned and gave herself to him. She said nothing and her eyes were closed, but she let him remove her nightgown and locked her arms around his body. It was a passionate primitive union, as wild and erratic as boughs rubbing in a strong wind, and punctuated by small cries.

When it was over she wept and held him tightly. Not understanding the tears but relishing the warmth of her embrace, Adam lay there, staring at the wall and mesmerized by the flickering pattern of the lace curtain. He was still awake when the streetlamp was extinguished and the first hint of sunlight entered the room. He was thinking about the property in Western Australia and wondering if it were still for sale.

For the rest of their stay in Manly they made love every night. The pattern was always the same. Some time before dawn she would half-wake and blend with him and be warm and soft and loving, but in the morning she would profess no knowledge of the act and flush with embarrassment if Adam tried to talk about it. So Adam said nothing. He was puzzled that Heather would not contemplate love-making when they went to bed, and yet turned to him with such passion at a time when most people were soundly asleep. Puzzled or not, he was happy to love and be loved so eagerly and found himself waking in anticipation. He even heard the horse again. It was a regular pre-dawn visitor. The man with the cart must collect empty bottles from the hotel, he reasoned, and as he listened to the sounds the horse made he

350

thought of the bush and longed to return.

TEN

The decision to go to Western Australia was a sudden one, made only three weeks after Adam and Heather returned to Nyngan and inspired by a chain of happenings. First, they found a plague of mice had reached the town and their new home was infested with the creatures. Some of their wedding gifts – linen, a wooden tray, the handle of a jug and even the cardboard storage boxes – had been gnawed through. Adam killed forty-three mice the first night, and next day Heather stormed back to her parents' home, vowing she would not return until the mice were gone.

She came back almost immediately because she and her mother had argued. Normally, Heather did the talking and her mother listened but this time Mrs Maguire snapped back. Heather, not knowing how to cope with such a situation, came running home, saying she wanted to leave town as soon as possible. Heather had started the argument, but that was normal. She had assailed her mother for letting the wedding gifts be damaged. Mrs Maguire, however, was not in the mood to worry about mice in someone else's home, even her daughter's, for Mr Maguire was much weaker and in constant pain and she had just endured the humiliation of a visit by a tradesman demanding money for past services. It was one of several similar visits in recent times. Mr Maguire was no longer able to work, of course, and, as Mrs Maguire put it, 'the maggots are after the body.' Then followed a discussion about who should bear the burden of the Maguires' financial responsibilities and what had begun as a one-sided tirade by the daughter ended in a bitter row.

Then there was a letter. Heather's friend Pam Stevens had written from Nevertire seeking news about the honeymoon and mentioning, in a most casual way, rumours about Mr Maguire's financial plight. Pam had, of course, *deplored* the stories and offered sympathy to Heather, who must be suffering *most dreadfully* under the weight of such *spiteful* and *untrue* talk. Heather was furious. She knew her friend was actually enjoying

351

the gossip, and resolved never to speak to her again.

Next came the arrival in town of Mr Abraham Steinbach, who was to replace her father as stationmaster. As if the name were not enough, Abe Steinbach proved to be a man attracted to the offerings of the hotel where he stayed. It was not just the drinking. Within a few days of his arrival there was talk of a liaison between Steinbach and one of the barmaids. To make things worse, people in town were laughing about him. About his looks (he had an unfortunate nose and they called him 'Stone-beak'), about the affair with the barmaid, and about the way he hovered, vulture-like, waiting for Maguire to die so that he could move into the house.

The man was a *creature*, said Heather, and his behaviour demeaned the position her father had filled so honourably.

She was already talking about her father as though he were dead. Seeing him was proving a distressing experience so she visited him infrequently; his face was gaunt and his skin a shiny grey and the room where he lay was dense with sickly air. It was not a place where a young, healthy woman should be, watching death close its grasp on an old man. So she behaved as though the man in her parents' bedroom were a stranger and continued to elevate her father's memory to a plane appropriate to someone who had been near-perfection.

Adam had never liked Mr Maguire. He had found him a pompous snob. The men at the railway station did not like him either, and reckoned Abe Steinbach was a fairer man to work for. At least Abe didn't have them doing private jobs, like watering and weeding the garden, or doing the shopping for his wife when the weather was too hot for women to venture out of doors. Adam said nothing to Heather, of course. He could imagine how dreadful it would be waiting for a parent to die, and if she chose to be like a child playing games of pretence to disguise the ugliness of reality then he was happy to let her prattle on about the fine man her imagination had made of her father.

But one day, something happened that he could not accept. He was buying meat – a simple order of sausages – and the butcher presented him with a bill for eighteen pounds, nine shillings and sixpence. Adam presumed the man had made a mistake and then, seeing him persist, thought he was joking. The butcher looked embarrassed, but he was serious.

Heather was waiting at the front door of their rented house, one hand aloft. Dangling from her thumb and forefinger was a mouse whose neck was caught in a trap. She held the mouse by the tail, grasping it firmly yet managing to suggest that, somehow, she was not quite touching it. Before she could speak, Adam wrenched the mouse from her hand, prised it from the trap and flung it into the trees lining the front fence.

'The house is still full of them,' she complained, but Adam ignored her.

'I have been to the butcher's,' he said. She blinked. 'He gave me a bill for more than eighteen pounds. Said it was for meat your mother has been buying.' He thrust the sausages at her.

'Nonsense!'

'It's not nonsense. He said it was for orders going back six months and more.'

'The man's mad.'

'He showed me the accounts.'

'How dare he!'

'Don't blame him. The poor bloke only wants his money. But do you know what really got me? Do you know what really made me mad?'

She stared at him, face shocked and with the sausages pressed to her body to protect her from the next onslaught of news.

'Your mother told him to give the bill to me!'

'She did what?' Her hands dropped to her sides.

'Told him I'd pay.'

'That man is unbelievable.'

'Your mother's unbelievable.'

'You don't believe him?'

'He showed me the note from your mother.'

'Mother wrote to him?'

'She said I was handling all financial matters because Mr Maguire was so sick. And listen to this.' He slapped his hands. 'She said I'd been given the money to settle the accounts.'

Heather lifted her head. 'How do you know mother said those things? You can't read.'

Adam blushed. 'I can read a bit. It was her note all right. In any case the butcher wouldn't lie.'

'Yes, he would. He's just out to rob us. I'll never do business with him again.'

'Heather, stop it!'

'Stop what?'

'Trying to sidetrack me. Whenever I try to say something you don't want to hear, you start blaming someone else for something else. I don't care about meat and whether you buy from that butcher or not.'

'Well, I do. I'll never do business with him again. I mean it.'

He took a step nearer her. 'It's not the butcher I'm angry with. It's your mother.'

'I'm sure she will never buy meat from him again.'

'I don't think he'd sell her any. He told me she can't have any more meat until the money's paid.'

Heather faced the wall. 'Oh, what a horrible thing to do! And with my father so sick.'

'The horrible thing was what your mother did. It was bad enough telling him I was responsible for all your family debts. But teling him she'd given me the money to pay the bills! Jesus!'

Her face turned towards him. Her eyes were frightened.

'Did you know about this?' he said.

She shook her head.

'If your parents want me to pay the family debts, that's fine. If they're in trouble and I can help, that's all right. But I'd like to be asked. I resent, my God, I resent your mother telling the butcher to give me her bill. Just like that. Eighteen pounds! For God's sake, that's nearly ten weeks' wages these days! What did you eat? Fillet steak every day?'

'Of course not.' She lowered her eyes. 'Are you blaming me for this?'

'Why would I blame you?'

She left the wall and put her arms around him.

'It must have been very embarrassing for you. I mean, having the man say those things to you.'

'It was.'

'Were there other people in the shop?'

'No.'

She offered her cheek and he kissed it.

'Well, that's something. What did you do?'

'About what?'

'The bill. Did you pay it?' She asked the question in an offhand way. He looked at her quizzically.

'Are you sure you don't know anything about all this?' he said.

'That is a simply awful thing to suggest. I merely asked what you'd done. That man, I think, has made the whole thing up.'

354

'No, he hasn't. He was genuine. Your parents owe him money.'

'I can't imagine how that could be. There must be some mistake. Mother may have overlooked settling the account because of all the worry she's had. I suppose that's possible.'

'He told me something else.' He paused, making sure he had her attention. 'He told me your family owes money all over town.'

'The man is a liar.'

'He said your father owes hundreds of pounds.'

She walked to the edge of the verandah. It was a sunny day with a cloudless sky, and she gazed up, squinting in the glare. 'Isn't it amazing?' she said slowly, searching the unblemished sky for an impurity to match her thoughts, 'A man of strength, a man of honour, someone every decent person respects, takes ill and is known to be … to be near the end, and immediately – immediately – some people start spreading malicious stories. Gossip of the most evil kind.'

She turned, smiling sadly. 'It's just envy, I suppose. People, knowing themselves to be inferior, invent stories to drag someone else down to their level. They certainly wouldn't dare say such things if father was well.'

'The butcher was talking about legal action.'

'What do you mean?'

'He said he would see his solicitor if I didn't give him the money.'

'And you didn't?' It was a question that longed to be contradicted.

'No, of course not. But he wants the money in a week.'

'What are you going to do?'

'See your mother.'

'No! Don't do that. She's had so many upsetting things happen lately. Let me see her.'

'You'll tell her what happened?'

'Of course.'

Heather went to her parents' home that night. She did not enter the bedroom where her father lay, but took her mother by the elbow and led her into the kitchen and closed the door.

'Well, you certainly botched that nicely, mother,' she began.

While Heather was away, Adam went to George Curran's house to see Jimmy and Josef. They talked on the back verandah.

Jimmy was in surprisingly high spirits.

'I've earned a bit of money,' he announced breezily.

'Doing what?' Adam asked. His friend looked thin but the smile, while emphasizing the new lines on his face, was genuine.

'Catching mice.'

'You're joking!'

'Fair dinkum. I've gone into business as a mouse catcher. This plague's a stroke of luck. I made seven bob today.'

'It's true,' Josef said. 'He's gone to the school and the nursing home and a couple of houses and they all want him to come back.'

'I charge threepence a dozen.'

'And you made seven bob?'

They all laughed. It wasn't just the mice or the money. It was that Jimmy was doing something and was happy.

'How the devil did you catch so many?' Adam asked.

'You mean with one arm?' There was a flash of triumph on Jimmy's face.

'No. I couldn't catch that many if I had four arms.'

'Well, mate, it's easy. I was always quick on my feet. I just run them down and stamp on them.'

Jimmy had a few seconds to enjoy Adam's look of astonishment.

'He does not!' Josef said, grinning. 'He borrowed George's dog which can smell a mouse at half a mile, and he carried a sugar bag and a lump of wood, and the dog rounds the mice up, just like a kelpie working sheep, and Jimmy belts them with the piece of timber and then puts them in the bag. It's the funniest thing you've ever seen.'

'Yeah, but it works,' Jimmy said.

'Sounds like hard work,' Adam said.

Jimmy shrugged.

'Not feeling sore?'

'Not as sore as the mice.' They all laughed.

'What are you going to do when all the mice are gone?' Adam said.

'I'm going to buy me a stud farm.'

'A what?'

'Stud farm. I'm going to breed mice. There's more money in them than there is in wool.'

They talked and laughed a lot and Adam felt more relaxed than he had for weeks. Elated in the company of his friends, he re-opened the subject of the property in Western Australia. Jimmy had not heard of it, so Josef ran through the details, his enthusiasm growing as he recalled the features. Another advertisement had appeared, he said, and went off to search for the newspaper.

'Would there be a job for a one-armed abo?' Jimmy asked while Josef was absent.

'Depends how many mice there are on the place,' Adam said, and they both grinned. Then he became serious. 'There's more than a job. Joe wants a share. Why don't you become a partner too?'

'Oh, I haven't got any money, mate.'

'Doesn't matter. Neither has Joe. I think I've got enough for the deposit. We can borrow the rest. Joe's going to work for his share.'

'Well, that rules me out.'

'No, it doesn't. There are things you could do.'

'Like what?' Jimmy picked up an old tennis ball and began squeezing it. It was an exercise he did regularly to strengthen the grip in his right hand.

'Lots of things. You can still ride a horse, can't you?'

'Don't know.'

'Bet you could, and as good as ever. You're better with one hand than most people are with two.'

'Yeah.' He squeezed the ball a few times. 'The hand's getting strong.'

'I noticed.'

He let the ball drop, and kicked it under his bed. 'I'd rather just work for you. That way, if it didn't work out, you know, if I couldn't do the sort of things I had to do, I could just piss off and do something else.'

Adam scratched his scalp. 'I'd like you with me, Jimmy.'

'Yeah.'

'We've been together a long time. Be nice to share something like that.'

Jimmy stood and adjusted the shirt sleeve around the stump of his arm. 'It still aches sometimes. Funny thing, it doesn't hurt where I've got any arm left but it aches down here.' He pointed to a spot near his trouser belt. 'Right where my hand used to be. Just now my fingers are hurting.'

Adam said nothing.

'You came down that bloody well to get me out, didn't you?'

Adam looked surprised. They had never discussed the accident.

'Never thanked you for that,' Jimmy continued. 'Must have been a mess down there. Joe tells me you nearly got killed.'

'Joe exaggerates.'

'Yeah. Anyhow, thanks.'

'That's all right. You'd have done the same for me.'

'Sure. How's the new missus?'

'Heather? She's good.'

'Working out all right?'

'What do you mean?'

'You know what I mean, you silly bugger! Are you happy? Is she treating you right?'

'Sure.' Adam said, but felt uncomfortable for Jimmy was staring at him and his eyes were bright, as though he knew all that had happened between them.

'She happy to go to the west?'

'She suggested it.'

'That rocks me,' Jimmy said. 'I'd never have picked her as a lady who'd want to go bush. I thought she'd have you packed up and heading for the city within twelve months.'

'She's full of surprises,' Adam said.

Joe returned, talking as he walked and bubbling with enthusiasm. The price of the property had dropped and the vendor was now offering better terms.

'They've arranged finance. It's only five hundred pounds down now. You can pay the balance off over ten years. We could do that, Adam.'

'Could you handle that?' Jimmy asked, arching an eyebrow at Adam. 'Five hundred quid's a lot of money.'

'I've saved a fair bit these last few months and I'm pretty well in with the bank manager.'

'So you should be. You must be the only bloke for a hundred miles who's made money in the last year. But listen, you two.' He wagged a finger at his friends. 'Don't rush in. If the bloke's asking for five hundred, he'll probably take four. Offer him that.'

So that night, Josef wrote a letter expressing interest in the property but saying four hundred was the maximum deposit they could pay. Adam signed it.

'I've asked Jimmy if he'd like to be a partner,' he said,

examining his signature with pride.

'And I've said no,' Jimmy said.

'Why?'

'I just want to see how good I am with this one arm. I'd rather just work for you two for a while, and see what happens. If it's a good property and there are things I can do around there, then maybe we'll talk about me having a share. But not now.' He smiled brightly. 'Supposing this bloke accepts your offer. What are you two going to do next?'

'I suppose we'd have to go over there and look at the place,' Adam said. 'We can't buy until we've seen it.'

'The advertisement says they'll take people out to the property for an inspection,' Josef said.

'Where from?' Jimmy asked.

'I don't know. Perth, I suppose.'

Jimmy turned to Adam. 'Can you afford to get to Perth?'

'I think so. I'm not sure how much three train fares would cost.'

'Are you taking your wife?'

'No. You, Josef and me.'

'Don't worry about me,' Jimmy said, searching under the bed for the tennis ball. He resumed squeezing.

'You're going to have the strongest right arm in the country,' Adam said.

'Yeah.'

'I'd like you to come. Have a look at it. See what you think.'

'No, I won't go there yet. Matter of fact, I thought I might go back home for a while and see some of the family.'

'In South Australia?'

'Yeah. Few people I'd like to see. Just take it easy for a while, you know. Then if you decide to go ahead with buying this place, let me know and I'll come and join you.'

Jimmy flicked the ball to Josef, who caught it and threw it back.

'You could come with us as far as Port Augusta,' Josef said. 'The train goes through there on the way to Perth. We'd have to go down to Orange, or maybe Parkes and pick up the train to the west. It goes through Broken Hill and Port Pirie and then up to Port Augusta.'

'Good old Port Augusta,' Jimmy said without enthusiasm.

'Oh, that's right!' Josef said. 'Would it be safe for you now?'

'Safe as houses. Specially with this.' He wriggled the stump of his arm. 'Anyhow, I wouldn't spend any time there. I'd go on up to Beltana.'

'How long would you stay there?' Adam asked.

'Long as it takes.' Jimmy began bouncing the ball. 'Tell me, mate, are you sure your missus wants to go to the west?'

'That's what she says.'

'Why?'

'She wants to get away from here. It's mainly because of the gossip. People are talking about her father owing money.'

'The old bastard owes hundreds,' Jimmy said. 'It's not just lately either. He has for years. At least, that's what people tell me. Do you know what, mate?'

Adam waited.

'I hope that wife of yours isn't like her father. From what I hear he's a scheming old bastard who uses people and doesn't give a donkey's turd for what they think or who he hurts.'

He bounced the ball vigorously a few times.

'You know Nugget Bennett?' He waited for the nods which meant they knew one of the local aboriginal men. 'Nugget did a job for Maguire and never got paid and when he kicked up a fuss Maguire reckoned he'd stolen something – a rake or something – and had him put in the slammer for three months. It's one thing not to pay people even when you owe them, but what sort of bloke would have someone put in gaol just to shut him up? It was only a five bob job, too. To put it politely, he's a nasty old cunt and the sooner he's dead and buried the better.'

Josef looked shocked. 'That's an awful thing to say!'

'He's an awful bloke,' Jimmy said.

For the next few days, Heather refused to return to her parents' home. She and her mother had argued, she explained to Adam, because her mother had misled her. Yes, there were some outstanding debts but only trivial ones, including one with the butcher. It was as Heather had surmised. Her mother had been so engrossed in the care of her father that she had overlooked these things. Normally, her father handled such matters. Her mother was a perfect goose when it came to money or business affairs. Even so, her mother should not have deceived her by saying there were no debts when there were. That deception had caused Heather to mislead Adam, however innocently, and she had been very cross with her mother because the last thing she wanted was to deceive her husband. As a punishment, she was not going to visit her mother until the weekend.

And the letter to the butcher? The man was obviously a scoundrel. Yes, there had been a letter but it had been merely a note apologizing for having overlooked the account and explaining that Mrs Maguire had been preoccupied with her husband's illness and the marriage of her daughter. She had mentioned that she found it difficult to leave the house and might ask her son-in-law, who was a most obliging type, to deliver a cheque on her behalf. That was all.

Several things had puzzled Adam but he let them pass. He had been excited about sending the letter to Western Australia and told her about it. She had not asked any questions but had smiled and said again she was anxious to leave town as soon as possible.

'When I see mother, I will tell her we are planning to leave,' she said, sitting primly with her hands crossed on her lap and relishing the thought of passing on such news. 'She will be most upset, and that will serve her right.'

Three weeks later, a letter came back from Perth. It was from the agent who said the lower deposit was acceptable and urged Adam to travel to Perth so that he could inspect the property and sign the contract of sale. He would be delighted to see them and would offer any assistance they required. Adam saw his bank manager and had him mail the agent a bank cheque for four hundred pounds.

Josef bought three rail tickets – Nyngan-Perth and return for himself and Adam, and Nyngan-Port Augusta for Jimmy.

Heather was shocked.

'Why are you going by train?'

'Because there's no other way, except by sea.'

Adam was still excited by the news. He was now virtually the owner of his own property.

'Where in the name of heaven is this place?'

'Near Perth.'

'Perth!' She collapsed on a chair. 'In Western Australia? You never told me that!'

'Yes I did,' Adam said and searched his memory. Maybe he hadn't said Perth, but he had definitely said 'in the west'. He recalled being surprised by Heather's desire to move and he also recalled being reluctant to be too specific in case she changed her mind. 'I said in the west,' he said. 'That's where Perth is.'

'I thought you meant somewhere out there.' She waved her

hand. 'And hour or so away. Somewhere where we could go by car.'

'You said you wanted to get right away from this town.'

'You've certainly done that. You could scarcely have gone any further. Perth! I don't even know anyone who's ever been there.' She fanned herself. 'And you say you've paid a deposit on this land?'

'Four hundred pounds.'

'Oh, my heavens!'

'I get it back if we don't like the land.'

'We?'

'Josef is going with me.'

'That young German man? What would he know?'

Adam's upturned hand swept the air, searching for the answer. 'He's going to be a partner in the deal,' he said. 'He should see the place first.'

'A partner? You mean we're not going to own this property?'

'I'll have the biggest share.'

She stood and walked to another room. Adam stayed where he was.

'When are you going?' she called.

'Next week. The man's going to meet us and show us the property. If we don't like it, we don't buy and we get our money back.'

There was a long pause. He heard water running from the tap.

'How long will you be away?' she called.

'I don't know. Maybe a month or so.'

A glass fell and smashed on the floor. She re-appeared at the door.

'You're going away for months?'

'Maybe a month. I don't know.'

'Exactly where is this property?'

'North of Perth.'

'Half the world is north of Perth. Do you know exactly where?'

'It's on the advertisement. It's got the name of the property. It doesn't seem to be too far from town. Do you want to see the ad?'

'No, thank you.' She turned her back on him. 'You're not really thinking of taking me to Western Australia, are you?'

'Well, I'm not going to go and live there without you!'

'You might have to.'

362

'You *said* you wanted to leave! You said you wanted me to have my own station. I told you about this place, I said it was in the west, and you said "get it". That was back in Manly.'

'I was upset.'

'And you are now?'

'Yes.'

'Does that mean I shouldn't take any notice of you when you're upset?'

She turned her head to glare at him.

'Because if that's the case, I wouldn't take any notice of you most of the time.'

'What do you mean?'

'I think you can work it out.'

She strode from the room and he followed.

'I don't know what to make of you, Heather. You marry me in a rush and then you treat me like dirt. I come back and get caught up in all this drama about the butcher and his bills and you give me some cock-and-bull story about your mother forgetting to pay because she's been so worried. Your family never pays. It's all around the town. Your father's tighter than a ... than a ...' He was going to say 'sheep's arsehole' but changed his mind. Cool down, a voice told him, but anger overwhelmed reason.

'He's a skinflint and a cheat who doesn't pay anyone unless he can help it.'

'You bastard!' she said.

'Oh, here we go again! Back to the number one naughty word. Where did you learn that? Behind the dunny at the ladies college?'

'How dare you say things about my father!'

'Because it's time, and because I'm copping some of the rubbish from people he's cheated.'

'He is the most honest man this town's known.'

'Baloney. Do you know a man called Bennett? Nugget Bennett?'

She frowned. 'A black man?'

'He did some work for your father.'

'He stole something from the shed.'

'Your father didn't pay him for a job.'

'He was a thief.'

'The people of this town reckon the thief was your father. They say he made up the story about Nugget stealing something so he wouldn't have to pay the man five bob.'

363

'Who says that?'

'Everyone. They say your father cheats people, they say he diddles the railways and hasn't paid his debts for years. Wake up, Heather! People here don't respect your father. They say he's a skinflint and a bludger.'

'And you agree with them?'

Adam sat down. He had never spoken to her like that. When he spoke again, he was calmer. 'Look, Heather, come down out of the clouds. Your father is what he is, not what you'd like him to be. And I don't want you turning out to be like him.'

'So you think I'm a ... What did you call him? A skinflint and a bludger?'

'You've been lying to me.'

'How dare you!'

'Oh, don't go on with that high-faluting rubbish! You have been lying to me and you know it. Your family's been in financial trouble for years. Everyone in town knows it, so you must have known. And don't go blaming your poor silly old mother. She does what you tell her.'

'That's absurd.'

'It's not. You boast about it. It was your idea to get married so that you'd have someone to pay the bills, so you and your mother could go on living this phony, social life of yours.'

'That is a hateful suggestion!'

'The hateful thing is what you did to me. I can hear you talking to your mother. "Don't worry, mother, I'll just choose someone big and strong. Someone who doesn't drink and doesn't swear and someone who won't have the brains to see what we're up to. Someone I can boss around. Someone who has enough in the bank to get us out of trouble and who might make money one day." Is that how it went? You didn't care what sort of husband you landed as long as he didn't have a big Adam's apple like the man your silly girlfriend with the tennis court got engaged to. Some sort of friendly, good-looking pet you could lead around on a rope and show off to your friends and bully at home. Is that why you married me? It certainly wasn't because you loved me. It wasn't because you wanted to hop into bed with me.'

'It certainly wasn't!' she screamed. 'But that's the sort of girl you wanted, wasn't it? You wanted a tart. A slut! A common whore.'

Suddenly Adam felt tired. He should have said these things

long ago and now, having said them, he felt the weariness of someone who has carried a burden for too long.

'Are you calling yourself a slut, a whore? Because I wanted you, I married you. I didn't want a bad girl. I wanted a good wife. Someone I could love and honour. Not someone who's always scheming, always complaining. Not someone who tells me lies and tries to make me look foolish. Don't you understand, Heather?'

Her face showed anger, not understanding.

'You can't understand how angry I was over that business with the butcher, or how frustrated I've been over the way you've been treating me.'

'You're using a great number of big words,' she said. 'For someone who can't read or write.'

Adam shook his head. 'I used to think you were so clever. So educated. Now I'm beginning to feel sorry for you. You may know how to read and write but you don't know much about life. The more phony someone is, the more you seem to admire them. Real people are a mystery to you. You don't know what the real world's all about.'

She had been waiting for him to pause. 'And you do, I suppose?'

'No. But I'm willing to find out. You've made up your mind and the world you like is full of fakes in fancy dress.'

She shook her head violently. 'I can't believe I'm hearing all this. My own husband, saying dreadful things about me and my family.'

'What I'm telling you is that I've had enough of the way you've been treating me.'

She began to leave and he seized her wrist.

'Are you going to beat me now?' she said, facing him defiantly.

'I'm going to tell you something. I want you to change. Not just for me but for you.'

'Oh, how noble!'

He shook her, then stopped. 'No, I'm not going to let you provoke me.'

'My!' she said. 'Another big word.'

'You'd really like me to hit you, wouldn't you? That would make you feel superior. Brains over brawn, or something like that.' He released her. 'You'll have to change, Heather. You can't go on like some twittish schoolgirl who wants her own way in everything she does. It's about time you tried being fair dinkum.'

'I hate that expression. It's vulgar.'

He looked at her with pity. 'I used to think it was funny when you said things like that. I thought you were joking. Now I think you're serious.'

'I am.'

'I know. It's terrible. You know what I think the trouble is? You've got the meanness of your father and the brains of your mother. It's a bad combination.'

'How dare you!'

'You always say that when you don't know what else to say.'

'The sooner you leave the better.'

'I'll be off next week. I'll go and see the estate agent and tell him we're moving out.'

'Of the house? What about me?'

'Do you want to come to Perth?'

'Definitely not!'

'Well, go back and live with your mother. You can bully her while I'm away.'

ELEVEN

A few days before Adam's departure, Heather seemed to change. Quite suddenly one night she declared she was sorry for the things they had said. It may not have been a complete apology (it was what *they* had said, not what she had said) but even so it represented a major change in her attitude. Until that time she had not spoken to him since the argument but had maintained a frosty silence. And despite her vow to 'punish' her mother by not visiting her, she had spent much time at the Maguires' house, even sleeping there on several occasions. Adam had assumed that Heather would not speak to him before he left for Perth. He accepted that. He was not going to withdraw any of his accusations because he felt that what he had said was true. He tried once to talk to her, to assure her he still loved her and wanted them to share in his new venture in the west; what he had said needed to be brought out in the open, but it did not change his feelings for her. She ignored him, and he did not try again.

He was surprised when she suddenly came to him. She had been at her mother's and normally when she returned she would be in a worse mood than ever. She would scowl and deliberately bump objects and even throw things across the room, but never speak.

This time, however, she came to him, smiling shyly and saying that they were silly. It had been a lovers' quarrel and neither had meant the things they said. Adam kept quiet because she appeared to be contrite and loving and he did not want to spoil the chance of making up.

She touched him gently, almost nervously, as though fearful of his reaction, and when he did not move away she put both arms around him, kissed him and began to cry. They both said they were sorry they had argued and she led him to the bedroom and they made love. It was the first time in Nyngan, and Adam almost burst with love and joy that his wife had returned to him.

Afterwards, as she lay in his arms and he gazed at the ceiling and wondered how he could endure the next few weeks without her, she asked him not to go to Perth. She lay beside him, talking into his breast, and quietly, calmly and logically listed the reasons why he should not go.

It was the way she spoke that chilled him. Her voice was not sad, or even sobbing with the out-of-control emotions of a woman who cannot bear to be parted from her lover. There was something calculating in her words. It was a planned speech, rehearsed with care and delivered at the crucial moment, when she was soft and naked and filled with his love and he was caring and spent and vulnerable. She delivered her lines like an actress playing a scene, and he realized that this was why she had come to him; not to love him, but to sway him.

Don't go, she said. It's so far. I'll worry about you. I'll miss you. Then the tone changed. Just think of the risk, she said, her whisper earnest and conspiratorial. You don't know these people. They may steal your money and then you will have nothing left. *We* will have nothing. And you shouldn't be going now, not while father is so ill. What if he dies while you're away? I won't know what to do. Who will make the arrangements? And we shouldn't let this house go. Where will we all stay, particularly if you don't like this land out the back of beyond? It's all so risky, so uncertain, so worrying. Why not stay for a while and look for a place nearer here? Maybe even closer to Sydney? We could even think about moving to the city. Just for a while, maybe a year or so, and then you could look around for a property. There was lovely land around Moss Vale. You should look around there before rushing off to Western Australia to go and live among the blackfellows. And how would mother get on if we both went to this new place? We can't just abandon her. There are some debts to pay – only small ones – but ones she might have difficulty meeting, keeping in mind all the expense of the wedding and all the cost of the coming funeral. And how could they even help a little bit if all their money was spent on land in some God-forsaken wilderness? Did Adam want to see her mother in the poorhouse, or taken to court simply because Heather's father had died with his affairs in an untidy state? Her mother would need help. It would be unthinkable to desert her.

'You mean you want me to stay so I can pay all the bills your family has run up for the last six months or more,' Adam said.

She pushed herself away from him. 'I thought you loved me!' she said, her voice throbbing with hurt.

'And I was starting to think you loved me. But it's the same old thing, isn't it? Who's going to look after your mother and who's going to pay all those bills? For God's sake, if you want me to pay all the family debts just tell me! Don't give me yards of tripe. Don't pretend to love me. Was that little speech something you and your mother have been rehearsing?'

'You can go to hell!'

'I'm going to Perth.'

'You don't care what I want, do you?'

'You wanted to go away from here. You wanted me to buy my own property. You wanted me to go to the west.'

She pulled a sheet around her body.

'Heather, if I like this place, and if I sign the contract of sale, you will come with me to Western Australia and we will live there together. Not you and me and your mother, but you and me. Your mother can go and live with her sister in Parramatta and sleep in the junk room with the cat and pretend she's Queen Mary and let them pay for her meat and her fancy clothes.'

'You're not taking all your money with you,' she said, squinting with concern. 'Are you?'

'I've already paid the deposit on the land. I've paid for the train ticket. There isn't much left.'

'You're deserting me! And my mother. You are abandoning my mother. You might as well be condemning her to prison.' She began gathering clothes. 'I will not see you again before you go on this crazy journey of yours. I shall go to my parents' place and stay there. But I warn you.' She turned, clutching garments to her chest. 'If you don't send me money, I will have you arrested.'

'I'm sure you will.'

She shook both fists. 'I'm serious!' she yelled.

'That's your trouble. You always are serious. The problem is that you get serious about the wrong things.'

Only George Curran came to see them leave Nyngan. He brought his dog and, because he was not allowed to take the animal on to the platform, he said goodbye at the wooden gate that marked the entrance to the railway station. Jimmy lingered, scratching the dog behind the ear and encouraging it to catch more mice.

'Your wife not well?' Curran asked Adam, who shook his head, and Curran said he was sorry to hear that. He repeated his promise to advertise the truck and drilling gear for Adam and to give him a list of any potential buyers when he returned.

'You are coming back?' Curran said.

'I think so. Unless the place is so good we start working it straight away.'

'Well, no worries, mate. I can sell the stuff for you if you like.' He left and the dog went with him but it was a twitching, halting departure with Jimmy's hunting companion stopping to look back.

'Knows I'm leaving, doesn't he?' Jimmy said. 'Good dog, that.'

Adam watched Curran and the dog depart. They were the only figures on the street. They passed the Maguires' house and Adam watched for a long time in case Heather appeared. She had been staying there since the previous day. He could see the brown wooden fence and the front gate, and the line of shrubs hanging over the dusty footpath and the roof of the house and the taller trees in the garden. He wondered if the parrots were in the trees. It was a lovely garden.

He saw no sign of his wife.

Josef and Jimmy sat on their luggage and gazed down the tracks, and said nothing. The train came, a black locomotive puffing smoke and hissing steam and hauling a row of brown carriages from which curious heads projected. The three friends were the only new passengers. A whistle blew, the engine blasted a response and Nyngan slid into the past.

BOOK FOUR

Cobargo

ONE

It took nearly ten days to reach Perth and in those long days of travel Adam had plenty of time to think about Heather. On the first day the three young men had to change trains twice, once at Narromine to head south through Peak Hill and again at Parkes, a major rail town where they were to board the train to the west. The land grew progressively more undulating and green. As the country softened and a stark horizon gave way to the smudge of hills, so did the fierceness of Adam's resolution wane. He began to wonder if he had been wrong. Wrong in deciding to buy the land. In accusing the Maguires and in arguing with Heather. In leaving her for so long. At first he gazed out of the window, eyes wide and unfocused, seeing not the land rolling past but images of the past weeks. He found himself reliving the most worrying occasions. He conducted endless debates with Heather, presenting with great eloquence all the arguments he should have made while still in town. An occasional flash of substance through the window of the carriage would bring him back to reality: a ploughed field with a team of horses working in the far corner; logs piled together and burning as a farmer cleared the land; or a cluster of concrete silos on the outskirts of a town.

Adam was beginning to doubt the wisdom of leaving on such an extravagant journey. He had been impetuous. Normally he did things after thinking about the consequences for a long time, and weighing the advantages against the disadvantages. This time he had rushed. It was partly his own desire to own a property and partly the infectious and urgent enthusiasm of Josef, but the main reason had been Heather. He had to get her away from her mother. They had to live on their own if their marriage was to work, and far better to be on their own property than renting a house. And then, when all the arguments had started, he had gone ahead like some stubborn bullock set on a course through rough country, and the more Heather had tried to talk him out of it the

373

more he had been determined to go.

The train stopped at a platform filled with people. An old woman stared at Adam. 'You're running away and leaving your wife,' she seemed to be saying. The woman kept looking and Adam felt bad. The train moved on again and he covered his eyes, pretending to sleep.

He wasn't running away. He was going to the west to establish himself on the land. The move was for the two of them, even if she didn't want to be part of it.

What if the property was no good? Almost all the money he possessed was committed to this deal. Maybe Heather was right. And God, why was he leaving her for so long?

He would have gone home at that moment.

As the train continued, light streamed through the window and the noise dropped to a comforting rattle. He saw a man on a fine horse and, a few seconds later, a row of trees leading to a homestead on a hill. It had an iron roof painted red and a wide verandah with white posts and trees on the western side to shelter it from the fierceness of the afternoon sun. Not big, but a good house. The sort he would like. One that was on a hill, so you could see it from a distance, with a wide verandah where you could sit in the evenings and look out over the land.

The line turned and the homestead merged with reflections on the glass, and was gone.

When they got to Parkes, he saw an eastbound train on the next platform. It was going through Molong to Orange. He could catch that train and connect with another train through Dubbo, Narromine, Trangie and Nevertire to Nyngan, and be back with Heather early on the afternoon of the next day. For a while, he played a mental game of tug-of-war, balancing one set of destinations on one platform with the other, but he knew he had made the decision a long time ago. He had dreamed too much, spent too much and said too much. He had to go on.

That first night became the clearest in Adam's recollection of the journey. The rest were blurred in a succession of long and uncomfortable hours spent rumbling and swaying through a cavernous blackness. There were occasional stops, of course. They paused at platforms where grey figures shuffled past, their shoulders hunched and their soles scraping gravel. And several times each night, it seemed, they would halt at some remote siding until an oncoming train had passed. Often the waiting took hours.

Those were the worst times. The cold and discomfort and monotony could be endured if the train were moving, but when it stopped it was as though the world had been overwhelmed by boredom and was pausing for breath. Sometimes the train jolted and clanked as it shunted from one position to another but usually it just waited. Within the carriages the lights were reduced to sleeping level and their half-glow added to the sense of timelessness. They shone dull and yellow and coated the interior with the tarnish of an old oil painting, finding lustre in brass luggage racks and richness of texture in cracked leather seats. Sleeping figures, heads bent unnaturally and muscles wracked by discomfort and cold, were transformed to soft shadows.

Occasionally, someone would cough. A child would cry. The engine would steam a hiss of frustration. And they would wait.

The days were as long and as monotonous but at least the land could be seen to be rolling past.

Josef was gazing to his right where long flat paddocks rose to meet the shadows of a mountain range. They were heading north from Port Pirie. They were on another train, the fifth of the journey.

'What are the hills?' he asked Adam, without looking at him.

'He's asleep, mate,' Jimmy answered.

'Oh.'

'They're the Flinders.'

Josef's look said he was surprised that Jimmy should know the answer.

'Adam doesn't know everything,' Jimmy said gently and kept looking out of the window. 'Matter of fact, I don't think he's ever been down this way. I spent a lot of time around here.'

'Big hills, aren't they?'

'They get bigger. They start here and go all the way north for a couple of hundred miles. Beyond Beltana where I was born.'

'How long are you going to spend up there?'

'Don't know. Few weeks maybe.'

'Why are you going back?'

'My mother's still at Beltana. At least I think she is. I'd like to see her.'

The steady rattle of wheels on the rail changed as the train crossed a bridge. A line of fat gum trees followed a sandy creek bed towards the ranges.

'When are *you* going home to see your mother and father?'
Jimmy asked.

'One day.'

'You should go back. Just for a while. They're nice people.'

Josef nodded. 'When I get set up.'

'Don't leave it too long. They're not getting any younger, you
know.'

'What do you mean?'

'People die.'

'Jesus, that's a nice thing to say!'

'Well, it's what happens. Christ, if you want to get a drunk to
cry, just ask him about his mother.'

Josef laughed.

'No, it's true. Most of the drunks I know spent half their lives
staying away from home and the rest of their lives regretting it.
You can learn a lot from drunks.'

'Like what?'

'Tons of things. You'd be surpised how many drunks were
clever men who hit the grog because they're sorry about
something.'

Josef laughed. 'Jesus, you lecture me a lot!'

'You need it.'

Josef crossed his ankles on the seat next to Jimmy. 'Is that why
you're going back to see your mother?'

'Yeah. To stop me turning into a deadbeat.' He threw a mock
punch at Josef. Although the fist did not come within a foot of the
younger man's chin he recoiled in slow motion.

'You still hit hard,' he said.

'Too right. I could beat you with one hand tied behind my
back.'

Josef didn't know whether to laugh or not, so he looked out the
window.

'I wish you were coming to the west with us,' he said
eventually.

'Yeah, well, not this time.'

'Why don't you want part of the property?'

'I don't feel like settling down.'

'It's not the arm, is it?' Josef was still looking out of the
window. When Jimmy did not answer he turned. The other man
was smiling at him.

'It's not the arm. It's just me. I'm not ready to settle down.

376

Have you ever known a blackfeller who could stay in one place?'

'Oh, cut it out, Jimmy! You're not like the others.'

'Yes, I am. Anyhow, what's wrong with being an abo?'

'Nothing, you silly bugger! It's just that ... oh, I don't know.'

'Don't worry, kid. I know what you mean. But I've just got something in me that makes me want to keep on moving. It's all right for you white blokes. You can build yourself a house and never move and be happy. Not me.'

'You will come and work on the place if we buy it, won't you?'

'Sure.'

Josef took his feet from the other seat. A thought had just occurred to him. 'How are we going to let you know where we are?'

'Write to me. Keep it simple so I can follow it.'

'Where do I send it?'

'Beltana. Or Port Augusta. I might come down there.'

'Any address in particular, or do I just write to "Jimmy Kettle, either of Beltana or Port Augusta, South Australia"?'

Jimmy scratched the side of his nose. 'For a feller who's been to school you aren't too smart at times. To start with, you write to Jimmy Black, not Jimmy Kettle. I don't think my real name would be a good idea around this part of the world for a while. Then you send one letter to me care of the post office at Beltana and another one care of the post office at Port Augusta. In about a month's time when I hear from you, I'll know what to do.' He stopped, for Josef looked worried. 'What's up, Joe? Want me to give you the tuppence for the extra stamp?'

'It's not that.' Josef did not smile. 'You will come, won't you?'

'I'll come.'

'How do you reckon Adam's going to be?'

Jimmy shuffled to an upright position. 'How do you mean?'

'With Heather.'

Jimmy let the tip of his tongue explore the gap in his front teeth. It made his lips balloon. He often did it when he was thinking about something.

'Don't know,' he said.

'I don't think I like her.'

'Lucky it wasn't you she married, then.'

'I mean I don't think she's good for Adam.'

Again Jimmy's lips swelled as his tongue probed the place where his teeth had been. He checked to make sure Adam was still sleeping.

377

'Have you said anything to him?' he said softly.

'No. I wouldn't. Oh, we had a bit of a discussion when we were first talking about the land but that was all.'

'Well, that's good. The best way to lose a mate is to interfere in his love life. You tell someone you don't like his girl or his wife and see how much longer you get invited home for Sunday dinner.'

'I don't get invited now.'

'You know what I mean. Just don't interfere.'

Josef removed a boot and massages his toes. 'I'm still worried. I can't see her living on a sheep station in the middle of the bush. She's not Adam's type.'

'That was the big attraction.'

Josef raised his eyebrows, wanting more.

'She's so different to any other woman he's ever known. Not that the poor bastard's known many, but look at what happened. We spend more than five years roaming the Never Never, keeping away from people and seeing no more than a dozen reasonable-looking sheilas in all that time. And then, while you and me are finishing that job on the railway, Adam goes off down to town on his own and meets this girl who looks like something out of a dream. Blonde hair, blue eyes, good legs. Takes a bath regularly, smells of perfume and talks like a lady. And let's face it, the girl is beautiful. Now if I'd seen her first and so much as smiled at her, there'd have been a shotgun up my arse so fast it wouldn't have been funny, and if you'd seen her first they'd have hung you for attempted rape because you're as mad as a donkey with sheilas.'

'Oh, cut it out, Jimmy!'

'It's true. Remember that Phyllis, the young sort you had out in the bush up in Queensland?' Jimmy used his hands to outline Phyllis's most outstanding assets. They grinned at each other.

'Well, that's you and that's me, too, if I get the chance, but it's not Adam. He's not like us. He respects women. He's very old-fashioned. He's probably always had a dream in his head about someone with big eyes and long hair and who dresses like a lady, and he arrives at Nyngan and there she is. He likes her. She likes him. Jackpot.'

Josef put his feet back on the seat. 'I don't think she does.'

'What? Like him?'

'No. That's the trouble. I've heard her talk to him. She bosses him around.'

'All women do that.'

'Not the way she does. She puts on this fancy voice of hers and tries to grind him down. You know, make him some kind of slave or something. She doesn't nag like a lot women I've heard. She just talks softly, but she makes him sound like some sort of gig.'

'Which he is not,' Jimmy said.

'No, he certainly isn't. I think he's too good for her.'

Jimmy looked quizzically at his friend. 'You haven't got your eye on her yourself?'

Josef looked offended. 'Shit, no! I think she's a toffee-nosed little twerp.'

Jimmy looked doubtful. 'Maybe, but she's the best-looking sheila you or I have ever seen. And that's the trouble. Adam was just bowled over.'

'But what if she won't come to the west?'

Jimmy spent some time gazing at the distant ranges. 'She won't be the first wife living in town while her husband's out in the bush.'

'Adam won't do it.'

'Won't do what?'

'Leave her on her own. If she won't come to this property, he won't stay.'

'Even if he buys it?'

Josef shook his head. 'You were right when you said he was different to us. You and me would tell her to piss off but Adam won't. He'd give up everything just to do the right thing by her. He's got a funny sense of what's right and what's wrong.'

'So why's he going to Perth?'

'Because she told him she wanted him to buy the place.'

'Well, what's the problem?'

'She doesn't mean it.'

'Who says?'

'I do. I don't trust her. She doesn't want to live in the bush. She wants a house in the city, where she can go to parties all the time.' There was a pause. 'What are we going to do?' Josef asked plaintively.

'I'm going to Beltana to see my mother. You're going to Perth with Adam. And you're not going to tell him he's married to a scheming little bitch. He's got to find that out for himself.'

Adam was still sleeping when the train reached Port Augusta. 'Don't wake him,' Jimmy said, taking the bag that Josef had lifted from the rack. 'Just tell him I said goodbye and I'll see him in a month or so. Don't forget to write, kid.'

Jimmy left quickly, not turning or waving as he walked along the platform. Not that he could wave, for his one arm was burdened with the single bag that carried all his possessions.

TWO

The real estate agency was in a street just off St George's Terrace, Perth. Adam and Josef went there after leaving their bags in the cheapest guest house they could find. The agency had windows painted brown, with the name of the business in gold lettering. The door was difficult to open. It dragged on the floor as Adam tried to push it.

'You have to lift it,' a woman's voice called. It was an unfriendly voice, brimming with scorn for the person outside who did not know the correct technique.

'You'll scratch the lino,' the woman added tartly when Adam had half-pushed, half-carried the door into the office. It was gloomy inside. The woman sat behind a high wooden counter. She had grey hair that had been forced into a pattern of tight curls and wore severe glasses. Her teeth were bared in what may have been a smile but it gave her the look of a savage and underfed watchdog.

'Can I help you?' she said, eyeing them with distaste.

'We'd like to see Mr Ritchie,' Adam said.

'We're the ones who are buying Cobargo Station,' Josef added.

For a moment her eyes registered surprise. Then the teeth were bared once more. Thin lines, faint as cracks in drying mud, spread from the ends of her mouth. It *was* a smile but not necessarily of welcome.

'Please wait,' she said and disappeared down a corridor.

Adam and Josef looked around them. One wall of the room was covered in notices.

'Mortgagee Sale,' Josef saw repeated many times. 'There must be dozens of them,' he said. 'What's it mean?'

'I'm not sure,' Adam said, studying the curious word. 'How do you pronounce it?'

'Mor-ga-gee.'

'I think it means someone's had to sell their land because they can't pay their debts.'

'Gee, that's rough.'

Adam nodded. 'I wonder if our place is a mortgagee sale?'

'Hadn't thought about that. I mean, you don't think of someone else's bad luck being good luck for you.'

The woman emerged from the shadows of the corridor.

'Mr Ritchie will see you,' she murmured, as though regretting the necessity to utter any words. 'Second door on the left.'

The door opened as they approached. 'Come in, come in,' a voice commanded, and the door closed behind them. Mr Ritchie was against the wall, framed by a large map of metropolitan Perth. He was a bald man who had oiled what hair remained on the left side of his head and swept it across his skull so that it covered the skin like a wet and shredded leaf. His head was tilted forward to examine them over the rim of his reading glasses.

'Which one is Mr Ross?' he said. Adam offered his hand. 'I must say you're a little younger than I expected,' Ritchie said, shaking hands with a surprisingly strong grip. He waved them towards two chairs. 'Sit down, sit down. And who are you?' He tilted his head at Josef.

'Josef Hoffman.'

'Are you two partners in this venture?'

'In a way,' Josef said.

'Good. Great opportunity for two strong young men. My God, you've got a bargain, Ross! This is the finest investment opportunity I've had on the books in years. You've brought the money with you, I trust?'

Adam shuffled nervously. 'I sent you the deposit.'

'Of course, of course. I mean the balance. So we can conclude the deal.'

'Well, I haven't got cash. I've arranged to borrow it through the bank.'

'Excellent. That's fine, that's fine. By the way, I hope you'll forgive me if I say you two look a little weary. Worn out, in fact.'

'We've just got off the train,' Adam said.

'From the east?'

'Yes. We've been travelling for ten days.'

'And you came straight here? Well, obviously you're anxious

381

to get this contract signed. Very wise too, because I can assure you there are others after it.'

Ritchie sat behind the desk. His chair was much larger than theirs. It had a high back, lushly padded with leather and with woodwork carved in geometric patterns. He picked up a sheaf of paper and ran his thumb across the ends. 'Yes, indeed. There are literally dozens of people who would like that property.'

'But Adam's paid a deposit,' Josef said.

'Of course, of course. But that's just to hold it temporarily. The sooner you sign the contract, the sooner you can rest in peace. With so many people interested in this property, goodness knows what the vendor might do.'

'Who's he?' Josef said, confused by the term.

'I'm sorry, Mr Hoffman, but I can't reveal the names of our clients.'

Adam and Josef exchanged glances. Each was alarmed by the news of other would-be buyers. Ritchie adjusted his glasses.

'You say the bank has approved the loan?'

Adam nodded.

'Well, I suggest we get straight down to business. After such an expedition on your part, let me not delay you.'

Adam scratched his chin. 'I'm a little confused, Mr Ritchie. If there are other people wanting to buy this place, why did you put so many ads in the paper?'

Ritchie tilted his head, seeking the correct angle of focus. 'Ah yes,' he said, smiling. 'Well, that was just normal business practice. We have to enter into advertising contracts with the newspapers concerned, you see.'

When it became obvious they did not see, he continued. 'We made a commitment to advertise a certain number of times. Despite the response from potential buyers, we could not cancel the other advertisements.'

'But you dropped the price,' Adam said.

'Printer's error,' Ritchie said. 'Mind you, we will stick by it but it was his mistake. And your good luck.' He took off his glasses and began polishing them. 'You're getting an excellent property at a bargain price. But you must be tired. I'll get Miss Thurwood to bring in the contracts and you can sign them and go back to your hotel and have a good rest. You have a hotel?'

'We booked in at a guest house,' Adam said.

'Good. I always admire thrift. Much better to save the pennies for the important things in life. I'll get Miss Thurwood.'

He was up before Adam could raise his hand. 'We have to inspect the place first,' he said.

Ritchie stopped. He scrutinized Adam, as though seeing him for the first time, and then removed his glasses and polished their lenses vigorously. 'Of course, of course,' he said and, replacing the glasses, went to a cabinet. He extracted a large folder.

'Forgive me. Of course you want to see the plan. Well, here we are.'

He spread the paper in front of them. It showed a series of boundary lines, with distances marked on them, the erratic course of a river, some hills, and the location of the homestead and its outbuildings. Adam and Josef stood and studied the plan intently. Ritchie went to the door.

'Miss Thurwood!' he called.

'When can we go there?' Adam asked.

'I beg your pardon?'

'When can we see the place?'

Ritchie closed the door. 'What do you mean?'

'I mean we've got to inspect the property. We can't sign anything without seeing what we're buying.'

'But you paid a deposit.'

Josef stepped forward. 'Your letter said we could inspect the property before buying and if we didn't like it, we could get our – Adam's – money back.'

Miss Thurwood knocked on the door. 'You wanted me, Mr Ritchie?'

'Go away,' he called. 'I might need you in a minute or two.' He returned to his high chair. 'Now, gentlemen, let me make certain that I understand you. You, Mr Ross, have paid a deposit and you have arranged with your bank for a loan to cover the full amount. Is that correct?'

'Yes.' He showed the other man the letter from his bank in Nyngan authorizing the loan. Adam was feeling out of his depth. The surroundings were intimidating: sombre walls of brown timber panelling, certificates with large red seals on them, and photographs of old men with mutton-chop whiskers and grey beards.

'You are aware of the legal implications of all that you have done?' Ritchie continued.

The portraits lining the walls seemed to glare at Adam. 'I think so,' he said.

383

'That deposit was an indication of your intention to purchase. You do want to buy Cobargo, don't you?'

'Of course. If it's as good as you say.'

'Well, to purchase you have to sign a contract. The deposit is nice but all it does, Mr Ross, is prevent me selling Cobargo to one of a number of other interested parties, pending your arrival. Now, I could have sold Cobargo any number of times since receiving your letter,' and he shuffled the papers on his desk once more. 'As you can see, there are many people interested. But I didn't sell, to keep faith with you. Had I sold, I would have merely been required to refund you the deposit. Now it's different, of course.'

'What do you mean?' Josef said.

'Well, gentlemen, now you're here.' He arched his eyebrows. 'Do I make myself clear?'

'No,' Adam said.

'Your letter and the subsequent deposit was a declaration of your intent to purchase. Now you've made a considerable journey, as further evidence of your intent to purchase. If you now change your mind – that is, put new conditions on our agreement or even decide not to honour your promise – then your deposit is forfeit.'

'You mean you keep it?' Josef said.

Ritchie shrugged.

'All we want to do is see the property,' Adam said. 'Would you buy a new shirt without looking at it?'

'This is hardly a shirt, Mr Ross.'

'That's my point. For heaven's sake, Mr Ritchie, no one I know would think of buying land without looking at it first, and no one I know could expect to sell land like that. You'll excuse me saying so, but I think you're trying to hurry us into signing.'

Ritchie looked shocked.

'Is there something wrong with the property?' Adam added.

Ritchie laughed and, as he laughed, he held the pile of papers high in one hand. 'All these people aren't fools, Mr Ross. Most of them would be a good deal older than you and possibly a little wiser. They know a fine property when they hear of one. They know a bargain.' He tilted his head forward, letting the glasses slide to the end of his nose. He leaned forward, resting on both elbows. 'Now I'm not going to pretend that there isn't some work to be done on the property. There is. The former owner let things

384

get a little run down. Some of the fences. Things like that. That's one reason why the price is so good. So outstanding. That and the times we live in, which, as I'm sure you'll know, are severe. I'm sure things are just as bad in the eastern states as they are here. But as they say, one man's misfortune is another man's gain. In this case, the poor fellow who has been running Cobargo has fallen on lean times and the result is you have gained an outstanding property at a price that would have been unthinkable just a few years ago.'

Adam put his hands on the table. He studied them intently. 'When can we see Cobargo?' he said.

Ritchie sighed. 'It will waste so much time, so much unnecessary time.'

Adam concentrated on his hands. He dared not look at Ritchie or the row of bewhiskered portraits.

'Could we see it tomorrow?' Josef asked. 'That's only another day.'

Ritchie's face succumbed to astonishment. 'It will take a great deal longer than that,' he said.

'To do what?' Adam asked. 'To see it or to get there?'

'To arrange things.'

'What things?'

Ritchie shrugged, a movement performed so slowly he could have been moving the burdens of the world. His face suggested he was.

'Just where is Cobargo?' Josef asked, producing the advertisement which had inspired his interest. 'The drawing here makes it seem pretty close to Perth.'

Ritchie smiled but his face had gone deathly white. 'Artist's licence,' he said.

'What does that mean?' Adam said.

'It's a little farther than it seems. That illustration was just to establish Perth for people in other states and to make it clear that our office was here.'

'Well, how do we get to the property?'

'Do we catch another train or take a bus or what?' Josef added.

Ritchie made a tent of his hands. He used it to support his forehead. 'You are determined to follow this pointless exercise and travel to Cobargo Station?' His eyes peeked at them through latticed fingers. 'Believe me, gentlemen, I can give you all the information you could possibly need and save us all a great deal of time and needless expense.'

'I won't buy unless I see the place,' Adam said.

'I could call the whole deal off. Take one of these other offers and not be required to refund you your deposit. You understand that?'

Josef produced Ritchie's letter accepting their offer. 'We have your promise in writing to let us see the place and to give us back the money if we don't like it.'

'I didn't write that letter. Miss Thurwood did. She was mistaken to say those things.'

'You signed it,' Josef said.

Ritchie stood up. He polished his glasses. 'In any case, we are only talking about trifles. You want to buy the land. I am anxious to sell it to you.' He put on his glasses and smiled. 'We are not in dispute. But if we are to inspect the property, there are arrangements I must make. I will have to ask you gentlemen to give me some time.' He withdrew a gold-plated watch from the fob pocket of his waistcoat. 'You could return at four?'

They spent the time wandering along the banks of the Swan river. It was a short walk from the office. They bought sandwiches and threw the crusts to the seagulls and discussed the meeting with Ritchie.

They decided they liked Perth but did not like Ritchie. He was too pushy, too much of a 'city' type. The most extraordinary feature of the whole meeting, they decided, was that they still did not know exactly where the property was. Just somewhere north of Perth. Josef guessed it would take them two hours to reach Cobargo and they would probably go by train. Adam was less confident. It could be even further, he thought, and they both laughed for in two hours of travel from Nyngan you could pass through a string of fine, and large, properties.

At a quarter to four, they walked back from the river, leaving the hordes of wheeling, shrieking gulls to search for other benefactors, and, right on the hour, presented themselves to Miss Thurwood. This time Adam had lifted the door, but she seemed no more pleased to see them. Without comment, she ushered them to the second door on the left.

'Ah, gentlemen,' Ritchie said, 'right on time, right on time. I admire punctuality. The sign of a tidy mind.'

'Mr Ritchie,' Adam began, 'we've been wondering if you could tell us exactly where Cobargo is.'

386

'All the details are here,' Ritchie said, handing Adam a sheet of paper. It was adorned by a dozen lines of lavishly embellished handwriting. 'Where we are going and, more important, where, and when we are to meet.'

Adam stared at the paper, not able to read the writing.

'As you can see,' Ritchie continued, 'we are to meet tomorrow evening at six. I trust that will be convenient?'

The two friends looked at each other and nodded.

'The sooner the better,' Josef said and grinned.

'As you can imagine, such a journey is not cheap but I have managed to arrange a special rate for you. You will need to have six pounds fifteen shillings each when you turn up. That will be no problem, I imagine?'

They shook their heads.

'Well, you must excuse me. I have been neglecting my other duties and have many things to do. I will see you tomorrow at six. You can find that address?'

Adam looked at the paper and nodded. 'You're coming with us?' he said not knowing what else to say.

'Yes. By a happy coincidence, I have other business interests I should attend to in that area. So we will all be travelling together. Roebourne will be warm but very pleasant.'

They left the office. Adam was flushed with embarrassment.

'Where's Roebourne?' Josef asked.

'I haven't a clue. It's probably on this.' He thrust the paper at Josef. 'What does it say?'

'It says Cobargo is via Roebourne, wherever that is. Oh, Christ!'

'What's wrong?'

'Do you know where we've got to meet him? At a wharf, at some place called Fremantle. We're going by ship, Adam!'

THREE

Fremantle was only seven miles from their guest house. It was the port of Perth and lined the mouth of the Swan river with a cluster of old and elegant stone buildings. They went there by train. The rail fare was modest and each had sufficient change from a shilling to buy himself two lamingtons at a cake shop near the station. Carrying their bags in one hand and the lamingtons in the other and trying desperately not to waste one shred of coconut as they walked and ate, they headed for the dock area. It was easy to find, for a tall stone tower and a forest of masts and four funnels projected above the roofs of the town buildings.

The ship they were to catch was the *Mary Elizabeth*. The only motorized water craft on which Adam had travelled was a Manly ferry, and he imagined the *Mary Elizabeth* to be similar. It might be painted green and cream and have two decks with seats at the front and back, so that the passengers could sit in the sun and look at the scenery. He wondered if there would be musicians on board.

He and Josef were excited. Some of the negative feelings from the meeting with Mr Ritchie had gone, dissipated by rest and their resurgent enthusiasm for buying Cobargo. The main damper was Roebourne. It was certainly not close to Perth for they had asked a few people and most had not heard of it. One old man knew the name and thought it was 'up the coast near Broome where the pearls come from'. But that didn't help much because he wasn't sure how far it was to Broome, except it was a long way. There were Japanese up there, he added, as though that explained everything.

The woman who ran the guest house was intrigued that they were going by ship and suggested their destination might be on Rottnest Island, which could be reached by a ferry from Fremantle. She had been there once as a girl and could remember small creatures that looked like kangaroos.

They were directed to a wharf which seemed at first to be deserted. There was no crowd of passengers waiting to board, no turnstiles for them to pass through as there had been at Manly and, most important of all, there was no sign of a ship. Then they walked to the water's edge and looked down. At the far end of the wharf and moored below the level of the timber on which they stood was a squat and ugly vessel. It was covered in equal proportions of grease, peeling paint and rust. It seemed to be rotting in the water for its hull was surrounded by a bilious mix of oil stains and rubbish.

'Looks like a dead steer in a dam,' Adam said.

'I wonder where the *Mary Elizabeth* is?' Josef asked, scanning the port.

'I have a horrible feeling we're looking at it.'

388

'That thing?'

'There are two words across the back. Can you read them?'

'*Mary Elizabeth*. Oh, shit!'

'Don't keep using that word.'

'I think it's spot on.'

Adam laughed. 'Come on,' he said, and walked towards the vessel. A man emerged from the shed near the truck. He wore a peaked cap.

Adam raised his hand in greeting.

'Do you think I'm a Red Indian?' the man said.

'I beg your pardon?'

'That's the way Red Indians greet each other. They lift their hands and say "how". What can I do for you?'

'Maybe you can help me.'

'How?' said the man.

'How,' said Adam, and raised his hand once more.

The man smiled. 'One to you. What do you want to know?'

'Is that the *Mary Elizabeth*?'

'What's left of her.'

'Is she going to Roebourne?'

'No. That'd be too hard.'

Adam's expression forced the man to smile again. 'But she goes close. Roebourne's inland, you see. We stop at the port a few miles away, and unload there.'

'We're supposed to catch the *Mary Elizabeth* and go to Roebourne,' Josef said.

'Are you the two young fellows travelling with Mr Ritchie?'

'Yes.'

The man looked at them, doubt creasing his face. 'Could I ask you what your relationship is to him?'

'We're not related at all,' Josef said quickly.

'We're buying land from him,' Adam said.

'Oh, I see,' the man said, taking off his cap and scratching his head.

'And this land you're buying is up at Roebourne?'

'Yes.'

'Ever been there?'

'No.'

'Used to living on the land, are you?'

Adam nodded.

'The real outback?'

'You could call it that.'

'I hope so. The country's rough up there. The blacks still throw a spear or two.' He replaced his cap. 'Anyhow, my name's Benson. I'm the captain.'

They shook hands and introduced themselves.

'Is that all the gear you've got?' he said and waited for their nods.

'That's good. There's not much room. Come on board and I'll show you where to stow your belongings.'

'It's very small, isn't it?' Josef said.

'That's the kindest word that's been said about this tub in the last twenty years. The truth is, she should have been scrapped years ago. Only greed keeps her afloat. Powerful influence that. They say love makes the world go round and it might have given it a spin to start things off, but it's greed that keeps it going. You know, love of this stuff.' He rubbed his thumb and forefinger together.

'Is it your boat?' Josef asked.

Captain Benson paused. 'If I knew you better and you knew me better, sir, I would be mortally wounded by that remark. The answer is no. I do not own the *Mary Elizabeth*. I just keep her afloat. Sustain the misery, you might say. Watch your step.'

He led them on board, and down to a tiny cabin near the engine room. It had two bunks, one above the other, and a small metal wardrobe. A triangular fragment from a broken mirror hung from a wall. There was no porthole.

'We're below the waterline down here so don't get alarmed when we get under way at all the noise. That's just the water rushing past. And the engines, of course. It won't be quiet and it won't be comfortable but at least it will be warm, which would have been an advantage if it was going to be cold, which it won't be. Not in a couple of days' time, when it will be real warm.'

Adam slung his bag on to the top bunk. 'Aren't we leaving tonight?' he asked.

'In about three hours' time.'

'But you said it was going to be warm in a couple of days.'

'That's right.'

'Well, how long is it going to take to get to Roebourne?' He sounded alarmed.

So did Josef when he spoke. 'And just where is Roebourne?'

The captain extracted a pipe from his hip pocket. He began

filling it with tobacco, eyeing them as he did the job. 'Didn't Mr Ritchie tell you? Hasn't he shown you a map or something?'

'There was a map on the advertisement for the land,' Josef said.

'It showed the property to be just to the north of Perth,' Adam said.

Captain Benson lit his pipe, twisting his face so that, somehow, one eye seemed to be watching the flame while the other scrutinized them.

'He didn't tell you exactly where it was?' His eye aimed the question at Adam.

'No. He just said it was via Roebourne.'

'The lady at the guest house thought it might be on Rottnest Island,' Josef said.

'Jesus Christ!' the captain said. 'So he just sent you down here without letting you know where you were going or how long you were going to be at sea. Well, gentlemen, it's not for me to comment on the morality of all this. Let me just explain. Roebourne – or more accurately Port Robinson, where I'm heading for – is way up north, well and truly into the tropics. Port Robinson, in fact, is the fourth stop we make. We call in at Geraldton, Carnavon and Onslow before we reach there. Then I go on to Port Hedland and Broome, unloading and picking up cargo, and then I turn around and come back again. This old tub, believe it or not, is what is laughingly called a coastal trader and I trade along most of the damned coast. The reefs are littered with the wrecks of old ships and every time we get back to Fremantle, I get down on my knees and give thanks that we made it back. And that's something because I don't believe in God. Let us just pray, gentlemen, that we get as far as Port Robinson so you can get off and start raising cattle or sheep and fighting off the wild blackfellows.'

'How far is Roebourne ... I mean Port Robinson?' Adam asked. The low roofline forced him to stoop. He had one hand against the inner plates of the hull and when he moved, his palm was covered in rust.

'Don't take any notice of that,' the captain said, smiling around the pipe stem. 'it's only rust that holds the *Mary Elizabeth* together. How far are you travelling with us? Well let's say you wouldn't see any change out of a thousand miles.' He paused, relishing their stunned expressions. 'It'll take us six days, God willing. God and the wharfies.'

391

'Wharfies?'

'The men who load us. They put things on and take things off. What part of the bush are you from?'

'Nyngan.'

'Never heard of it.'

'Near Bourke.'

'Heard of that. Fairly civilized out that way, isn't it?'

'We spent a lot of time up in the north-east of South Australia and in far Western Queensland.'

'Ever been to sea before?'

'I've been on a Manly ferry,' Adam said and immediately regretted it, for the captain did not look amused.

'When's Mr Ritchie coming on board?' Josef said.

'Just before we sail. He usually leaves it to the last minute.'

'He's travelled with you before?' Adam said.

'A few times. He's got a lot of business interests up the coast.'

Josef looked around the cabin and grimaced. 'They must be important if he puts up with a room like this.'

'Don't call it a room, sonny. It's a cabin. And you're right. It's about as bad as civilized man can tolerate. By the way, the lavatory is down there.' He pointed to his right. 'If this is the first voyage for both of you, you'll probably be needing it fairly regularly.'

Adam looked puzzled.

'The stomach can get a little upset. It soon passes.'

'How long does it take?' Josef said, eyes alarmed.

The captain cast undertaker's eyes over Josef's body, measuring him precisely. 'On this tub, maybe twenty years.'

They both smiled and the captain smiled in return, but his smile was sad.

'Where is Mr Ritchie sleeping?' Adam said.

'In the owner's cabin.'

'Is that good?'

'Best on the ship.'

'Lucky Mr Ritchie. Just as well the owner isn't on board.'

'What do you mean, lad? Mr Ritchie *is* the owner.'

Ritchie boarded the ship at sunset. Adam and Josef were on deck, watching men load sacks into a hold at the rear of the ship. Ritchie nodded, said he hoped they were comfortable, and went to his cabin. An hour later, the *Mary Elizabeth* sailed.

Adam and Josef were sick all the way to Geraldton. Once the ship rounded the Fremantle breakwater it began to roll. A steady swell moved in from the south-west and she wallowed and yawed without relief for thirty-four hours. The plates in her hull creaked and the steam engine thumped and shuddered, and the whole vessel stank of oil and past cargos.

The ship stopped within sight of Geraldon and lay side on to the swell, pitching violently.

Ritchie came to their cabin.

'I hear you haven't been well,' he said, leaning to fit through the doorway. 'The captain tells me we've had to stop with engine trouble. Shame. It'll be rougher than ever for the next hour or so.'

'It's going to get worse?' Josef said. His face was as grey as the pillow slip.

'Afraid so. Sure you wouldn't like to try some breakfast? They have very good bacon on board.'

Josef turned away.

'How about you, Mr Ross? Bacon? Some fried eggs?'

'No.' Adam had difficulty controlling his mouth.

'Nasty being sick. I suffered myself the first couple of voyages but you get used to it. I like the rough weather now. By the way the captain tells me we're in for a big blow north of here. It'll make what we've been through seem like a mill pond.'

Josef glanced at him. 'Isn't there any other way to Roebourne?'

Ritchie moved one step closer. 'You could go by horse. Take you a couple of months. Cost you a lot of money for a good horse.'

'How about the train?' Josef was facing the wall again.

'It doesn't go that far.'

Adam managed to sit on the edge of his bunk. He had to bend forward to avoid the roof. The ship pitched violently and he almost fell. Ritchie steadied himself. 'I hope we can repair the engine,' he said as though talking to himself. 'If we break down north of Geraldton with all that rough weather coming ...'

He stared at Adam.

Sick as he was, Adam knew the man had more to say.

'The train runs as far north as Geraldton,' Ritchie said and paused, having dangled the bait. The ship lurched violently.

'We could be ashore in an hour,' he added.

Another wave raised the ship and sent it sliding, side-on, down the far side.

'Oh, Jesus!' Josef said and retched. There was nothing left to vomit and he clasped his stomach.

'It would be very simple to sign the papers when we go ashore,' Ritchie said when Josef was calm again. 'And then you two could go back to Perth on the train.'

Someone came to the door but stayed out of sight. Ritchie withdrew for a moment to speak to him. 'I'll tell you when,' he said and re-entered the cabin. 'This is what I was frightened of,' he said. 'A rough trip in this small boat can be most uncomfortable, most uncomfortable. Why don't we just conclude the deal here and now and then you can avoid all the misery of another week at sea in rough weather.'

'How long?' Josef said.

'A week. It could easily be that long. Storms do delay things you know.'

'Oh Jesus, I couldn't stand another week of this,' Josef groaned.

'Oh, it will get worse, my young friend.'

'If we do sign now, how are we going to get to Cobargo later on?' Adam said.

'You wait until the weather is calmer and then catch a larger and more comfortable ship. I'll tell you what.' He stepped forward, as though impelled by a sudden thought. 'You do that and I'll refund you the money from this trip. Now I couldn't be fairer than that, could I?'

The ship corkscrewed down the swell. The sound of metal crashing against metal echoed down the corridor. Someone shouted. Josef began retching again.

'This is really the most unnecessary torment you are subjecting yourselves to,' Ritchie said.

'I wouldn't mind going back on the train,' Josef said.

'Same here,' said Adam, lowering himself to the bunk. 'But I want to see that land before I sign. We've come this far. We might as well stick it out.'

'It's entirely unnecessary,' Ritchie said, his voice a whine of concern.

'Are you going on?' Adam said, raising himself on an elbow.

'Unfortunately I have to.'

'So do we.' And Adam fell back in the bunk.

A few minutes after Ritchie left the engines resumed and the *Mary Elizabeth*, back under control, headed for its berth at Geraldton.

*

They stood on the wharf at Geraldton, letting the sun drench them and watching fishermen work around the crayfish boats moored nearby. They could not walk properly. The wharf seemed to be swaying, so after a while they sat on a wooden rail. Captain Benson came from the ship.

'How are you feeling?' he said, pausing to fill his pipe.

'I'm still rocking,' Adam said.

'You will for a while. If I was you, I'd try and get some food inside me.'

'I couldn't eat a thing,' Josef said, grinning.

'You should try. You'll only get worse without a feed inside you. We'll be here until two. Have some toast and a cup of tea. Drink a bit of flat lemonade. There's a cheap café just across the road.'

Adam nodded his thanks but his face expressed doubt. 'I hear we're in for rough weather,' he said.

The captain looked surprised. 'No. It should be good from now on. Smooth as glass.' He started to walk away but turned, and winked.

'You didn't change your mind, did you?'

'About what?' Adam said.

'About that land of yours.'

'No.'

'You're still going to have a look?'

'Yes.'

The captain slapped his thigh. 'Good on you! Serves the bastard right.'

FOUR

The sea became calmer and the night and the next day passed pleasantly. Josef was sick early in the night but Adam felt better and, on the following day, spent much of the time on deck. He became friendly with Tabby, one of the three crewmen on board. Tabby was part-Japanese, part-aboriginal, and came from Broome where his father had been a pearl diver. He had curiously arched eyebrows and high but wide cheekbones and when he smiled, which he did often, his face looked remarkably like a cat's.

When he had free time, Tabby joined Adam at the rail and pointed out features on the land. Early in the morning they passed Steep Point, the westernmost projection on the Australian mainland. A squadron of dolphins joined them, leaping and tunnelling and playing around the ship until its slow progress bored them and they sped away.

The colour of the water changed from a deep ocean blue to a creamy green, and the air came to them warm and laden with aromas. Low in the water and shuddering from the vibration of the engines, the *Mary Elizabeth* laboured along the shores of Dirk Hartog Island. It reached Cape Inscription and changed course for Carnarvon.

'This is Shark Bay,' Tabby said, indicating a vast stretch of water. A low island was on the horizon to the north but the mainland was out of sight. 'It's full of the bastards. Up north once I saw a shark fighting a crocodile. In the sea, but just off an island.' He glanced at Adam to make sure the rarity of his experience was appreciated.

'What's a shark?'

The seaman spent several moments with his head touching his arms, which were cradled on the rail. 'You having me on?'

'No. I've never seen one.'

'But you know what it is?'

'No.'

'Bloody hell. I thought everyone knew what sharks were. You're not pulling my leg?'

'No.'

'Where've you spent all your life? Out the back of beyond?'

'Yes. That's exactly where I've been.'

Tabby shook his head. 'I wouldn't have believed it. A shark's a fish. A big bastard.'

'Like those ones who were jumping around the boat?'

'A bit, only bigger. And meaner. Dolphins are friendly. Sharks are bad.'

'What do they do?'

'Eat you.'

'Why?'

The other man looked puzzled. 'I've never thought about that. They just do. I suppose it's because they're hungry.'

'How big are they?'

'Depends. There are big ones and little ones, but the little ones are big and big ones are bloody huge.' Tabby turned and leaned against the rail with his arms folded across his chest. 'I hear you're going up north to buy some land.'

Adam copied his pose. 'Yes.'

'Know anything about cattle and sheep and those things?'

'Yes.'

'Seen the land before?'

'No. Joe and I are going to have a look.'

'Buying the land from Mr Ritchie?'

'Yes. If we like it.'

'And if you don't like it?'

'We don't buy it.'

'Have a good look, won't you?'

'Certainly. Tell me, Tabby, how well do you know Mr Ritchie?'

He shrugged. 'Seen him a few times. He comes up here often. Do anything for a quid.'

'A good businessman, I hear.'

'Wouldn't know. I wouldn't like to owe him money. I tell you, mate, that bloke is so hungry for money he'd scrape the shit out of a dead horse if he thought he'd get an extra penny for it.'

Adam laughed.

'No. I'm serious, mate. Watch your step with that bloke. The more money he makes, the more he wants. I was telling you about sharks. Remember?'

Adam nodded.

'Well, there are two sorts. The sea shark and the land shark. They both eat you. Ritchie is a land shark and, mate, they're the worst kind.'

The *Mary Elizabeth* reached Carnarvon late in the afternoon and berthed at a wharf whose tall wooden piles were stained black from the embrace of twenty thousand tides. The town fanned from the port. It was a low and sleepy place, studded with trees and flashing colours from gabled iron roofs.

Two men lounged on either side of a bollard. Because the tide was falling, the ship's deck was below the level of the wharf and Josef, the first person off, had to scramble up with the aid of a rope.

One of the men straightened. He was wearing a wide-brimmed

hat, blue singlet, blue trousers and riding boots. 'You one of the crew?' he asked casually, his thumb hooked to his trouser belt.

'No,' Josef said, turning to help Adam gain the wharf.

'How about your, mate?'

Josef turned to the man. 'No. Why?'

'What are you doing here then?'

Josef was still feeling weak and was hungry and in no mood for trivial conversations with strangers.

'Same as you. Standing on the wharf,' he said.

The second man joined the other. He was dressed similarly but without a hat. His shoulders were covered in curly black hair.

'What have we got here, Alf?' he said. 'A pair of young scabs?'

'Reckon so.'

Adam stood beside Josef. 'What's up?'

'What are you doing here, Snow?' the second man said.

'Just visiting,' Adam said. 'Why? What's the trouble?'

'Where are you two from?'

'New South Wales. Why?'

'Bloody hell. They're bringing them from everywhere these days, aren't they, Alf?'

'Reckon so,' the man with the hat said. 'Ever done any shearing?'

'A bit.'

'Where?'

'In Queensland. Why?'

'Just get back on the boat and piss off back to New South bloody Wales.'

'We're going into town to have a meal,' Adam said. 'So just get out of our way, will you?'

'Step off this wharf and we'll put you back on the boat in a wooden box.'

Tabby had climbed to the wharf to loop a rope around a bollard. 'What's up?' he called.

'Are you one of the crew?' the second man said.

'I wouldn't be doing this if I was Don Bradman.' He walked to join them.

'Just keep out of this, shit-face!' The man stepped forward and pushed Tabby hard on the chest. He stumbled on a rope and fell.

'Jesus!' Josef said and struck at the man. It was a wild blow and hit the man on the shoulder-blade. He turned and whacked Josef in the stomach.

'Young bastard,' he grunted. 'I'm going to have you for dinner.'

Josef had fallen to his knees, grasping his stomach. The man bunched a large fist and prepared to hit him again. Adam, the only one of the three still standing, ran forward and kicked the man on the back of the knee. He fell heavily, gasping with pain.

The man with the hat advanced on Adam. He had picked up a short but stout piece of timber. 'See how you like wearing this where your teeth used to be, scab,' he said and swung.

The man's aim was hasty and poor. Adam stepped back and, when the man was off balance, darted forward. The other man raised his hands to protect his face. Adam bent low, hooked an arm through the man's widespread legs and, lifted him to his shoulders. He spun him around a few times.

'Let me down, you bastard!' the man shouted his voice pulsating with each gyration.

'Delighted,' Adam said. He walked to the edge of the wharf, just beyond the grimy stern of the *Mary Elizabeth*, and threw him in the sea. It was a long fall, and the man hit the water flat, his arms and legs outstretched as though crucified.

The man with the hairy shoulders was on his feet but was bent low, holding one knee. 'Alf can't swim,' he said weakly.

'Well, you'd better help him.'

The man let go his knee. 'What do you mean?'

'Jump in.'

'Like bloody hell.' He raised his fists and limped towards Adam. He swung hard and Adam swayed easily out of range. Adam kicked and caught the man behind the knee again.

'Oh, shit!' he screamed and fell, writhing, with his bent leg clasped in both arms. 'That's my crook knee again!'

'What a shame,' Adam said and grabbed the man by the singlet. He pulled him towards the edge of the wharf.

'What are you going to do?' the man shouted, trying to struggle but wincing as long splinters drove into his skin. 'Oh shit, mate, stop it, stop it!'

He brought the man to rest on his hands and knees on the raised timber edging the wharf.

'Can you see your friend?' Adam said, and the man looked over the side. Alf was splashing frantically. His hat had drifted towards the ship. 'I think he needs a hand,' Adam said, and putting the heel of his boot against the man's haunches, pushed him over.

Tabby was helping Josef to his feet.

'Still feel hungry?' Adam asked his friend.

'I feel bloody sore. What was all that about?'

'Wouldn't have a clue. Are you all right, Tabby?'

'Thanks, mate. I wasn't hurt. I just tripped.' Tabby pulled a splinter from the seat of his trousers. 'By the way, what are you like with your hands? I mean, bloody hell, you take on two big buggers and you throw them both in the water and you never even use your fists.'

'Yes, you weren't too bad,' Josef said. He was still short of breath.

'I'd just like to know what that was all about,' Adam said. He wiped the palms of his hands. They were sweating. Now that the fight was over, he was shaking.

'They called us scabs,' Josef told Tabby.

'Probably thought you were shearers. That what it was. They thought you were scabs one of the bosses had brought in.'

'Scabs?' Adam said, scratching at an imaginary wound on his arm. 'Dried blood?'

'No, mate. A scab is a strikebreaker. There's been a big shearers' strike up here. The blokes on strike have been trying to make sure no other shearers come in to do their work. They get a bit touchy.'

'So we saw. What's the strike about?'

'Wouldn't have a clue. I think they've all forgotten what started it. Now it's just one side against the other. You know the sort of thing? All they want to do now is break a few heads.'

Josef rubbed his stomach. 'Well, it doesn't concern us. Let's go into town and get a feed. If I don't put something in my stomach soon, my backbone will come through my belly button.'

'What about the two characters in the water, Tabby?' Adam said. 'Will you make sure they don't drown?'

The seaman sauntered to the edge of the wharf. 'They're both hanging on to one of the piles.' He gazed down for some time, like a fisherman surveying his catch. 'I might let them stay there a bit longer. I don't like being called shit-face.' He turned to the others. 'Don't worry. I'll keep an eye on them. When they look a bit weary I'll get one of the other blokes to get a boathook and fish them out.'

He looked down at the men in the water. 'I wouldn't kick like that,' he called to them. 'It only attracts the sharks.'

He winked at Adam. 'That should keep them quiet for a few minutes. Why don't you go and get something to eat?'

'How about you?'

'No, I think I'll stay on board.'

Within an hour Josef and Adam were wishing they had stayed on the ship too. They reached the main street – a dusty thoroughfare of extraordinary width, built to allow the camel trains hauling wool from the hinterland to turn in one sweep – and walked along it until they found an eating place. It was a small café with an alley on one side and a vacant paddock overgrown with grass and weeds on the other. The building was all white. The front weatherboard wall was painted white. The door was white. Even the window was coated white. The word 'café' had been signwritten in a red crescent across the glass but the paint was blistered and large flakes had fallen away. The sun had set and a single globe glowed from the awning.

A man stood in the doorway. He was fat and wore an apron.

'Are we too early?' Josef asked. He was now ravenous.

'What for?' the man said, looking not at them but down the street, where long shadows were merging in the early night.

'A meal.'

'No. Come inside.' He stepped back, rubbing his hands on his apron. 'Not many people about, are there?'

'No,' Josef said, following. 'Got any steak?'

'Yep.'

'What's it like? Good?'

'Depends what you call good. The last bloke who ate some walked out of the place on his own legs and from what I hear he's still alive. You new in town?'

'Just got in.'

'Got money, I suppose?'

'How much is the steak?'

'One and six. That's with potatoes and one egg. You want an egg?'

'Sure. Yeah, we've got enough.' Josef rattled the money in his pocket.

'Sit down then. You want steak too?'

Adam shrugged. 'Why not? It's been a long time since I had a steak.'

The man rubbed his hands on his apron. 'You can have it

without the egg if you like. Save yourself threepence.'

'No. I'll have the works.'

The man went into the back room. He returned almost immediately. 'How long you staying in town?' he said.

'One night. We're on a ship. We're leaving in the morning.'

The man nodded. 'Not shearers, are you?'

'No. We've already been through that.'

'What do you mean?'

'A couple of blokes met us when we came off the boat and called us scabs.'

The man looked interested. 'What happened?'

'He threw them in the sea,' Josef said and laughed.

'What? Both of them?'

'Too right.'

'What did they look like?'

'Wet.'

The man appeared to laugh but no noise came from his mouth. He walked to the front door, looked both ways along the street and moved back inside. 'This strike's a silly bloody business,' he said. 'All they talk about now is solidarity. Solidarity. Shit, most of them wouldn't know what the word means.'

'What does it mean?' Adam asked.

'It means bloody fighting and bloody trouble, that's what it means. I'll put your steak on.'

About ten minutes later they saw a mob of men walking down the middle of the street. One detached himself from the others and came straight to the café door. He put his head inside, blinked once in the light, and withdrew immediately.

'They're here,' he shouted and within seconds four men had filed into the room. Others waited on the footpath. One of the men who had come into the café was Alf. He was without his hat.

'That's the bastard,' he said, indicating Adam.

'Get up,' the leader said. He was about fifty and as lean as a greyhound.

Adam pushed himself from the table and stood. 'We don't want any trouble.'

'I bet you don't. Just step outside. We don't want to wreck the joint.'

Josef got up slowly and stood behind his chair, gripping it to use as a weapon. 'We're not scabs,' he said.

'We're not shearers,' Adam added quickly. 'We're just on our

402

way north to buy some land. We'll only be here tonight.'

'You won't even be here that long,' Alf said. 'We're going to throw you out of town now. Let's get 'em, Harry.'

The leader held out his arm to restrain Alf.

'Who brought you in?'

'We came on a ship.'

'That wasn't what I asked you. Who are you working for?'

'No one.'

Alf pushed his shoulder against Harry's back. 'They came on that junk boat, the *Mary Elizabeth*, Harry. She don't carry passengers. Someone must have brought them up.'

The café owner re-entered the room, carrying two plates of food. 'Bloody hell,' he said, 'what do you blokes want?'

'We want these scabs out of your place,' Harry said.

'They're not scabs.'

'How the hell would you know? Just get back in your kitchen. This doesn't concern you.'

'Like bloody hell it doesn't! This is my place. They're my customers. If you don't want a feed, get out.' He put the plates on an empty table.

'It's our place for the next ten minutes,' Harry said. 'Just get back in the kitchen and you won't get hurt.'

Alf picked up a chair and the two men nearest him did the same.

'I'll show you whose place it is,' the man in the apron said. He moved from the room with surprising speed for a man so large and reappeared holding a shotgun.

'All right,' he said, his face flushed, 'who wants to be on tomorrow night's menu?'

Alf dropped the chair.

'Put that gun down,' Harry said, retreating as he spoke. 'It might go off.'

'You're bloody right it might. Who are you anyhow, mate? I've never seen you around here before.'

'He's come to give us a hand,' one of the men said.

'Well, he won't have a bloody hand left if he doesn't get out of here and take the rest of you stupid drongos with him. Now march out of here before I turn your backsides into sausage mince. Come on!'

'You haven't got the guts,' Harry said.

'You won't have any guts in a minute.' And the two men faced each other, neither moving, and neither taking his eyes from the other.

'I think things would be a lot better if we left,' Adam said to the man with the gun. 'Is there a way out through the back?'

'There certainly is,' the man said and breathed deeply, relieved to have a solution presented to him. 'In fact that's the most sensible thing I've heard in the last five minutes.' He inclined his head without taking his eyes from his target, who was now watching Adam intently. 'Straight through the kitchen and out the store at the back.'

Alf turned and ran to the front door. 'They're going out the back!' he yelled. 'Quick! Head them off.'

In an instant the café was deserted, save for the owner and Harry.

'I won't forget this,' Harry said, and turned to follow the others.

'You'd better not,' the owner shouted after him, and sat down at the table where he had put the two plates. Gingerly, he placed the shotgun beside one plate. 'Bloody hell,' he said softly, 'with all the world going mad, why did I have to join it?'

In the storeroom behind the kitchen, Josef was moving so quickly he bumped a stack of cans and sent them crashing to the floor. A cat which had been in the far doorway took fright and ran outside. A dog barked. There was the sound of a chase. With a stuttering crash, something fell and banged against an empty drum.

'I can hear them,' a man called, from somewhere to the side of the café.

Adam steadied his friend. 'Wait a moment. They're all racing around the back.'

'Well, for Christ's sake, let's hurry!' Josef said, trying to tear himself from Adam's grip.

'But if they're all going around the back, why don't we go out the front?'

Josef grinned and turned. They heard a thud and the skid of a body on gravel. Someone in the alley had fallen.

The café owner looked up at them in surprise. 'I thought you'd gone,' he said as though the thought had been his most fervent wish.

'No one out the front?' Adam asked, staying in the kitchen doorway. The man rose, cradled the shotgun in his elbow and walked to the door. He looked both ways.

'Not a bastard in sight. Come on.' He need not have bothered with his last words for they were already at the door. 'Cross the road and keep in the shadows. Go on, quick! They'll be back soon.'

'I owe you for the steak,' Adam said.

The man looked at him strangely. 'I've had plenty of blokes try to nick off without paying for something they ate but you're the first that's ever tried to pay for something he didn't have. Just piss off. And thanks.'

They ran across the road. They had just reached a tree growing on the edge of a vacant allotment when one of the striking shearers returned to the front of the café. The owner was still in the doorway.

'Where are they?' the shearer demanded. He was breathless from running.

'How the hell would I know?' He moved the shotgun to his other hand. The shearer stepped back.

'Well, they're not out the back.'

'And they're not here.'

A second man arrived, breathing heavily. 'Harry said to stay around here in case they double back.'

'See anything?' the first man asked, looking along the wide street as he spoke. There were lights at the far end, near the waterfront.

'No. Blacker than a bull's arsehole out there now.'

'They might be on the roof,' the café owner said helpfully.

'Yeah?' the second man said and stepped back a few paces to take himself clear of the verandah posts. He looked up. 'Can't see nothing,' he said.

'They might still be inside,' the first shearer said.

'They're not.'

'Well, let me have a look.'

'I said they're not. If you go inside, you're calling me a liar and if you call me a liar, those are the last words your teeth are ever going to let slip out of that pretty little mouth of yours. Now, I'm telling you they're not inside.'

He rested the shotgun against the door and clenched his fists. His hands were extremely large.

'Harry just said to wait outside,' the second man said, and his companion retreated.

'Who's this Harry?' the café owner demanded.

'He's one of us. A shearer.'

'Never seen him around here before.'

'He's from the south. He's a terrific organizer.'

'You blokes are fools. You should be able to settle your own problems without bringing in thugs from the south.' He picked up the shotgun and turned. 'And if you want to stay out front, get away from the doorway. I don't want you driving my customers away.'

Adam had lost contact with Josef. They had moved through the allotment away from the road and had become separated by the dense growth of grass and bushes. He called softly and heard branches parting in front of him.

'Is that you, Joe?' he whispered. A dog growled. It was not a savage sound, more the noise a dog makes when frightened. It sounded like a small dog.

'Go away.' Adam moved forward and the dog retreated, still growling. Adam could see a light ahead. He must be near another street.

'Adam?' It was Josef's voice, from somewhere on his left.

'Over here.'

'Wait there. I'll join you.'

'Careful. There's a dog in here somewhere.'

Adam crouched low, listening to the snap of wood that marked Josef's progress. The dog had stopped barking.

'Is there someone there?' It was a man's voice, high and hesitant. Adam could now see the looming shadow of Josef. He stopped moving.

'Come here, Neb!' the voice said, sharp and nervous. 'I said, is there someone there?'

It was not the voice of an angry shearer, Adam decided, and stood up. He walked towards the light. 'Only me,' he said. 'Me and my friend.'

He could see a man stooping to lift a small dog. He was near the streetlight and as he straightened Adam could see he was dressed in black, with a clerical collar. The man was small and slightly built. He seemed young. He retreated when he saw two tall men emerge from the bushes.

'What were you doing in there?' His voice, intended to be authoritative, emerged with a squeak.

'To tell you the truth, we were hiding,' Adam said.

'Goodness me!' the parson said (for Adam could see clearly now that he was a minister of religion). 'Is this some sort of game or are you serious?'

'Not a game, Reverend,' Josef said. 'There are men after us. They're shearers, I think, and they reckon we're scabs.'

'Oh, not more trouble!' the parson said. He put the dog on the ground. 'We had violence last week. It's been dreadful. They ganged up on some poor wretches who came up on a wagon to shear at the Morton place. There was blood everywhere. It was awful. What are you boys doing in town anyway?'

Adam smiled at the word 'boys'. The minister could not have been more than two or three years older than he was.

'We're on the way to Roebourne. We came in by ship today and we're due to leave in the morning. I think we should be moving,' he added, glancing backwards. 'There are a dozen men back there in an extremely nasty mood, and I think we should go somewhere else.'

As if to emphasize the point, a branch snapped nearby and a man uttered an oath.

'Goodness me!' the clergyman whispered. 'Quick! This way.'

He ran with the dog bounding happily at his heels. They followed and stopped when he leaped over a low metal fence.

'In here,' he said, pointing to a small wooden church. 'It's not mine, but it's the closest and it will certainly do.'

He led them to a back door. He opened it. 'The lock never works,' he said. 'Quick. Inside. This is a Catholic church so if you two are Catholics do whatever you should do and get in out of the open.'

He closed the door behind them. It was intensely dark inside. The minister spent some time regaining his composure.

'This is most irregular, of course, but I'm sure Father Ryan would understand. He's a good man. I'll go and get him in a few minutes.'

'There's no need to get anyone else mixed up in this,' Adam said.

'Oh yes, there is. You've got to get out of town in one piece without having one of those imported hoodlums break your head open. I'm new to Carnarvon. I don't know the best way to do it. Father Ryan would. He's been here a long time.' He giggled.

'What's wrong?' Josef said.

'I was just thinking how dark it was in here and I was tempted to light a candle. Father Ryan is a tolerant man but he might not approve of a Presbyterian doing that in his church.'

'We're right,' Adam said and felt the dog sniffing his leg. 'What's your dog's name?'

'Neb. It's short for Nebuchadnezzar. You may think it's a strange name for a dog but it's because he likes hanging around gardens.'

He waited for a titter of understanding. There was silence.

'I've only been here for six months,' he said. 'Neb adopted me the day I arrived. He was a stray and so, in a way, was I. Where are you two from?'

'Nyngan.'

'Where's that?'

'In western New South Wales.'

'My, you have come a long way. And you're not shearers come to work? Not that it matters, mind you.'

'No,' Adam said, scratching the dog behind the ear. 'We're on our way north to buy some land.'

'I see,' he said, and opened the door a little. 'It seems quiet outside. I'll go and get Father Ryan.'

While he was gone they heard some men pass. One of them must have been carrying a stick for they heard the rattle of wood against the metal railing of the church's fence.

FIVE

Father Ryan opened the door noisily and turned on a light.

'Just because we're in the bush doesn't mean we don't have electricity,' he said. 'I believe my young colleague has been keeping you in the dark. Typical of a Protestant, if I may say so. Now, what are your names?'

They told him.

'Either of you Catholics? No? Well, are you Presbyterians?'

'No.'

'Well, at least we're even. What are you?' He pointed a broad finger at Josef.

'I'm Lutheran.'

'German?' the priest said. He was a man who had once been larger than at present and his skin hung in folds, waiting for the flesh to blossom once more.

'Yes.'

'Well, God moves in mysterious ways, son. How about you?'

'I'm not sure,' Adam said. He did not like the inquisition. He was anxious to return to the ship, fearing it might sail without them.

'Don't you have parents?' And then he turned to the young parson. 'Roger, would you put that infernal dog of yours outside? A church is not a place for a mongrel to be roaming around, piddling all over the place.'

'I was frightened he might attract attention. He'd probably scratch around outside.'

'Well, kindly hold him. Tonight you can bless the beasts and I'll look after the children. Now,' he said turning towards Adam once more, 'I was asking you about your parents.'

'My mother died soon after I was born and my father died when I was nine.'

'Who brought you up?'

'An old friend of my dad's. We were out the back of Broken Hill, in the bush.'

'So you don't know what church you belong to, eh?' Wrinkling his eyes, he studied Adam's face. 'I think I see a bit of Celt in there somewhere, don't you, Roger? I mean, he could be Scottish but I think I see Irish. You could be Catholic, boy. How does that strike you?'

'Not as hard as one of those shearers will if they catch us.'

The priest lifted his head.

'Ha,' he said and the noise ricocheted through the wooden arches of the small church. 'He must be Irish, don't you think, Roger?'

'That sounded like a bit of Scots earthiness to me,' the younger man said, looking down deferentially. 'He is correct though, Father. Our main concern is not conversion but salvation.'

'Are you frightened of a fight?' the priest asked Adam. His tone was pugnacious.

Josef answered before Adam could speak. 'He threw two of them into the sea off the wharf before we even got on to the land.'

'Did he now?' the priest muttered, admiration icing his words. 'My heavens, Roger, he does sound like an Irishman, doesn't he?

Well, now, tell me, if you don't mind throwing people in the water, why were you hiding in the bushes when my friend found you?'

'There were more than a dozen of them.'

'Not a fair fight, eh?'

'Come now, Father, you know what these men are like. Since these new fellows arrived from the south there has never been any suggestion of fairness about the fighting. They just hunt in packs.'

'Well, that's just these new men. The local shearers are all decent fellows. I know most of them and they'd give you their shirts if they thought you were catching a cold.'

'We'd gone into a little café to have a feed,' Josef said. 'A mob of them came and reckoned we were scabs and were about to wreck the joint.'

'It must have been that little white place across the paddock,' the parson said. 'Run by the big fat man.'

'Bill Gowrie,' the priest said, as though the name should strike a chord. 'Big man. Big stomach, big hands. Biggest hands I've ever seen on a man. Good fellow. He'd stand by you, wouldn't he?'

'Yes, he was good.'

'Did you finish your meal?' the parson asked, smiling.

'We didn't even start it,' Josef said. 'Matter of fact, I haven't eaten since we left Perth.'

The men of God exchanged glances. 'I think the expression is "Your place or mine?" ' the priest said.

They ate in the priest's house because it was closer and because a woman was there to prepare the food. She was old with a bent back and she said nothing. She shuffled in and out of Father Ryan's dining-room, serving them cheese and cold sausage and bread and when they had eaten that, dry fruit cake and tea.

'It's not what you'd get in Bill Gowrie's café but at least no one's going to come busting in and threaten to bash you over the head.'

The parson, who had introduced himself as Roger Montgomery, had left his dog on the priest's verandah.

'How are we going to get them to their boat?' he asked.

'I dislike stealth,' the priest said, joining the tips of his fingers, 'but I believe it is justified if it avoids violence. We cannot expect our young friends to walk down the main street. We cannot expect them to walk along the wharf for this new man … what's his name, Roger?'

'Harry Mills.'

'... Harry Mills will certainly have put some of his men there. So we will have to go by the only other way.' He paused, enjoying his performance. 'We shall go by water.'

'How?' Josef asked.

'I think I know,' the Reverend Roger Montgomery said, his face beaming. 'Father Ryan is an avid fisherman. He maintains a boat, for those moments when he desires solitude.'

'And when I can't stand any more of old Ethel's tinned meat,' the priest said. 'It's a very modest craft, a rowing boat which one of my parishioners was kind enough to present to me a few years ago.'

'He left it to Father Ryan in his will.'

'A practical thought. I trust the dear man has already been rewarded. I've certainly done what I can to smooth his reception. The one problem with my boat, Roger, is that it will be sorely pressed to carry four of us. Do you intend coming?'

'Certainly. Your eyes are not good enough to find your way back in the dark.'

'Well, you must leave that confounded dog of yours. He would bark or get under my feet and I would be sorely tempted to reverse the sermon on the mount and offer him to the multitude of fishes.'

'I shall leave him on your verandah, if I may, Father. He seems to be nicely cowed by your cat. I doubt that he will move.'

'Excellent. Then we'll go when you finish your meal.'

'You don't think these men will just get tired of looking for us and go to bed?' Adam said, drinking some tea to soften the fruit cake in his mouth.

'Not with Harry Mills in town. He is not an ordinary man.'

'He was brought here to cause trouble,' the parson said. 'That's right, isn't it, Father?'

'Unhappily, yes. One scoundrel, with his own interests at heart, brought this Mills and a few other toughs up from the south to make sure the strike was perpetuated.'

'What do you mean?' Adam said.

'This man who employs Mills wants the strike to continue. He doesn't want it settled. Not until the time is right for him. So Mills's job is to increase bitterness, to stir up talk about scabs and solidarity — we used to call it mateship but that's the word he's brought up with him — and what he's done is turn decent, hardworking men, who had a reasonable cause, into men who

411

hate and will bash anyone who's on the other side. They don't know they're being duped.' He paused and winked. 'I hear a lot in my position, you know. The story is that someone wants to buy the Morton property, and if he can stop Bob Morton shearing, he'll get the place for a song. Morton's in financial trouble, you see, and he needs the money from the clip. If the strike were to end, Morton could shear his sheep and stay in business. Or if he could get other labour, he'd be all right. But if he doesn't get that wool to market he will be forced to sell. And this other creature who is stirring all the trouble will get the property.'

'What a bastard,' Josef said.

The priest turned owl-like eyes on him. 'Very likely,' he said, managing to scold and forgive in only two words. Then he stood and excused himself, to return wearing a pair of overalls. 'I'm wearing my most religious clothes,' he said.

'He means they're very holey,' Roger Montgomery explained smiling. 'He always goes fishing in them.'

The priest smiled, pleased that the joke had been told and that he had not had to tell it. 'I've told Ethel we're going out in the boat,' he said. 'She is convinced I'm as nutty as a fruit cake so she said nothing. She never says anything. She may well be a deaf mute for all I know. I must ask her one day. Shall we go?'

He stepped on to the verandah but retreated almost immediately. 'The street is full of unpleasant shadows,' he said. 'A gang of men is passing, so it might be prudent for us to wait a few minutes.'

They waited, and when the sound of the men had faded they followed the priest to the place where he moored his boat. The journey was short. The rowing boat was strung to a rickety pier projecting into a shallow inlet. The air smelled of mud and mangroves.

'It's low tide, so we'll have to be careful where we go,' the priest said. 'I will row. Roger, would you be kind enough to sit in the bow and guide me? The basic idea is to keep Australia on the right, but there are some subtleties such as channels and mud banks which I would like you to observe and attempt to distinguish, one from the other, for they will be vital to our progress. What is the name of your ship, gentlemen?'

'The *Mary Elizabeth*,' Josef said.

'Goodness me! Is that still afloat? At least she'll be easy to board. She's not much bigger than my boat.'

'What do you want us to do?' Adam asked.

'Sit in the back and keep your heads down and try to look like fishing nets or sacks of mullet or something suitably non-human.'

For an old man, Father Ryan was a remarkably skilled oarsman, guiding the boat deftly and making little noise as they left the jetty and followed a winding channel up the inlet. He rowed in silence, getting an occasional word of warning from the parson in the bow. They rounded a spit of land and the lights of the port came into view.

They drifted with the breeze, sliding across the water with quiet and economical strokes. The water was oily and slick with reflections. Several ships were moored there, but the *Mary Elizabeth* was easy to distinguish.

She sat low in the water, drenched in shadows from the tall wharf to which she was moored. A bright light shone from the ship's rigging, illuminating steps up to the wharf. A row of crates that had been loaded during the day lined the deck.

They did not see the men at first. It was the voices they heard, loud voices, at first indistinct but obviously arguing. Tracing the sound they saw two men, as vague as the piles and masts and railings but moving a little, and standing in the bow of the ship where the shadows were the deepest. Cautiously, Father Ryan changed course to pass the ship beyond the reach of the mast light, and with the intention of approaching from the stern. The voices became clearer.

'They'll have to come eventually,' one of the men said.

'I don't want any trouble within sight of the ship.'

'What's it matter?'

'It matters, you fool, because I don't want to be involved and if any fighting takes place near here again, I could be involved. Are you sure they can't be found?'

'The men are still looking.'

'Well, go back and help them. I don't want them back on this ship. Just put them in the nursing home for a couple of days. That would be ideal. Then we could pick them up on the way south and I can make sure things are settled properly. Now get back there and get on with the job.'

One man walked towards the light and began to climb the steps. The other man lit a cigarette. He was still at the bow. 'Mills!' he called, and the cigarette glowed as he inhaled deeply. The man on the steps hesitated. 'How are things with Morton?'

'Under control.'

'Good. I'll be back in a few days. Now see you find those two and take care of them.'

The man on the ladder left. The one in the bow drew on his cigarette several times and then threw it in the water. He walked towards the ship's bridge and passed under the light. Adam saw him clearly. It was Ritchie.

Father Ryan rowed well beyond the *Mary Elizabeth* before turning. He waited until they had entered the darkest shadows of the wharf before speaking.

'That was Harry Mills,' he whispered. 'Do you know the other man? The one who mentioned Morton?'

Adam was still shocked. 'He's the one who's selling us the land. His name's Ritchie.'

The boat nosed into a pier. Roger Montgomery held the slimy timbers while the priest paddled with one oar to turn them, so they were completely under the wharf.

'Ritchie,' Father Ryan said, damning the word. 'That's the name I've heard. The man is a monster.' He pivoted in his seat. 'Well, what do we do now, Roger?'

'Take them back, I suppose. They could stay at the manse with me. I've room.'

'What are you talking about?' Adam said.

'Your fate, dear boy,' the priest said.

'But we'll go back on the ship.'

The priest reached out to touch Adam's shoulder, to help him absorb what he was about to say. 'You may not have understood all we heard,' he said, searching for Adam's eyes in the darkness, 'but those men were talking about you and your friend. They want you hurt, injured, incapacitated. In hospital. I'm not sure of the reasons, but they are evil. Now, lad, this is the same man who is out to buy the Morton property and who is bringing in thugs to cause trouble and prolong the strike. You can't possibly climb on to that ship now.'

'I think it would be the safest place for us to be,' Adam said. The priest removed his hand.

'How can that be?'

'Ritchie himself is not going to hurt us. He gets others to do the bashing. Right?'

'That seems to be his method.'

'The crew seem to be all right. I reckon the real danger is ashore, not on the ship. If we get on board, Ritchie won't dare touch us.'

The priest spun around once more. 'The lad makes sense. What do you think, Roger?'

The young parson leaned forward. 'Would you still go north and buy your land?'

'Adam's paid four hundred pounds deposit,' Josef said loudly.

'Keep your voice down!' Father Ryan hissed. They sat there in silence, listening to the lap of water. A bird flew low, passing between them and the ship.

'I think you're probably right,' the priest whispered. 'You won't be truly safe anywhere, but you'll be safer on the water than you will be in town. Just take care.'

'And you're still going to buy the land?' the parson asked, his voice high again.

'Why not?' Adam said. 'We know what Ritchie's like but if the land's any good, we'll go ahead. I'm not going to be bluffed out of my property by some land shark.'

'Well said,' the priest said. 'Now, how are you going to get on board?'

'By climbing up the back. There's a ladder.'

The priest manoeuvred the boat into position. All four shook hands.

'I don't know how to thank you,' Adam said.

The priest winked. 'You could always consider becoming a Catholic.'

They reached their cabin unchallenged and stayed there until dawn, when they heard the sounds of the ship being prepared for sailing. Trying to appear casual, they sauntered to the deck and enjoyed the look of consternation on Ritchie's face. He was standing near the bridge, watching the wharf. When he saw them, his mouth opened and his face grew red, but he said nothing.

'Good morning,' Adam called. Josef waved a greeting. Ritchie raised a finger weakly in response and turned and went to his cabin. They scarcely saw him for the rest of the voyage.

The *Mary Elizabeth* stayed only three hours in Onslow for the ship had no more than a few drums of fuel and lubricating oil to unload. They took on water and headed for Port Robinson.

The coastline now swung to the north-east, but Captain Benson headed north for a while, steering well away from land to avoid the reefs and Islands snagging the coastal waters. They passed Barrow Island and the Montebello Islands and the sea teemed with life.

They saw more dolphins. Terns and gulls stalked the ship, screeching and wheeling. Turtles appeared, snake-heads swivelling as they broke the surface. Seeing the ship, they dived in alarm, spiralling through the transparent waters like blackened and battered pans sinking to the bottom. Occasional studs of coral coloured the water and everywhere were fish, tumultuous shoals of them, flashing banks of mirrors as they turned in formation.

While the Montebellos were still on the horizon, the captain swung towards the east, cleared the farthest islands of the Dampier Archipelago and turned again towards Port Robinson. They came in after sunset and anchored offshore. Adam and Josef rowed ashore the next morning. They were surprised to learn that Ritchie had left earlier and wondered what sort of reception might await them, but when they reached the landing the agent was waiting with a car and driver. The car was a black Ford which had suffered so much from exposure to the sun that the paint on its mudguards and roof had crazed. The cracks had grey edges and, from a distance, the car appeared to be covered in mosaic tiles. Behind the car was a trailer, piled high with drums and cartons and covered with a tarpaulin. The driver stayed well back, his face anonymous in the shade of a large hat.

Ritchie was wearing a pith helmet and carried a leather brief-case. He was smiling. 'I didn't want to keep you waiting so I came on ahead to organize things. George will take us out there.'

The brim of George's hat tipped, acknowledging the introduction. Ritchie put his briefcase on the front seat. He rubbed his hands and looked up at the sky. 'Well, gentlemen, this is the big day. Cobargo. Get in the back and we'll be off.'

They jolted down a rough track to Roebourne, turned at a signpost to Port Hedland and Broome, and crossed a river. Ritchie explained that he had another visit to make during the day and intended dropping them at Cobargo so that they could inspect the property. He would return later. He wanted them to take their time. There would be no hustling, he assured them. He had removed the pith helmet and, as he spoke, smoothed the strands of oiled hair that covered his skull.

The country was sandy and sparsely covered with vegetation.

Low hills, as bald as Ritchie's head, rimmed the horizon to the south. As though reading Adam's mind, Ritchie put on his helmet.

'Good sheep country,' he said. 'You need plenty of land out here, but you've got it, of course, and the rain's dependable. You've got access to a good port too, so there's no problems getting your wool to market.'

'What if we want to raise cattle?' Adam said.

'Excellent cattle country. Excellent.' And he settled back in the seat and went to sleep.

The driver turned off the Port Hedland road and went south. For some time they followed a river but then the track became rougher and climbed into hills that bristled with rock. Mounds of spinifex and a few hardy eucalypts, their trunks as bright and polished as white marble, softened the scene, but the country would be cruel for any hoofed animals. Adam could see no grazing stock, no fences, no buildings.

'How far to go?' he asked George, but the driver did not answer.

They crossed a ridge and entered a valley that could have been the centre of some gigantic and ruined castle, for the hills that surrounded them were topped by towers and sheer ramparts of shattered stone. The track left the valley by following a dry creek whose bed was a jumble of boulders and uprooted tree trunks, and then swung to the east.

They came to a junction and took the left fork. The track had been badly eroded by rain and for a while the driver avoided the wheel ruts altogether and made a path through tall grass that was as bleached and brittle as straw. They came to a fence with a wooden gate across the track. George got out and opened the gate. It moved with difficulty for one of the hinges had broken. He returned to the car, drove through the opening and then went back on foot to close the gate. He had to carry it and had difficulty with the catch, which was a length of fencing wire that had to be looped over a thick post. Adam had watched the operation through the car's rear window and the driver, aware of being observed, lowered his head so that the brim of his hat obscured his face.

'What a queer bastard,' Josef whispered.

'So would you be if you drove on these roads all your life,' Adam said and they both grinned. The journey may have been appallingly rough but at least they were nearing their destination.

417

'When do you reckon the country's going to improve?' Josef said, peering through his window.

'Soon, I hope. You couldn't raise anything on this except blisters.'

The track turned north and wound through low hills. The car travelled slowly, juddering from one rocky outcrop to the next. They came to another fence and another gate. This gate had been broken and lay on its side. Weeds grew through it. They swung to the east, cresting a low rise near the ruins of an old stockyard. On the ridge the driver stopped the car and touched Ritchie on the shoulder.

'Ah,' he said, sitting up and looking around him. He pushed his hair into place. 'Thank you, George. Well, gentlemen, here we are. Welcome to Cobargo Station.'

SIX

'Where is it?' Josef said. He turned in a circle, tucking his shirt in his trousers as he scanned the country around him. He kicked a stone. The country was as hard as flint. Adam said nothing. Biting back his disappointment, he walked towards the stockyard. The posts had been rough hewn and were powdery with age. There were no traces of hoof marks around the yard. Weeds grew high in the open gateway.

'Not frightened of hard work, are you?' Ritchie called after him. Adam turned. The agent was spreading his hair across his skull before fitting the helmet. He came towards him, smiling. 'A man who's good with an axe and a few simple tools would soon have this place spick and span. In any case, Mr Ross, you're not buying fences and stockyards and things like that. You're buying land. A priceless, irreplaceable commodity. When the good Lord made the first lot, that was it.' He had been sweating and he pulled the collar away from his neck. 'No more. The man who gets in early and buys land is the man who makes his fortune. Particularly up here. This area is in for boom times, mark my words. You might face a few months of hard work,' he said, waving around him, 'but then you'll be sitting pretty. I reckon a smart operator here, someone who knew the land and knew how to husband his resources wisely, could be a millionaire in ten years.'

'What happened to the last owner?'

Ritchie took off his helmet and wiped the inner lining. 'Sad case,' he said replacing the helmet and squinting towards the sun. 'Very sad case. An alcoholic. You don't drink, do you?'

'No.' Adam was studying the land. There were bigger hills to the south and they seemed to be well covered with timber, but the land nearer him had few trees and was crusted with rocks. Many had cracked from ages of heat and wind and rain and coated the iron-hard ground in tumbled disarray.

'Well, then, you'll have no problem. As you can see, he let the place go a bit. Great shame.' He nodded towards the stockyard, 'A lot of work has been put into this place.'

'Those yards haven't been used for twenty years.'

'Well, this is the old part of the property,' Ritchie said, walking back towards the car. 'The homestead and all the new yards and sheds are down this way, beyond the ridge.'

'What are they like?' Adam followed carefully picking a path through the sharp-edged rocks that covered the ground.

'You'll have the chance to see for yourself in a moment. They're quite extensive.' Ritchie reached the Ford. George had begun refuelling its tank, filling it from a drum carried on the trailer.

Josef had been further along the ridge. 'I can't see any sign of a homestead,' he said.

'It's about a mile away,' Ritchie said.

'Where's the river?' Adam asked.

'There's not just one river. There's three.' Ritchie beamed. 'The Yule's over that way,' and he pointed to the east, 'the Sherlock's in the other direction and down south is the Fortescue, one of the noblest streams in all the state.'

Adam was surprised. 'Do they all run through this land?'

'Not exactly, but where you have major rivers you have rainfall and run-off and other such desirable things.'

'Mr Ritchie, are the rivers on this land? Your advertisement showed a river. Which one was it?'

'It's a tributary of the Sherlock.'

'Does it have water in it?'

Ritchie smiled. 'Mr Ross, rivers do have water in them.'

419

'Not most of the ones I know.'

Ritchie mopped his forehead. 'Well, we're wasting time. It's extremely hot and there's a lot to do. George and I have business just down the road.'

'Down what road?' Josef asked, gazing about him.

'Back the way we came. You saw a fork in the road?' He waited for Josef to grunt recollection. 'Along the other road. I have rather urgent business at a property there.'

The drive had filled the tank. He started the engine.

'You're going now?' Adam asked.

'What I was thinking was this, Mr Ross. I'll go and attend to this other matter. You and your young friend might care to stroll down to the homestead and have a good look around. There are things you'll want to see on your own and discuss, I'm sure. We'll be back in about three or four hours' time. What do you say?'

'And just leave us here?'

'It's your place. You want to see it, don't you? I mean, we came up here at your insistence to inspect the property. Don't tell me you don't want to inspect it now that we've got here?'

Adam noticed George standing beside the driver's door. He seemed taller than before, and he was looking straight at him. There was a suggestion of menace in the man's pose.

'I've never heard of anyone selling land by nicking off and leaving the buyer on his own,' Adam said.

'You must appreciate, Mr Ross, that I have gone to a great deal of personal inconvenience to bring you here like this. Now please be reasonable. All I want is the chance to attend to some other business while I'm in the region. Is that not a reasonable request?'

'You will come back?' Josef said anxiously.

Ritchie laughed and moved to the car. 'Is that all that's worrying you? Don't worry, young man. I've never been known to leave a client alone until I have his signature on the contract. I'll see you this afternoon. We'll meet you back up here.'

He drove off.

The walk down the ridge to the homestead was difficult. The track was clear enough to follow but it was rough everywhere and partly overgrown in places. Obviously, it had not been used for a long time. Several seasons of heavy rain had sent water cascading down the wheel ruts, scouring them into deep trenches and undermining large rocks, leaving them bare-sided and poised to topple.

The closer they moved to the homestead, the more depressed Adam became. Cobargo was an abandoned wilderness.

The house was partly concealed by a stand of low trees but even looking through the trees they could see it was derelict. One wall had been burned by fire, many of the roof's wooden shingles were missing and a corner post of the verandah leaned at an angle. Bushes grew through the floor boards. Near the house were two sheds, one of which had partly collapsed and had a young tree growing through a hole in the roof. There were some smaller outbuildings, a windmill with a trough and tank, and a collection of yards with posts and railings angled in various directions.

They passed the trees and jumped a small creek. It was lined with boulders and rounded pebbles. In one hollow, the muddy bottom seemed damp.

'I think this is our river,' Adam said. Josef sat on a boulder. He was too disappointed to speak. They could see the homestead clearly now. It was tiny with no more than two rooms. The front door was missing.

Adam began to laugh. When Josef turned, he said: 'I was just trying to imagine Heather living here.' He searched for a smile on his friend's face but it would not come. He tried to perpetuate his own smile, to disguise the awful disappointment welling within him, but it would not last. One pathetic attempt at humour was all he could manage and even then his laugh had come darkly tinted.

Heather would never live here. Not in that ramshackle ruin of a house; not in the tent he would have to string between trees down near the creek while he built a new homestead; not on these cruel rocks in these desolate hills. This would be the living equivalent of hell to her, the antithesis of what she understood or could accept. She would go mad.

Adam could cope. He had worked in difficult country. He could survive here. But this property would be almost impossible to work. Not only was it run down to the point of ruin but it was in an area which would be incredibly hard on men or beasts. Sheep or cattle, whatever was attempted here, would need a huge area for grazing so they could search out pockets of feed, and he would need half a dozen men to keep track of the stock in the hills.

Suddenly he felt thirsty and extremely tired. Bring Heather here?' Imagine the parties she could throw. Or maybe tennis. He looked for a site for a tennis court. There was no possibility of them living here, but he looked, realizing a place for Heather's tennis court had been in his mind since he began the journey. There was plenty of flat land beyond the creek but none of it was without an outcropping of harsh rock and a thick crust of loose, sharp stones. He wondered how the ball would bounce. Pam – was that the name of Heather's idiotic girlfriend at Nevertire, the one with the lighted tennis court? – she would be busy if she came here for a weekend tennis. Adam imagined her chasing a wildly bouncing ball. She would show her knickers as she bounded over the rocks after a flyer, he thought, and smiled again.

Josef was looking at him, and the smile caused his head to tilt in curiosity.

'Nothing,' Adam said, coming back to reality.

'I just can't believe it,' Josef said, standing and raising and lowering his arms several times, like a bird trying to fly in slow motion. 'I mean ... shit!' He sat down again, defeated. 'This is nothing like the advertisement. We've been tricked.'

'Maybe not,' Adam said, not believing what he said but hating to see his friend look so crushed. And hating to admit what he knew to be true. He had made a dreadful mistake. He began to walk towards the homestead and heard the sounds of Josef following, deliberately kicking stones as he went.

This was his own fault. Yes, he had been misled. But the fault was essentially his. He had been the fool. Gullible to the point of idiocy. Eager to buy, he had behaved like the rawest amateur and had rushed to impale himself on the hook that Ritchie had dangled. And he knew why. That was the effect she had on him. She had knocked him off balance. With his deal, he had ignored all the principles he knew he should have followed. And all because he had married a woman he did not understand and could not please despite his best efforts; because he had been so upset by her family's duplicity; and because he did not know what to do back in Nyngan, and had rushed out here, to this dreadful, impossible place on the other side of the continent. And because of Josef's wild enthusiasm. No. He could not blame Joe.

He stopped and shook his fist at the pathetic collection of buildings.

'Bloody hell!' he screamed.

Josef stopped, astonished. 'I've never heard you swear before.'

'I've never felt like this before.' He felt better. Not good, but a little less angry. He continued walking.

'How could they have said the things they did about this place?' Josef said resentfully, but Adam's jaw was too tightly set for conversation.

He should have demanded more information. He should have found out exactly where Cobargo was located, and been given precise details about the property and nature of the country. He thought about the way he had rushed in and blushed with embarrassment. He could never tell anyone what had happened. They would laugh at him. How could he have been so simple?

All he knew about the area was what Tabby had told him on the voyage north. He had learnt the rainfall was seasonal, with the wet season being in summer and the rest of the year usually dry. That could account for the withered look of the land at the moment. It was almost certainly greener in February, when the dry little creek was probably a raging torrent.

But Tabby had said the rain didn't penetrate far inland. This could be marginal rainfall country, getting the tail-end of a cyclone one year and nothing the next.

Tabby had also told him there were a number of mines in the area for substances like tin, copper and even gold. He studied the serrated hills surrounding this place. He wouldn't like to be a miner here. The hills were dry and rough and hostile, and would be ferociously hot later in the year.

That was the sum of his prior knowledge; that and the advertisement.

He reached the house. It seemed so forlorn, so abandoned, so forgotten. He wondered what sort of people had built it, lived in it and, finally, left it. They would have come here with dreams, just like he had. And suffered and failed and gone.

He saw a grave away to his right, near the trunk of a dead tree, and walked towards it. The ground at the grave was humped and formed of carefully selected stones of small but uniform size. Nettles grew through the stones. A wooden cross had been erected at the head of the grave but it had fallen down long ago and was splintery and rotten. A name had been cut into the crosspiece, but time and weather had blurred the letters. Adam could distinguish a 'T'. Nothing more. Who was it? The man who built the house? His wife? A child?

A noise made him turn. Josef, who had wandered casually into the house, had suddenly emerged stumbling backwards. He landed so heavily on the verandah that he broke through a floorboard. He pulled his foot clear, shattering more of the board, and jumped awkwardly to the ground.

Adam ran back. 'What's up?' he shouted.

'Have a look for yourself.' Josef tried to laugh, but it was the noise a man makes when he has had a fright and wants to conceal his shock. 'Just don't go beyond the door.'

Adam hesitated but Josef, wild-eyed and flirting with a smile, was daring him. Cautiously, he climbed the verandah. He avoided the newly broken floorboard, moved past a bush sprouting through another gap, and stood in the open doorway. Spider webs framed the opening and covered much of the inner roof of the building in a lattice of neglect. It was dark inside. Shafts of sunlight, white with dust and speckled with insects, cut across the remains of a table.

The floor moved. A large brown snake was sliding through the beam of light. On the edge of the beam, the snake's path was interrupted by some obstruction that caused it to rise. Adam looked more closely. The snake was crossing the coppery back of another snake.

As his eyes grew more accustomed to the darkness, he saw more snakes against the far wall. Two were coiled in the dust and rubble of a stone fireplace.

'Don't come back too quickly,' Josef called with just a hint of a mocking laugh, and Adam turned. A smaller snake had emerged from the hole through which the bush grew. Adam withdrew gently, circling the protruding bush and taking care not to apply sudden pressure to any board for the building seemed to shake with each step.

'How did you like that?' Josef said, feeling better now that he could see Adam was as shocked as he. 'I went straight in and nearly trod on the big bugger near the table.'

Trying to appear casual and back in control of his nerves, he moved to the edge of the verandah and, with one outstretched arm, leaned against the corner post. It moved. Unbalanced, Josef put more of his weight against the post. It snapped at its base. The wood, rotten from termites, made a dull popping sound and began to topple. It came down in slow, wrenching stages and as it fell, it dragged the verandah roof with it.

Adam just had time to jump clear. He landed on stones and fell forward, glimpsing Josef stumbling away from a cascade of timber and iron and dust.

The sounds of the collapse shuffled to the hills and returned in booming echoes. Pancakes of dust rose from the ruins.

Josef was on his hands and knees. He looked up at Adam. 'I've never done that before,' he said and began to giggle.

After a while, they went looking for water. They found some in a rock hole in the creek. Having drunk, they rested in the shade beneath the branches of a gnarled tree before walking back to inspect the property further.

The windmill did not work. It was a tall unit, with a metal derrick surrounded by drums and cans and lengths of water pipe. A heap of mechanical refuse was piled against one leg of the mill. At the top of the structure some blades were missing giving the appearance of a circular mouth with gaps in the teeth. The tail, bearing the faded words 'Southern Cross', had been locked at right angles to the blades but the cranking mechanism that allowed it to be adjusted had rusted in place.

The trough was dry and partly filled with dust.

They inspected the yards. The fences were crudely made, being roughly cut from local timber, and while the posts could be shaken and some rails had come loose, the wood seemed sound. Someone had started to build a wire fence near one yard. A row of posts ran across a stony paddock. Two coils of wire lay on the ground. They were overgrown with weed.

Being wary of snakes, they approached the first shed cautiously. It could have been the oldest of the buildings, for the wood had been cut differently and more expertly, and was white with age. It had never been more than a flimsy structure, probably having been used as a temporary residence before the homestead was built, and one wall and the roof had collapsed. A tree grew in the corner. They used a long stick to poke at a bush growing around the collapsed wall and withdrew hastily when the bush responded with hisses.

The second shed was larger and intact. It was a newer building and of massive construction compared to the other. Sections of tree trunks had been used as the main uprights. They were so stout a man could not wrap his arms around them and touch fingers. The boards were rough paling nailed vertically. The walls had been whitewashed repeatedly but the layers had flaked and in some places it was possible to count the coats of lime.

On the wall facing the house were two doors. They were

secured, one to the other, by an enormous metal bolt. They were big doors and obviously they sagged on their hinges because the area in front of them had been graded into two fan-shaped grooves. Smooth ground marked the zone where the doors had scraped clear space for themselves and beyond, like a cutting on a carved road, was a wall of stones.

The door bolt was reluctant to move. Adam had to use a stone to hammer it free. Between them, they dragged one door open.

They might have expected ruin or weeds or snakes. They did not expect what they found.

Piled in front of them were pieces of old machinery. There were large and rusted gear wheels, rollers, boilers and engine blocks. Bins full of nuts and bolts and washers. Axles and shafts. Canvas belts and hoses. Radiators with yellow-brown streaks. Large metal cases with mysterious seals and levers and shafts projecting from them. Broken packing cases. Cardboard boxes stained with oil.

The pile rose almost to the shed's rafters. An alley had been cleared to the right of the door. They entered it, Adam leading and carrying a stick in case of snakes. Through towering rows of worn metal they came to a clearing in the corner of the shed. There were shelves along one wall, and a bed made from boughs and animal skins. A rotting shirt and a threadbare pair of trousers hung from nails on a rafter, the two garments linked by spider webs.

Another corridor went to the left, along the back wall of the shed. It was lined on the inside by a tall row of wooden crates. Against the wall had been nailed rough shelves and on these were racked rows of opened jam tins, jagged at the top and rusted on the sides. They were filled with old and bent nails, screws, nuts and bolts of all sizes and thread types, split pins, springs, old tyre valves and other treasures of a fanatical hoarder.

They followed the corridor to the other end of the shed and came to a curtain formed by lengths of chain hanging from a rafter. They parted the chain and stepped into a larger area. The floor had been levelled and raked clear of stone. The walls were lined with old fan belts, tyres, pumps, roller chains, gaskets, hoses, pipes, tubes, cables and the worn, punctured and broken debris of many departed motor vehicles.

There were even two cans of polish, both of which had been left open so that the substance that remained resembled hardened glue, and a large and bone-dry chamois.

In the middle of the cleared space was an old car.

It had once been a sports model. It had seats shaped in rich red leather and a small glass aero screen in front of the driver's seat.

The mudguards were flared and painted black to contrast with the crimson bodywork. A spare wheel was fixed across the tail of the car by a thick leather strap, which was strange because the other wheels were missing. The car was supported on four blocks of wood, two under each axle.

Even like that – immobilized, incomplete and surrounded by rusted, oil-stained junk – the car had a proud, haughty appearance.

'What is it?' Josef whispered. There was no need for quietness but the car demanded respect, even reverence.

'I don't know,' Adam said, his voice hushed too. 'I've never seen anything like it.'

'It looks like a racing car.' Josef approached the front, and stooped to identify the name on the badge.

'Alfa-Romeo. What's that?' He turned but Adam was shaking his head. Josef looked again at the badge, which had a third word at the bottom, beneath an embossed laurel wreath. 'Milano,' he said. 'That's Italian. It must be an Italian car.'

They studied it for a long time, looking into the open cockpit at the large wood-rimmed steering wheel and the row of circular instruments all neatly framed by polished metal bezels. The floor pedals were shaped plates, worn and polished from use. The handbrake lever was missing.

They opened one of the hinged engine covers and gazed in admiration at the motor.

'It's got six cylinders,' Adam said, counting the spark plugs. He touched the polished metal covers on the top of the engine. 'It must have overhead cam shafts.'

'What's that mean?' said Josef, who had returned to look inside the cabin.

'That it's fast. But what the hell would it be doing out here?'

As neither could answer that question, they continued to examine the car in silence. Several things were missing: a cap on the radiator, the dipstick, and, of course, the handbrake lever and the four road wheels. They spent another twenty minutes in the shed, examining the car and fingering some of the things stored there before walking outside again.

It was hot in the sun and they squinted in the bright light. For some time, they walked among the buildings. They checked the windmill and tried once more to crank the tail back into place, to see if it would steer the blades into the wind but the rust had bound the pinion teeth together and the winding handle would not move.

They walked back to the rock hole for another drink and then ambled along the creek, searching for more water.

The creek was lined with rocks but gave little sign of water flow. The rocks were square and knife-edged, not rounded and polished as river rocks usually are. A line of trees followed the path of the creek. They were irregularly spaced, and gnarled and stunted from ages of withering heat. In places, low bushes dotted the banks, like embroidered patterns on a rumpled and dirty tablecloth.

Adam found dingo tracks on one patch of sand and, curious to find so many, followed them to a mound of softer earth on which a younger bush was struggling to survive. He was about to pass the bush when he saw something projecting from a hole dug by the wild dogs.

It looked like a long strand of human hair.

With a stick, he poked around the edges of the hole. Bone was revealed. 'What have you found?' Josef said.

'I'm not sure. It might be a skeleton.'

'Of some animal?' Josef got a stick and began to dig with enthusiasm. Adam stopped, some half-forgotten memory forcing him to back away.

Part of a human skull came into view.

'I bet it's an aboriginal,' Josef said, digging with more enthusiasm. 'This is probably an old burial ground. Could be hundreds of years old.'

A mouth, empty of all but three teeth, smiled at them.

'Joe, don't!' Adam said, but his friend was on his knees, digging hard.

More of the skull was revealed. It was on its side with the eye sockets facing them. There were still fragments of skin and flesh stuck to the bone.

Josef stood. 'Jesus,' he said, 'this is new. It can't have been buried for more than a couple of months.'

He poked at the skull with his stick, a little frightened now but

428

curious to know more. He cleared dirt from the top of the skull, where wispy grey hair still rose through a layer of dry and peeling skin.

In the centre of the forehead, framed by splinters of bone, was a bullet hole.

SEVEN

Ritchie was late. Adam and Josef had been waiting on the hill for more than an hour before they saw the faint trail of dust that signalled the approach of the black car. As it drew closer, rumbling and clattering over a long stretch of loose stones, they could see the car no longer pulled a trailer. George was driving. He stopped about fifty paces from where they stood and pulled the brim of his hat low across his face. Ritchie got out. He adjusted his hair and put on the pith helmet.

'I must apologize,' he said, projecting his voice so they could hear him clearly. 'I forgot to leave you some food for lunch. You must be hungry.' He walked towards them. He carried no food; only his briefcase. He reached a large rock halfway between the car and the two young men. He stopped, resting one foot on the rock.

'I have to be back in Roebourne tonight,' he said, using his raised knee as a platform for his briefcase, and beginning to unbuckle one of its two straps. 'Therefore, the quicker we get all the formalities over with, the quicker I can be on my way.'

'We've been talking,' Adam said, not sure where he should start, 'and we've decided not to go ahead with the purchase.' They had, in fact, decided more than that. They had decided there was something distinctly frightening about Cobargo and the deal, and the sooner they headed south, the happier they would be.

Ritchie did not bother to look up from the briefcase. 'Oh you can't do that,' he said jovially. 'You'd only lose your deposit and we wouldn't want that, would we? Now, I think if you, Mr Ross, were to sign here we could be on our way.'

Adam stared in amazement. 'I said I wasn't going to buy.'

'You have bought.' Still Ritchie did not look up. He pulled

some sheets of paper from his bag.

'When you sent your letter and your deposit for this land, that constituted an agreement to purchase.' He put on his glasses and lowered his nose to study Adam above the rim. 'I hope you understand what I'm saying. You have, in the eyes of the law, agreed to purchase this property. If you do not sign the contract, you are in breach of the law. I could take you to court. At the very best, you would merely lose your four hundred pounds deposit. I think it is likely, however, that you would also be found liable for the balance of the money, plus my not inconsiderable costs in travelling here to show you the land. To deliver you to the site, so to speak.'

He closed the briefcase and leaned on it with one elbow.

'As you will have to pay all this money, Mr Ross, it would be much simpler, and certainly in your interests, to sign now and become the legal owner of the land.' Ritchie fixed a vulture's eye on his prey.

Had Ritchie been standing there in silence, Adam may have been tempted to laugh. He looked as out of place as a kangaroo in the main street of Perth. With his city man's suit, his half-moon glasses and that pompous pith helmet, he looked ludicrous; a comedian thrust into a villain's role without time to change costume.

'You will sign,' he said, producing a pen, and there was no suggestion of a comedian in the way he delivered the words.

'How long is it since you've inspected the homestead?' Adam asked. He moved towards Ritchie. He saw George, still at the car, open a back door and reach for something.

'Why do you ask?' Ritchie said.

Josef stepped forward. 'Because it's bloody well fallen down! The roof fell in on top of us.'

Ritchie straightened. 'If you've caused damage to the property, you will be held responsible.'

'Don't give us that bullshit,' Josef exploded.

'The crass turn to profanity when they have nothing to say,' Ritchie said.

'The bloody place collapsed,' Josef shouted.

Ritchie closed his eyes, waiting for the storm to pass.

'What was left of the homestead was full of snakes,' Adam said.

'Australia is full of snakes, Mr Ross.'

'And serpents,' Josef said.

430

The corners of Ritchie's mouth twitched acknowledgement. There was a cough, a signal from one man to the other, and George emerged from the back of the car holding a rifle.

'What's that for?' Josef said.

'Snakes,' Ritchie said and smiled. 'Now, Mr Ross, I suggest you sign.'

Very slowly George raised the barrel of the rifle.

Adam licked his lips. 'I have two questions for you, Mr Ritchie,' he said.

'Yes?' Ritchie was reading the document. He did not look up.

'What will happen if I don't sign?'

'You will lose your money and you will not own the land.'

'That's not what you said in your letter,' Josef shouted.

'What letter?' Ritchie asked, his brows knotted as though genuinely puzzled. 'I haven't seen such a letter. Have you seen a letter, George?' He turned to the man with the rifle. The hat shook.

Ritchie stroked his chin.

'Could you possibly mean some letter you left in your bag, a bag which, I should point out, you no longer possess?'

'Jesus Christ! Where are our bags?' Josef said.

'On the trailer. Which is safe.' Ritchie's smile almost stretched beyond his control. 'Now, Mr Ross, I believe you had a second question?'

Adam breathed deeply. 'Who's the man buried down by the creek?'

The smile vanished. Ritchie swallowed, spun briefly to face George and then turned again. He removed the helmet and wiped his head. 'What man?' he said.

'The one with the bullet in his head.'

Ritchie turned sharply. He stood still for a moment with his back to Adam. He looked once up at the sky, once back towards Adam and once at George and then strode towards the car. Adam could hear him speak to the driver but could not distinguish the words. Obviously they were critical, because George wriggled in discomfort. He said something, lifting his shoulders as he talked to ward off whatever accusations Ritchie was hurling at him.

Ritchie faced Adam once more. He took off his glasses, polished them carefully and put them in their case. He coughed to clear his throat.

'Are you going to sign the contract, Mr Ross?' he said.

'No.'

'Do you realize what this means?'

'It means I'm not going to buy the land.'

They faced each other in silence.

'Who is the man buried down there?' Adam said. 'He's a white man, he was shot in the head and he hasn't been buried very long.'

Ritchie looked at his watch. He manufactured a yawn.

'Was he the last fellow you tried to sell land to?' Josef said, expressing a theory he and Adam had been discussing.

'Or was he the previous owner?' Adam said.

Ritchie put his hands in his pockets. 'I don't see why I should be concerned about some lost or lonely old man who committed suicide,' he said, letting his foot toy with a stone as he spoke.

'I didn't say he was old.'

Ritchie continued to play with the stone, rolling it backwards and forwards.

'How did you know it was an old man we found, Mr Ritchie?'

'This part of the world is full of failures,' Ritchie said. 'Most of them are bitter old men.'

'Well, if this man shot himself,' Adam said quickly, 'I don't think you could call him a failure.'

The foot paused at the point of sweeping the stone to one side.

'You see, Mr Ritchie, he's the first dead man I've heard of who was able to bury himself.'

Ritchie was silent.

'We only found him because the dingoes had started to dig up the body.'

Ritchie put his hands back in his pockets. 'Troublemakers aren't liked up here, Mr Ross.'

'Who's the troublemaker? Me or that man?'

Ritchie walked to the front of the car. 'No one's going to believe you,' he said. 'Because no one's going to see you again.'

George had raised the rifle. For the first time, Adam could see his face clearly.

'No, you clot,' Ritchie growled. 'You've done enough damage. Just get in the car.'

'They're going to leave us,' Josef cried.

'That's absolutely correct,' Ritchie said. 'No need to do anything else. You're one hundred and five miles from the nearest house. No one'll ever see you alive again. Ross, to put it bluntly, you've become a pain in the arse. The same applies to your coarse

432

young friend. I've spent too much time and money on you already to justify this enterprise and I'll be damned if I'm going to waste a couple of bullets on you. Enjoy your stay at Cobargo.'

The car drove away.

Josef spent some time shouting profanities at the departing car. When he grew tired of that he was surprised to find he was on his own. Adam was already walking down the hill towards the creek and the homestead. Josef ran after him.

'What are we going to do?' he called out.

Adam squinted towards the sun. There was, he reckoned, about two hours of light left. He wanted to use that time to search for things they would need. Something to hold water. Any food. Maybe a few old cans in the shed. Somewhere to sleep. Something to hunt with.

'You're not planning to live here?' Josef said, when he had finally reached his friend.

'No, but we're not going to die here, either.'

'What are we going to do, Adam?'

'Find the things that will keep us alive. Then decide the best way to get out of here.'

They went back to the newer shed. They fossicked through the shelves, around the bed, but found no food. They moved to the other side of the shed, where the car was stored. They found a bucket and a variety of cans and open containers. They became excited when they discovered two heavy, unopened cans without labels but when they used an old screwdriver to punch a hole in the lid of one, they discovered it contained lubricating oil.

Adam examined the Alfa-Romeo once more. Having satisfied himself with what he saw, he stood on the car's seat to get a better view of items on the top of the pile of mechanical debris in the middle of the shed.

'What are you looking for?' Josef asked.

'Anything that might be useful.'

He then got off the car, wiping his boot marks from the leather, and searched the walls for a rifle, an axe or some other weapon. There was none. He found the head of a pick but could not find a handle. Eventually, he selected a long and rusty piece of steel rod. One end had been flattened into a chisel point.

'This'll do,' he said, examining the sharp end.

'Do for what?'

'A spear.'

'You're not serious!'

'Do you want to go hungry?'

'No, but you won't catch anything with a spear.'

'All right. I'll go looking for food with this and you go to the nearest shop and we'll see who eats first.'

Holding the metal rod lightly in his right hand, and having slipped the screwdriver into his belt, Adam walked back through the dark rows of junk.

'What are you going to hunt?' Josef asked, following him. 'Kangaroo?'

'I thought of something a bit easier.'

'Like what?'

'You'll see.' The sun had just dipped below the hills as Adam walked to the old homestead. With great care, he picked his way over the remains of the fallen verandah roof and entered the house. Josef heard the creak of the boards, and imagined a violent slithering.

'You are crazy!' he shouted.

He heard a thud, a human grunt of exertion and then more boards creaking. The long metal rod emerged from the doorway. It was held horizontally and on its end writhed a large brown snake. Adam followed.

'Dinner,' he announced.

They slept by the creek, at a place where there was soft sand and dead timber for a fire. In the morning, they scouted along the banks of the creek, following it for more than an hour until the watercourse ran into a rough and narrow gorge. They were looking for several things: more water, a track leading somewhere else, or wild fruit and berries. They discovered a little water but none of the other things. However, they did see many signs of animal life. They found fresh droppings left by kangaroos and rabbits and many lizard tracks and Adam felt more content. They would not starve. With water and plentiful game, they would always eat, for as a child he had hunted with aboriginal children and could throw a spear. He was not as good as a skilled aboriginal, but he could catch enough game to survive.

The discovery of a potential food source was vital, not just for the obvious reason of survival but to make feasible a scheme brewing in Adam's mind. He had been thinking about many things: staying alive, getting away from Cobargo and reaching civilization, and catching Ritchie. To combine all three desirable objectives was the purpose of his scheme but to make it work – and there was a gamble to it – required the two of them to stay at the property for at least a couple of days. And there was the risk. To have them stay at Cobargo for some days without nourishment would make them so weak they could not hope to have the strength to walk out. Adam estimated that walking back along the car tracks would take at least five days – hard days – and, because the country along the route appeared to be generally waterless, they probably would not survive. They could head for one of the rivers and track it downstream. That could take months.

Having found food along the creek meant he could try the plan he favoured.

He wanted to fix the old car and try to drive back to Roebourne.

First, there were things to find and the two most compelling items were fuel and wheels.

The fuel they found near the windmill. Most of the drums scattered near the structure had been used for power kerosene but one forty-four gallon container was stamped 'Neptune Motor Spirit' and gave off the smell of petrol. They shook the drum, listening to the slosh of its contents. They estimated it had about ten gallons left but, unhappily, the drum's cap was missing and water had mixed with the fuel. They solved the problem by rolling the drum to the shed and pouring the petrol through the old chamois they had found hanging on the wall. They found a couple of empty cans and poured the fuel from one to the other, using the cloth as a filter. The chamois allowed the petrol to pass through but trapped the water. They filtered the fuel several times, until they were satisfied no water remained.

It took them another hour to find the wheels. At first, Josef had climbed the pile of old parts to search among the chaos of bits and pieces, but the light was so poor that they stopped to open the second door. It proved difficult to budge and they had to dig away some earth to allow the door to swing out. When it did, they found the missing wheels. They were neatly stacked against the inside of the door, obscured from the view of anyone within the shed by a row of boxes.

The spokes and rims were sound and the hubs had splines to match up with the stubs on the Alfa-Romeo's axles. Each wheel had an eared cap to lock it in place. A hammer, or even a rock or lump of wood, could be beaten against the ears to tighten the cap. They oiled the splines and tried the wheels and found they slid easily into place. But if the wheels were all right, the same could not be said about the tyres. One had a rip in the sidewall.

'We can sleeve that,' Adam said and went searching for a strip of canvas or rubber. The main problem, however, was with the inner tubes. They had all perished. One had rotted at the valve stem. The others were sticking to the inside of the tyres and disintegrated at the touch of an exploring finger. Josef left the car in disgust and sat on a box.

'We're stuffed.'

'No,' Adam said, 'but you've used the right word. I want to check over the engine while you do something else.'

'What?'

'Collect grass.'

Josef waited for a laugh or something to indicate a joke but Adam was serious. 'We're going to stuff the tyres. My father did it once when I was a kid. We were out the back of Yunta and we'd had a series of blow-outs. We had one more puncture and there was no spare and no way to repair the tube, so he sent me out collecting grass.'

'And he put it in the tyre?'

'Jammed it in.'

'And it worked?'

'Certainly did. It stank a bit. You could smell the grass stewing but we went slowly and it got us there.'

'But we've got over a hundred miles to go.'

'It's better than walking.'

Josef scratched his chin. 'What are you going to do while I'm cutting grass?'

'Try to get the engine running.'

Josef grinned and went off to search for a bag.

Meanwhile, Adam found a rusted wrench, washed it in petrol and soaked it in oil until it could be persuaded to work, and then he used it to unscrew the engine's sump plug. A trickle of treacle-like oil ran out. He replaced the plug and poured fresh oil into the engine from the two cans he had discovered earlier that day. He had no idea if it was the correct oil, but it smelled and felt like engine oil and it was all he had. He had to guess when the motor was filled to the correct level.

436

He used his knife to shape a piece of wood which he then plugged in the hole where the dipstick should have been. He didn't want this precious, anonymous and irreplaceable oil pumping out of the opening.

He brought water from the creek and filled the radiator. He checked for leaks and spent nearly an hour shaping a piece of tin to serve as a crude radiator cap.

He poured a little petrol down the throats of the carburettors (as he had done many times with his old Essex when it had been reluctant to start) and cautiously swung the crank handle. The engine coughed, and, for a few stuttering moments, tried to run. A puff of black smoke emerged from the exhaust. Encouraged, Adam checked the petrol tank. Using the wrench, he undid the drain plug on the tank and let the fluid flow into a can. About half a gallon ran out. He poured it through the chamois several times, extracting a little water. Then he replaced the drainplug and put the petrol back in the tank. To it he added some of the precious filtered fuel they had found near the windmill. He cranked the engine again. Nothing happened.

It took him the rest of the day to get the motor to fire once more. The fuel line was blocked and removing and cleaning it was a laborious job with the few tools he had. With only an hour's sunlight left, he went hunting for food while Josef started a fire. Adam returned just after sunset with a three-foot perentie lizard impaled on his makeshift spear.

They roasted it in the coals of the fire. It was a cooler night but they slept soundly.

Back at the car next morning, Adam primed the carburettors and wound the crank handle. The engine coughed a great deal. He kept winding. With a shattering noise, the motor began to run. The sound of the exhaust hit the wall and blasted back. The building quivered.

Josef had spent most of the previous afternoon cramming grass into the tyres and then levering the outer beads into place on the wheel rims. When he had finished, the Alfa-Romeo still sat on squashed tyres but at least the rims were clear of the ground and the car rolled freely when they pushed it.

God, what a machine, Adam thought. With the right tools, he could rebuild it completely. Put the missing parts in place. Polish it. Then drive it, fast, with the raucous exhaust note chasing him and making people turn and stare in admiration.

437

But now the car was a sad sight, without headlamps and with the sun cruelly finding flaws in its crimson and black paintwork. And the tyres bulged, as unsporting as middle-aged spread. Inside the shed, shaded and mysterious, the car had dominated its space. Now that it had been rolled outside the building, with hills surrounding it and rocks threatening it, the Alfa-Romeo looked frail.

EIGHT

Before they left they did several things. They poured half their petrol into the car's tank and the rest into a can which they strapped to the spare wheel. Needing water, they filled two smaller cans. One, being reasonably clean, was for themselves. The other, being tainted by methylated spirit, was for the car, in case the radiator required topping. The only tools they had were the wrench and screwdriver, but to these Adam added the pick head and the tyre pump. He also took a selection of nuts and bolts, screws and nails, some small coils of wire and a length of chain. He put all these items in a sack and tied it with twine to a running board.

While he was preparing the car for its long and rough journey, Adam was thinking about the body they had found beside the creek. They could not leave it uncovered for the wild dogs to devour and scatter the bones. They'd have to take it to another place and rebury it, not only because of what dingoes might do but because of Ritchie. Once Ritchie learned they had left Cobargo he would send someone back to move the body. He would assume that Adam would tell the police or someone in authority in Roebourne about the dead man, so he would either have it burned or hidden where it would never be discovered.

The afternoon was still hot when Adam and Josef walked back to the shallow grave and looked around for an alternative burial site. But the ground was hard and they had no shade. Adam contemplated using the blade of his spear as a digging tool. He even tried a few strokes, thumping the rod into the rock-hard ground, and quickly gave up. Without the proper implements, he and Josef would work for two days or more trying to gouge a deep enough hole, and they could not afford so much time.

Instead they refilled the holes exposing the body and tried to disguise the site. They reasoned that only the killer would know exactly where he had buried the body and even he could be confused if the location looked different. Once the body had been covered, they carried a few large rocks to the bank and put them on top of the grave. They arranged the rocks to look as though they had been there for ages, even partly embedding the biggest ones and transplanting a few dry bushes to give an air of undisturbed tranquillity to the site. Then they covered the whole area with stones. It was heavy and hot work but the grave was transformed into a large rocky outcrop.

When the landscaping was finished, Adam walked north along the creek, counting the steps to a distinctively shaped tree. He cut a diagonal cross on its trunk.

'Why have you done that?' Josef asked.

Adam had been silent most of the day and Josef, being hungry and tired and content to let his friend do most of the thinking, had asked few questions. But the large cross intrigued him.

'So someone else can find the grave,' Adam said, beginning the long walk back to the car. Josef hesitated. He looked back down the creek to the rocky shelf that marked the grave.

'But I thought we didn't want anyone to find the old man,' he said, hurrying after Adam.

'We don't want Ritchie or one of his men digging him up.' Adam slowed to let Josef catch him. 'But we do want the policeman at Roebourne to be able to find the body. We'll tell him to look for a tree marked with a cross and then take thirty-seven paces to the south and dig under the big stones.'

'We're going to tell the police?'

'We certainly are. I want Ritchie arrested but the police can't arrest him if they don't find a body.'

Adam hurried on. He wanted to get to Roebourne as soon as possible to catch Ritchie in town before the *Mary Elizabeth* returned to sail south. Then the police could put him in gaol and come out to Cobargo and dig up the body. With that they would have the evidence to charge Ritchie with murder.

'You reckon they'll hang him?' Josef said, panting under the strain of climbing a ridge that lay across the direct route back to the shed

'I hadn't thought of it.' Adam was using the spear as a walking stick and was making better progress than Josef. 'Maybe not. He mightn't have killed him. That's up to the police to find out.'

Josef reached the crest and stopped for a few moments with his hands on his hips. 'Jesus, you're a funny bloke,' he said, breathing deeply. The lack of good food had left him weak. 'You and I both know the man's a crook. He's dudded us on this place, he tried to get us bashed in Carnarvon, he's paying for a couple of strong-arm men to stir up trouble back there, his gorilla George pulls a gun on us, and you still reckon he mightn't have had that old bloke back there shot in the head! If it was up to me, I'd just have him strung up to the nearest tree. He's a real genuine, twenty-four carat bastard.'

'If you hung all the real, genuine, twenty-four carat bastards in this world there wouldn't be room to stand under any tree.' Adam turned and noticed Josef had not moved. 'What's up?'

'I'm just tired.'

'I know, mate, but we've got to keep going. When we get to town I'll buy you a steak.'

Josef resumed walking. He grinned. 'What with? I've got no money and you've got no money. Everything we've got's in our bags, and Ritchie has pinched those.'

Adam, in triumph, withdrew a crumpled pound note from his pocket. 'Enough to buy you two steaks,' he said and waited for Josef to join him.

He was anxious to leave Cobargo that evening. With no headlights, the Alfa-Romeo could not be driven at night and he was not confident of the car's ability to keep running in the worst heat of the day. He had little idea of how the car would perform and so he could only risk driving when the day was coolest, which meant late in the afternoon and early in the morning.

They would take no food. He could possibly have speared something – another lizard or a snake – or even tried to snare a rabbit, but that could have taken the last of the daylight and meant another night at Cobargo.

He lashed his spear to the spare wheel. Josef cranked the engine into life.

Driving out of the property was to prove so difficult they almost gave up the idea of using the car. On the third attempt, the car scrambled out of the creek, only to face the climb up the hill. With growing concern Adam watched the needle rise on the water temperature gauge but, although the engine became hot, it did not overheat and they reached the top of the rise with the car still running well.

Adam now felt more confident. The climb had been a severe test and the car had mastered it. He reached beyond the windscreen and patted it, as he would a horse that deserved praise.

They passed the broken gate. The sun was setting.

The tyres were marshmallow-soft and inclined to wobble on the rims. Anything faster than a running pace was out of the question but that suited Adam. The track was so rough and strewn with rocks that a faster pace could break a spring or put a rock through the gearbox. By nursing his stuffed tyres he was also nursing the whole car and that improved their chances of reaching Roebourne. He put the gear lever into second, and let the Alfa-Romeo trickle along.

They tried to estimate distance and as each mile was reached, they ticked it off. At three miles, they disturbed a mob of kangaroos grazing near the track. The animals, unused to humans, hopped a short distance and them stopped, heads turned and ears twitching, baffled by the strange sight. After four miles it was so dark they could no longer see the track. Adam slowed, feeling his way through the ruts and stones until the dark outline of trees loomed above them. He stopped.

'We'll camp here for the night,' he said.

It was a miserable camp – the ground was rough, they had no food and a cool wind blew during the night. They had little difficulty in waking early and were under way half an hour before sunrise. They came to the second gate and found the ashes of a recent fire. While Josef struggled to close the gate (it being an outback ritual to shut all gates even if they led to an abandoned property with no stock), Adam walked around the fire, looking at recent tyre marks.

'There's been two cars here,' he called to Josef and they examined the ground together.

There were two distinct sets of tyre prints. In one place, they were jumbled together and trampled by many footprints.

'I think this is where Ritchie came to when he left us. You know, when he said he had another business engagement.'

They drove off. A kangaroo emerged from some scrub on their

left and hopped leisurely in front of the car. Adam touched the brake pedal and the front trembled as the tyres wriggled on their rims.

'I mustn't do that,' he said, 'or I'll put us off the road.'

'Better than hitting the bloody roo,' Josef said, twisting in his seat to watch two other kangaroos follow the first across the track. They travelled at a gentle pace, their bodies and long, curving tails rocking and flowing in perfect balance as they moved.

'Bloody beautiful things, aren't they?' Josef said.

'I don't know how you can swear when you talk about something you say is beautiful.'

'Bloody easy.'

'Your mother would be ashamed of you.'

He glanced at Josef and saw the quick smile. 'Anyhow, back to Ritchie. I've been wondering where he might have gone to when he drove off in the middle of the day. He said he'd gone to have a meeting with someone and yet, later on, he was telling us the nearest house was more than a hundred miles away. There was no way he and that character with the hat could have driven two hundred miles on roads like these in the time they were away.'

'So what do you reckon happened?'

'He met someone back at the gate. They made a fire and had a cup of tea and probably something to eat. I also reckon they went through our bags.'

'Bloody thieves!'

'And I reckon they put the trailer on the back of the other car. That's what all those foot marks were about. That was where they hooked up the trailer.'

'Why? I mean why would he give his trailer to someone else?'

'Because of what was in it. I don't know what Ritchie was carrying in that trailer but he must have been delivering it to someone else.'

'I thought they were drums of petrol.'

'So did I. But what if they were something else?'

'Like what?'

Adam shrugged. 'I wouldn't have a clue. It could be anything. In any case, he had more than drums on the back. Whatever it was, there's someone else out here in cahoots with Ritchie.'

'What the devil would he be doing out here?'

'What do you think? What's about the only thing anyone could do out here?'

442

Josef looked puzzled. 'You couldn't do anything.'

'Well, the fellow who was shot was doing something and it wasn't raising cattle. Do you recall what Tabby told us about this country? He said there was some mining going on.'

'Do you reckon this bloke Ritchie met was a miner?'

'Why not? There's supposed to be all sorts of minerals around here. Even gold.'

'So what are you thinking? Christ, Adam; you can be annoying! You take so long to say something.'

'Well, I'm wondering if the fellow who was shot, the fellow who owned this car, wasn't killed for the land.'

Josef said nothing.

'Supposing he was killed because he was a miner who'd discovered something? Something really valuable.'

The early morning air was cold with just a snap of moisture and, even travelling at such a slow pace, Adam and Josef clutched their shirt collars to their throats and shivered. But once the sun cleared the hills, the air became warm. For a while it was pleasant. The breeze was filled with bush smells, and it ruffled their hair and coaxed the cold from their bodies. But within an hour, the sun had bleached all colour from the sky and the air was thin and dry and hot. Their throats became parched, their lips cracked and their faces were stung by a bombardment of tiny insects.

With the speedometer not working and with neither possessing a watch, they were still estimating both the time and the distance they had covered. About nine in the morning, and when they thought they had driven thirty-four miles, they crossed a gully full of loose rocks. Deep wheel tracks had left a high centre ridge with a topping of upended, wedge-shaped stones. The car's axles graded the ridge, flicking stones in many directions. One sharp projectile struck the fuel tank.

Half a mile beyond the gully, Adam noticed the smell of escaping petrol. Because the track was so rough, he had been watching where he was going rather than checking the instruments and he saw to his horror that the needle on the fuel gauge was slowly sinking towards the 'empty' mark. He stopped the car and they both jumped out.

A fine jet of petrol squirted from a hole in the tank.

Adam slid beneath the car. The hole was small and flat, a split where the metal had been indented by the force of the stone. He pressed his fingers against the hole. The spray ceased. Petrol began running, very slowly, down his fingers to his hand, his wrist and his forearm.

'Get me a small stick,' he said. Josef had moved to the side of the car and he could see his face, upside down and wrinkled with worry. 'Just a twig will do.'

Josef reappeared with a selection of small sticks and passed them to Adam's free hand. Adam chose one.

'Come and change places with me,' he said, and, when Josef's finger was in place, crawled from under the car. With his pocket knife he trimmed one end of the stick, tapering the point to suit the hole. Satisfied with his work, he slid back under the car. Josef removed his finger, petrol streamed out once more, and Adam jammed the stick into the hole.

The flow stopped. Both on their backs, they watched intently. The stick became moist. A drop of petrol fell from its end.

'No bad,' Josef said.

'It'll get worse,' Adam said, trying to wedge the stick more firmly in place.

'What'll we do?'

'Get back in the car and keep going. We might as well use it as have it drip on the ground.'

The car ran for another half hour before coughing to a stop, out of fuel.

'We might stay here a little while,' Adam said.

'What do you mean?' Josef had stepped out of the car and was preparing to unstrap their spare can of petrol. 'We've got more. Let's put it in and keep going.'

Adam was on his knees, inspecting the leak. 'We wouldn't get to town,' he said. 'It's been dripping around the plug and if we put more in, we'll run out with thirty or forty miles to go.'

'Well, what are we going to do?' Josef sat on the ground.

'Make a better patch. Ever mended a petrol tank with soap or chewing gum?'

'You're kidding!'

'No, it works. There's white clay back down the road at that last creek. I'm going to get some. It should work like soap.'

First, they made a poultice of soft clay and threads from a small length of twine, ramming this fibrous mixture around the stick where it plugged the hole. Then they plastered the whole area with moist and well-kneaded clay. Finally, they rested under the car, out of the sun and away from the horde of flies.

They dozed, because neither had slept well the previous night. The hottest part of the day passed. The clay hardened.

It was mid-afternoon when they resumed their journey. They poured half their remaining petrol in the tank. When none leaked through the clay patch, they wound the motor into life and departed.

The road became smoother and Adam increased the pace. After two hours, and having covered possibly thirty more miles, he stopped and Josef added the rest of the petrol. The engine was reluctant to restart and when it did, it ran roughly.

'It's the plugs,' Adam guessed. 'They're oiling up.'

'Should we go slower?'

'We're not going fast enough. This thing's probably designed to run at high revs and the spark plugs get fouled up if they're not hot.'

'What can we do?' Josef shouted.

'Give it a bit of a thrash,' Adam said, putting the gear level in neutral and pumping the accelerator pedal. The engine coughed and fired rings of dark smoke from the exhaust pipe. Adam persisted. Gradually, the coughing was replaced by a stuttering snarl and finally, the snarl became a roar. The needle on the tachometer swung above three thousand revolutions per minute. Adam blipped the throttle a few more times and, on each occasion, the noise that answered him was loud and eager.

'Fixed,' he said and selected first gear.

A car overtook them, showering them with stones as it passed. Adam had been so intent on the problem with the engine that the sudden appearance of the other car made him jump in his seat. He caught a glimpse of the driver, a man with a long dark beard. He looked across at Adam but he was travelling so much faster that their eyes met for only a fraction of a second. Then the car had gone, chased by a cloud of dust and small stones. Adam did not have time to see what make of car it was. All he noticed was its canvas top, and the trailer it towed.

Josef coughed in the enveloping cloud of dust. 'Jesus, that gave me a fright,' he said, and tried to laugh over his coughing. 'If we'd seen him coming, we could have waved him down and got a lift.'

In his reaction to the shock of being overtaken, Adam had swung to the side of the road and he now struggled to bring the car out of a deep shoal of gravel. The car weaved atrociously, misled by its own sloppy tyres. It was only when he was back in the middle of the road and on hard earth that Adam spoke again.

'I'm not so sure that would have been a good idea,' he said.

'To get a lift? Why?'

'Did you see the trailer? It was the one that was on the back of Ritchie's car.'

NINE

The tyres were deteriorating. The grass and rubbish that filled them was being compressed and on two occasions tyres rolled off their rims. They drove on slowly, watching the tread on the front tyres meander with each revolution of the wheels.

Smoke poured from one tyre when its filling began to smoulder and they were forced to stop again, to sprinkle some of their precious water on the wheel. They resumed the journey but the steering was now so imprecise that the car wandered the width of the road, rolling on its ruined tyres like a ship floundering in a swell.

They passed some cattle and felt cheered by the first sign that another settler was near. With less than an hour of daylight left, they reached the main Roebourne to Port Hedland road and turned left.

The setting sun was in Adam's eyes and, at first, he did not notice the two cars parked at the end of a long straight. He had been concentrating on the fuel gauge, which now registered empty. Josef squeezed his shoulder.

'Two cars,' he said, pointing ahead.

One was the vehicle that had passed them. It still had the trailer attached. The other was the black Ford that had taken them to Cobargo. The cars were on either side of the road. Between them stood two men. One was the man with the beard. The other was George, still wearing his hat. He was armed.

Adam stopped well short of the men. George raised his rifle.

'What are you going to do?' Josef said, bracing himself against the dashboard.

'I'm not going to stay here and be shot at. Get down and hang on.'

446

'What are you doing?' Josef did not move. Adam pushed him off the seat.

'Get down and hang on,' he repeated, and lowered his own head. He selected gear and, for the first time on the journey, accelerated hard.

The engine roared, the back wheels spun and dithered on their flabby tyres but then gripped and, with a surge of power that astonished Adam, the car rocketed forward. He changed to second gear, and then third. The vehicle slewed from one side of the road to the other. Adam fought to control it but kept his right foot flat to the floor.

A rear tyre began flapping. Grass and rags spewed from the wheel.

He heard the rifle fire but the car was swerving and bucking wildly and there was no sound of a strike. Adam raised his head. George was taking aim once more. The back of the car slid wide, broadsiding into some stones and rebounding in the air. Adam was almost thrown from the seat.

The bullet ricocheted from metal, twanging somewhere beneath his feet.

Adam aimed the long bonnet at the gap between the parked cars. The bearded man ran. George, rifle clutched to his chest, backed away. Adam sawed at the wheel, desperately trying to control the Alfa-Romeo's swinging tail.

The car thundered through the gap. A cry of pain pursued them. The back of the car began hammering. Adam eased his foot from the throttle. Josef was up in the seat but facing backwards and grabbing whatever was available to prevent being thrown out. He was kneeling, not sitting, and when the car bounded through a rill he was catapulted over the seat and only stopped himself falling from the vehicle by grabbing the spare wheel. Adam braked and hauled Josef back to the seat.

'We've lost a back tyre,' he said, turning anxiously to see if one of the cars had begun a pursuit.

Josef brushed dirt from his shirt. 'George won't be chasing us for a while,' he said.

The road turned left around some low scrub. The other men and their cars were hidden. Adam slowed the car to a walking pace. The noise was dreadful. The naked rim rattled and bounced, rough as a wheelbarrow on blue metal.

'We won't last long like this,' he said, his brow furrowed, and

447

then added, as though he had only just heard his companion. 'Who won't be chasing us?'

'George. He got clobbered by the tyre. It came off as we went past him and flattened him. He went down like a man under a dozen wild dogs.'

Adam concentrated on dodging a line of stones. He tried to place the wheel on a ridge of dust. The noise and the shaking became less severe.

'He was knocked down?' he asked.

'Flat on his back.'

'He's a tough bloke. Let's say he's back on his feet by now. That gives us about twenty seconds to get off this road.'

'Shit!' Josef said, suddenly concerned. He looked about them. The road was passing through a region of dense scrub. It writhed in a succession of bends. 'Where are we going to go?'

'Anywhere,' Adam said and, seeing a flat and sandy patch on the inside of a bend, turned off the road.

'Quick. Get out. Grab a bush and wipe out our tracks.'

Adam did not stop, for there was a risk of the wheels bogging on the soft surface. Josef jumped from the car, uprooted a small shrub and ran back to the edge of the road. He swept away the deep grooves they had cut in leaving the corner and then, running backwards, obliterated their wheel tracks through the sand.

Adam was waiting for him at a place where a fallen tree and some dense bushes provided cover. The ground was firm and coated with small stones little bigger than ball bearings.

They heard the first car coming. It was going fast, scattering stones like shotgun pellets. Its dust trail swirled above the trees, but they could not see the car.

The second car passed thirty seconds later. It was travelling more slowly. They could hear its trailer bouncing and clanging as it followed the car through a succession of ruts.

Josef opened their can of water and offered it to Adam. 'What now?' he said.

'We can try driving for a bit. Then we might have to walk. I don't want to ruin the wheel.'

'Why not? Why don't we just drive the bastard until it won't go another foot?'

'Because if the wheel collapses we won't be able to travel an inch.' Adam passed him the water. 'Besides, it's such a good car I don't want to ruin it. And please, don't call it a bastard.'

The scrub covered a low hill. The road ran on one side of the hill. They went on the other, following the belt of fine red stones and aiming generally at the setting sun to maintain their westerly course. The land flattened to a plain bordered by clusters of low timber. It was a strange sight; a lagoon of stones surrounded by a reef of trees.

Adam stopped under the last line of trees and gazed at the plain. 'I wonder how firm that is,' he mused, sitting with his elbows resting on the steering wheel.

'I'll have a look,' Josef said and jumped down, but no sooner had his feet touched the stones than the Alfa-Romeo's engine coughed and stopped.

'Why did you turn it off?' he said.

'I didn't. We're out of fuel.'

It was nearly dark and they were halfway across the wide stoney plain. Josef carried the can of water, Adam had the spear. They heard the bicycle before they saw it. It was clanking and making a great deal of noise. So was the rider, who was out of breath and in distress.

It was a boy.

He rode close, not seeing them until the last moment and almost falling off in fright when he became aware of the tall figures in his path. He would have been no more than ten. His bicycle had no saddle, so that he was compelled to ride standing on the pedals. Behind the cycle was a crude trailer. It was a box, the sort that are prized for the bodies of billy carts, with an old bicycle wheel on each side and a beam which was attached to the bicycle by a rope. A series of wooden stakes projected from the box.

'Me trailer broke,' the boy said. His eyes were wide with fright.

'That was bad luck,' Adam said gently.

The boy nodded. 'Did me dad send you?'

'No.'

He stepped back, taking the bicycle with him. Its rear wheel bumped the trailer.

'What are you doing out here?'

'Same as you,' Josef said cheerily. 'Only we're walking.'

'Did you come to see the plane?'

'What plane?' Adam said.

The boy shuffled his bike to another position. One foot was poised on a pedal.

'I never seen you two before,' he said.

'I haven't seen you either,' Josef said. 'You wouldn't be carrying any food on you, would you?'

The boy looked confused.

'We were in a car that broke down,' Adam said. 'We had to leave it and walk.'

The boy, obviously used to hearing of cars having broken down, took his foot from the pedal. 'Where is it?'

'Not far,' Adam said. 'Just over in the trees.' He pointed.

'There's no road over there.'

'We know. Where is the road?'

'Back there.' The boy pointed behind his trailer.

'How far are we from Roebourne?'

'About six mile.'

'What happened to your trailer?' Adam said, not moving closer. The boy was as nervous as an unbroken horse. One wrong move and he would bolt.

'The tow bar broke. I had to tie it on with rope. It doesn't work very well. I'm late.'

'What this about a plane? You mean an aeroplane?'

The boy nodded. He looked worried again. 'It's coming in tonight. Me dad sent me to put the flares in place.'

'It's landing here?'

The boy lowered his bicycle to the ground. He went to the trailer and withdrew a stake and a mallet. He began to hammer the stake in the ground. 'Not till about ten o'clock,' he said, wielding the mallet fluently.

'Here, let's give you a hand,' Adam said and, within a minute, the boy was telling him the story. His name was Stan McKay. His father ran the garage in town. Mr McKay had been asked to refuel the aircraft, and to make sure that the landing strip was illuminated by flares so the pilot could find it and land safely. The plane was making the first flight on a new air mail service. It was flying down from Derby, Broome and Port Hedland. Stan's father would be bringing some drums of petrol and hand pumps later, after he had closed the garage. He had a truck. He had sent Stan ahead on his bicycle to set up a line of flares before sunset. The trailer contained wooden stakes, pieces of cotton waste, kerosene and matches. The broken tow bar had delayed the lad and he had arrived at the site panic-stricken that he would not get the job done in time.

'Before the plane gets here?' Josef said, surprised.

'Before me dad gets here,' the boy corrected.

They worked as a production team. Adam held the stakes in place. Stan hammered them into the ground. Josef dipped some of the cotton waste in the kerosene and tied it to the top of each stake. Stan's father had told him to put a stake every fifty yards.

'Is the plane staying here tonight?' Adam asked, when Stan was hammering in the fifth stake.

'No. I think they're only staying to take on petrol and mail. Dad's bringing out the postmaster in his truck. Mum wrote a letter to me Auntie Maude in Perth just so it would go on the plane.'

'Is the plane going to Perth?'

'Yeah, in the end. It stops in Carnarvon first, and I think at Geraldton too.'

'I've never seen a plane close up,' Adam said. They moved on to the next stake.

'It's real big. It's got two wings and windows down the side. It stopped here on the way north. It came in daylight but.'

'You were here?'

'Me dad brought me out. The postmaster asked him to bring petrol out for the plane then, too.'

'Did he now? That must have been interesting.'

'Yeah.'

'Are there any passengers?'

'What do you mean?'

'People. Has the plane got room for people? We want to go to Perth, you see, and I was wondering if there'd be room on board.'

'Dunno,' the boy said, straining to hammer the wood. He was finding it difficult to see the end of the stake. The boy looked agitated.

'What's up?' Adam said.

'Do you reckon we're halfway?'

'How far are you supposed to go?'

'Dad said about a quarter of a mile.'

'I think we're probably more than halfway.'

'I was supposed to light a bonfire at the halfway mark. I forgot.'

'What do you say we light one on the way back?'

451

'Do you reckon that would be all right?'

'I reckon. Why does your dad want the bonfire?'

'So's he can see where I am. The pilot asked for it too. He wants dad to park the truck next to it with its lights on, pointing the way the wind's blowing.'

'Why?'

'He said he had to land against the wind.'

'But there's no wind.'

The boy looked around him. 'No, you're right.'

'Gee, that's a shame, isn't it?'

'Why?'

'Well, he won't be able to land.'

Stan scratched his ear, then looked shyly at Adam, his face longing to burst into a smile.

'You're pulling my leg, aren't you?'

'Hope so,' Adam said. 'Tell me, when are you going to light the flares?'

'When we hear the plane. The postmaster's going to leave all the lights on in the post office so the pilot can find the town and then, when we hear the plane, me and dad are going to light the flares. We're going to start at the fire. Dad'll go one way and I'll go the other.'

They finished placing the stakes and then walked to the edge of the plain, on the side nearer the stakes, to gather firewood. When the fire was lit, the boy reached into the trailer and produced a bulging brown paper bag.

'I've got some sandwiches,' he said. 'Would you like some?'

Harold McKay arrived in a truck that carried drums of petrol, oil, hand pumps, long lengths of rubber hose, a small sack of mail and a cattle dog. The dog patrolled the back of the truck, unable to stay still for a moment. It was split by conflicting desires. The tail wagged but the mouth barked.

McKay got out and silenced the dog with one raucous command.

'Where's Mr Wilson?' Stan asked.

'The postmaster couldn't come, son. His wife's sick.' He was looking past the boy at the two strangers. 'Who are your friends?'

'They've been helping me,' Stan said and the man nodded thanks but his eyes remained narrowed by doubt.

Adam introduced himself. He told McKay their story. 'I'm not sure that it's safe to go into town,' he continued as McKay stood, rubbing his chin. 'That's why we were wondering if we could get on the plane.'

'That's up to the pilot,' McKay said, still stroking the stubble on his face. 'Have you got any money?'

Adam produced the pound note.

'That's all?'

'Ritchie's got the rest,' Adam said.

'Had anything to eat?'

'Your boy gave us some of his sandwiches.'

McKay took a box from the back of the truck, pushing the dog away as he did so, and carried it to the fire. 'I've got some more sandwiches and some of the wife's fruit cake if you'd like. It was for the pilot but the missus has packed enough for a football team. Help yourself.' He put the box on the ground. 'I'll make some tea.' When he had filled a billy can and cleared a space for it at the edge of the fire, he said: 'This bloke Ritchie. Has he got funny little glasses and hair that he brushes across his head?' His hand swept across his skull, imitating Ritchie's combing method.

'That's the bastard,' Josef said, bending to get a sandwich.

'Don't swear in front of the lad, please!'

Josef straightened quickly. He blushed and glanced at Adam who was staring into the fire with only a hint of a smile on his face.

'Sorry.'

The apology was waved aside. 'It's just that there are so many rough people around these days that it's hard raising children. I don't want young Stan growing up to speak like all the deadbeats you find around these days. No offence meant.'

Josef shook his head. He bit heavily on a sandwich.

'Now this Ritchie. I've seen him in town a few times. A big wheel from the south apparently. He owns a mine somewhere out to the east. Is that the one?'

'I don't know about a mine. He was trying to sell us a property,' Adam said.

'He's got a couple of men working for him. I'm not even sure what it is they mine. It's something big though. He comes up here every couple of months.' McKay crouched near the can and used a stick to lift its lid. The water was not boiling. He threw a few sticks near its base and poked at them until flames appeared. 'Where's this car you were driving? Far away?'

'Just over the other side in the trees,' Adam said. 'It's no more than half a mile away.'

'What's wrong with it?'

'Just about everything.' Josef laughed.

'It's out of petrol,' Adam said defensively. 'And it needs tyres.'

'How many?' McKay said. Adam could see the garage owner mentally checking the stocks on his racks.

'All of them.'

McKay stood slowly, holding his back and straightening in painful stages. 'Got a crook back,' he said. 'Four tyres, eh? What sort of car is it?'

'An Alfa-Romeo.'

'It's Italian,' Josef added hastily.

'I know what an Alfa is,' he said, rubbing his lower back. 'That's a rare car. I've only ever seen one of them up in this part of the world. What colour is it?'

'Red and black,' Adam said.

'Open car? Big high bonnet with an angled radiator?' McKay took his hands from his back to form an arrowhead with horizontal fingers.

'You know it?' Adam said.

'A prospector named Jimmy Sinclair had a car like that. Would have been about a 1925 model.' His eyes turned the statement into a question.

Adam shrugged. 'It looks about ten years old. What happened to this Jimmy Sinclair?'

'He went south. At least I think he did. That's what people said, anyhow. I haven't seen him for a year or so.'

'What was he prospecting for?'

'He didn't say. Some people reckoned it was gold. One bloke told me Jimmy had said it could be the biggest thing in the country. Apparently he needed money.'

'Where did he get the car?'

'He brought it up on a ship. He was a smart bloke. Used to be an engineer apparently. I think he raced cars, too. Ever hear of him?'

'No. I don't know any racing drivers.'

'They say he was good.'

The water boiled and McKay added tealeaves. Neither Adam nor Josef had mentioned the body near the creek at Cobargo. Now they told him of the grave and described the man they had found.

'You say he was almost bald?' McKay asked. His son was

standing behind him, fascinated and saying nothing.

'It was hard to tell. He'd been dead a while.'

'Jimmy was nearly bald. He had grey hair.'

'Well, so did this bloke.'

They drank their tea and ate Mrs McKay's fruit cake. McKay checked his watch.

'We've got time to go and look at the car if you like.'

McKay had a torch and they followed him across the plain to the trees. It took them some minutes to locate the Alfa-Romeo. It took McKay only three seconds to decide.

'That's it,' he said. 'I filled it a few times when he first came here. Looks a bit the worse for wear, doesn't it? What are you going to do with it?'

'Nothing,' Adam said. 'Just leave it here, I suppose.'

McKay walked around the car, inspecting it by torchlight. 'That'd be a waste, wouldn't it? Let's face it, if that is Jimmy Sinclair back there, this car's got no owner. Jimmy had no relatives or friends that I know of. And you say you'd paid four hundred quid deposit on the land?'

'That's right.'

'Well, you're not going to see that money again. And you say this Ritchie character stole your bags and they had the letters that proved you'd paid the money?'

Both nodded.

'Well, I'd keep the car. It's about all you're likely to get out of the deal and if you can nail Ritchie, then I reckon Jimmy would want you to keep the Alfa.'

'What'll you do with it?' Josef said to Adam.

'Leave it here. That's all I can do.'

'Let me look after it for you,' McKay said. 'I've got tyres and tubes in stock that'll fit. If you can't get on this plane, you can drive it south.'

'And if we get on the plane?'

'We'll work something out.'

'I haven't got any money,' Adam said. 'I couldn't pay for four tyres.'

'You'll have it one day. You can pay me then.'

'You'd trust me that long?'

McKay shone his torch in Adam's face. 'Yes,' he said simply. 'Let's get back to the fire. That plane might be here soon.'

TEN

They first heard the aircraft just before ten. It flew in from the east, following the curve of the coastline, and the drone of its engine came to them in bursts as faint and shallow as the swell of a drowsy sea. There was still no wind to ruffle clouds or stir the dust and their eyes scanned the sky, searching for a light. When they found it, the aircraft was lower than they had expected, a faint moving star that flashed just above the horizon. McKay estimated it was already within a mile of the town.

They had built up the fire and now each of them took a burning stick and hurried to light the flares. The dog ran after McKay, who first went to the truck and switched on its headlights. There being no wind, he had parked the vehicle parallel to the line of flares and in the stab of lights, the dog jumped and barked with the joy of sudden action. The animal quickly paid for its temerity. McKay snapped an order and the dog sat, wriggling in wretched frustration, while its master jogged off to light his share of the stakes.

The winking star changed direction. It came towards them, climbing gradually as it headed inland. They threw more wood on the fire and as the flames grew, so did the sound of the approaching engine.

Adam looked up, mouth open in awe, for he had never seen nor heard an aircraft flying at night, let alone had one coming straight at him.

The plane came in low, passing a few hundred feet above the fire. For an instant, a ghostly reflection of flames flashed in the sky. Then there was just the flat throb of the engine and even that faded as the pilot cut the throttle to signal his greeting.

The only sound was of air rushing across wire and fabric surfaces.

Adam searched for a shadow among the stars. The engine bellowed once more as the pilot restored power and turned to head for the end of the landing strip. The exhausts spat sheets of flame. A light blinked, bright and clear and headed away from them. The noise diminished. The four on the ground watched as the light grew distant and described a silent arc at the end of the sky.

The plane came in quietly, almost stealthily. The only sound to reveal its arrival on earth was the squeak of rubber and the jouncing compression of undercarriage struts. There was a pause as the aircraft bounced and then a thud and a constant rumble. The exhausts coughed and disgorged firecrackers and wild colours spun through the propeller.

The plane ran past them, its engine chattering. Adam saw a face and an upraised hand.

'We're to stay here,' McKay said, holding out an arm to prevent anyone running towards the aircraft. 'He was very particular about that. Said he didn't want someone being chopped up in the propeller.'

The pilot turned at the last flare and taxied towards the fire. Wheels bumping, body shaking, wings wagging, the plane emerged from the dark. The pilot drew level with them, ran the motor for a few seconds and switched off.

'G'day,' the pilot said. 'Bring the truck over, will you?'

The pilot was not as Adam had imagined. He had pictured a superhuman being flying such a machine – at least a large man, dark and with a moustache and maybe wearing a leather helmet and a long white scarf. Someone, in fact, like a drawing he had once seen of a fighter pilot in the Great War.

This man was not like that. He had ginger hair and he was thin. His cheekbones projected like boils and his eyes were surrounded by deep-set wrinkles, the scars of having flown into too many setting suns. He wore plus fours and a baggy leather coat that was too big and hung at awkward angles from an occasional projecting bone.

He sat on the aircraft, holding the end of a hose in the fuel tank while McKay worked the pump at the drum.

Adam was standing beneath the man's dangling legs.

'I'd like to, friend,' the pilot said in answer to his request, and for a brief moment his face appeared above his knees. He carried a torch and it shone across his face, deepening the lines into troughs of sadness. 'But I'm only carrying mail and freight. I haven't got any seats in the back.'

'That doesn't matter.'

'Yes, it does, friend. Mind you, I have got one other person on board but I don't think you'd like to change places.'

Josef had joined Adam. 'What do you mean?' he said.

'He's in a canvas bag.' The head reappeared, a smile

devastating the facial landscape.

The others looked up, not understanding.

'It's a stiff,' he said. 'A bloke who died in Broome. He wants to be buried in Perth. Well, he doesn't, I suppose, but his family wants him taken there. Great way to start an air mail service, isn't it? Just an aerial hearse. Still it's all money. You say you haven't got any?'

'The other bloke took the lot.'

'Yes, well, you've had hard luck but I'm afraid I can't help you.'

McKay had stopped pumping to change hands. 'If they go into town they're likely to get shot at,' he said.

'You believe that, Mr McKay?' the pilot said, using the torch to check the fuel level. His voice suggested he did not.

'They were shot at earlier today. I inspected the car. It's just over there in the trees. There's a fresh bullet mark on the chassis just below the driver's seat.'

'Yes?' He was still watching the fuel.

'And there's no doubt there are some nasty types in town. I don't know much about this Ritchie the young fellows were telling you about but I know some of the men who work for him. There's one cove called George Karloff that I wouldn't want the dog to bite in case he got poisoned.'

'The bloke who drove Ritchie's black Ford was called George,' Adam said.

'Shifty fellow.'

'Always wore a hat and never looked us in the eye, except when he pointed the rifle at us.'

'Sounds like him,' McKay said, changing hands on the pump once more. 'I hear that when he gets full he boasts of the men he's shot.'

The pilot looked at McKay. 'A lot of men talk when they've got a few drinks under their belt.'

'Maybe. How are you going up there?'

'Almost full.' He looked up suddenly, his eyes attracted by a flash of lights at the end of the air strip. 'You expecting any sightseers, Mr McKay?'

McKay stopped pumping. 'No. You said you didn't want a crowd out here. Why?'

'There's a car coming towards us.'

'What sort?' Adam asked. He and Josef were on the far side of the fuselage.

'Can't tell from here. All I can see are the lights. Tell you what.' He shifted his position slightly. 'Why don't you get inside the cabin? Through that door just to your right.'

'Why?' McKay said. He had stopped pumping and was peering at the advancing lights.

'Just in case,' the pilot said softly. 'I haven't lived to my ripe old age by taking chances.' He noticed that neither Josef nor Adam had moved. 'Do you fellows want to get in or not?'

Josef opened the door.

'Careful where you tread. And friends, this doesn't mean I'm taking you anywhere. I just want you out of sight, just in case those men you were talking about have decided to come looking for you. And you, lanky!'

Josef looked up. His hands were already seeking a grip inside the cabin door.

'You'll find a cover on the left. You and your friend get on the floor and pull it over yourselves. Lie alongside the other bloke. He won't mind. And cover everything.'

'What for?' Josef said, his body still bent with one long leg stretched to the ground. 'No one'll see us in here.'

'You'll get under the canvas because the stiff is starting to stink.' He waited until both were in the aircraft before adding: 'And because I'm not taking any chances. I had three good mates in the war, who were better fliers than me and braver than me and inclined to take more risks than me. And do you know what, friends?' His audience was McKay, the boy and the cattle dog. 'The last one died on Christmas Day 1917.'

Stan blinked, trying to comprehend.

'That might only be Santa Claus coming but I'd rather feel a fool than see His Majesty's Royal Mail shot full of holes. Give me a couple more pumps, will you, Mr McKay? We're almost there.'

The car stopped with its lights on the biplane. The passenger's door opened. Ritchie stepped out.

'Well, what have we here?' he said jovially.

'It's called an aeroplane,' the pilot said, closing the fuel cap.

Ritchie walked towards the drums. 'You're from the garage, aren't you?'

'Yes,' McKay said. He withdrew the stem of the pump and began resealing the drum.

'And what have you men been doing out here?'

'Working,' the pilot said. He tightened the belt on his jacket and was engulfed by folds of leather. 'How about you?'

'Oh, I was attracted by the lights. It's very late and very dark for this sort of thing, surely?'

The pilot breathed deeply, and dropped to the ground. 'This is the first flight of a new service, sir. We're carrying mail and freight and, because we believe we can offer a faster service than anyone else, we fly day and night.'

'I don't know that I like the idea,' Ritchie said, forcing himself to smile. 'I own a shipping line, you see. I suppose that makes us rivals.'

'There's a place for both.'

'Possibly, possibly. Actually I was looking for someone.'

'Out here?'

'Two young men. You might have seen them.'

'Are they lost?'

'Not exactly.'

'Did they jump ship?'

'You've got a good sense of humour,' Ritchie said. 'I like that in a man.'

'I'm so pleased.' The pilot approached McKay. 'Were you able to rustle up some food for me?'

'I've got some sandwiches and fruit cake. Would you like some?'

'I might take it with me.' He had his back to Ritchie.

'Mind if I take a look at your aeroplane?' Ritchie said.

'Go ahead. Please don't touch anything, though.'

'Are you on your own?'

'No. Mr McKay here's refuelling the aircraft.'

Ritchie coughed. 'I meant on the aeroplane. Do you have any passengers?'

'There are three bodies in the back.'

'Bodies?'

'Yes. That's one area where we can beat your ships, sir. We'll deliver our cargo in Perth in time for the funeral. On one of your ships they'd be full of maggots long before they reached Fremantle and no one would want to go to the funeral.'

'Have you really got dead men inside that aeroplane?'

'Do you want to have a look?'

'No, of course not. I mean, I don't want to look at dead bodies. I wouldn't mind inspecting the aircraft however ... if you don't mind.'

460

A door closed on the car.

'Would your friend like to have a look, too?' the pilot said.

Ritchie scowled at the car. The man who had stepped out was hidden by the dazzle of lights.

'Oh, George can wait. How do I get in?'

'Through the door at the side. Just be careful what you touch. I don't think the medical officer in Broome did a very thorough job of disinfecting everything.'

'What do you mean?' Ritchie said, hesitating.

'Well, with a thing like bubonic plague, you've got to be careful.'

Ritchie took a step backwards. 'They died from bubonic plague?'

'Got it from a Japanese diver apparently.'

'Well, I don't know,' Ritchie said, rubbing his hands together and laughing nervously. 'Well, maybe I should leave it till some other time.'

'Certainly. We'll be coming through regularly. Would you like a sandwich?'

'Ah, no thank you.' Ritchie looked around him, trying to probe the darkness. 'They were in a car. An open car. Painted red.'

'Who were?'

'Those two young men I mentioned.'

'Well, I didn't see them on the flight down,' the pilot said, 'And I'm sure I'd have noticed a red car. I don't pass many cars in my line of work. Did you see a red car on the way out from town, Mr McKay?'

'Didn't see a thing,' McKay said. 'Why are you looking for them?'

Ritchie continued searching the shadows. 'They're due to sail south on one of my ships in the morning. I was concerned that they hadn't arrived in town.'

'I'm beginning to think it's easier dealing with dead men,' the pilot said. 'They don't drive red cars and get lost.'

'No, indeed not.' He coughed. 'Are you staying the night?'

'I'm about to take off.'

'May we watch?'

'You'll have to move your car. You're on the airstrip. Park it near the fire.'

'Oh, of course. George!' he shouted. 'Drive the car over near the fire.'

A door slammed. The car turned and for the first time they could see it clearly. The black Ford stopped near the fire. George was behind the wheel. Another man was in the back.

'A lot of you are out looking,' the pilot said.

'Well, we are concerned.'

'Of course.' He turned to McKay. 'You give me the bill and I'll give you a cheque. Goodbye, sir.' He nodded towards Ritchie but did not look at him. 'Nice meeting you. If I pass you at sea one day, I'll do a loop-the-loop.'

A couple of flares had burned out and the boy went along the line, adding kerosene and relighting the cotton waste.

McKay spun the propeller to restart the engine. The boy, approaching from the back as he had been instructed, removed two stones that acted as wheel chocks. The pilot warmed the motor and checked the instruments. He waved.

The plane rolled to the last flare, turned and took off.

When it was above tree height, the pilot turned. 'How's the smell back there?' he said.

The mail plane reached Carnarvon at first light. The pilot followed the coast most of the way. It was longer but safer than the direct overland route for he preferred the prospect of a forced landing on a beach or in the shallows offshore than having to put down in the dark in the rough range country of Australia's western rump. He ate and talked a lot. It helped to keep him awake.

He owned the aircraft and was flying it all the way himself because he could not afford to employ another pilot. Maybe soon he would have the money for another flier, once he had proven the run to be fast and reliable.

He could not take them all the way to Perth, he said, because he was not licensed to carry passengers and there would be curious officials awaiting his arrival in the state capital. He would take them as far as Geraldton. A train ran from there to Perth. Alternatively, they might be able to hitch a ride south. There was a reasonable road to Perth.

Several people were waiting at the Carnarvon airfield. One of them was the Reverend Roger Montgomery. His jaw sagged in astonishment when he saw Adam lead Josef from the cabin. He could not speak but started to laugh, a high-pitched staccato peal of disbelief.

'What are you doing out here?' Adam said, stretching his

462

aching limbs. 'And where's your dog, Reverend?'

The minister brought brought himself under control. 'Neb is locked up at home. And please don't call me "Reverend". It's wrong.' He wrung his hands, squeezing the last of the nervous excitement from his body. 'It should be the Reverend Roger, which is silly, Mr Montgomery, which is pretentious, or just plain Roger, which I would prefer.' A giggle was stifled with a cough.

Adam imagined that had the young parson worn glasses, he would now start to polish them.

'You are the last persons on earth I would have expected to have seen step from this aeroplane. You may not believe this but just before dawn I was thinking about you two and praying for you.' He saw Adam's flush of embarrassment. He clasped his hands. 'And why am I here? Well, this is an historic occasion of sorts and I thought I should witness it. Besides,' and he smiled, about to confess a secret, 'I love aeroplanes. I think they are among the most marvellous of man's creations. As a matter of fact, when I was young I wanted to be a pilot. That was my first love, until I realized my interests were, shall we say, on an even higher plane.' He lowered his eyes. Like all shy wits, he could not bear to face his target squarely in case the bullseye deflected the dart. He risked a glance. Adam was smiling.

'Where's Father Ryan?' Josef asked.

'He didn't come when he heard the pilot was a Protestant.' Again he lowered his eyes but now they were sparkling. He was truly pleased to see them. 'No, actually he's out of town and won't be back until lunchtime.'

The pilot walked past carrying rocks to chock the wheels. 'You know these two, Reverend?'

'Indeed.' He could not stop smiling. 'The local priest and I smuggled them out of town less than a week ago.'

'Really? How did you do that?'

'In a rowing boat.'

The pilot looked from Adam to Josef. 'You two get around, don't you? Here!' He threw one rock to Josef and the other to Adam. 'Help earn your way by putting those in front of the wheels.'

While they wedged the chocks in place, they began telling their story to the young parson. They continued when they followed the pilot to the nearest bushes to relieve themselves, and concluded their tale while consuming tea, toast and bacon which

463

the local postmaster's wife had prepared over an open fire.

'What are you going to do about Ritchie?' the pilot said. 'The man sounds like a menace. He's got to be stopped.'

'My original idea was to go to the police in Roebourne,' Adam said.

'What, and complain about the way you were cheated?' the pilot said, his voice coated with cynicism. 'Without any papers or proof, you'd have as much chance of nailing this character as I would of flying to Perth without wings.'

'I know that. No, I was going to tell them about the body in the creek. If the police could dig the body up, then they'd have something to go on.'

'Well, we're no longer at Roebourne. Anyhow, you work out what you're going to do,' the pilot said, tightening his leather belt. 'I'm going to refuel this bus and then I'm going to sleep for twenty minutes. Have you got a watch?' he asked Roger who extended his wrist in acknowledgement. 'Make sure I don't sleep past seven thirty, will you?'

Drums of petrol had been brought to the grassy paddock outside Carnarvon and while refuelling proceeded, the three young men walked far from the aircraft, discussing what should be done. Adam gave Roger the names they knew: Ritchie, George Karloff and the prospector Jimmy Sinclair. He gave him the name of the ship and the address of Ritchie's office in Perth. Roger wrote everything in a small notebook he carried in his breast pocket. Finally, Adam repeated the directions for finding the body.

Roger stopped writing. 'I was shocked when I learned Ritchie was behind all the violence we've been experiencing here. But this is dreadful. He apparently has men killed for his own gain? I can't believe there are such monsters on earth.'

You should have met Mailey, Adam thought, but said nothing. He never mentioned Mailey.

'Why would he have had this Jimmy Sinclair murdered?' Roger said, curling the cover of his notebook.

'Maybe he was killed for the land,' Adam said.

'But you said it was worthless.'

'For grazing,' Adam said. 'He was a prospector, remember. Maybe he'd found something on it.'

'Gold maybe,' Josef said. He and Adam had been wondering about Jimmy Sinclair and had shouted theories to each other above the racket of flight on the long and cold journey from Roebourne.

'But if the land was valuable, why did Ritchie try to sell it to you?'

'Maybe Sinclair was just using Cobargo as a base,' Adam said. 'You know, somewhere to stay and keep all his equipment.'

'And maybe he found gold, or whatever it was, somewhere else,' Josef said.

'He needed money,' Adam said. 'Mr McKay told us that. Maybe he got money from Ritchie.'

'And got killed because Ritchie wanted the gold for himself,' Josef said.

No one spoke. They turned. The aircraft was still being refuelled. The pilot was standing on top. The sun was now above the aircraft, and the plane and the pilot were blurred outlines in the glare. From this distance, they could have been one weird creature: a giant grasshopper settled on the paddock. The insect's feeler twitched; the pilot had moved.

'There are a whole lot of maybes, aren't there?' Roger said, deep in thought. 'Never mind, I will go to the police station immediately it opens.'

He said he would emphasize how urgent it was to send someone to Cobargo immediately, but spoke with some uncertainty because he recognized the possibility of a hardened policeman not taking much notice of a novice clergyman – particularly one so young and so new to the district. If the police seemed reluctant to act, he would ask Father Ryan to go to the station immediately he returned to Carnarvon.

'He can move heaven and earth,' Roger said, 'and while moving a policeman may be a more formidable task, I'm sure Father Ryan has the necessary ability. In any case,' he went on brightly, 'the good Father knows everyone within five hundred miles. If the local constabulary seems tardy, I'm sure he'll make contact with the man at Roebourne. Have no fear. We'll get action.'

The refuelling had been completed and the pilot was now lying on the grass beneath the wing. Roger checked his watch. 'He can sleep longer than he thought,' he said. 'It's only five past seven.'

They walked back slowly, talking about many things.

Adam liked Roger Montgomery. He had, from their first meeting. In part that was due to the fact that he had been willing to help them immediately when they were in need of immediate help. More than that, however, had been the way he behaved. He liked the way Roger loved his dog, he liked the way he had been prepared to accept risks and he liked the way he had respected the priest. Adam did not know many men of God but he knew plenty of people who professed to love God but who seemed filled with hate for those who loved in a different way. He had assumed this was because priests and ministers hated each other. Yet Roger had sought help from Father Ryan and the old priest had given it willingly and obviously had affection for the younger man.

'Adam?' Roger said, looking at him anxiously.

'Sorry. I was thinking of something else.'

'I was asking what you are going to do now.'

'Get back to New South Wales, somehow, I suppose.'

'Do you have any money?'

'I have one pound between me and starvation.'

'Us and starvation,' Josef corrected.

'I don't have much,' Roger said, dipping into his pocket. Adam raised a hand in protest. Ignoring the gesture, Roger counted change from one hand to the other.

'Eight shillings and fourpence. A parson's stipend does not go far. That's why coming out here before dawn to see an aeroplane was such an entertaining prospect. Here, take it.' He extended the hand full of money.

'No. I couldn't.'

Roger poured the money into Adam's pocket. 'I have more at home,' he said, smiling, and then hesitated. 'I assume you are going on. You're not staying?'

'No,' Adam said and then thought, Why not?. He had not planned beyond this moment. All his energies had been devoted to the need to get away from Cobargo and now that he and Josef had been whisked through the night to a field more than three hundred miles to the south, his mind was numbed. It had been outpaced and disorientated by the confusion of reality.

The two men stared into each other's eyes. It was a moment when looks go deeper and show more than was meant to be revealed.

'The pilot's offered to fly us as far as Geraldton,' Adam said, and cleared his throat. 'It might be the only way for us to get to the south. And it's for free.'

Roger grinned.

'Would there be a bank in Geraldton?'

466

'Certainly,' Roger said.

'We should go there, then. I'll get them to wire my bank in Nyngan and see if they'll bail me out. We'll need money to catch the train to get back. We had tickets but they were in the bags Ritchie stole.'

And what then? he thought, pushing his mind to catch up with his words. Back to Nyngan and Heather?

ELEVEN

Travelling with the body of a dead man was acceptable in the dark. He – it – was merely a long lump in a canvas shroud. Just another piece of freight, like the crates and the smaller and dumpier bags that carried letters and parcels. The one concession, denied the crates and the mail bags, was that nothing was flung on top of the body. Even so, in the dark and lying along one wall of the narrow fuselage, the shrouded package could not be seen. The two passengers, sitting further forward where the pilot had said they should be to balance the weight within the aircraft, had found it simple to ignore and even forget. But that was in the dark.

On the flight to Geraldton it was different. Adam had tried to sleep, resting with a hip on one clear section of the floor and his shoulders against a mail sack that had been put on board at Carnarvon, but the sun was streaming through the port windows and the fuselage vibrated and the engine droned its shattering song. And every time he sat up, he could see the canvas bag with the projections where the feet were.

'Can't sleep?' the pilot shouted.

'No,' Adam said and rubbed his face. Josef yawned. He was hunched against the other side of the cabin, using his knees as a chin rest. 'Why didn't they put the body in a coffin?'

'Weight.'

Adam had been examining the structure of the aircraft. The frame was a mixture of lightweight metal and wood. The wings were covered in fabric. It looked flimsy.

'Would a heavy coffin break through the plane's body?' he said.

The pilot pushed back his cap. 'It's not strength that's the problem, friend. It's money. I'm like the grocer or the butcher. I charge by the pound. So the people who are paying decided they only wanted the flesh, not the wood. Follow?'

He turned his head to make sure Adam understood. 'There'll be a coffin waiting at Perth. How's the smell?'

The cabin was full of the pungent smells that radiate from hot machinery.

'All right.'

'He'll just about make it, I think. Just as well you're getting off next stop. By this afternoon, I think he'll be letting me know he's there.'

Adam tried not to look but his eyes were drawn to the tapering canvas around the head. 'How did he die? Was it truly that thing you told Ritchie?'

'Bubonic plague? No way. He was thrown from a horse.'

'Old feller?'

'No. Twenty-eight. His family's in Perth.'

They must have loved him, Adam thought, and was envious. Not for whoever it was under that humped canvas but for the family he had known. He changed position, to look the other way. They were flying over the coast. To the east, a great brown land, wrinkled with age, stretched into a haze of dust and sky and cloud. Nyngan was a couple of thousand miles beyond that smudged horizon.

Suddenly he felt lonely.

'I wonder how Jimmy is?' Josef shouted, coughing as he spoke.

Adam wriggled into a more upright position. His eyes turned to the window. Jimmy was out there somewhere, far beyond the place where the brown earth and a mottled row of clouds met. Probably having a good time with his family. He'd been away from his own people for a long time.

'Don't know,' he said, still looking out the window.

'I wonder where Nellie is these days.'

Adam turned slowly towards his friend.

'Ever think of her?' Josef added.

'No,' he said, matter-of-fact, and wondered why he had lied. He thought of her often, when he was lonely and wanted someone to talk to. She was an easy person to talk to; she didn't analyse your words and twist them and spit them back at you. And he thought of her when he burned for a woman. That shocked him for he

468

realized then that at such times his thoughts went to Nellie rather than to his wife.

He let his head rest against the fuselage. Aircraft noises chattered and buzzed through his cheek. He closed his eyes, thinking.

A storm was approaching Nyngan. Heather stood at the front window of her parents' home and watched the black clouds slowly bubbling on the horizon. Lightning jagged the sky. A gust of wind ripped grit from the street and hurled it at the glass. It would probably rain soon, she thought, and was not pleased. The garden ached for water; shrubs were wilting and some of the prized azaleas were already dead. Well, let everything die. Why should that slimy creature Abe What's-his-name get their beautiful garden? Let it die, along with her father.

Another cloud of dust enveloped the house and the window rattled. The door to her father's bedroom opened and a small, stout man in clerical garb emerged. He smiled. The smile was intended to suggest understanding and compassion but, she thought, it gave his face the expression of a dog having its belly tickled. That was appropriate, she decided, for in intellectual terms the reverend Cyril neville had the brains of a dog. A bloodhound, with the ability to detect freshly brewed tea or baked cakes. He always called when there was food about.

'Your father continues to be very brave, Miss Maguire.'

'Mrs Ross,' she corrected. It had not been a mistake and while she accepted his mumbled apology, her eyes flashed contempt. The man always called her by her maiden name. It was his way of perpetuating a protest at her marrying in another minister's church. And of reminding her of her husband's continuing absence.

'You will have to be brave, too,' he said, mistaking her emotion for anguish.

Brave? Another word to add to the list of things she had needed to be in the last weeks.

'I must be going,' he said, hoping to be contradicted.

'You should hurry. It might rain soon.'

'Well yes, I must I suppose,' he said, stretching the words to allow her time to offer tea and maybe some of her mother's cake. There was fruit cake. Mrs Maguire had mentioned it when he arrived.

A long pause.

'Well, I'll be off.'

'Goodbye.' She did not look at him.

The doorknob rattled. Wind curled into the room and ruffled the curtains. There was a knock and a man's voice, low and apologetic. Angrily she turned. 'I have no time to fetch cake.'

But it wasn't the Minister. Another man stood in the dorrway, his body partly obscuring the figure of the departing parson. It was the owner of the general store. He blushed.

'I'm not the Minister,' he said

'How perceptive of you.'

'I've come to see your mother, miss.'

She blocked the passageway. 'To pay your respects, no doubt. Unfortunately, you're a few days too early. My father has not yet died.'

The man spun his hat in hands that trembled with nervousness. 'It's not that, miss.'

Heather knew why he had come. He was the third businessman to call this week. All wanted money.

'I'd like to see your mother about the account. May I come in?'

'To seize some furniture perhaps?' The last man had threatened to do that and had engaged in a brief tug-of-war over a lounge chair. She had won by pretending to faint.

'I don't want to take anything. I just want my money. I'm not a rich man and if people don't pay their accounts I won't be able to carry on.'

'How tragic.' She advanced, forcing him to retreat to the verandah. 'I'm sure my mother has told you already, but let me repeat the fact that all such accounts are now being handled by my husband. Send him the bill, and leave two women, who are preparing for the death of a loved one, alone. Do you understand? Alone.'

'People say your husband's not coming back.'

'That is absurd.'

'Do you know where he is?'

'How dare you ask such a question!'

'Nothing personal, miss, but this state's full of women who can't tell you where their husbands are. All gone looking for work but gone, none the less.'

'Kindly leave.' She pushed the door closed.

'You'll hear from my solicitor,' he called, his voice suddenly confident now that he was hidden from her. She waited, her back pressed against the door, until she heard his feet on the verandah steps. 'You may come out now, mother,' she said.

Mrs Maguire's head appeared from the bedroom doorway. 'Is he gone?'

'Of course. As always, trusty Heather has repulsed the invader.'

'Will he come back?'

'How would I know? But I presume so. They all come back.' She paused and her expression became venomous. 'Oh, how I hate him.'

Mrs Maguire was surprised. 'The storekeeper?'

'Don't be ridiculous. You know who I mean.'

Mrs Maguire pressed a finger to her lips, admonishing them for having allowed so foolish a question to escape.

'And he will pay,' heather continued. 'He will suffer for making us go through all this humiliation.'

'But my dear, he is your husband.'

'And he is not here. He abandoned us when we needed him most. He took all of his money which we could have used to get us out of this predicament. He is selfish and heartless and he will suffer for what he has done to us. If I do nothing else in my life, I will make him pay.'

Adam had been dozing. He woke with a start.

'I've been thinking,' Josef announced.

'What about?'

'Everything.' He straightened his back and stretched his arms. 'About the last few days. About all the money you've lost. About it all being my fault.'

'No, it's not.'

'Yes, it is. I pushed you into it.'

Adam shook his head. The country outside seemed not to have changed. 'Lot of land out there,' he said.

'Yes. And none of it is ours.' He shuffled his legs, seeking a more comfortable position. 'I've been thinking about Adelaide. I've been thinking about my mother and father and Anemone. And I've been thinking about him.' Josef angled a thumb in the direction of the corpse.

'Makes you think, doesn't it?' Adam said. 'I've never travelled with a dead man before.'

471

'Me neither.' Josef glanced out a window on his side of the cabin. The coast was a creamy line of beaches, more an edge to the land than an end to the sea.

For a moment, he was reminded of a tablecloth. The land was a linen cloth, a brown one speckled with regular stitches of low vegetation, and its border, finely worked with a crochet needle, was the beach. So even, so continuous, so dazzlingly white. The surf formed lines of lace. Strong parallel threads where the breakers curled, and fainter patterns linked in chains where the current drew the froth back out to sea. The colours were intense. Blues, greens, shades he had never seen. Beyond the surf, the water was a deep blue. The sea was flecked by white caps but nothing seemed to be moving. Even a ship that was two or three miles from shore appeared to be static. Its bow wore a beard of white foam but there was no suggestion of motion. That was what surprised him most. He had imagined flying to be like falling but never hitting the ground. He often dreamed he was flying. He soared just above the ground with the air rushing past his body, and it was always quiet and filled with sensations of speed and of swooping past trees and rivers and upturned faces. This was nothing like that. He was sitting still, feeling cramped and suffering from nausea, being bombarded by noise and not getting any sensation of rapid movement.

And yet he was flying, travelling at a speed beyond the imagination of most people.

Flying, he decided, was standing still in mid-air while the world slid beneath you. It was not as he had expected; but then, few experiences were.

'That could be me back there,' Josef said, inclining his head towards the body.

Adam smiled. 'How?'

'I could have been hit by one of those bullets when George shot at the car. Could have been me that got hit, not the chassis.'

'Or me.'

'More likely me.'

'Why?'

'Because I'm unlucky. You're not.'

'I haven't been doing too well lately,' Adam said. He had been watching the pilot. The man had not moved for a while and Adam was wondering if he had gone to sleep. The aircraft was steady. The engine note was constant. And then the pilot, like some sort of slow-motion machine, reached out with his right hand and touched a lever. He did not move it. He touched it, comforting himself with the knowledge that it was still where it should be. Adam looked across at Josef.

'Do you wish it had been you?' Josef said and gazed at the sea. The ship was still not moving but it was behind them now.

'What do you mean?'

'Don't you ever wish you were dead? I do sometimes. I wouldn't mind being dead now.' He avoided Adam's eyes. 'I mean, it doesn't matter what we do, we're going to die sometime and there are times when it would be more convenient than others. Now would be a good time. It'd be a rotten time to die if things were going well for you and you had all sorts of things to do. Do you know what I mean?'

He did not look to see if Adam understood.

'Like when?' Adam said.

'Well, say if you were the pilot and you were flying us south on your first air mail run and you were going to make a lot of money, it wouldn't be a good time to die, would it?'

'Not for us.'

Josef picked up a sack and pretended to throw it at Adam. 'You know what I mean. I'll give you another example. You'd just bought a fine spread with ten thousand head of sheep all ready to be shorn and the market for wool has just risen like mad. Now, that wouldn't be a good time to die, would it?'

'Why not?'

Josef thought he saw a hint of a smile.

'Because it would be so frustrating,' he said, speaking more loudly to make sure Adam realized he was serious.

'If you were happy, you'd die happy,' Adam said.

'No, no, no! That would be awful! Like winning some big prize and then falling flat on your face just as you were about to collect it. Better to die when things were crook. Then you wouldn't mind.'

'And you wouldn't mind now?'

'No. Things are crook. You've lost all your money. We don't have the land. When we get out of this plane we're going to be stuck in Geraldton with one pound eight and threepence ...'

'Fourpence.'

'Oh, well, things aren't as bad as I thought then.' Josef stroked the side of his face. 'It's just that we may never get back to the east, because we've got no money, and we'll never do anything

473

over here because we haven't got the money to get started.'

'You said you were thinking of Adelaide.'

'Yeah, well, that's if we ever get some money.'

'You told me once you didn't want to go and see your parents until you'd amounted to something.'

Josef let his forehead touch his bent knees. 'That's never going to happen, so I might as well go and see them.'

Adam stared out the window. A dry river bed spread across the plain like a lizard skin nailed out to dry.

'I've got a feeling things are going to get better,' Adam said.

'Why?'

'Because it's about time,' he said and rearranged a bag so he could sleep.

A crowd was waiting at Geraldton. The landing field was near the coast, between a long sandy ridge and a thick stand of scrub. As they landed, Adam counted eight cars, one cart and a few horses near the group standing beside a row of drums. The pilot saw them too and taxied to the far end of the clearing.

'I'm going to ask you two to do something for me,' he shouted, opening the throttle to increase power for the turn. 'I want you to get out up here, not back there where all the people are.'

Both Adam and Josef tried to rise, each hampered by cramped limbs.

'There are too many official-looking people back there. You know, men with suits and hats.'

'How do we get out?' Adam said, his voice loud so as to be heard above the roar of the motor. The plane was lumbering to the right. Dust and scraps of grass whirled past the cabin.

'Just open the door when I tell you. What I'm going to do is complete this turn ...' his feet prodded the pedals, '... and then stop. When I tell you to get out, I'll give the engine a bit of a rev to stir up the dust so no one'll see you. Just get out and get clear and then lie down. And for heaven's sake, don't go anywhere near the propeller.'

'What do we do then?' Josef said.

'Wait till the crowd's gone. The town's down that way.' He pointed with his thumb. 'By the way, I've got something for you. Harold McKay gave it to me when I was paying for the petrol back at Roebourne.' From his pocket he took a slip of paper.

Josef took it. 'It's his name and address,' he said.

'He said something about a car.' He turned towards Adam. 'He said that's where your car would be. Does that make sense?'

Adam nodded.

'OK. You two ready to hop out?'

'I wish we could pay you,' Adam said.

'So do I. Now get to the door or they'll be wondering what the devil I'm doing up here. Don't forget, keep down, crawl clear of the tail, and don't go near the front of the plane.'

Josef went first because he had a clearer path to the door. Even so, he stumbled on a sack and fell on his back on top of the corpse. He struggled to get up.

'Jesus, friend,' the pilot said, 'give the poor bloke a fair go! A horse has already rolled on him. Don't make things any worse.'

Josef scrambled to his hands and knees and crawled to the door. He opened it and dropped to the ground.

'Now you, friend,' the pilot said.

Adam reached for his hand and shook it. 'I don't know your name,' he said.

'Taylor. Arthur Taylor.'

'Adam Ross.'

'OK, Adam. Out. And don't forget to close the door.' He opened the throttle and the propeller raised a fury of dust.

Adam dropped to the ground, latched the door and crawled after Josef. The plane taxied away, its tail fin waggling. Grit and chopped grass peppered them.

They were not far from some bushes and they moved there, taking care to stay low until they were hidden by the thick leaves.

'What do we do now?' Josef said.

'Wait for him to take off. Then we walk to town.'

They heard the engine cough and backfire and then stop. They heard the chatter of voices. A dog barked. It was hot and they crawled into a shadowy hollow within the bushes. Both were tired and within minutes, they were asleep.

The cry of a galah woke Adam. He had been sleeping with his face resting on the palm of his hand and he was now wet with perspiration. He sat up, wiping his cheek. If he got to town before three o'clock he would go to the bank and see if they could persuade the Nyngan bank to advance him some money. Roger Montgomery had also given him the name of the Presbyterian minister. He might make contact with him. He wasn't so sure. He didn't want to appear to be begging and he didn't like asking strangers for help.

Once they had walked into town, Adam headed straight for the bank. He had done his best to brush his clothes and polish his boots but he was still conscious of his scruffiness. He need not have worried. The bank manager sent a telegram to the Nyngan branch and promised all the help he could give.

He had a reply the next day. It said there were funds in the bank and a letter was on the way. The letter took two weeks to reach Geraldton.

After a week, Adam went to see the Presbyterian minister. He was out of town. Adam spoke to his wife who offered tea and cake and insisted on noting where he was staying in case her husband wanted to make contact. This he did two days later but it was a brief and almost hostile meeting. The man came to the guest house, complaining how busy he was and how inconvenient it was for him to have made the call. His face bore an expression of disappointment from the moment he cast his eyes on Adam, as though the subject were unworthy of his attention. And when he discovered Adam carried with him nothing more important than the greetings of a novice parson from a parish more remote than his, he lost interest and left, with the feeblest gesture of farewell.

The letter, when it reached the bank, seemed small for so long a wait. Even so, it had good news of sorts.

There was certainly money in Adam's account. George Curran had found a buyer for the truck and drilling equipment at a price only slightly below what Adam had wanted. He had proceeded with the sale, presuming (correctly as it transpired) that Adam would be needing cash quickly. There was now a credit in the Nyngan bank of one hundred and twenty-seven pounds. The Geraldton branch was authorized to pay all or part of that sum to Adam Ross, on his signing the appropriate form. A specimen signature was attached.

The not-so-good aspect to the news was that Adam now had no business to which he could return. George Curran had acted in good faith, but now Adam had some money in the bank and no means of earning more.

'Why bother going back?' Josef said, as they left the bank.

They walked towards the jetty, where seagulls perched to await the return of fishing boats. 'It'll only cost us money and there's nothing there for us.'

'Except Heather.'

'I hadn't meant it like that,' Josef growled and they walked in silence. Adam had written to Heather on their second night in Geraldton. He had needed help from Josef because the letter had been so long. There was no answer yet, of course, but Adam was not sure he would get a reply no matter how long he waited. The news in his letter would not please her.

A strong breeze blew. Ahead of them, gulls rose on the wind like flotsam on a sea swell. Used to man but barely tolerant of him, the birds lifted gracefully from the wooden rails as the two tall figures approached, hovered on the wind for the few seconds it took the intruders to pass and then settled gently back in place.

'What I mean,' Josef said, angling his head into the wind, 'was that there's no business reason for us to go all the way to Nyngan. It's a hell of a long way. It would be better and cheaper for Heather to come to us than for us to go to her, and then for the three of us to go somewhere else.'

They sat on the boards, looking towards the port and dangling their legs over the water.

'I've been wondering what to do,' Adam said. 'The part of this country I know best is where I've spent most of my life – in the northern part of South Australia and around Broken Hill.'

'It's crook country.'

'Not if you know it.'

'There are better stretches of land than the places you know,' Josef said. A seagull had settled near him, hoping to be fed. 'This may surprise you, but there are parts of Australia where they have green grass on the ground and the rivers have water in them. Why don't we got to a place like that?'

'Two reasons. I know the dry country. It's where I was born. I was raised in it I feel at home in it. I like it.'

'And the other?' Josef offered the gull his finger. The bird, which had been dancing to retain its place on the boards, allowed the wind to carry it away.

'I still want my own place. I'll never be able to afford a property down south. That would take thousands and I haven't got that sort of money and I'm not ever likely to have it. But up north in the country I know it's different.' He had been watching some men load bales on a ship at the far end of the port. He swung his legs a few times, cranking himself to speak again. 'Up in the north is the driest part of this country. There's not much water, not

477

much feed and not many people who want to live or work there. Do you know something? That's lease land. One day, I could afford a property up there. I could have a big place and I could handle it.'

'You mean we're going back to South Australia?'

'Why not?'

'Straight away?'

'I'm not sure. I've got to work out what to do about Heather. Maybe I should go to Nyngan and bring her back with me.'

'That would cost money.'

'I know.'

'What would we do?'

'Work for someone, I suppose. I can't afford a property now. So I'd have to work.'

'*We'd* have to work.'

'You said something about going to Adelaide.'

Josef shrugged. 'One day,' he said.

'OK. *We'd* work,' Adam said and then suddenly grew still.

'What's up?' Josef said. The seagull had returned and Josef offered him his finger once more.

Adam climbed to his feet. 'I've just realized something,' he said. 'I've been looking at those men loading that ship at the end of the far wharf.'

'So what?' Josef stood too. The bird flew away.

'That ship. It's the *Mary Elizabeth*!'

TWELVE

Tabby was on the wharf, fishing. He was sitting on the edge with the line trailing from his right index finger. He had his back to the town and, from that side, it would have been easy to assume he was asleep. He was bent forward and did not move. Only an occasional drift of smoke from the cigarette between his lips suggested a mind wakeful enough to respond to a nibble on the other end of the line. He saw two shadows and turned.

'Well, I'll be buggered!' he said, almost swallowing the cigarette in his surprise. 'Where the hell did you two come from?' He threw the cigarette in the water and looked up, his broad face lopsided as a smile began.

'It's a long story,' Adam said, looking across to the ship. 'When did you get in?'

'Last night.' Tabby got to his feet and started reeling in his fishing line.

'Caught anything?' Josef said.

'No. I was just filling in the time. By the Jesus, you're the last blokes I would have expected to see down here! I thought you were buying land up at Roebourne?'

'So did we,' Adam said. 'The land was no good.'

'Ritchie tricked us,' Josef added. 'The man's a crook.'

Tabby busied himself rolling a cigarette.

'Seen him about?' Adam said.

'Why?' he said, grinning. 'Do you want to give him a belting?'

Adam was not smiling. 'You're not the only blokes looking for him,' Tabby added hastily, 'but to tell you the truth I wouldn't have a clue where he was. I haven't seen him for a couple of days.'

'What do you mean? Who else is looking for him?'

'The cops.' He flattened the end of the cigarette and lit it. He inhaled deeply. 'Mr Ritchie got on the ship all right but must have got off somehow before we got to Carnarvon. That's where the cops were.'

'And he wasn't on board?'

'No.'

'You didn't see him get off?'

'No.'

'Did the ship stop anywhere?'

'No.'

'What did the police want him for?'

'Dunno. They just asked if he was on board and could they ask him some questions. They were real polite.'

'What did you tell them?'

'I didn't speak to them. The captain did. He said Mr Ritchie never got on the ship.'

'But you said he did.'

'Oh, he did all right. I saw him come aboard just before we sailed. I said I never seen him get off.'

Josef interrupted. 'Why didn't you tell the police?'

Tabby examined the end of his cigarette. 'I've got two golden rules, mate. Never volunteer information to the police and never volunteer to get sacked. What do you think the captain would have done if I'd rushed up and told the cops that the skipper was telling them a lie? He might have kicked my arse but he wouldn't have kissed it, I can tell you that.'

Josef frowned. He always seemed to ask the questions no one else needed to ask.

'Where do you think Ritchie is?' Adam said.

'No idea.'

'Haven't you wondered?'

'A bit. He's a funny bloke, though. He's been on the ship sometimes when I didn't know he'd come on board so I didn't take much notice. Why do you reckon the police wanted him? Have you put them on to him about the land?'

'No. It might be about something else.'

'Like what? What happened up there?'

'We found ...' Josef began.

'We got dudded for our land,' Adam said and there was an awkward silence.

'How the hell did you get down here?' Tabby said.

'Different ways,' Adam said. 'We hitched a lift into Geraldton.'

'Didn't you have return tickets?'

'Ritchie pinched our bags,' Josef said.

'You're joking!'

'He took everything. Our clothes, money, tickets, the lot.'

'What a rotten bastard.' They nodded solemn agreement.

'Did the police search the ship?' Adam asked.

'No. They just spoke to the captain.'

'Could Ritchie have been hiding on board?'

'I suppose so. It's only a small ship, though. If he'd have moved around I'd have seen him.'

'Could he have gotten off in Carnarvon?'

'You mean before the police came? No. They were watching for us.'

'Could he have gotten off afterwards?'

Tabby sucked deeply on the cigarette, marshalling his thoughts. 'I suppose so. We were there all right. I was in town, so I suppose he could have.'

Josef jabbed a finger. 'Could he have stayed in Roebourne?'

'I saw him get on.'

'But could he have got off again, before the boat sailed?'

'I didn't see him get off. I suppose he could have, though.'

'So he could be in Roebourne or Carnarvon,' Adam said. 'Or he could still be on board.'

'No. He's definitely not on the ship now. I cleaned the cabins out this morning and Mr Ritchie is not on board. I can guarantee that.'

'Could he have got off last night?'

'Suppose so.' Tabby grinned. 'What's the bastard done? Murder someone?'

When there was no answering smile, Tabby's grin faded. 'I've been thinking about getting a job on another ship,' he said, dropping his cigarette and grinding it under his heel. 'Might have to anyhow. The captain was saying this could be the old tub's last trip.'

'When did he tell you that?'

'When he told me not to answer any questions about the boss.' Again, his face lurched into a smile.

'Why did he say it might be the last trip?'

'Dunno. I just do my job and don't ask any questions. But I do think, and what I think is that Mr Ritchie might be going to sell her. Given half the chance, I reckon he'd sink her for the insurance money. He's the sort of bloke who'd put his mother on the ship, just so it'd look fair dinkum. I never thought he was a crook, though.'

'The man's a real bastard,' Josef said bitterly.

'Yeah. But who isn't?'

'When are you sailing?' Adam said.

'For Fremantle? Tonight. When are you heading off?'

'We thought we'd catch tomorrow's train. We've done all the business we have to do here.'

'Why don't you come on the ship?'

'Because,' Josef said, 'I want to eat lunch tomorrow.'

The guest house was an old wooden building. It had a verandah at the front and windows down both sides, and an iron roof that had once been red but was now either faded to whorls of pink and white or surrendered to columns of rust. The house was built high on tall wooden piers. The theory had been to provide a space for air to keep the building cool in summer but the reality was that the area beneath the floor had become choked with grass and weeds. The woman who owned the guest house shared only one room with the guests. That was the kitchen which was a huge common room. It had a large table at which everyone ate or wrote letters or sat after meals to play cards or talk. In the centre of the table was a permanent decoration consisting of an embroidered lace cloth, yellowing with age, an arrangement of dried flowers in a toby jug, salt and pepper shakers which had been issued to commemorate the opening of the Federal parliament in Canberra and were adorned with portraits of the Duke and Duchess of York, a Holbrook's Worcestershire sauce bottle whose label bore the splash marks of a score of eager but inaccurate diners, a jar of Keen's mustard, a sugar bowl with a spoon marked 'souvenir of Geraldton', a bottle of tomato sauce with its lid cemented in place by a thick red mortar, and packets of Weetabix and Kellogg's corn flakes. Letters for any of the guests were left on the kitchen table, propped against the corn flakes.

There was a letter for Adam.

It had been brought to the house by the Presbyterian minister, a method of delivery which greatly impressed the landlady. She had been hovering near the table, waiting for Adam to return and read a letter which was obviously of great importance, having been carried, as she saw it, by God's nearest available messenger. She was astonished when Adam handed it to Josef to open and disappointed when they retreated to the front verandah.

The letter was from Roger Montgomery and had been addressed to Adam, care of the Geraldton parson.

' "Many things have been happening in both Carnarvon and Roebourne," ' Josef read, after he had disposed of the letter's early formalities. He paced up and down, walking no more than four steps each way and speaking softly so that only Adam could hear. ' "To start with, the police were not greatly interested so I had to unleash Father Ryan, who very quickly stirred them into action. He is an amazing man with simply astounding influence in this region and not just among people of his faith which I, personally, as a broadly based Christian, find most encouraging. But to keep the story as short as possible, Father Ryan – who really is most incensed about the things this man Ritchie has done – not only got the local police to make contact with their colleagues in Roebourne but he too got in touch with them. The result is that a policeman and an aboriginal helper were despatched to Cobargo with instructions to recover the body you and Josef had found. To their surprise (and I am sure to your delight) they found George Karloff, one of the names you gave me, at the property, armed with a shovel and a pick and busily digging holes along the creek bank in a desperate and, I gather, rather confused search for the remains. This Karloff put up some sort of struggle but was eventually overpowered, although not before he had laid low the poor aboriginal with a blow from the shovel. This Karloff was, apparently, at first reluctant to talk to the police but I understand the officer who arrested him is noted for his powers of persuasion, and by the time they had returned to Roebourne, Karloff had given them many of the details they required.

' "To start with, the dead man has been identified as Jimmy Sinclair, once quite a noted mining engineer, I understand, but, in recent years, something of an eccentric who had devoted himself to prospecting. It seems that he found something big – no one is quite sure yet but there is talk of an immense deposit of iron ore – and that he, needing financing, became involved with Ritchie. There must have been some dispute between them. I think you, with your knowledge of Ritchie, could speculate that the man tried to cheat Sinclair. Whatever it was, Sinclair was shot. Karloff says Ritchie killed him but the police, I gather, think it more likely that Karloff did the shooting on his master's command. The Roebourne police, unfortunately, were not able to apprehend Ritchie. The ship had sailed but they intend arresting him as soon as the *Mary Elizabeth* reaches Carnarvon in a day or so. The other man you mentioned, the one with the beard, seems to have disappeared and there is a search on for him. Such excitement!

' "By the way, I have also had news about the car. It seems Father Ryan knows Harold McKay rather well and he has elicited the following information, which I think you will find interesting. Mr McKay managed to retrieve your vehicle and has carried out certain repairs which, he assured the good priest, he was happy to do at his own expense. These were, I gather, mainly to do with the wheels which were a trifle bent. Father Ryan tells me, incidentally, that Mr McKay is a most capable and dedicated mechanic so we can be sure the work was well done. He has fitted new tubes and tyres and has driven the car and reports that it performs well although it is still in need of a few items which he cannot easily acquire." '

At this point in the letter, Josef paused. 'Jesus,' he said, 'this Mr McKay is a beaut bloke! Or does he just want the car for himself?'

Adam looked worried. 'Is there any more in Roger's letter?'

'Yes,' Josef said and scanned the lines rapidly. He began to shake his head.

'Well, what does he say?' Adam said, trying to follow the letter over Josef's shoulder.

'Listen to this. "Mr McKay has been concerned about getting the car to you,"' Josef read, '"and not knowing your address but knowing you were heading south, he arranged to ship it to Perth. He spoke to the freight agency which handles all the transport arrangements for the tyres, parts and oils and other things he buys from Perth to ship the car south. It is going on the *Roebuck Star* and should be in Perth about three weeks from now."'

Adam stared in disbelief. 'He's sending the Alfa to Perth?'

'There's more,' Josef said. 'Listen to this. "Father Ryan and I were concerned that you might not get to Perth for some time or, in fact, that you might even have passed through. Therefore, rather than have the car on the wharf at Fremantle or be stored at considerable cost awaiting collection, we suggested to Mr McKay that he consign the car to my father, who lives in Perth. He is a widower and he has a large and empty garage behind the house. His name and address are at the bottom of the letter.

'"I am not certain, of course, whether you will have received this letter so please be kind enough to drop me a note. If I do not hear from you in one month, I will write to you at Nyngan, NSW, in the hope that that address will be sufficient to reach you. (I have just re-read that last sentence and realize how absurd it is. If you *are* reading this letter, it is meaningless. Still, it does indicate I had another plan although I'm not sure how my father would have got the car to you!) While Mr McKay has done a considerable amount of work on the car on his own initiative and expects no recompense, there are items, such as the tyres, tubes and, of course, the shipping freight, for which he would be grateful to receive money ... at some stage. He understands your financial plight but I rather think he has done this as some sort of test of character. Do you understand? He has a great faith in you and is prepared to put his faith to the test. I am sure he will not be disappointed. The amount involved (one could not describe it as a bill) is attached to the car in a letter he has glued to the base of the driver's seat.

'"I hope we may all meet again some day, although I suppose that is unlikely in such a large country. I shall pray for you both

484

and hope that you are able to recover from the difficulties that Ritchie's criminal behaviour has caused you." '

Josef lowered the letter. 'And then he goes on to ask you to remember him to me and spells my name wrong, and then gives his father's address. What an amazing letter!'

Adam took the sheets of paper. Roger's handwriting was of a flourishing style and he had difficulty in distinguishing the individual letters.

'I don't know how you can read it,' he said. 'It looks nice but it's not clear, like printing.'

'My mother used to write like that. A lot of educated people do.' Josef smiled at his friend. 'Well, Adam, it looks like you own a car and it's being delivered to you in Perth.'

'I didn't believe in Santa Claus,' Adam said, trying to decipher Roger's signature. 'Now the place seems to be full of them.'

The train to Perth left Geraldton early the next morning. Adam bought two second-class one-way tickets to the capital and then joined Josef, who had already selected their seats in a carriage near the locomotive. They knew enough about train travel to realize that the closer one sat to the steam engine, the less likely one was to be showered by soot. That happened further back, where wind could swirl the smoke down to the carriages. Josef had a window seat. Adam sat opposite him. They were among the first people on the train. A wind was blowing strongly from the sea and most of the arriving passengers were huddled against the cold.

They watched people join the train. A woman with two young children, both wrapped in tweed overcoats, their heads sealed by warm berets, clambered on to the train. A man and woman, both struggling with heavy suitcases, walked towards the middle of the train. They looked poor. Their cases were bound with rope. A young man wearing riding boots and a hat stained with perspiration and fingermarks limped past their windows. He had a canvas sack over his shoulder. Adam watched him swaying as he walked on uneven legs. A horse did that, he thought. He'd seen many bushmen with one leg shorter than the other.

Two women walked past, dressed so differently that one was obviously travelling and the other was saying goodbye to her. An old woman, stooped and carrying two string bags, shuffled past. She looked up into every window, her face twitching with anxiety.

Adam smiled. She looked away. She was searching for empty seats, not occupied ones. A man passed with head down and turned away from the carriage. He was wearing a navy duffel coat and a sailor's peaked cap. He carried a leather briefcase. Two boys ran along the platform. One bent to pick up gravel and threw it to the other. A man and a woman following them both shouted and the boys, laughing, kept running.

Adam opened his window and leaned out. He looked towards the rear of the train.

'What's up?' Josef asked.

'Did you notice that man?' he said, slumping back in the seat. 'The one with the big coat and the cap?'

Josef's brow knitted in concentration. He had been looking but not remembering. 'Wasn't he a seaman or something?'

'That's just it. What would a seaman be doing catching a train?'

'Why not? All he's got to do is buy a ticket.'

'But why not go by ship? After all, this is a port and that fellow looked like an officer. It'd be like a train driver going on a ship.'

'I thought you only got like this later in the day,' Josef said grinning. Outside their windows, the two boys had returned and were still throwing gravel at each other.

'There's something else,' Adam said, pressing his shoulder into the padded leather seat.

'What?' The grin was a taunt.

'I don't know. Just something niggling in the back of my mind.'

'You're sure it's not hunger?' Josef said. 'I could do with another breakfast.'

Adam stood up. 'You're always hungry.'

'And you're always worrying about something.'

'I might go for a walk.'

'Jesus! The train's due to leave in ten minutes.'

'I won't get off the platform. I'll just go for a bit of a stroll. Want to come?'

'No. I'll stay here and mind the seats.' Josef shoved his hands deep into his pockets.

Adam walked to the end of the carriage and stepped on to the platform. The wind was cold and he pulled his collar around his throat. He walked slowly down the line of carriages, watching his reflection flit from one window to the next. He was looking for the sailor. There was something about the man, something that

486

jarred, and he could not think what it was.

He had reached the third carriage before the thought came to him. It was the briefcase. Why would a sailor be carrying a briefcase? Not a bag over his shoulder or a suitcase, but a leather briefcase? At that moment, he saw the man. He was sitting in the corner of the carriage, with his head slumped forward as though he were sleeping. Reflections mutilated the image but Adam could see the man's cap and coat and briefcase, which he carried on his lap with his arms folded across the top. The train guard walked along the corridor. The man looked up and said something to the guard and then, yawning, looked out the window. He stared straight at Adam.

It was Ritchie.

He blinked. Both hands grabbed the handle of the briefcase. He looked around him within the carriage and then back at Adam. He stood, clasping the briefcase to his chest. The guard turned and spoke to Ritchie.

Adam ran for the door. He entered the carriage to see Ritchie trying to force his way past the guard. Other passengers looked up in alarm. Locked together by panic and confusion, the guard and Ritchie fell to the floor of the corridor.

Ritchie's cap had fallen off. He sat up, brushing his hair in place and looked up at Adam. He raised one hand.

'Don't hit me!' he said.

The guard was on his hands and knees. He had lost his glasses and blinked profusely.

'Get the police!' Adam said.

Naturally, they missed the train. Much of the first day was spent at the police station, giving an account of what had happened at the railway station and, of far greater interest to the police, of what had happened in earlier weeks. Adam, unexpectedly, found the experience pleasant. The police treated him kindly. In fact, there was a suggestion of respect which bordered on awe, for he had recognized and apprehended a man who was wanted on a number of major charges including murder. But there was one point in all the report-giving and question-answering that had Adam nervously clenching his knuckles.

The sergeant had scratched his head and said, 'One thing in all this confuses me, Mr Ross. You've given me the date on which you first met Mr Ritchie, and the date on which you sailed north, and you've told me when it was that Mr Ritchie's employee, Mr Karloff, allegedly fired at you and your friend. Now, what I can't understand is how you got from Roebourne, which is a devil of a way to the north, to Geraldton in just one day. It is just not possible.' And the sergeant had sucked the end of his pen and looked everywhere except into Adam's eyes.

'I made a promise to Mr Taylor,' Adam said softly.

'To the pilot?'

'Yes.'

'Is it the sort of promise you wouldn't want made public?' he said and Adam nodded. 'Well then, Mr Ross, why don't you tell me what it was in private, and then between us we'll decide whether the information is so important that it has to be made public. What is it?'

'Joe and I got a lift on the plane from Roebourne to here. Mr Taylor gave us a free lift to help us out. We had hardly any money, you see. But he was frightened that someone might find out and then he might have lost his licence. So when we landed here, Joe and I jumped out at the far end of the strip and just stayed low in the bushes while he went back to get fuel and take on more mail.'

The sergeant stopped his smile by inserting the top of his pen in his mouth. 'I suppose Mr Taylor is now concerned about such things as insurance.'

Adam scratched his knee. 'I believe so.'

'And he probably prefers not to be mentioned in our report?'

'I think so.'

'I'm sure so.' The sergeant tilted his head to gaze at the ceiling. He seemed in danger of swallowing the pen. 'And frankly, I can't see any reason why he should be. We know all we need to know and I can't see why we should cause Mr Taylor any distress. How much longer are you staying in town?'

'We were leaving this morning.'

'Which means you want to get away as soon as possible. Are you staying in Perth?'

'A few days.'

'Give me an address where we can reach you, just in case there are more details that may be needed. I'm sure the detectives down there will want to talk to you. Just tell them what you think they should hear.' He winked.

Adam showed him Roger's letter and the sergeant wrote down

the father's address. At the door, he shook Adam's hand.

'Well, thanks for your help,' the sergeant said, retaining his grip. 'You seem to attract adventure. Let me know if you're ever coming back this way.'

'I will.'

'Good,' said the sergeant. 'It will help me plan my holidays.'

THIRTEEN

On the day they arrived in Perth, the two friends contacted Roger Montgomery's father who immediately invited them to stay with him. On the second day Adam wrote to Roger, explaining all that had happened. Josef helped with the letter and then wrote two brief letters to Jimmy Kettle. He addressed them to Jimmy Black and sent one to the post office at Beltana and one to the post office at Port Augusta. The letters said they hoped to be in Port Augusta in three months' time. On the third day the *Roebuck Star* berthed at Fremantle and on the fourth day they went with Mr Montgomery to collect the Alfa-Romeo. The car had no fuel in its tank and they had to buy a gallon of petrol and carry it to the wharves, but once started the car ran well. Harold McKay had fitted a proper radiator cap to the cooling system and had crafted a cap for the oil filler. He had also made an improvised dipstick, curling the end of an aluminium rod to form a handle, brazing a sealing rim halfway along its length and filing grooves in the rod to correspond to the maximum and minimum oil levels. The tyres had seen some service but so little that the manufacturer's stickers had not worn away. Under the driver's seat was a note which stated, in almost apologetic terms, that the tyres, tubes and freight had cost a total of twenty-eight pounds, sixteen shillings and sevenpence.

Adam spent the weekend tinkering with the car and polishing it and admiring it. On the Monday, he went to a bank and arranged to have twenty-eight pounds, sixteen shillings and sevenpence paid to Mr Harold McKay of Roebourne. That day Mr Montgomery saw a friend of some influence who was able to handle the delicate but essential matter of registering the car for road use. And in the afternoon a telegram arrived requesting Adam and Josef to contact a Detective Flanagan in Perth.

This they did the next day. The detective wanted further details about the bags Adam and Josef had lost, as a man answering the description of an associate of Ritchie had been arrested near Port Hedland, and he had a number of articles, including several bags, in his possession. They spent an hour at the station, signed a declaration, and left.

After two weeks in Perth they were ready to leave. They shook hands with Mr Montgomery, climbed aboard the car, and set off to drive across the Nullarbor Plain to South Australia. They were facing a journey of more than one thousand, five hundred miles.

For the first three hundred and seventy-one miles the road followed both the railway line to the east and a pipeline carrying water to the gold mining centres of Coolgardie and Kalgoorlie. That was the easy part of the journey. At the goldfields, they had to turn south away from the railway to pass the great expanses of salt that were Lake Lefroy and Lake Cowan and drive one hundred and five miles to another gold mining town, Norseman. There, they had to turn to the east once more and cover just on four hundred and fifty miles to reach the old telegraph station at Eucla, set among the rolling sand hills near the beaches of the Great Australian Bight. The South Australian border was only a few miles to the east. From the border to the port of Ceduna was nearly three hundred and twenty miles. Beyond Ceduna, the country ripened into wheat fields and, after another two hundred and ninety-two miles of undulating monotony, the road reached Port Augusta.

The journey took nine days, and for most of it the road was rough with deep troughs of dust. There were sharp ridges of limestone in some areas and washboard corrugations almost everywhere else. When it rained near Eucla the dust turned to mud. The sixth day of their journey was notable because they passed two other vehicles.

For such a difficult trip, their tyres performed exceptionally well. They had to repair only six punctures and replace one tyre whose sidewall was slashed by a rock.

When the sun set on the ninth day they were passing Iron Knob but, being so close to Port Augusta, pressed on to reach their destination that night. Josef drove into town. Adam had been sleeping and only woke when the flash of streetlights disturbed him. They crossed a long bridge at the head of Spencer Gulf with Adam, still not fully alert, trying to identify the site of the circus where he had first met Jimmy.

Josef stopped opposite a café.

'I feel hungry,' he said. 'I am sick of tinned meat and sardines. I am tired of cold food. I want a grilled steak.'

'You're as dirty as a chimney sweep,' Adam said, 'and I suppose I'm the same.' He rubbed his cheek.

'You've got rid of the dust but you've put grease on your face,' Josef said.

'They'll probably throw us out.'

'I'm so hungry that if someone touches me I'll bite their hand off.'

Adam rubbed his hands vigorously on his trousers. 'All right,' he said. 'If you're game, I am too.'

The café had six tables. Two were occupied. They sat in a corner, where the light was weakest. A menu was scribbled in chalk on a blackboard.

'Don't need to read that,' Josef said, studying it all the same. 'I'm going to have one steak, two eggs and anything else they can fit on the plate.'

A waitress emerged from an inner room. She bore a tray laden with plates of food and stopped at a table where three men were seated. She put the plates in place, left, and returned with pots of tea and a jug of milk.

Adam felt like sleeping and sat with his forehead resting on the palms of his upturned hands.

The waitress moved to their table. With an effort, Adam straightened. He was aware of slim dark legs. 'What'll you have?' she said, and he looked up into the big, enquiring eyes of Nellie.

He stared at her, not knowing what to say. She was thinner than he remembered, her cheekbones a little more prominent. She blinked recognition. Her mouth was open, not in a smile but rigid with surprise.

Josef had not looked up. He had discovered another menu, a typed sheet under the glass which covered the table. 'Steak, well done, and two eggs for me,' he said. 'Whatever vegetables you've got, and lots of onions.' He looked up. 'Jesus Christ!'

'Josef?' she said. 'Are you young Joe?' She avoided Adam's eyes. Josef stood and knocked over his chair. He turned, apologizing, and bent to recover it.

'Hello, Nellie,' Adam said.

Her lower teeth nibbled a lip. 'You look older,' she said.

'I am.'

Her hands fidgeted with the empty tray. 'I didn't recognize Joe at first,' she said. Josef was sitting again and she smiled down at him. 'He's grown, hasn't he? What are you two doing here?'

'We've just driven in.'

'Where from?'

'Perth.'

Her eyes widened. They were such big eyes. Larger and even more striking than he remembered.

'You've driven from Perth?' She bent to look out of one of the café windows. Josef had parked the Alfa-Romeo under a streetlight. 'Is that your car, the funny-looking one without the roof?'

Adam's face dropped. 'I don't mean funny like "ha-ha",' she said. 'I mean unusual. Different.' She touched Adam's shoulder. It was just a brush, the slightest contact, but he stiffened.

'It looks lovely,' she said. 'Very expensive. Are you two rich or something?'

'We're one stage removed from being dead broke,' Josef said.

A man walked from the kitchen and stood in the doorway, wiping his hands on a tea towel. He glared at Nellie.

'Better get working,' she said. 'What'll you have?'

'Steak, two eggs ...' Josef began.

'That's right. And everything else. Adam?'

Adam's eyes swept into hers. Many times in the years since they'd left Coober Pedy he had thought about such a moment. Even practised things to say. Sometimes he had been angry. That was when he was short of money and thought about the opal and all that he could have bought with it. He had polished the angry phrases, turning them on the sharp edges of his bitterness. At other times, the words had been soft and passionate. That was usually when he was lonely. Tired and unable to sleep and staring at ice-cold stars and wanting her. Saying tender words of forgiveness and sorrow and longing.

'I'll have steak, too,' he said.

'With everything?'

'I suppose so.'

'Do you want a wash? There's a room out the back.'

'Yes. That would be good.' Adam rose. He towered above her.

He was bigger than when she had known him. Deeper in the chest, thicker in the arms and a little lined by the sun and wind and disappointment.

He smiled and he was a boy.

'It's that way,' she said, pointing, and hurried to the kitchen.

They had finished the meal and she was clearing the table.

'Are you staying in town?' she enquired, looking at neither of them.

'I suppose so,' Josef said, looking to Adam for confirmation. 'We certainly intend staying in the area for a few days.'

'Got a place?' she asked, stacking the dishes on a tray.

'No.'

She started to laugh, a small private laugh.

'What's up?' Josef said.

'It's you. I can't get over how big you are.'

'I did my best to stay small,' he said. 'Tell me, what are you doing working at a place like this?'

'Trying to make money. What have you been doing?' Her eyes went from Josef to Adam.

'Seeing a lot of the country,' Adam said.

She readied herself for departure. Tray high, body aimed at the kitchen, but face still turned towards him, she said in as casual a voice as she could muster, 'At the place where I stay there's room for you both. I've been there a few months now and it's clean.' She glanced briefly towards the kitchen in case the man was watching. He was not and her body relaxed a little. 'It's cheap. Even got running water. Not like the old days.'

A smile flashed. Gently, nervously, briefly. She's changed, Adam thought, recalling a younger woman, maybe not so beautiful but brazen and more certain of herself. How long ago had she stood before him, laughing and taunting, naked and flashy and with her skin glistening from a few splashes of water? Was it six years? Only that long? So much seemed to have happened.

'What do you think?' Josef was saying, anxious to see approval on Adam's face.

'Sounds like a good idea,' Adam said, wondering why he had said that, but too weary to think clearly. He was sure it was not a good idea to stay in the same house as Nellie but here he was, saying one thing and thinking another. His mind was no help. It was shuffling thoughts ceaselessly, playing them over and over

493

but finding nowhere to put them. He had once loved her. She had stolen from him. She was black. He was white. He was married.

He didn't trust her. No, that was wrong. It was himself he doubted. His body was stirring. Just like it had in the cave. He and Josef should go somewhere else. Just say goodbye. Be polite. It was a nice surprise seeing you. Good luck and see you again sometime. Who knows where, eh? Then get up and leave.

'Is it far?' he said.

'No. It's real close.' Her eyes moved across his and reluctantly descended to the tray. She busied herself stacking knives and forks. 'I'll give you the address when you come to the counter to pay your bill.'

The address Nellie gave them was across the bridge on the northern side of town. They stopped outside a small hotel. It was a squat building set flush with the road. The walls were made of stone but they had been roughly whitewashed and allowed to peel, converting what might have once been rugged or attractive or even quaint into a façade of neglect and seediness. The front door, centrally placed and as predictable as a child's drawing, was partly open.

The bar was on the side of the building, halfway along a corridor lit by two bulbs that hung naked from plaited cords. There were three men in the bar. One was the owner. He left a glass of beer and a partly smoked cigar to show them a room. They followed him from the stone building into a back yard. They passed a laundry and a bath house and came to another building. A row of wooden doors stared blank-faced at them.

'Last two on the right,' the man said and struggled with the lock on the first door. It sprung open and he ushered Adam in, switching on the light behind him. The room was tiny. An iron bed filled most of the space but there was also a wooden chair and a small table with an enamel basin. A towel, striped and threadbare, was on the corner of the bed.

'You can hang your clothes here,' he said, pointing to a row of nails on a wall. 'Breakfast's at seven, served in the dining room. The bar's closed but if you want a drink I can fix you up.'

He showed Josef to his room and Adam was left alone. He lay on the bed. The mattress was thin and lumpy. It was covered by two sheets, one grey blanket and a thin red cover, and felt cold. He was worried about the car, for it had no hood and the night was cloudy. It could rain and that would saturate the interior. He

494

jumped up and caught the publican on his way into the main building.

'Yes, mate,' the man said, pausing with the flyscreen door ajar, 'just drive around the corner and in through that gate and park it in the old stables over on the right. There's no doors but no one's going to pinch nothing and you've got a roof which is all you need. What sort of car is it?'

'An Alfa-Romeo.'

'What's that?'

'An Italian car.'

'You're not a dago, are you?' He asked the question pleasantly.

'No.'

'Didn't think so. Not with that hair. What are you doing with a dago car?'

'Driving it.'

'Ask a silly question, eh? What's it like?'

'Good. We drove it from Perth.'

'Yeah?' He scratched his stomach. 'Well, if you can drive it around the corner, you can leave it under cover.'

'Does it cost any more?'

'No, mate. We have a house rule in this pub. Anyone who drives an Italian car from Perth can park it for free. Don't forget, if you want a drink I'll be in the bar.' He moved inside the doorway. 'By the way, if you feel like a hot bath, there's a chip heater in the bathroom. You know how to use one of them?'

Adam nodded.

'Good. I had an Indian staying here a couple of weeks ago who almost burned the bloody place down. The wood chips are in the bucket. Try not to use too many and don't splash water into the bucket if you can help it. See you later.' He closed the door.

Adam had trouble starting the car and made a note to clear the fuel filter. When he finally persuaded the engine to fire, he drove into the hotel yard and parked the car in the old stable building, close to a stone wall lined with old paint tins, brooms, mops and buckets. The wall had been used to clean paint brushes and was a patchwork of colourful slashes.

Josef was waiting. 'Thought I might have a scrub,' he said, 'but there's only one gent's bathroom.'

'Toss you for the first bath,' Adam said, and lost. He waited in the yard. He had stayed in country hotels before; not often, but often enough to understand the need to queue.

A breeze thick with moisture and laden with sea smells drifted through the night. A light from the edges of the bath house door angled across the yard.

Adam thrust his hands in his pockets and tried not to think of Nellie. He leaned against the wall. It was thin and vibrated with sound. He heard the rush of water into a bath, the 'woomf' of the heater being lit and the gasp as Josef stepped into water too hot to bear. The tap ran faster. Josef cursed. He never could adjust chip heaters properly.

Light poured from the main building as a door opened. A man stepped into the yard and walked towards Adam.

'Someone inside?' he said.

'Yes.'

'You waiting?'

'Yes.'

He went back into the hotel, pausing only to spit.

The longer Adam waited, the dirtier he felt. There had been no opportunity to bathe since leaving Mr Montgomery's house and his skin was sheathed in a coarse coating of dust and sweat and grease, and his hair was peppered with the carcases of insects. He stank. The body normally protects its wearer from its own excesses but Adam could smell himself, and he smelled vile. And he chafed and ached.

'This is bloody beautiful,' Josef called out.

'Well, hurry up!'

'Another five minutes.'

'Make it two.'

'How about three?'

'Two or I'll come and pull you out.'

'Two and a half.'

'You'd better be clean when you come out.'

Adam walked away from the light. He went to the old stables and groping in the dark, ran his hand over the back of the car. At least he had something to show for the journey to the west. He wondered what Heather would say about the car. And when she would say it. Would he ever see her again?

Until that moment he had never doubted it, but now, for the first time, he thought about not going back. About just staying here, or going somewhere else and letting Heather and her crazy family and snobbish friends all go to hell.

He folded his arms across the top of the spare wheel and

lowered his head. 'I must be going off my head,' he said out loud, the noise muffled by his arms. Of course he would see her again. He was married to her. He had to. It was what a man was supposed to do.

But not what he wanted to do. That realization shocked him, but it was true. He had no desire to go back to Nyngan; no urgent, desperate feeling of love for Heather. God, it seemed so long since he had been with her, argued with her, left her.

'Something wrong with the car?'

Adam turned to see Nellie near the entrance. 'No,' he said, 'I was just waiting for Joe to finish his bath.'

She was a silhouette outlined by the light from the bath house door. She swung one foot behind the other. 'You were both pretty dirty,' she said.

'We'd come a long way.' He stayed with the car. 'I feel filthy.'

'It's honest dirt,' she said. Her foot still swung, back, forwards, back, forwards.

'Have you finished work?'

'Yes. Until tomorrow.'

'Good job?'

'Not bad.' The foot found the ground. She moved towards Adam. 'Which is your room?'

'Second from the right. Which is yours?'

'Last on the left. No palace, is it?'

'No. I suppose not. Still, it's a place to stay.'

She stopped. 'I've thought about you a lot. Did that policeman ever catch up with you? What was his name ... Mailey?'

'Didn't you hear?' He was out of the stables and standing beside her but not looking at her. 'He died.'

'Mailey? How?'

The water was being drained from the bath.

'The story we heard was that he got lost in the desert. An old Afghan found his body.'

She said nothing.

'I heard he caught you,' Adam said. 'Gave you a bad hiding.'

'How did you hear that?'

'I forget,' he said, cursing himself for not thinking. They had heard from Mailey. 'Somebody mentioned it.'

'It was a long time ago. I'm glad he's dead.' She had turned towards the light. 'Where did you go when you left Coober Pedy?'

'Oh, all over the place. We found our way to William Creek

and then down to Marree. Then we went north for a few years.'

'Did you ever think about me?'

He could hear Josef singing as he dried himself.

'Yes. A few times.'

'I've often wondered what would happen if we met again. I thought you might give me a belting.'

'I'm not like Mailey,' he said and started to walk to the bath house. 'I think I'll have a bath.'

'See you about.'

'Yeah. See you.'

She was gone before Josef appeared.

FOURTEEN

Adam was nearly asleep. He heard the door handle rattle, the lock click and wood scrape on wood and sat up, expecting Josef. Nellie came into the room. She was carrying something.

'Are you awake?' she whispered and then, seeing him, advanced to the side of the bed. She handed him a parcel.

'This is yours,' she said and left. The door squeaked. The lock grated and clicked.

Adam turned on the light. The parcel was heavy and about the size of a loaf of bread. It was wrapped in weathered newspaper and tied with string. He put it on the bed. It took him some minutes to untie several knots, and to unwind the coils of string.

He knew what it was before he removed the last layer of paper and saw the flash of opal.

He tried to sleep but could not and, an hour later, put on his trousers and shirt and went to her room. Her door opened easily. He closed it behind him. He had intended to call her name softly, to wake her without frightening her, but he knew she was already awake. He could not see her, he could not hear her move, but he knew she was alert and waiting for him.

'I don't want you to say anything,' she whispered.

'I never really believed you'd stolen it,' he said. There was a long silence.

'I took it to a dealer,' she said. 'It's worth a lot of money.'

Again, there was silence. Adam could see nothing and, as sometimes happens when the body is isolated in a vacuum of darkness, he had the sensation of floating, of moving, of being unattached to his surroundings. He reached out and touched the wall to steady himself.

'You'd better go,' she said, hearing the sounds of movement.

'I just wanted to say thanks,' he said from the darkness.

'That's all right.'

His hand was still on the wall. He moved forward a step and stumbled on something.

'One of my shoes,' she said.

'Sorry.'

'That's all right. I drop things everywhere.'

He reached down and put the shoe to one side. He took another step. 'Why didn't you sell the opal?'

'It wasn't mine.'

'There must have been times when you needed money.'

Her laugh was soft. It seemed to run along the wall, tickling his imagination.

'You could have sold it,' he said. 'I would have understood.'

There was another long silence. He had spent the time in his room thinking of things he should say but now that he was here, in her room, he could find no words to add. The bed creaked. He heard her sigh.

'It was yours,' she said. 'I didn't mean to steal it. I just got angry with you and Jimmy and went off with the bag and then we got separated.' Another pause. 'That was some night, wasn't it?'

'Yes, it was.'

'You were burnt. You could hardly walk. Were the burns bad?'

'No. They were crook for a while, but they got better.'

'No scars?'

'Only on my knees.'

'Everyone's got scars on their knees.'

'That's right.' He leaned against the wall conscious of the tumult within him. He was two men. One wanted to do the decent thing and just acknowledge his gratitude for the remarkable thing she had done and then get out. The other was thinking of Nellie in the cave at Coober Pedy, and wanted to stay. His fingers tapped the wall.

'What are you doing?' she said.

499

He stopped tapping. 'Leaning against the wall.'

'Do you want to sit down?'

'No. I'd better get going.' The bed springs groaned. She was standing.

'Bad luck about Jimmy,' she said. 'I mean, losing an arm.'

'How did you hear?'

'Joe told me. I saw him while you were having a bath. Jimmy going to be all right?'

'I think so. He's up this way now.'

'Yes, so Joe said. I hear you got married.'

Adam cleared his throat. 'Yes.'

'What's she like? Good-looking?'

'Yes. She's in Nyngan.'

'So Joe said. Is it a big town?'

'No. Oh, it's big for the district but it's not a big town.'

'I never heard of it before.'

'It's on a river.'

'Oh.'

Some distance away a dog barked. Another responded. It was not a challenge but a lament. Adam heard a board squeak. She had moved.

'What's her name?' Nellie said, her voice soft but closer.

'Heather.'

'I knew a girl called Heather once.' The dogs were still barking. It was the melancholy sound of one animal separated from another by an unbridgeable distance. 'She worked at Port Pirie.'

With you in the brothel, I suppose, Adam thought and felt the curious mix of revulsion and excitement that always came when he thought about Nellie and the way she had earned money before they had met. Her hand touched him.

'There you are,' she said and he stayed still, pressed against the wall and trembling. 'You're cold.'

He closed his eyes and his head reeled.

'It's spooky talking to someone you can't see,' she said. 'It's like being with a ghost or something.'

A ghost or a memory – of her, all those years ago in the underground house. Naked. Wet. Moving. 'I just came to say thank you,' he said and moved away from her, stumbling on the shoe again.

'You really did think about me?' she said.

His outstretched hand had reached the door. 'Yes.'

'Because I had the opal?'

'No.'

'You mean you just thought of me? Not of getting your opal back or wanting to belt me or anything like that? Just me?'

'Yes.'

'Often?'

'I suppose so.'

'I've thought of you a lot too. I've been a good girl since those days. Do you know what I mean?'

'I think so.'

'I've given all that up. Do you know why?'

'No.' His hand strayed reluctantly across the door handle.

'Because of you. You changed me. Funny, isn't it?'

He said nothing.

'You were different. You showed me some respect and I think you liked me. No one had ever done that before. And then when we got separated and I didn't see you again I just thought about you and felt that I'd be letting you down if I ... no, I'd be letting *me* down, too.' She coughed. 'I'm not saying this very well. Do you understand what I'm trying to tell you?'

'No.'

She laughed softly. 'Neither do I. You'd better go or something'll happen and you won't believe a word of what I've been saying.'

He opened the door slightly and felt the touch of cold air. 'Thanks again for the opal,' he said, marvelling at how flat and controlled his voice seemed, wanting to say other things but finding no words to express the confusion of thoughts tumbling through his brain. He walked out, heard her murmur something and closed the door without looking back. He stayed outside her room for some time, gazing at the stars, breathing deeply, and trembling.

Only one dog was barking now. It was a mournful, lonely sound.

FIFTEEN

So many things happened in the next seven days that Adam, in later years, would have difficulty recalling the sequence of events. Whatever the order, it was to be a week which profoundly

501

affected his future. There was the return of Jimmy Kettle, news of the ballot for the land in the far north, the selling of the opal, Josef's communication with his family, telegrams to and from Heather and, of course, further meetings with Nellie.

Jimmy Kettle very nearly bumped into Josef at the Port Augusta post office.

On their first morning in town Josef had walked to the post office to see if there was a letter from Beltana or whether, in fact, his own letter from Perth had been collected. As he attempted to enter the building, a swinging door, hit sharply to force it open, compelled him to step back and, to his astonishment, he was confronted by the emerging figure of his one-armed friend. Both men halted, speechless. The door swung back, clouted Jimmy, and was thrust open again.

'How long have you been in town?' Josef said when surprise had ebbed sufficiently to expose his voice.

'Since yesterday,' Jimmy said and laughed, and the floodgates of conversation opened. They talked all the way along the footpath as Josef led Jimmy to the hotel. Jimmy had travelled down from Beltana with an uncle and one of his cousins, plus a girl who, although a cousin too, did not rate the same status, being only a girl. Jimmy was bruised around one eye. He had been in a fight.

Josef was horrified. 'With one arm?' he said.

'Well, I wasn't going to tie it behind my back,' Jimmy said, and explained. 'There's this big abo up at Hawker I used to know as a kid. He never could beat me in a fight although he'd tried a few times. Even had a go at me with a piece of wood when he was full, a few years back. Anyhow, we ran into him at Hawker on the way down. He's become a real piss-pot and he saw me and laughed at me and started sticking his fingers in my chest. You know what I mean?' He demonstrated, jabbing his fingers at Josef. 'I hate that, don't you? So I told him to shove off but then he just landed one on my eye.'

Josef examined the swollen eyebrow. 'Did he knock you around much?'

Jimmy looked amused. 'That's all he landed. And I only hit him once, too.'

'What happened?'

'I think they expect him to wake up about next Tuesday.'

'You knocked him out?'

'King hit him.' Jimmy brandished his right fist. 'I've been working on this arm. I reckon it's as strong as the left used to be. Maybe better. It certainly felt good to flatten someone again!'

That night they ate at the café where Nellie worked. It was there that Adam heard about the land.

Adam, Josef and Jimmy had talked so much during the day that there seemed little left to discuss and the meal was a quiet affair, made more so by Jimmy's reluctance to talk whenever Nellie approached their table.

Her returning the opal had shaken him. He did not know what to say, so said nothing. His silence, however, had a bitter, accusing edge to it as though she had betrayed him by doing something so unexpected and so shockingly honest. And as Jimmy thought about it, that was how he felt. Betrayed. This woman was always doing the dirty on him.

First, she had left him. He could not forgive her for that. Not because he cared for her – he did not. It was because she had gone to his best friend; it was because Adam was a white man and that hurt; but most of all it was because no other woman had ever left *him*. He left *them*. He had shed himself of many a woman. Ones who wept copious tears and ones with hard faces who said they couldn't care less and went off hunting for another man. It didn't matter what sort of women they were, he left them. They never walked out on him.

Until Nellie.

Therefore, when it appeared that she had stolen the opal he felt a certain pleasure, a satisfaction that she had betrayed Adam just as she had betrayed him. True, the theft affected him because he owned a share of the rock, but she had physically taken the opal from Adam, and that made him feel good. It confirmed that she was rotten and it made him and Adam even.

Jimmy had thought about Nellie many times in the last few years, and always with a certain pleasurable bitterness. It was a bitterness which nourished him in his most trying moments. He had been hunted by Mailey, made the degrading transition from being a famous fighter to a nameless drifter, and lost an arm, and he had found ways to blame Nellie for all those disasters. He had enjoyed his vision of her perfidy. It had become the foundation on which the rationale for all his failures and troubles were based, and now she had cracked that foundation. For him, it was like

503

learning that something he cherished, something he believed in implicitly, was false.

He hated her.

'You're very quiet,' Adam said. 'What's up?'

'Just tired,' he said, and looked up as a man approached their table. The café was crowded and there was a spare chair only where they ate.

Adam was used to people who slurred their words, for mangled speech was as common among bushfolk as chipped fingernails, but this man was a grand master of the art.

'Jamine diffeye s'darn?' he enquired. Adam was about to say 'no' because he certainly did not mind if the stranger sat down at their table, but the man sat before he could answer. He studied the menu, arching his eyebrows so radically that the skin on his forehead narrowed to a series of deep furrows.

'Bide a cheeses,' he began, eyeing Josef who was beside him and rapidly translated the words into a mild oath, 'I reckonat Smithy's dunnidat larse, tone chew?'

'Done what?' Josef said.

'Kill dimself,' the man said and looked at the menu once again. 'Was a stay klike?'

'Good,' Josef said. He was eating it and the steak was good. 'Who's killed himself?'

'Smithy.' The man looked around for the waitress, 'Lease tit seem sew.'

Adam was about to ask who Smithy was, but Josef spared him the embarrassment.

'You mean the flier?' he said, and the man explained that Sir Charles Kingsford-Smith was missing on a flight from England to Australia and was presumed to have crashed in the Bay of Bengal. He looked at Josef in some surprise, for the news had dominated the papers. Ships and other aircraft were looking for his missing plane. It was a big search.

'Do they need help?' Adam asked.

The man searched for a smile. 'Inner Bayer Bengal?' he said and then, deciding Adam was joking, allowed a half-smile. It was not the sort of subject people laughed about but he felt required to show a polite response.

They began to talk about land. The man told them that he, too, had been looking at land, but in South Australia. He had just returned from the north of the state, having inspected land in the

504

Flinders Ranges and beyond Marree.

Some large properties were being made available for lease, he said, and explained the system.

A person did not have to buy the property. In fact, that was not allowed. The land was available for lease at an annual rental of so much per acre. What the government required was that the person be prepared to occupy the land within a specified time, carry out certain improvements like the erection of buildings and fences and, above all else, be able to make a go of it. Well, the man added smiling, not above all else: the person had to be able to stock the property and pay the annual rental. Everything comes down to money, he said, and they nodded slowly, firstly trying to untangle his words and then to assay the wisdom of his remark.

'What's the land like?' Adam asked.

'Bloody awful,' the man said. It was the clearest statement he had made. He was acting as agent for someone else and had looked at several places on offer. All were in arid country. Some had been worked before, and abandoned. One, near Lake Eyre, had been a government camel-breeding station. Another, adjoining it, had no buildings, no surface water and little grass. All it had was size. It could be large enough for a skilful operator to raise sheep on, he said, but then added, with the twinkle of experience in his eyes, that it would be an impossible place to raise sheep. He waited for one of them to ask why.

Because it was north of the dog-proof fence, he said, and dingoes would destroy a flock within months.

'How would you apply for land like this?' Adam asked.

Just put your name down, the man said, and then ordered his dinner. When Nellie had gone, he continued. The government would select suitable candidates and then hold a ballot. First name out of the hat would get the land. He would recommend that his client look at one of the properties in the Flinders. The others were useless.

Adam asked about the two properties near Lake Eyre.

One was called Muloorina. That was the old camel breeding station. It was on the Frome river, although the river was dry most of the time. He understood a couple of men were interested. Crazy fools, he reckoned.

And the other place?

The man laughed. Not even blackfellow country. He glanced at Jimmy who smiled benignly at him. No one had applied or should.

He described the location, more to emphasize the hopelessness of such a property than to define it but, as he talked, Adam realized he knew the area. The man was talking about the land where Saleem Benn had taken them. The place where he had fought Mailey. A place which had a fine but secret source of water.

He was busy that night, spinning images of that land with a homestead and shearing sheds, and shade trees, and fences, and sheep and horses. It was dry and inhospitable land, he knew, but he could live there and he could work it and make it pay.

Jimmy did not stay with them that night but camped on the edge of town with some of his uncle's friends. Adam had suggested he stay at the hotel but Jimmy refused. He no longer liked big towns and he had never liked hotels. He didn't drink and didn't like what alcohol did to aborigines. A hotel, therefore, was the focus for his concern about the way liquor was degrading his race.

Adam had not thought about it much. He knew Jimmy could not drink at a pub, but as Jimmy did not drink and he himself did not drink, it didn't seem to matter much. Adam also knew that Jimmy would almost certainly be refused where an aboriginal was either not allowed or not welcomed. A hotel bar scored on the first count and a hotel room on the second. While he did not like such ways, Adam had never thought seriously about them. They were just things that were part of the way life was. His own reaction, a quiet, unnoticed and unintended personal revolution, was to ignore such rules. That was why he invited Jimmy to share his room. He had no intention of telling the manager. Free accommodation and a soft kick in the tail for the people who represented such injustices seemed fair enough. Jimmy, however, said he could not be bothered and opted for the bush camp, which he preferred anyhow.

Before leaving, Jimmy spent some time talking to Josef. They talked about Beltana. It was a conversation that ran around the edges, for there was much that had happened in the time Jimmy had spent with his family that he would not talk about.

He had had a bad time up there and had seen things that shamed him. The problem essentially was to do with liquor. A sly grog operator had set up a shanty on the eastern perimeter of town and was pumping booze into the tribe. The man, a seedy white named Cavendish, was ostensibly a storekeeper who offered flour, sugar, salt, tea, and packaged and tinned goods to the aborigines and some of Beltana's poorer whites.

In fact, he made his money from importing cheap booze and then adulterating it either with sugared water, vinegar, methylated spirit, or cleaning fluid. Whatever was available, whatever was cheap and whatever had the required taste or impact was offered. Cavendish was becoming a rich man, and the aborigines were becoming babbling rabble.

Most of Jimmy's family had become drunks. Their days began in squalor, with violent headaches and the smell of dried vomit on their lips, and ended late at night in wretching convulsions. They had always been a people who did things together and they expected Jimmy to join them. When he would not, they subjected him to increasing abuse. At first they taunted him. 'You think you're too good for us!' they had shouted, slurring the oaths that accompanied the taunts. Then they had started to mock him, calling him a white man's lackey and laughing at his one arm. In the end, they had made him an outcast, ignoring him and talking around him as though he were not there, and that had hurt him deeply. He had gone back to Beltana to seek some balance in his life, to regain a sense of purpose which he had hoped to find among his own people, but they were not the men and women he remembered. They were strangers: dribbling, giggling, filthy, incomprehensible travesties of the people he had once known, and their only purpose in life seemed to be self-destruction.

His mother was one of the worst, and that had shocked him.

Like many a person who leaves home for a long period, Jimmy had created memories which were polished by desire rather than tarnished by fact. He had, somehow, buried certain recollections of the way his mother looked and behaved. She had lost some teeth and her hair had turned grey and her skin was wrinkled but these were just part of the normal process of ageing. What he had forgotten was her shrill voice, the fact that she liked to be with other men, that she could burst into a violent temper with little provocation, and that half a bottle of weak wine was sufficient to reduce her to a chattering, amorous harridan.

She had been one of Cavendish's first customers and the word around the camp (which was passed on to Jimmy with glee when the taunts were flying) was that she slept with the man to pay for her grog. She must have slept with him many times because Jimmy never saw her sober in all the time he was at Beltana. One night he had tried to carry her from the creek bed near

507

Cavendish's shanty back to the camp, but she had fought him and bitten and scratched him and called him a one-armed bastard, and he had let her fall and gone to the camp on his own. He had wept all night, not from any injuries she had caused, but from shame and shock and, above all else, from a sense of loss.

So when Jimmy talked to Josef about Beltana, he talked about the way the town had changed and how a mine had closed down, and about the trains that rattled through on their way to Marree, Oodnadatta and Alice Springs, and about the Australian Inland Mission station there – a small stone building that was as hot as an oven on a warm day – and about the minister who always wore a waistcoat and collar and tie; but he didn't talk about his family or his mother.

Josef mentioned Nellie and Jimmy felt the anger rising in him.

'I was watching the way she was looking at you,' Jimmy said, knowing what he was going to do and not liking it, but not being able to stop.

'What do you mean?'

'Jesus, you're innocent, kid! How long since you've had a woman?'

Josef blushed.

'Have you had one since that sheila up in Queensland? The one with the big dongers.' He sketched an outline in case Josef was not able to recall her large breasts.

'Oh, cut it out, Jimmy!'

'Why?' He punched Josef lightly on the shoulder, just as he had when Josef was only a boy and Jimmy had had two fists.

'It's normal to want a sheila. Nothing to be ashamed of.'

'I know, but not Nellie.'

'Why not her? Jesus, she's had more men than you've had breakfasts.'

'Don't say that!'

Jimmy looked innocent. 'But it's true. That's how she makes her money.'

Josef blushed again.

'Didn't you know? Flaming oath, she worked this coast for years. There wouldn't be a man over eighteen within fifty miles who hasn't slept with her.'

Josef turned away.

'What's up, kid?'

'Nothing.'

508

'Do you like her or something?'

'What about Adam?'

'What about him?' Jimmy felt his throat constricting.

For a moment Jimmy saw Josef's eyes. Hurt, bewildered. 'I thought she was Adam's girl.'

'You're forgetting something. Our mate's well and truly married.'

Josef looked as though he had forgotten. 'But he liked her, didn't he? And she kept the opal for him.'

'Look, Joe, she used to be my girl for a time until I kicked her out. But that doesn't mean nothing to me, and it was a long time ago that Adam had anything to do with her. No, I was just thinking when we were eating. You're a grown man now. Big and good-looking.'

Josef grinned, and Jimmy tapped his shoulder once more.

'No, it's true. And she only knew you as a kid. A boy. A child.' He held out his hand, measuring the height of a small boy.

'Ah, cut it out! I was bigger than that.'

'Maybe, but only a kid. Now you're a man and to her, you're a different person. I saw the way she looked at you.'

Josef scratched his cheek. 'I think Adam still likes her.'

'Bullshit! Oh, maybe he's surprised about the opal but you can bet she had some reason for doing that. Women are like that, kid. They never do nothing without some reason and you can bet a hardened tart like that one had a good reason for doing what she did.' He stood and yawned. 'Gees, I'm tired. I'll be on my way.'

'See you in the morning.'

'Yeah, see you, Joe. Why don't you wander around and see her?'

'Who? Nellie?'

'Why not? Listen to one who knows. I saw the look and I know what she wanted. You. She was giving you the eye, Joe. She would just love to have you crawl into the cot with her. Wouldn't be half bad. Maybe not as good as that young sheila you barrelled up in Queensland but still ...'

'Ah, Jimmy, cut it out!'

'Yeah, OK. See you tomorrow. Have sweet dreams.' He left, conscious of a different expression on Josef's face, and he felt pleased.

The next day was an important one for Adam. In the morning he sold the opal. Nellie had told him an opal buyer was in town.

Adam saw him soon after eight o'clock, when the man was still in his hotel room. The buyer admired the rock and said it would probably have fetched well over a thousand pounds, maybe twelve hundred, a couple of years earlier. However, the market for opal had fallen disastrously. It was the depression. Opal was a luxury and people weren't paying the prices they had willingly offered in the past. Then he said nothing for some time, but merely turned the rock in his hand and observed the way its colours changed in the light streaming through the window.

Adam sensed the man was going to buy, and steeled himself for a low offer. He had no idea what the opal was worth. The man might well have been telling the truth. The bottom had fallen from everything; it was a common story. Still, there was something in the man's face that showed he wanted the opal, that he recognized something special.

Adam had been thinking about the property up north and calculating what he would need. He could build a house. It would be small and rough but sufficient for a few years. He could get Saleem Benn to haul the material in, and knew he could count on the old man's help. He could drill a well or two, build fences, and stock the place with hardy sheep. Animals were going cheap. He would need about a thousand head, he reckoned. He could probably borrow the money to purchase those from Elders or one of the stock and station companies. To build a house, and put a few things in it – furniture, a bath and maybe even one of the new kerosene refrigerators – would take about six hundred pounds more than he possessed.

He looked at the opal buyer intently.

'I have to say, Mr Ross, that this is a beautiful specimen,' the man said. 'It will be worth a lot of money one day. When did you say you found it?'

'About six years ago.'

The man sighed. 'You should have sold it. You'd be a wealthy man today. Why didn't you sell it then, when the market was high?'

Adam shrugged.

'Yes, I know what it's like,' the buyer said, nodding in sympathy. 'If everyone made the right decisions all the time the world would be full of rich men. Which it isn't. Tell you what.' He put the opal on the table. 'I'm going to be honest with you. At the peak of the market, such a big and unusual and, frankly, such a beautifully coloured specimen as this could have fetched a couple of thousand pounds from the right buyer. You know what I mean? The sort of person who wouldn't just break it up into a hundred brooches or tiepins but would keep it like it is. A real collector. You follow me?'

Adam said he did. He had never met a collector of opals but could imagine such people. He had heard people collected paintings and they were of no practical value, so why not opals?

'If I were to sell this today, I'd be lucky to get five hundred pounds. That's from a conventional buyer, the sort who'd turn it into little bits and pieces that would look pretty but would end up lost down drains or buried in the bottom of grandfather's trunk. You follow me?' He kept on without waiting for Adam's reassurance. 'This specimen is too good for that. Somewhere out there, in Adelaide or Sydney, or in London or New York or Hong Kong, somewhere out there is someone who wants this opal and still has the money to pay for it. I'm prepared to take a gamble and try to find that person.' He took a deep breath. 'I'll give you seven hundred and fifty for it.'

Adam held his breath. It was more than he needed. But some of the money was Jimmy's. How much? They'd never discussed it. He tried to divide seven hundred and fifty by two. He stared out the window.

'It's a good offer,' the man said. 'A very fair offer in these times.'

'You'd sell it for more?' Adam asked.

'Of course. That's the way this business works.'

'There was a buyer I met up in Coober Pedy,' Adam said slowly, taking care not to say when he had met the man, 'He was prepared to pay more than a thousand.'

'Look, son, I'd be looking for someone to pay me a thousand quid for it too. That's being very frank. But I'd have to buy it from you and then travel to other places looking for someone to buy it from me. All that takes money. Sure I'd be looking for a thousand. But I'd have expenses and I need to make a profit. You understand that, surely?' He picked up the opal and carried it nearer the window. 'You know something?' he said, not looking at Adam. 'I think that is the most beautiful opal I've seen.'

He examined it for a full minute, saying nothing. Adam was silent. The man put the rock back on the table.

'Eight-fifty,' he said. 'I can't go higher, believe me.'

*

With Josef, Adam then went to the land office and lodged an application for his name to be included in the ballot for two of the blocks of land. One, his first choice, was for the property known as Muloorina. The second was for the undeveloped land, known only on the form as Lake Eyre West, Lot B. Josef helped him fill in the forms.

He was advised that the ballot for Muloorina would be held first, in a week's time. He would not win two blocks of land so, if he were successful for Muloorina, his name would automatically be withdrawn from the ballot for Lot B. If, however, he was unsuccessful in the first draw, his name would remain in the ballot for the second property.

After that they went to the post office, where each found a telegram waiting for him. Josef had advised his mother he was in Port Augusta. The telegram was from her. His father was ill. Not seriously but enough to make work difficult. She wanted him to come south for a few days, to discuss the family's future. That's what it said: family's future. Josef was intrigued.

Adam's telegram was from Heather. Josef, still puzzling over his mother's cryptic message, read it aloud. 'Father passed away Tuesday last week stop all town remarked on your absence funeral stop have sent letter with important personal news stop please await its arrival Heather.'

SIXTEEN

Adam found it difficult to talk to Jimmy about the money. His friend seemed uninterested, almost belligerent, when he tried to discuss the division of proceeds from the sale of the opal.

'Whatever you think's fair,' Jimmy said and shrugged.

'Half each, then.'

'No. That's too much.'

'Why? We worked the mine together.'

'But you found it. I wasn't there that day, remember?'

'What's that matter?'

Jimmy had tried to talk about something else and it was only

512

with difficulty that Adam brought him back to the subject.

'Look, it was your mine,' Jimmy said, as though the topic angered him. 'The lease was in your name. I was just the abo giving you a hand.'

Adam knew these moods. 'What's happened, Jimmy?' he said. 'Something here, or was it up in Beltana?'

Jimmy rolled his eyes, avoiding Adam's. 'Nothing. I just don't want any of the money. Not from that opal that that rotten shiela's been carrying around.'

'Nellie? Is that it?'

'No! Of course not.' They were near the post office where Adam had been to check for any mail and Jimmy spun around to watch a car that had passed. 'Ford V8,' he said. 'I'd like one of them one day.'

'You could buy one with your share of the money.'

'Don't want half. That's not fair. We've been through all that. I'll take some, if you like, but not half. Let's not argue about money, for Christ's sake.'

They crossed the road in silence. Jimmy paused to remove a stone from the sole of his bare foot. When they reached the footpath, Adam said: 'What's this about Nellie?' He spoke gently, as though the question did not matter, and looked in the window of a shop that sold hats and boots and riding gear.

'Nothing,' Jimmy said, eyeing a pair of brown elastic-sided riding boots. 'I just don't trust her. She's up to something. Must be. She always is, or was.'

'People change,' Adam said, studying the same boots. Jimmy couldn't tie shoelaces properly now, and the boots would be good for him.

'Not many of them. Where are you going?'

Adam entered the doorway.

'Just wait a moment.' He returned with a boot a few moments later. A man, bearing a box in one hand, was staring from the shadowy interior of the store. 'Size ten,' Adam said, thrusting it at Jimmy. 'Your feet haven't got any bigger, have they?'

'What's this for?'

'A little present.'

'Why?'

'Because I'm glad to see you again. Try it on.' The man in the shop was moving forward, concern on his face. Adam casually blocked the doorway. 'Does it fit?'

513

'Like a glove.'

'Not like a boot?'

'Silly bugger. How much is it?'

'Who cares? We're rich.' He turned. The man was about to speak. Adam took the box with the other boot. 'I'll buy them,' he said, and counted out four pounds three shillings.

'You're mad, you know that?' Jimmy said when the storekeeper had retreated. He was admiring the reflection of his new boots in the shop window. 'How much are you going to need if you win one of those blocks of land?'

'About six hundred.'

'That's on top of what you've already got, not counting the opal?'

'That's right.'

Jimmy lifted one leg and glanced along the line of the boot. 'And this opal buyer gave you a cheque for eight hundred and fifty?'

'Right.'

'Well, if you gave me half like you've been saying, you silly bugger, you wouldn't be able to afford the property.'

'I could raise some money. Sell the car. Do a few jobs.'

'Yeah, and gum trees are going to start sprouting ten bob notes! I'll tell you what. You give me a hundred quid and keep the rest.'

'No. That's not enough.'

'Yes, it is. Just shut up and listen. If I had more, I'd have to share it with every relative I have, and there are dozens of them, and the way things are at the moment I know who'd end up getting all the money.'

'Who's that?' Adam looked puzzled.

'A prize bastard called Cavendish, but that's my problem, not yours. And I told you to shut up, so shut up or I'll kick you with my new boots. No, here's the deal. A hundred for me, but you put it in the bank where no one can touch it. You use the rest of the money to start up your property. That's if you get it. If you do,' and he held up his hand, for Adam was about to interrupt, 'give me a job on the new place whenever I want one. A job, free tucker and a place to sleep.'

'You can have a share of the place,' Adam said.

'Oh, Jesus, we've been through all that! I told you before I don't want to own a property like you do. I don't want to be tied down to any one place. I want to be free to come and go as I please. That's how I am. I'm different to you.' He danced a few steps, as he used to in the days when he boxed. 'Just a hundred in the bank and a job when I feel like it.'

Adam was torn between feeling that the deal was grossly unbalanced in his favour and recognizing that with this arrangement he could afford to go ahead with the land.

'I don't know,' he said.

'I do,' said Jimmy. 'It's settled. By the way, thanks for the boots. No one ever bought me boots before. Not even my mother.'

Nellie did not work in the afternoons. She saw Adam enter his room and, a few minutes later, followed him. He turned in surprise.

'Just wanted to talk,' she said and sat on the end of his bed, clasping her hands on her lap. She looked very young, like a child waiting to be told a story.

'It's hot outside,' Adam said. 'Like some water?' He had put clean water in the basin on the small table.

'No thanks.'

Adam drank some, scooping the water with one hand.

'Not very elegant,' she said and laughed.

'Hands were made before cups,' Adam said, smiling but feeling embarrassed. 'In any case, there are no cups.'

'No. It's not much of a pub, is it?'

'No. It's all right though.'

She crossed her ankles. 'Is something wrong?' she said, eyes on her feet.

Adam wiped his lips. 'Why?'

'No one's talking to me.'

'We've been busy,' he said and, not knowing where to move, sat on the table. It creaked violently and he stood again.

'Not made for a big man,' she said and crossed her ankles the other way. 'I know you've been busy but even when you're not busy no one talks to me. Everyone avoids me.'

'No, we don't.'

'Jimmy's behaving like a pig.'

Adam lifted one shoulder. It was a 'you know what Jimmy is like' gesture.

'I don't know what's wrong with him but he treats me like I was some sort of disease. It doesn't worry me, mind you. I couldn't

515

care less if he never spoke to me again. It's just the way he does it. He turns his back on me, talks over me or just shuts up until I go away.' She stood quickly, adjusted her dress, and sat down again. 'The trouble is, he's affecting everyone else.'

'How do you mean?' Adam sat on the other end of the bed, beyond touching distance.

'You haven't given me more than two words since the other night and even Joe's shut up in the last day or so. He gives me the queerest looks.'

'Like what?'

'I can't explain. Just strange looks, as though he's expecting me to do something.'

'He's got some things on his mind. He may go home to Adelaide for a few days. His father's sick.'

'It's nothing like that. It's something to do with me. I find him staring at me when he thinks I'm not looking. He doesn't say anything, though when you first reached town he wouldn't stop talking. It's weird. I feel real uncomfortable.'

Adam let his head rest on the pillow. 'I don't know what it is,' he said, counting flies on the ceiling. Three were entangled in a spider's web in the corner above him. 'Joe's very much influenced by what Jimmy says.'

'And what's Jimmy saying?'

'Nothing.'

'I've noticed.'

'Oh, he talks a bit. I think you surprised him by returning the opal.'

'So? Would he rather I'd stolen the thing?'

'Yes. I think he'd have found that easier to understand.'

'He's crazy! He might get on all right with men but he hasn't got a clue about women. About how they feel, what they want. About anything. He thinks he knows, mind you. Like all men ...' and she looked at him and hesitated, '... like most men he thinks he knows everything about women, but he knows less than most, which is saying something. And since he gave up boxing, the most exercise he gets is jumping to conclusions.'

Adam laughed.

'I feel sorry for Jimmy,' she said and swung her legs vigorously. 'Sorry, and mad at him. If he's to blame for all this silent treatment I've been getting, and it's all because of the opal, I wish to heavens I'd never held on to it. I wish I'd lost it or something.'

516

'Did I tell you I'd sold it?'

Her ankles locked across each other. 'No.'

'I saw that buyer you told me about. He said it was a beautiful specimen but he said the market has collapsed for opal.'

'Everyone says that about everything these days.'

'That's what I thought. Still, he gave me eight hundred and fifty pounds for it.'

Her eyes grew unnaturally wide.

'He said it was worth more and would have fetched more a few years ago, when prices were higher.'

'I should have sold it,' she said, smiling.

'Yes.' He covered his eyes with one arm. A thought had occurred to him. 'Would you like some of the money?' he said, and realized that he had said it in such a way it sounded obvious he wanted her to say 'no'. Hastily, he added: 'I mean, you looked after it all those years and we ... you know ... up in Coober Pedy ...'

He was conscious of her embarrassment. 'I kept the opal because it was yours,' she said firmly. 'I'm sure you could use the money. You know, being a married man and all that.' She paused, sorry to have said that. 'You've had bad luck. Maybe the money will change things for you.'

Adam told her about the ballot for the land. He found it easy to talk to her about such things.

'It sounds like a hard life,' she said. 'Do you think this Heather of yours could live in a place like that?'

'Why not?' he said, manufacturing confidence. 'It's the only way we'll get a start. I certainly can't afford to buy an existing property, so we'll just have to build our own.'

'You won't be satisfied with a small place,' she said.

Adam sat up. She was not looking at him but into him, and he shifted, feeling uncomfortable.

'You'll want a big place,' she said. 'You'll make it big. You'll make it the best property in the area. I know you. I know you better than anyone. You'll be a rich and successful man one day with a property so big and so good people are going to look at it and gasp and say they don't believe it. You'll do all that.' She stood and faced him. 'The trouble is you'll need help and I don't know if this Heather of yours is good enough for the job.'

She walked to the door. 'It's been nice to talk to someone at last,' she said. 'I was beginning to think that all those things that happened all those years ago didn't really take place at all. I'm going to lie down for a while. I've got a long night. By the way, I know you're married and all that, but if you want to come to my room I wouldn't mind.'

She left the room. Adam gazed at the ceiling. There were four flies in the web.

He thought about what she had said, and about the land up north and about Coober Pedy and went to her room. She was on the bed, covered only by a sheet. Her bare arms were folded behind her head.

'I'm glad you came,' she said.

He sat at her feet and talked about the land. What he would do if he won one of the ballots. The sort of homestead he would build. What trees he would plant. The type of sheep he would raise. His voice was a rushed whisper. She let him talk.

When he was silent at last, she sat up, allowing the sheet to fall around her hips. She reached out and stroked his cheek.

'It was so long ago,' she said. 'You've no idea how I've missed you.'

He touched her shoulder and let his hand slide gently to her breast.

He had loved her and lost her and given her up and found her again, and now that he was with her, the burning that had been buried within him flared up.

He began gently but the fire raged and consumed them both.

'I don't know if I should have got married,' he said, lying beside her. The ceiling of her room was clear of spider webs.

She laughed softly. 'You sound like some fat old man saying his wife doesn't understand him.'

'I didn't mean it that way.'

'I know. You'd be surprised just how many men, once they've been with a woman, have to say that they didn't really mean to do it, and they wouldn't have if only their wives were different.'

Adam looked hurt.

'I know you didn't mean it that way,' she said. 'It was because of what I said back in your room. I understand that. I think your wife sounds like a bitch but that's only my opinion and I hope I'm wrong. You need someone who knows the bush and is tough and loves her man and won't complain when he comes home stinking under the armpits.' She was about to add, 'someone like me' but thought better of it. She touched his wrist. 'And I didn't want to give you the impression I'd been sleeping with men again. I haven't, not since the old days. I used to do that and I'm not proud of it, but still I did it and that's in my past and that's that. Believe me, since we left Coober Pedy, since I met you, I haven't done anything like that.'

'It doesn't matter,' Adam said gently.

'Yes, it does. You do believe me, don't you? It's important to me.'

'Yes.'

She kissed his shoulder. 'You've got lovely muscles,' she said.

She finished work in the café at eleven. Just after midnight Adam went to her room. He heard a noise, a sharp scuffling sound, as he approached the door. Inside, shadowy figures were struggling. Two of them: Nellie and a tall man.

He grabbed the man and wrenched him clear before realizing it was Josef.

Nellie was naked and nearly choking in her effort to stifle the noises bubbling in her throat. 'I'm not hurt. I'm not hurt,' she said, grabbing Adam and then, realizing what she had done, pushing him away and covering herself with her bedspread.

'What the hell's happening?' Adam demanded and turned on the light. Josef was white with shock. He was trembling and blinked rapidly in the bright light. Blood trickled down his cheek.

'Turn off the bloody light!' he said, his voice high. He darted to the wall and pressed the switch himself. 'Jesus!' he breathed, touching his face, 'I'm bleeding.'

'Nothing happened,' Nellie said, and then repeated the words, her voice as out of control as flotsam on a raging torrent. 'I didn't know who it was. I didn't know it was Joe.'

'Yes, you did!' Josef growled. 'I'm going!' He pulled the door hard but checked himself at the last moment and closed it quietly behind him.

'Don't turn the light on,' Nellie said, her voice steadier. She sat on the bed. 'Oh, that was awful!'

'What happened?'

'I don't know! I mean, I don't know why it happened. He just came in here.'

'When?' Adam felt his heart racing. He was breathing heavily, as though he'd been running. He sat beside her.

'I don't know. A few minutes ago. I thought it was you at first.'

'What did he do?'

'Calm down!' she said, reaching across to pat his hand. 'Nothing happened. I'm not hurt.'

'Joe's bleeding.'

'I didn't mean to do anything to him. It's just that he's very strong ...' One hand touched Adam's, the other was braced across the top of her chest. 'He knocked and came straight in. I couldn't see him properly and I thought it must have been you. He was all strange. Stiff and awkward, like some sort of clockwork toy, but he came in as though I was expecting him.'

Her fingers tightened around Adam's hand.

'I haven't said anything to him or done anything. Honest! He just walked up to me and grabbed me. I was half-undressed and he tore the rest off.' Her voice was out of control again and Adam patted her, feeling foolish and not knowing what to do.

'Jesus, just like the old days!' she said eventually, forcing the joke and trying to smile, though her cheeks were stained by tears. 'Why Josef?' she asked. 'Why did it have to be him?'

She let Adam pull her into his arms. He stayed until she was calm.

'Where are you going?' she said when he rose.

'To see Josef.'

'You won't hurt him?'

'Should I?'

'No. He didn't do anything. It was just the shock of it all. I didn't expect it, but he didn't hurt me. Please don't do anything to him! Adam?'

But Adam was gone.

He found Josef outside in the shadows near the car.

'What are you doing here?' Adam said.

'Nothing, and I don't want to talk to you.' With a fingernail, he picked at the raised lettering on the wall of the spare tyre.

'What was all that about?' Adam said.

'What's it matter to you? You're married. You've got a wife. You don't own all the women in the world.'

'You've been drinking.' Adam could smell the liquor.

'Why not? I'm old enough.'

'Where'd you get it?'

'For Christ's sake, you can get it anywhere! I'm free, white and old enough to go in a pub.'

'You've been in a pub?' Josef had not eaten in the café that night.

'No.' He strode angrily to the other end of the car. 'For Christ's sake, leave me alone! You're a bloody pest. Bad as my bloody father.'

'Who were you drinking with?'

'Do I have to drink with someone? I haven't got a woman of my own, not like you with as many as you want, so why do I need someone to drink with?'

Adam stayed at the back of the car. Josef blended with the deepest shadows.

'I was with Jimmy,' Josef said.

'Jimmy doesn't drink.'

'He has friends and they drink.'

'You bought the grog?'

'What are friends for?'

'Are they black?'

'Of course. Jimmy hasn't got any white friends, other than us. Other than me. I'm his best friend.'

'You could have got yourself put in gaol.'

'What, for buying my friends a drink?'

'It's against the law and you know it. So does Jimmy. I've never known him to do that before.'

'Do what? He didn't do a thing except sit with us and talk.'

The sky was filled with stars. Adam walked a few steps from the shelter. He could see Orion, the hunter.

'What made you do what you did to Nellie?'

'I didn't do a thing. She scratched my face with her nails.'

'But why did you go into her room?'

'She likes me.'

'She likes a lot of people.'

'Too bloody right she does! She fucks for a living. She's a whore. A bloody trollop!'

'Who told you that?'

'No one.'

'Well, she's not!'

'You're just saying that because you want her all to yourself. Jimmy says she's been rooted by every bloke within fifty miles. I just thought it was my turn.'

521

'Jimmy told you that?'

'Don't you try and blame Jimmy! He's my best friend.'

Josef walked from the shelter and stood under the stars but turned his back to Adam. 'Do you know what she called me when I walked in?' he said. 'Adam. She called me Adam. Oh shit, I feel sick!'

He went back in the shadows. Adam could hear the sound of retching. He found Josef on his knees, near the nose of the car.

'I haven't dirtied the Alfa,' he whispered.

'That's all right.'

'How's Nellie?'

'She was a bit frightened, that's all.'

'Jesus! What have I done, Adam?'

'Nothing. You just gave her a big shock, that's all. She does like you, but I think it's like a brother. Do you understand?' He had his hand on the back of Josef's neck and he felt the head nod.

The next morning Josef announced that he was going to Adelaide for a few days to see his parents. He avoided Nellie.

The ballot for Muloorina took place. It was won by the Price brothers of Peterborough. The draw for Lake Eyre West, Lot B, was held the same afternoon. It was done with formality but there was little point. Only one person had submitted his name.

'Congratulations, Mr Ross,' the presiding officer said. 'You've won yourself a large parcel of land surrounded by a great deal of nothing. What are you going to raise? Sand?'

Adam smiled and was still smiling as the officer read through all the obligations associated with winning the lease.

The letter from Heather arrived two days later. It was short and contained one essential point. She was pregnant. The baby was due the following winter.

BOOK FIVE

The Empire

ONE

The wind began to blow before dawn, as it usually did at this time of the year. It was cold and carried fine grains of sand and it stung and chilled the mare, causing her to shiver and stamp in bursts of irritation. Normally she was the most placid of horses but she hated the wind. She could tolerate the heat, ignore the yapping of dogs or the mindless bleating of sheep and even withstand the tickle of flies with no more than a weary flick of the tail to show her displeasure, but the wind needled her to the point of madness. Knowing this, Adam Ross turned her head from the wind and stroked her flanks as he finished tightening the saddle's girth strap.

He had covered a mile before the sun rose. The horse was pleased to be moving. She followed the line of the sandy creek bed by habit, crossed at the place where the old burnt tree had fallen and followed her own tracks around the ends of the sand dunes. With the sun up it seemed even colder, and the mare stepped high, prancing like some fancy show pony; not to show off, for no one could see her in such a remote place, but to keep her fine muscles warm and supple.

She passed a clump of squat acacia trees, leaves grey and trunks tortured and wrinkled from the struggle to survive. The trees were misshapen, even ugly, but they cast long shadows that stretched slender and graceful, like dreams of what might have been in a gentler land. Near the point where the shadows ended, the horse turned and began the slow climb up a sand ridge. The deep hoof marks from previous crossings had softened into a jumble of craters. It was hard work. The mare snorted and snuffed and slid and occasionally had to stop to regain balance. When she reached the top she paused, her flanks swelling with charges of fresh air, while Adam stroked her and spoke soothing words. The ridge was wide and flat on the top and studded with low bushes. Weaving an erratic path to miss the grasping thorns and to find firmer footing, they crossed to the other side. There, Adam stood in the stirrups and gazed down on the place where Jimmy Kettle was camped.

Sunlight reflected from bare metal where the new water trough was being built. Pipes, timber and pieces of scaffolding, partly assembled but not erected, lay on the ground. A crude bough shelter was nearby. Smoke whisped from the ashes of a small fire. No human was in sight.

It was a flat and narrow valley hemmed by sand hills. The ground was covered by stones so small and finely meshed as to give the impression of a mosaic floor.

The dunes that surrounded this valley were beautiful in the early light. The breeze had brushed the sand into minute ripples and the surface glowed bright orange or a moody red, depending on the fold or the stripe of shadow. Clumps of needle grass coated the hills. At the base of the dune, where salt bush formed a border as precise as a planted hedge, the sheep were grazing. Having little grass to eat, they nibbled the bushes and the line of grey-green leaves bobbed under the onslaught.

Adam rode down the hill. The sheep were nervous. They broke from the salt bush and wheeled in flocks, as aimless as a series of willy-willies stirring the dust. Adam eased the mare to her slowest walk to calm the sheep and searched for Jimmy.

A black dog with a collar of white hair came bounding towards him, twisting through the bushes and scattering sand as it ran. Jimmy followed. He half ran, half stumbled down the hill. His shirt, open to the waist, billowed in the air. His pants were ragged and he wore a pair of well-worn brown boots. He was carrying an old .22 rifle. He looked tired but managed a smile.

'Had another bastard of a night,' he said when he reached Adam. 'Lost another two. Over there.' He waved the rifle towards the end of the mosaic valley. 'I got the bugger, though. Big feller.'

'Do you think he's the one who killed the other sheep?' Adam dismounted and moved the mare behind a bush, out of the wind.

'No doubt. Got the biggest belly I've seen on a dingo. That one's been eating better than we have. Not that that's saying much.' He grinned ruefully.

Both Adam and Jimmy were as lean as working cattle-dogs. The last year had been hard and good food had been scarce. Adam had started with one thousand head of sheep, borrowing the money from a stock agent at Peterborough and buying the animals at an auction there.

As his future depended on the amount of wool he could sell and the quantity of wool depended on the number of sheep shorn and as every dead sheep was one less fleece to be weighed, he had slaughtered none for meat. The only mutton he and Jimmy had tasted in nearly twelve months had been salvaged from the ripped carcasses of sheep killed by dingoes. Sometimes the dogs only tore the throat from a beast and then Adam or Jimmy butchered the rest. On such occasions they ate with a guilty relish, always bemoaning the loss of the sheep, never saying how good the meal tasted, but attacking the roasted flesh with zest.

Otherwise the only meat they ate was from what creatures they could catch. They had supplies of flour and tea, sacks of sugar, salt and baking soda, and a few tins of biscuits and cans of jam, but mainly they hunted for their food. They shot an occasional kangaroo or lizard. Usually they ate cockatoo or galah. Many parrots lived in the area. While easily alarmed by humans, they were not difficult to shoot. Jimmy had perfected an imitation of the cry made by an injured galah. The birds had one fault which minimized their chances of eluding a determined hunter – they would not abandon one of their kind when it was wounded. Shoot one and only wound it, and you could take your time and shoot the whole flock. So Jimmy would utter his plaintive screech and galahs would come to investigate and he would cull enough for dinner. He had a magnificent eye and even with one arm was a deadly shot. He held the light rifle like a pistol with his hand extended and stock resting along the forearm. Shooting a bird in flight with a rifle bullet is an almost impossible shot, but Jimmy did it regularly. Naturally, he shot most of the parrots when they were at rest, because his hunger demanded that he fire when he was most likely to fell a bird. He killed to eat, not for sport, which usually meant firing when a flock was resting in a tree or grazing for seeds, but when his belly was not twitching with emptiness and he felt like demonstrating his prowess (even if only to the dog) he would shoot a bird in flight.

Eating galah was often less satisfying than shooting it. There was an old bushman's tale about the recipe for cooking the bird: throw the galah in a pot of boiling water and simmer for a week, then add an old boot and simmer both for another week, then throw the galah away and eat the boot. Adam and Jimmy had devoured hundreds of the birds.

They ate some damper which Adam had cooked the day before, and drank tea. Adam had brought with him enough supplies for several days. After breakfast, Jimmy slept for a while. He was exhausted, having been awake for most of the night. Adam resumed work on the trough and windmill. He had discovered underground water in this arid valley and had drilled a bore, using old equipment Saleem Benn had found abandoned on a property east of the Flinders Ranges. The Afghan had been a frequent visitor and a great friend, hauling supplies, usually for nothing or at rates that were lower than his normal charges, and often bringing gifts, like the pieces of drilling equipment, odd lengths of timber, old sheets of iron, an occasional roll of fencing wire or a bag of nails. Saleem Benn insisted the items were things he had found on other properties where, as he put it, their need no longer existed. He swore they had been honestly acquired and, as he was an honourable man who would have found argument or doubt offensive, Adam never argued and tried not to doubt. The gifts were priceless.

There was good top feed in this area. Little grass grew but the bushes were plentiful and the sheep had developed a taste for them. Moreover, the bush would survive when grass died. The plants, he had reasoned, would be an essential factor in his survival and, eventually, his success on this property. They were native to the region and well able to grow where the ground either was as hard as rock or as loose as driftsand. They could withstand the hottest summers and all but the most cruel droughts. They were even the right height for his sheep. The animals would graze happily on these miserable bushes, stripping the foliage without bending their necks. Whether that mattered Adam was not sure, but he liked to persuade himself that a sheep that ate comfortably would grow better wool.

The salt bush and the blue bush and all the other edible plants that managed to grow on the vast spread of land he now owned were assets as precious as gold bars in the bank. They were plants as suited to their environment as camels to sand or birds to the air. Where there was little water, they gained what they needed by absorbing dew or by burrowing long roots into sandhills to search for the faintest trace of moisture. The root systems were often marvels of tubes and branches and hair-like ends, greater in size, more complex in structure and more beautiful in appearance than that part of the bush compelled to exist above ground.

The roots of certain plants acted as reservoirs, storing sufficient fluid to sustain the bush in dry times. Adam had known these plants all his life. As a child, he had been taught to recognize those that held water underground. He knew where to dig for their roots and many times had slaked a raging thirst by getting on his knees in sand and wrenching out a long, thin, tubular root and cutting himself a two-foot length and drinking from it, raising it above his head and sucking like a child trying to extract the last delicious drop from a drinking straw. The roots were full of grit and he had to draw through clenched teeth to filter out the dirt, but the water was sweet.

Adam had gained the lease to a huge tract of land: his property covered an area of one thousand, three hundred and thirty-seven square miles. Awesome though it was in size, it was not the biggest in the country or even the largest in the area. Spreads farther to the north dwarfed his but it was still a grand total. One thousand, three hundred and thirty-seven square miles! Not acres, he had to tell people when he had been south buying stock, but square miles. There were many parts of his property he had not yet seen. It was just too big for him to cover in only a year.

There were things he had to do in those twelve months to honour the terms of his lease. "Improvements", they were called in the quaint language of officialdom – fences and sheds to erect, a homestead to build, bores to drill. Meeting these obligations and trying to make money as soon as possible meant concentrating on the most promising parts of his property. He would inspect other areas next year or the year after.

The eastern boundary was formed by the shoreline of Lake Eyre. Adam had been to the lake once. He had half expected to find water, even though he knew the salt lakes in the northern part of South Australia were almost perpetually dry. Even so, the first sight of the lake shocked him. He had ridden to a bay on the western shore, following the line of a watercourse until the ground around the creek became too soft for the horse. He had then ascended a flat-topped hill whose sides glistened with black boulders, and from the hill saw the lake.

It was dry. In the distance the salt was hard and as bright as a mirror, but closer to the shore the lake was rimmed by a murky rainbow of colours. Shoals of slate-blue mud, as deadly as quicksand, bruised the surface. Between them lay pavements of pink clay, dried and cracked and tilted into crazed, uneven patterns. Where the bay curled between two headlands, its edges carried a variety of water marks: a network of white lines where salt had hardened into crystalline ridges, yellow stains where sulphurous pigments had been swept across the salt, and black lines where vegetation had gathered and dried and decayed. Tiny islands of brown pimpled the surface, some bearing crusty rims of salt as bright as painted fences. Near the tip of the bay was a circle of dense grey where fish had been trapped in a flurry of despair and died and rotted.

The low cliffs edging the lake were splotched with muted tones. The crust was brown or pale yellow. The exposed sides were scored with ridges of grey silicrete or bands of kaolin, as brilliant as white enamel. Shards of gypsum, dumped like truckloads of broken glass, flashed silver relections.

Adam did not ride beyond the hill. The shore looked soft and sour and evil. The mare would sink to her withers in that treacherous region. He withdrew and had not been back.

He was well aware of the reason why his holding was so big. It was to give him a chance. Up here, size was the only counterbalancing weapon in the settler's battle against nature. The authorities knew it; the more difficult the land, the larger the area of the lease they granted. With a truly big parcel of land, there was a chance that a shower of rain might dampen one corner even if the rest of the property was scorched by drought. Or, if no rain fell, a wise and energetic operator might just keep his stock alive by moving them from one desiccated paddock to the next, and thus find enough feed to keep his flock or herd on its legs.

There had been occasions, particularly during the long summer when the horizon drew close and buckled and danced with constant heat hazes, when Adam had doubted the wisdom of coming to Lake Eyre. In weak moments he had wished that this place – his place – had been farther south where rain fell and grass grew and normal things happened. But those had been weak moments and they had been rare. They were idle wishes. Stupid dreams. They happened when he was more tired than normal or reeling from a day that had provided more than the usual dose of frustration and disappointment. Like the time some sheep strayed and dingoes took six of them in one night, or the time the drill broke and jammed one hundred and fifty feet down and, being unable to retrieve it, he had to abandon all that equipment. Or when a gust of wind lifted sheets of iron from a partly completed roof and flung them so far and bent them so badly it took him a day to recover and straighten them. No, the reality, Adam knew, was that his property was in the driest region of Australia. The average annual rainfall was about four inches a year. That much rain could fall in one night and be followed by two years of drought. It was that sort of country: either stricken by drought or ravaged by flood. It was a land of extremes where the only certainty was that life would be hard. He had to accept the fact that his property was on the western side of the continent's biggest salt lake in a region of sand dunes and clay pans and marauding dingoes, where rain rarely fell and grass grew reluctantly and he was there, essentially, because no one else wanted the land and it was the only place he could afford. He was a man of the outback. The back of beyond. The Never Never. Call it what cliché you liked, this miserable patch of semi-desert on the western side of Lake Eyre was his type of country and if he were to succeed in life, to do the things he had always wanted to do, it would have to be here.

As far as he knew, the property had only one source of surface water. That was the mound spring to which Saleem Benn had taken them all those years ago. It was a prolific source and the water was good and it was there that he had decided to build his house. However, the venture would fail with only one source, no matter how abundant the supply. His stock would be limited to eating the feed they could get within close range of that water, which meant he would be wasting more than one thousand, three hundred square miles of land.

He needed more water, in new locations. Nature had provided the potential food. He had to provide the water, and that meant digging for it.

If Adam was an expert in one field, it was in finding underground water and bringing it to the surface. That had been his father's profession, and Adam had learnt it with him and practised it after him. He had been drilling, burrowing and scraping for water for as long as he could remember. Other boys' first memories were of simple homely things – the room where they slept, a pet dog, smells from the kitchen, the pattern on a rug, a favourite toy, brothers and sisters. Adam remembered drilling-rigs. Not a house or a room or a family, but tall gaunt towers of metal tubes, rearing above some bare paddock. Tall rigs and his father's anxious face as he came to check that his infant son was all right. And the clank of machinery and the sweet smell of deep, damp earth being spilled on the surface.

He had thought deeply about the matter of underground water and was convinced it must exist beneath his land. The bed of Lake Eyre was below sea level and the whole area was in a low basin which drained water from a huge slab of central Australia. The lake itself covered four thousand, eight hundred square miles. It might be dry most of the time but it was a lake and there were watermarks around its shores and that meant it sometimes held water. The water might come down rivers from Western Queensland or the Northern Territory but, wherever the floods came from, they filled the lake, and a deep lake that spread across four thousand, eight hundred square miles could contain an enormous amount of water. Some of it would have evaporated but some of it must have soaked into the ground. There could be, should be, millions of tons of water under the ground all around the lake, so that if you drilled a hole in a likely place you should strike water. He was certain it was there.

He drilled a few holes in promising places and found water in two. Choosing the location was a matter of experience of studying the surrounding country – the jut of hills, the angle and placement of rock outcrops, and other clues to what might lie beneath the earth's crust – and then sinking the bit above the spot where he judged impervious rock had trapped a reservoir of good, salt-free water. A second and more important requirement was to sink the hole where water was needed.

It was this need which posed the biggest problem and demanded the most planning.

On a normal sheep station, where dams stored water and creeks trickled through the hollows, the animals could drink where and when they wanted. But at Lake Eyre West, Lot B, a delicate balance existed. The sheep could only eat within a certain range of water, for five miles was about as far as they could walk. They could drink, walk five miles to graze, walk five miles back and drink again. But if it was six miles or more to the nearest feed they would probably die of thirst on their return journey. If Adam tried to operate his station with just the mound spring as a source of water, the sheep would gradually strip all the top feed until the spring was surrounded by a five-mile-wide circle of bare earth. And then they would die and he would be ruined.

He had worked out that he needed a minimum of two bores, and they had to be sufficiently distanced from each other to open up the maximum amount of land for grazing. They had to be less than a day's walk apart and situated where plenty of feed existed. They also had to be away from the spring. That was where he had decided to build the homestead, and he had no desire to share his water with nearly a thousand head of bleating, stinking, defecating, fly-attracting sheep.

Adam stayed at the site of the second bore for two more days until work on the trough and windmill was completed. Neither man had much sleep, for dingoes prowled the hills at night and the sheep were restless. On the third morning, Jimmy followed the trail of a wild dog that had come particularly close. He saw it loping through the bushes nearly a hundred yards away and felled it with a single shot through the chest.

Later that morning, Adam rode back to the homestead to prepare for the arrival of Heather and his infant daughter.

TWO

Trailing a long stream of black smoke, the locomotive hauled its string of carriages through the Pichi Richi Pass. It curled through the narrowest gap in the hills, chuffing with exertion. It followed a twist of sand that was a river. It ran under the shadow of a cliff and emerged into the speckled light filtering through the leaves of a strand of white-trunked gums. Gradually, the hills eased in height and other larger hills could be seen in the distance. The line swung to the right and the carriages rocked and tugged at their couplings. The train clattered across a wooden bridge.

Inside the leading carriage, the conductor was making slow progress down the corridor. He walked with the gait of a sailor used to rough seas, with his legs splayed wide to brace himself against the swaying and the jolting.

'Just a little rough through here,' he said, and smiled down at the young woman with the baby in her arms. She struggled to find her ticket.

'No need to rush,' he said and bent to look out the window. A blur of timber rushed past. 'How far are you going?'

'William Creek.'

'Oh, well you've got a long way to go yet. How's the young fellow enjoying the ride?'

'Young girl,' she corrected, and handed him her ticket, 'Very well, thank you.'

'Long trips are hard on babies,' the conductor said.

'It's harder on the mother.'

He laughed, managing to inject a massive dose of sympathy in

533

the sound. 'We'll be at Quorn soon. You can get off for a few minutes and stretch your legs.'

'Would you like to mind the baby?'

He looked at her, trying to determine if she were joking, but was baffled by her hard stare. 'I'd love to,' he said eventually, 'but I don't think my masters would appreciate it. They think I should do other things, you see.' He touched his cap and moved on.

Heather Ross brushed a fly from her daughter's face.

Cassandra Elizabeth Ross, as dark as her mother was fair and nearly three months old, was asleep. She had had a disturbed night. The train into Port Pirie had been as cold as an icebox, there had been a long delay while they changed trains, rain had swept the station and her mother had coughed a great deal, both from a cold and from the pungent fumes drifting from the town's smelter.

Cassandra had been born with long and soft black hair. That hair had gone within the first month, to be replaced by a crop of equally dark hair that was spreading from the crown. It tended to stick up. Heather licked her fingers and tried to smooth the offending projections in place. She would be glad when the hair grew longer and softer and covered the scalp completely. She licked her fingers once more to smooth down one particularly obstinate strand which projected from the back of the scalp like a fine black feather. The baby's cheeks were fat and looked even fatter as she slept with a blanket framing her face. Heather adjusted the blanket and smoothed Cassandra's cheeks. With that fat face and black hair and smooth, olive skin, she looked disturbingly like ... well, she didn't dare express the thought but people had called her a 'little darkie'. Only in jest, of course. But she was so dark! How could that be, Heather wondered, when both she and Adam were so fair? She had thought about it many times and some of the possibilities were worrying. She meant to discuss them with Adam ...

Adam had not seen the baby. He had travelled to Nyngan last year soon after he had received the news that Heather was pregnant. He had not stayed, of course, Heather reminded herself, but had rushed back to start developing this new property to which he had committed them. Why he wanted to bury them in some remote place she had no idea. She had pleaded with him to move to Sydney and to live a normal ordinary life where she would be close to some of her friends, but he had this bee in his bonnet about establishing his own sheep station even if the only

534

land he could afford was in the most God-forsaken part of the country. You'd think he'd have the sense to give up after that disaster in Western Australia. Other men would, and do what their wives wanted them to do. Not Adam Ross. Why, she asked herself, did she have to be the one who had married a man who was so perversely stubborn, who was so ... different?

The train rattled over a long bridge. Jolted briefly from her thoughts, she saw trees, all gnarled and knobbled and lining a creek with real water. Sunlight was striking the water, sparking mirror flashes from its surface. Beyond the creek was a field of wheat as brittle and stark as upturned brooms. Above it wheeled a flock of cockatoos.

She turned, seeing nothing that pleased her.

She had thought of remaining in New South Wales and forcing Adam to stay with her. Other women would have done that. They would have put their foot down. Those other women would not have tolerated their husband running off to the west just after they were married, or losing all that money on some addle-brained venture to buy land, or not even being at her side when the baby had been born. Not to mention buying or leasing, or whatever it was, some land somewhere in South Australia.

She had heard Adelaide was nice. A lot of churches and pretty parklands. William Creek was a long way from Adelaide, though, and she didn't like the look of the land they were now passing. It seemed just as dry as the country around Nyngan. There were more hills but they seemed rocky and all the land had a harsh look about it. Maybe Lake Eyre would be better. She had looked it up in the school atlas. It seemed very large. Maybe they could go swimming or boating. Adam hadn't mentioned that. It could be nice. She was trying very hard, she assured herself, to be fair. No one could say she would not try to like this new place.

Adam had mentioned, in one of his clumsy little letters, the possibility of giving the property a native name, but that seemed absurd. She rather liked 'The Dunes'. Adam had written that there were sand dunes on the land. She had seen *The Desert Song* on stage in Sydney once and gone to the movies to see Rudolph Valentino in *The Sheikh*. The desert seemed such a romantic place and in those moments when she had rather missed Adam and let her mind ramble a little, she imagined herself in sumptuous luxury within a huge tent and Adam bursting in, dressed like Valentino.

Maybe they could have a tennis court. Adam had not been to

the land when he had last seen her but he said he was sure there would be plenty of flat spaces for a court. A court – boating on the lake – soft sand dunes, glowing gold in the setting sun. It could be all right.

The train was slowing. That would be for the next station. What was it called? Quorn. With her free hand, she straightened her hair.

Why was she travelling to join Adam? Her face, reflected brightly in the glass of the carriage window, demanded honesty. Because she had no choice. After her father's death, after the way they had been hounded for money, after the dreadful things people had started to say about them, after her mother's own sister had refused to let them live with her, there was simply no alternative.

Heather turned at the sound of someone approaching.

'You've been a long time,' she said.

Her mother was still drying her hands.

'There were two people waiting in front of me,' Mrs Maguire said, 'including one wretched man who looked as though he had been drinking. Are we stopping?'

'Yes. There's a station here where we can stretch our legs. Do you feel like some exercise.'

'I feel maybe I should get off the train and go back home.'

'You have no home, mother.'

'You know what I mean,' she said, sitting beside Heather and peering at the baby, her face soft with concern. 'I feel terrible about this.'

'Nonsense!'

'No, it's not. You should have told Adam I was coming with you.'

'What difference would it have made? You are my mother. You have nowhere to live. So you will live with us.'

'You still should have told him.' She said the words softly, anxious to have the final say but not wanting to provoke an argument. Her voice trailed into a series of grunts as though she were continuing the discussion in the deepest recesses of her body.

'You are impossible, mother!' Heather said and turned her attention to the approaching railway platform. Brakes grinding, the train rolled into Quorn station.

Nellie watched the train stop. She picked up her bag and walked towards the nearest second-class carriage. The man who had been standing beside her followed, hesitating near the doorway.

'You're being very foolish,' he said.

'I know,' she said and turned. She extended a hand. 'Thanks for all you've done. You've been really good to me in the last six months.'

The man shook his head. He was thick-set with skin of a dusty brown colour and eyes that bore a hint of Chinese ancestry. He was about forty, with a touch of grey in his hair. He was wearing his best clothes.

'I don't want to shake your hand,' he said his voice curling with misery.

She moved forward and kissed him lightly.

'And I don't want you to kiss me goodbye, either. I just want you to stay. You're being crazy. You've got nothing to go to.'

'Maybe,' she said. 'But you know me, Norm. Always restless. When I feel I have to do something, I have to do it.'

'You've got a good job here. Or you had a good job.'

'I know. Thank you.'

A man squeezed past her to enter the carriage.

Norm rubbed his hands in anguish. 'And you know how I feel about you.'

'Goodbye,' she said and, smiling, turned to enter the carriage. It had many empty seats. She chose one and put her bag beside her to discourage anyone from sitting there. She wanted to be alone. She ignored the man on the platform.

Instinctively she knew he was still there, rubbing his hands and rolling his head in anguish. She should never have gone to work for him. He was a good, decent man and he seemed to be making money from his guest house. She had slept with him a few times and why not? She had feelings and desires like other women and just because she loved another man didn't mean she had to live like a nun.

Except she couldn't stand it any longer. Norm had suddenly got serious and that had made her feel bad. If he had been some sort of half-drunken slob, or just a lecherous louse like so many men she had known, she could have tolerated things. She could play games as well as anyone. A bit of bedding to relieve the tension was all right – like a safety valve. Only you had to do it with someone who didn't matter or didn't care.

Norm didn't matter much but he was a decent man and he did care. And that made her think even more of Adam. So much that she could no longer stay here and wonder how he was, and whether he was working too hard, and whether that cold fish of a wife of his had gone to join him and was helping him.

She hadn't seen Adam since that day last year when he had received the letter from Nyngan. He had been so confused. A little shocked, a little proud and terribly guilty. Guilty because he had left his wife for so many weeks and she had been pregnant with his child, and guilty because he had slept with another woman. Men, she thought, were such helpless children, inclined – indeed almost destined – to stray and yet tormented by such misery when they did. They were slaves to a sense of duty they didn't understand and couldn't explain and Adam, being more perfect than any man she had ever known, was a perfect example.

He was stupid to behave the way he did and to go back to a wife who, Nellie judged, was totally unsuited to him. It was that weird sense of duty, of doing what was 'right', of doing what other people expected of him, not what he himself wanted to do. And all because of the most natural thing in the world: reproducing.

She had stayed away from him until he had left town. That was just silly – her own strange sense of doing what was 'right'. We are all crazy, she told herself. Men or women, we do things we don't want to do, worry about what other people expect us to do, and hurt ourselves and those we love by saying nothing when we should speak, doing nothing when we should act, or doing one thing when our instincts and desires screamed at us to do something else.

She had to see Adam again. Or at least be close to him and find out what was happening to him.

I am crazy, she said to herself, and smiled happily. That is why I have chucked my job, broken Norm's heart, and bought a ticket to Marree. I might get a job there or I might not. Who cares? All I know is I want to do it.

The whistle blew. Passengers who had been strolling along the platform scurried for their carriages. A tall young woman, strikingly good-looking and carrying a baby, hurried towards the front of the train. Norm had not moved. His face was torn between the hope that Nellie might still walk from the carriage and the growing certainty that she was leaving.

She closed her eyes and thought of Adam. The train began to move.

Josef Hoffman came into the house, his face flushed with anger. He had argued with his father once more. He stormed into the kitchen. His mother backed against the sink. She had heard the two men shouting.

'That bastard ...' Josef began.

His mother blinked. She could absorb angry words but not profanity. 'You will not swear,' she said.

'I fucking well will if I feel like it!' he roared and immediately regretted it. He had never used that word in front of his mother.

She said nothing but her face was bleached of colour.

'I'm sorry,' Josef said, 'but he keeps on treating me like a child, and an idiot at that.' He breathed heavily, trying to control himself.

'He is trying to teach you the business.'

'No, he's not! He's trying to show me how much he knows and make me look like a fool.'

'You must make allowances, Josef. He's not well.'

'You can say that again! He's mad.'

Mrs Hoffman started to protest but her words were interrupted by the arrival of Josef's father. He strode into the kitchen, his face red with fury.

'Did I hear you swearing at your mother, you foul-mouthed young dog?'

'The word is pup. You should learn to speak proper English,' Josef said.

'How do you dare say that?' he shouted.

'Easily.' Josef was out to hurt now. 'You've been here all these years and every time you open your mouth you make a fool of yourself.'

Mrs Hoffman moved between them. 'Stop! This is awful.'

'Out of my way, woman!' Hoffman said, his eyes burning.

'Don't you touch mother!'

'And what will you do, pup?'

'Please!' she shouted, but Hoffman pushed her away.

'What will you do, eh?' the older man taunted, his hands raised. Josef lifted his fists but then stopped and took a step back.

'You'd love that, wouldn't you?' he said. 'You know I could flatten you, you silly old crock, but if I hit you, you'd go around and say I was a brute and that'd make you feel good. It'd make you right and me wrong and you'd talk about it forever. You're just a silly old turd.'

'Josef!' His mother spun towards him.

'Oh, for Christ's sake, every time I say something wicked it's "Oh, Josef!"' He mimicked her cry. 'You're as bad as he is. If he's not complaining, you're pestering me. I'm not a child any more, mother. I'm a grown man, or haven't you noticed? I came back to help you two out for a few days and you've kept me down here for the best part of a year. Every time I wanted to leave, it was "Oh Josef, you can't go because your father's not well. He needs you to run the business." And when I try to help, he keeps on nit-picking and criticizing and treating me like the village fool.'

'Don't speak to your mother like that,' Hoffman said.

'What is this? The anti-Josef society? I can't please either of you.' He stalked from the room, halting beyond the doorway. 'That's it this time. I'm off!'

'Where to?' the man mocked. 'You'll be back in a week begging for a meal and a blanket to sleep under.'

'Bullshit!' Josef said. 'I'm going back to join Adam.'

'Adam! That's all you talk about. Young Adam's all right, but he's wasting his life and you want to rush off and join him?'

'I'm going to.'

'What? In the middle of nowhere? And what does he know about living on the land? He's just a boy and ...'

'He's not a boy!' Josef shouted. 'Jesus Christ, you annoy me! He's a grown man and he knows a bloody sight more about raising sheep than you do about growing grapes.' Josef turned, conscious that his mother was crying. 'Just because you couldn't make a success of something doesn't mean he can't. Or I can't.' Without looking back he went to his room. He collected his belongings and left without saying goodbye.

THREE

The house was not impressive. No matter how Adam looked at it – from the shade of the beefwood tree which grew in regal isolation two hundred yards from the front door, from the mound spring on one side of the building, from the eroded bank that was the first step in the climb up the low hills far to the back of the house, or from the gathering of coolibahs which gave protection from the prevailing winds and laid gentle shadows to ease the worst of the afternoon's heat – it was not impressive. The most remarkable thing about it was that it was there at all. But only someone who had seen the area before the house was built and who had witnessed Adam's labours and who understood the problems he had overcome would appreciate the near miracle he had wrought.

He had built the homestead virtually on his own. Jimmy had helped him on occasions, but Jimmy's main job was to look after the sheep and to help with the construction of the bores and that had left him with few opportunities to assist in house-building. Saleem Benn had occasionally lifted something to help Adam during his work on the house or used one of his camels to haul heavy items into place, but the Afghan was only there every few weeks and, although he sometimes stayed a few night because he enjoyed the company, his sessions of work were rare. No, this was a house built by one man, and by a man who had not built a house before.

And it looked like it.

To start with, the building was small. It had to be, because he lacked the materials, the expert assistance and, above all, the money to build a large home. He would construct another, larger house when he was established. He had heard that Parliament House, opened in Canberra only nine years earlier, was also a temporary structure to be replaced by a permanent building at an appropriate time, so he felt he was following a worthwhile precedent.

Nor was the house straight. That did not matter, he told himself every time he looked at the bend in the roof that it reminded him of the sway in a lame horse's back. Nothing in nature is dead straight so he had merely given the house a natural look. The sway was caused by the fact that he had to use what materials were available, and the bend in the roof line just sort of happened. It was strong enough.

He made two walls of mud brick, using a style of construction he had seen some years before on old mission buildings around Lake Kopperamanna on the Birdsville Track. He used the bricks on the western wall, where the need for heat insulation would be greatest, and on the eastern end to provide symmetry. The front and back walls were a mixture of stone and timber. He had made two windows at the front and one at the back. There was no glass, but he had made wooden shutters and bag curtains. He had divided the building into two rooms, using bags stretched across light wooden frames. There was one bedroom and a living room/kitchen, in which he had installed a wood-burning stove and

541

his pride and joy, a new kerosene refrigerator.

Near the spring was a wash house with a bath he had cut from a forty-four-gallon drum and tubs made from the same source. A lavatory with a door and a seat, built above a deep trench he had spent three days digging, was beyond the spring.

He looked at the house and wondered what Heather would say. He had not seen her for nearly nine months and, as sometimes happens when a person is isolated in a harsh environment where the nights are often lonely, his image of her had blurred. In the blurring it had softened and Heather had, through bearing his child, become a more loving and caring creature. She understood what he was trying to do and would help him while things were still tough. He was looking forward with intense enthusiasm to working with his wife to develop this place, even savouring the prospect of years of hard work with his wife at his side. And he was yearning to meet his daughter.

He had received just two letters from Heather – one announcing the birth and the other advising him of the details of her journey to William Creek. The letter had contained little more than basic information about the baby. He knew the name (he had not been asked what names he liked but rather fancied Cassie) and he knew she was a big baby with dark features and long dark hair, and he longed to see her for himself, to hold her and feel her tiny fingers grasping his. He did not think of her as a baby who might cry or vomit or foul her nappies. She was, he was certain, a perfect child, a sort of younger version of Shirley Temple whom he had seen at the pictures before leaving Port Augusta. He had been so moved by that story he had cried.

Cassie's birth had awakened deep feelings within him, and helped to straighten him out. He felt older, more responsible, and he was determined to be a good husband. He had tried to wipe away the memory of some of the things he had done. Particularly with Nellie. He was ashamed about that.

He often dreamed of Nellie and that worried him. Sometimes they were loving dreams, a series of placid images of the two of them sitting, touching, talking. Others were wild and erotic and he would awake sweating with guilt. He would try to change the fantasy, to expunge the lead character and substitute Heather, and then go back to sleep and resume the dream with Heather doing the loving and touching and talking, and Heather sharing the erotic moments. But it never worked.

*

542

Knowing Mrs Ross was due soon, Saleem Benn rode from William Creek, bringing some stores and a present: seeds for vegetables and flowers. 'You will want to keep your wife busy while you are not here,' he said. 'The flowers are a vanity but women like such things and in truth the house could do with some colour.'

'What do you think of it?' Adam asked him. 'Be honest.'

'The house?' The old man scratched his nose. 'It is a fine dwelling. Cleverly thought about and very strong. It will be comfortable and keep out the dust and the heat and even the rain – if we ever see such a thing again. Your wife will be overjoyed.'

Adam too scratched his nose. 'It's not square.'

Saleem Benn let his finger slip to his chin. His eyes lingered over the uneven roof. A hint of amusement quickly vanished. He examined the twists in the main wooden uprights which Adam had fashioned from knotted tree trunks. True, they rambled from the floor to the roof but the timber was bonded to the stones of the wall by mud which had been applied in such a way as to suggest a vertical line. And while the stone walls slanted, it was because Adam had run out of large stones and been forced to put the big ones at the bottom and use a jumble of little ones at the top. The result, inevitably, was that the wall leaned inwards. Still, it was extremely strong.

'Who would choose to live in a square house?' he said simply, opening his arms to amplify the stupidity of such a thought. 'In any event, my friend, this is merely a shelter, a place to eat and sleep and to take refuge when the weather would drive us from beneath the roof of our creator. Let me assure you, it has far more substance and grace than the tents I have been forced to use for most of my years,' he said, shaking his head at past memories. 'No, it is a fine building, but that's not really important.'

Adam looked at him quizzically.

'What matters is what you have out there. Your land. Your water. Your animals. The food they must eat. And the things you have built which will make you money.' He gestured toward the stockyard and shed, both hewn from local timber, which Adam had sited north of the spring. 'You have not come here to live in a grand house but to make money. That is something you must not forget. Those structures which will help you earn money are far more important than a simple dwelling. Even so,' he added, grasping Adam by both shoulders, 'you can be very proud of the house you have built here, where man has not lived before. It will

543

provide a handsome shelter for your child and wife. Mrs Ross will be full of admiration.'

Adam hoped Saleem Benn was correct, that Heather would like the house, and would praise him for what he had done. It was important to him. He was establishing the property for himself because it was his dream, but he was building the house for his wife. He could have lived happily in a tent for a few years, or made himself a crude bough shelter as Jimmy did, and spent his time building stockyards and fences and bores and troughs, but he couldn't expect his wife and infant daughter to sleep in the open. He had built the best house he could and while he was honest enough to see flaws in its appearance and knew it was essentially little more than a rough hut, he was proud of what he had accomplished. 'Do you really think she'll like it?'

The years had not dimmed Saleem Benn's proclivity towards grand gestures. He raised a palm to the sky, 'Are the heavens blue?' he said, searching for a sign that he might be wrong. Finding none, he allowed his hand to sweep the horizon. 'Are the sands coloured? Does a man need a woman?' he winked. 'And woman need man? My friend, you are as nervous as a groom who has never laid eyes on his bride. But you have known this woman and she has submitted to you and borne you a child. A daughter, admittedly, but nonetheless a child. Of course she will like this home, over which you have laboured for so many months. She will fall at your feet and marvel at the deeds you have performed.'

Adam smiled.

'Why do you laugh?'

'I can't see Heather doing that.'

Saleem Benn looked puzzled. 'She should. You have done miracles. You have never faltered in your resolve or your labours. Is she obedient?'

Adam was trying to think of an appropriate answer when Saleem Benn, obviously feeling the question required no response, continued: 'You will need many sons to work this property. It is a great pity your customs do not allow a man to take more than one wife. It would be so practical, but still, there are many things about your country that I do not understand. Tell me, is this single wife of yours a resourceful woman? Will she know how to make the best use of the seeds I have brought?'

'I think so,' Adam said, trying to sound convincing. 'Her family had a beautiful garden.'

Adam recalled the trees and shrubs and blooms of the

544

stationmaster's shady yard at Nyngan. Saleem Benn contemplated a vision of vines and furrowed earth and nodded in satisfaction.

'How are things with you?' Adam said, anxious to change the direction of the conversation.

'We are in difficult times with poverty as prevalent as drought, but sometimes I feel the authorities take delight in making our lives even more tiresome.'

'Why?' Adam said. 'What's happened?'

'It is called progress, but I believe it is the hand of the devil.'

'What is?'

Saleem Benn breathed heavily. 'As you know, the railway line was extended from Oodnadatta to Alice Springs seven years ago. Your Bible talks of seven good years and seven lean years. You're aware of that?'

Adam shook his head.

'Really, you must learn to read your own bible! A man without belief is like a ship without a rudder, or that fancy red car of yours without a steering wheel. In any case, those seven years have been lean years for those of us who operate camels. Now, virtually everything to the north goes by the railway. Did you know that twenty years ago there were fifteen hundred camels in Marree alone? The way things are going, there will be none left in another twenty years.'

'All because of the railway to Alice Springs?' Adam asked.

'No, no, no! We could survive with the steam train. There are still many people like yourself who live far from the railway line and needs goods and supplies brought to them. But the authorities are now starting to give mail contracts to men with trucks rather than men with camels.'

'For short hauls?'

'No. A gentleman with the curious name of Ding has been granted the mail contract for the Marree to Birdsville run and he will use a truck.'

'You're joking!' Adam said, knowing that the other man was not. 'And this Mr Ding is going to take the mail to Birdsville regularly?'

'Every fortnight.' He smiled ruefully. It was the smile a sportsman uses to cover the hurt of a defeat. 'They will use a six-wheeled truck.'

'But that's almost impossible country for a truck. To do it regularly, that is. What about when it rains, or when it's dry and the sand's too soft?'

'It is called progress, my friend. And, of course, it is all to do with money. In good times, a truck is faster and cheaper.'

'It won't work.'

Saleem Benn looked sad. 'It will, in time. My friend, I remember the camels of thirty years ago and they were precisely the same as the camels I have today. I also remember the motor vehicles of thirty years ago. They were the toys of the rich men and they were evil-smelling, spluttering devices that were always breaking down. Today, the motor vehicle has improved a hundredfold and it is used by men of all classes – even mailmen. Within ten years it will be even more reliable and within twenty ...' His eyes fluttered in distress. 'The railway was the beginning of the end. This latest move, I feel, is the end.'

'What will you do?'

Saleem Benn said nothing.

'You could buy trucks,' Adam suggested.

'No.' He scratched his back and then spent a few moments examining his fingernails for the source of the irritation. 'I do not understand motor vehicles,' he said evenly. 'They are the future. I am of the past. In any case, I am growing weary of all the travel I have to peform just to earn a modest living. So I am at the point of making a decision. I think I will become a shopkeeper.'

'A shopkeeper?' Adam could not imagine him behind a counter.

'Why not? I sell goods to people now. They are people who live in outlying places. I go to them because they cannot reach the store in town. But soon they will all have motor cars and when that happens, the only customers who will greet me and my camels will be those few benighted souls like you who live in impossible places. The rest will drive in their fine motor cars to the store in town, so I thought it an opportune time to become a storekeeper.'

'And sell camels?'

'Who would buy them?' He gestured hopelessly, but it was such an exaggerated movement that Adam knew more was coming. 'Unless I could find someone with a genuine need for such animals. Someone who could use them and profit from them and care for them.'

'Someone who lived in country like this?' Adam dared not look the other man in the face. He was thinking of the ways a camel could be used on his property. In exploration, to start with. A camel could take him to all parts of the land and help him search for another spring or other patches of good feed. And the beasts would be marvellous for hauling things. His mind raced.

Saleem Benn was smiling. 'I will keep some. The best. I could not part with them. Nor would I cease to operate a transport service entirely. I would still service some of my better customers, until someone invents a mechanical camel and puts me out of business entirely.'

'You'll come here?'

'Of course. Now tell me, my dear young friend, do I detect a glimmer of interest on your part in acquiring some of my animals?'

'Certainly! If I could afford them.'

'Ah. We will talk about that later.'

'This store you want to start,' Adam said, 'where will it be?'

'I may open more than one. I have reasoned that if I cannot compete against the railway, I might as well make use of it. Therefore, I am considering opening stores in Marree and up this way at William Creek. I can get my supplies by rail, serve the local communities and use the stores as depots from which to operate my depleted fleet of camels.' He scratched his nose once more. It was a prominent, demanding nose on which he lavished much attention. He sniffed, and let his nose sample air from several directions.

Adam watched, amused. Saleem Benn was an entertaining man to observe.

'There could be a storm,' the old man said absent-mindedly. 'Not today. Tomorrow or the day after. Yes, you know, Adam, the more I think of the prospect of becoming a simple shopkeeper, the more entertaining I find the idea.'

'When are you going to do all this?' Adam asked.

'Soon, my friend, soon. Now, are you going to force an old man to stand out in the sun or will you invite him to inspect the interior of your fine new house?'

The railway line split the town of Marree in half. To the right, where a flat plain ended in a bristle of low scrub, was a collection of huts and shanties, made of wood and iron and hessian and ringed by debris. Scattered beyond them were several crude wurlies. Between the shanties and wurlies, some camels grazed. Close to the line, and visible only as the train slid into the railway station, were a series of water tanks and a row of stone buildings. They were railway buildings: an office, a storeroom and a few residences for staff assigned to work in this outpost where the way to the north forked – Birdsville and Queensland to the north-east, Alice Springs and the Northern Territory to the north-west.

Nellie frowned. This was not what she had expected. There was no proper town and without shops and buildings and people with money she could not get work.

She could not see what was on the other side of the line for a few moments because two men were standing in the train corridor and blocking her view. They were struggling to free a saddle from an overhead luggage rack. When they moved, muttering profanities, she saw a wide and dusty road lined on its far side by a row of buildings. A store, by the look of the sacks piled against its front. Some other buildings that could have been shops. A two-storeyed brick structure with a wooden verandah on the first floor. This was better. She stood and walked to the door.

A railway official waited outside. He helped a white woman with her bag and then watched Nellie attempt to leave. Her bag jammed in the doorway.

'Come on, you're blocking the door,' he snarled.

She retreated a step, straightened her bag, and left the carriage. 'Thanks for the help,' she said.

'You're a cheeky one,' he said, pushing up the brim of his cap. He smiled but it was not a pleasant smile.

'I thought you were supposed to help ladies,' she said.

'I do. Come on, get off.'

Nellie was hot and tired and hungry. She prepared a few words that might startle this man but thought better of delivering them. 'Is that a hotel across the road?' she asked, not looking at him.

'Yes, but you're not allowed in there. Are you staying in town?'

'I might be.' Other passengers brushed past, glancing at her with curiosity.

'Well, you go over there.' He pointed toward the wurlies on the gibber plain. 'That's the abo camp.'

'I don't want the abo camp,' she said and began walking to the back of the train, so she could cross the line and head for the town.

'You'll end up in the slammer,' he called after her. She ignored him. She walked towards the hotel. A man was sitting on a bench. His knees were crossed and he sat with his shoulders pressed against the wall, scrutinizing her as she approached.

'Where do you think you're going?' he said. A cigarette was stuck to his lower lip. He spoke with the utmost economy of muscular effort but the slight lip movement set the cigarette wobbling.

'Inside,' Nellie said, but despite her brave tone, she stopped on the road. A young woman, dark but not black, was approaching, carrying a small sack in her arms. She too stopped, apparently unwilling to get involved in the impending confrontation. A child followed, dragging a cotton reel on the end of a piece of string.

'Inside the pub? Like hell you are,' the man said. His voice was slurred. 'Go on, go back on the other side of the line.'

'Why?'

'Because I'm telling you.'

The railway man had appeared at the tail of the train and was watching with interest. 'She's a cheeky one, Harry!' he yelled.

'Bloody oath!' the man said. 'What are you after anyhow? Do you want a drink or a man or what?'

'I want a room,' Nellie said, firing each word slowly and deliberately at the man.

'Oh, you want a room, do you?' he said, mimicking her voice. 'Well go over and get a room with your friends on the other side of the line. Go and sleep with the dogs, like they do.' He laughed and looked about for any audience who might have appreciated his wit. Only the woman with the sack and the child with the cotton reel were within range and neither seemed entertained by his remarks. The woman now moved again and headed towards Nellie.

'Come with me,' she said simply. 'Otherwise there will be trouble.'

'But I want a room in the hotel,' Nellie said. 'I have money.'

'That doesn't matter,' the woman said. 'Just follow me. Don't stand here arguing with that man. He's drunk and he'll cause trouble.'

'Who are you calling drunk?' he said. 'Go back to your camels and take the gin with you.'

Nellie glared at the man. 'I thought you must have been the town idiot,' she said. 'Now I see you're just the town drunk.'

The man tried to stand, but slipped back on to the bench.

'Let's clear out,' the woman said.

'Yes, clear out,' the man said loudly. 'We don't want abos over here and we don't want your type in town.'

'I suppose you want more of your type,' Nellie shouted. 'I wonder why? Is the town short of donkeys or something?'

Awkwardly the man pushed himself to his feet, took one step and stopped to adjust his trousers which had slipped beneath the bulge in his stomach.

The woman hissed a warning. Sensing urgency, the child gathered the cotton reel and ran to its mother. 'Come,' she said to Nellie and began to walk along the street, away from the hotel. Nellie picked up her bag and followed.

The man at the railway yards had been watching. 'Good on you, Harry!' he shouted and waved. The man at the hotel spat and sat down.

'Bloody cheeky gin,' he muttered to himself. 'I'd shoot the lot of them.'

Nellie had to hurry to catch up to the woman. 'That man was a mongrel,' she said.

'You shouldn't answer him back like that,' the woman said but, despite the chastizing tone in her voice, her eyes shone with admiration.

'No one talks to me like that,' Nellie said. 'Who does he think he is?'

'He's white. That's enough.' She continued to walk rapidly. The child ran and skipped and looked up at Nellie with large, liquid brown eyes.

'Where are we going?' Nellie asked.

'Over the line.'

'Where to?'

'My place. What are you doing in town?'

'Looking for work.'

The woman paused. 'Why here?'

'It's a long story and it doesn't make much sense.'

'A man?'

'In a way.'

The woman put the bag over one shoulder. With her free hand she grasped the child's arm.

'Where've you come from?' she asked Nellie.

'Quorn. I was working in a guest house. I worked in a café in Port Augusta before that.'

'Married?'

'No. How about you?'

'Where do you think I got this boy from?' She smiled. She had a slim face and large soft eyes. 'Are you planning to stay long?'

'Depends.'

'We've got a shed at the back of our place. You can sleep there for a while if you like.'

'I don't want to put you out.'

'You won't do that. There's plenty of room. I hope you don't

550

mind camels.'

'Why? Are they in the shed too?'

The woman laughed. She was about Nellie's age, but taller. She walked with a catlike grace despite the weight of the sack. 'No, but there are a few of them in a paddock just behind the shed. They smell and make a bit of noise. My uncle has a lot of camels.'

'Are you Indian or something?' Nellie asked.

'Afghan,' the woman said, and changed direction. 'Follow me. We cross over the railway line here.'

FOUR

Adam scarcely slept the night before Heather's train was due at William Creek and when he did sleep, it was a rest disturbed by thoughts and dreams of Heather. Heather with him looking at the new house; Heather riding with him to inspect the number two bore; Heather and him walking among the sheep with him calming them and her patting the occasional lamb. She was no longer that hazy figure of recent dreams, his wife. This was Heather, clear and distinct. The dreams were confusing. Sometimes Heather was smiling and loving, her cheek pressed into his chest and her eyes warm with admiration for the things Adam had created in her absence. When he dreamed that, he felt good. But at other times, and with an awful clarity, Adam remembered the way Heather had reacted to some of his other achievements and then he thought of her looking at the house and laughing, a hurting, scornful laugh, and of her being frightened of sheep.

He had meant to clean the Alfa-Romeo so it would flash red and black where it was enamelled and sparkle silver in the bright places and look sensational parked on the dusty space outside the William Creek railway station. However, before leaving in the morning, Adam rode out to help Jimmy move the sheep back to the bore nearer the homestead and some of the flock strayed. The journey took two hours longer than Adam had scheduled and so there was no time to clean the car.

On the long drive to William Creek, across the hazardous Douglas creek system, Adam merely ran in his own wheel tracks, made on previous journeys to and from the railway. A back tyre punctured on the way. The wheel was difficult to remove and even harder to replace and the repair cost Adam almost an hour. By the time he had restarted the car he was filthy, with grease embedded in his nails and skin and hair grey with dust.

Not knowing the precise time, he was concerned that the train might reach the station before him and he drove hard, haunted by the spectre of Heather, baby in arms, pacing the tiny platform and with each step being more convinced her husband had finally deserted her. However, when he first saw the distant outline of William Creek – the water tower, the hotel, the spidery lines of the cattle yards – it was obvious that the train had not arrived. The place just slept. He slowed down. He knew where the people would be – in the hotel or at the station. They would be out of the sun, resting and waiting.

The station was a small building, flanked by fettlers' cottages. They flared heat, simple buildings as uninviting as tin boxes in an oven. Nearby, a line of peppercorns squatted on pools of shade. The cattle yards were empty but a visiting troop of cockatoos lined the upper rails and performed somersaults on the wires that braced the posts. They enjoyed the heat and the lack of human activity. Two dogs were sleeping in the street. Adam found a man sitting on the railway platform.

'Train not in yet?' Adam inquired.

'Be a couple of hours.'

'Running late?'

'Always late. Not as late as usual, though.'

Adam went to the water tower. He washed himself, even removing his shirt and using the long hose to shower the upper part of his body. He then brought the car over to the tower and washed it and wetted a cloth to wipe dust from the seats. Then he went to the hotel and drank a sarsparilla and ate a sandwich. He walked to the station and waited.

The air was still but thick with the threat of a storm. Adam searched the western horizon. Nothing yet. Only a faint darkening at the very bottom of the sky gave a hint of what might come. The dogs were stirring in the street. The cockatoos had gone from the cattle yard rails. The line to the south ended on a heat haze that appeared to turn the rails into wavering strips and played tricks with the eyes of those staring into its mysteries. One moment the distant rails would twitch, like a snake flicking the tip of its tail, then they would disappear under a sheen of haze. When the train first came into view, it too appeared as a series of surreal images, steamy shapes that puffed smoke and rose into the air and inverted themselves and stretched and compressed and danced on that moving set of rails. Then the images solidified. A real train puffing real smoke emerged from the vapours, and soon the line began to vibrate. The locomotive blew its shrill whistle. Several men joined Adam on the platform.

The train came in slowly, hissing and grinding and trailing steam and sparks. Behind the locomotive clanked a succession of goods trucks laden with crates and drums and bulges shrouded in canvas. Behind them were four carriages. Weary faces protruded from the windows.

A man wearing a blue cap watched the train stop. 'William Creek!' he shouted, above the clanking of buffers and couplings, and strode towards the guard's van at the rear of the train. A man descended from the first carriage, brushed his coat, and turned to help another passenger. Heather appeared. Baby in arms, she stepped cautiously on to the platform.

Adam ran to her. He stopped a few feet away, seeing for the first time the small face nestling in his wife's arms. The eyes were closed, cheeks chubby and squashed out of place by the blanket wrapped tightly around her. A strand of dark hair had strayed across the forehead.

'Thank heaven's that's over!' Heather said. 'We have had the most awful trip.'

Adam moved closer. He felt he should kiss her but instead said, 'How are you, Heather?' He removed his hat and played nervously with the brim.

'Tired. Filthy. Worn out. Otherwise fine.'

'And this is Cassie.' He was bursting with feelings but that was all he could say.

'Cassandra. Please don't call her Cassie.'

'Oh, Jesus, Heather!' he said, and kissed her. 'I've been thinking about you all the time.'

She seemed embarrassed and looked to see who was watching. A tall man with bowed legs and a hat satined by grease and dust was greeting a younger man who wore a city hat. Neither was interested in them.

'Would you like to hold your daughter?' she said.

Adam extended his arms. She stepped back. 'Your hands are so dirty,' she said, pulling the baby into her body.

'I had a flat tyre on the way in,' Adam said. 'I've washed them.'

'Well, I suppose it's all right if you don't touch her face.' She offered Cassandra Elizabeth Ross to her father. 'Just hold her in your arms and keep your hands away from her.' She prodded his arms into position and, for the first time, Adam held his daughter.

'I'll help with the bags,' Heather said.

'I'll do it.'

'No. You hold the baby.' Heather was looking beyond Adam. 'By the way, how far are we from the town?'

'This is it.'

'William Creek?' Her voice suggested some trick; that the train had stopped short of its destination just to torment her.

'That's right.' Adam grinned, sharing the joke with Cassandra who had opened her eyes and was struggling to focus them on the strange face above her. 'Isn't it, Cassie?' he said and, forgetting his instructions, stroked her cheek.

'I'll give you a hand, mother,' Adam heard Heather say. He looked up to see Mrs Maguire clambering from the train.

For several seconds, Adam was speechless. At first he thought he must have made some mistake; not understood something Heather had once said to him or not read correctly something she had written in one of her letters. But she had said nothing and written nothing. Of that he was sure. And Heather was behaving as though Adam should be aware that her mother was travelling with her. And I suppose, he added to himself, staying with them. Living with them. Then a thought occurred to him. She must have come to help Heather with the baby on the long train journey. That was it. She would probably return on the next train south.

Mrs Maguire busied herself looking elsewhere.

Heather reached for the baby. 'Maybe you should help mother with the bags,' she said, taking Cassandra and brushing the hair from her face. 'They're too heavy for me.' Adam went to the carriage door and took a suitcase.

'Hello, Mrs Maguire,' he said. 'Nice of you to help Heather like this.'

Mrs Maguire looked at him in astonishment.

It was only when he saw the two extra bags that Adam's doubts returned. 'Where will I put these?' he asked.

Heather had walked to the edge of the platform in case the main part of the town had been hidden behind the station's small shelter shed. She turned, still perplexed by the ghostly emptiness of William Creek.

'Why, with the others, of course. In the car. You've brought the car?'

Adam pointed to the Alfa. It was glinting in the sun. From this distance it looked remarkably clean.

'Oh, you've still got that funny car!' she said. 'Will it hold us all?'

The first growl of resentment rose within him. 'Well. I wasn't expecting so many people,' he said pointedly.

'Really, Adam, I had hoped you would have got rid of that ... Whatever it is ... and bought something larger and more modern and infinitely more practical.'

With dismay, Adam recognized the tactic. When he broached a difficult subject, Heather changed topics and attacked. He put down the bags he was carrying. 'I was saying,' he said firmly, 'that I didn't expect your mother to arrive on the train with you.'

'Well, never mind,' Heather said, walking towards the car. 'It will do, I suppose. Is it far to the house?'

Adam had not moved. Mrs Maguire stopped. She looked away.

'What is going on?' Adam asked. 'Is your mother expecting to live with us or something?'

'Of course,' Heather said, turning. 'Do you expect me to look after the baby on my own?'

Adam didn't know much about babies but he had always thought a mother looked after her own child. He hesitated, wondering if he were being unreasonable.

'Mother also has nowhere to stay,' Heather continued. 'Some simply dreadful things have happened since I last saw you. Had you been around, had you been with your wife as a husband is supposed to be, you would be aware of that. You might even have been able to help.' She looked at him, not accusing but lecturing.

'What happened?' Adam said, unable to prevent himself being sidetracked.

'Ghastly things. I'll tell you about them later. Now, we must hurry because I have to feed the baby soon. I asked you before but you didn't answer – how far is it to the house? Is it nearby?'

'Reasonably close by the standards around here,' he said, picking up the bags again. 'It's still a couple of hours away.'

'We may have to stop on the way. If the baby wants to be fed, I will have to feed her.'

'What will we give her?'

The first suggestion of a smile softened her face. 'Not we,' she corrected. 'Just me. I will give her milk.'

Adam's face reddened.

'You are a silly goose!' she said. 'And I am pleased our house is two hours away. This is such depressing country. I'm sure it's much prettier near the lake. Can we go sailing some time?'

'Where? On Lake Eyre?'

'It looks huge on the map. Do many people go sailing there and has it got nice beaches?'

'Are you serious?'

'Of course. Do you remember the lovely beaches at Manly?'

'Heather, Lake Eyre is a salt lake.'

'Really, Adam, you are a dummy! The sea is salt water too, and it was the sea that we saw breaking on those beaches. So …' She smiled, happy with her triumph, and adjusted the baby's blanket.

'A salt lake is a dry lake,' he said. 'It has a bed of salt.'

She looked up. 'What do you mean?'

'Lake Eyre is dry.'

'You mean it has no water?'

'None.'

'Then why do they call it Lake Eyre?'

'Because they do,' he said, exasperated. 'How did we get on to this subject? We were talking about your mother.'

'We were, but we had finished.'

'No, we hadn't!'

'Don't shout. You'll disturb the baby.'

'I'm not shouting, Heather, your mother can't stay with us.'

Heather passed the baby to him. 'Hold her for a moment,' she said, 'I have to change her nappy. Your daughter can be a dirty little grub.'

Adam held her on outstretched arms. 'What do I do with her?'

'Not drop her. Just hold her while I get a fresh nappy and I'll do the rest. Men are so helpless when it comes to doing things.'

'Heather,' he said, watching her remove the pins holding the dirty nappy in place, 'your mother can't stay with us because there is no room for her.'

'That is a cruel thing to say,' she said, her voice muffled by a pin held between clenched teeth. 'Of course we will make room for her. She is my mother.'

'There is just *no room*!'

'Of course there is!'

'You haven't seen the house. How the hell would you know?'

She removed the pin. 'I had hoped that you would have lost your passion for profanity.'

556

'Stop trying to change the subject! My God, Heather, I thought you'd left all that behind in Nyngan.'

'I don't know what you're talking about. You may pass Cassandra back to me now. By the way, do you like the name? I think it has a classical sound to it, don't you?' She held out her arms for the baby.

'We are talking about your mother. She will not fit in the house. There is no room. It is a small house and there is no room for another person. Do you understand me?'

She blinked. 'What do you mean, small?'

'Small. Not big.'

'Do you mean to tell me you bought a small house for us to live in?'

'I didn't buy a house. I built it.'

'But you can't build houses!'

All of Adam's worst dreams seemed to be coming to life. God, what will she say when she sees the roof and the leaning wall? He recalled Saleem Benn's prediction about her falling at his feet and marvelling at the miracles he had performed.

'What are you grinning at?' she asked.

'Just something someone said.'

'When?'

'When he saw the house.'

'It sounds marvellous, I don't think! You say it's too small, and some person sees it and bursts into laughter!'

'I didn't say that. I didn't say he burst into laughter.'

'Well, you're laughing. Did you really build this house yourself?'

'Yes.'

She studied him. The look was as critical as the moment. 'It must be awful,' she said.

Adam turned away. A dark line, as striking as a brush mark on clear canvas, stained the horizon but he did not see it. His eyes were moist.

'You may not be a house builder but you were always a gentleman,' Heather said to his back. 'Mother is still over there with a suitcase that is far too heavy for her to carry.'

No knowing what to do or what to say, Adam walked to Mrs Maguire. He reached for the case.

'I'm sorry,' she whispered, her face wretched with worry. 'This was not my idea.'

557

FIVE

The stain on the western horizon grew into an advancing dust storm of gigantic proportions. Like a creeping tidal wave of grey and red, it stretched beyond the limits of sight and rose thousands of feet into the air. The storm was devouring the land and its wild winds tore up dry earth and leaves and anything light and loose that had covered the ground in its path. And yet, from a distance, it seemed a majestic and eerie thing for it travelled with such stealth behind folds of solid colour that it seemed not to be moving at all. It was only when it drew closer, and the dust blotted out half the sky and the howling could be heard, that its menace was felt.

All birds had long gone. The nimble and fleet animals had fled. The slow had burrowed beneath the surface. Only a car moved. It crossed a wide plain, trailing a corkscrew of dust that was a puff compared to the fury approaching.

They had been driving for almost an hour. At first, Adam had hoped the storm might pass to the north but it had changed direction and would soon engulf them.

He raced for the shelter of some trees in the lee of a dune. He wanted time to stop and rig a shelter from a tarpaulin he carried in the car. There was no question of his trying to drive through the storm. He would not be able to see, the car would be buffeted and blown off course and everyone on board would be stung and cut by the flying grains and debris. That's if they stayed on their wheels. Out in the open, the wind could snatch the car and tip it on its side. No, he had to stop and make some sort of shelter for the baby and the women. He knew dust storms. They were frightening, hurtful things. He had suffered many since coming to Lake Eyre but this threatened to be the worst.

At a place where the trees curved in a shallow arc, he stopped and removed the tarpaulin. He took it to the front of the car, unfolded it and spread it on the ground. Heather had experienced dust storms in western New South Wales but never one as ferocious as this promised to be. To the left of them she could see the first waves of the storm looming over the dune. She grew frightened and clutched the baby tightly. Her mother, white with fear, sat unmoving in the back.

'What on earth are you doing?' Heather shouted. 'Why have we stopped? Why don't you try to get away from it?'

'Because we can't!' Adam replied and then, seeing Heather trying to get out, added, 'Stay there! Don't move till I tell you.'

But Heather got out and began to run with the baby around the back of the car. Adam chased her and dragged her back. 'Get in and stay in!' he roared. The first strong wind bent the trees. The day became dark.

He leaped into the car and drove its left set of wheels over the edge of the tarpaulin. Heather, mesmerized by the red wall curling above them, began to get out of the car again. He grabbed her roughly.

'Do what I tell you! Stay here. Lie down. Cover the baby's face.' He turned to Mrs Maguire who was staring imploringly at him. 'You too. Down on the seat. Cover your face.' She did not move. He reached over and pulled her down. 'Have you got a handkerchief?'

The back of her head bobbed an acknowledgement. 'Use it. Breathe through it.'

Heather sat up again. He pushed her down, covering the baby. Cassandra was crying. It was the first time he had heard his daughter cry.

The wind was ruffling the free side of the tarpaulin and whip-cracking the ropes tied to its corners. Jumping to the ground, Adam grabbed one rope and dragged the canvas across the front of the car. He stretched the corner over the bonnet of the Alfa and tied the rope to the spokes of the wheel. The other rope flicked savagely in the wind.

It lashed him twice before he caught its knotted end and hauled the rest of the tarpaulin over the vehicle. He tied the rope to the back wheel and then, as the first cruel gusts of grit stung his face, dragged the cover across the windscreen and both seats until the top of the car and the side facing the storm were encased in canvas. The air turned red. Coughing, he opened the driver's door and crawled to the floor.

He had learned to deal with dust storms. The first few after the death of his father had been nightmares but old Tiger had belted him into a routine of survival, and now he knew what to do and did it quickly. Like taming a bucking horse or catching a deadly snake. They too could kill you if you did the wrong thing or panicked. It was merely a question of practice. And luck.

'I can't breathe!' Heather shouted.

'Yes, you can! It's just dusty. It's worse outside.'

The car rocked. The front of the storm had reached them.

'We'll turn over!'

'No, we won't.' The baby was screaming. 'Have you got something over Cassie's face?'

'Of course I have,' she said. 'And don't call her Cassie!' She tried to rise, pressing her back and head against the canvas.

'Get down,' Adam shouted. He was on his side, head near her feet and looking up at her.

'I can't breathe! It hurts! I've just had a baby, in case you don't remember, and I can't bend like that.'

'You might get hit!'

'Are you threatening me?'

'Oh, for God's sake,' he began, but heard the split of timber and the thud of a branch hitting the ground near them. 'There are things flying around. Get down!'

Something hit the side of the car and it shook. 'What was that?' she said, her eyes wide with fright. She was still up and had lifted the baby.

'Give me Cassie,' Adam said. 'She'll be safer down here.'

Heather, holding the baby even more tightly, straightened her back in defiance. She glared at Adam. Her head, bent forward under the pressure of the tarpaulin, formed a tent-like peak in the canvas.

'Please, Heather!' Adam begged. 'Bend down. Get behind the door. Lie along the seat. Do something! Just get down or you'll both get hurt.'

From the back Mrs Maguire called out: 'What on earth are you doing?'

'Nothing, mother,' Heather snapped.

A salvo of small stones peppered the lower parts of the car. The howling of the wind intensified. An edge of the tarpaulin began to flap. Fine dust swirled into the car. Another branch split, making the ripping sound of a close strike of lightning. The car shuddered as something struck it. There was a softer, duller thud and Heather fell forward groaning. The baby fell. Adam tried to catch her but he was lying awkwardly and could not move fast enough. Cassandra hit the floor.

'I've been hit,' Heather said, surprise in her voice. Her eyes glazed, she stroked the back of her head until she caught sight of the baby on the floor. Adam had scooped her up. She was screaming.

560

'Are you trying to kill the baby?' Heather cried. 'Is that why you brought us here? So we could be killed!'

'She's all right,' Adam said, feeling along the child's plump limbs to be certain he was correct. 'She just got a fright.'

'You could have killed her!' Heather examined her own fingers, searching vainly for signs of blood.

'You dropped her,' Adam said quietly. He had turned the baby on to her back. She was still crying, but not as loudly.

'You were the fool who brought us here.'

'What happened?' Mrs Maguire's voice drifted over the seat.

'I was hit by a falling tree.'

'Maybe not a tree,' Adam said.

Heather wiped her face with violent sweeps of her hand, 'You're making fun of me.'

'No, I'm not. But if it was a tree you wouldn't be talking about it.'

She felt the back of her head again, and searched once more for the stains of injury. 'I could have split my head open,' she accused.

'Let me have a look.' He touched her hair.

'Don't touch me! I had hoped you'd change but I can see you're still the same selfish person you always were.' She used the handkerchief which had been covering her nose to wipe her eyes. 'You only think of yourself. You only do what you want to do. You certainly don't think of me.'

'I've been thinking of you all the time,' Adam said, but it was merely a statement of fact, not an emotional outpouring, and he said it so coldly that she looked at him in obvious disbelief. 'I have,' he said, looking away. 'I really have. I built the house for you. Everything I've done, I've done wondering what you would think of it.' He stroked Cassandra's forehead. The baby's cry had subsided to a whimper.

'What are you doing to her?' Heather said.

'Patting her.'

'I asked you not to.'

'I'm her father.'

'She doesn't know that.' She paused to blow her nose. 'Your hands are dirty.'

'So is the floor. So is the air. So are you. Everything's dirty.'

Adam heard her blow her nose again and gasp.

'What's wrong?' he asked.

'I am discharging mud.'

He came perilously close to laughing.

'Oh, my God!' she said. 'I'm full of mud.'

'That's normal. You only have to start worrying when you get so dry you can't make mud.'

'You say the most disgusting things!'

'There's nothing disgusting about it. All that's happening is that the dust is mixing with the wet stuff in your nose and when you sneeze, you get mud.'

It was dark under the canvas but he could see her eyes clearly above the handkerchief. They carried warnings of anger and something worse: hatred.

An hour later, the storm blew away, heading for the emptiness of the lake. Adam crawled from the car. The sharp ends of a broken branch clawed at his back. He got to his feet and pulled the limb from its resting place on the tarpaulin. Another, larger piece of a shattered tree was leaning against the windscreen. The canvas shroud that had protected the car was covered by fine debris. Broken twigs, shredded leaves and chopped spinifex formed a coating to the dust that filled all the hollows.

A deep wedge of sand trailed from either side of the car, forming an orderly ridge like the walls of a moat. Beyond the canvas-covered mound that was the Alfa lay a wilderness of uprooted bushes and broken branches, all linked by freshly sculptured swirls of sand.

To the east, where the storm had gone, the sky was foaming red, but around the car the air was muffled by faint breezes and streaked by trails of pinkish brown, where the lightest particles of dust were settling back to earth.

Adam blew his nose. Mud. Just like Heather. Just like anyone who had been through that. He breathed deeply, tasting the dust in his mouth, and went to work removing the tarpaulin. With the cover off the car, Heather sat up. Before Adam could drive the Alfa forward to free the tarpaulin, she left the car. Limping slightly, one hand holding the back of her head, one arm clutching the baby to her breast, she went to the nearest tree and sat down. She offered the baby milk. Mrs Maguire also got out but walked in the other direction, not looking at her daughter, not looking at Adam, just wiping her eyes constantly.

Adam drove the Alfa off the tarpaulin. Keeping his back to Heather, he cleaned the canvas as well as he could, plucking thorns and seeds and the spiky ends of spinifex from its fibres and then folding it and packing it in the back of the car. He opened the bonnet and made sure the carburettor inlets were clean and checked the oil. The sun was shining in a sky bright and pale and clear of dust. He walked towards Mrs Maguire and stopped behind her.'

'It's a lot better now,' he said.

'Yes.' She turned, flustered and blinking. She dabbed her eyes and looked down.

'They're rotten things, dust storms.'

'Yes.' She brushed dirt from the front of her dress. 'Do they happen often?'

'Every now and then. They're worse when things are dry and we've got a real drought on at the moment. This is the windy time of the year too.'

'Have you had many? I mean, while you've been up here on your own?'

'A few.'

She was not looking at him. 'Things must have been very hard for you these last few months.'

'There's been a lot of work. Are you all right? You weren't hurt or anything?'

'No. No.' Obstinately, she kept her eyes away from his.

'It's funny how they come and go. Storms, I mean. They're so wild when they're blowing but when they've passed by …' Adam stopped, thinking Mrs Maguire was not listening.

'We had dust storms at home,' she said, her voice vague. 'My husband used to get one of the men to come and clean up.' She wiped her eyes again and faced him. 'Did you really build a house for Heather? All on your own?'

'Yes.'

'You are a very clever boy. Will it be full of dirt now?'

'From the storm? Probably. It might have missed the worst of it. But there'll probably be a foot of dust in it.'

'There'll be a great deal of work.'

'Not that much.'

'Can you get someone to help you?' She saw the answer in his face and turned away embarrassed to have asked such a question. She walked a few steps. Adam followed.

'It's very difficult on your own, Adam.'

'Yes.'

'Of course. You'd know, poor boy. Does the country get better?'

'It's much the same.'

'Oh.' Her face was a mixture of surprise and pity. 'But Heather was talking about some lovely lake.'

'I'm afraid the lake is a dry salt lake. It's not very nice.'

'Goodness me! Can you live out here?'

'Yes, if you know what you're doing.'

'And you do?'

'I think so.'

'I'm sure you do,' she said, but sounded unsure. 'You didn't want me to come here, did you?'

'I wasn't expecting you.' Adam said the words slowly, not wanting to hurt. An hour ago he had been angry with her for the trick he presumed she had played on him. Now he was sorry for her.

Some birds flew past, chasing the storm and searching for insects unsettled by the winds.

'Is it really a small house? I didn't mean to eavesdrop but I couldn't help overhearing what you were saying – at the station.'

'It's very small. It was hard getting material to make it with. I'd have liked to make it bigger but, well, you know ...'

'Of course. I should go back to New South Wales. It's very unfair.'

Adam felt he should put his arms around her. She looked frail and in need of comforting. 'Where would you go?'

'Somewhere. Who knows?'

'Couldn't you stay with your sister?' Immediately Adam regretted the question for Mrs Maguire began to cry. She did not hide her grief but lifted her face and let the tears stream down her cheeks. She shook her head.

'Unfortunately,' she said, coughing a little, 'that is not possible.'

Adam patted her shoulder. He was about to say, 'But she's your sister,' but stopped himself in time when he realized the extra pain he would cause.

'Don't worry, Mrs Maguire,' he mumbled, feeling foolish at saying something so meaningless but not trusting any other words. He withdrew, confused. What am I doing? he thought. Here I am with no room for her and I'm at the point of asking her to stay. Yet I can't throw her out.

Near the car Adam looked back, suddenly concerned that he might be the victim of another Maguire trick, another acting performance to gain some advantage. But Mrs Maguire was still gazing into the sky and weeping and looking thoroughly, genuinely miserable.

He felt intensely sorry for her, and then just as angry for allowing himself to feel that way. He could not be weak. She could not stay. It was not that he didn't like her. There was nothing personal. Not now. Not with her howling her eyes out. It was just there was absolutely no space for her in the house. He would like to be able to offer somewhere to live. He really would. He sat behind the wheel of the car once more. Heather was still feeding the baby. She looked so soft, so attentive and loving, and so out of place. How could she look so soft and be so hard?

How could he have been so foolish, so wrong? How could he have brought her here? What was he going to do? Gently, he let his forehead settle on the rim of the wheel.

They reached the house late in the afternoon. The storm had passed through and piled a brush fence of tumbleweed against the western wall. The front door had blown open. The floor was buried in layers of talcum-soft dust.

Heather stayed in the car examining the homestead and saying nothing. Adam still found himself worrying about her reaction. After all, this was the house he had built for her. He had spent months – sweated and strained, bruised and cut himself, and worried if she would like it. He was still worried, and the longer her silence persisted the more he began to hope, absurdly, illogically, that she might change, that she might understand. That she might want to share his life out here. That she would like the house he had created for her.

She got out of the car.

'It would have been better,' she said, 'if the storm had blown that ugly little shack out of sight.'

SIX

The first thing that Adam did was go to the mare. The storm would have terrified her and he was frightened that she might have hurt herself. She normally stayed outside but he had left her in a makeshift stall he had built in the corner of the shed. She had, apparently, lashed out during the storm for her hind leg was grazed and a couple of boxes had been kicked across the shed. She was still agitated and he spent several minutes calming her.

Adam cleaned the house, on his own and in silence. He had no broom because he had not thought of buying one, so he used a shovel to scoop out the worst of the dust and then took an uprooted bush to sweep the floor. He carried out the table and chairs he had made and tipped them on their sides to dislodge the dust, and bundled up the blankets he had purchased from Saleem Benn and shook them until he could see the original grey colour. Mrs Maguire came into the house and used a cloth to dust the refrigerator and stove and to give the tables and chairs a final wipe, but she spent most of her time staring through the open doorway. She did not speak. Heather did not enter the house. She had walked as far as the door, looked inside, and then taken the baby to the edge of the spring. While Adam worked, she sat there with the baby lying in her shade and with one hand dangling in the cool water.

When Adam had finished, Mrs Maguire was outside and Heather walked to the house. She carried the baby awkwardly above her left hip, a position which exaggerated the limp she had developed since leaving the car. She passed the baby to Adam.

'Are you hurt?' he enquired.

'I don't see why you bother to ask since you obviously are not interested in what happens to me. I detest hypocrisy.' She slowed, enjoying the bemused expression on Adam's face. 'Oh, I forgot. You don't understand anything but the basic English of the working man. Which is all you are.' She hesitated.

'And talking of that, I've something to ask you,' she continued. 'It's something that's been concerning me since I first saw Cassandra.'

'What is it?'

'Who were your parents?'

'What?' He looked at her in disbelief.

'Your parents died when you were very young. Who were they? What sort of people were they?'

'You want to know this now?' Cassandra was firmly gripping his little finger. It was a thrilling sensation.

'Well, the baby's so dark and yet I'm fair and you're fair.' She paused, 'Don't you understand what I'm getting at?'

'No,' he said.

'People are calling her darkie.'

'I prefer Cassie.'

'Be serious. Do you remember your father?'

'Yes.'

'What was he like?'

'Nice. I liked him.'

'I don't mean that! Was he fair or dark?'

'He had brown hair.'

She had trouble in delivering the next words. 'Was he a white man?'

Adam laughed. 'As far as I know.'

'Be serious! Was he white?'

'Well, to be truthful, he was a bit brown from the sun.'

'You are making a difficult conversation extremely awkward.'

'Oh, I'm sorry.'

'What about your mother?'

'Dad got her in exchange for a string of beads and three goannas. She was the favourite daughter of King Billy.'

'Who?'

'King of the Umbergumbies. Best man with a boomerang I ever saw.'

Her voice was firm and measured. 'I don't think I understand. Are you trying to tell me your mother was some kind of aboriginal princess?'

'Would that be all right?' he said, no longer finding the conversation amusing. 'I mean, you wouldn't like my mother to be an aboriginal but you wouldn't mind it so much if she had blue blood. Is that what you're saying?'

'Was she?' Heather shouted.

'Black or a princess?'

'Either! Oh, my God, how could you have done this to me? You have shamed me.'

'You don't love the baby any more?' he said.

She reached for Cassandra. 'Oh, how could you have done this to her? If you knew you had that sort of blood in you, you should have kept away from decent folk. You should have killed yourself or married a black woman, or done something like that.'

Free of the baby, Adam sat heavily on the ground. 'I was only joking because I'd hoped you weren't serious, but you are, aren't you? All this business of colour is terribly important to you.'

Heather had dropped her handkerchief and was weeping, her tears flooding the baby's face. 'You are a deceitful, horrible man!'

'My mother was not an aboriginal princess.'

'You said she was!'

'I was joking.'

'That is not a joke.'

567

'You're right. The whole matter is very serious and the most serious thing about it is that you're treating it all so seriously. Heather, I don't know whether my mother was a princess or not. I don't remember her. My father never said to me: "Adam, your mother was black". He didn't tell me she was white, either. Frankly, I don't think it would have mattered to him. She could have been brown, yellow or green and it wouldn't have mattered. He loved her and he missed her like hell when she died.'

'There is no such thing.'

'As what?

'As missing someone like hell. That is like saying someone is a devil of a good fellow. You cannot be a devil *and* a good fellow. The two are not compatible. You do talk such nonsense.'

Adam thumped his forehead. 'Heather, you're doing it again!'

'What?'

'Changing the subject.'

'A poor command of English is no excuse for continually picking on me.'

'I'm not sure whether you're very, very silly or very, very clever.'

'What are you talking about?'

'Heather, tell me one thing. Why did you come up here?'

'I have no idea.'

'Was it because you loved me?'

She said nothing but pressed her face close to the baby.

'Was it because you had to be with me?'

'Hah!'

'What does that mean?'

'It is a short expression, used by people who understand the language, to display contempt for a thought.'

'I don't know what you mean. Now, would you like to answer my question?'

'I don't recall any question that deserved an answer.'

'I asked why you'd come here.'

'And I said I had no idea.'

'Which was a stupid answer.'

'Stupid! Is it any more stupid than bringing me up to this stupid country, and getting off a stupid train that stops at a stupid town where there is no town, and getting into a stupid car with no roof and heading for a stupid house built by a stupid, stupid man? Now, does that make me stupid?'

Adam covered his eyes. 'In the last year, I've thought about you all the time. I guess I'm a dreamer because I thought about you not as you were but as I'd like you to be. Do you understand that? I wanted to be a good husband and I wanted you to be a good wife and I sort of changed you in my mind so you became the kind of wife I wanted. Am I stupid?' He wiped his eyes. 'I *am* stupid, and blind. I should have remembered what you were like. I was blind when I married you because I didn't see what you were like, was stupid to have let you come up here. I used to think you were the most beautiful, the cleverest girl I ever saw. Well, you certainly are beautiful. But you're a fool and a nasty one at that, and I'm just sorry you had to come all the way up here for me to find that out.'

'How dare you say that!'

'Quite easily. It took a while for me to work it out but now I see it quite clearly. I know what you are.'

'And what am I?'

'A snob and what is commonly known as a bitch.'

She smiled and her face had a hardness Adam had not noticed. 'There's one thing you forgot,' she said. 'I am also the mother of your child.'

'Which you think is part aboriginal.'

'She could be. You don't know.'

'And that worries you?'

'It should worry you. Oh my God, you could have anything in your blood and you pass it on to me and that poor, poor child has to bear the stigma. And me, as her mother.'

'You're sillier than I thought.'

'And you are so shallow, so unconcerned, that I just cannot understand you. You defy logic. Happy-go-lucky, spreading your poison, contaminating pure blood.'

Unable to contain her curiosity any longer, Mrs Maguire joined them outside the house. 'What's up, dear?'

'Nothing!'

'Heather thinks Cassandra is part aboriginal,' Adam informed her.

'What?'

'She thinks she has black blood.'

'Oh. Is she bleeding?'

'No, mother,' Heather said. 'It's to do with ancestry.'

'Yes,' Adam butted in, mischief in his voice. 'Is it true Mr Maguire's grandfather was a blackfellow?'

'Well, I don't know,' the older woman said and stroked her chin

569

in confusion. 'I never met him but I saw a photograph of him. He had white hair and a white beard but he did have a very dark face. Mind you, it was a very old photograph.'

'Mother!'

'You didn't see that photograph, did you, dear?'

'Will you shut up?'

Adam was startled at the venom of her words.

'How long have you been speaking to your mother like that?'

'That's none of your business.'

'Maybe not,' he said. 'But tell me. Whose idea was it that your mother should come here?'

'Mine,' she said immediately. 'And if she goes, I go. And, of course Cassandra goes too. Just think about that.'

'But Heather,' Mrs Maguire began, 'you're being very ...'

'I said be quiet. Take the baby for a walk.'

'Heather, please!'

'Show Cassandra the tree.' She pointed towards the solitary beefwood. 'Let her see the wonderful garden we have here in our lovely new home.'

Mrs Maguire did not move.

'Your mother's tired,' Adam said.

'You stay out of this. Go on, mother, before the baby starts crying.'

'Really, Heather!' Mrs Maguire said, her protest already acknowledging the certainty of defeat.

'Goodbye, mother. Take your time.'

'You're very cruel,' the older woman said in a whisper, as though she were trying to shield the baby from the truth. Then in a louder, cooing voice, she addressed Cassandra. 'Come on, my love, Nana will show you the beautiful tree. Do you want to see the beautiful tree?' And she walked away.

'That's a good word for you,' Adam said. 'Cruel.'

'Really?'

'I feel sorry for your mother.'

'Good. That makes two fools who are sorry for each other. I must admit, however, that you were right in one thing.'

'Was I?'

'You said the house was too small for us all. There is only room for me and the baby and mother. Where will you sleep?'

'I built this house for you,' Adam said, then stopped, realizing he was about to pour out his unhappiness. She would enjoy that.

'Good,' she said brightly, and for the first time entered the building. 'And as it's such a small house with no room for you, may I suggest you keep out. Apart from there being no room, you're filthy and I don't want you touching anything. Now, I've had a long and exhausting journey and I'm hungry. Where do you keep the food?'

'Do you need it for the baby?'

'Of course not. She's far too young for solid food.'

'Good.' He started to walk away.

'Where's the food?'

'It's your house. Find it.'

She ran after him, her limp gone. 'How dare you say that! Do you want us to starve?'

He was heading for the shed and the mare. 'I don't want you to do anything.'

'Is there food here?'

'I told you. Find it yourself.'

'How will I cook it?'

'Isn't that what you brought your mother for? To do the work for you?'

She slowed and the limp returned. 'You're the one who's cruel. You are unbelievable. You drag me and your baby daughter out here to live in a ramshackle hut in the middle of the desert and you have no food for us and you expect me to fend for myself. You want us dead. I don't know why. I never could understand you but you want to see me dead. You are a madman!'

'I'll take you back to William Creek tomorrow,' he said, turning, 'I'll put you on the first train south.'

She smiled. 'Oh, that's it. You want to keep the baby and send me away.'

'No,' he sighed. 'But you're mad and you're not staying here.'

'Aren't I? Why do you want to get rid of me so badly?' She looked around. 'Where are the sheep? I thought you had sheep here?'

'They're at the bore.'

'Where there's water? Is it far?'

'A few miles.'

'How many sheep did you say there were? A thousand?'

He didn't answer.

'Is it good where they are?'

Again he said nothing.

'A thousand sheep. That's a lot. That's a huge number of sheep. The people I know – knew – with that many sheep were very wealthy. Have you made a lot of money?'

'Yes. I'm a millionaire. You can see for yourself.'

She turned, examining the country. 'You've only shown me this, the worst part. Are you trying to get rid of me and keep the baby because you're making a fortune you don't want to share with me? Is that why you hate me so much?'

'Oh, for Christ's sake, Heather!'

'You know I despise profanity.' She rubbed her skin and then suddenly stood erect. 'Is there another woman?'

'What?'

'Is that it? Have you found someone else?'

'Heather, you are as silly as a rabbit.'

'I've been on my own, suffering in a way that you would never comprehend, putting up with the most outrageous insinuations from people who are simply despicable, and going through the agony of bearing your child, and you've been living here with some other woman, some bush slut … Is that it? I suppose the two of you have been laughing at me. Well, I'm not going to leave. I'm not going to play into your hands.'

'Heather. Stop it.'

'Where is this slut? Is she at the place where you've hidden all the sheep? Have you built her a big house? You give me this tumbledown shanty while she lives in luxury!'

Fuming, Adam resumed his march to the shed. She limped after him.

'You stop this instant and tell me the truth!'

'The truth is,' he said, still walking, 'that you are off your head.'

'I will make you suffer!' she screamed.

Adam reached the mare and began saddling her.

'I will!' she said. 'I will make you pay.'

'Do you know what you can do?' he said, stroking the horse, which had become agitated. 'You can get stuffed.'

He had never said that to anyone. He felt good.

Adam rode into camp just after sunset. The dog ran out to greet him and returned, happily trotting behind the horse. Jimmy had a small fire burning. He stood and scratched his head.

'Got any tucker?' Adam said as he dismounted.

'Shot a roo.'

'Big one?'

'Big enough.'

'How are you cooking it? Blackfellow way or proper way?'

'Same thing. Want some?'

'If you've got enough.'

'More than I can eat. Staying the night?'

'Yes.'

'Train come?'

'Yes.'

Jimmy used a stick to prod at a lump in the coals at the edge of the fire. 'That Heather of yours, she hasn't changed?' he said, still concentrating on the fire.

Adam grunted. 'I don't have to tell you a thing, do I?'

'She's a woman, mate. That's enough. How do you want your meat?'

'Any way you like.'

'If you were a blackfellow I'd say grab a chunk now. Seeing you're a poor miserable white man, I reckon you should wait another half an hour.'

Adam fell into a troubled sleep that night. He dreamed an old dream, that he was pursuing his mother and she would not stop for him. She turned during this dream and he saw her face clearly. It was black and ugly. Wide-nosed, broad-lipped, pock-marked, wrinkled and leering at him. Heather was there too, mocking him. They were both laughing at him. Nellie was somewhere in the background, a slim hazy figure who drifted in and out of focus. He awoke, sweating.

Jimmy had little sleep. He spent most of the night setting traps for the wild dogs. Despite being tired, he had a good night for he was pleased to have Adam in the camp with him.

Saleem Benn was astonished. He did not have much time for women, especially young and good-looking ones who were usually more interested in men than work, but the black girl whom his niece had befriended seemed exceptional. The day she had arrived in Marree she had helped unload bales of wool and seemed to have the staying power of a man, and a good man at that. Now she was saying she wanted to work in one of the stores he was planning. Incredibly, she did not want to go to the biggest town she could, like all the other girls, but seemed to prefer the outback. Why, she had even said she would like to work in the store he was planning at William Creek. No one ever wanted to leave Marree for William Creek. Certainly no woman. Truly, she was an unusual woman. His brother's younger son was in need of a wife. Unhappily this girl was an aboriginal, or at least part black, but still, women were scarce and good women who were not frightened of work and who did not mind the isolation of the bush were even scarcer. And he was thinking of sending his nephew to William Creek to operate the new store. He would think about it when he came back from his next trip to the north-west.

In the morning, Adam rode back to the homestead. It was a slow journey because the mare was sore from the leg injury and he walked beside her for much of the way. As he neared the house, the sounds of an argument and of the baby crying drifted to him. Then the arguing ceased and only the baby cried. Heather appeared in the doorway.

'Why are you walking?' she said.

'The mare has a sore leg. She was frightened by the storm.'

'I have a sore leg and I was terrified by the storm. Obviously you care more about your horse than you do about me.'

Adam led the horse to the water. Heather followed, moving with a pronounced limp. 'Stop trying to bait me all the time,' he said.

'The trouble is, Adam Ross, you cannot bear to hear the truth.'

'Really? Is that the trouble?'

'That's one of your problems. Have you been to your other house?'

He sighed. 'Oh God, Heather, there *is* no other house! It's taken me all of my time and energy to build this place.'

'It doesn't say much for the way you use your time or your energy. I'd be inclined to say you had wasted both.'

'Would you?' he sounded uninterested.

'Yes, I would. So would you if you were totally honest. Have you been to see your other woman?'

'Where I have been there *are* no other women. There are dingoes, about a thousand head of sheep and a one-armed aboriginal named Jimmy.'

'Is that creature still with you?'

'He is not a creature. He is my friend.'

She moved closer and stroked the horse's hindquarters. 'I don't like him.'

'He doesn't get many compliments like that. I'll have to let him know.'

The remark sailed past, leaving her unruffled in its wake. She continued to pat the mare. Adam was curious; it was such an unexpected gesture. A warm thing in the midst of all the hostile remarks. It was as though she were saying, 'There is something about you I like even if it is only your taste in horses.' But what she actually said was different.

'I find that black friend of yours rather slimy. I know the poor wretch only has one arm but it make him look so lopsided. And he's so black he always strikes me as being dirty. I do wish you'd choose your friends more carefully. I want to make it clear that if I'm to live here I would not expect this Jimmy friend of yours to be around the house.'

Adam faced her. 'Does that mean you're going to stay?'

'I thought I made that clear yesterday.'

'Nothing seemed very clear yesterday.'

She walked along the other side of the horse, which twitched nervously when Heather touched its neck.

'You must realize I was extremely tired. It was such a long journey and everything seemed so strange, and that dust storm was frightening.'

Adam had endured what could have been the most miserable night of his adult years. His hopes for a good life with Heather on his land had, it seemed, dissolved. His dreams had been false and, worse, foolish. He had eventually accepted that Heather had no love for him, that she in fact despised him, and that she would be leaving and taking Cassie with her. He had come back to make sure they had food and to find out when they would be leaving. And now here was Heather talking like a reasonable person and even, in a roundabout way, offering an apology.

'Yes, of course,' he said and waited for her to complete her journey around the horse. She was at the head, gently running her fingers along the nap of fine hair on the mare's nose. She emerged from behind the animal.

'Do you think I could ride him sometime?'

'Her. It's a mare. Of course.' He patted the horse's neck, loosening a fine cloud of dust. He tried to restrain a smile but could not. 'She's got a sore leg at the moment and is a little lame. But when she's right in a few days ... Sure. I didn't know you could ride.' By now his smile was one of pure delight. Yesterday had been a nightmare but it was past, and Heather had been just tired, and not herself. It was natural. The long trip. The baby. The worry. The shock of being in such arid country. The dust storm. He should have realized.

'I learned at school.' She smiled modestly. 'It was one of the things they taught us. And, of course, some of my friends had horses.' One hand reached out and almost touched him. The fingers stopped short and fell away, slowly, gracefully. 'I'm sorry about yesterday.'

'That's all right. I mean, I'm sorry for what I said too.'

'No, it was my fault. Mother has been telling me I was very unfair.'

Adam didn't know what to say. He felt like singing. He patted the horse again. 'Your mother seems very unhappy,' he said at last.

'She's been through a bad time, of course, but it's been extremely trying for me. She's done a number of things that have caused me grave embarrassment.'

'Oh?'

'I won't bore you with them but I've had to assume responsibility for all family matters. She's done some things that were, well, silly.' Her eyes were intense, probing him for understanding. 'Frankly, I think she's suffering from senility.'

Adam looked concerned.

'Do you know what that is?' she said.

'Too much salt?'

She had been moving to the side of the horse, and the animal lifted its head, breaking the contact between their eyes. When Adam saw her face again, a faint smile was playing on the corners of her mouth. 'You are still the same,' she said. 'A dreadful tease. Or are you just being sweet and trying to make an unpleasant fact more acceptable?'

Adam returned her smile. It seemed the safest thing to do.

'No,' she said, turning from him to shield her face. 'The sad fact is that mother is old and she was greatly affected by father's death and she is not as ... bright ... as she once was. I shall just have to bear with her but there are times, particularly when I am tired myself, when I find the strain too much and say things I regret. I'm sure it's normal and I'm certain you understand but I still regret it. You do understand, Adam?'

'Yes.'

'You are sweet.' Adam had begun to walk towards the house. She followed him. 'Now,' she said brightly, 'you must show me where the sheep are.'

'They're a few miles away.'

'It doesn't matter. We can drive. Mother will look after the baby. We can be on our own.'

'We can't drive there. There's no road.'

'Well, there was no road from William Creek and that didn't seem to stop you.'

'That was different. The ground was much firmer. The sheep are in sandhill country. We just wouldn't get there in a car.'

'I see.' She looked at him earnestly. 'The sheep are where the dunes are?'

'Yes. There's a chain of dunes all through there.'

'Is it pretty country?'

'I think so. The sand's lovely in the morning. You get beautiful colours at dawn.'

'I see.' She walked quickly past him and turned. 'What are you going to call this place? I like "The Dunes". It sounds romantic, don't you think?'

He stopped, facing her. 'I suppose so. I thought we should give it an aboriginal name.'

She wrinkled her nose in distaste. 'They either sound like children's games or they are unpronounceable.'

'No, they're not.'

'They are. Tell me one nice aboriginal name.'

'What about the place where you used to live?'

'Nyngan? That's not aboriginal.'

'Yes, it is.'

'You are being absurd.' The severe tone had crept into her voice. He didn't answer and, when she spoke again, her voice was more controlled and milder. 'Well, it doesn't sound like a black name.'

'No,' Adam agreed, and waited for Heather's face to register pleasure at her vindication. 'But there are some really beautiful aboriginal names, like the one I thought of calling this place.'

'Which is?'

'Kalinda.' He waited, transparent in hope.

'It sounds like a calendar and that would be silly.'

'It means a look-out or a view.'

'Well, that's even sillier. There's nothing to see.'

'Oh, yes, there is! Do you feel like a walk?'

'To see the sheep and the dunes?'

'No. To see the look-out. It will take only five minutes. There are hills behind the house. We have to go there.'

Adam led her towards the low hills and, as they walked, he described what he had done in the past year. She said nothing, absorbing his stories about the building of sheds and fences and bores without comment. When they reached the first hill, he helped her climb over a shelf of crumbling earth and up the side of a slope made treacherous by loose stones. She held his hand tightly and Adam enjoyed guiding her through some of the roughest parts. When they were near the top, Adam ran ahead and waited on the crest, arms outstretched to help his wife join him.

She was short of breath. 'Where's the view?' she asked, gently pushing him away.

'All around.' He looked surprised that she should ask. From such a moderate elevation the view was remarkable. In all directions, the land ran to interesting conclusions. A row of dunes that stitched the sky to the earth with a ruffle of colour. Distant salt lakes that frizzled like fat in a pan. Even the black hills that rimmed the lake. He could see them all in an area large enough to have contained a city. And it was all his. Maybe that was the thing that appealed most of all, but he would not mention that. Not yet. Not till she felt the same excitement at owning so much land.

'So this is your empire,' she said slowly.

He grinned. 'You can see for miles.'

She pivoted through a full circle, stopping at each quarter to examine the view. 'What's the point? There's nothing worth seeing.' Her nose twitched in ladylike distaste. Noticing the disappointment on Adam's face, she added, 'I mean there are no buildings to look at or forests or lawns or gardens. It's just ...' She fluttered her fingers, trying to find the words. 'It's just nothing. But I'll admit there's miles and miles of that.'

He dug his thumbs into his pockets. 'I like it,' he said stubbornly. 'And one day this land will make us a fortune.'

She found a clean shelf of rock and sat down. 'How?' she said, gazing at the view beyond the home. Her mother was walking near the beefwood tree, carrying the baby high in front of her. She was cooing baby talk. The sound drifted to them.

'With wool. I know everyone says you can't raise sheep north of the dingo fence, but I can.'

'I don't mean that.' She had picked up a small stone and was examining its bright colours. 'I mean, how can you make any money at all, let alone a fortune, when there is just no grass for these mysterious sheep of yours to eat?'

'They eat the top feed. The bushes. And what do you mean, mysterious?'

'I haven't seen a sign of them. I'm beginning to wonder if they exist.'

'They're at the bore.'

'Oh, yes, the bore. You will let me see it one day?'

'Of course. I want to show you all of the property.'

'Of course. It's a shame the car can't drive to this bore and the horse is lame so I can't ride to this bore. I presume when the horse is fit again, you'll want to ride it so I'll never get to see anything but this God-forsaken part.' She stood up. 'Where is this bore where all the sheep are hiding?'

'They're not hiding! They're eating and, I hope, growing wool.' He pointed towards the distant dunes. 'It's over that way.'

'There's grass there?'

'Some.'

'And another woman.' It was a statement, not a question.

'Oh, for God's sake, we're not back to that!'

'We're not back to anything. Just tell me. Is that where you're hiding her?' The question was all the more venomous because of the pleasant way it was asked.

'Heather,' I thought you said those things yesterday because you were so tired.' Adam tried to touch her arm but she pulled away.

'I *was* tired. I was also aware that you have such strong animal urges that you could not possibly have gone for twelve months without ... without doing what seems to be on your mind all the time.'

'You mean ...?'

'I don't want you to say it. I remember vividly how coarse you can be.'

He began to descend the hill.

'Where are you going?'

'Back to do some work. The sheep are due to be shorn in a couple of weeks and I've got to finish a shed for the shearers to shear in.'

'You're not going to tell me, are you?' she said, following him. 'About the other woman. Or were there other *women*?'

'Yes, hundreds of them,' he said, still walking. 'They come out of the lake at night and go back before sunrise, otherwise they turn into frogs.'

'You are not going to distract me by being ridiculous. My friends told me what you'd be up to.'

'Your friends? Where? Back in New South Wales?'

'Yes. They know what happens when men like you are away from their wives.'

'Your friends are twits.'

'You always become rude when you have something to hide.'

Adam turned. She had stopped with her hands defiantly on her hips.

'Heather,' he said, and she avoided his eyes. 'I have been out here, on my own or with no one but Jimmy for a companion, since I last saw you. I have not got a woman hidden in the sandhills. I have done nothing but work on this place, and it has been hard work, and I have done it because I want to succeed. To get on in this world. And I want things to be good for both of us. Like I said, I built that house for you.'

'I'm sure you did,' she said, still looking at other things. 'It's such a small, mean house it summarizes very well how much you really care for me. How long did it take you to make? One week? Two? What did you do for the rest of the time you've been here?'

'Heather, I spent months building that place.'

She strode down the hill past him. 'Then you must be even less efficient than I thought.'

'What is wrong with you?' He shouted after her. 'Everything I do, you criticize! You're nice one minute, rotten the next. I can't follow you.'

She stopped and, for a moment, he thought she was about to shout at him. He could only see the back of her body, and it quivered. But then she turned, wiping her face as though to rearrange her expression. A contrite look emerged. 'I'm sorry. I am still weary. I am still a little … surprised by this place. Can you understand that?'

'Yes.' He walked to her, choosing his path through loose stones. 'But I still find it hard to know what you want. Tell me, are you going to stay or not?'

'I'm still your wife,' she said, looking away when he reached her.

'What does that mean?'

'Exactly what it says.'

He breathed heavily, exasperated. 'Do you want to stay?'

'What else can I do? You won't move to Sydney, will you, and live the sort of life normal people live?'

'No.'

'You see? I have no choice. You are my husband, for better or for worse. I would have preferred it to be for the better, but if it has to be for the worse, so be it.'

'We can live a good life here.'

'Can we? If it's all like this,' and she gestured with her hand, dismissing all she could see, 'if it's all just wasteland like this, with no grass, no decent trees, no proper hills, then I don't see how we can possibly do well. Frankly, I think it would be an awful life here.'

'No, you don't understand,' he said, eager to have her share his enthusiasm for the land. 'Sheep can do very well here. We can grow fine wool. We can make a lot of money. I can build you a bigger home one day, with all the things you want. All I need is time, and your help. I can't do it on my own.'

'You want me to shear the sheep?'

'Of course not. There are men who do that.'

'I see,' she said, and was silent for a few moments. 'Well then, you can't want me to mow the grass because there is none, so what do you want me to do? As far as I can see, there isn't that much to do. You just have sheep and they have wool and you cut it off and sell it. So what do you want me to do?'

'Just support me. Maybe give me a hand every now and then. Do the cooking.'

'For you?'

'Yes.' He looked surprised. 'You'd do that, wouldn't you? I've been cooking for myself for a long time now. I had hoped you might do that.'

'Mother will cook. She realizes she has to earn her keep.'

'What will you be doing?'

'Raising your daughter. Obviously, you have no idea of what's involved in attending to a baby. And I thought I might get the opportunity to see something of the property.'

'You mean with me?'

'Do you object?'

'No.' He was surprised.

'You don't seem wildly enthusiastic about the idea of me seeing anything else. You've taken me to a look-out where you can't see anything. You won't let me see your sheep. You won't take me to this bore of yours.'

'What the hell are you getting at?'

'That you're hiding something from me.'

'Like what?'

'Why don't you tell me? Look, Adam, I'm not a fool. You've been here for a year and you expect me to believe that all you've done in that time is knock together a miserable shack which you present to me, in all seriousness, as a house.'

'I sank two bores, built those yards ...'

'Oh, how amazing! And those sheds too?'

'Yes.'

'My father had a man from the railway yard come and build a shed in our garden. It was made of high-quality timber and painted cream and green. It looked very smart, and that man did the whole job in one week. I must say it looked neater than the house you built, let alone those awful, rough sheds.'

'Really?' Adam said, trying to control his anger.

'Yes. It was something you could proudly show your friends. But still,' she added brightly, 'each of us can only do our best and I suppose that was your best. Now, you said you were going to build another shed or something?'

'I have to finish a shearing shed.'

'Will you be wanting lunch?'

'I've gone without a few things in recent months but I still like to eat.'

'I'll have mother prepare something, although there seems precious little variety in the food you left for us. Oh, I should have asked earlier,' she had resumed moving towards the house, and paused briefly, 'have you had breakfast?'

'Yes. At the bore with Jimmy.'

'Ah yes. Of course. With Jimmy.' She set off again. 'I'll have mother prepare you a nourishing meal of flour and tea, which seem to be the two items you have in the greatest abundance, while I shall probably go without. But then that's a wife's duty, isn't it? Shall I have mother deliver the meal to the shearing shed?'

'Why don't I come to the house?'

'Because I'm still trying to tidy up. You would simply devastate it. By the way, I found a packet of seeds. At least I think they're seeds. It's a large packet and there are many of them. What are they?'

Adam laughed. Not at the recollection of the gift from Saleem Benn but because he remembered the old man's prophecy about Heather's reaction to the house. Rather than fall at his feet, she had knocked them from under him. 'They're a gift from a friend,' he said. 'You're right. They are seeds. Some are vegetables, some are flowers. They are for you to start a garden.'

'And they are from a friend?' She emphasized the final word. Adam nodded. 'You must thank her for me,' she said. 'That's if I ever get a chance to meet her.'

582

'Saleem Benn is hardly a "her", but he should be here in a week or so. You can thank him then.' He reacted to her puzzled look. 'He's an Afghan trader. He brings supplies on camels. It was a very thoughtful thing for him to do, giving you seeds.'

'He would expect me to plant the garden myself, I suppose. Presumably, he is a man's man who likes his women to work in the fields.' She smiled, oozing sweetness. 'Is that what you meant by having me help you? Do you want me to work on the land, digging gardens and planting crops? Is that what you had in mind?'

'You're always asking questions and the more questions you ask, the sillier you get. I don't know where Saleem Benn got the seeds from but I'm sure he went to considerable trouble to get them. And he thought you'd like the flowers.'

'How sweet of him,' she said, her voice heavy with irony. 'I can just see it now. A lovely bed of roses in the middle of all the sand. And I suppose you expect me to dig the garden, with all the other things I have to do?'

'Saleem Benn won't say anything, but when he comes he will expect to see a garden and he would like to hear you say thanks. So would I.'

'I'm sure. But nothing would grow here.'

'There's a good spot for a vegetable garden over near the spring and you could plant the flower seeds around the house.'

'Good. You can dig the gardens and you can thank this what's-his-name for his lavish gift. Now if you'll excuse me, I don't have time to waste in talking like this. The house is a shambles from the storm and an even bigger shambles from the way it was built and there are things I must do. If you're not busy, I am. I'll have mother bring you lunch.'

She entered the house. 'Don't follow me,' she said when Adam seemed to be doing that. 'You're filthy. I noticed you smelled of the horse. It would be a good idea if you went over to the water and bathed. Even in isolation, a man should not abandon hygiene. After all, cleanliness is next to godliness.'

She closed the door and waited behind it until she was certain Adam had gone. Her mother was standing against the far wall. She was still nursing the baby. 'I hope you've got over your hysteria,' Heather said.

'I was not hysterical, Heather,' she said softly. 'I just think I should go. It's not fair.'

'Fair to whom? You or me or Adam?'

'Adam. I feel terrible just blundering in here, uninvited, like this. The poor boy has worked so hard to try and make a start for the two of you. He was right. There is no room for me here.'

'You're not going. That's all there is to it and there'll be no more arguing.'

'But a man should sleep with his wife. This is awful, the way it is.'

'If he wants a bed for himself in the house, he can build another room for you. I'll get him to do that, maybe, but until he does you stay in here and he stays outside. I'm going to make him pay for the suffering he's caused me. And you.'

'He hasn't caused me any suffering.'

'If he'd been in Nyngan instead of gallivanting around half of Australia, he could have handled all that nastiness that followed father's death. He could have paid those bills, for instance.'

'But they weren't his.' She put the baby on the bed.

'Is she asleep?' Heather asked.

'Yes. She's so sweet.'

'She likes you.'

'She knows I love her. Children can always sense that.'

Heather had gone to a window and opened the rough curtain. She could see Adam, carrying a long piece of wood over his shoulder.

'He's up to something,' she said.

'I'm sure he always works hard.'

'I don't mean that. He's trying to trick me. He has all his sheep out at some place where he won't let me see them. Apparently there's water there and grass. In other words, it must be much better than here. I think he's got another house out there and I think, mother, that he has another woman out there.'

'Oh, Heather, how do you know that? What has Adam said?'

'Nothing. That's just it. He will not answer. He refuses to take me there. He didn't want you to come here – you know that – and he was telling me he expected me to go back and leave him here.'

Mrs Maguire sat down. She fanned herself. She was not hot. It was merely her reaction to a situation she could not understand. 'But why?' she said.

'Money. I think he must be making a great deal.' Slowly, she turned from the window and gazed at the ceiling, making calculations. 'He let a few things slip. Apparently some men are going to shear the sheep soon, so they must be men who work for him. Where are they and where are they living? Over at this other place, I'm sure. And do you know how many sheep he says he has?'

'I couldn't possibly guess,' Mrs Maguire sounded too exhausted to try.

'A thousand. Can you imagine a thousand sheep? Do you remember when we used to go down to Nevertire to play tennis at Pam's? Well, I never saw more than a dozen or so sheep at their place and they had so much money it positively dripped from them.'

'Oh dear, I don't know whether that's right,' she protested. 'I think they had a great deal of sheep somewhere else. They did have a very large area of land.'

'Not as much as Adam has. I think he's about to make a great deal of money and wants to get rid of me so I don't get any. That's why he went to the trouble of building this awful shack in the worst possible place so I'd think it was horrible and rush off and leave him.'

'Why? I don't understand why.'

'Because he wants the money for himself! And because of this other woman.'

'How do you know there's another woman?'

'I know. There has to be, to explain the way he's behaving. Besides, I know Adam. All he ever thinks of is women. All that's on his mind ...' She turned so that her mother would not see her face. 'I think you know what I mean and I know he could not possibly survive for a year without, shall we say, female company. And I can see it in his eyes. When he's talking to me, I can see that he's thinking of another woman. I've looked at him, mother. He positively burns with guilt.'

SEVEN

Three weeks later, Josef arrived. He came with Saleem Benn, who used two camels to haul a dray laden with supplies for Kalinda. Josef rode on the dray, sitting cross-legged on a pile of sacks. He jumped to the ground before the camels stopped near the yards where Adam was working, and earned a mutter of disapproval from the Afghan because his sudden action caused the younger camel to shy. While Saleem Benn tried to soothe the animal, grabbing its halter and making loud clucking sounds, Josef ran to Adam.

'Jesus!' Adam said, lowering the adze he had been using to shape a post. 'I'd given you up for lost.'

Josef stopped and looked as though he were deciding whether to laugh or cry.

'Haven't they been feeding you?' he said, and wiped his eyes. 'You're as lean as a drover's dog!'

'You've been eating all right,' Adam said, sizing up his friend. 'You've put on half a stone.'

'Yeah. Plenty of food and good German wine.'

The two men almost embraced but, self-conscious at the last moment, stopped short of such an emotional greeting and shook hands.

'Why didn't you write?' Adam said. He was almost gurgling with joy and had difficulty speaking.

Josef withdrew a letter from his pocket. He gave it to Adam. 'I did. This was waiting for you at William Creek. I wrote to you a few weeks ago.'

'I don't get in there very often. Saleem Benn is my mailman. Is it a good letter?'

'Terrific. Do you want me to read it to you?'

'Later. Are you staying?'

'If you'll have me.'

It was all decided with smiles. They talked for a few minutes until Heather appeared at the door of the house. She remembered Josef and greeted his arrival with more enthusiasm than Adam might have expected. She displayed the baby with a modest pride, remembered to make a show of thanking Saleem Benn for the gift of seeds – a little speech which she delivered with simple elegance – and withdrew discreetly to allow the men to talk further. Adam was surprised. He and Heather had maintained a peace of varying uneasiness in the past weeks. She still needled him with suggestions of another house and another woman but such exchanges were rare. She constantly criticized the property and the house, but in milder terms than she had used in the early days. It was as though she was growing to like the place but was still too proud to admit it. He had decided to wait and get on with the work he had to do, and see what happened.

One change was that he entered the house whenever he felt like doing so. Heather had tried to keep him out several times, but he

586

took no notice of her. Once he lifted her bodily from his path and she had said nothing after that. He ate his meals and cuddled Cassie when he came into the house – usually in the evenings before Mrs Maguire served dinner – but he did not sleep there. Not until that night. After Heather had been re-introduced to Josef and after the men had helped Saleem Benn unload the dray, she came to Adam and quietly suggested that he should move his bed, which was in the shed near the car, to the house. It wouldn't be proper, she suggested, for another man to discover they weren't living beneath the same roof. Adam recalled that Jimmy was aware of his sleeping arangements but realized he was not important to Heather. What a black man thought was of no consequence. Josef was different. No suggestion must be allowed of anything scandalous or unconventional.

That night, Josef slept in the shed and Adam put his bed roll near the stove in the house. Heather would not allow him to put out the bed until Josef had gone to the shed and she only let Josef go after apologizing profusely for not having room for him in the house. Josef would happily have slept in the bush at Jimmy's camp but Jimmy had moved the sheep to the number two bore and that was too far away to be reached that day.

Josef's arrival was fortuitous. The first team of shearers to visit Kalinda was due in a few days, and Adam was behind in some of the preparations for their arrival. He had been forced to spend several days at the most distant bore when the pump had failed, and he still had some fences to build around the new shearing shed. Josef's hands had grown soft and soon carried large blisters but he worked with gusto, pleased to be back in the bush and to be working with his friend.

The shearing was to be the culmination of Adam's year of work. From the clip, he would earn his first money since coming to Lake Eyre. He had many things to do with it: some horses to buy; some more sheep dogs to procure; more material to extend the house, and erect quarters for Josef and Jimmy. And, of course, money for Jimmy and clothes and food and anything else they needed to survive until he could sell his next clip.

The shearing shed had a different meaning for Heather. The arrival of the shearers, in a train of dusty cars and a solitary truck bearing a portable shearing plant, meant much work for the women. The men were a hungry lot who not only ate great quantities of food but were particular about what they would eat and, more important, what they would not. It soon seemed to

Heather that they were an unreasonable lot for they happily accepted the crude conditions in the shearing shed, even complimenting Adam on the work he had carried out.

Yet they expected their food to be perfect. Her mother did the cooking, of course, and there was no doubt the stove was on the small side for so big a job, but at least her mother could stay in the house and just cook. She, in her eyes, had the far more onerous job of carrying the food to the men, which meant she had to hear their complaints. They always seemed to be complaining. One man in particular, a small person with a sharp face and the nickname of 'the Ferret', was constantly complaining. He never spoke to her but grumbled to the other men and that, she felt, was worse because he ignored her and behaved as though she were not present. The Ferret complained if his meat was cold or his tea too hot, he whined about stale bread and butter that was melting, and he rarely had a good word to say about anything. The gravy was too salty or the apple pie – which she herself had helped make from canned apples in that last expensive shipment of supplies from that creepy camel man – was too sweet and the pastry too soggy. He was simply dreadful.

But he was talkative and so she chose him as her target. He was lingering over his tea one night. A lamp glowed on the table. Other lights showed from the tents which the shearers had erected around the spring.

'Bloody tea's cold,' he said and then, noticing her, apologized for the language but not the observation.

'Oh, that's all right,' she said sweetly, busying herself with clearing the table near him. It was a rough table which Adam had built and she had made presentable by covering with dyed hessian.

'How long have you worked for my husband?' she asked.

'What do you mean?' he said, his face contorted from the misery of having to drink lukewarm tea. Another shearer was leaving but he stopped, surprised that the boss's wife would speak to the Ferret. He was a notorious grumbler and none of the other men bothered with him.

'Well,' she said, confused by his reply, 'Have you been here long?'

'Too long, missus.'

'Oh, I see,' she said, excited at the prospects revealed by his words. 'You spend most of your time working at …?' and she hesitated, not being sure of what words to use, '… at the other place?'

He looked puzzled. 'You mean other places.'

'There are more than one?'

'Too right. We're usually pretty busy.'

'I see.' He had finished his tea and she collected his cup. 'Is there water at the other place? I mean places?'

'Well, we wouldn't be in business if there wasn't any water, would we?'

'No, I suppose not. Is there grass too?'

He scratched his nose. 'What is this, missus?'

'I was just wondering. You know, about the other house and the woman in it.'

'What house?'

'Well,' she said, brushing crumbs from the hessian, 'the one at the bore.'

'The last one we were at?'

'Of course.'

'Well, the house is small but it's pretty nice.'

'I'm sure it is. And the woman?'

'Well, I hardly met her. Not to talk to anyhow. She's a good cook though.'

'Really? Is she a good-looking woman? Young, attractive? You know.'

'It's hard to say.'

'I'm sure you noticed.'

He scratched his nose. He was anxious to leave. The conversation was idiotic. Better to finish it dramatically, he thought, and stood up. 'Matter of fact,' he said, 'she's the best-looking woman I've ever seen.'

Heather's flushed. 'Is she fair or dark?'

'Dark.'

'Long hair?'

'Very long.'

'Blue eyes or brown?'

'Brown.' This woman is nuts, he thought, and began to retreat.

'Tall?'

'Yes.'

'Is she ...?' Her hands made a clumsy effort to outline a woman's figure.

'Too right. Excuse me, missus, I've got work to do.' His walk accelerated into a run.

She stayed at the table, burning with jealousy and yet feeling good. She had known there was another woman, and now she had the proof. She stayed there so long, planning what to do next, that her mother came looking for her.

With all the sheep in the homestead yards and the shearers at work, Kalinda became a bustling, noisy place. The sheep were always moving and sawing the air with their plaintive bleats. The shearers had brought dogs and they yapped constantly, nipping the sheep into squads. The men shouted or swore or laughed or sang. Machinery clattered. Dust rose and covered everything.

The nights were calmer, but still less tranquil than they had been. The sheep were always stirring and the dogs were restless, for dingoes were around and they could sense it and pulled and jerked at their leashes.

The dingoes had followed the sheep. There were a lot of them. They howled every night, mournful sounds that woke Heather and her mother and kept them trembling with fright. There were no attacks on the sheep because the dogs and the smell of so many humans kept the dingoes away, but in the morning the men could see tracks around the water and close to the yards, where the bolder animals had ventured.

'Why don't you just shoot them?' Heather asked after one particularly frightening night.

'Because they're too clever,' Adam said. 'They're interested in the sheep. When the shearing's over and we move the mob out, they'll go away. Even so,' he cautioned, 'don't leave any scraps lying around. If they find food around buildings, they'll expect it in future and come back looking for it.'

'Are they dangerous?'

'Not to humans.'

'You mean adults?'

Adam pondered the implications of the question. 'I wouldn't leave Cassie out of your sight.'

'As if I would!'

'And I wouldn't wander too far from the homestead. The drought's getting worse and there's not much for the poor blighters to eat out there.'

'You're not sorry for those wild creatures?'

'I'd shoot one rather than have it kill my sheep, but I don't hate them just because they're wild dogs. In fact, they're a beautiful animal in many ways. And let's face it – this is where they've always lived. This is their country. We're the newcomers. They were here a long time before we were.'

She looked at him in astonishment. 'So were snakes and blackfellows.'

'That's right.'

'Really, Adam, you say the most foolish things! Sometimes I think you'd rather live with those wild creatures than with civilized human beings.'

'Sometimes I would,' he said and left the house.

Saleem Benn returned a few days later, bringing with him two camels. He presented them to Adam. They were not his best animals, he admitted, but they were reasonably placid and easy to ride. That was an important consideration, he said with a wink, now that Josef had rejoined him, for that young man possibly was the worst rider ever to have survived a long journey by camel. The animals could also be persuaded to carry or haul heavy loads, which would be a useful attribute in moving bales of wool to the railway.

Adam was moved by the gift and offered eloquent thanks in Pushtu, which greatly pleased the old man.

'You have a remarkable memory for words,' Saleem Benn said and shook his head sadly. 'It is a matter of profound regret to one who has a deep affection for you that you have not used that facility to learn to write or read properly in your own language.'

'I haven't had the time, or the teacher.'

'Is it possible that your wife has had the opportunity denied to you, even though she is but a woman?'

'Do you mean can she read?' Adam said, smiling at the discreet way Saleem Benn had asked an awkward question. 'The answer is yes. She is very well educated.'

'Ah, then you have the solution to your problem. The most delightful way to learn a language is on the pillow, as an uncle of mine who had travelled widely once told me.' He depressed the pliable tip of his nose. 'There is one problem, which I'm sure you as a strong man would overcome, and that is that you would have to put yourself in the role of a student with your wife as teacher. That could be difficult, or amusing, depending on the couple.' He made the statement a question, arching his generous eyebrows to indicate he expected an answer.

'It should be very entertaining,' Adam said, and the Afghan was pleased. 'Tell me,' he added, posing the question that had intrigued him since Saleem Benn's arrival, 'I am pleased to see you with this generous gift but how have you managed to return so rapidly from Marree? It is such a long journey.'

The other man flared his nostrils in delight. He had been anticipating the question. 'It is because I have not been to Marree. I am in the process of establishing my store at William Creek.'

'Already?'

'Indeed. The building is humble but the goods themselves are of the highest quality. I have selected a site not far from the hotel. That is why I was able to return today. I have been at William Creek all this week, to ensure a successful start to the business.'

'Who's going to run it for you?'

The old man sighed. Adam thought he was going to rub his nose once more, but instead his long fingers came to rest on his cheek. For such a hard-working man, he had graceful hands.

'One of my nephews,' he said. 'He is a young man for whom I have some hope. He has considerable talent, balanced by a lack of enthusiasm for this project.'

'He sounds a bit of a risk.'

The hand slid down the cheek and reached his beard. 'I think responsibility will make a man of him. That and the assistant I have chosen for him.' Seeing the enquiring look on Adam's face, he winked and added: 'The assistant is a female to whom my nephew seems to be considerably attracted. I am told that she is extremely pleasing to lay eyes upon. What concerns me is that she has some intellect and a great deal of energy and initiative. She is, if you like, the bait I am using to lure my nephew to success. His, and ultimately, mine too.'

'Your cunning is matched only by your generosity.'

Saleem Benn tilted his head. 'There are times you sound more Afghan than many of my people. You are wasted as a white man, but still ... Before I go, you must make me a promise.'

'Yes?'

'Next time you want stores – modest items that can be carried on one camel – you come to William Creek to collect them. It will be cheaper for you and simpler for me, and it will also give you an opportunity to meet my nephew.'

'And this intriguing young Afghan girl you have employed?'

'Oh, she is not one of us.' He flattened the end of his nose and managed to smile at the same time. 'And she lacks this distinctive appendage. 'Hers is a little wider, perhaps, but infinitely shorter. And she is even darker than we.'

'She's aboriginal?'

'An unusual one. Perhaps part white and, I suspect, extremely clever.'

*

592

Mrs Maguire had been hanging clothes on a line strung at the side of the house. It was near the place where Adam and Saleem Benn had been talking. When the Afghan had gone, she approached Adam. She began nervously.

'I always seem to be eavesdropping on your conversations. I'm sorry. I don't mean to.'

Adam smiled. He had grown to like Mrs Maguire. They rarely spoke but she worked harder than Heather and did things for him without being asked. And occasionally, when the women argued and he heard fragments of their conversation, it seemed the mother was on his side.

'That's all right,' he said. 'There was nothing private.'

She squirmed with nervousness. 'I heard that man say you were going in to William Creek.'

'Yes. He wants me to. He's starting a store there.'

'Would you take me with you?'

'Do you want to do some shopping?'

She glanced around her, checking that no one was near. 'Well, actually, I'd like to get on the train.'

'You're leaving?'

She nodded.

'Heather hasn't mentioned it,' he said, his voice trailing off as he realized what he was saying.

She nodded. 'She doesn't know. And, please, you must promise me you won't tell her.'

'But you don't have to leave.'

'Yes, I do.'

'Look, I'm sorry about what happened when you arrived here. I know you got the impression you weren't wanted and I apologize for that.'

'No, no. It's not that. You're a sweet young man and you've done your best to make me feel at home.' She gave his wrist a motherly pat.

'I was going to build another room on the house.'

'I'm sure you were, and that's very kind of you.' She gripped his wrist. 'But I simply have to leave. The situation has become intolerable. If I stay, it will cause damage to you and Heather and ...'

She stopped. Heather was approaching.

'Say nothing,' Mrs Maguire whispered. 'Please?' And she walked back towards the house. Heather followed, firing a look at

Adam that somehow managed to combine curiosity with hostility. The two women entered the house and, as Adam walked away, he heard Heather's voice, loud and harsh.

That night, Heather came to Adam's bed. He was asleep and woke with her hand on his shoulder.

'I want to talk,' she whispered.

'What about?'

'You and me. Do you realize that since I came here, you haven't once tried to sleep with me?'

Adam sat up, rubbing his face. His bed was on the floor. Heather was on her knees beside him.

'Well, you haven't,' she repeated.

'You haven't exactly made it easy for me.'

'Sh. Speak softly. Mother will hear you.'

Adam pulled off the blanket. 'Do you want to get in with me?'

'No. But I want to know why you haven't tried to force yourself on me like you used to.'

'You want me to walk into the other room where your mother's sleeping and make love to you?'

'You used not be able to control yourself.'

'You never did understand, did you?'

'Understand what?'

'That I loved you.'

'Sh. Mother will hear.' She rocked back on her heels. 'That wasn't love,' she whispered. 'You were an animal.'

'No. You're wrong. I did that because I loved you.'

'Loved?'

'Yes. I used to love you.'

'Does that mean you don't love me now?'

He paused long enough to be conscious of noises. The sheep stirring. A dog rattling a chain. A man coughing. 'Yes,' he said.

'Yes what?' The whisper was almost inaudible.

'Yes, it means I don't love you now.'

'Why? Is it that other woman?'

Adam pulled the blanket over his body again. 'I don't love you because of the way you behave. I tried to love you. I can't. You won't let me.'

'And what about Cassandra?'

'I love her, of course.'

'Of course. But you don't love your wife.'

'You don't behave like a wife.'

Heather rose, a pale figure in the black of the house. 'I lowered myself by marrying you. You know that, don't you? And I only married you because my family was in a desperate financial situation.' She had moved away and her voice barely reached him. 'Had you been a man of honour you would, of course, have responded by taking over some of the burdens which eventually killed my father.'

'Really?' said Adam. 'So now I helped kill your father?'

'Yes. A gentleman would have behaved differently. Your reaction was to run away and abandon your pregnant wife and her family. And leave my father to die.'

'You have a marvellous way of changing the facts.'

'I haven't changed anything. As I've noted repeatedly, you just can't accept the truth. I have also discovered, Adam Ross, that you may not be clever in the civilized meaning of the word but you are cunning, and I know that you are making a great deal of money ...'

'Me? Those sheep out there have got more than I have!'

'Wouldn't you like me to believe that! And now that you have money and realize that I have discovered that fact, you are trying to get rid of me. Which is what all this sham of yours is about.'

'I am not trying to get rid of you.'

'Yes, you are. You are deliberately trying to shock me, to upset me so much that I will go away so that you can keep everything for yourself and that whore of yours.'

'Oh, yes, the woman in the sandhills.' Adam lay back and rested his head on clasped hands. 'You haven't mentioned her for a day or two.'

'You may try to joke about it but I will not let you make a fool of me.' She walked away, then returned quickly and bent low, so her head was near his. 'Do you hear me? I will never let you sleep with me again. I will make you pay for all the misery you've caused me. And I will find this other woman, and make you suffer for having people laugh at me.'

EIGHT

Mrs Maguire kept away from Adam for the next few days. She was still anxious to leave but even more concerned not to be seen talking to him. She could not bear the thought of another vituperative lecture from her daughter. She hated being spoken to in that way. No that she minded being told what to do. Someone else had always done the thinking for her, always firmly, but mostly kindly. She had lived with strong people: her mother, her husband and now her daughter. She had never questioned their right to map her life for her. If they thought it was best, it probably was.

When her husband's awful illness tightened its hold and he had become positively doddery, Heather had taken over the running of the family. But instead of merely helping and guiding her through a difficult period, her daughter had become some sort of tyrant. She had become such a hard young woman. It frightened her. Heather made impossible demands and enjoyed seeing her suffer. No, she reassured herself, she was not imagining it – her daughter had become an unreasonable, harsh and even cruel person.

Her hands were chafed and cut from the work she had been required to perform in these last weeks. Her mind was battered from Heather's constant verbal assaults. She did not mind Kalinda, rough, dusty and isolated though it was, but she could not bear to be there and be treated the way she was by her own daughter. So she had to go. Where to, she had no real idea. Maybe to Parramatta, to see if her sister would look after her. Somewhere. It was, she knew, a simply dreadful thing to have to do at her age but she could not stay. She was frank enough to acknowledge that her primary motive was selfish: she could no longer tolerate being treated the way she was. And yet there was also a genuine concern for the future of Heather and Adam. They were not happy and she was sure her presence contributed to the friction between them. If she left they might stop arguing, because she was certain most of the arguments were over her. She had heard the term 'that woman' and it made her cringe with shame. There was the chance that Heather would change if the major problem in her marriage – the presence of her mother – were to disappear.

However, she had decided against asking Adam once more to drive her to William Creek. Heather would find out and accuse Adam of having thought of the idea and then there would be a terrible argument. No, she would ask one of the other men – either young Josef, who seemed very pleasant, or the one-armed aboriginal who was always smiling, although he spent most of his time away from the homestead.

Adam saw her, and she was alone.

'I'm going in to William Creek in a day or two, Mrs Maguire,' he said. 'I have some stores to collect. I don't want you to leave but if you still feel you should go, I'll take you.'

'No, it's all right, thank you, Adam.'

'You've changed your mind?'

She nodded, not daring to speak the lie.

'Good. I'm glad for two reasons. One is that you're staying.' Mrs Maguire smiled, but kept looking about her in case Heather was in sight. 'And the other,' he added, 'is that I would have had to take the car. I want to take the camels. Give them a try out.'

'That will be nice,' she murmured.

'It'll be rough,' he laughed. 'I haven't ridden a camel for a long time. Still, I'm looking forward to the trip.'

'How long will you be gone?'

'Two days. Maybe three.'

She mumbled good wishes for his journey and began planning her own departure. It would be better to leave while Adam was away because then Heather could not order him to pursue her and bring her back. Yes, she decided, she would leave Kalinda while Adam was in town.

Adam was caught in another dust storm on his way to William Creek. He saw it coming and had time to search for shelter. He found a clump of low bushes on the edge of a faint and powdery watercourse and, dismounting, led the animals to the spot. There he brought them down, putting them parallel to each other but side-on to the forthcoming blow. He sat hunched against the undulating side of his riding camel. The beast was young and nervous and breathed more vigorously as the storm drew nearer. When the first sharp waves of sand lashed them, the camel began to tremble as well so that Adam, pressed to its flank, rocked and shook with each intake of air or quiver of muscles. The other camel, older and heavier and fitted with a wooden frame Adam had fashioned to carry stores back to Kalinda, simply turned its head and closed its eyes and rolled its jaws.

The storm was brief. Adam shook dust from his hair, brushed his clothes, drank some water and remounted. He reached town in the middle of the afternoon and went directly to the new store. It consisted of two buildings. The larger was a shed which served as the main storeroom. The other fronted the road. The smaller building had three walls of corrugated iron and an open front, which could be closed by lowering two rolled strips of canvas. The entrance to this building was through a gap in a wall of produce.

597

On the left, racked like a line of sandbagged defences, were sacks of potatoes, onions, rice, flour, salt and sugar. On the right were a few prized boxes of fruit, mingled with an assortment of shovels, picks, drills, axes, buckets, cans, tins of various oils and stout packets of nails and screws. Above the lot hung a collection of boots, hats, whips, belts and leather pouches of varying size and purpose. Inside was a shadowy collection of items, ranging from cotton shirts to enamel baths.

A young man with greased hair and a lean, dark face was sweeping dust through the opening. He recognized the camels and he remembered the rider, much to Adam's surprise. He had been at Marree in 1929 when his uncle had brought Adam there to recover from his burns.

'You would not remember me,' he said, and introduced himself as Saleem Goolamadail. 'I was one of a dozen boys there at the time. I have grown up but you have merely grown older.'

It was the first time anyone had ever referred to Adam as being old. The remark was one that only a very young man would make. Adam tried to estimate the age of Saleem Benn's nephew. Maybe twenty-one or twenty-two. The youngster's eyes flashed confidence.

Yes, Goolamadail was aware that Mr Ross had established credit with his uncle. He would be happy to supply any item in the store. He even had fruit and vegetables from the south, fresh from yesterday's train. Adam gave his 'maybe' look and entered the building. He admired a Schneider saddle strung over a rafter. He would need saddles when he purchased extra horses, which he would have to do soon. Not Schneiders. They were beyond his means although he could admire the craftsmanship. He found small items he needed: a round pocket stone to sharpen his knife; a rasp and hoof knife for completing the kit he needed to shoe the mare; boxes of ammunition for Jimmy's rifle. He liked to wander through places like this, among familiar objects with rich new smells. He touched flannel garments and leather boots, balanced an axe in his hand and even tried on a hat he had no intention of buying.

He had not thought about Goolamadail's assistant.

Nellie was in the storeroom at the back, removing the seals she had stuffed around windows and doors to keep out dust from the storm. Despite her efforts, some dirt had penetrated the building and swirled over everything and it took her an hour to sweep or shovel it out. The building was old with wooden walls whose boards flexed in a strong wind and presented a score of new openings with every gust. She spent another half-hour dusting the boxes and cans but ignored the sacks. They always looked dusty, so what did it matter?

When she had finished, she walked to the front building. She saw the two camels tethered to a post and taking it in turns to gnaw each other's neck, and wondered if Saleem Benn had returned unexpectedly. The front of the shop, she observed, was still coated with dust. Goolamadail was lazy and would expect her to clean up.

A man was in the store. She saw his back, the broad shoulders, the long and unkempt fair hair, and suddenly had difficulty breathing.

'Oh, there you are,' Goolamadail said, emerging from a shadowy recess. He was carrying a box which he put on top of some sacks, arousing a swirl of fine dust. 'There's still a mess in here,' he said, managing to imply that she had caused it. 'You'd better clean this up. Oh, by the way, this is my uncle's friend, Mr Ross.'

Adam turned. His mouth opened. His tongue touched his lips. He managed to nod.

'Nellie Arlton,' the young man said. 'She helps me here.' And then to Nellie: 'Mr Ross owns a big property up near Lake Eyre. He's a good friend of my uncle.'

'Hello,' she said.

'Pleased to meet you,' he said and swallowed hard.

'You might help Mr Ross, Nellie. He wants a few things so maybe you could get them together for him. Do you want them loaded on the camels?'

'No,' Adam said, shocked back to the conversation. 'I'll do it myself but I won't want most things until tomorrow.'

'Well, just get what he wants,' Goolamadail told her. 'I've got some paperwork to do. My uncle's very particular about that.' Now he was talking to Adam. He seemed pleased at the prospect of avoiding physical effort. He excused himself.

'Where's he gone?' Adam said when they were alone.

'There's an office in the storeroom. He hides there whenever he can.' She smiled shyly. 'You look thin.'

'I haven't had much time for eating.'

'How's it going? The new property, I mean?'

'Good. What the devil are you doing here?'

She plucked at a projecting strand of jute on a bag. 'You sound as though you're not pleased to see me.'

'I'm just surprised. I can't believe it. I always seem to be running into you when I least expect it.'

She smiled. 'Must be fate.'

'How are you?'

'I'm fine. A bit dusty at the moment. That was a big storm. Did you get it?'

'Can't you tell?' He brushed his sleeve.

She had thought about this moment for so long and now she didn't know what to say. 'Would you like some oranges? We got some in yesterday. I'm not supposed to sell more than a dozen to any one person but you can have a case if you like.'

'I'd like one now, if I could.'

'Help yourself.'

He peeled an orange, looking at her as he removed the skin. 'Would you like some?'

'Just a little.'

He gave her a quarter and bit hard into his similar piece. Juice trickled down his chin. 'I'm not used to these things,' he said, wiping his face and leaving a mud stain.

'They're nice, aren't they? We've got potatoes too.' She giggled. He was still dribbling. 'How long since you've eaten one of those?'

'Long time.' He swallowed. 'Nellie, what the hell are you doing up here?'

His voice wasn't harsh. It was miserable, and she knew he was pleased to see her but didn't know how to express his feelings. And he looked so worn and sad. She wanted to hold and comfort him. She turned away and blew dust from the lid of a biscuit tin. 'It's a long story,' she said. 'I've been moving around a bit since I last saw you. How's the baby? Have you seen it yet and what is it?' She faced him, smiling.

'A girl. She's good.'

'What's her name?'

'Cassie. Cassandra's her full name but I prefer Cassie.'

'That's nice. Is she a blondie like you?'

'No, she's dark. More your colour.' The words were out before he realized what he had said and he blushed.

'That'll take some explaining,' she said, enjoying his embarrassment.

'I mean her hair. Oh, God, you know what I mean!'

'Yeah. She's not blonde.'

'Right.' They smiled at each other.

'How's Heather? That's her name, isn't it?'

Adam raised his shoulders and eyebrows in unison. 'OK.'

'OK?'

He cleared his throat. 'She's good.'

'That's good.'

'Yes. Where are you staying?'

'Here.'

'No, I mean where do you live? There aren't exactly a lot of houses in town.'

'I sleep in the storeroom. It's much bigger than this. I have a bed behind a row of car tyres.'

'You're joking!'

'No, I'm not. That Goolamadail has a purse that's as big as a mouse's ear. Mind you, he's staying at the pub until they build a room on the back of the store. I think his long-range plan is to have me move in with him.'

'Marry him?'

'I don't think so,' she said, laughing. 'What he has in mind is for me to visit him at night. You know, sneak in when no one's looking and creep back to my bed among the tyres before dawn when he has to get up to pray.'

'He's very young,' Adam said, knowing that a young man of his Afghan background would regard marrying an aboriginal as anathema.

'He's stuck up. He thinks he's God's gift to women. Or Allah's gift, or whoever it is he keeps praying to.'

'What are you going to do?'

'If he comes sneaking around the tyres after I go to bed? I've got a pick handle there and I'll flatten him with it. And then apologize and say I thought he was a burglar.'

Adam was thinking about Saleem Benn's conversation and how he had planned to use a woman as a lure for his nephew. A woman in whom his nephew had already shown interest. He fidgeted with a leather strap hanging from the roof. 'Didn't you know it would be like this? I mean, you must have known him in Marree.'

She nodded.

'Well, there are only the two of you up here. It's really putting temptation in his way.'

She pulled the strap down so he could no longer play with it. 'What you're trying to say,' she said, looking into his eyes, 'is, why did I come here to this out-of-the-way place with a randy young horror like Goolamadail?'

'Well, yes.'

'Don't you know?'

'No.'

'That's your trouble, Adam. It takes you a long time to understand the obvious.'

Heather would have said the same words, he thought, but made them sound bitter. They flowed from Nellie's tongue as smooth and soothing as soft laughter. The thought produced a gentle smile. 'I don't follow you,' he said.

'I know you don't. Let me tell you something. After you left Port Augusta, I worked there for a while and then got a job in Quorn. It wasn't a bad job but I quit it to come to Marree and I got a job with Saleem Benn's family and when I heard they were opening this store, I applied for this job. I'd have worked with Jack the Ripper to come here. Don't you know why?'

Adam squirmed.

'That's right,' she said, staring at him frankly, all pretence gone. 'I came here to be closer to you.'

He brushed past her. At the entrance to the store he turned, rubbing his chin and confused. 'Nellie, I'm married.'

'You're not happy.'

'How do you know that?' he said gruffly.

'I can tell.'

'Rubbish!'

'All right. Tell me I'm wrong.' She had retreated to the back of the store where she merged with the shadows. 'Tell me you're happy.'

The sacks at the front seemed to hold a fascination for Adam. He stared resolutely at them, refusing to look Nellie's way. Nearby, the camels dozed at their mooring, heads bobbing slightly as though riding a faint but persistent swell. He heard Nellie move towards him.

'I'm not happy either,' she said.

'Who is?'

'I didn't have any plan. I mean, I wasn't going to go anywhere else or do anything special. I was just going to stay here until I saw you. Silly, wasn't it?'

He neither answered nor moved. He was aware she was near him.

'Are they your camels?' Her voice was bright again. It was a

602

signal that it was safe to talk freely.

'Yes.'

'They're nice. Did they cost you a lot of money?'

'Not a zac. Saleem Benn gave them to me.'

'What are their names?'

He turned, confident to face her once more. 'That is a typical woman's question.'

'Why?'

'Well, a man wouldn't ask that. He'd want to know how old they were or what they could carry or if they had bad breath. Things like that. Not their names.'

'If it was a typical's woman's question, does that make me a typical woman?'

'No,' he laughed. 'Definitely not! Do you mind if I have another orange?'

'Go ahead.'

'I'll pay for it.'

'You certainly will. I'm counting. You're up to two.'

He selected an orange, peeled the top and bit into it. Again, juice ran down his chin. 'The camels don't have any names,' he said, leaning forward to avoid the dripping liquid.

'Every camel should have a name. Why don't you call one Saleem and the other Benn?'

'I don't think the old man would be flattered,' he said, approaching the younger camel. It opened its eyes wearily.

'I worked with a man called Khan in Marree,' she said. 'He was a camel man. Why don't you call one Khan?'

'What about the other one?'

She twinkled with mischief. 'Tin.'

'What?'

'I think they go well together. Tin and Khan. Get it?'

He swung away, attempting to hide a smile and suppress a fresh cascade of orange juice. It seemed such a long time since someone had joked with him. He wiped his face carefully before confronting her. 'I think we should call them serious names. They're very serious animals. But I think we can leave it till later. I think I should get the things I need and go. You probably have other things to do.'

'I suppose so. You're leaving tonight?'

'No. I'll probably go back in the morning.

'Where are you staying?'

'I'll camp somewhere.'

'I'd like to talk to you. Maybe later?'

He hesitated for such a long time she thought he hadn't heard her. 'Sure,' he said eventually. 'I'd like that.'

Josef was mending a puncture in one of the Alfa's back tyres. It was a slow leak which had been gradually deflating. He had jacked up the car, removed the wheel and prized the tyre from the rim. He had taken out the tube, pumped it up, and was now passing it like an endless sausage through a drum of water, searching for air bubbles to reveal the leak. Heather walked from the house. To his astonishment, she invited him to join her for afternoon tea. He had entered the house before, but only in the company of Adam. Heather had never asked him. She rarely spoke to him.

'I'm very dirty,' he said, displaying hands stained by grease and dust.

'That's quite all right,' she said pleasantly. 'Just give your hands a wash and come and have some tea. Mother has baked fresh scones. You'd like some of those?'

She was almost the same age as he, Josef thought, but she spoke like a much older woman. He washed quickly in the drum and followed her, drying his hands on his pants as he walked.

In the house, the table had been set for two. Mrs Maguire stood beside the stove, drinking tea and occasionally stirring something in a pot. Heather sat at the table. She indicated Josef should join her. He hesitated, looking at Mrs Maguire.

'No, no, she's busy,' Heather said and her mother gave a thin smile.

'I'm sorry we haven't had a chance to talk before but I've been so busy.' Heather offered Josef black tea. 'I hope you like your tea without milk because we don't have any. Adam is trying to get some of this new powdered milk from William Creek but really, the thing he should do is have a few cows. Don't you agree?' Before he could, she went on: 'Have you ever heard of a farm without cows? It's like a beehive without honey. Or a man without a woman.' She smiled sweetly. 'Do you take sugar? We have some of that.'

He dipped his spoon in the bowl. 'It might be hard to keep milking cows,' he said, stirring vigorously. 'They usually like grass.'

'Well, we could keep them at the bore.'

He glanced at her, not understanding.

'It sounds very nice there.' She sipped her tea without milk and pulled a face that was still highly attractive. 'The water here has such a strange taste.'

'It's got a few minerals in it. At least you don't need to put as much salt on your food.'

She laughed, somehow managing to suggest great amusement without making a sound. Josef relaxed. She seemed nicer than he remembered.

'Would you believe that I haven't been to the bore since we arrived?' she said.

'You've been very busy,' he said, echoing her earlier remark.

'Oh, it's not that. Adam won't take me.'

He helped himself to a scone. There were times, he knew, when it was better to say nothing and he sensed their conversation had entered such a zone. Since he had come to Kalinda, Adam had never spoken to him about his wife. Josef suspected they had quarrelled.

'It sounds beautiful,' she said.

'Which one, Mrs Ross?'

'Please call me Heather, Mr ... may I call you Joseph?'

'Joe.'

'No, Joseph. It suits you. It's ... biblical. There are many Joes but not many Josephs and you, very definitely, are a Joseph. It's that last "s,e,p,h" that makes the difference.'

'It's spelled with an "f",' Josef said, collecting a crumb that had fallen on the table.

'Really?' She dabbed her lower lip. 'That's much more refined than the normal way.'

'It's German. My family came from Germany.'

'How interesting!' The smile was intense. 'But you were telling me about the bore. Did you say "which one"?'

'Yes. There are two.'

'Well, I suppose Adam was talking about the one with all the grass. It does sound beautiful.'

Josef concentrated on his tea, trying to think of an answer to please. 'That'd be number two bore,' he pronounced, because he recalled seeing some grass near the windmill. There was not much and it was dry and tufty and would certainly not support dairy cattle, but it was grass. Of sorts.

'You will have to take me there sometime,' she said and offered him another scone.

'I'd be pleased to,' he said, beaming. 'I'm not sure how we'd get there, though. It's a few miles.'

'We could drive in the car.'

Josef had only been to that bore once, and he had walked. Brow furrowed, he tried to recall what the ground was like. A great deal of sand was near the bore.

'You *can* drive?' she asked, with the faintest suggestion of a smile.

'Of course,' he answered quickly.

'Good. Shall we go tomorrow?'

'Well, I don't know. Adam's away and it's his car.'

She waved aside the objection with an elegant sweep of her hand. 'Oh that's all right. Isn't the car working? I saw you doing something with the wheel. Can you fix it?'

'Oh, sure.'

'You must be very clever with mechanical things. Much more than Adam, who is not very good with his hands – as you can see by this house.' There was no malice. Just a statement softened by a smile. 'Shall we say tomorrow, then? I'm so looking forward to seeing it.'

She had terminated the conversation and Josef, worried about the undertaking he had made, went back to repairing the punctured tube. He was replacing the wheel when Mrs Maguire entered the shed.

'I heard my daughter say you were going to drive her somewhere,' she said, her voice trailing towards silence. She backed into the shed's darkest corner.

'That's right, Mrs Maguire.' Josef stood with his hands clasped respectfully in front of him.

'Well,' she said, her eyes darting nervously about her, 'I was wondering if you could take me somewhere too.'

'To the bore?'

'No. To town. I want to go to the railway station.'

'I don't know. Adam will be back in a day or so. He could take you, Mrs Maguire.'

'No. Adam mustn't know. Oh!' She had heard footsteps and pressed against the wall.

Heather approached. 'Have you seen my mother, Josef?'

He didn't know what he should say. His eyes went from Heather to her mother and back again. Heather strode forward, saw her mother, and smiled benignly. 'Go back in the house, dear,' she said. Her mother reminded Josef of a trapped animal. She was in the corner, face bleached by fear, an arm spread along each wall.

Heather advanced and took one arm. 'Come along. You have some things you should be doing.' She pushed her towards the house. The older woman walked a few steps and stopped. 'Keep going.' Heather waited for Mrs Maguire to move again and then crossed to Josef.

'I hope she didn't bother you,' she said softly.

'No, not at all.' Mrs Maguire was pursuing a wobbly course towards the house. 'Is your mother all right? She seems very unsteady.'

'Oh yes, she's all right. What was she saying?'

Again, Josef had the feeling that this was a good time to say nothing. 'She just got here.'

'You'll have to forgive her. She's a little ...' and she put her finger to her head and described a circle. 'It's just old age. I have to watch her all the time. You can imagine how difficult it is, what with the baby and all the other work.'

'That's all right.'

'The car will be ready for tomorrow?'

'Yes.' He felt he should say, 'Why don't we wait until Adam gets back?' but she had such a contented look that he said nothing.

'Good. I'll take some lunch, shall I? Or will we be able to get something to eat there?'

'At the bore?'

'Yes,' she said, waiting for him to make a slip. She was certain Adam would have forbidden him to talk about the other house or the other woman. But this young man could be tricked into saying things.

'No,' Josef said, wondering what on earth she expected to find at the bore.

'I'll pack a nice lunch then. I'm really looking forward to tomorrow, aren't you?'

'Yes,' he said lamely and wished Adam had not gone to William Creek. One crazy old woman was bad enough but he was beginning to think there was something strange about her daughter, too.

NINE

Adam tethered the camels near some trees. Around sunset he made a small fire, boiled a billy of water for tea, opened a can of meat and roasted two newly purchased potatoes in the ashes. He ate another orange. He left the camels happily chewing some prickly bushes and headed back to the town.

The air was warm. A gibbous moon flirted with clouds, making the night a flickering succession of bright images or shadowy mysteries. When the moon was out he strode confidently across the plain, but when the clouds ensnared the light he stumbled into bushes or kicked unseen rocks, as vulnerable as a ship drifting in a sea of reefs.

William Creek was small, even by the standards of the bush. It was shown on maps in reasonably large type but that was because there was little else to put on that part of the paper and cartographers were loath to leave empty spaces. Stranded between Marree and Oodnadatta – one hundred and thirty-six miles north-west of one and one hundred and twenty-seven south-east of the other – it had little to recommend it, except as a base for a scattering of cattle and sheep stations. It had a railway station and a hotel and now a store, and it was a logical place to pause for rest on the way to somewhere else.

In the dark that night, William Creek seemed tiny and almost ephemeral; dim lights and hazy shapes hovering on a plain that stretched to the other side of infinity.

One of the lights moved. Someone with a torch was approaching. Adam stopped, the natural reaction when facing an encounter with a stranger. The light flashed brightly and then grew dim as the person shone the torch in several directions – down, forwards, to the side – trying to determine the best path to take. Adam resumed walking. There was no point in waiting for whoever it was to run into him. As he drew near the light, he heard the other person stumble. The torch clattered on the ground and went out. There was a grunt of pain.

'Are you all right?' he called out. Silence.

'Have you hurt yourself?'

'Who is it?' It was a woman's voice, shaky with pain and fright.

'My name's Ross.'

The woman laughed, an artificial sound thinned by stress. 'Come and give me a hand, will you, Adam? I'm stuck.'

'Nellie?'

'That's me.' The voice was more normal.

'Are you hurt?'

'Don't think so. Just stuck in a hole.'

'I'll come and give you a hand. Just hang on.'

'I'm not going anywhere.' She giggled and then groaned. 'Oh, I've got a sore leg!'

Adam fell into a bush. He struggled to his feet.

'Are you all right?' she called.

'I'm OK. Just can't see a thing.' Arms outstretched, he negotiated the journey around another bush. 'I think I've run into a forest.' He blundered on, snapping branches until he was finally clear of the patch of bush. 'How bad's your leg?'

'Don't know. I can't see it. My foot's down a big hole of some sort.' There was the sound of sliding stones. 'No. I can't move it. You'll have to help me. What are you doing out here, anyway?'

'Coming to see you.'

'Good.' She waited for him to reach her. The moon reappeared. Misty clouds streaked its face and a wan light bathed the plain. Nellie was sitting near a bush. Her left foot and ankle were caught in a rabbit burrow.

'Well, what are you doing here?' he said, standing above her.

'Same as you. I was frightened you mightn't come.'

'No, I was on my way,' he said, suddenly feeling shy. He bent to dig the earth trapping her foot. A broad cloud slipped across the moon. She faded into the night. He could hear her breathing.

'This is weird,' he said. 'I can't see you any more.'

'I'm still here.'

He had his hand around her ankle. 'Does that feel sore?'

'It feels wonderful.' Her hand touched his shoulder. He kept digging.

'Do you think you could stand?'

'If you help me.'

He stood and offered his hand. 'You'll need both hands,' she said. He bent, grasped her and lifted. She came up in his arms.

From the hotel came the clink of bottles being thrown on a heap. A man growled at a dog. A door slammed. The sounds were close, threatening.

'How's the foot?' Adam whispered. He lowered his arms as a signal that she should try to walk, but she left her hands on his

609

shoulders.

'It's the ankle. It's a bit tender.'

'It's dangerous out here on your own in the dark.'

'Yes. I'm glad I'm with you.' She joined her hands behind his neck. 'You're not sorry I came to this town? You're not angry with me?'

He let one of his arms slide around the small of her back. He shook his head. 'No. Do you want me to help you back to your place?'

'In Rubber Row? No, thank you. I'd like to see where you're staying.'

'It's over among the trees. It's a fair walk. Do think you can make it?'

'If you help me.'

She took his other hand and pulled it around her. She felt him tense but held him in place until he began to relax. 'I'm glad you were coming to see me,' she said. He made a noise as though he were about to speak but had strangled the words before their escape embarrassed him.

'You don't really mind me holding you like this?' she said. 'I mean, I know you're married and all that, but deep down you don't feel bad because I've got my arms around you? Please say no! Please.'

She thought she felt his ribs shake, as though a puff of laughter had disturbed them. 'No,' he breathed.

'Can we be honest with each other?'

'Sure.'

'Have you missed me?' When he didn't answer, she added: 'Have you thought about me then?'

'Yes.'

'Often?'

'Yes.'

She squeezed him. 'I've thought about you too. Oh, God, I've missed you, Adam! Back in Port Augusta, I made up my mind how I felt about you and then you went away. You've no idea what that did to me.' His muscles tensed. 'Before you say anything, there's something I've got to tell you. It's like a confession,' she added and breathed deeply to prepare herself. 'I missed you but I tried to forget you. I really did. I knew you were married and that wife of yours was going to have a baby. I knew you were white and I was coloured.'

'You know that doesn't matter.'

She turned her head side-on to his chest. 'I know, I know, but let me finish. We're being honest with each other so let me tell you something. I got a job with a man in Quorn and I slept with him a couple of times. It was only because I was trying to forget about you. I didn't love him although he was a good man.'

'You haven't got to tell me this.'

'Yes, I have.'

He stroked her hair. 'Have I ever told you you get more beautiful every time I see you?'

'No,' she said, her mouth buried in his shirt.

'You were so beautiful when I saw you in the store today I could hardly speak.'

'I looked like a golliwog.'

'And I was as dusty as one of the camels. Do you think you could make it to the camp?'

The clouds drifted to the other side of the sky and the moon was on its own, bright and bulbous and lighting their way across the plain. They kept to clear ground, avoiding the dark splotches which were either rotund bushes or deep burrows. Nellie's ankle hurt and she limped. They stopped several times for her to rest. Adam had one arm around her. He began to hum a tune. Very softly, but loud enough for Nellie to look up.

'I don't think I've ever heard you sing,' she said.

'I'm not singing.'

'Hum a tune then.'

'I feel good.'

'So do I.'

They reached the camp. The camels shuffled their legs and pulled at their ropes. The older animal emitted a sound like mud sloshing in a geyser.

'That settles it,' she said. 'That one has to be called Rumble.'

'All right,' Adam said, spreading his groundsheet. 'What about the other one?'

'You mean you like Rumble?'

'Sure.'

'Don't you want to discuss it? How about Rumbles? Or Gurgles?'

'No. Rumble. Here.' He took her hand. 'Sit down and take the weight off your ankle.'

She sat on the groundsheet and kicked off her shoes. 'Now the other one.'

'Bozo,' he said.

'Why Bozo?'

'Why not?'

So the names were decided and he sat beside her and they talked about Kalinda. He talked about sheep and fences and bores and the house and she sat, silent and attentive.

'Is it going to work out?' she said. 'I mean, it's terribly dry country and this is an awful drought. Will you make any money? Enough to live?'

'I think so.'

'Well, if anyone can do it, you can.'

The moon shone, cold and accusing, daring him to make comparisons.

'Heather has this crazy idea that I'm making a fortune.'

'But can't she see for herself?'

'She thinks I'm hiding things from her.'

'Like what?'

'Another house.' With Nellie, he was able to smile.

'But didn't you build her a house?'

'She's convinced I've got another one, bigger and better, hidden away somewhere.' He scratched at the ground beside the canvas sheet. 'She also reckons I've got a woman hidden away somewhere.'

Nellie, who had been bending towards Adam, straightened her back. 'Where? Here in town?'

He dug a furrow in the dirt. 'No. Out at the bore.'

She allowed herself to topple slowly until her back was resting against him. 'She sounds as silly as a snake,' she said happily.

'I certainly don't understand her.'

'Do you think having the baby affected her? I mean, some women do turn a bit funny after they've had a kid.'

'I don't know. I think she's always been a bit hard to understand.'

Nellie rested against him, not daring to say more. In the old days, she'd heard many a husband complain about his wife and the woman's lack of understanding. This was different, but she'd learned when to be quiet.

'Anyhow,' Adam said, 'let's not talk about Heather.'

'Good.' She reached for his hand. 'Have you had anything to eat?'

'Yes. How about you? I could cook you some of the things you sold me today. Potato. A bit of meat.'

612

'No thanks. I've eaten.'

'Wouldn't you like an orange?'

She laughed.

'Where do you have your meals?'

'I've got a space near the bed.'

'Among the tyres?'

'Where else? That's my own little spot. It's very cosy although it stinks of rubber.'

'How do you cook?'

'I've got a primus. Gooly lets me take food from the store.'

'Who?'

'Goolamadail. The young drip who thinks he's Rudolph Valentino. He's not that bad, I suppose. He lets me choose what I want but he counts everything and makes a note of it. Every single baked bean.'

'Do you have to pay for it?'

'Not that I know of. I guess it depends on whether I ever have to hit him with that pick handle or not.' She squeezed him. 'No, I think it's free. They don't pay enough for me to buy meals and it's better than having their number one worker starve to death.'

'Like some tea? I could boil a billy.'

'All right.' She drew her knees into her body and sat there, arms wrapped around her legs, while he rekindled the fire. She watched him, chin on her knees, and felt a surge of joy. She was with him, he was happy to be with her – really happy, she could tell – and his wife, that blonde girl from the east whom she'd never met but was sure she'd hate, sounded like a prize drip. That made her happy but then, as she thought more, it worried her too, because Adam had to live with her and a woman like that could ruin him. Physically, mentally and financially.

'Adam,' she said, 'I know you don't want to talk about her but is this wife of yours going to stay out there at Kalinda?'

'I think so,' he said, throwing another piece of wood on the fire. Sparks showered from the ashes. 'She reckons she's not going to be cheated out of all the money I'm making.'

'From this fortune of yours?'

'That's the one. The million or two I've made in the last nine months.'

Their eyes met, smiling and understanding.

'What about this other woman she reckons you've got out there? There isn't one, is there?' She saw the pained expression on his face and added quickly: 'I'm sorry. Forget I said that. You'll think I'm as nutty as she is. What's she going to do about this imaginary lover of yours? Search for her?'

'I suppose so. Once she gets hold of an idea, she doesn't let go.'

'That'll keep her busy. How big did you say this place of yours was?'

'More than thirteen hundred square miles.'

For a delicious moment, Nellie envisaged Heather on foot, combing the land for her phantom rival. She could be away for years ...

'Tea's ready.' Adam filled an enamel mug. He offered it to her.

'What about you?'

'I've only got one cup.'

'That's a bit rough for a millionaire! Still, we'll share it.'

She took his hand and drew him closer. 'Don't go away from me again,' she said. She sipped some tea and gazed at him, her face partly obscured by the mug. She had enormous eyes.

Adam sat beside her. He stared into the fire. 'I've been such a fool,' he said.

She drank some more tea and offered him the mug. 'In what way?'

'Many ways. I can do some things right.' He sampled the drink without taking his eyes from the flames. 'But when I do something really important I foul it up.'

She touched his arm where a fresh scar stood proud from the skin. 'You've hurt yourself,' she murmured and he grunted acknowledgment. He'd cut his arm while tensioning fence wire a few months before.

'I shouldn't have gone to Western Australia,' he said. She put her head against his shoulder. 'That cost me all my money and weeks of lost time.' He drank more tea and passed her the mug. 'I shouldn't have left Jimmy to work on that well with only Josef to help him. That cost him his arm.'

'That wasn't your fault.'

'Yes, it was! And I shouldn't have got married. I made a real blue there.'

She said nothing. In the fire, a stick hissed boiling sap.

'I guess I was ... the trouble was ...' He took the mug from her. He drank deeply and returned it. 'I don't know what was wrong but it was wrong.'

'I've done bad things all my life too.'

'Not stupid things like me.'

'I let men fuck me when I was fourteen.'

614

He closed his eyes. 'Don't say that.'

'That's what it was.'

He covered his face and spoke through his hands. 'Do you know what the worst moments for me were, when Jimmy and Joe and me were roaming the bush? You know, in all those years after Coober Pedy?'

She pressed harder against him.

'The worst times were when I thought of you and imagined you were with other men. I used to dream of that. Of other men ... being with you. We were in some pretty out-of-the-way places and I used to lie under the stars at night and feel so lonely I used to ache, and I thought of you. And then I'd imagine you with some other bloke and ...' He lowered his hands. 'That was the worst mistake I ever made.'

'What was that?'

'Leaving you that night, when we were being chased by Mailey.'

'You didn't have much choice.'

'I should have tried to find you.'

'It was a mixed-up sort of night.'

'I should have waited around and searched for you.'

'You'd have been caught.'

'Maybe.' He was silent for a long time. Beyond the fire, the camels rested as immobile as sandstone carvings. There was no noise other than the crackling of the fire. No human voices. No dogs barking in the distance. No insects chirping or buzzing. No wind stirring the trees. They could have been the only creatures on earth.

Nellie moved, to ease the pressure on her hip. Her body swayed against his.

'If I'd found you that night,' Adam asked softly, in tune with the silence, 'would you have come away with me?'

'Yes.'

'We just wandered the bush for a few years. It wasn't very pleasant. We didn't make much money. Didn't eat all the time.'

'It wouldn't have mattered.'

'Wouldn't have been easy.'

'Wasn't easy as it was.'

He sighed. 'Want some more tea?'

'If you'd like some.'

He stood and walked to the fire.

'What did you do about women while you were away all those

years?' she said, leaning forward to rub her ankle.

He broke a dead branch and threw the pieces on the fire. 'Thought about them. Thought about you.'

'Didn't you find any nice young things so you could do something more than think?' She tried to smile.

'Joe got himself a young girl up in Queensland. I think it was his first.'

'I was your first, wasn't I?'

He grinned. 'I thought that was obvious!'

'Was I good?'

'Gee, you say some funny things!' He took the can from the fire, removed the lid and poured more tea. He offered her the mug. 'Be careful. It's hot.'

'You're just not used to people who say what they think,' she teased. 'Was I good?'

It had been so long since he had made love to a woman. You could forget, he thought, specially if you worked hard and long hours and there was no woman around. But when you were with a woman again, and you loved her ...

'Well, tell me!' She said. 'I want to know.'

'I said I used to think of you.'

'How did you remember me?'

With both hands, he rubbed his forehead. 'Like you were in the dugout.'

'That first time?'

He swallowed clumsily. 'Yes.'

She stood and slowly, sinuously, removed her dress. Adam looked the other way.

'There's no one out here,' she said. 'We're on our own.'

He kept his head down.

'Look at me,' she said. And when he did: 'Is this how you remembered me?'

'No,' he said, his voice rasping.

She limped to the fire, her back to Adam, and removed her brassiere. She was directly in front of the flames, a black shape with tantalizing swells and an edge of flickering light. Slowly she turned to face him.

'Like this?'

'No. You had nothing on.'

'Is that how you remember me?'

'Yes. Sometimes.'

'Most times?'

'When I was lonely.'

With a slow, flowing motion, she removed the pants. She stood erect and moved slowly towards him. 'I used to dream of you, too,' she said.

'Oh. How did you remember me?' Adam managed to say.

She started to unbutton his shirt. 'You were very tall and fair and strong. And very shy.' She pulled the shirt from his shoulders and let her fingers track lightly across the muscles of his chest. 'You're stronger now.'

Gently, she stroked his nipples.

She unfastened his belt and then the buttons on his trousers. Delicately, she freed him of his remaining clothes.

She stood against him.

'This isn't a dream,' she said. 'Don't you want me?'

TEN

Mrs Maguire cooked the dinner while Heather bathed the baby. Both women talked to Cassandra, exchanging coos and gurgles with her, but neither talked to the other. The meal was eaten in silence. Mrs Maguire was agitated and frequently bumped or dropped things. Heather was calm. She ignored her mother and ate as though alone. Only when the meal was over and Mrs Maguire was clearing the table and stacking the dishes in a large enamel basin did Heather speak. She knew the signs. Her mother was nervous and fretting in anticipation of being questioned. The longer she waited, the less controlled would be the older woman's reaction.

'All right, mother, what's worrying you?'

Mrs Maguire jolted upright, as though the basin she was touching had transmitted an electric shock.

'Nothing!'

'Really?'

Mrs Maguire tried to lift a plate but could not grasp it properly.

'Why did you walk out of the house today and speak to Josef?'

Mrs Maguire put her left hand on her breast to suppress the noise of her pounding heart. 'I just felt like a walk.'

'You're not allowed to go over there. You know that. You are not allowed to speak to anyone.'

'Really, Heather! I think you're being very cruel. Besides, I didn't say anything.'

Heather leaned forward in confrontation. 'I told you before, you are not allowed to go over there and you must not talk to other people.'

'Really, you treat me like a child!' She avoided her daughter's eyes.

'It is dangerous.'

'It seemed perfectly safe.'

'There are wild animals all around here and the men cannot be trusted.'

'Oh, Heather, that is going too far. Josef seems a nice boy.'

'He speaks well.'

'Yes. He's obviously well educated.'

'What were you talking about?'

'Oh dear.' Mrs Maguire put her hand to her mouth.

'I will not have you lying to me, mother!'

Mrs Maguire took the kettle and poured hot water in the basin. Her hand shook and she splashed water across the table.

'I can tell when you're lying and you're lying to me now,' Heather said. 'You are like a child. What were you and Josef talking about? Were you talking about me?'

Mrs Maguire seemed surprised. 'Goodness me, no! Why should we?'

'Are people talking about me behind my back?' she asked, grabbing her mother and spinning her towards her. 'Look at me when I speak to you!'

'Heather, dear, this is awful. Please stop!'

'Was he talking about me? Were you both laughing at me?'

'We weren't saying anything about you. I was just asking ...' Once more, her hand blocked her lips.

'You might as well go on. I've already spoken to Josef. I know what it was.'

Mrs Maguire looked more distressed than before. Her eyes implored the roof to fall on her.

'I know,' Heather repeated.

'And you're very angry.' She looked down, resigned to her punishment.

'What do you think?'

'Heather, my dear, I have to. I have no choice. It's best for you and it's best for me.'

Heather waited.

'If I stay, you and Adam will continue to argue ...' She could not finish the sentence. She started to wash a plate.

'You're leaving?'

'It's best. If Josef can drive me into town, I'll catch the train.'

'You are not leaving.'

'I must.' She used her fingernail to scrape a stubborn piece of food.

'You are not leaving,' Heather repeated, her voice firmer. 'I need you here.'

'I should never have come. It was wrong. I shouldn't have listened to you. It was a dreadful mistake.'

'Did Adam put you up to this?'

'He had nothing to do with it.' Her voice shook with conviction.

'I'll bet he did. He wants to get rid of you and then me.'

'Heather, I think you're making a terrible mistake. Your husband is a fine young man.'

'He is an uncouth, illiterate peasant who's plotting against me.'

Mrs Maguire attempted to put the wet plate on the table but dropped it. It rolled and clattered on the wooden surface but did not break.

'You clumsy, useless old thing!' Heather screamed. 'Can't you do anything right? You make me so ashamed of you.'

Mrs Maguire took one step back and threw the dishcloth on the table. She did it with no great passion. It was a gentle protest but a protest nonetheless. 'I will not be spoken to like that,' she said in a tone that was almost inaudible. 'And I am going to leave tomorrow. I will speak to Josef and he will drive me to the railway station.'

'You are not leaving! Now pick up that cloth and finish the dishes.'

'I will not.' She clasped hands in a vain attempt to stop them trembling. 'And I will not have you treating me like you do and I am sick and tired of doing all the work around here.'

Heather's legs were widespread. 'Oh, are you?' she said slowly.

'Yes.' She nodded several times, each stroke boosting her new determination.

'You old fool! I am ashamed of you, just like father was.'

'What?'

'Surely you knew? You were a dreadful burden to him.'

Mrs Maguire lunged forward. 'How dare you say that?'

'Easily.' The women were face to face. 'Because it's true.

Father was such a fine man and you dragged him down with all your dithering and waffling …'

She didn't finish. Mrs Maguire slapped her face. Heather stepped back, blinking from shock.

'You'll regret that!' she hissed. In the corner, near where Adam slept, was a stockwhip. Heather strode there, one hand to her cheek. She took the whip and let it uncoil. It was long and heavy.

'You are staying here, mother,' she said, 'and you are helping me.'

'I am not.'

Heather tried to swing the whip but it caught in her feet. She tried again and lashed a table leg.

'What are you doing?' Mrs Maguire retreated to the wall.

Fuming, Heather attempted to free the whip. Its end was tangled around the table leg. She jerked and the table moved. She threw the whip on the floor. Running the few steps to the table, she picked up the basin of dishes.

'Are you still thinking of leaving?' she shouted.

'Heather, please!'

'Are you?'

'I have to. It's best.'

She threw the basin – water, dishes, everything. The basin hit the wall. Water and some plates struck her mother.

'Oh, I'm scalded!' she moaned, covering her face.

'You are not, you old fool. You've been plotting against me, haven't you?' She stepped closer.

'No, I haven't! Please! Don't do anything else.' Mrs Maguire sheltered behind her upraised hands.

Heather grabbed her wrist. 'You're not going, are you?'

'No.' She shook her head vigorously.

'You're not going to talk to anyone else, are you?'

'No. No one else.'

'You'll do what I tell you, won't you?'

'Yes. Yes.'

Heather stepped away. 'You can start by cleaning up this mess.'

An hour before dawn, when a faint breeze ruffled the trees and a hint of colour washed the sky, Adam escorted Nellie back to the town. She still limped slightly. They walked with arms around each other. Near the back of the store she stopped.

'I'll be all right now,' she said. 'You'd better not come any further. Gooly gets up early.'

'I'll be over later,' he said. 'There are still a few things I have to collect.'

'I'll have them ready for you.' She pulled away from him, holding his hand so that their arms were almost at full stretch. 'When will I see you again?'

He grinned. 'In a few hours.'

'You know what I mean.'

'I don't know. As soon as I can. There are always things I need. Now that there's a store here, there'll be plenty of reasons for me to come to town.'

'You'll be back soon?'

'As soon as I can.'

Only their fingers were touching. 'I'll miss you,' she said.

He nodded. 'I don't know what's going to happen, but I do know I'm glad you came up here.'

'So am I.'

'It must be awful for you working in that place. What are you going to do?'

'Wait for you.' She turned and walked away. He waited until she had disappeared behind the building and then slowly walked back to his camp.

The days were becoming hotter. At Kalinda, the sun had been up for an hour and a half and the air was thin and dry and the flies were thick and menaced every moving creature. Josef had backed the car from the shed. He had filled a bucket of water at the spring and wiped the car with a wet rag and then gone over the leather seats to make sure they were free of dust. When he had finished, he retreated into the shed, where the flies were not so bad, and sat against the wall and waited. He was nervous at the prospect of taking Adam's wife to the bore. He didn't like the idea of driving the car without his friend's knowledge. He wasn't familiar with the track. And he was uneasy at the thought of travelling alone with Heather.

He saw her walking towards the shed and jumped to his feet. She was carrying the baby. He hadn't expected that. He walked to meet her. She had a basket in her other hand and passed it to him.

'Something to eat in case we feel hungry,' she said. She was wearing a large hat that flopped around her ears but allowed her hair to spill across her shoulders. She seemed happy. She chatted about the heat and the flies and how shiny the car looked and how she had seen him washing it. Cassandra was wearing a hat and trying to grasp the mosquito net that enveloped her in a loose anti-fly shield.

'That's a good idea,' Josef said and took the baby so that Heather could climb in the car. With his free hand, he helped her up. She slipped and fell lightly against him, laughed, and climbed in. Ratty or not, she was a very good-looking woman, he thought, and walked around the back of the Alfa.

Josef had become extremely aware of women while down south. Two girls who lived near his parents' winery had become interested in him. One was not so good-looking, but liberal in the way she was prepared to share her body. The other was better-looking but less generous, although he had taken delight in trying to convert her to the other girl's point of view. Neither girl was aware of the other's interest and that had given Josef many energetic and sometimes frantic nights. He often missed those girls, especially the good-looking one. He had enjoyed the challenge.

He started the car and drove slowly from the homestead. He chose a pace that was fast enough for the windflow to sweep flies away but not so rapid that the noise of the engine or the rush of air would hinder conversation. Heather had the baby on her lap with one arm across her. The other hand held her hat in place.

'It's so lovely with the breeze in our faces like this,' she said. 'Oh, and it's so good to get out of the house for a while!'

He smiled understanding. His mother used to say things like that. Heather talked a lot – about picnics she had been on during her years in Nyngan and about things she had done at school. He was concentrating on the country ahead of them and looking for firm ground. He noticed horse tracks crossing a sandy ridge on his left and drove another half-mile before turning around the final spit of sand.

'Tell me about you,' she said, changing hands on her hat. 'How long have you known Adam?'

So he talked about Coober Pedy. He found it easy to talk to her. She laughed a lot and had this nice habit of touching his arm when she laughed. He didn't mention Mailey or Nellie or the opal Adam had found, just stories about the underground houses and the characters they had encountered. She was laughing and touching his arm when he stopped the car.

'I think I should have turned back there,' he said, and reversed until the car rolled abreast of a scraggy collection of trees, from the roots of which ran a carpet of sand. It looked familiar but it was difficult to be sure; he had only been to the bore once. He searched for animal tracks. He was aware of Heather studying him, an inquisitive smile on her lips. She looked beautiful when she smiled.

He turned and drove around the trees and told her a story about the days when they were in western Queensland. As he talked, his eyes roamed the barren landscape in front of them, searching for a familiar mark. Some birds were circling on the far side of a low ridge. There were always birds at the water trough so he angled the car towards them. She was telling him about a tennis party at Nevertire and gripping his arm all the time.

The baby slept. She was a remarkably placid child. When Anemone was a baby she had cried all the time. To stop himself thinking about his sister, Josef told Heather about the two girls down south. He hadn't meant to and he didn't tell her that he used to sleep with each of them whenever he could, but she had asked him something about girlfriends and he just found himself talking. She was good at making you talk and saying more than you intended to say.

'I suppose Adam had a lot of girlfriends,' she said pleasantly. When he didn't answer, she touched his arm and laughed. 'I had so many boyfriends. Simply droves! It was marvellous.'

He relaxed. 'I don't think Adam was much of a ladies' man.'

'Oh, he must have been.' She waited, and prodded. 'Surely, with those broad shoulders and good looks of his?'

'No. In fact, he was usually the one getting me out trouble.'

'Really? You were the Lothario of the team?'

The car began to labour in soft sand. Josef had not noticed it. Christ, there was sand all around him! He engaged a lower gear and accelerated.

'Were you often in trouble?' she asked sweetly.

I'm in trouble now, he thought, as he felt the wheels floundering for grip. He aimed for a patch of dry grass. 'No,' he said, and attempted to laugh, but the effect was spoiled by the juddering of the car and the laugh came out in staccato bursts.

'What's wrong?' Heather said, looking around.

'Sand,' he said and the car shuddered to a halt.

She stood, lifting Cassandra to shoulder height and bracing herself against the windscreen. They were in a region of forbidding emptiness. To the right was a low ridge of sand. It bore a fuzz of tortured vegetation. Birds were still circling on the other side of the ridge but they were mere specks. Ahead of them and to the left the land vanished in layers of shuffling heat haze. Behind them was a distant line of scrub and more low and miserably dry ridges.

Josef got out of the car. He sank to his ankles in soft sand. The wheel tracks left by the car made him groan in despair, for they were of the worst kind – not sharp and clear but soft plough marks, which meant the sand was deep and powdery. He would have to dig a long way down before he found a firm base. If he had a shovel, which he did not. Josef Hoffman, he said to himself, you are going to have a bloody hard time getting out of here.

'Are we stuck or something?' Heather said.

'I wish it was something,' he said, trying to sound cheerful. 'I'm afraid, however, that we are stuck.'

'Will you have to push?'

I couldn't move this on my own if I was as strong as a bullock, he thought. The car was deep in sand and, even with a shovel, he would have had a devil of a job getting out. He had blundered into the trap and, worse than the hard work he faced, worse than the inconvenience they were both bound to suffer, was the fact that he was going to look so damned foolish. He should not have taken the car. He recalled now that Adam rode to the bore. He never took the Alfa. And yet he, Josef, trying to be the big man, had wheeled off over a route he didn't know and stuck the thing in the world's largest patch of sand. With Adam's wife on board, plus the baby! Jesus, the wife was enough to worry about out here but what about the baby?

Heather was expecting him to do something.

'Should I get out of the car?' she said hopefully.

'No. Just sit down and take it easy for a while. I want to have a look around.'

'Will we need help?'

'I don't know.'

'Should you go on to the bore and get them to come and give us a hand?'

'The bore?' he said, not comprehending. 'There's no one there.'

'But what about ...?' she began but then thought better of it. Adam would certainly have ordered Josef to tell her nothing of the house, the woman and whatever else was there. 'What about the sheep and that aboriginal friend of Adam's?' she said instead.

'Jimmy? No, the sheep are at the other bore now. He and Adam have been building a yard there, so that they can pen them at night to keep them safe from dingoes.'

'The other bore? Well, why on earth are you taking me to this one?'

'Because you wanted me to.' He was getting sick of this conversation. 'Now, you hang on for a minute and let me have a look around.'

Heather got out of the car, leaving Cassandra on the seat. The baby, sensing her mother's agitation, had begun to stir and now she kicked and screamed. Heather looked around her, waving away the first horde of flies to discover her presence. The country looked awful. Where on earth had Josef been taking her? There could not possibly be a house with water and lawns and trees out this way. Had he taken her the wrong way and deliberately bogged the car in sand? Or pretended to? She moved around the car, kicking at the sand. Josef had walked to the place where the deep wheel tracks began. He seemed to be doing nothing. He had his hands in his pockets and was just standing and looking at his feet. This, she decided, was Adam's doing. He had told his friend to bring her here, pretend to be in trouble and show her nothing. Well, two could play games.

The more Josef looked at the scene, the worse he felt. How could he have driven so enthusiastically into this trap? It was so soft, so obviously a hazard when you walked across it. He squatted and looked back towards the car and comforted himself with the observation that the sand *was* deceptive. Wind had smoothed it and coated it with brown dust so that the whole area looked like hard earth. Until you looked closely, which he had not done. He had been too busy talking.

He returned to the car, ploughing ankle-deep through sand, and knelt beside the rear wheels.

'What are you doing?' Heather had picked up the baby.

'Digging sand away from the tyres. I'm going to try to reverse it out.'

'Will it take long?'

He was not in a good mood and was inclined to answer that the job would take less time if she helped. But he said: 'I can't say,' and kept digging. The flies were tormenting him, crawling over his face, in his ears, up his nostrils.

'Would you like something to eat?'

'No, thanks.' He brushed a swarm of small flies from his eye.

'I brought some sandwiches.'

'No, I'm OK.' He was scooping down to the depth of the tyre's tread and then extending the trench backwards, so that he could drive out gently without spinning the wheels.

'If you'd like me to drive the car for you, tell me.'

He stopped digging and poked his head around the wheel. 'How do you mean?' If I can't drive it, I'll bet you can't, he thought. She saw his flushed face and assumed it was from exertion, not anger.

'Well, maybe I could sit behind the wheel and drive it backwards when you tell me to. You could push and I could drive.'

'Can you drive?'

'Of course.'

He moved to the other wheel. 'I didn't know your parents had a car.'

'They didn't. But I had a girlfriend at Nevertire and her father had a car. He had everything. They had sheep and they were just so rich. Anyhow, she used to let me drive her father's Oldsmobile around the paddocks. They said I was a very good driver.'

'Well, maybe. We'll see. It's going to be tricky getting out.'

'They told me I was very good at changing gears.'

'Great.' He busied himself digging sand.

'Aren't the flies awful?'

'They certainly are. Is the baby OK?'

'I've got her covered by the mosquito net. I don't want her getting that dreadful eye disease that all the black children seem to have. I forget what it's called.'

'Sandy blight?'

'That's it. It makes children look so ... unclean. Don't you think? Are you sure you wouldn't like a sandwich? I had my mother make some for you.'

'Not just now.' He clawed at the sand, burrowing like a dog. 'I might have some later, although we ought to save some food, just in case we can't get out of here.'

'What do you mean?' For the first time, she sounded alarmed.

'There's nothing to worry about,' he assured her. 'It's just that if I can't get the car out we'll have to walk for it, or wait for someone to come and find us.'

'You're serious?'

'Afraid so.'

'Well, Josef, I am certainly not walking.'

'No, I suppose not. Not with the baby.'

'Even without the baby.' She walked to the rear of the car, holding Cassandra against her body and waving constantly to

626

drive away flies. 'But surely you're being a little dramatic? After all, it's only sand. I mean, you're digging it away with your hands.'

'That's precisely the problem,' he said, wiping sweat from an eyebrow and continuing the movement to fan his face. 'It's so soft the wheels can't get grip.'

'Why did you drive into it, then?'

He found this a difficult question to answer and paused to remove a thorn from his hand.

'I mean, it's very easy to see,' she continued. 'It's all around us.' She waved her free hand to indicate the extent of the trap in case Josef had missed the view.

'Yes, well, I didn't see it in time.'

I'm sure you didn't, she said to herself. You knew this was here and you deliberately drove straight into it and now you're going on with this song-and-dance so that I can't get to see what's at the bore. She smiled sweetly. 'Is it far to the bore?' she said.

'Not far,' he said, not bothering to tell her he had no idea where they were, let alone where the bore was.

'Could we walk there?'

'There's nothing there. Except a windmill and a trough. You wouldn't even like the water. The sheep rather fancy it but I think you'd find it a little bitter. It's full of minerals.'

You really are trying desperately hard to stop me going there, she thought.

Josef stood, holding his back as he straightened. 'Maybe I will have one sandwich. How many have we got?'

'Tons. I told mother you had a healthy appetite.' She brought him a sandwich and he ate quickly. 'What do you think of Kalinda, Josef?'

His mouth being too occupied to utter words, he nodded.

'Will it make all the money Adam says it will?'

He shrugged.

'He's apparently done very well already,' she continued. 'What with all the work he's done, all the buildings he's erected, all the sheep he has.'

He swallowed the last of the bread. 'He certainly has.'

'He's told me all about it. He talks for hours. About everyone. Even that … shall we say … other person?' She glanced away, not daring to show him the eager expression on her face.

'Who?' Josef wiped his mouth and walked to the front of the car. He knelt again and resumed digging. She followed and stood behind him.

'You know. The one he doesn't like talking about.' She waited, not daring to say any more. She had been careful not to mention the word 'woman'. Men were sensitive about such things. She wanted him to talk freely, not be frightened into silence.

Josef was still digging, but his action was slow. What the hell was she talking about?

She had to say something. What? Something to play on his ego. 'It must have been very hard for someone like you. I mean, you're such a decent sort of man that there must have been times when you found it very difficult to remain silent.'

He dug.

'I mean, you didn't even say anything to me.'

'I haven't had many chances to talk to you.'

'I know, and I'm sorry about that. And I do respect you for your silence about ... well, about that other person. It must be terribly hard to keep such a secret. I mean, we're near the very place where ... well, where it happened.'

Mailey? he thought. Is that who she's talking about?

'Adam's told me all about it. You can imagine how difficult that was for him, but he's told me everything.'

'He has?' He could not control his surprise. It must be Mailey, but they had agreed never to mention what had happened here to anyone.

'I think that's the only way for a husband and wife to behave, don't you?' she said, anxious to let the bait be swallowed. 'In a spirit of absolute trust.' A long pause, waiting for the bite. 'With each telling the other person absolutely everything.' Another long but non-productive wait. She kept on talking. 'The way Adam and I are with each other. The way we've been about this ... situation.'

Without looking at her, he stood and walked to the other front wheel.

'I think Adam feels very guilty about it,' she said, sauntering after him. 'I've told him that's natural and that he shouldn't. I've told him I understand.'

'He had no choice, really,' Josef said, settling himself into a digging position.

Well, that's one way to put it, she thought. Trust a man to say that about another man. I suppose they understand male lust and therefore have to support each other. 'No,' she agreed. 'That's what he said. I suppose he asked you to keep quiet too?'

'Oh, we agreed to say nothing.'

I'm sure you did, she thought, but said: 'I think that was wise. Very discreet. How are you with names, Josef?'

The question surprised him and he stopped work, sat on his haunches and wiped his face. 'Names?'

'Yes. I'm always forgetting them, aren't you?'

'Always.'

'I keep forgetting the first name of ... that person.'

'I don't think I ever knew it.' He bent forward and scraped a trench from the tyre. 'We just knew him as Mailey.'

Mailey? Him? Oh, for heaven's sake, what has he been talking about? In frustration she walked from the car. She would have to start all over again. She stopped. Josef was still talking, his voice sounding curiously disembodied as it came from under the car.

'That was just an awful day. He was going to kill me. Adam saved my life, I'm sure of that, but what happened then was terrible. I'd never seen a man killed before.'

She moved closer, fascinated.

'I try not to think about it.'

'Of course not,' she said, her voice little more than a whisper.

'He was the most evil man I've ever known. Amazing that he was a cop.'

'Cop?'

'Sorry. Policeman.'

'Oh, yes.'

'He was such a big bloke. I thought for sure he was going to kill Adam but, well ...'

'Adam killed him.' The words were flat, with no inflection to betray her.

'Yes, and thank God for that or none of us would have been here now. It's funny for him to talk about it again. We never discuss it.'

'No.'

He was standing on the other side of the car. She had been staring at the horizon, seeing nothing and trying to assemble the facts he had been scattering.

'I'm going to give it a go,' he announced. 'Do you want to hop in?'

Still dazed by what he had said, she climbed into her seat. Mailey. A policeman. Adam had killed him. And here, on this property. Josef had been present. But how could that be? Josef had only arrived recently.

He started the engine, selected reverse and stalled. He restarted, increased the motor's revolutions and let in the clutch. The car jerked a little, the rear wheels spun and then stopped. He got out and inspected the sand at the back of the car.

'We've dug in again,' he said wearily.

'What does that mean?'

'It means I'll have to do some more digging.'

'Why don't you try again? You were scarcely at the wheel for thirty seconds.'

'It wouldn't do any good.'

You must I think I was born yesterday, she thought. You are going to try to keep me out here all day so that I never get to this bore and see who or what is there. And this story about a policeman ... What was that? Some nonsense to throw me off the scent?

The engine was still running. Carefully, she put the baby on the seat and slipped across to the other side of the car. Josef saw her behind the steering wheel.

'What are you doing?' he said, moving clear of the car as the engine beat increased.

'I'm going to drive out,' she said triumphantly.

'No, please don't!'

'You wouldn't like that, would you?' She struggled to push the gear lever into reverse. It made a gnashing noise, but went in.

'You'll make things worse!' he called.

'Just stand clear,' she said, and took her foot from the clutch pedal. The wheels spun viciously. The car did not move. The tyres dug deep into the sand. She pushed harder on the accelerator. The wheels became blurred discs and twin spurts of sand shot into the body of the car, which vibrated and weaved from side to side and gradually lowered itself until the differential and springs were buried. The engine backfired and stopped.

'Oh, *Jesus*!' Josef said, walking a tight circle in his fury. 'What the hell did you do that for?'

She looked back, not comprehending what had happened. 'It won't go,' she said.

'You never bloody well spoke a truer word!' he thundered.

She blinked. 'There is never any excuse for profanity.'

'Jesus, you're unreal! Do you know what you just did? You buried the bloody thing! You might as well say prayers and send flowers. Holy bloody hell!'

'Please don't swear!'

'Why not? I can't do anything else.'

'Should we walk to the bore?'

'No!'

'You don't want me to go there, do you?'

'Abso-bloody-lutely not! I don't want you to do a thing.' He pointed a finger at her. 'Now listen, I'm going to walk back to the homestead and get something to pull us out. Do you want to come with me?'

'No.'

'Good. Then stay here. Look after your baby. Eat your mother's sandwiches. Do anything you like, but don't leave the car. Whatever you do, stay with the Alfa. I'll be back as soon as I can but it won't be for a few hours at the earliest. Now, have you got that?'

She refused to look at him, let alone speak.

'And for Christ's sake, don't try and drive again or you'll burn out the clutch.'

He tramped along the car's tracks, muttering to himself and wondering when Adam would return with the camels. And not liking the prospect of what Adam would say.

Heather waited several minutes and then got out. Slowly, she walked around the car and wondered what he had done to make it sink in the sand like that. All she had done was try to drive it. Maybe he had let the air out of the tyres. He had been doing something at the back wheels, where she couldn't see him. She kicked a tyre. She wondered how far she was from the bore. And then she began to think about that extraordinary tale Josef had been spinning about a policeman named Mailey.

ELEVEN

Adam returned to a deserted homestead. He knew Jimmy was at the number one bore but there was no sign of Josef, of Heather and the baby, or even of Mrs Maguire. The car was gone. He presumed they had all gone driving, but where, and why? He unpacked the freight from the larger camel and stored the items temporarily in the shed. He left the riding saddle on Bozo and led both animals to the spring. While they drank, he went back to the house, searching for any note or other indication of where the

631

people had gone. The house was a mess. Dishes were scattered across the table and unwashed pots rested on the stove. He went outside and, leaving Rumble tied near the spring, rode the younger camel to the hills. He secured the tether to a bush and climbed to the top of the ridge. He scanned the country in segments, searching each part with great care before turning to the next. On the last segment, he saw Josef.

He was still at least a mile from the homestead, a solitary figure wavering in the heat haze. He was moving slowly, a tired man who had walked a long way. Adam returned to the camel and rode swiftly to meet him.

Josef stopped when he saw the camel loping towards him. He was tired and extremely thirsty. He had covered about six miles, longer than he need have but, not knowing the direct route back to the homestead, he had followed the car's tracks. He had hurried because he dared not leave Heather and the baby exposed to the sun for too long. It had taken him half a mile of fast walking to get over his anger at Heather's stupidity and for the rest of the journey he had worried about how he was going to extricate the car. He would ride back on the mare; her leg was still tender but she could be ridden, and he would try to carry some rope, a shovel and a few planks. The mare was no draught horse and wouldn't be able to pull out the car, especially working in soft sand where she would flounder and possibly hurt herself even more. And digging and jacking up the car, and planking the wheels back to solid ground, was going to be a long process that could take the best part of a day. He had resolved to get more food and water and to leave a note for Adam – a simple, printed note that he could understand if he returned while they were still away. Josef had hoped he could have got Heather and Cassandra back to the safety of the homestead before Adam rode in from William Creek. It would be far less embarrassing to explain the episode with everyone safe and the car back in the shed. But Adam had come back. Well, he could use the help.

He stood still and rested his legs and wiped his dry and cracking lips and watched the camel approach with apprehension.

The meeting was an anti-climax. Josef told Adam what had happened and Adam, saying nothing, hauled him on to the camel and rode back to the spring. While Josef drank and bathed and filled a metal container with water, Adam saddled the second camel and loaded the rope, shovels and planks. Only when they were riding side by side back to the car did Adam ask the question

Josef had been dreading.

'What the devil were you doing, trying to drive to the bore?'

'Your wife ... Heather ... wanted to go there.'

'But you can't drive there! There's too much sand.'

'I know that now.'

'Heather knew that too.'

'Yeah?' The word burst from him in a gush of breath as he bounced roughly in the saddle. Josef was not a good rider and Rumble was not a good camel to ride.

'I told her,' Adam continued. 'She had a bee in her bonnet about going to the bore and I said it was too sandy for the car. Whose idea was it?'

Josef looked miserable. 'Her's.'

'Did she pester you into it?'

'Not really.'

'What do you mean?'

'Well,' he said, holding on tightly as the camel stumbled through a patch of rough ground, 'she sort of said it in such a way that I couldn't say no.' He shook violently as Rumble negotiated more broken ground. 'Jesus Christ, what a ride! No, it's hard to explain, but by the time she'd finished she made me feel that I'd be the world's greatest bastard if I said no. It's probably hard for you to understand.'

Adam smiled wryly. 'Oh, I think I know what you mean.'

'What have you told her about the bores?' Josef said, his tone full of curiosity.

'Why?'

'Because she seems to have a funny idea of what she's going to find there.'

Adam pulled his mount to a halt. He leaned to one side, head down, studying the tracks. 'Did you go straight on here?'

'I suppose so.'

'You should have swung left.' He pointed beyond a clump of acacia with limbs as gaunt as dry firewood. 'The bore's over that way.'

'Oh. I wasn't sure. I'd only been there once before.' And having said that, he thought: Jesus, what an excuse, and from someone who's spent years in the bush! He said: 'I'm sorry. I was mad to go. I should have made her wait for you to come back.'

'Not much chance of making her do anything reasonable once her mind's made up,' Adam said, searching ahead for a sign of the car. He could see the tyre marks and, parallel to them, Josef's footprints, but the twin trails led only to floating mirages, and they were thin and flat and smoky grey. Just sand hills. Not the narrow, oddly coloured and shimmering pimple on the horizon that could have been a motor car. 'She wanted you to take her while I was away,' Adam added. 'She can be pretty hard to resist.'

'She certainly can. I didn't say I would take her. She just didn't give me a chance to say no.'

Both men felt better: Josef because Adam was not angry and seemed to understand, and Adam because it was good to find another man who could be engulfed and befuddled by Heather.

'She thinks there's another house at the bore,' Adam said.

'You mean a shed?'

'No, a house. Bigger and better than the homestead.'

'Who was supposed to have built it?'

'Me. She thinks I'm keeping another woman out there.'

Josef twisted in the saddle to see if Adam were joking. Obviously he was not and Josef straightened, frowning. 'She said some very strange things to me.'

'She was probably pumping you. Trying to find out about this imaginary woman.'

She's nuts, Josef said to himself but considered it unwise to express such a thought. Adam glanced at him briefly and his face was wreathed in misery. The man was begging for sympathy.

'Has she been giving you a hard time?' Josef said.

'She's been impossible.'

They rode without speaking until they reached the place where the wheel tracks reversed and then turned left across a spit of sand. 'You were giving them a good ride,' Adam said and Josef grinned sheepishly. His friend understood and he felt good. In fact, he felt closer to Adam than at any time since coming to Kalinda. This was like the old days.

'You said they had food?'

'Yes,' Josef said, snapping back to the purpose of the ride. 'Mrs Maguire cut some sandwiches.'

'She's not such a bad old sort.'

'Your wife's mother?'

'She wants to leave. She asked me to drive her to William Creek.'

Josef was surprised. 'She asked me too!'

'When?'

'After you left.'

'Poor old thing must be desperate. I think my dear wife has been giving her a rough time.'

634

'Heather reckons she's a bit touched.'

'I think she's just sick and tired of doing all the work. How was she when you left?'

'I didn't see her this morning.'

Adam stopped the camel and Josef jerked to a stop beside him. Rumble made an obscene gurgling noise.

'You mean she's not in the car?'

'No, of course not. There's only Heather and Cassie. Mrs Maguire's back in the house.'

'No, she's not! The house was deserted.' Adam turned in the saddle and scanned the country behind them. The land danced in the heat.

It was undignified to sit on the ground but there seemed no alternative. The tree offered the only shade for miles and it was extremely hot, so Mrs Maguire sat on a well brushed square of dirt and removed her hat. She used it to fan herself, to keep the flies away and to provide a little cooling air. She checked the bag she carried. Her jewellery was there. Some rings, a brooch that had belonged to her grandmother, and a necklace given to her by her husband. It had three small diamonds and a gap where a fourth had been. She had lost the fourth stone seven years before but had never told her husband. He would have been furious. It had been a very expensive gift, he had said. She fingered the space where the diamond had been and tried once more, as she had many times in the past seven years, to imagine where it could have fallen. She had not worn the necklace after the stone disappeared. It was simpler than risking her husband's anger.

She put the jewellery back in its little black box, made certain the lid had snapped shut, and then wrapped the box in a woollen jumper. It would be safer there. She hoped the local people were honest but she had not met any, other than the strange man with the towel around his head who rode a camel and brought them supplies, and therefore she was not going to take any chances. If some thief should open her case, he wouldn't easily find her jewellery.

She had a few clothes, some money for the rail fare, a sandwich wrapped in a damp tea towel and a bottle with water. She unscrewed the cap and drank a little. She wasn't sure how far it was to William Creek. She wasn't even certain of the direction she should be taking but she thought she was going the right way. Reaching the station was not her main concern, for she had little

635

understanding of the bush and thought that if she kept on walking she would reach the railway line or some house, and then she would be all right. There would be kind people who would look after her. The thought that frightened her was that Heather would follow and force her back to Kalinda. Heather had gone driving with Josef. When she found her mother had gone, she would probably make Josef pursue her in the car.

So she sat in the shade where she would be out of sight. Her ankles were swollen and her feet ached. She took off her shoes and, feeling drowsy, was soon asleep.

The car was first a black speck that hovered above a horizon of steam. Then its shape jumped and fizzed, as lively as spitting fat in a pan. Finally, as they rode closer, the image solidified through the gaseous boundary of this hot land and they were able to distinguish form and colour.

'You walked a long way,' Adam said with admiration and Josef, who had been sore from walking and now ached from the jolting ride, grunted agreement. As they drew closer, both men became alarmed. There was no sign of Heather or the baby.

'I *told* her not to leave the car,' an anxious Josef said. Adam had already spurred his camel into a run. He took his animal fast through the soft sand, paused to look down into the open vehicle, and then slowly followed a set of footprints running to the north. He dismounted.

'She went this way,' he said, standing astride the track. She was carrying a heavy load, by the depth and close spacing of her shoe marks. He ran back to the car in case there was some clue as to where she had gone. He leaned against the door and recoiled. The metal was so hot it almost burned the palms of his hands. How would the baby be out there? And Heather? If she collapsed from the heat or hurt herself, Cassie couldn't survive for long. He looked up at Josef, who had brought his camel close and was leaning forward along its neck.

'What was Heather wearing? Did she have on a hat and good shoes?'

'Yes. Well, she had a big hat on. I'm not sure about the shoes. I didn't notice.'

'And Cassie? Was she well covered?'

'I think so. She had a big hat and was covered in a net to keep the flies off.'

'Thank heavens for that! How long ago did you leave them?'

'Four, five hours. I'm not sure.'

Adam climbed back on Bozo. The animal lurched to its full height and, prodded into motion, set off at a steady run to the north. Josef followed, grunting with each bump of Rumble's rough ride.

Heather had covered almost a mile and a half. She had entered a region of stones and wandered towards a thick stand of scrub which rose above the plain like a desert island on a red sea. Adam lost her trail on the stones but headed towards the scrub as a place where someone might seek shelter. He saw a dark shape beneath a larger tree. Bozo walked slowly, carefully choosing where to step to avoid the larger stones. Heather walked from the tree.

Adam slid from the saddle and ran to her. Her face was red and she wiped her lips constantly. He took her by the arm and led her back to the shade. He helped her sit down.

'Is the baby all right?' he asked anxiously.

'You're not concerned about me?' she croaked.

'Yes, of course, but I can see you're alive and able to walk. Is Cassie all right?'

'I suppose so. My God, what dreadful country! Do you have any water? I'm dying of thirst.'

'Joe has water. He'll be here in a minute.'

'I must have a drink.'

'Soon.' Adam could see Josef unstrapping the water container. 'Has the baby had water?'

She rolled her eyes, admonishing him. 'Babies do not drink water.'

Cassie was on her back with her eyes closed. She was breathing rapidly in brief, painful bursts. Adam knelt beside her and touched the baby's cheeks. They were burning. 'What has she drunk?'

Heather didn't answer.

'Has she had milk?' Adam said, grasping Heather by the shoulders.

'What?' She looked confused.

'Milk. Have you fed the baby?'

She stood, staggering a little and grabbing him for support. 'What on earth are you talking about? Where is the water?'

Josef arrived with the container. He poured water into her hands. She drank voraciously.

'More.'

'Take it easy,' Adam cautioned. Josef had poured water into Adam's cupped hands and he let it trickle on to Cassie's lips.

'What are you doing?' Heather said.

'Giving her a drink.'

'Your hands are dirty.'

'Don't be a fool, Heather!' Adam said.

She slapped him, a hard blow between the shoulder-blades that sent water spraying across his shirt. 'I will not have you speak to me like that!' she screamed and hit him again. He moved out of range, taking Cassie with him. Josef tried to restrain her and, for the first time, she noticed the man bearing the water container.

'You! So you came back.' She turned to Adam. 'He abandoned me! He left us and just …' She stopped, blinked rapidly, looked from one man to the other, and sat on the ground. 'Oh, God, this is dreadful country!' she moaned.

Josef gave her more water. Adam carefully removed Cassie's clothing and rubbed her body with his wet hands. Heather drank a lot and wet her face and wrists.

'Please give me Cassandra,' she said. 'I'm all right now. I'll look after her.'

Adam handed her the baby. Josef had gone to catch his camel, which had wandered in search of food.

'I do not want you to keep that man on the property,' she said in a hushed voice.

'Joe? Why not?'

'He uses vile language. He swore at me in a most uncouth manner.'

'You might have given him good cause to swear.'

'I might have expected such a remark from you. You are coarse but I suspect he is even coarser. He used the most disgusting language and then just walked away and left me there. I could have died.' The baby whimpered, reminding her of her presence. 'We could both have died.'

'He went for help. It was a long walk.'

She began dressing the baby.

'Why did you leave the car?'

'Did you expect me to stay there and fry in the sun?'

'Josef said he told you not to leave the car. It was a very foolish thing to do.'

'Here we go again! I'm a fool, am I?'

'You could have died.'

'That would have worried you, wouldn't it?'

He said nothing.

'Oh,' she breathed, stretching the sound. 'Is that what all this was about? You had your henchman take us out in the desert so we could die. So you could get rid of us. So you could spend all your time and your money with that other woman?'

'Oh, Christ, Heather, not now!'

'Do you want to know why I walked from the car? Do you? It was to get to the bore. So I could see for myself what's there and what it is you're trying so desperately hard to hide from me. This woman of yours and whatever else you have there.'

'Heather, you're as nutty as a fruit cake.'

'And do you know what?' she said, ignoring him, 'I don't think he ever intended to take me there. Are we anywhere near the bore?'

'No.'

'Well, at least you're being honest now.'

'Joe got lost.'

'Of course.' She sneered.

'It's true! He's never driven to the bore. He didn't know the way.'

'What rubbish! First you try to keep me from seeing what's going on at Kalinda and then you try to have me killed. It was obvious that you were most disappointed to find I was still alive.'

The baby started to cry.

'It might be an idea if you gave Cassie some milk,' he said. 'She's only had a few drops of water.'

'I don't need you to tell me such things. I am, after all, the child's mother.' She turned her back. 'Kindly move away and do not look.'

'There's one other thing,' he said. 'Do you know where your mother is?'

'Back at the house. She has things to do.'

'She's not there. I searched everywhere but there was no sign of her. Did she say anything to you about going away?'

'Leaving? What an absurd thing to suggest!'

'I thought maybe she wanted to go back to New South Wales.'

'Of course not. Have you suggested that to her?'

'No.'

Her head angled towards him. 'You have, haven't you? You and she are plotting against me, aren't you?' The baby was crying louder but Heather kept talking. 'Was it your idea that she should go? Have you taken her away? Are you going to kill her too?'

He walked away. 'For Christ's sake, just feed the baby!'

'Are you going to kill her and then me? Just like you killed that policeman?'

Adam pivoted, his face white with shock. She saw the expression, smiled and bent to tend the baby.

*

639

She knows about Mailey? Adam walked towards his camel, stumbling on stones because he wasn't seeing them. How? How could she have learned about Mailey? Josef was heading towards him, leading his camel.

'Is she better now?' he said.

'She knows about Mailey,' Adam said, still dazed. He focused on Josef. 'Did you tell her?'

'No!' Josef looked offended. 'You did.'

'Me?'

'That's what she said.'

'I've never mentioned it. I haven't even hinted at it.'

Josef bristled. 'But she said you told her everything! She said there were no secrets between the two of you and that you'd told her the whole story.'

'We have never discussed it. For heaven's sake, Joe, why would I? She'd be the last person I'd tell, anyhow.'

'Well, she knows.'

'Everything?'

'I don't know. She seems to know an awful lot though. She just started talking about it while we were driving in the car.'

'Did she start the conversation?' Adam said slowly, probing.

Josef gazed at the pale, hot sky, seeking inspiration. 'Yes,' he said. 'I forget how it started but she just began talking about it and saying what a dreadful thing it must have been for all of us.'

'And she mentioned Mailey?'

'Yes.' Josef searched for the same spot in the sky. 'Although I'm not sure if she said his name. She certainly knew he was a policeman because I remember her saying that.'

'Well, I didn't tell her, and you didn't tell her.' The second part of the statement was more of a question and Josef shook his head in confirmation. 'That leaves Jimmy and Saleem Benn.'

'I don't think Jimmy's had two words with her since she arrived,' Josef said.

'He wouldn't say anything. And Saleem Benn hasn't done anything more than bow and touch his forehead. In any case, she's frightened of him.'

'Well, there's no one else who knows.'

'Only Nellie,' Adam said, and immediately regretted it for Josef looked at him with interest and wore a 'But how would she know?' expression which demanded explanation.

'I told her when we were in Port Augusta.'

Josef turned to his camel. Nellie at Port Augusta was still a painful memory.

'She had a right to know,' Adam explained. 'She helped you get us out of that gaol and she copped a hiding from Mailey. And she brought back the opal.'

'Yeah, that's all right. Anyhow,' he said, facing Adam once more, 'She wouldn't tell anyone and she's probably five hundred miles away.'

Adam coughed. 'There's something you should know. Nellie's turned up at William Creek.'

'What?'

'She's working in the new store there. Saleem Benn gave her a job there. I ran into her the other day. Got the surprise of my life.'

'What's she doing up here?'

'Looking for work, I suppose. She had a job for a while in Marree.'

'Jesus! You never know where people are going to turn up.' He pawed at a stone. 'Is she all right?'

'Yes. She seems good. I think it's a hard job, though. One of Saleem Benn's many nephews runs the place and she does all the dirty work.'

'Times are tough.'

'She asked to be remembered to you.' She hadn't exactly said that but she had asked about Josef and said she didn't hold any hard feelings for what had happened, so that was almost the same thing.

'Really? After ... ah ... what happened?'

'You didn't do anything.'

'Yeah, but still. Jesus, that was a bad night.'

'We all have bad nights. We all do things we don't mean to do.'

Josef nodded. 'And she's all right, eh?'

'Yeah. Good.'

He scratched his nose. 'Well, she hasn't seen Heather so she can't have told her about Mailey.' He glanced quickly at Adam. 'Are you going to tell Heather about Nellie?'

'Tell her what?' The thought jarred.

'That we knew her in the old days. That she used to be Jimmy's girlfriend.'

'No, I'm not,' Adam said, relaxing again.

'Me neither.' He saw Heather stand. 'I think she's ready to move on. How are we going to travel?'

'I'll take Heather and Cassie with me.'

641

'Are you going to say anything to her about Mailey? Find out who told her?'

'No. She's a great one for leading people into traps so I'll just shut up.'

'And what about her mother? I wonder where she is?'

'She might just have gone for a walk. If she's not back at the house, we'll have to try and find her.'

'Only a few hours of daylight left,' Josef said, squinting at the sun. 'We've got a long way to go, a car to get out of the sand and an old woman to find. Going to be a busy evening.'

It was a rough ride back to the stranded Alfa-Romeo. Bozo was tired and did not appreciate the extra load and so walked poorly, jerking and bobbing excessively. Adam nursed Cassie in one arm, holding her against his chest and managing to insulate her from the worst bumps. Heather, sitting behind and compelled to hold Adam around the waist, had a wretched journey, frequently crying out from the shock of meeting the camel rising when she was descending. Josef led. He had dismounted by the time Bozo reached the car.

'Thank God,' Heather said wearily when the camel stopped. She straightened her back, expecting to dismount.

'You're not getting off just yet,' Adam told her, and beckoned to Josef. He handed down the baby. 'Do you mind playing mother for half an hour or so?'

Josef, holding Cassie awkwardly, shook his head. 'No, she'll be all right. What are you going to do?'

'Why have you given Cassandra to him?' Heather asked.

'Because you and I are going somewhere.' Ignoring her, he bent close to Josef. 'Can you put the baby on the front seat while you work on the car?'

'Sure.'

'Where are we going?' Heather demanded.

'To see the bore that's been worrying you so much. It's about fifteen minutes away over the sand hills. Hang on tight. See you later, Joe.' And he urged Bozo into a gallop.

With the sun having lost the worst of its heat, the distorting hazes had gone and the land around the car had been resolved into clear images of low vegetation and distant dunes. The last view Josef had of the departing couple was of the camel climbing a towering sand hill. He could no longer distinguish Adam or Heather but he could still hear her shrieking with fright in that mad gallop across the plain.

Adam eased the pace over the last few dunes. Even so, they swayed violently across the ridges until he halted the camel above a steep descent to a valley strewn with stones. To their left, almost in the centre of the flat area, was a pipe gushing hot water, a windmill with its blades unmoving in the still air, and a low tank spilling water into a long drain.

'There it is,' he said.

'What?' She had difficulty breathing.

'The bore that you wanted to visit. See the windmill?' She didn't answer and he pointed. 'There. The windmill.'

'What about it?'

'Well, just behind it is the house I built. Isn't it big? I like the red roof, don't you?'

Behind the mill stretched a flat and empty expanse of gibbers.

'What are you talking about? There's nothing there.'

'Oh, and you know the woman who lives here? The one you're always talking about? There she is on the verandah, waving. Give her a wave, Heather!'

'What are you talking about? There's no one there.'

Adam pretended not to hear. He spurred Bozo to tackle the descent. Heather screamed and clung tightly to him. Slithering, jolting, swaying, they ploughed down through the sand. At the bottom, Adam ordered the camel to its knees. Heather slid from its back and fell to the ground. Adam vaulted to her side.

'Well, here we are. Welcome to my other, bigger and better home.'

'There's nothing here!' she said, close to tears that were due partly to anger and partly to humiliation.

'That's what I've been telling you,' he said softly and walked towards the windmill. 'This is just a place where there is underground water. We need it for the sheep. They drink it.'

'I know that.' She stood and brushed dust from her clothes.

'There is no house here; there is no woman hiding here; there is merely this contraption which pumps water up from under the ground and lets the sheep get a drink.'

She examined the surrounding country. The camel was heading for a patch of salt bush. She could see nothing else but stones and sand. 'Josef said there was grass,' she said defiantly.

'Well, there is.' Adam indicated a patch of weedy growth, the colour of bleached bones, at the foot of the dune opposite them.

'That's not grass.'

'It's what we call grass.'

'Grass is green and lovely. That's awful.' She spun around. 'And Josef said this place was beautiful.'

'In a kind of way it is. It depends on what you call beautiful.'

'And you call this beautiful?'

'The colour of the sand can be beautiful. The shape of the dunes can be beautiful, particularly when the wind has blown and left little ripples all over them. Even the gibbers can be beautiful. Look at the shades of red you can see in this late afternoon light.'

She walked some distance from him, with her head down and one hand nervously playing with the other. And she thought: Is this what he calls beautiful? Is he truly so warped? Dry sand, a flat bed of small stones and grass so parched and miserable-looking it could be straw? Is he serious? She risked a glance at him but he was looking at her and so she quickly turned away. No, he *couldn't* be serious, so what was he up to? The windmill looked old. The tank was old – she could tell by the weathered appearance of the metal. All the parts looked secondhand and no one would use second-hand pieces of iron and pipe to build new things, so the bore and the windmill and the tank must have been there for a long time. Adam had not built them. He was still trying to deceive her.

She walked back to him. 'Where are the sheep?'

He had been examining some fresh dingo tracks in the soft soil edging the bore drain. There was also a clear set of emu prints. 'At the other bore,' he said.

'Oh, the *other* one! Of course. I should have known. And what would I find if I went to this other bore?'

'A thousand or so sheep, Jimmy and his dog, a bore, a windmill. Much the same as here, except that we've just finished a yard to pen the sheep. There are more dingoes over that way.'

'I find it strange,' she said, looking around with the studied indifference of a potential buyer trying to disguise an appreciation of what he sees, 'in fact, I find it very strange that wherever I go on this property, or, more correctly, wherever you take me, there is absolutely nothing to see.'

Adam folded his arms to help contain his temper. 'Well, I see water running out of the ground and that wasn't here a year ago. I wouldn't call the pipe we sank in the ground nothing. I wouldn't call the windmill nothing.'

'Really? And you built all that with your own little hands?'

'Me and Jimmy.'

You must think me a fool, she thought. Everything here is so obviously old and decrepit. This has been here for years. 'You must feel so proud,' she said.

'It took us nearly two months of hard work.' Adam breathed deeply. He liked it here at the bore. It was peaceful. 'If you've seen enough, I think we should head back to the car and help Joe pull it out. Then we've got to get back to the homestead and see if your mother's back.'

'Oh, yes. You say she's not there?'

'She wasn't when I got back from William Creek. I'm worried about her,' Adam added, noting her apparent lack of concern.

'That's very touching, and you, of course, have no idea where she might be?' she said, her voice heavy with sarcasm.

'Jesus Christ!' Adam muttered, his patience ending. 'Come on. Get back on the camel.'

'You are not to go fast. I will not get on if you are going to ride that thing like a lout.'

'You can walk,' he said and waited for her to scramble on to Bozo's back. 'And we will go slowly,' he said, when she was securely in place.

'I'm pleased to see some small sign of concern.'

'I'm concerned about the camel. It's tired.'

TWELVE

They reached the car to find Josef had already jacked it clear of the sand. He had put the planks under its wheels to form a short wooden railway to start it on its journey out of the trap. The men backed the camels to the rear of the Alfa, attached ropes between the animals and the back axle, and hauled. The car came out easily. Josef then got into the car with Heather and the baby and started the journey home. Adam followed, riding one camel and leading the other.

All the way from the bore, Heather had been planning what she should do. She had to find out more about Kalinda, more about what Adam was doing, maybe even more about the policeman Josef had mentioned. Josef was her most likely source of information.

'I'm sorry I got the car stuck in the sand,' she said as soon as Josef began to drive away.

He was surprised. He had anticipated an unpleasant journey, but she was smiling.

'That's all right,' he said, relieved that she seemed so jovial. 'It wasn't really your fault. I got the car stuck in the first place.'

Quite right, she thought. And obviously at my husband's instructions. You even went back looking for him, to find out what you should do with me next. But she said: 'I must have caused you a great deal of extra work. Thank you for walking so far.'

Jesus, she can be nice, he thought, and looked at her. She returned his gaze, her eyes shining with gratitude. The sun had set and the last flush of daylight coloured her face. She glowed.

'What did you think of the bore?' he said, looking away and feeling unsettled by the intensity of her stare.

'Oh, you were right. It's lovely country.'

'Well, I wouldn't call it lovely exactly.'

'It depends on what you call lovely,' she said, making sure she presented her most attractive angle. Chin up, face a little to one side, hat off to allow the wind to jostle her hair into playful loops of gold. 'But I imagine it would look beautiful now, with all the colours in the sand. The dunes are magnificent, aren't they?'

'Yes,' he agreed, his face still stretched in surprise. 'How did you enjoy the camel ride?'

Was that another possible means of having me killed? I hadn't thought of that. How thorough you two are ... She laughed, a lovely light sound. 'It was awful! I'm sore all over.'

'Me too. I hate the things.'

She smiled again and waited for him to drive through a small but rough watercourse. 'It must be getting difficult for you to see where you're driving.'

'Yes.'

'Do you like driving?'

'Yes.'

'A shame you can't practise where there are proper roads.'

He nodded. He switched on the lights and pale beams spread across the gravelly ground in front of the car.

'Did you help build the bore?' she inquired.

'No. It was done a long time before I got here.'

A very long time, she thought, and felt good. It was so easy to trap this young fool into telling her the truth.

'I should like to see the other bore some time,' she said.

Oh, Jesus, he thought, this is where it all started.

She laughed. 'Don't look so alarmed! I'm not going to ask you to drive me there now. It's just that I do so want to see what Adam has on our property and he seems so reluctant to show me anything. It's almost as though he were trying to hide something from me.' She was still smiling – not protesting but trying to understand her husband and not being treated quite fairly.

It was a difficult blend of emotions to convey, but she thought she had formed the expression rather well.

Adam could be a difficult bastard to understand, Josef thought, and returned her smile. She let her face turn into the wind so that streams of air tossed her hair and plucked at her blouse. Josef swallowed awkwardly. This woman was twenty times better-looking than the good-looking girl down south. He began to judge one set of features against the other and then felt ashamed at the thoughts that were creeping into his mind.

It was dark when they reached the homestead. Adam arrived twenty minutes after the car, finding his way by the full moon. There was no sign of Mrs Maguire. Adam and Josef searched the area around the house and then each took a camel and rode in opposite directions, checking a half-mile square from the building. They returned to find Heather waiting.

'She took her bag,' she said. 'She's taken some of her clothing, her jewellery and even some of my money.'

'She must be trying to walk to William Creek,' Josef said.

'Why do you say that?' Heather asked.

'Because she asked me to drive her there.'

'She asked me too,' Adam said. 'We'll have to try and find her. She could have suffered sunstroke if she's been out all day.'

'Would she have got to the station?' Heather asked, alarm in her voice.

'No way. She'd have been lucky to have covered ten to fifteen miles in the heat.'

'I'll get the car out again,' Josef said.

'You're not both going,' she said. 'I refuse to be left here on my own.'

Josef raised his hand, forestalling any argument. 'That's all right. I'll go.'

'I don't think you'd find the way,' Adam said. 'It's not that easy in daylight let alone at night. You stay here and I'll go.'

'I'll get the car for you,' Josef said, pleased to have the decision made for him. He was extremely weary. 'It'll take me just a few minutes. You'll need spare water. I'll put a drum in.'

When he was gone, Heather said softly: 'You and mother planned this, didn't you?'

'I knew nothing about this. I don't know where your mother's gone.'

'You planned it, and while Josef had me stuck out there in the car you took her off somewhere. Where is she?'

'Heather, will you stop making up these fairy stories? Your mother is missing. I don't know where she is. I'm worried about her. She could have broken her leg or collapsed in the heat or anything.'

'I'm warning you! You'd better bring her back. You've either hidden her somewhere or you've forced her to run away because of some threat you made. Either way, you find her and bring her back.'

'Or you'll leave too?'

'Oh, you'd like that, wouldn't you? No, I'm not leaving, but you go and get her and bring her back to me or ...'

'Or what?'

'Or I'll go to the police and tell them about that man you killed.'

From the shed, the lights of the car flashed and moved towards them.

Mrs Maguire saw the lights approaching. They were visible from a great distance and, at first, she did not recognize them as a car's headlamps. They could have been from a torch, just a single beam held by a man on foot. It was a strange effect, a bobbing beam that sometimes flashed and sometimes glowed and seemed to come no closer. She became frightened, thinking someone was walking towards her. When the light split into two and she heard the faint noise of a car engine, she became calmer. She had been expecting the car all day.

She had slept for much of the afternoon. She had not felt like walking in the heat but it was pleasant now and the moon was bright so that she could find her way easily. For a moment she thought of standing up and being seen so that she could be taken back to the house, where she could drink and eat as much as she liked. But no, she would be strong. She was thirsty but she had a little water left and while she had eaten all her food she wasn't really hungry.

She was not going back.

She moved towards the trunk of a small tree that had died and toppled to the ground and been half-buried by drift sand. With difficulty, because she was stiff from walking, she lowered herself beside it. Hidden from the approaching car, she waited.

The driver was travelling slowly. A thought occurred to her: supposing it was someone else? Another car that could take her to William Creek? No, there were no other cars out here. At least she didn't think so. A quick glance confirmed it. While she couldn't identify the vehicle, the driver, quite obviously, was looking for her because he was swerving first one way and then the other, so that the car's beams covered the greatest possible area.

She had played hide-and-seek as a child and had been rather good at it. She giggled at the memory. The light swept across the fallen tree. Scarcely able to stop herself laughing, she stayed low. The lights went and the noise grew fainter. She stood up, carefully brushed her clothes, and resumed walking.

Half an hour later, she saw the lights returning. She hadn't expected that and felt frightened until she realized it was merely Adam or Josef or whoever was driving Heather – she was sure her daughter would be in the car, distraught with worry and searching for her – heading for home. A low bush offered some shelter so she hid behind that, being careful to cover her face with her hat. The bush was ragged so she needed to cover her face; that was something she had learned in hide-and-seek. Her sister had caught her once because she had seen her face, pale and bright, peering from under a bush in their backyard.

To her surprise, the car stopped almost opposite her hiding place. Had she been seen? She was about to stand, pouting with the disappointment of being discovered, when she heard Adam shout her name. He wasn't calling out as though he had seen her; it was the call of a man still searching for someone. She stayed down.

The car drove away. She stayed behind the bush, still not daring to look and waiting for the sound of the car to fade. Something moved near her. It made a thumping sound and she closed her eyes, too terrified to look or move. Two kangaroos passed behind her.

When the noises had ceased, she stood and resumed walking. William Creek would have to be *very* close, she assured herself. She wasn't certain how far it was from the homestead because the journey by car from the railway station had been so confusing, what with the sand storm, but she had been walking for such a long time that it couldn't be much further. She tried to guess how much longer she would have to go on before reaching the town. Maybe an hour? She might arrive in time to have dinner with some family. She'd heard the people of the outback were nice. Even if she were too late for a meal, they would certainly give her a cup of tea and make some toast. She'd like that.

She began searching for house lights.

Josef was in the house. He had been invited to have a cup of tea while Adam was away. He had drunk one cup and then Heather had excused herself and gone into the other room. Josef went to the stove and poured himself more tea. He searched for something to eat and found a slice of bread. He went back to the table, ate the bread, drank the tea. He waited. He didn't know what to make of Heather. She had performed a bit out in the sand when they were stuck, but that was understandable. She had the baby with her and any mother would have been upset out there. But she had been so nice coming back in the car and in the house.

What had Adam said? She was impossible. Maybe to Adam, but he could be a bit strange himself and possibly he wasn't trying hard enough to help her adjust to Kalinda. It was all right for him. He was used to living like a bushie because that essentially was what he was. Heather was different. She had class. She could be a bit irrational and hard to follow but all women were supposed to be like that. He hadn't been too keen on her at first, back in Nyngan, but he had to admit he didn't know her well. Right now, he suspected he liked her a lot.

What if she and Adam split up? Married couples did that sometimes. He'd known a man who lived near his parents' winery and that man's wife had run off with another bloke and then the man brought another woman in to live with him. Everyone talked, but still, it happened ... What the hell was he thinking of? Adam and Heather were married and Adam was his best friend.

The door to the other room was a slim affair, a bag stretched over a wooden frame. It swung open, as if by accident. He saw Heather near the door, her back to him. She was brushing her hair and she was bare from the waist up. She turned and, for a brief time, looked straight at him.

She closed the door.

He went back to the stove and poured more tea. My God, what

a woman! Such a figure with those big, full breasts. And she'd looked at him without a suggestion of surprise or shame or resentment. She'd just stared at him with her face wearing a lovely, placid, almost inviting look. He drank the tea rapidly.

He'd been imagining it. She would not come out of the room. She would be too ashamed of having been seen like that.

The door opened and she walked out, tucking a blouse into her skirt.

'Well, Cassandra's well and truly asleep and I've washed myself and given my hair a good brush and I feel marvellous,' she said and then laughed, once more managing the feat without making a noise and without wrinkling her face in the wrong places. 'Although I'm just a little sore from the camel ride. How about you?'

He realized he had been standing with his mouth open. He put the teacup on the table. He managed to smile. 'Me too. I hate camels.'

'Obviously we're kindred spirits. We do seem to have a lot in common.' She undid the top button of her blouse. 'It's so hot. How on earth do men like you put up with the heat?'

He shrugged. It wasn't a particularly hot night.

'You're modest,' she teased. 'And shy. Now, it's a lovely night outside so why don't we wait out there?'

She led the way but turned suddenly in the doorway so that they collided. 'Oh, excuse me,' she said with just a trace of a laugh. 'I've forgotten something.'

Josef walked out, brushing his chest where they had made contact. He stood beneath a brilliant sky. He heard her approach.

'I hope Adam finds your mother all right.'

'Yes. So do I.'

She wasn't touching him but he knew she was close; so close his skin tingled.

Adam was deeply worried when he returned. He had seen no sign of Mrs Maguire and he had driven further than she could possibly have covered on foot. That means, he reasoned, that she was either walking in the wrong direction or she was somewhere off the track and injured. He presumed she had no water. She could not survive more than a day or two. She might not even be heading for William Creek as they were assuming. She might have wandered off – lost her memory and gone walking. She could be anywhere.

He spoke to Josef and they agreed on a plan. Jimmy was the best at following tracks so they needed to bring him into the search. Before dawn, Josef would take the camels to the bore where Jimmy was camped. Josef insisted he knew the way for he had been to that bore several times. Jimmy would then return to the homestead, search for tracks and follow them. Josef would ride back to the homestead in a loop that would take him through country to the east – just in case she was out that way. Adam would take the mare and cover a quadrant of land to the north-west. When one found her, he was to make smoke from a single fire if she were unharmed. If help were needed he was to light two fires, well separated so that the columns of smoke could easily be distinguished.

Heather listened to them planning with some amusement. It was, she was sure, an act for her benefit to make her think her mother really was in danger. Her mother was probably safe somewhere, well fed and in bed and laughing at the discomfort she had caused her daughter. It was her way of getting even for last night. Heather had worked out what this was all about. Adam wanted her to leave so that he could have all the money for himself and that other woman of his. Her mother wanted to go away and, because she couldn't exist without Heather, she wanted her daughter to leave the property too. So Adam and her mother had got together. It was all so obvious – scare Heather, and make her think this was a dangerous, unpleasant place. They'd tried today with that ridiculous episode in the sand and now they were trying with this manufactured drama about her mother being missing.

She went to bed, half-expecting to find her mother hiding in the room. She even searched under the bed. Now I'm being ridiculous, she told herself. They wouldn't hide her here. She would be somewhere far away.

The men were still talking in the other room. Somehow, they managed to retain a note of concern in their voices. I have to admit, she thought, that they are extremely good actors. They sound convincing. And for the first time, doubt jostled with her convictions. Was it possible that her mother truly was lost out there somewhere? Supposing it was true? Supposing her mother had hurt herself or was dying of thirst? What if her mother died? How would she manage by herself, without her mother helping her in this frightful place?

Jimmy was surprised to see Josef arrive so early in the morning. His dog barked at the two camels and Jimmy laughed when the leading camel shied and almost threw its rider.

'You look as comfortable as a lizard on a push bike,' he said, as his friend tried to dismount. Josef had never mastered the technique. He was riding Bozo because he thought the smaller animal would be simpler to handle than the more powerful Rumble but, at a crucial moment in his descent, Bozo rocked sideways and Josef fell on his knees.

'Ever thought of letting the camel ride you?' Jimmy asked. 'You know, giving it a piggy-back ride? It might be easier.'

'Very funny.' Josef dusted himself. He explained why he had come. 'I reckon Mrs Maguire's trying to get to William Creek. She asked Adam and then me to take her there. Heather says the old lady's a bit touched.'

'Yeah?' Jimmy was checking Rumble. Water and food were packed in a pannier bag. There was also a small tin of burn cream. 'What's this for?'

'Adam thought she might be sunburned.'

Jimmy squinted at the sun. 'Good idea, I suppose. I keep forgetting you whites are such a delicate lot.' He climbed into the saddle. 'You're going back to the homestead?'

'In a roundabout way. I'm going to search the country over in this direction.' He pointed to the east.

'Well, if I'm not back by this afternoon will you come out here again and look after the sheep tonight? It's bad enough losing an old sheila but we can't afford to lose any more sheep.' He smiled, but Josef wasn't sure if he were joking or not.

'And you reckon she's heading for William Creek?'

'If she knows the way.'

Jimmy nodded. 'Well, that could take me all day.' He shouted a command and the camel rocked to its feet.

'Hey, before you go, guess who's at William Creek?'

'William?'

'Don't be a goat, Jimmy! No, Nellie. Adam saw her the other day.'

Jimmy jerked at the rope. 'What's she doing there?'

'Working at the new store.'

The camel had turned in a half-circle and Jimmy pulled it around again. 'How long's she been doing that?'

'Don't know. Only a few days, I think. Amazing, isn't it? Of all the places in the world for her to turn up at.'

Jimmy's lip curled. 'Jeez, you're innocent, kid! You don't think it's an accident, do you?'

'What do you mean?'

'If that bitch is at William Creek, she's there for some reason and I bet it's not a good one. Don't forget the sheep tonight.' He rode off. His dog ran after the camel, yapping and nipping at its heels.

Jimmy went back to the homestead. He slowly circled the buildings, searching for a solitary set of footprints. There were many tracks but they became jumbled with others and usually returned to one of the yards or a shed. The way to William Creek had become marked by wheel tracks and the imprints of camels. It was clearly defined. Jimmy presumed that if Mrs Maguire wanted to go to town, she would have had no trouble in following the track in its early stages. He let the camel amble along for a mile, the gentle pace pleasing his dog which was still following. When he came to the place where the track first crossed the Douglas, he dismounted and searched the creek's banks. He found footprints well to the right of the wheel tracks. He was sure they were hers. No one else went walking out here. He followed them to a tree. She had apparently rested in the shade, sitting on the trunk of a tree which had fallen against a larger one. He found heel marks in the sand and many ants which had apparently been attracted by fallen particles of food. She had rested and had something to eat. So she had food with her. Good. She knew what she was doing.

He went back to the camel and led it for some distance until the tracks left the creek and followed the tyre marks across a flat expanse of hardened clay. The dog had begun to limp so he picked it up and remounted Rumble. The tyres had made little impression on the clay so he rode quickly to the end of the pan where wheel ruts stood out clearly on a ridge of sand. There he resumed his search for the woman's track.

He found it about three hundred yards to the left. The track wandered across the sand. She had gone in several directions, apparently searching for the wheel marks, but eventually she had swung to the right along a narrow gully and at last intersected the proper route. Jimmy smiled. The old sheila had a few brains.

She must be really tired now, he thought, because her trail began to weave. He followed her path to a place where she seemed to have rested for some time. He could see where she had levelled the sand and stretched out full length. She had eaten again here. A fragment of bread remained. It had attracted a long trail

654

of ants. He went on. He found a place where she had urinated. Good. She wasn't dying of thirst. He noted how discreetly she had relieved herself and grinned. It was behind a bush and, to get there, she had detoured at least two hundred yards. He looked around him. It was as deserted and as private a place as you could find and yet she had hidden behind a scrawny fragment of vegetation rather than expose herself to the world. With the dog obediently lying across the camel at the front of the saddle, Jimmy stood in the stirrups and peed on the sand, enjoying the noise his water made from such a height.

She was staggering now. He found another place where she had apparently rested on her knees behind a bush. This puzzled him. She had not urinated or sat down; just kneeled and put her hands on the ground. He also found the marks of kangaroos. He couldn't work it out. Was she hiding from the 'roos?

From that point, her track and the wheel marks began to diverge. For some distance she walked roughly parallel to the road but then, at a place where the wheel ruts turned right and skirted the edge of a salt pan, she had gone straight across. Her feet had broken through the crust in a couple of places. She had fallen once. He tracked her to the edge of the salt and found clear footprints entering a region of dunes.

He found her in a valley between two dunes. She was walking towards him. He could see her footmarks climb the dune and then return, a hundred yards to the right. She had begun to walk in circles. She stopped. She was covered in dust and had torn the hem of her dress. She was still carrying the suitcase. Her face was flushed.

'G'day, Mrs Maguire,' he said.

She took one step backwards. 'You're not going to hurt me?'

'No. It's me. Jimmy.'

'Oh.' She dropped the case and slowly, like an inflated toy losing air, sank to the ground. She clutched her forehead. 'I thought you were a savage.'

'Not me.' He brought her water. The dog licked her face and Jimmy kicked it out of the way. She swallowed water and wiped her face.

'Is this William Creek?'

'No.'

'Oh. Where are we?'

'I don't think it's got a name.'

She realized her dress had risen above her knees and hastily covered her legs. 'I'd like to go to William Creek, please.' She could have been buying a train ticket.

'I think I'd better take you back to your daughter.'

'No.' She shook her head firmly, not opening her eyes.

'Come on, Mrs Maguire. I'll put you on the camel and take you back.'

She attempted to stand. 'I will not go back,' she said, her voice croaking but defiant. 'My daughter will kill me.'

'No, she won't. Come on.'

'She tried to beat me with the whip. She threw hot water over me.'

'Jesus!'

'She did. You mightn't believe me but she did.'

He gave her more water. Her lips were cracked and he remembered the ointment. He passed it to her and offered her food. She refused.

'Am I near William Creek?'

'No,' he said gently.

'But I've walked so far and the country is so difficult to walk in. It is a simply dreadful road.'

'You've wandered a bit off the road.'

'Oh, I see. I'm not very good at finding my way.'

'You did pretty good.' He drank some water. 'Adam came out looking for you in the car last night. Shame you didn't seem him.'

'Oh, I saw him. I hid. I didn't want to go back.'

'It can't be that bad, Mrs Maguire.'

'It is. I will not go back. I'd rather die.'

Jesus, he thought, a man hasn't got much choice. If I take her back she'll only walk off again and if I leave her here she'll die. 'What will you do if I take you to William Creek?' he asked.

'Catch the train. I want to go back home. I have money for my ticket.'

I wouldn't mind going on to William Creek, he thought, just to find out what that slut Nellie's up to. 'Can you ride a camel?'

'I don't know.'

'Well, if you're prepared to give it a go, we'll soon find out. You can't be any worse than Joe. You just sit there for a minute and get your strength back.' He gathered a few clumps of dead wood, stacked them in a heap, and set fire to it. A thin column of smoke rose in the air, straight and unruffled by any breeze. No bastard will see that, he thought, but felt better for having done what he was supposed to do. He walked to Mrs Maguire.

'Come on,' he said and helped her on to the camel. He nursed her suitcase. He said to the dog: 'And you, you stupid mongrel, are going to have to walk.'

Josef was the first to return to the homestead. He rode in, soon after ten o'clock, having completed a futile semi-circular sweep of the country. He checked with Heather, who was doing something with the baby in the house. She had seen Jimmy on the camel but had not spoken to him. No, she had no idea if he had found her mother's trail. Josef thought about going out again. He should, and make a wider search of the land between the homestead and the bore, but what was the use? Adam had been out for hours and might have found her. In any case, Jimmy would probably pick up her trail and track her down. They were both better bushmen than he was.

He was sore, stiff, tired and filthy. He still ached from yesterday's exertions and he had been so tired last night that he'd gone to bed without washing. He stank and chafed at the joints. He went to the spring, carried water to the wash house and filled the cut-down forty-four-gallon drum that served as a bath. Undressing was difficult, for his back hurt, but when he was naked he climbed in the drum and began soaping himself.

He thought of the south. He missed four things: his mother's cooking; his mother; the two girls who had provided him with so many ecstatic and dramatic moments; and water. Right now, he reckoned water was the thing he liked most of all, and he tried to submerge himself in the crude bath. It was awkward because the drum, resting on its side, rocked against the bricks that held it in place and water splashed over the side. He had to lift his legs in order to cover his shoulders and head. After a few such contorted immersions he felt better and thought about the other things he missed, and decided the girls deserved second place. He concentrated on them one at a time: the good-looking one who had been such a challenge and then the plain one who had been so extraordinarily willing. He became excited and put his head under the water again.

Through the water, he heard a voice. Heather's voice.

'My, you are having a good time,' she said and he struggled to sit up, splashing the floor. 'But you do seem to be having difficulty in washing all of you at the same time.'

He rubbed his eyes. She was in the doorway.

'So many parts seem to be projecting from the water,' she said.

He folded his hands across his partly submerged lap. 'I didn't see you.'

'Obviously.' Now she was beside the drum, arms folded across her chest and her face crinkled in the smile a mother gives a child caught in an embarrassing but funny escapade. 'I came to see if you wanted something to eat. Maybe I should scrub your back instead.'

He tried to laugh but no sound emerged. He lifted his knees and wrapped his arms around them. What was she doing? She had picked up a can and was dipping it into the bath water near his feet.

'I'll wash your hair.'

'No, I'm all right, thanks.'

'Nonsense. It's full of dirt.' She tipped the water over his head and refilled the can. 'I'm very good at this. I wash my daughter's hair every day.'

'I'm not the same as Cassie.'

'Please call her Cassandra.' She had found the soap and was lathering his hair. 'And the only difference is that you have more hair and it is many times dirtier than hers has ever been. Now, doesn't that feel good?' With long and gentle fingers she was massaging his scalp. He stretched his neck, pressing his head into her hand. I'm like a cat being tickled, he thought, and it is good.

'It's been a long time since anyone's done that to me,' he said.

'Too long,' she said, working more soap into his hair. 'It's not natural for a person to be on his own, like you are out here. Or like I am.'

She poured another can of water over him. He gasped and rubbed soap from his eyes. 'What do you mean?'

'About me? Oh, I'm lonely. I have the baby but it's not the same as ... as an adult.'

He pressed his knuckles against his stinging eyes.

'You're probably saying to yourself "But what about Adam?" Here, take this.' She pressed a towel into his hand. He wiped his face. "Now close your eyes. I'm going to pour more water over you.'

'But what about Adam?'

She giggled. 'I knew you would say that! All he seems to think about are sheep and bores. I hardly see him.'

'But that's only in the day. He's got to work then.'

'I don't see him at night, either.' She was lathering his scalp again, and his head tingled with delicious sensations. 'Oh, I know he makes a great pretence of being with me but … oh, what's it matter. You don't want to hear all this.'

On the contrary, he did want to hear but he said nothing. She stroked his forehead.

'Would you believe,' she continued, 'that he sleeps in the other room? On the floor. Rather than be with me or even be near the baby he actually chooses to lie on the floor in the other room. I think he's become as strange as one of those dingoes he's always talking about.'

Her fingers had strayed to the sensitive area behind the ears. They moved with supreme delicacy. This is such a gentle, sensuous woman, he thought. What was wrong with Adam? And no wonder she flew off the handle occasionally! A woman had to have a bit of sex and without it she was liable to do all sorts of strange things. Adam had said she was impossible, but he sounded crazy. Maybe it was a result of all those months of being out here in the heat. Isolation and hard work and too much sun could affect people.

More water cascaded over his head. Her fingers slid gently down his neck and out along his shoulders. 'There we are,' she said, still touching him. 'If you would like something to eat why don't you come on over to the house?'

She left. Josef followed ten minutes later. His hair was still wet and hung across his forehead. He sat at the table and she poured him a cup of tea that was thick with tealeaves. She went to the other room and returned with a large comb.

'You look like a little boy with your hair all over the place,' she said. Standing behind him, she proceeded to comb his hair. She did it slowly and, Josef imagined, lovingly.

'You've got beautiful hair,' she said. 'Very fine and such a rich colour.'

Josef had never thought about his hair.

'Do you like it here?' she asked.

'Yes. It's good. It's very big.' He wiped away water that had trickled behind his ear.

'Adam thinks he's going to make a lot of money here.'

'Yes. He reckons he'll be a millionaire.'

The comb stopped for no more than a second. 'Yes. And straight away. Is that what he tells you too?'

Josef just grinned, but it was a strange expression, she thought. Like someone who realizes he's been caught out by a smarter person and knows he has revealed more than he meant to say.

'You know Adam,' was all Josef said.

'Yes, I certainly do.' Try as she might, she could not stop smiling with satisfaction.

THIRTEEN

Having found no trace of the missing woman on his search to the west, Adam rode to the Douglas and intersected Jimmy's camel tracks and those of Mrs Maguire. He followed them for some distance but then, growing concerned about the mare's need for water, returned to the homestead.

He went straight to Heather, presuming she would be growing desperate for news of her mother. She was talking to Josef.

'Jimmy has picked up her track,' he told her. 'I'm sure he'll find her soon.'

'Did you see them?' Josef said.

'No. Just their tracks. But you can be sure she'll be all right.'

'Good,' Heather said calmly. 'When will she be back?'

'It depends on what sort of condition she's in and how far she went on foot.'

So this little charade is almost at an end, Heather thought. I wonder what you have planned now, my dear, deceitful husband, to cheat me of all the money you are making?

Jimmy delivered an exhausted Mrs Maguire to the hotel at William Creek. She managed to summon enough strength to take a room and bathe, using water from the enamel jug on the dressing table. Then she checked the bag to make sure her jewellery was safe and fell asleep. The first train south was due the following night.

Jimmy went to the store. A young Afghan met him. 'You want something?'

'Yeah,' he said, looking around him. There was no sign of Nellie. 'You got a black girl working here?'

'Yes. Why?'

'How much do you charge for her?'

Saleem Goolamadail stiffened. 'What are you talking about?'

Jimmy flashed a conspiratorial smile. 'You know, mate. How much?'

'I don't know who the devil you are but you might as well shove off.'

'But isn't this the local brothel?'

'It certainly is not!'

'Well, what the hell's she doing working here?'

'Look, clear off.' He advanced on Jimmy, fortified by the discovery that the aboriginal only had one arm.

'Good-looking sheila? Tall, not quite full blood? Calls herself Nellie?'

Goolamadail stopped.

'She worked for the biggest brothel in Port Pirie. Then she moved to Coober Pedy. They say she was rooted by every Chinese miner in the place. In fact, it was a chow who told me she was here.' Jimmy saw the shock on the young man's face. 'He reckoned a whole lot of Chinese would move up this way if they knew Nellie was here.'

The Afghan had to lean against a box. He detested the Chinese. And he had been contemplating inviting Nellie to his hotel room that night. He felt ill.

'Didn't you know?' Jimmy asked, beaming innocence. 'Seeing she was working here, I thought this must have been the local tart factory. Where is she, anyhow?'

'Out the back in the store.' He wagged a slender finger at Jimmy. 'Don't you go near her. I don't want any dirty stuff around this place.'

'No, that's all right. She's probably rotten with the pox by now anyhow. See you later.' He ambled away. Once out of sight, he walked briskly to where he had tied the camel. The dog waited obediently, but could not control its joy at seeing him return. Jimmy kicked it out of the way. He felt rotten.

It was too late to return to Kalinda that day and he had no intention of staying in town. He no longer liked being with people. He rode out of William Creek, searching for a good place to camp. The dog limped behind.

Heather stood near the house, watching the sunset. A ruffle of clouds fringed the horizon and she had to admit the colours were beautiful. At least, she corrected herself, the sky was stunning but the land beneath it was as hostile and ugly as ever. She was nursing Cassandra and feeling lonely. Josef had gone to tend the sheep. Adam had driven down the track towards William Creek, to search for Jimmy and, if needed, bring back Mrs Maguire in the car. Heather turned and walked to the front of the house. She did not feel like going inside. The house was so tiny and depressing. Instead she walked towards the beefwood tree and searched for a sign of the returning car. She did not want to be on her own after dark. She was relishing the prospect of his return, not to see him or even her mother but to listen to whatever fanciful concoctions spilled from their lips. They will be out there now, she thought, talking about me and plotting something between them to make me go away.

She heard the sound of the returning car. Adam had driven back slowly, almost reluctantly. 'No sign,' he said simply.

'Of whom? My mother, your aboriginal friend, or the camel?'

'Of anyone. I had to leave the road at one place and walk quite a long way. It was across a salt pan and then through sand hills. I could see your mother's tracks and those of the camel. The trouble was there'd been a wind and the tracks are pretty well filled in.'

'Of course. The wind adds to the mystery.'

He ignored the irony. 'I came to a place where they could have met up. It's hard to say. It's possible Jimmy put her on the camel.'

'Well, they're not here,' she said.

'And I didn't pass them on the way back.'

'It's very curious. Maybe they've eloped.'

Adam was tired. He stroked his chin. 'Heather, this is serious but you're going on like it's some sort of game.'

'You mean it's not?'

'Do you understand that out here, people who get lost can die?'

'I thought you said she was with that grotesque one-armed black friend of yours.'

'I think she's with Jimmy, but I'm not sure.'

'And you think I should be frantic with worry over all this? Possibly not sleep tonight? Be in a fine state of hysteria so that when mother does return, I'll be weak and weepy and ready to do whatever you suggest? Is that what you want?'

'I only want to find your mother.'

'How noble!'

'Heather, do you remember how you were feeling when we found you yesterday? You could hardly think, you were so dry. Your mother's been out there for two days. I don't want to alarm you but you should face reality. She could be in a very bad way.'

'I'm quite aware of what you two have been up to. I have a good idea of where she's been staying. And I know how you'd like me to react because I know what your motive is. But you're not going to win. Let me repeat, Adam, in case you're in any doubt: you are not going to cheat me out of what is lawfully mine.'

'I was not talking about the pair of us and whatever's going on in that scrambled egg of a brain of yours. I was talking about your mother, and your mother has been missing in dry country for two days.'

'I'm quite aware of what you've been talking about. And talking about mother, why don't you put an end to this ridiculous game of yours and just bring her back? Have her here by tomorrow. The house is in the most awful mess and I need her here and I will not tolerate this charade any longer.'

'You *are* nuts!'

'By tomorrow, or I will go to the authorities and tell them something I would have great shame in disclosing, but would be compelled to, nonetheless.'

'You'd tell them what?'

'You know.'

'Tell me,' he taunted.

Now she wasn't sure of the man's name and she cursed herself for her poor memory. Was it Bailey or Mailey?

'About the policeman,' she said.

'Heather, what are you talking about?' He tried to sound baffled and as unconcerned as he could, but his voice shook.

'The one you killed.' She remembered something else. 'The one who almost killed Josef.' She enjoyed the look on Adam's face, and the way the colour had gone from his cheeks. He was shocked, but there was something else. Doubt. He was not convinced she knew all. It was time for a gamble. Bailey or Mailey?

'I know all about Mailey,' she said and she knew she had scored.

Adam walked away. He left the car where it was and went to the yard where the mare stood. He checked that she had food and water and felt for tenderness in the injured leg. She shivered nervously, for she could feel his hand trembling.

The sun had set behind the clouds. They were rain clouds, Adam noted, and tried to calm himself by analysing their importance. He felt happier with animals and clouds. Yes, they were definitely rain clouds. He wondered if they were in for a storm in the next few days.

Nellie was surprised to find Saleem Goolamadail waiting for her. Normally he did the bookwork at this time of the day, but he was at the front of the shop and so agitated that he found it impossible to be still. One hand wrestled the other. His eyes looked at everything but her.

'What's up?' she said.

'There are questions I must ask.' His right hand seemed to have gained control of the left but a twitch had developed in his shoulders. The nervousness spread to Nellie.

'Like what?' Her hands shook. She folded her arms to stifle the movement. What on earth had happened?

'Where did you come from?'

'I've been out the back ...'

'I do not mean that, foolish woman. What did you do before you came up here and worked for my uncle?'

'You know. I've told you before. I worked in a guest house.'

'Oh, is that what you call it?'

Puzzled, she said nothing.

'What sort of guest house?'

'Just an ordinary sort of guest house. A house with guests in it. What other sorts are there?'

'The sorts you worked in. Oh, you dreadful woman, you have betrayed me!'

She relaxed a litle. 'Have you been drinking?'

He jumped to his feet and, for a moment, she thought he was going to hit her. 'You know I do not drink!' His hand remained aloft, poised to strike. He held it there for so long it became obvious he would do nothing. Feeling foolish, he bent the hand and ran the fingers through his hair. He turned from her.

'I came to see you the other night. You were not in your room.'

'Did you look behind all the tyres?'

'I am not joking. Where were you?'

'Do I work for you all night as well as all day?'

He ignored the answer. 'Were you selling your body to some man? A yellow man perhaps?'

'What are you talking about?' she said, each word bracketed by a growing apprehension.

'You are nothing but a common prostitute.'

'How dare you call me that!'

'I dare because it is true. You were a prostitute in Port Pirie.' His voice had gone flat. 'And then a prostitute in Coober Pedy. And now you are trying to be a prostitute here. Well, you will have to leave. We cannot have that sort of thing here.'

She sat on a sack. 'Who's told you these things?'

'What does it matter? They are true and you must go.'

'Who have you been talking to?'

'Someone who came looking for you. He was seeking your favours. I threw him out. He has gone away.'

'I am not a prostitute. For God's sake, how could I be a prostitute in a place like this? There's no one here.'

'Were you at Port Pirie? Were you at Coober Pedy?'

'I've been to a lot of places.'

'And you shared the bed of every Chinese worker on the opal fields?'

'That is a lie!' Suddenly, she remembered a similar accusation. 'Who told you that? Was he a black man?'

'It does not matter. You cannot work here any more. You are fired.'

'Did he only have one arm?' she asked, and saw that the question jolted the young Afghan. 'He did, didn't he? I know who it was and if you listen to him and take any notice you're as crazy as he is. That bastard is mad. I don't know why but he wants to get me.'

'You were a prostitute?'

'Yes, but that was years ago.'

He fell against some sacks and pounded his head. 'Oh, you have no idea how much this revelation has hurt me! I had such plans.'

'Like what? Rooting me?'

'You see! You speak like such a woman. It is all coming out.'

'The only thing coming out is that you're an idiot.'

'That's it!' he shouted, jumping up and raising his hand again. 'You are dismissed! Go now.'

'You can't dismiss me again. You sacked me only a minute ago.'

'Well, go! Out! Now. I do not want filth here.'

'The filthiest thing around here is your mind.' She walked from the shop.

'Where are you going?' he shouted when he saw that she was heading towards the storeroom.

'I'm going to that place you jokingly called my room. I have nowhere else to go, or would you rather I slept on the railway line?'

'You are not to set foot on these premises again.'

'I am going to cook my tea and I am going to go to sleep on my bed. Tomorrow I'll leave, but not tonight.'

'I will throw you out!'

'If you so much as come near me, so help me I will split your head open.'

For many days, Goolamadail had been preparing himself for the delight that had brought him to this remote place: the prospect of going to bed with Nellie. He was a young man who found more comfort in imagination than in reality and so he had not broached the subject with her. He had merely thought about it. He had dreamed at nights and constructed little plays in which each scene of masterful seduction had grown progressively more erotic. Always she had been eager. Never was there a suggestion that she would or could reject his advances. He was, quite simply, irresistible.

He thought about what the black man had said and, for the first time, felt excitement and curiosity pushing against the revulsion that had swamped his thoughts. She was a filthy, mercenary woman, but so extraordinarily alluring and attractive. Her body had been bought by many men – but what a body! She had slept with men for money – which meant she must know secret ways to delight a man.

He went to his hotel room and thought about her for several hours. She would be gone soon. His life would be a misery. He would have to work harder and he would have no woman to dream about or to warm his nights. He sat up in bed. He had had enough of dreams. Tonight, he would take this woman. She was only a prostitute. She had no honour. She would submit to him without resistance. She might even be good. No, she would be a delight. Possibly he would beat her afterwards. Then she would plead to stay and he would force her to submit again – she would be only too eager to do what he wanted because she would be desperate to get her job back and be with him. She would beg him. He would beat her again. Only mildly – just enough to show he was superior but had a sense of mercy, and she would squirm at his feet, pleading for his forgiveness. She would be naked, of course. He wiped his lips.

He dressed and went to the storeroom. He had difficulty finding his way and bumped into several things.

'It is me,' he whispered, just before the pick handle hit him across the back of the skull.

The sky was grey with cloud when Jimmy returned to Kalinda. He arrived early in the afternoon, carrying the dog on his lap. Adam saw the single figure on the camel and, alarmed, ran to meet him. The two men talked for several minutes and then Adam walked back to the house. Heather was in the doorway.

'Still missing?' she said, examining her fingernails.

'No.'

An expression close to alarm jolted her face. 'You're not going to tell me she's dead?'

'No. She'll all right.'

'Well, where is she?'

How do you tell your wife that her own mother is frightened of her? Adam wondered. That she'd rather die in the desert than come back to live with her?

'Oh, for heaven's sake, Adam, I know you've had this planned for ages, so just tell me what it is that the pair of you have cooked up now. To start with, where is she?'

'There's nothing cooked up, as you call it! Your mother was lost but now she's safe. Jimmy found her wandering among some sand hills about eleven miles out.'

'Did he? And I suppose she was delirious with thirst, dying of hunger, burned by the sun and about to be attacked by savage dingoes?'

'I don't know why I bother trying to be gentle with you. Your mother wouldn't come back. She said she was frightened of you. She said she would rather stay out there and die.'

'Even for you that is absurd.'

'She told Jimmy you'd attacked her. Tried to hit her with a whip or something.'

She had been taunting him with a smile of disbelief, but now the smile dissolved. 'That, of course, is an absolute lie. Where is she now?'

'William Creek.'

'What's she doing there?'

'Waiting for the next train south. She intends going home. That's what she told Jimmy. I presume she means back to New South Wales.'

Now there was no suggestion of a smile. 'You put her up to this. First there was the other night when she said those ridiculous things. Now this. This is your doing.'

'Can't you understand this is your mother's own decision and that she made it because of the way you've been behaving?'

'Oh, I understand all right. I know precisely what you're up to and believe me ...' She stopped in mid-sentence. 'You haven't killed her, have you? I mean, you tried to have me killed the other day and I know your record for murder is an excellent one.' She stared at him with an intense curiosity. 'Is she dead?'

'Your mother is alive and waiting for the train. And the only person who's tried to kill her, according to what she said, is you.'

Heather presented her back to him. She sometimes did that when she had a demand to make. Adam wondered what it might be.

'Take me to her.'

'No.'

'I demand you take me to William Creek!'

'And put you on the train?'

'No. Bring my mother back here. I will not have her running off like this. I need her here. I cannot run this house without help, so get the car and take me there this instant!'

'If there was a lake here I would tell you where to go and jump.'

'You won't take me?'

'No.'

'All right. I shall drive myself.'

'Good. But don't expect us to come looking for you. Jimmy and I will be busy away from the homestead. We have a fence to put up.'

'You are going away at a time like this?'

'Just to the bore.'

'Of course, of course. Everything's at the bore. The mythical bore that I have yet to see.' He was striding away rapidly and she could not keep up. 'Are you really going to go away for some days?'

'Yes. There's a lot of work to be done out there.'

'Will you all be working there?'

'Just Jimmy and me. I'll send Joe back.'

She stopped. A plan was already forming. 'Send him back quickly,' she called. 'I hate being here on my own.'

Josef was late. He walked the final miles to the homestead, leading Bozo and preferring the possibility of tired leg muscles to the certainty of aches in every other part of his body. He found Heather waiting for him. She was dressed for travel. She had prepared a basket of food.

'We're going to William Creek,' she announced. 'Please make sure there's enough petrol in the car and that everything works. It's most urgent that we get there tonight.'

Josef knew about Mrs Maguire. Adam had said she should be left alone.

'Oh, Adam hates her. You weren't here when mother arrived but it was awful. Please, Josef, the train is leaving tonight.'

'The trains up here are always late,' he said, as though that were a reason not to go.

'No matter. We should still hurry. Mother is not well. She should not be left on her own.'

'Jimmy said she didn't want to come back.' He licked his lips, not wanting to disappoint her, but Adam had been clear: Mrs Maguire was to be left alone.

'The poor thing is terribly confused. She needs medication. I have it with me. Without it, she gets terribly sick.'

'Adam didn't say anything about medicine.'

'I can understand that,' she said reasonably. 'He doesn't want her here but I'm afraid he is being more than a little ... selfish. He resents her being here. Many husbands would feel the same way, but tell me, Josef, do you hate my mother?' She reached out and touched his arm. Her fingertips were ice-cold and marvellously soft.

'No, of course not.'

'She can't be left on her own. Without her medicine she could die. Specially on that long, awful train ride.'

He was nodding agreement.

'I didn't dare argue with Adam. He gets ... well, violent, and I'm so weak and, well ...' Her fingers were still on his arm. 'I do get so frightened.'

'Oh, he's all right.'

'I was going to drive myself,' she said.

'You can't do that.'

She bent forward and almost kissed him. Her lips were close. He felt the soft puff of her breath. 'Oh, Josef, that's so kind of you! I'll run back to the house and get the baby while you put some petrol in the tank. I'll only be a minute.'

Josef scratched his head, wondering what he had said. Whatever it was, the matter was decided. Adam would be angry. But, Jesus, if Mrs Maguire was likely to die ... That was justification for going. He couldn't let the old lady die. But as he walked to the shed he knew he was not going to William Creek because Mrs Maguire was without her medicine but because he had been manipulated.

He reached the car and thought for a while. To hell with all this, he decided, and turning quickly walked back towards the house. I will tell her I'm not going. Adam said not to and, besides, it will be dark before we get there and the track is dangerous at night. And I'm not going to be talked into doing things I don't want to do.

She saw him approaching and ran to meet him. 'Oh, I'm so glad you came over,' she said, touching his arm. 'I have a special favour to ask. I was wondering if you would let me drive the car.'

A protest formed on his lips. She blocked it with cool fingers. 'No, no, not all the way.' She laughed lightly and allowed her finger to move from his lips to his cheek. 'Just at first. Let me drive the car just a little way and then you can take it all the rest of the journey. Please?'

Her hand was still on his face and her eyes were large and warm and pleading.

'Yes, sure.' He grinned and she kissed his cheek.

'You are a darling,' she said and ran back to the house. Slowly, he returned to the shed to put fuel in the car.

FOURTEEN

Nellie had spent most of the day at the camp where they had made love. It was shady but not quiet. Cockatoos were in the trees and they squawked and chattered constantly and sent down regular showers of stripped leaves and broken twigs. She liked the birds. They reminded her of young children playing and arguing and eating. They seemed to have no cares beyond today.

She didn't know what she was going to do. She had come to the camp-site straight after the affair with Goolamadail. She had hit him good and hard and, while she hadn't knocked him unconscious, she had sent him pitching to his knees and then, when he had tried to get up, she attacked him again and he had run from the building. What a silly twit he was, sacking her one minute and expecting her to sleep with him the next! She wished she'd hit him smack on the face rather than on the back of the head so that he would have had something to admire when next he indulged in one of his long sessions in front of the mirror. A flat nose and black eyes would have been a reasonable reminder of how unfair he'd been to her.

She left immediately after that. She didn't know what he might do. Come back with a gun or one of those long knives he had. So she had gathered all the things she could legitimately claim as hers, plus a little food and water, and walked to the camp-site. And this time, she reflected with a wry smile, she hadn't put her foot down a rabbit hole.

What was she going to do? Not stay here, sharing a stand of trees with a bunch of parrots. And that was about the only decision she could make. No point staying in town. There was no other work in such a small place. Maybe she should go back to Marree? Or even further south? Was she being a fool for wanting to be near Adam? Yes, but what of it? If you spent your life only doing the things that weren't foolish you wouldn't do much. She even contemplated going to Kalinda. But how? She couldn't walk. And when she got there, there was nothing she could do. She could hardly bowl up to the mistress of the house and say, 'I'm the woman your husband truly loves so, if you don't mind, I'll sleep down by the waterhole until you wake up to yourself and clear out.' She couldn't do that, much though the thought entertained her, so, late in the day, still not knowing what to do, she walked into town, lugging her suitcase with her. Possibly she would catch the train south, at least as far as Marree where she might be able to find some work. She headed for the William Creek Hotel. That was the only other business in town. There was just a chance the publican might give her a job.

The man was out the back, chopping firewood.

'If I had enough money to hire help, I wouldn't be doing this,' he said cheerfully. 'No, I'd like to help you, love, but I can't.'

'I can chop wood,' she said.

'That's not a woman's work.' He split a log with one stroke.

'I'd work for just my board and keep.'

He leaned on the axe. 'The truth is, love, I couldn't employ you. You had a run-in with one of my guests.'

'Gooly?'

'He tells me you attacked him with a lump of wood.'

'That's right. He was trying to climb into bed with me.'

'Oh, I see. He tells it another way.'

'I'll bet he does!'

'Do you know where you went wrong?' the man said. 'You didn't hit him hard enough. The blokes who drink here call him Bluc, which stands for big, long, useless ... and I'd better leave the rest to your imagination. Anyhow, whatever the rights or wrongs of it, I can't give you a job.' He split another piece of wood. 'What are you going to do?'

'Don't know.'

'Going back south?'

'Probably. Don't want to, though.'

'Got any money?'

'Little bit.'

'Enough for the train fare?'

'Just.'

'You'll be all right then. Tell you what. If you've got nothing to do for an hour or so you might like to go and give some comfort to an old lady who's staying here. She's catching the train tonight but she's in pretty poor spirits. She could do with a hand and she might be good company on the train.'

'Oh?' Nellie was not enthusiastic.

'It's a funny business. She's only been up here a few weeks. She's the mother of Adam Ross's wife. You know, the young bloke who runs that new property up near Lake Eyre.' The axe had jammed in hard wood and he struggled to free it. 'She came in yesterday, on her own and very distressed. She's been howling all day. I wouldn't know what to say to her. Maybe you could have a bit of a talk to her. You know, calm her down.'

Nellie's thoughts raced. The mother of Heather, Adam's wife?

'It would help the poor old soul,' he added. 'Me too. You can hear her from the bar. Puts everyone off their beer. Tell you what, if you'll have a talk to her and see if you can quieten her down, I'll give you tucker for the night. How's that?'

'It doesn't matter about the meal but I'll gladly see if I can help her. Where is she?'

'Through the door. Second on the left. Her name's Mrs Maguire.'

The door was ajar because it had fallen on its hinges and would not close properly. Inside, the curtain was drawn and the room was dark. Nellie could see the woman on the bed. At first she thought she was asleep but the woman sat up.

'Heather?' she said, alarm in her voice.

'No. My name's Nellie, Mrs Maguire. I just came by to see if I could help.'

Mrs Maguire swung her feet over the edge of the bed. 'Oh, I don't know,' she said, sounding flustered. 'What is it you want to do? Someone swept the floor earlier today.'

Nellie smiled. 'I don't want to do any work. I just thought we might talk.'

'Goodness me!' She groped for her shoes. 'I don't have any tea to offer you.'

'That's all right. I believe you've been having a pretty rough time.'

'Have I? Well, I suppose I have. You haven't seen my other shoe, have you?'

Nellie found it under the bed.

'Oh, that's very kind of you. What did you say your name was?'

'Nellie. Nellie Arlton.'

'Thank you, Miss Arlton.' Mrs Maguire, shoes in place, walked to the window and pulled back the curtain. She raised the blind. It rose halfway and jammed. She tried to free it, gave up and turned. She took a step backwards.

'What's wrong?'

'You're black.'

'Yes.'

'I'm sorry. Forgive me. I just didn't expect it.' She placed her hand on her chest and managed to squeeze out a noise which was meant to be a further apology. Other small sounds followed, her lips moving but issuing no words. Then she laughed nervously and the words poured out. 'How silly of me! It was like expecting to see someone else but then seeing someone else. Oh dear me, I do say such foolish things!'

'That's all right. I'm surprised you could see me at all.'

'I beg your pardon?'

'Well, the room's still quite dark.' Nellie laughed and Mrs Maguire laughed a little too, stopping when Nellie stopped.

'Yes, I can see what you mean. I can also see you're a very pretty girl.'

'Thank you.'

Mrs Maguire sat on the bed and blinked rapidly. 'Now, why did you say you came to see me? Did someone send you? My daughter, perhaps?'

'No.'

'I was wondering if she was well.'

'I wouldn't know.'

'No. I do worry about her, you know. Do you know my daughter Heather?'

'No, Mrs Maguire.'

'But you know my name.'

'The man told me.'

'Oh. He's a nice man.'

'Yes.'

'My daughter is cruel.'

'Is she?'

'She tried to whip me.'

Nellie stared at the room's darkest corner, trying to imagine the woman with whom Adam lived.

'She made me do all the work. Do you know, young lady, that when you came through the doorway I thought you were her, coming to take me back, and I was frightened.' She used her fist to muffle a cough. 'Tell me, why did you come?'

'I just heard that you'd been upset. I came to see if you felt like a chat.'

So they talked. At first it was of inconsequential things – the size of the town, the long distance to the next town, the weather. Nellie had heard there might be rain. But after a while, Mrs Maguire closed her eyes and rested on her pillow and talked about the things that had happened at Kalinda. She talked about Heather and about Adam. She was still talking when the publican knocked on her partly opened door and said it was time for dinner. The train, he added, was due in an hour and a half.

As the two women left the room, he winked at Nellie.

The stationmaster at William Creek knew the train was running late but it was still a couple of hours later than he predicted. There had been heavy rain near Oodnadatta and the train had been forced to run at reduced speed due to some local flooding. Anticipating an earlier arrival time, Mrs Maguire and Nellie sat on the tiny platform from eight o'clock until twenty past ten before they saw the first glint from the approaching locomotive's light.

It was cold. Nellie had spread her blanket across their laps. With the train in sight they stood, glad to stretch cold and cramped muscles. The stationmaster hurried past, rubbing his hands. 'You'll soon be out of this cold wind, ladies,' he said.

He pulled a lever at the end of the platform. A signal clanked into position. He returned, still rubbing his hands. 'Be here in about five minutes.'

'Thank you,' Mrs Maguire said and, when he was gone, she looked at Nellie and took her hand. 'Why don't you come to

674

Sydney with me?' she said and began to cry.

'I can't do that.' Nellie squeezed her hand.

'I have enough money for both of us.'

'It's not that. I just have to stay up this way.'

'Family?'

'Something like that.'

Mrs Maguire dabbed her eyes. 'I'm a foolish, selfish old woman. All I've done for the last few hours is talk about my problems. I'm sure you've got your worries too.'

It was a question posed discreetly and requiring no answer. Nellie smiled.

'Is Marree a big place?'

'No. It's bigger than here, though.'

'My dear, are you sure you'll be able to get work there?'

'No, Mrs Maguire, but I'll try.'

'I wish you'd come with me,' the older woman said softly. 'It will be very lonely without someone.'

'You'll have your sister.'

'Yes. Yes, of course.' There was no conviction in the words and Nellie took her other hand.

'Are you sure you want to go? Maybe things would be better if you went back to Kalinda.'

'No. I couldn't do that. I feel that, in many ways, I've contributed to the problems there. I fear my presence has helped to ruin my daughter's marriage. That's a dreadful thing for a mother to have done, isn't it?'

'I'm sure it wasn't your fault.'

'Oh, it was. Heather has changed and it's all my fault. She used not to be so cruel, so cold, so ... I don't know, she's just changed. I know I couldn't possibly stand being treated the way she has ... Oh, here I go, sounding like a selfish old woman again.' She released the grip and wiped her face. 'No, it's better for me to go away. Heather might change with me away. Did I tell you about her husband?'

'Not much.'

'He's a nice man. He works hard. I must confess that when I first met him, I thought he was beneath my daughter's class.' She gazed into Nellie's dark face and twittered nervously. 'But then, I've been so wrong in so many things. Do you know something? You are the first black woman ... do you mind if I call you that?'

'What's wrong with it? It's the truth.'

'I just didn't want to sound offensive.'

'I don't think the word black is offensive.'

'No. Of course not. Dear me, I am clumsy! What I was trying to say was that you are the first black woman I've ever spoken to.'

'Was it difficult?'

Mrs Maguire became more flustered. 'Certainly not. You are sweet and I think we could become such good friends. It's just that I have been a fool over so many things.'

They could hear the train now. Nellie turned and noticed lights approaching from the north-east. It was a car. Its lights were bobbing on a rough track. It was near the town and it was coming from the direction of Kalinda.

The train arrived before the car. The locomotive hissed past the two women, who were the only passengers waiting on the platform. From the footplate a man in blue overalls stared at them. His face was stained with sweat and coal dust. Nellie turned her head to avoid the cloud of steam spreading beyond the wheels. She closed her eyes and felt damp heat envelop her, then pass on. When she looked again, still with her back to the train, she saw a car sliding to a halt on the loose gravel beside the platform. The lights shone in her eyes. There were two people on board. One jumped out – a woman carrying something. She ran into the lights and Nellie could see she was carrying a baby. The woman had been travelling with a scarf across her face and it unwound as she ran. She went to the far end of the platform, saw Mrs Maguire, and moved towards her.

'Oh, my heavens, it's Heather!' Mrs Maguire said and began an incoherent mumble. The train stopped. Mrs Maguire picked up her bag, put it down again and covered her mouth with one hand.

'My daughter,' she said to Nellie, as though a formal introduction were necessary. Nellie stepped back, distancing herself from the confrontation.

Still retreating, Nellie watched open-mouthed. So this was Adam's wife! She was a beauty, even with dust streaking her face and hair. A past moment nudged her memory. Surely she'd seen her before? Like this, hurrying with a baby on a railway platform. Then she heard her speak.

'Thank God we got here in time! Pick up your bag. We're going back.'

The mother bent as though caught by a wind. 'No, please, Heather! Just let me go.'

'You pick up that bag and keep your voice down.' She glared at Nellie, willing her away.

I don't like you one little bit, Nellie thought, staring back until the blonde looked away. If you talk like that to your mother, what on earth are you like with my Adam?

'I brought Cassandra. She's very tired. You take her and I will carry your bag to the car. Please hurry. People are watching.'

'No.' Mrs Maguire grasped the bag with both hands, using it as a barrier.

Nellie retreated towards the car. The driver was still at the wheel. He switched off the lights. She had expected to see Adam and jumped with surprise when she recognized Josef. He was almost breathless from the long and hard drive. He sat with both hands across the steering wheel.

'You look as though you've run all the way,' Nellie said, walking to the side of the car.

'That was the hardest bloody drive I've ever had,' he said, as though talking to himself, and then smiled. 'I heard you were in town. How are you?'

'Good. You nearly missed the train.'

'I think she'd have had a stroke if we missed it. Then skinned me.'

'It was close. Lucky the train's running late.' She put her hand on the top of the door, bridging the gap between them. 'It's good to see you.'

He pulled his hands away.

'I mean it. We're still friends, aren't we?'

'Sure.'

'That other business ...' He looked away. 'Joe, I know you didn't mean any harm. I've forgotten about it.'

He nodded.

'Sorry I scratched you.'

He grinned but did not look up. 'So am I.' He cleared his throat. 'Adam told me you were here.'

'Adam looks thin.'

'He's been working hard.' He inclined his head towards the two women. 'Were you talking to Mrs Maguire?'

'Yes. She's going all the way to Sydney.'

'Not now. Heather will get her to stay. She's not well. She needs medicine and she needs someone to look after her.'

'She was telling me her daughter gives her a bad time.'

'Oh, that's all baloney. Actually, the old girl's not all there. You know, a bit loopy.'

'She seems nice.'

677

'She tried to run away. She just went off on foot. She would have died, only Jimmy found her. He brought her here.'

'I thought he must have been in town.' She breathed angrily. 'Did you hear I'd lost my job?'

'But you've only just got here.'

'And now I've been sacked. I was going to catch the train as far as Marree.'

On the platform, the stationmaster approached the two women. 'Are you getting on the train, lady?' he asked Mrs Maguire.

'Yes, I am.'

'No, she's not.'

'Well, I don't know what's going on but if you don't make up your minds, the train'll go and you'll have a couple of days to think about it.'

'I am going,' Mrs Maguire said and backed towards a carriage door.

'Don't you dare! You just cannot do this to me.' Heather was speaking softly, intimidated by the presence of the stationmaster. She followed her mother to the door. 'We just cannot argue like this in front of strangers. It is so vulgar. Now stop this nonsense and come with me this instant!'

'No.' Mrs Maguire put her bag on the train. A man, watching the discussion with interest, extended his hand to help her.

'Stop that!' Heather commanded and the man backed away.

'I am not coming back with you, Heather. I am sorry, but I am simply not getting off this train.'

The stationmaster intervened. 'Have we decided who's going?' he said cheerfully.

'I am,' Mrs Maguire said.

'She is not.'

'I think you're wrong, lady,' he said to Heather. 'She's on the train and she's over twenty-one and she's got a ticket.' He addressed the mother. 'Where's your friend? You know, the young dark woman.'

'I really don't know,' Mrs Maguire looked about her in confusion. 'She must be on the train already.'

The man had been carrying a lantern. He began to swing it, signalling the driver to move off.

'You can't go,' Heather said, trying to grasp his arm.

'Just stand clear,' he said, gently pushing Heather from him. The wheels started to turn.

'What am I going to do?' Heather cried, struggling to hold the

678

baby and keep up with her mother in the accelerating carriage.

'Please, Heather, just try to make things work out here. You've got a fine husband in Adam.'

'This is his idea, isn't it?'

'No, it's mine.'

'How much did he pay you?' She had reached the end of the platform. 'How much?' she shouted. Moving faces, weary from travel, rolled past. When the train had gone and there was just a fading rattle, and the twin red lights of the guard's van were drawing together in the distance, she turned and said to no one in particular: 'What am I going to do?'

Josef had been watching. Leaving Nellie, he hurried to the end of the platform. Heather had not moved. He took the baby from her.

'She went.'

'Yes. I saw her,' he said. 'Did you give her the medicine?'

She stared past him. 'Adam did this. He made her leave.'

'Oh, I don't think so. She just wanted to go.'

'No. He paid her to leave.'

'Adam did?'

'She told me.'

He muttered an obscene expression of disbelief and immediately apologized. She seemed not to have heard.

'I wouldn't have believed it,' she continued. 'My own husband doing that. And doing it to my mother.'

'It doesn't sound right.'

'Oh, Josef, thank heavens for you!' She gripped his arm. 'You're the only person left I can trust. What are we going to do?'

'Well, I don't know,' he said, baffled by developments. He not only didn't know what to do, he had no idea what the problem was. He waited.

'It's an awful thing,' she said, and he rather liked the feel of her hand on his arm. She started to cry, a pathetic howling sound like a cat issuing a quiet meow. Obviously some new thought had occurred.

'He will force me to leave, too.'

'What do you mean?'

'I can't do all the work by myself. Not with the baby and that primitive house.'

'Is there much?' he asked gently.

She pulled her hand away. 'You sound callous, just like Adam. He's always saying I have nothing to do. No meals to cook, no house to clean, no clothes to mend, no baby to feed and raise.'

'I wasn't being callous.'

She judged him from eyes supported on columns of tears. 'Truly?'

'Of course not.'

'I believe you.' She took his arm again. He had had a marvellous time on the long drive from Kalinda. She had laughed a lot, touched his arm or knee to emphasize things she was saying, and had been full of praise for his driving.

'Even so, he has won.' She was talking more to herself now. 'I could not possibly continue out there on my own. There is just too much to be done.'

Josef guided her to the car. He was alarmed at the thought of her leaving. 'Do you need help?'

'Indeed I do, but there's none to be had. You certainly can't do all the things I need. Is that what you're suggesting?'

Nellie was watching, fascinated by the way Heather was touching Josef. He was talking: 'I was thinking there's someone here who could help you.' He signalled to Nellie. She moved towards them. 'This is an old friend of mine,' he said, and thought, Jesus, I hadn't meant to say that. But it was too late; he had to go on. 'I just ran into her a moment ago and she was saying she was on her way south to look for a job.'

'An old friend of yours?' Heather had released his arm.

'Yes, I knew her ... she used to work for my parents.'

'Really? Doing what?'

Josef looked to Nellie for inspiration. She had heard the last part of their conversation and said: 'The housekeeping and cooking. I'm a very good cook. I even taught young Mr Hoffman's sister English.'

Josef's eyes bulged. Why shouldn't I lie too? Nellie thought. I've heard some great stories here tonight.

'You were a governess?' Heather said, eyes wide in surprise.

'For many years.'

'How extraordinary.' Heather had difficulty in controlling her lips, which were busy wiping her teeth. 'But aren't you ... aboriginal?'

'Partly.'

'Her father was a sea-captain,' Josef said. 'He was from Sweden.'

'Finland,' she corrected. That was one thing she couldn't lie about.

'He was a war hero,' Josef said, warming to Nellie's spirit of improvization. 'He was the last man killed at sea in the Great War. He deliberately rammed a U-boat. He went down with his ship. Did he get a medal, Nellie?'

'No. All he got was killed.' Her mother had never told her what had happened to her father. She liked Joe's version.

'How extraordinary,' Heather repeated. 'And your mother?'

'She was not in the navy.'

'No, I meant ...'

'Was she aboriginal? Yes. She was black as the ace of spades.'

Josef could see a twitch developing on Heather's face. 'They'd been married less than a year when he died,' he said, and saw the twitch vanish. A half-caste woman would be difficult for Heather to accept but an illegitimate one would have been impossible. 'Nellie was very popular with my parents,' he said, moving to safer territory. 'Mother thought the sun shone out of her.'

'Really?' One eyebrow arched. 'And what did the son think of the maid?'

He hadn't expected that. There was a suggestion of jealousy. He was pleased. 'I never thought about her,' he said and could see she was placated.

'Is she a good cook?'

'Out of this world.' At least, he thought, I hope her food's good because, with a bit of luck, I'll be eating a fair bit of it from now on. After tonight, he expected to be dining with Heather more often.

Heather considered Nellie as she might have examined a bunch of fresh vegetables at the market.

'This could be a propitious meeting. Do you know what that means?'

'Yes,' Nellie said, guessing that it meant good.

'How splendid. And you can, of course, read and write?'

'Yes.'

'Please say "Yes, ma'am." '

'Yes, ma'am.'

'I might even ask you to help my husband. You may find it hard to believe but my husband, who owns a vast area of land and no fewer than one thousand sheep, cannot read or write.' She paused, awaiting an expression of horror, or sympathy for her, or both.

'A lot of men can't,' Nellie said softly. 'Not out this way. They seem to be too busy doing other things.'

'That's very charitable of you. You are looking for work?'

'Yes, ma'am.'

Josef grinned. He'd never heard Nellie being so polite.

'Well, I doubt whether I can afford to pay you much. Shall we say food and lodgings to start with, and then we'll see how much is left over?'

'Yes, ma'am.'

Heather turned to Josef. 'I think we have had a stroke of luck. Adam thought he had beaten me by getting rid of my mother but I think when we all turn up at Kalinda, he's going to get a very big surprise.'

FIFTEEN

They had to travel to Kalinda that night. It was a long and tiring journey. Heather slept a little and thought a great deal. She had given the baby to the half-caste woman and travelled more comfortably without the burden of Cassandra. Heather was in a curious, mixed-up state: part anger, part elation. The anger was because her mother had defied her; the elation because, by the merest chance, she had found a black girl who would be a servant at the house. How marvellous! Someone who would cost nothing and could sleep out in the open like all natives did and who could do all the unpleasant things that had to be done. She was young and strong and could probably do more work than her own frail mother. She even seemed to have a way with the baby. She thought of her good fortune and felt like laughing. Adam would be furious.

Nellie held Cassandra close, shielding her from the dust and the biting wind. The baby was so dark. Adam had said she was but Nellie had imagined a child with light brown colouring. This baby's hair was black and her skin was a lustrous olive. She will grow up to be a beauty, she thought, and pretended Cassandra – no, Adam preferred Cassie and so did she – was hers. From there it was a short step to wondering what her own child would look like. Her child and Adam's, if they ever had one. Like this probably, with even darker skin. Or maybe not. She'd known quarter-castes with skin so fair they looked positively unhealthy.

She was stunned by what had happened. A few hours ago she had been wondering if she would ever see Adam again. Now she was being driven to his house. She was even nursing his daughter. What would he say? Her first thoughts had been exciting ones. They would be close again. But, as the miles droned by, she began to worry. Being there with Heather was going to cause awful problems. She was too tired to think clearly but she was sure there would be trouble.

So what if there was? This woman was a bitch and she was doing her best to ruin Adam. He could do with help, even if it took him a while to realize that fact.

There were times on the journey when Josef wished the car would break down so that he might never have to return to Kalinda. Jesus. Adam would explode when he found out they'd been to William Creek. Still, the old lady had gone and that was apparently what he wanted. Not that Josef was too sure what Adam wanted these days. On most subjects he said one thing and his wife said something else, and Josef was inclined to believe Heather. He felt sorry for her, too. She was having a rough time and not getting the sympathy or understanding a woman like her deserved.

Maybe the marriage had ended. It had certainly gone sour and while people rarely got divorced, except in America, it did happen occasionally and it could happen here. Adam seemed to have given up. She was trying her best, but getting nowhere.

She was lonely. So was he. They were good friends. She liked him, obviously, and she was attracted to him. Jesus, the way she'd come up to him in the wash house!

He drove for a while and saw a pair of kangaroos lazily rocking on their massive hind legs as the lights interrupted their grazing. Then he thought about Nellie. He hadn't meant to suggest that Heather should give her a job but thoughts just kept popping into his head and he'd said things without thinking too deeply. And it had been fun making up stories about his family and Nellie's family. He'd always enjoyed himself when Nellie was around. At least, back in the old days.

I suppose, he told himself, the reason I suggested she work out here was because I was scared ... scared that Heather would leave. I would miss her. I like talking to her. It's like talking to my mother. She cares about me, says nice things. Things men don't talk about, like what your hair feels like.

Adam used to be keen on Nellie. He thought about the balance this situation could create. Heather and Adam didn't get on. Adam even preferred to sleep in another room. Nellie would turn up and Adam could have her.

That left Heather free.

Not conventional. Not nice. Not the sort of thing you'd talk about. But it could be good. Bloody hell, they were so far removed from society and civilization that normal rules didn't apply. And there were only two women up here, Heather and Nellie. Nellie for Adam; Heather for him. He glanced at her, slumped in the seat beside him, sleeping. My God, she was ... hang on, hang on, this is madness! People don't do things like that.

His hands tightened on the steering wheel. Jesus, it was a long way.

I won't rush things. I'll just take my time. Let things happen. And they certainly will as soon as Adam sees Nellie again.

Dawn was less than two hours away when they drove into Kalinda.

Adam stayed at the bore for two more days. He and Jimmy were extending the yards there, and it was slow, hard work made worse by lack of sleep. Every dingo within a hundred miles seemed to have moved into the area and the men's nights were spent in constant patrols, either setting traps or making sure the wild dogs were kept away from the sheep. The dingo had been in Australia for ten thousand years or more. A shy animal, it preferred to hunt far from the dreaded scent of man, but the twin temptations of water and the tantalizing smell of flocks of woolly-coated meat had brought a score of them to the site of the bore.

Jimmy reckoned the dogs were becoming cheekier and cleverer. He set his traps along the bore drain, where overflow water ran into the wilderness. He caught one that way, but only one. From then on, the dogs would drink beside a trap – he could see their tracks – and even turn circles in a confusion of temptation and caution, but they would not take the bait.

Jimmy and Adam had stopped work for lunch. They were sitting against a fence post, back to back, each sheltering under his hat. They had been talking about the likelihood of rain. A few spots had fallen during the night. It was just enough to raise their hopes but the fall had been no more than desultory spitting; nature taunting them but holding back her favours.

Good rain would bring on fresh growth and see them safely through the summer, Adam said. It would scatter the dingoes, Jimmy said, because there would be water and food for them in their traditional hunting places, where no man ventured. Jimmy had developed a love-hate feeling for the animals. All night he would curse and hunt them and if he killed one he would dance with glee, but when his blood lust was down he talked of dingoes with respect, even affection. One hunter, one killer, one true-born Australian admiring another.

He had even found two pups and was raising them.

'You're a funny bloke,' Adam said. 'You kill the mother, but you save the pups.'

Jimmy was nursing them, as he did most of the time when he was resting. He was trying to provoke one into biting his hand.

'Are you going to shoot them when they grow up?' Adam asked.

'Course not. Neither would you. You're softer than I am.' The pup had given up trying to nip his elusive fingers and attacked the other pup. Jimmy undercut its feet so that it rolled on its back. 'I reckon they'll make good pets. I might train them.'

'I'm told it's illegal to keep a dingo.'

'So are most things that are a bit of fun. Here, have one.' He passed one of the dogs to Adam, who held it up so that its body dangled from his hands.

'Do you ever get lonely out here, Jimmy?'

'Me? No.'

'It's a funny life, though.'

'That's all right. I'm a funny bloke. You said so yourself.'

'But it's a lot different to the old days. You know, when you were in the boxing troupe. You were always in a different town and mixing with people. Girls. All that.' He pretended to throw the pup and collected its scrambling legs in his hands. 'You know what I mean.'

'Yeah, well, things were different then.'

'You don't miss all that?'

'Not a bit of it.'

Two hawks circled high above them. Adam watched, envious. If there was such a thing as being born again, he'd like to come back as a bird.

'How about you?' Jimmy said.

'Oh, I've never spent much time in towns so I don't miss them much.'

'I don't mean that. I mean do you ever get lonely out here?'

Adam was concentrating on the birds. They were spiralling in independent circles. They were like two people on earth, sharing the same space, intent on the same things but moving in different planes. Jimmy reached for the pup. Adam passed it back. He wiped his hands.

'I like it here,' he said.

'You can like a place and still be lonely. Do you want me to tell you what I think?'

'Go ahead.'

'You mightn't like what I'm going to say.'

Adam turned to find Jimmy facing him. 'That's never stopped you saying anything in the past.'

Jimmy grinned. 'No, you're right.' He took a couple of slow breaths, like a smoker inhaling the first puffs of a cigarette. 'I reckon you ought to give that missus of yours the arse.'

Adam had lost sight of one of the hawks. The other was still high above them. He said nothing.

'She's about as good for you as a dose of weed killer.' Jimmy let the pups go and searched for a pebble. He put one in his mouth. 'I never liked her. I don't think much of sheilas, anyhow.'

'I've noticed.'

'But she's real strange. I think, mate, that all she cares about is herself and anyone else can go and get nicked.' He took the pebble from his mouth, examined it with distaste, and threw it away. He selected another one. 'She's been giving you a hard time, hasn't she?'

'Oh, I don't know,' Adam said, floating the sentence on a sigh.

'Well, I do. You come away from her sometimes looking like some bastard's just shot your horse. Know what I mean? And she treats me like garbage on legs. That's all right. I don't mind what she says to me because I've had experts insult me and I don't give a stuff any more, but I'm not married to her and you are, and she treats you like you were some sort of piss-potting no-hoper. For crying out loud, mate, I'll tell you what – I wouldn't like her for my enemy if she goes on like that with her own husband.'

'She knows about Mailey.'

Jimmy slumped against the post. 'Jesus! How?'

'Did you tell her?'

Jimmy got on one knee. 'Shit, no! I wouldn't tell her if the sun was up, let alone something like that.'

'Maybe you said something accidentally. You know, something

686

to give her a clue. She's very clever at piecing things together.'

'I think the longest conversation I've had with her was when she said "Get out of my way," and I said "Sorry." ' He put his hand on the post. 'You didn't say nothing?'

'Not a word. She talked to Joe about it the other day. Joe said she told him I'd told her all about it.'

'Which you hadn't?'

'I certainly had not.'

'Saleem Benn?'

'No way.'

'Well, that only leaves Joe,' Jimmy said. 'You didn't. I didn't. Saleem Benn didn't. Doesn't leave a lot of other people.'

'Joe insists he didn't say a thing. He said she started talking about Mailey and seemed to know all the facts.'

'That'd have to be bullshit. I reckon Joe told her. He probably didn't mean to, but if she's as clever as all that she probably wheedled it out of him and now he's not game to let on.'

'He was very definite about not telling her. He said she knew already.'

'Well, it has to be Joe who told her. She wasn't there and Mailey's not saying anything these days. No, mate, it was Joe.'

'But how?'

'I think she could get anything out of him. Haven't you noticed?'

'What?'

'That he's a bit soft on her.'

Adam sat upright.

'Jesus, don't look so shocked! He's only a bloke and not a very smart one at that. Not where sheilas are concerned, anyhow.'

'And they're keen on each other?'

'I didn't say that. I don't think she could give a stuff about him but Joe's a bit starry-eyed about any good-looking sort and you've got to admit, your missus is a very good-looking sort. For a white sheila, anyhow.'

The attempt at humour didn't ease the shock. 'Yes, but Jimmy, not Joe and Heather,' Adam said, shuffling uncomfortably on the ground.

'Oh, don't look so miserable! There's nothing going on. It's just that he's a bit ga-ga with her and she could twist him around her finger. Which is probably what she did. She might have got some hint that something happened here and dragged it out of him without him even knowing what was going on. She's as cunning as a snake and Joe's as simple as a rabbit, so there's no prize for guessing who the bunny was.'

Adam had begun to scratch a pattern in the dust.

'Anyhow,' Jimmy said, 'if I was you I'd piss her off before she really causes trouble. The longer she stays, the worse she'll be, the worse you'll feel and the sillier Joe will get. No, she's got to go.'

'I can't just send her away.'

'Yes, you can. All you have to do is put her on a train and make sure you don't buy a return ticket.'

'What about Cassie?'

'Keep her if you like. You like her, don't you?'

'Yes, of course.' Adam couldn't imagine himself without his daughter. It was strange. He had spent little time with her. He hadn't seen her for a couple of days now but he could put up with that. Knowing she was in the house, living on his property, made it a pleasant, close thing. He didn't have to see her or hold her all the time. Just knowing she was there was sufficient. But if Heather took Cassie and went away the loss would be unbearable. It was a strong feeling but he couldn't explain it, so he made no attempt. 'Of course I would,' he repeated, 'but I couldn't take her away from her mother.'

'Why not?'

'It wouldn't be right.'

'You're a funny bugger. I'd just take the kid and kick the sheila out.' He leaned around the post to see if Adam was looking at him but his friend was staring at the ground and tracing lines in the dust. 'But then you and me think differently about all sorts of things.'

'Yes.'

Jimmy moved away. 'I hear Nellie's in town.'

'Who told you?'

'Joe, when he was out here the other day. Said she was working at the new store. How is she?'

Adam wondered what he should say. Wonderful? We spent the night together and, Jimmy, I'm sure now she's the woman I really love? He couldn't say such words, not even to his friend. 'She's OK,' he said, hoping the curious mix of excitement and love and guilt he felt when thinking about Nellie wasn't being revealed in his voice. 'Didn't you run into her in town the other day?'

Jimmy had walked a few steps from the fence. 'Didn't stay long. I didn't bother going into the store.' He didn't turn because he was ashamed of the rotten thing he'd done. He did the worst things he'd ever done when Nellie was around. He tried to justify his action at William Creek by telling himself Nellie would only cause harm to Adam if she stayed. He wanted to convince himself that his action had been her fault and not the result of his own vindictive spite; the less real cause he had to despise her, the more he needed to believe she was contemptible to bolster his vanity.

He turned. Adam was staring at him in a strange way, as though he had guessed what Jimmy had done.

'You don't like her, do you, Jimmy?'

'Oh, I don't like any sheila. You can't trust any of them but you can't trust her most of all.' He swung away, feeling transparent. He stopped to pick up the pups. And then, because the silence was becoming threatening, he said: 'You're not keen on her, are you mate?'

It was something to say, a jocular taunt that needed no answer.

'Yes, as a matter of fact I am.' Adam was glad. He had been bursting to say it.

In alarm, Jimmy regarded him. 'Just keen, or real keen?'

Adam shrugged.

'Oh, Jesus,' Jimmy said, interpreting the gesture and covering his face. 'Real keen.'

'I don't know how to explain it. We just seem to get on real well with each other.'

Jimmy's expression shuttled between astonishment and disgust. 'You mean you like rooting her and she likes it too. Well, that's all right.'

For a moment, Jimmy thought Adam was going to strike him. He lifted the pups, shielding his face with them.

'Jesus, don't get upset!' he said, backing away.

'Well, it's not like that!'

'No?' Jimmy put the dogs on the ground. One of them attacked his foot. He felt more confident. The blaze had gone from Adam's eyes. 'That's all it usually is, mate. People talk about love or being keen on someone or any of that crap, but all they usually mean is they like fucking each other.'

'Jimmy, that's a rotten thing to say!'

'Well, it's a rotten world.'

Adam was now leaning against a new fence post with his forehead on his clenched fists. Jimmy walked to the next post and put his back against it. One pup had followed him. The other was smelling a trail of sheep's droppings. 'Is that why you want to get rid of your missus? Because of Nellie?'

Adam had been hurt by Jimmy's words. He had spent days trying to convince himself that his longing for Nellie had little to do with sex. His own conscience had been needling him and now his friend had dug into the wound. 'It has nothing to do with her,' he said. 'Yes, I'm not getting on with Heather. Yes, I would be happier if she went away. And yes, I am keen on Nellie. But the things aren't related.'

The pup at Jimmy's feet was gnawing the toe of his boot and he flicked it away. 'You're getting yourself on dangerous ground, mate.'

'I know. I can't help it.'

'She's black.'

'So are you. Anyway, she's half-caste.'

'That's even worse.'

'It doesn't worry me.'

'I know that, Adam, but shit, if you get rid of your missus and shack up with Nellie, the whole world will give you a hammering. You won't have a friend left.' The second pup had joined the other and they both attacked his feet. He kicked them away and snarled at them and they sat, puzzled. Eventually the newcomer returned to the dung. The other followed. Jimmy leaned against the post once more. 'No white bugger'll talk to you. They'll reckon you've gone native and cut you dead. The blacks won't want you. They'll think you're just after a cheap fuck.' He saw Adam move and held up his hand. 'Now don't get riled up! It's true. That's what people'll think.'

'I don't care what people think!'

'You will.' He let his body slide down the post until he was sitting. 'How long've you been keen on her?'

'Nellie? I don't know. It just sort of built up.'

'You've never talked about it,'

'Yeah, well, I don't talk about those sort of things.'

'Jesus, Adam, you don't know her all that well. You've hardly been with her enough times to do any talking. Coober Pedy, Port Augusta a year ago. And then the other day. That's not much. When did it build up?'

'I thought about her a lot when we were away, roaming the bush.'

'We were away for years and you were only a kid and everyone thinks of a sheila like that. That means nothing.'

'It did to me.'

'It does to everyone, but it still doesn't mean nothing.'

'Who did you think of?'

I thought of Nellie too, Jimmy thought, but not like you did. I only wanted to throttle the bitch and make her pay for what she'd done. 'No one,' he said.

'You must have thought of someone.'

'No. I'd had enough. I'd had more women than I could handle when I was young and you get to the point where you get sick of them. You can't stand them. All their lying and nagging and wanting things gets on your goat. I didn't need women any more. So I didn't think of them.' He offered one toe to a pup and when it advanced he kicked it. Not hard, but with sufficient force to make it yelp and scamper away.

'We never talked about it,' Adam began, and waited until Jimmy was looking at him, 'but you weren't still keen on Nellie yourself, were you?'

'Shit, no!' Jimmy said and laughed.

'You seemed pretty fond of her when I first met you.'

Jimmy wiped the end of his boot, which was moist from the dog's saliva. 'I was fond of a lot of sheilas. One week here, another week there. That sort of thing, but nothing serious.'

'But she travelled up to the opal fields with you.'

'That was just because of the way things happened. It wasn't because I wanted her or anything.'

'And you didn't mind it when …?' Adam couldn't complete the question but there was no need. Jimmy smiled, the gap in his teeth prominent in a row of flashing white.

'She was your first, wasn't she?'

Adam looked away.

'Jesus, you're a funny bugger. There's nothing wrong with rooting a sheila. I'd been doing it all my life up till then.'

'It was more than that.'

'Yeah, but a lot of blokes say that, mate. No one ever says he gave the ferret a run just because he felt like it.' He was still smiling broadly. 'Look, it's as natural as having breakfast. There's nothing to be ashamed of, just as there's no need to feel you should fall in love with the first sort you slip the old feller into.'

Adam's brow wrinkled in distaste. 'You make it sound dirty.'

'Not dirty. Just natural. Animals do it. We do it too, because we're animals.' He sighed, sorrowing for the frailty of man. 'Even so, mate, I'm surprised about you and Nellie. I thought you had more sense.'

'You mean because I was married?'

691

'No. That's got nothing to do with it. I mean getting involved with someone like her. If you had to get caught up with another woman, you could have done a lot better.'

'I wasn't looking for another woman.'

'Yeah, well, you couldn't have made a bigger mistake than get involved with that little one.'

'I think you're wrong about her.'

'Yeah, well, it mightn't matter much.'

'What do you mean?'

Jimmy clicked his fingers, summoning the pups. He picked them up before speaking. 'I reckon she'll piss off before long.'

'But why? She just got here.'

'Why would she stay? You know why she came here, don't you?'

'She said it was to be near me,' Adam said quietly.

Jimmy issued a series of grunts which could have passed for a laugh. 'She came to start a whorehouse. I didn't see her the other day but they were talking about her in town. Oh, for Christ's sake, mate, don't look so hurt.'

'I don't believe that.'

'You mean you don't want to believe it. But it's true. She came up here to work the town, but it's such a small place she'll have been rooted by every bastard there inside a week and then she'll be off. She's probably gone already.'

Suddenly Adam was angry again. Jimmy skipped away.

'If you don't stop talking like that I'll thump you!' Adam growled.

'Oh, take it easy,' Jimmy said, raising a hand to seek peace. Adam was red-faced and still advancing.

'She is not like that!'

'OK. OK. That's good. I'm pleased. It's just what people are saying and if they're wrong, I'm pleased.' And to himself: pleased that the bitch will be thrown out of William Creek and sent running down south where Adam will never see her again. And where I won't have to see her, either, because if I see her again and she and Adam get together, so help me, I don't know what I'll do.

SIXTEEN

On her first day at Kalinda, Nellie worked like a slave which, she soon realized, was precisely the role assigned to her. The house was filthy, not having been swept for days, and she cleaned it. She cooked, served food and scrubbed dishes. She washed clothes and mended torn garments. She bathed the baby. And she watched Adam's wife, to see what she was like and what she did.

Heather did little. She fed the baby, although Nellie noticed she wasn't like most mothers. She didn't talk to Cassie in the sweet, nonsensical chortle that most mothers used with infants. She addressed her. Her words were short and sharp and seemed to lack affection. She was preparing her daughter to take orders.

Most of the time Heather stayed in her room with the door closed. Sometimes she came to the table and drank tea, which Nellie made for her. She was demanding, but did not ask Nellie to do unreasonable things. It was just that Nellie did everything. That didn't matter, Nellie told herself. The important thing was that she was at Kalinda. Also, Adam's wife seem to grow more pleased as the hours passed. Maybe it was because Nellie was a good worker and this would make it easier for her to justify hiring a maid when Adam returned and ... well, she wasn't sure what would happen then but it would certainly be better if Heather really wanted her to stay. So she worked hard, did what she was asked to do and even sought out work.

She was not allowed to sleep in the house but she had no desire to do so. The thought of sharing such a small building with Adam and his wife, even though she knew he slept apart from Heather, was unbearable. She slept in the shed. Heather gave her a blanket and she made a bed of bags in one corner.

On the second morning she cooked and did more cleaning and then was given the task of altering some clothes left by Mrs Maguire so that they would fit Heather. She stopped that work to prepare lunch, and after lunch watched the baby while Heather rested. She rested a lot and was easily irritated by the child. Nellie wondered how she would react to the extreme heat of summer.

After two hours, Heather emerged from the bedroom and asked Nellie to plant the seeds Saleem Benn had given her. She was to put aside the sewing until the seeds were planted. Nellie knew little about gardening but she was aware you had to dig holes in the ground and bury the seeds and water them. So she went outside and looked for a suitable place to start the garden. She chose ground near the house. Digging was extremely hard work but at least the weather was cooler with thick clouds covering the sky.

Heather watched for a while, not speaking but observing her in the manner of someone who knew what should be done. She's a real fox, Nellie decided. She wouldn't know which end of the spade to dig with but she's standing there like the inspector of gardens, watching a poor labourer at work. Well, she thought, I can be as good an actress as she is and I'm not going to let on I don't know what I'm doing.

So Nellie dug holes and planted seeds and added water from a can. Heather watched. Nellie dug. Never once did Heather offer to help: to pass the seeds, to pour in some water, to refill the can.

Nellie stopped to wipe perspiration from her face.

'It's much cooler,' Heather said. 'You're lucky it's such a nice day.'

'Yes, ma'm.'

'Will they grow soon?'

'I hope so, ma'am.'

'What colour will they be?'

'All colours, ma'am.'

'Oh, that will be lovely.'

'Yes, ma'am.' Nellie resumed digging.

'I had a beautiful garden at Nyngan. It was by far the finest in the district. We had the biggest azalea bush in town.'

And I'll bet you were the biggest twit, too, Nellie thought. You talk like a gramophone record when you get wound up.

'Do you know what azaleas look like?'

'Very beautiful,' Nellie guessed.

'We might plant some here. They might hide this disgusting little shack I'm forced to live in.'

Disgusting? I thought it was amazing for one man to have built on his own, out here. Can you imagine what Adam must have gone through to put this place up? No, you can't. She sneaked a glance at Heather. This woman, she decided, believed the centre of the universe was where she stood and that all wisdom radiated from her mouth.

'What do you think of the house, Nellie?'

Be careful. She's testing you. 'Well,' she said, smiling innocently, 'I've seen worse.'

694

'But not much, I'm sure. I think there's another house on the property, a larger and better one. Adam – my husband – has built it as a surprise for me. However I don't like surprises and I would so like to see it soon. He's such a tease. Do you think men can be teases, Nellie?'

'Yes, ma'am. Some of them.' Adam's right, she thought. She is mad.

'I hope you haven't been teased too much in your life, have you, Nellie?'

'No, ma'am.' For crying out loud, I'm older than she is and she's treating me like a kid, and not a very bright one at that.

'That's good. You're lucky. I have had a very difficult life. Things have been very hard for me. My father died. Did you know?'

'Did he, ma'am? I'm sorry.' And mine just sailed away. I'd like to have met him. I could even have put up with him dying if only I'd known him for a few years.

'That's kind of you, Nellie. I think you're sweet and I'm sure we'll work well together.'

'Thank you, ma'am.' As long as I do all the work. It's a nice arrangement for you. You talk; I work. You feel good; I feel tired.

'Nellie.'

She stopped digging and wiped her face again.

'If you hear the men talking about this other house, you'll let me know, won't you?'

'Yes, ma'am.'

'It would be so nice for the two of us to spoil their little game. Now you stay here while I take the baby for a walk.'

You make it sound like I'm resting while you do all the rotten jobs, Nellie thought, and smiled as sweetly as she could. She drank some water from the can. How could Adam have married a person like that? she wondered, and immediately began answering her question. Easily. Heather had looks and that gave her a flying start. She might be selfish and a chatterbox and have more bees under her bonnet than a hive with a hat on, but she was clever. No, cunning was a better word. She could probably act well enough to go on the stage and when she wanted something, she just turned on a performance.

Nellie had seen the way she had been charming Josef at the railway station. Touching him, leaning against him, laughing. The act had been sickening and obvious to another woman but Josef hadn't a clue. He'd fallen for it like a mouse sticking its neck into a trap. Adam would have been the same. Fresh from the bush, he would have been an easy victim. She knew what Heather had wanted from Adam because he'd told her – money to pay the family debts and security after the father died. Where she'd miscalculated was in assuming Adam would do what he was told.

What did she want from Joe? Her type never turned on an act without expecting to be paid.

'I'm going now.' Heather had reappeared holding Cassie, who was blinking in the bright light. 'I'm taking Cassandra for a walk, just so I can get out of the house.'

'Yes, ma'am.' You poor dear, you must be worn out from watching me do all the work. 'What time will you be wanting dinner?'

'Oh, not till late, Nellie. I don't feel like eating early tonight. And try and finish the garden off tonight because there are things I want you to do tomorrow.'

'Yes, ma'am.' I'll bet there are. Maybe you'd like the house moved a few feet to the west, or something simple like that.

The girl is working out rather well, Heather thought. She seems industrious and knows what she's doing. Adam can't possibly object. Not that his objections would matter. She would insist that the girl stayed. He had coerced and bribed her mother to leave so he couldn't possibly argue about the fairness of her engaging someone to help with the housework. And the girl was cheap. That should appeal to his miserly instincts.

She walked towards the hills. It was a dull afternoon, not cool but lacking the fierce heat of the previous days. The sun was hidden behind cloud and it was difficult to tell how much daylight remained.

It would be fun, she thought, if this girl could find out about the other house and the other woman. She might be able to persuade the one-armed aboriginal to tell her; he might find her attractive. They could perhaps indulge in some grubby little liaison behind the shed and he could be persuaded to talk. How fascinating. She looked forward to the next few days. They could be positively entertaining.

Rather than climb the hills she walked around them, following a spur of rock which jutted into sandy soil. The ground was criss-crossed with animal tracks. She walked on, not concerned about tracks but wondering how much longer she would be forced to stay here.

The baby was asleep and heavy. She moved her to the other

side, but both her arms were tired. She came to a rock with soft sand at its base and put Cassandra down. She sat on the rock.

She had no intention of staying at Kalinda for one day more than she had to. She detested the place. But she was equally strong in her determination not to leave without money. Adam was making a million. She would have her share. At least half. Preferably more.

She stood and walked a few paces, hands behind her back. Most certainly, she thought, she was not going to wait for him to be generous. He would just have to sell up and give her the money. There was a huge amount of land which must be worth a great deal and he had all those sheep. She had no idea what they were worth but wool was expensive. Her mother had knitted jumpers and her father had always complained about the cost of a single skein, so heaven knows how much all those sheep would be worth. Many, many thousands, judging by the way her friends at Nevertire had lived.

And if Adam wouldn't sell?

She would threaten him. She would try to find out more about this Mailey business and, if the information was promising, force him to do what she said. What was the word? Blackmail. She would blackmail him. And if he still refused, she would go to the police and have him arrested. With him in gaol, she could sell the place, surely, and take all the money. A felon had no right to property, her father had once told her. If Adam were arrested, she could get everything.

The day had become cool and grey. It was a good time to walk and think.

Adam rode back towards the homestead ahead of Jimmy, who was travelling with some of the sheep. A few drops of rain moistened his skin. He searched the sky hopefully for the signs of a storm. Even with his hat removed, no more drops brushed his face and the ground was as parched and untouched by raindrops as ever. The clouds seemed high. He pressed on, wanting to reach the house before dark.

Josef wandered over to the house and, finding no one inside, walked around the back to where Nellie was digging.

'What are you doing?' he said and took the spade from her. She explained her job. He went back to the shed and returned with a pick. 'Too tough with a spade,' he said and began carving a trench in the hard soil.

She was tired and sat near him.

'Where's Heather?' he asked.

'Gone for a walk.'

He blasted another hole and Nellie, on her knees, planted the seed. 'What you need is a seed box,' he said.

'What's that?'

'A box for seeds. You get them to germinate and then you plant them.'

'Do we have one?'

'Not that I know of.'

'Will they grow without one?'

'I suppose so.'

'Well, let's keep going like this. I don't think it matters whether anything grows or not. This is just a job to keep me busy.'

He swung the pick a few more times. 'Where did she go?'

'Over towards that hill.'

'With the kid?'

'Sure. Hey!' Josef had showered her with dirt. She wiped her eyes and lips. 'Why did you want to see her?'

'Oh, nothing special. Just to talk.'

Nellie watered a row of seeds. 'What's she like?'

'Good. I don't think she likes it here much but she's giving it a go.'

'Do you reckon?'

'Yeah. Adam gives her a rough time.'

'He gives *her* a rough time?'

'Yeah. Why do you say it like that?'

Maybe Adam hasn't talked to Joe about it, she thought, and said: 'I just can't imagine Adam giving anyone a rough time.'

'Oh, he's changed. It's all the work and being on his own so much of the time. He says some really strange things to her and acts really weird.'

'How do you know? I mean about what he says to her?'

'She told me. I'm about the only one she can talk to.' There was a boyish pride in his voice.

'Do you think she might be having you on?'

He looked offended and swung the pick with more strength than was needed. 'I know you find it hard to think Adam can do any wrong but, believe me, he's been giving this girl a rough time. She's not perfect,' he said, swinging again and grunting with exertion, 'but she's trying really hard and he's not giving her a fair go. They're not even living together. Can you imagine that? She wants to but he sleeps on the kitchen floor, like the bloody house dog.'

'Really?'

'I tell you, he's changed and she's copping it.'

'You sound as though you like her.'

He leaned on the pick. 'What's wrong with that? You're keen on Adam.'

'What's that supposed to mean?'

'You are, aren't you? That's what that business in Port Augusta was all about.'

'I don't think we should talk about that,' she said, and went to the spring to get more water. When she returned, Josef had finished digging but not talking.

'You only went on like that because of Adam, didn't you?'

'Joe, this is silly.'

'No sillier than you accusing me of being keen on my best mate's wife. But he's not pure. I know what he was up to. Jimmy told me all about it.'

'Jimmy! I might have guessed he'd be behind all this.'

'Oh, Jesus, don't go blaming Jimmy!'

'Why not? He got me fired from my job at William Creek.'

Josef stopped for a moment, his mouth open in surprise.

'Yes, your good friend Jimmy,' she went on. 'He saw Gooly – he's Saleem Benn's nephew – and apparently told him I was setting up a brothel. He told Gooly I'd slept with every Chinese miner in Coober Pedy. He told him the most awful things.'

'Jesus!' Josef played with the pick handle. 'This was when Jimmy took Mrs Maguire to catch the train?'

She nodded and wiped an eye.

'Did you and Jimmy have a fight or something?'

'I never even saw him!' she shouted and then paused, trying to control herself. 'He must have just sneaked in while I was in the storeroom and told all his lies to Gooly, because as soon as I came out he sacked me.'

'Where was Jimmy?'

'He'd gone.'

'Why would he do something like that?'

'Who knows? He's crazy.'

Josef rubbed his chin. 'Oh no, he's not, Nellie. He's a good bloke.'

'He's a good bloke to blokes but he's a crook with women. Do you know why I think he hates me? Because I gave Adam back the opal. He was certain I'd stolen it and he can't stand being proved wrong.'

'That doesn't make sense.'

'You're right. I told you he was crazy.'

'He'll probably be back here in a day or so. What are you going to do?'

'I'll just behave as though I've never seen him in my life.'

The light was fading and Nellie was becoming worried. Heather had not returned. She had the baby and if she was not back in fifteen or twenty minutes the sky would be so dark she would never find the way back to the house. And it looked like rain. She started to walk to the hill.

Josef stood in the doorway of the wash house. 'Where are you off to?' he shouted. No one left the homestead without saying where he or she was going.

'Mrs Ross's not back. I thought I'd give her a hand with Cassie.'

Josef waved an acknowledgement and went inside to wash.

Nellie walked to the hill. She was about to start climbing, assuming Heather had gone to the look-out, when she heard a faint sound to the right. She stopped and listened. A child crying? It was hard to tell. The noise was as thin as the cry of a distant bird, but it was no bird. She walked around the spit of land, looking for tracks but finding it difficult to distinguish any marks in the murky light. She came to the jumble of rocks which marked the end of the hill and paused. It was so hard to see anything other than the looming shape of the hill and the outline of scrub on the flatter horizon to her right.

The sound came again. It was to her left now, and it was a cry. She hurried, stumbled on a stone and stopped to rub her foot. She heard another sound. It was an animal. Moving. Somewhere to the left, too. The baby cried again. It was definitely the baby.

'Cassie?' she called out, softly because she was frightened, and then felt foolish, both for being frightened and for expecting the baby to answer.

'Mrs Ross?'

The response alarmed her. It was a scuttling of animals. They were nearby. Big ones. She could hear them move, startled by her voice.

'Cassie!' she screamed and began to run, keeping close to the darker shadows which were formed by a line of rocks spilling from the hill. A dingo ran in front of her, accelerating towards the open space on the right.

'Oh, my God!' She stopped, terrified. The noises were all around her. The baby cried. There was another sound, a dragging noise as sand and stones were moved. It was in front of her, 'Cassie?' She stepped forward, frightened of what she might find.

There were shapes. Dark, blurred outlines, moving around her. Cassie was shrieking. Somewhere in front, two shapes melted into the dark. A third remained. The tugging sound, and the pitiful, terrified crying continued. The noises were coming in bursts. A deep, throaty sound. A grunt of exertion. Something sliding on the ground. And the crying, also coming in bursts as though the baby were being choked.

A dingo had her. She could see it. A big dog, dragging an object. Now it turned and was backing away, trying to free itself. Its teeth were caught in something. It was so big and so close.

Nellie's foot hit another stone. She bent, picked it up and ran for the dingo. It was backing away, still hauling the baby along the ground. It was a huge thing and it shook its head violently, trying to free its teeth which were hooked to the baby or its clothes. The blanket was trailing behind the baby. She trod on the blanket and then grabbed it and, for a few seconds, engaged in a deadly tug-of-war.

The dingo had gone berserk in its effort to free itself. It was stronger than Nellie and began to drag her too. She was screaming now, terrified of this dark monster but determined to hang on.

Suddenly the dingo slipped and Nellie dashed to it, the stone raised in one fist. It thrashed to its feet and she clubbed it. She felt its jaws snap on her leg. With both hands on the stone she struck again. The teeth bit deeper. Claws scratched her. She hit with all the strength she had and heard the grisly sound of cracking bone. She hit again and again until she missed and grazed her own leg, for the dog had slumped lifeless to the ground.

The baby was still crying.

Cassie was partly out of her clothes. The dog had grabbed her by the blanket and the collar of her jacket and its teeth had become enmeshed in the wool. Nellie picked her up and felt her. The child was bellowing and quivering with fright but seemed to be unmarked. Nellie pressed her to her chest and saturated her face with her own tears.

The dog near her feet twitched and she stumbled back. She

turned to walk away but could not. Her left leg would not move. She felt her knee, which was sore in a numb, vague way, and lifted a hand wet with blood. She hopped a few steps and then fell, saving the baby but jarring her spine. She sat up, put Cassie on her lap and felt the leg. It was torn from the knee to the shin. There were a few holes too – deep puncture wounds with blood oozing out and joining the stream from the open gash. She should bandage it. She had no handkerchief. She thought of tearing a strip off her skirt but she had so few clothes … The baby's blanket. It was already ripped and sticky with saliva or blood. She tried to tear a bandage from it but couldn't start the tear and instead wrapped the whole blanket around her leg.

She pulled the baby close to her body. 'There, there, you're all right,' she said and gently stroked the child's hair, brushing strands from the forehead. 'Where's your mummy?' she whispered and searched the shadows for any sign of another human. A terrible pain was searing her leg. Rain began to fall.

The rain was marvellous. Adam dismounted and stood with his hat off, allowing the water to patter on his head and stream down his face and tickle his neck as it ran into his collar. This was real rain and there was more of it coming. He stood with hands upraised. He felt like singing, but he just stood there with his arms lifted to the storm and laughed and enjoyed the delicious sting of fresh raindrops on his tongue and lips. And then he remounted the mare and rode on to the homestead. It was now dark but the path was easy to find and, in any case, the mare had an unerring sense of direction.

Josef was waiting at the house. He had hung a lantern on a rafter of the verandah roof.

'Isn't this wonderful?' Adam said, not bothering to get off the horse. His face was wet and glistening with happiness, in contrast to Josef who was dry and drawn with worry.

'Heather's not back.'

'What?' Adam swung his leg over the saddle. 'Back from where?'

'She went for a walk. Took Cassie and went to the hills.'

'How long ago?'

'I'm not sure. An hour. Two hours. Nellie didn't say.'

'Nellie?'

Josef bent like a question mark, his eyes avoiding Adam's. 'Yes. She went out looking for her just before sunset.'

'You mean ... our Nellie?'

Josef straightened and peered into the darkness behind Adam. 'Yes. She's working here.'

'What the hell are you talking about?' Adam said, under shelter now and shaking water from his hat.

'It's a long story but Heather gave her a job.'

Adam had gone inside to get a torch. 'How did Nellie get here in the first place? And when did all this happen?'

Josef continued to look miserable. 'She didn't come here. We went there. She'd been sacked from her job at the store. Adam, I think we should go and get them. They'll be wringing wet.'

Adam returned with a torch and the strip of canvas he used as the basis of his bed. He slung the canvas across the mare's saddle. 'And how did Heather get into William Creek?'

'I drove her there.'

'To get her mother?'

'Yes. Mrs Maguire wouldn't come back, though. She caught the train.'

'I asked you not to go into town.'

'Heather talked me into it.'

'For heaven's sake, Joe, can't you ever say no?'

A squall of heavier rain swept across the house. Adam turned from Josef who had been staring silently at the floor, and untied the mare's reins. 'The baby'll be soaked to the skin,' he muttered.

'And your wife. Don't you care about her?' He looked up to see Adam standing in the rain, glaring at him from behind a fine wall of water cascading from the brim of his hat. 'Well, you sound as though you don't give a stuff about her.'

'And you do.' No question. Just a flat statement. He mounted the horse and swung away from the verandah. 'I'll go ahead on the mare. Do you want to stay here in case I miss them and they come back another way?'

'No. I'll follow you.'

'Bring the lantern then. And get a coat or something to cover them.'

'Yeah.'

'You said she went to the hills?' Josef nodded. 'See you out there then.'

'Sure.'

'We'll talk later.' The mare's hoofs splashed in fresh pools of water as Adam rode off.

Josef watched him leave. You bet we're going to talk, he said, and I'm going to say what I think. I'm sick to death of being treated like a boy around here and I shall tell you exactly what a bastard you've become, Adam Ross.

Nellie woke, spluttering and coughing. With a start, she realized she must have fainted. The pain from her leg was intense. Rain splashed on her face. That was what had stirred her. Water was trickling into her nostrils. Gasping for breath and feeling giddy, she tried to sit up. She wiped her face and breathed deeply. The pain was awful. Where was the baby? Beside her. She had rolled to the ground and was lying beside her, whimpering and kicking. Nellie lifted the baby and held her so tightly she cried. But Nellie continued to hold her just as firmly because she was frightened and the baby gave her a feeling of comfort, of being with someone. Heavy rain was falling. She leaned forward to shelter Cassie. She could hear sounds. Water gurgling. Things moving. Maybe animals. The dingoes could have returned and be out there, circling around them. She had no idea whether they were inclined to attack humans. All she knew about dingoes was that she was scared of them.

She heard more noises. There was something out there. She tried to stand, bending forward, lifting herself to one knee and then pushing herself upright and all the time clutching Cassie in one arm. She heard something hard strike a rock.

'Mrs Ross?' she called. No answer. 'Heather?'

The sound was lost in the thud of rain.

Can't stay here all night, she said to herself, and began to hobble towards the end of the hill, or where she guessed it to be. She bumped into a large rock. A little more to the left. She hummed a tune for the baby, to comfort her and comfort herself. Having to worry about someone else made her do something; otherwise, she'd have stayed on the ground, weeping and holding her leg.

'Heather!'

It was a man's voice from far away. To her left, she saw the weak flash of a light.

'Over here!' she shouted and began to shake violently. 'Over here, please.'

The light grew brighter. It was high above the ground. Someone on a horse. Adam. He was calling out.

'Heather?'

'No. It's me. Nellie. I've got Cassie. She's all right.'

He dismounted and led the horse towards her, using the torch to pick a path between large rocks. The beam touched her. 'My God, what's happened?'

'The baby's all right.'

'I mean you! Nellie, what's happened to you?' His torch was on her leg. The blanket, her ankle and shoe were a watery red. He ran to her.

'Take Cassie,' she said and slumped to the ground.

He took the canvas from the saddle and covered her. He put the baby under the cover with Nellie and removed the bloodstained blanket. The cut had opened and a strip of flesh hung below the kneecap. Ugly puncture wounds, bruised and swelling around cores of thick blood, rimmed the cut.

He wiped water from his eyes so he could see the injury more clearly. 'What did that?'

'A dingo. I was trying to get the baby away from it.'

'Cassie!' he cried, flashing the torch on the child.

'She's all right. She just got a hell of a fright. Like me. I can't stop shaking. Oh, Adam!' She held out her arms. 'Hold me. Please!'

'I'm awfully wet,' he said but already she had her arms around him. Still kneeling, he kissed her and then gently pushed her away. 'Let me look at that leg,' he said and with his handkerchief began wiping dirt from around the wound. 'You've lost a lot of blood.'

She nodded. 'The dingo was dragging the baby away.'

'Where was Heather? And where is she now?'

'I've got no idea.'

'Weren't you together?'

'No. She'd taken the baby for a walk and hadn't come back so I went looking for them. It was just on dark and I was getting a bit worried.'

Adam tore a strip from his shirt.

'Anyhow, it was pitch black when I got round here and I heard the noises and there were dingoes all about and then I saw this big shadow dragging something and I could hear Cassie crying her little heart out.'

She gasped with pain. Adam was bandaging the cut.

'Sorry,' he said, but kept winding the strip of cloth around her leg. It was not long enough and, while she held the bandage in place, he tore another piece from his shirt.

'What happened then? How did it bite you?'

'I grabbed the other end of her clothes and we started pulling

705

and it slipped over and I hit it on the head with a rock.'

'You hit the dingo?'

'That's when it bit me. They're still around, Adam. I can hear them. I was so scared.'

He finished bandaging the leg and stood up, shining the light around them. From the side of the hill, small stones rattled.

'Well, don't worry,' he said slowly. 'They won't come near us. Although I must say you were lucky the dog ran away once he got a taste of your blood.'

'He didn't run away. I killed him.'

He shone the torch in her face. She had picked up Cassie. Four eyes blinked at him.

'You killed the dingo?'

'Yes. It's just over there. I was frightened it was going to eat Cassie or something.'

Adam left her to search for the slain dog. He found it about a hundred yards away. It was lying on its side with blood trailing from its mouth and ear. He touched it with his boot and it wobbled, still soft before the onset of rigor mortis. It was a big female. He'd never heard of a dingo attacking a human, even a small one. It probably thought Cassie was a small animal, maybe a rabbit. That meant Cassie had been left on the ground. Where was Heather? He called her name several times and flashed the torch before returning to Nellie.

'You didn't see her?' he said.

'Your wife? No. Would the dingoes ...?'

'No,' Adam said, frowning. 'They'd never attack an adult. But why would she leave Cassie and where would she go?' He bent down. 'And while we're asking questions, what the hell are you doing here?'

Josef arrived on foot a few minutes later. He had a sheet of canvas across his head and shoulders and carried the lantern. He had seen the torch. Adam explained what had happened. Heather was still missing.

'I'll go looking for her,' Josef said.

'No. You stay here with Nellie and Cassie. I'll find Heather.' His expression made it clear there would be no arguing. 'Leave the lantern out in the open so I can find you again.' Adam rode off.

He moved slowly along the side of the hill. Hunched against the rain, he shone the torch up the hillside, ahead of him, and to the

706

right. He called her name. He rode half a mile before hearing a response.

She was standing among rocks at the edge of the slope. Her hair was bedraggled and streamed across her shoulders. Her dress was stuck to her body and undergarments. He spurred the mare towards her. She backed away, her hand protecting her eyes from the glare of the torch.

'Josef?'

'No.' He leaped from the saddle and the torch flashed across his face.

'Where have you been?' she exploded, shaking both fists. 'I have been here on my own for an hour or more in this dreadful rain and in the dark and there are creatures moving around.'

'You're all right now.' He pulled her against him so that his head and hat covered her. She pushed him away.

'I cannot find Cassandra.' It was not a wail of distress but an accusation, as though he had hidden the child.

'She's safe.'

'What do you mean, safe? I'm telling you I cannot find her. I put her down somewhere among these rocks and she's gone. Don't you understand that? She's been moved. Someone must have taken her.'

'Heather, Cassie's all right. Nellie found her about half a mile back. You've been looking in the wrong place.'

'She's all right?'

'She's wet and miserable but she's not hurt.'

'Half a mile away? That's not possible.'

This would be a great place to start an argument, Adam thought, and said: 'Come on, get on the horse and I'll take you back.'

'You say that girl took her?' she said as Adam helped her into the saddle.

'She didn't take her. She found her.' He decided to say nothing about the dingo. Not until they were in the house where such things would not seem so frightening.

'What was she doing out here? I left her in the house.'

'She got worried about you and came looking for you. Just as well she did.'

'I suppose you're thinking of terrible things to say to me.'

'I just want to get you all back inside the house and out of this rain. Nellie's been hurt.'

'Really.' There was a pause and she leaned towards Adam, who was walking and leading the horse. 'You called the girl Nellie.'

'She told me that was her name,' he said and headed back to the others.

SEVENTEEN

The one good thing about tonight, Adam thought, is that it's still raining. The ground would be saturated, the natural waterholes would fill, shoots of fresh growth would appear all over his property, the sheep would thrive. Even the dingo menace would ease as the dogs head into the more remote regions, following the small creatures who would feed on the whole new cycle of life started by the rain.

A heavy shower rolled a drum break on the roof and, when it eased, Adam searched for leaks. There were none. He felt good. He had built a sound house. He took the kettle of hot water from the stove and put it on the table near where Nellie was sitting. They were alone in the room.

'The creeks will be up,' he said, pouring the water into a basin. 'I don't think we'll be moving too far from here for the next day or so.'

'Not me, anyhow,' Nellie said. Her injured leg was outstretched and supported on a stool.

'Do you know what I'm going to do when the rain stops and things settle down?' he said, dipping a cloth in the water. She seemed more interested in the steaming cloth than in his question and braced herself for the sudden application of heat as he tried to clean the wounds.

'I'm going to go out to the lake.'

'Lake Eyre?' she said, temporarily unclenching her teeth.

'Right. I've never been on it.'

'Will it be full?'

'No. Not unless it rains for another month. Hang on. This might hurt.' He wiped along the jagged edges of the cut. 'This doesn't look like a bite.'

'The dog scratched me.' She groaned.

'Sorry. I'll try not to hurt.'

'That's all right.' She put her hand on his shoulder to brace

708

herself against the pain.

'No,' he continued, 'the rain will make the sand firm and I could get to places you'd never reach when it was real dry. You could even drive the car to the lake. I might take the horse and go up north for a couple of days. There'd be plenty of feed and water for her.'

Heather had been in the other room with the baby. She joined them, closing the bag door behind her.

'Well, this looks cosy,' she said.

Adam did not look up. 'Is Cassie all right?' he said, wiping a fresh trickle of blood from the cut.

'Cassandra is perfectly well, thank you. And how's the leg?'

'It'll be all right, thanks,' Nellie said.

'Ma'am.'

'Ma'am,' she repeated, and when Adam looked at her she gave him a 'don't you dare say anything' glance. She took her hand from his shoulder.

'I must say you two seem to be getting on extremely well.'

Adam ignored the jibe. 'This cut should be stitched.'

'Well, there's no chance of that. Just clean it up and let her get on with her work.'

Now he looked at her. 'Heather, this cut is a bad one. The bites are even worse. They're deep and God knows how much damage they've done. They'll be hurting like hell.'

'Don't blaspheme. You'll have to excuse him, Nellie. Whenever he gets excited or finds events too much for him my husband lapses into bad language and it's usually the Lord who suffers.'

Nellie had closed her eyes. She had been feeling faint but the insult to Adam acted like smelling salts. She sat up straight. How have you put up with this spoiled bitch? she thought.

'She won't be walking tonight,' Adam said, 'and she certainly won't be doing any work.'

'Oh, for heaven's sake, they're just scratches and she's only ...'

Adam turned towards her. 'Only what?'

Heather smiled and searched the ceiling for support.

'Well ... black.'

'So?'

'Well, they do that sort of thing to themselves all the time. I mean, every time you see an aboriginal he's covered in scars and most of them are self-inflicted. And they don't feel pain like we do. I've heard it said ...'

'Oh, for heaven's sake shut up!' Adam said. 'This girl saved

709

Cassie's life and you're going on as though she were some sort of rag doll.'

Heather stamped her foot. 'I will not be spoken to like that! I've been through a dreadful ordeal and I will probably end up with pneumonia but have you shown any concern for me? Not one bit.'

'You weren't savaged by a dingo.'

'And what was this, this ... servant doing with Cassandra? I know precisely where I left my baby and yet this girl followed me there and took her away to this place where all those mad dogs were.'

'No, I never,' Nellie said softly.

'Quiet!' Heather snapped. 'You have shown reckless irresponsibility. If you hadn't already suffered some pain I would have to think of an appropriate punishment for you.'

Adam straightened and stared at his wife. 'You will not talk to her like that. She did not *take* the baby. She saved it, and to do it she had to kill the biggest bitch of a dingo I've ever seen.'

'Do not use that word "bitch".'

'Oh, keep quiet! And she did not remove the baby. She found it where you left it. *You left it.* At night and in dingo country. I can understand you getting lost, Heather, because anyone can get lost in that sort of country, but I cannot for the life of me understand how you could put a baby on the ground and just walk away.'

Heather was white-faced.

'I had things to think about!' she shouted. 'And I did not get lost. This girl took her from where I put her.'

'I did not.' Nellie said. 'I just saw the dingo dragging her away and I grabbed her.'

Josef stamped into the house, shaking water from his hat. 'Jesus, it's raining,' he said, and looked at Adam and Heather confronting each other. 'What's up?'

Heather turned so he could not see her face. She drew a handkerchief.

'Thank heavens you've come,' she said, anguish in her voice. 'These two have been teaming up against me.'

'Oh, for heaven's sake!' Adam growled and turned his attention once more to the injured leg.

'How do you mean?' Josef said, gripping his hat in both hands and shaking water from his shoulders. Heather angled her face towards him.

'I am just so shocked,' she said, her voice wavering.

'What have they been saying?'

'Nothing, Joe,' Adam said. 'Just keep out of it.'

He was walking on the spot. He put his hat on his head. 'I'll go back to the shed,' he said.

Heather moved towards him. 'No. Don't go. I don't feel safe.'

'Oh, Jesus,' Adam said.

Heather took Josef's arm. 'That woman took Cassandra from the place where I left her. I don't know what her motive was. She must have been sneaking behind me.'

'I was not,' Nellie said, shuffling in the chair.

'You were lost, Heather,' Adam said.

'You see? They're both against me. They're behaving like old cronies, as though they had all this planned.'

'Heather, you're nuts,' Adam said, not looking at her but preparing to bandage the leg.

'Don't call her that,' Josef said.

'Well, you try and persuade her to stop saying stupid things. Cassie could have been killed tonight and it would have been her fault.'

'You see?' Heather said, gripping Josef more firmly. 'That girl steals the baby and I'm blamed.'

'I did not steal the baby.'

'You speak when you're spoken to.'

'Adam's right,' Nellie said. 'You're nuts.'

'How dare you!'

Josef stood in front of Heather, protecting her from the onslaught. 'Yes, you shut up, Nellie.'

'Don't you tell me to shut up. And don't be a young drip.'

'By the Jesus, if you were a bloke I'd flatten you!'

'You can have a go,' she said, grasping the kettle.

Adam stood and sighed wearily. 'Joe, you're being used. Just don't say any more. Go back to the shed. I'll come and talk to you later.'

'Yes, Joe,' Nellie said. 'Nick off.'

Adam put his hand on her shoulder to restrain her.

'You see?' Heather said. 'He's touching her. When I came in the room she had her arm on him.'

'Stop it, Heather,' Adam said.

But she was away. One hand grasping Josef, the other carving the air in oratorial strokes, she said: 'It's wonderful, isn't it? I employ a black woman out of the kindness of my heart. To help a person without a job and in distress. And after a couple of nights

711

in my house, she tries to seduce my husband. Or is it the other way round?' She was waving both hands now. 'Is it my husband who was doing the seduction? Tell me, Adam, do you prefer dark women to white? Is that why you've spent all your life away from civilization, so you can engage in your sordid little night-time escapades with black sluts like this?'

'Don't you call me a slut!' Nellie said, trying to stand. 'And we weren't touching each other. Adam was trying to fix my leg.'

'Oh,' Heather said, returning to Josef and standing beside him so he could only see her profile. 'It's Adam, is it?'

No one spoke.

'And out there tonight, when my gallant husband finally came to my rescue, having, of course, first come to the aid of the new maid,' she said, turning slowly as she spoke, 'he referred to her by name. He didn't say the girl or the lubra or the gin or any of the things you might have expected, he said "Nellie". She faced Josef. 'Don't you find that strange? Having met her once, and under what one could only describe as bizarre if not unbelievable circumstances, my husband calls this little black servant girl "Nellie". And now here she refers to this stranger, whom she barely knows, as "Adam".'

Still no one spoke. Heather studied each face. 'Obviously it was a conspiracy. To steal my child. That was what it was all about, wasn't it?'

'That's an insane idea,' Adam said, trying to speak as calmly as he could. 'And the sillier your ideas are, the more you believe them.'

Again her fingers were touching Josef's arm. 'You see? When he's frightened, he always calls me insane. But it's all becoming very obvious. He's been trying to get rid of me since I came here. To make me unwelcome. To make me uncomfortable. To make me frightened. He wants the child. He doesn't want me. So tonight we had this little staged drama. I'm surprised he came looking for me at all. It would have been so much more convenient if I'd just been left out there to die.'

'You weren't much more than a mile from the house,' Adam said.

She ignored him. 'Tell me, Josef,' she said, letting her fingers run along his bicep, 'was Adam making any effort to search for me when you arrived on the scene and found him with Nellie and my baby?'

Josef took his hat off and let the brim touch his nose. 'Well, I don't know.'

'You're loyal and I admire that but you shouldn't be foolish. Had my husband started looking for me?'

712

'No.' He avoided Adam's eyes.

'You see?' she said triumphantly.

'Joe, I'd just got there myself,' Adam reminded him.

'I couldn't walk,' Nellie said. 'I'd fainted.'

'I'm sure you had,' Heather said. 'You'd followed me, stolen the baby, brought it back and were having a nice long chat about what to do next. If you hadn't been bitten by that dog you'd have merely brought the baby back here and left me out there on my own.'

'That is bullshit,' Nellie said loudly.

'My, my, you're really showing your breeding now,' Heather said. 'I can see you and Adam must have a lot in common.'

She stopped. There was a noise on the verandah. Jimmy appeared in the doorway. 'Anyone home?' he said and shook his head. Water sprayed from his hair. 'I heard this was the local picture show. Still got a seat left?' Smiling, because he knew this was normally forbidden territory when Heather was in the house, he took one step. He stopped and the smile vanished. He had seen Nellie. 'Bloody hell, what are you doing here?'

Having seen his expression Heather turned quickly to Nellie. Dismay was spreading across her face.

'You know her?'

Jimmy blinked. He rubbed his forehead. 'I'd better be going back,' he said. 'I just called in to let Adam know I was here.'

'I'll see you later,' Adam said.

'No, don't go,' Heather said, her voiced laced with sugar. 'We hardly ever see you and it's such a miserable night. Come on in. We're about to have tea.'

Jimmy's eyes had been darting from Adam to Nellie. 'No, I'll be going.' He left the room.

'But you'll get wet,' Heather called after him.

'I've got a dry place,' he said as he ran out into the rain.

Heather stood in the doorway, listening to the sloshing sounds of Jimmy's hurried departure. A strong wind was blowing and fragments of the downpour dampened her face. She breathed deeply, trying to calm herself and conscious of the silence of the others. Despite the shocks of the night, she was enjoying the situation. Things were happening that were helping her piece together the puzzles of the past weeks. It would all be resolved in the way she had imagined, she was certain. And she felt in control. Even with her back to the others, she could sense the tension in the room. It was time to say the unexpected.

'I think we should have something to eat,' she announced.

'That's a good idea,' Josef said, relaxing and moving to the table. He put his hat down.

Heather walked back into the room, smiling at him but addressing Adam. 'How long before you're finished with that leg? If we're going to eat, someone will have to prepare the food, and that's what the maid is paid to do.'

'I thought you said you weren't going to pay me?' Nellie said.

'I will not tolerate insolence,' Heather said softly.

'And I won't tolerate you going on like this,' Adam said. 'This girl is not going to get tea for us.'

'So it's "this girl" now, not Nellie?'

'She can't walk around on that leg,' he said.

'I'll get something,' Josef said and was rewarded by a smile and an outstretched hand with cool fingers tantalizingly close to his hand.

'That's sweet of you, but let her do it. She's not as bad as my husband would have us believe. By the way, Josef, did you notice the way Adam's black friend reacted when he saw the maid?' She spoke as though the others had left the room. 'I'd swear he knew her.'

Josef swallowed awkwardly.

'Now I thought only you knew her. Wasn't that right? She used to work for your family? But she calls my husband Adam, he calls her Nellie, and that black man stares at her as though he's seen a ghost. Don't you find it all rather strange?'

'The only thing that's strange,' Adam interrupted, 'is the way you're behaving. You're the one that left Cassie on the ground and almost got her killed and now you're going on as though everyone else is to blame.'

'You see?' she said to Josef, still speaking softly. 'Things are always twisted to make me a villain. And you notice how cleverly my husband tries to change the subject whenever the conversation becomes awkward? But I will not be put off. You all know each other, don't you?'

Adam faced her, his hands on his hips, but said nothing. He wished he could have been calm. He would like to have smiled and told her everything and held Nellie's hand and said, 'I'm sorry it's turned out this way. I didn't plan it like this. I tried to make our marriage work but it hasn't, and I don't love you any more but I do love this woman, and that's the way it is.' But he faced

714

her and felt guilty. And no matter how he tried, he couldn't stop his hands shaking.

Josef picked up his hat, put it down and then picked it up again.

Nellie touched the bandage on her leg.

Heather raised her chin. The silence was telling her more than words.

'Don't tell me, my dear husband, that this is the woman you have been hiding from me!'

'I haven't been hiding anywhere,' Nellie said quickly. 'What are you talking about?'

'Oh, you know. Well, well! So at last we're face to face. I must say I'm disappointed, if not surprised. I had thought, Adam, that she would at least be white. This is all very humiliating for me.' She faced the wall. 'You've all been laughing at me, I'm sure.'

Josef moved towards her. 'No, we haven't.'

'Not you, Josef?'

'No. Of course not.'

'You haven't conspired against me?'

Adam walked to her and pulled her around so that she faced him. 'No one's conspiring, you silly woman!'

She wrenched herself from him. 'Are you going to hit me now?' She moved against the flimsy bedroom wall, facing them all. 'This is what he does, Josef. My husband does not have many words at his disposal and when he runs out of them, he starts hitting me.'

'Oh, for God's sake, Heather!'

'Blaspheming again.'

'Keep away from her, Adam,' Josef said in a strained voice.

'Do you think I'm really going to hit her?' Adam said, his voice high as though he were about to laugh.

Josef licked his lips. Heather's eyes were boring into his, drawing him towards her. 'Just don't hit her,' he said flatly.

'Don't be such a drongo, Joe,' Nellie said. 'Can't you see what she's up to?'

'You stay out of this,' he said and waved his hand at her. 'This is your fault.' He had taken his eyes from Heather and realized with a start that she was now beside him.

'They are conspiring against me,' she said. 'How long have they known each other?'

He found it hard to speak.

'We met years ago,' Adam said.

Heather's fingers curled around Josef's arm. It was the touch of someone who needed a friend, he thought. You're the only one

715

who can protect me, she was saying. It's those two against me. You and me.

'It was at Coober Pedy,' Adam continued. 'That was a long time ago.'

Heather looked up at Josef but he said nothing.

'And how long have you two been hatching this plot against me?' she asked Adam.

'There is no plot.'

'Ha!' It was a discreet protest, suggesting pain borne with dignity. 'I suppose this woman just turned up here out of the blue. You expect me to believe that?'

'I was working in the store,' Nellie protested. 'I got sacked.'

'Of course.'

'You gave me the job. I didn't ask for it.'

Heather glanced at Josef and released his arm. 'It was you,' she said, hurt swelling through her voice. 'You suggested I should employ her. Are you part of this too?'

'Jesus, no,' he said and then, noticing the offence he had caused, added: 'Sorry. I didn't mean to say Jesus like that. No, I had nothing to do with it.'

'There *is* nothing, Joe,' Adam said. 'There is no plot. This is all nonsense.'

'The woman's a nut,' Nellie said. 'Stop acting like a lovesick galah.'

'Jesus, Nellie, will you shut up!' Josef shouted. 'I wish to hell you'd caught that train.'

Heather touched his shoulder, restraining him. 'But that was not part of their plan, Josef. Was she on the train with mother? Do you recall?'

Josef had become confused. He concentrated hard, but no thought could be squeezed out.

'No, she wasn't, was she?' Heather said. 'She was not even on the platform. She had no intention of leaving. She had, in fact, been with my mother all afternoon and my mother, I'm ashamed to say, was a part of this whole grubby business.'

'Jesus,' Josef said softly and did not apologize.

'My mother was paid to leave.'

'That is rubbish,' Adam said.

'It is *not!*' she shouted, stamping to emphasize the last word. Her movement startled Josef. 'You paid her, Adam. You gave her money to abandon me and leave.'

'Oh, for Christ's sake, Heather, that is a lie and you know it.'

'It is not. She told me. My own mother told me before she left. She confessed. And how dare you stand there and deny you paid her? She told me. She shouted it out. You bribed her!'

'She left because she wanted to. She was frightened of you.'

'I loved her and needed her and you drove her away.' She grabbed Josef. 'You heard her, didn't you? The last thing she called out was that my husband had paid her to leave. You heard, didn't you, Josef?'

'Well, I ...' he began.

'You see? Josef heard her.'

'That's not what she told me,' Nellie said.

Heather raised her hand to block the words. 'No one is interested in what you have to say because no one would believe one single word you uttered. You are a harlot.'

'She's the only lady in the room,' Adam said.

'How dare you!'

'Yes, take that back,' Josef said, laying his hand across hers.

'Joe,' Adam said, 'don't make a fool of yourself.'

'By the Jesus, will you stop treating me like a kid!'

'I'm not doing that.'

'Yes, you are,' he said, advancing and trailing Heather whose hand was still clasped in his. 'You think I'm still just a little German kid who does whatever you say, but I've had enough of that. I am no kid.'

'Well, stop behaving like one.'

'I'll thump you!' he said, moving another step.

'You and who else?' Nellie said.

Heather pulled Josef back. 'He's trying to trap you,' she said. 'He'd love nothing better than a fight. He delights in hitting people.'

'Look, Joe,' Adam said, as evenly as he could, 'I know what my wife's up to. I've seen her play these mad games before. I don't want you to be tricked into doing something you're going to be sorry for.'

'Stop blaming Heather,' he demanded.

She patted his hand. 'That's all right, Josef. He always does that.'

'It is not all right. Jesus Christ – I'm sorry – you are a much changed man, Adam. You're blaming this poor woman for everything and you're not giving her a fair go. You've done the weirdest things.'

He could feel her hand tightening in his and it gave him more

717

strength. 'You're at fault here, not her, and you won't admit it.'

'Have you spoken to Jimmy?' Adam said, trying to stay calm. 'He picked up Mrs Maguire. He said she was terrified of her own daughter and would rather die than come back. Talk to him.'

'Do you believe anything that man would have to say?' Heather said, squeezing his hand. Josef blinked. He usually believed Jimmy. Or he used to, just like he used to believe Adam. 'He is with them in this,' she continued. 'The three of them. First they get rid of my mother. Then me. And then you.'

'Do you think we should cut her throat now?' Nellie said and flashed a smile that found no response.

'You see?' Heather said.

'Oh, for crying out loud, it was only a joke. The whole thing's so ridiculous. Why would I plot against this mad bitch? I only met her for the first time the other day and I'd be happy if I never saw her again.'

'Oh, you won't see me again, I can promise you that,' Heather said. 'You're fired.'

'I'm having a good week for getting the sack,' Nellie said and grinned broadly.

'They talk of murder in one breath and laugh the next,' Heather said. 'These people are so brazen they're unbelievable.'

'She uses a lot of big words,' Nellie said.

'Jesus, Nellie, shut up!' Josef said.

'I killed a wild dog earlier tonight,' she said, grabbing the kettle again. 'Come on! I could handle you.'

'You see,' Heather said. 'She's as violent as my husband. All they understand is bash and kill.'

'Oh, she was only talking,' Josef said, turning away and frowning. He needed time to think and things were happening too quickly for that. 'She's like that. She was always getting hot under the collar. She doesn't mean half the things she says.'

'Oh, yes, I do.' Nellie tried to stand and the stool fell over.

'She's a vicious little thing,' Heather said, appearing amused. 'But frightful to look at. I can't understand why my husband would bother with her, can you, Josef?'

Josef was concentrating on his feet. 'No,' he said.

'He must have been desperate,' she said, 'just like an animal.'

'You might use big words,' Nellie said, 'but you've got a very dirty mouth.'

'This has gone far enough,' Adam said. 'Joe, I think it would be a good idea if you went to your quarters.'

'Do you?' he said without moving.

'And I think it would be a good idea if you took your hands off my wife.'

Heather gripped Josef more firmly. 'Now he's jealous. We've had rage and hatred and now jealousy. What's next, I wonder? Murder?'

'Joe, are you going to let go?'

'And what are you going to do?' Heather taunted. 'Hit him and then hit me? Is this how you planned to get rid of me? Kill me in a sordid fight and then say it was all a lover's quarrel?'

'Joe, you're being a fool,' Adam said.

Heather had pulled herself close to Josef who held his free hand in front of him, fist clenched.

Nellie struggled to her feet and tested the left leg. 'I've got a good idea,' she said. 'Why don't we leave mad eyes and the handsome prince together and go outside where there's nothing to worry about except the rain?'

Adam breathed deeply several times. He'd have loved to give Josef one good hit and see if he could knock some sense into him. More than that, he felt like hitting someone. He knew Heather was lying. He knew what she was trying to do, but he was no good at arguing and it made him angry as a bull to see his friend there smiling like a twerp and hanging on to his wife's hand. He didn't love her but she was still his wife. He took a step forward.

Nellie caught his shirt. 'Let's go. You could smear them over the wall and all you'd do would be to ruin the appearance of this place.' She tugged the shirt. 'I need a hand. My leg's hurting.'

He stepped back. 'I'll carry you.'

'Don't you dare go with her,' Heather said, moving away from Josef. But Adam had lifted Nellie in his arms and walked past them.

'Have a good night,' he said and strode out into the rain.

Josef prepared a meal. Heather seemed unable to do anything and hardly spoke. He could understand that. She had been through an ordeal.

When they had finished eating she said: 'I want you to do something for me. It's awful of me to ask but it's very important.'

'Sure. What is it?'

'I want you to go to your black friend. What's his name?'

'Jimmy?'

'Yes, him. Ask him to come and see me. It's most important.'

'Now?'

'Yes.' She turned the full power of her look on him. 'If you'd be a darling and do that I'd be most grateful.'

'Well, I'm not sure where he is. Normally when he's here he sleeps out in his little lean-to but with so much rain ...'

'Please see if you can find him. And please – not a word to the others.'

'I don't want to talk to them again.'

'Good. And Josef – I must talk to Jimmy alone.'

Doubt clouded his face and she rushed so soothe him. 'It's very important. For both of us. What I want you to do is get him to come here on his own and for you to stay there.'

'Where?'

'Wherever you find him. Wait until he comes back and then, Josef ...'

'Yes?'

'I want you to come back here. On your own. To me.'

'Oh. You don't want Jimmy to see the two of us together?'

She lowered her face in what could have been a blush. 'I'll be waiting for you,' she said. 'Do you understand what I mean?'

Josef nodded and left. Adam was correct, she thought. He is a boy.

It was still raining heavily.

Adam helped Nellie to the running board of the car. He searched for some dry rags. 'They're not towels but you might be able to dry yourself with them,' he said and turned his back while she took off her clothes.

'I don't mind you looking,' she said but he did not turn.

'I'm not doing all those things she's saying,' he said.

'I know.'

'I just can't understand her.'

'I wouldn't bother. She's a basket case. I don't know how you've put up with her.'

'I haven't been very fair. I've been away a lot.'

'So what? When you're around she behaves as though she was practising to run a lunatic asylum. You mind passing me my bag? It's got some clothes in it.'

He brought the bag. She was naked but for the bandage. He turned away.

'Don't like me in bandages?'

'It's not like that, Nellie. I'm just upset by everything.'

'Do you still love her?'

'No.'

'Do you love me?'

'Yes.'

'Enough to live with me? Sorry, I shouldn't have asked that question. You might have a loony for a wife but you're still married to her. For better or for worse, or whatever it is they say.' She pulled on a dry jumper and spoke while it was still over her head. 'What are you going to do?'

'I don't know. I'd like her to leave.'

'She won't until she wants to.'

He sat next to her on the running board. 'Nellie, please be careful. She's dangerous and I don't want her doing anything to you.'

She laughed. 'I was handling tougher women than her when I was fifteen.'

EIGHTEEN

Jimmy entered the house cautiously. He did his best to dry himself on the verandah so he would not drip water in the room. He moved through the door, rolling his eyes. She was at the table.

'Please come in.'

He moved to the table. He was barefooted. He preferred to go without boots in wet weather and she looked at his large, flat and still wet feet in distaste.

'Sit down there.' She pointed to a stool. 'Thank you for coming. It's still raining outside, I see.'

He smiled, showing her the gap in his teeth, and she looked away.

'It was good of you to come to the house and I'm sorry you had to get so wet. What I wanted to talk about ...' She stopped, suddenly thinking of something. 'Oh, you do speak English?'

'Yes.' It was a fair imitation of the soft, throaty sibilance of the genuine bush aboriginal.

'Good. You understand me?'

'Yes.'

She wondered if she should offer him something to drink. Tea perhaps, although she would have to make it. But did he drink tea? Probably not. He looked so … primitive … sitting opposite her with his hair all knotted and sparkling with droplets of water and his mouth open in that idiotic smile showing the revolting space where his teeth had been knocked out. Her father had said aborigines drank methylated spirits but she could hardly offer him that.

'It was about the girl you saw in this room earlier tonight,' she said, speaking slowly and enunciating each word. 'The one called Nellie.'

'Yes.'

I wish he would stop saying that, she thought. Maybe it's the only word he knows. 'I am not pleased with some of the things she has done. In fact, I am thinking of dismissing her. Do you understand?'

'Yes.' Jimmy's smile broadened.

'Now I know you know her. You were all friends a long time ago at that opal place.'

'Coober Pedy.'

Ah, she thought. Two new words. Well, at least that part of Adam's story might have been true. 'But I thought from the way you looked when you saw her tonight that, possibly, you did not like her very much.'

She watched him intently. He blinked. Nothing else. The smile remained. The man must be a moron.

What's she after? Jimmy wondered. She's talking of sacking Nellie. Good. But what does she want from me?

'I don't want to dismiss someone without good cause. I don't want to be unfair. Do you understand?'

'Yes.' Was she fair dinkum? Was she just asking him, as someone who knew Nellie of old, whether she deserved to be sacked?

If he says 'yes' once more I shall hit him, she thought. 'One of the things she did,' Heather continued, 'very nearly cost the life of my daughter. She tried to run away with the baby. Only the fact that she was later bitten by a dingo – or that's what she says – prevented her from getting away.'

Jimmy closed his mouth. What the hell had Nellie tried to do?

'Now Jimmy, I know that my husband and this girl are quite good friends. I'm fully aware of all that's been going on, just as I'm sure you are. I understand that. I do not blame Adam. He's been on his own a lot and I know how men behave when they live

722

under those circumstances.' She thought Jimmy looked baffled. She had used big words. She smiled tolerantly. 'I know ... what men do ... when they are away ... from their wives ... for a long, long time. Do you understand me?'

'Yes.'

She breathed deeply, reinforcing her patience. 'Because of this friendship, I cannot expect my husband to say things that incriminate ... to say bad things about her. But I must know the truth. It would be unfair to dismiss this girl if this was the first time she'd transgressed ... done the wrong thing. Has she ever stolen anything before?'

Jimmy was tempted to say the opal, but Nellie had brought that back and besides, it was a complicated story and he wasn't going to give this woman too much information. She smiled and looked pretty but there was something in her eyes that reminded him of a snake. So he said nothing.

'Nothing?' she asked.

'No.' Just ask me if she's done anything rotten, he said to himself, and I'll tell you a story that will curl your hair, and Nellie will be thrown off this place before breakfast. I'd even drive her to the station and give her a kick up the arse to get her on her way. Go on, lady, ask the right question.

'Where did you first meet her?'

The wrong question, he thought, but I can lead her into it. 'Port Pirie.' He was still using his hushed voice and she had to lean forward to hear him. Just ask me where she was when I met her and I bet you'll blush.

'Is that where Adam met her?'

Wrong question again. 'No.'

'Where did he meet her?'

'Later.'

'At Coober Pedy?'

'Yes,' he said, and the warning alarms were jangling. She's not concerned about whether Nellie was a thief or anything like that. She's trying to pump me. The cunning bitch. She's trying to trap me into telling her about Nellie and Adam.

'Were they always good friends?'

'We all were.' Let her untangle that.

'What do you mean?'

'We were friends.'

'I see.'

No, you don't. What's coming next?

723

'Why don't you like her?'

Play dumb. He shrugged.

'Did she do something to you?'

He shook his head.

'Did she do something to Adam?'

His eyes narrowed.

'That's it, isn't it? Was it because of what happened between her and Adam? Is that why you don't like her?'

He lowered his face. 'Something like that,' he mumbled.

'What do you mean?'

'Well, Adam's my best mate.'

'Yes. Go on.'

'Well, I didn't want him getting into trouble.'

'And she's trouble?'

'Yes.'

'Because he was a married man?'

'Yes.'

She stood and walked around the table, slowly rubbing her hands together.

'How long has she been out here?'

'How do you mean?' What was she getting at? Nellie must have just arrived. Although Adam had said something about Heather thinking there was another house and another woman on the property . . .

'How long? You know, what period of time?'

Jimmy blinked a few times. I'm stupid, lady. Give me a few more clues.

'Did she come out here when my husband first arrived?'

A year ago? She thought that? He licked his lips, as though reluctant to answer.

'She's been with him all the time? Since he first came to Kalinda?'

He let his head hang almost to the top of the table. I'm not lying, he told himself. Just let her believe what she wants to believe. She'll have Nellie out of here in the morning and I won't have said a thing.

'Where has she lived? Where, Jimmy? I know there's another house.'

He tried to look as though she had torn the answer from him. 'On the lake,' he said.

'The lake?' She seemed astonished. 'The big salt lake? But Adam said there was nothing there.'

He smiled, still trying to look uncomfortable which, he reflected, required no great acting ability.

'Isn't the lake dry? Just salt?'

'Yes.'

'Then where is the house where Nellie lived? On the shores of the lake?'

'No,' he said, deciding that if he were to deceive her he might as well do a thorough job.

'Then where?'

'On the lake.'

'*On* the lake? But where?'

'In the middle.'

'What? That's impossible.'

'No. The salt's hard.'

'But you can't live on salt.'

'The house is on an island.'

'There are islands?'

'Yes. Many.'

'And the house is on one. A big one?'

'The biggest.'

She could not hide the expression of triumph. Now she knew. After all the deceptions and lies. 'Where is the lake?'

He pointed in the correct direction. 'Where the sun rises.' He was pleased with that answer. It sounded like the sort of thing a genuine bush black would have said.

'You mean the east?'

'Yes.'

'Due east?'

'Yes.' Why not? She could spend years searching for the house. She was smiling and he came perilously close to smiling too.

Josef waited for Jimmy to return and then walked to the house. He did not go directly there, for he had told Jimmy he was going to the shearing shed, but followed a wide detour via the wash house. Rain was still falling but not so heavily. He entered the verandah on the side farthest from the shed where Adam and Nellie were resting. He could see a lantern glowing in one corner of the shed near where the mare had been stabled.

He stood on the verandah for more than a minute. He took off his hat and the canvas cover he had been wearing as a raincoat. He scraped mud from his boots. And he stayed, searching the night for any sign of movement. There was no one out there; he

725

knew that. Only three other people were on the property and he knew where each of them was. But he felt as nervous as a boy about to meet his first girlfriend. No, it was worse than that. He felt guilty, as though he were about to steal something. And the night pressed against him, wet and black and bleak, imprisoning him with his fears.

He went in the house.

'Is that you, Josef?' Heather called, her words little more than a whisper. She sounded nervous too. He felt better for that. She was in the bedroom with the door closed. Josef had never been in that room. He recalled the time when the door had swung open and he had seen her, staring at him and half-naked. It was a signal. She had been giving him signs for a long time. He had been a fool to ignore them. It was his concern for Adam that had restrained him. Well, Adam had shown how much he thought of him. And of Heather. Adam could go to hell. He cleared his throat.

'Yes.'

'Good. I was frightened.'

Josef hesitated, staying on his side of the wall. A candle burned in the other room. He could see its light fluttering through seams in the hessian.

'Did the meeting go all right?'

'With your friend? Yes, thank you.'

He waited. What would she say? 'Please come in,' or 'Would you care to join me?' or something like 'Josef, I need you'? He walked to the water bucket near the stove and filled a cup. Strange, it was so wet outside and yet his throat was dry.

'It's still raining,' he said.

'I beg your pardon?'

'I said it's raining.'

'Yes. I can hear it.'

She's waiting for me, he thought, and I'm pussy-footing around like an old woman. She's testing me. Leaving it to me to make the first move. Judging me against Adam, who preferred to sleep out here and leave her on her own.

He strode to the bedroom door, which was a simple wooden frame with bags stretched across the members and nailed to them. It was surprisingly difficult to open.

'What are you doing?' She sounded alarmed.

'Trying to open the door.' He laughed, an apologetic sound.

'There's something against it.'

'Oh.' He waited for the shuffle of her feet as she came to

remove the obstacle. There was no sound.

'Heather?'

'Yes.'

'I can't get in.'

'I told you. There's something against it. It won't open.'

'Well, how am I going to get in?'

There was a noise now. The bed squeaked.

'What do you mean?'

'Just that. If I can't open the door I can't get in. Do you want me to climb in through the window?' He was feeling foolish and very young. What should he do? Rip the hessian and walk through? Is that what she wanted?

There was a footstep and then another. But only two. Something rattled.

'Josef, I don't want you to come in here,' she said. Her voice was firm but angelic. She could have been on the outskirts of heaven, explaining the ultimate secret of life to a newcomer. Nothing harsh. No suggestion of passion or criticism. Just the 'but surely you must have known' inflection, the merest hint of mockery.

He turned his back on the door. Bloody bastard, everyone's playing me for a fool. He had tears in his eyes. Not from sadness, not even from frustration, but from bitterness. Every bloody body took him for a fool. He kicked the door with the back of his foot.

'Not yet anyhow,' she said, and he turned.

'When?'

'There are things I must do. You know, with the baby.'

He scraped his fingers across his forehead. Jesus, I am a fool! Of course. I'd forgotten the kid. 'I'm sorry,' he said and the flush of anticipation banished his despair. 'Later?'

'Yes.'

It was a sweet sound.

Adam could not sleep. He had tried lying on some bags of feed near the mare but it was too uncomfortable, like stretching out on river-washed stones. Besides, his brain was swirling with thoughts. Nothing substantial that he could ponder and solve, just froth whisked from the waves of a high tide of problems.

The mare was restless too. She had been quiet when the rain was heavy, cowed by the tumult of water falling on and around the shed. But now that the storm had been reduced to sharp squalls and gusts of wind that carried strange, wet smells, she

727

stirred and rattled her hoofs in a constant restless patter on the earth floor. Occasionally she provoked a squeaking of wood as she brushed a plank or a rail. Adam sat up.

'Can't you sleep?' Nellie said from her bed near the car.

'No. How's the leg?'

The cut was throbbing and the bites were burning deep in her leg as though a row of pokers had been wired to her knee, but she knew Adam would know that. 'Not bad,' she said, which meant she could tolerate the pain, because – as again they both knew – there was no alternative.

'It should be stitched,' he said.

'No thanks. I'm a coward with doctors. Do you want to sit over here?' she added.

He thought for a long time. 'No. Well, yes, I do, but I shouldn't. I mean, I want to but I don't think it would be right.'

'I'm sure your wife thinks we're together and going hammer and tongs.'

He laughed. Heather would be tormented by images of what they were doing. Not so much, he reckoned, by thoughts of the two of them engaged in wild couplings, because she had little concept of what such things were all about. Love, to her, was a cold thing: a handsome prince swearing eternal love to a beautiful maiden and then going off to fight dragons. The physical side was what animals did, and 'hammer and tongs' to her would be Adam pursuing Nellie and mounting her like a rampant bull. The sort of love where you touched and thrilled and felt the burn of passion was unknown to her. If she thought of them doing it she would feel only disgust, not envy or a lustful and jealous hatred. No, Heather would be more worried about what they were saying about her, and what they were planning. Which meant, he reasoned, that if she was convinced they were plotting against her, she was certainly plotting against them. What was she up to?

The house was in darkness. And what about Josef? Adam had seen him sneak in some time ago. He'd cooled down now and felt sorry for the bloke. Josef didn't know what he was doing, what anyone else was doing, or whom he could trust.

'What are you thinking about?' Nellie said.

'Joe. The poor fellow doesn't know which way is up at the moment.'

'I'm not sorry for him. He's being a fool. The trouble with Joe is that his brain has split into two and fallen down to hang between his legs.'

Adam grunted, half protest, half laugh. 'You've got a nice way of saying things.'

'Well, it's true. He's playing right into her hands. Maybe he can't help himself but he could sure try.'

'I think he's confused.'

'Who isn't? He thinks he's a real red-blooded man but he's got so much blood in his head he can't see out.' Nellie moved her leg, seeking a more comfortable position. Adam heard the hiss of pain.

'If he was just confused it would be all right,' she said, 'but he's turning against you and siding with her.'

'Yes,' he sighed.

'How can you be so calm? I mean, this is your friend and your wife.'

'Who said I'm calm? I'm just saying I can't really blame him. I know what she's like. She'll be working on him, leading him up the garden path, trying to use him or get something from him that she can turn against us.'

'Yeah, she'd do anything. I know her type. Will she have him in bed with her?'

He didn't answer.

'Women do that sort of thing, you know.'

'Not her.' A pause. 'At least I don't think so.'

'It doesn't worry you?'

He thought about it. 'I don't think she'd do it. Not because of any loyalty to me or anything like that. She just doesn't think that way.'

'Really? What if she did? What if she had Joe in bed with her now?'

There was a long pause.

'She wouldn't.'

'But what if Joe was with her? Would you worry?'

Another long silence.

'No,' he said.

'Honest?'

'Yes. I wouldn't like it, but mainly because of Joe. Not her and me.'

'Come off it.'

'It's true. I've got no feeling for her. He can have her. But she'd ruin him.'

'She didn't ruin you.'

The horse bumped a rail and shied in a flurry of dirt. Adam was thankful for the interruption. He got up, calmed her and then nuzzled her, enjoying the tickle of her fine hairs against his nose and cheek. God, animals were simple to understand.

'Adam?' Nellie called softly and almost hesitantly. Obviously it was a prelude to a difficult question.

He let his hand run down the mare's neck and walked back to the sacks. 'Yes?'

'I reckon you married her because she seemed such a lady and it took you a while to discover she was a bitch and a hard one at that. I never have been a lady and I probably never will be, although I wouldn't mind trying.'

In the following pause, he could not suppress a chuckle.

'What are you laughing at?'

'You. You're about as hard to see through as a mosquito net.'

He heard her move, heard the gasp of pain as she changed the position of her leg. She was sitting up.

'Is that why you won't come over here? I'm all right in a creek bed or in some dingy room in a crummy hotel, but you don't want to come near me in your own place? Even in the shed?'

He walked to her, feeling his way around the front of the car.

'You don't have to,' she said petulantly.

He squatted beside her. 'Look, I love talking to you. I love being next to you. I'm proud to be seen with you.'

'Why didn't you come over before?'

'Because of her, lying over there and thinking we're sleeping together or something. I didn't want her to be right.'

'Who cares?'

'I don't know. I'm all mixed up.'

She reached for his hand. 'That's the first sensible thing you've said for a while. I'm mixed up, too.'

'I don't know how all this is going to end up,' he said.

'Neither do I.'

'Do you want to hang around and find out?'

'Why not?'

Adam leaned to kiss her. To his surprise, she began to giggle.

'What's up?' he said, drawing back.

'I was just thinking how well I've done. Instead of being without a job on some creek bank I'm here without a job in the middle of the desert. What would you call that?'

'Being different.'

'You're right.' She pulled him towards her. 'You can kiss me now.'

730

NINETEEN

Awaiting his summons to the bedroom, Josef tried to stay awake but fell asleep at the table. He stirred, stiff and cold, just before dawn. There were noises in the other room. The baby was crying, not loudly but with the squeak of early morning hunger. Heather was moving and talking softly. He heard a slight bump, more talk and a sucking sound. All was quiet.

He thought of making tea but instead walked to the door, not bothering to muffle the noise. He wanted her to know he was awake.

The rain had stopped. The air was damp and cool and he breathed deeply, letting the charge scour the debris of sleep from the back of his throat. The sky was dark but clear with only the brightest stars still shining. He tried to judge how long it would be before sunrise. Maybe half an hour. From somewhere behind the house birds began to chortle. His back ached. He flexed his shoulders, touched his toes – it was an exercise his father had forced him to do all through his childhood – and took some more deep breaths. He went back inside the house and waited.

He heard occasional sounds. Heather uttering a few soft words. A patting noise. A few steps. More words. The baby gurgling. The bed compressing. Brushing. Silence.

He went to the door and knocked on the wooden frame. 'Are you awake?' he called.

There was a soft rustling and she was on the other side. 'Don't call out,' she whispered. 'I want Cassandra to go back to sleep.'

'I still can't open the door.'

'Oh.' He heard a scraping. The door opened. She was in a long nightgown with her hair, golden and glossy from brushing, curling around her shoulders.

Josef ran his fingers through his hair. 'You must have gone to sleep,' he said, the faintest suggestion of protest in his words.

She smiled and gently pushed him back so she could walk through the door. She closed it behind her. She touched his upper arm, running her fingers around the muscle. 'I was so tired. I'm sorry. I must have just dropped off.'

He reached for her hand but missed.

'Did you sleep well?' she asked, moving away.

'I went to sleep sitting in the chair.'

'Oh, you poor thing! You must be stiff and sore.' She ran a hand along his back. 'Would you like me to give you a massage?'

'No, it's all right.'

'No, let me. Sit down.' Now she took his hand and led him to a chair. With both hands she pressed him into place and then stood behind him. 'You really should take your shirt off. I can't do it properly like this.'

'Oh, I'm all right, really, Heather.'

'What's the matter? Are you frightened to undress in front of me?'

He began to remove his shirt but, in his haste, caught it around his head. She helped him undo a button but left her hand on his skin, lightly touching his chest.

'There, now, you have to relax,' she said. 'You feel all tense, as though you really are frightened of me.' She put both hands on his shoulders. 'That's better. There's no need to worry. I'm really very good at this. I used to do it for my father and he said I had the best touch he'd ever felt.'

She ran her fingers down his spine, playing chords on his imagination.

'How was that? Make you feel more relaxed?'

He could not speak.

The fingers rose, their touch so light that he twitched. They stopped at his neck. Her hands caressed the long muscles to his shoulders. He let his head fall forward.

'You must be tired,' she said. He could feel her body against him. She must be bending. Surely those were her breasts against his shoulders?

'I hardly slept,' she continued and he didn't bother to doubt her. 'I kept thinking about that man Mailey.'

Josef lifted his head.

'Just relax.' Again the body brushed his bare skin. 'You know how it is when you start to worry about something? You just can't stop and your mind races along and you can't sleep. I started to think about Mailey and that was it. I came out in the middle of the night but you were asleep.'

'I was?'

'Yes. In the chair. Poor dear, you looked so uncomfortable.'

'You should have woken me.' He tried to stand. She eased him back into the chair.

'No. You were worn out. I wanted to talk to you about ... well,

732

that time. I was so worried for you.'

'Me?'

'Well, it seems there's going to be some sort of investigation.'

'How do you mean?'

'Please relax. I can't do this if you keep jumping about.' She let her hands lie on his chest until he was calm. 'There always has to an investigation into something like that. I'm not concerned about Adam any more, obviously, after the things he's said and done, but I am worried for you. That's why I was so restless. Oh, Josef, I'm so worried.'

One hand stopped on his shoulder. He put his hand across it.

'What about?'

'Well, I understand that you might be blamed.'

He stood and faced her. 'Me?'

'So Adam was saying.'

'When?'

'Before you arrived here. When he was telling me about what happened.'

'He says he's never mentioned Mailey to you.'

She had backed against the wall. She smiled 'I don't know what's happened to Adam. He's changed so much.'

'He certainly has. But what about me? How am I going to be blamed?'

'Well, that's what I don't understand. He just said that if – when – the investigation comes, you'll be in a lot of trouble. He made it sound as though the matter was all your fault.'

'But I didn't kill the bloke. It wasn't me who broke his neck.'

She lowered her head. The top buttons of her nightgown were undone. She took a deep breath and the gown opened a little. 'Josef, I have been so terribly frightened for you.'

'But why are they sending anyone now, after all these years?'

She turned quickly to face the wall. All these years? What is he talking about? Adam has only been here twelve months. 'I really don't know,' she said, her head tilted so that her hair fell spectacularly down her back. 'All I know is that the way Adam puts it, the whole affair was largely your doing, and that the police will want to talk to you or even arrest you. And, Josef, that frightens me. I know what a clever liar Adam is. How he can fool his friends. All I've got is his account of this business. I can't believe that you'd kill a man.'

'I didn't. I don't know why he'd say that.'

'Adam killed him?'

'Yes.'

'Thank heavens for that! I knew it couldn't have been you. But you were there?'

He didn't answer and she was frightened she had pushed him too hard. Josef was a slow thinker, so she shouldn't allow him too much time to work out what she was doing. Quickly she added: 'Could that be enough, Josef? Could they arrest you for just being there?'

'I don't know. The man was a bastard. Sorry, but I don't know a better word to describe him.' He paused. 'Evil. He was a genuinely evil person. He was going to kill us.'

'All of you?'

'Yes. He had the other two roped up. He had me digging their grave. He didn't know Adam was there, of course, but he was dead set on killing the rest of us.'

She was trying to store all the information he was giving her. Three people plus Adam. Josef, Jimmy, and who else? The girl, Nellie? Of course. They had all come here some time ago. Maybe they had even built the house on the lake then. But when had all this happened, and where had Mailey come from? What had they done wrong to have a policeman come here?

She turned slowly, shaking her head so that her hair partly covered her face. It gave her, she thought, a mysterious yet vulnerable look. The gown had slipped off one shoulder.

'What I couldn't understand from Adam's story was what Mailey was doing here in the first place. He made it sound as though the man were after you.'

The gown slipped a fraction more. Josef stared and she didn't seem to mind. He coughed, a signal that if she wanted to lift it back into place, now was the time to do it. She brushed the hair from her face and her eyes were inviting him to do something. Or say something. He looked away, not sure what the invitation meant. He said: 'Mailey was after all of us. Mainly Jimmy and Adam though, because they were the ones who'd got out of the gaol.'

They had broken out of prison? Her husband was an escaped convict? This was awful. No, she quickly corrected, this was good news. With this information, she could gain almost any concession from him. He would have to do what she wanted now. If he refused she would have him put back in prison. And if he went to prison, she would get ownership of everything.

'Adam didn't tell me much about that,' she said, moving from the wall and standing beside him. He tried to move to face her but caught his feet in the chair and sat down heavily. Before he could rise, she had placed a hand on his arm. The movement exposed her other shoulder and he wondered how long it would be before her chest was bared.

'And how did you get involved in such a terrible business?'

'I got him out of the gaol and then showed him the way out of town,' he said and looked up. 'Nellie and me nearly burned the place down.'

So Nellie *was* the other person. And she and Josef had got them out of gaol. Good. She had information she could use against all of them. She could send them all to prison. That was a tempting prospect. Adam and Nellie in cells for years, unable to see each other. Marvellous. And if Josef and Jimmy were in prison too, so much the better. None of them could interfere with her plans, then. She could sell the place without anyone making poisonous accusations.

'Was it big, this prison?' she asked, and her fingers tightened on his arm.

'No,' he laughed, not feeling amused but unable to control the shake in his voice. 'Nellie got in Mailey's car but she couldn't drive and backed through the door. You should have seen the fire. The car blew up, you see.'

'Blew up?'

'The petrol tank went up. That's how Adam got burnt.'

She had seen Adam's burn scars. 'But that was when he was digging opals,' she said.

'At Coober Pedy,' he said. She was looking shocked. 'What's wrong? Didn't Adam tell you that?'

So this had happened about six years ago. Mailey must have been the policeman at Coober Pedy. They had broken out of prison, Mailey had followed them, somehow they had come to this place and Adam had killed Mailey. They were all criminals. Two had been in gaol, the other two had broken in, they had destroyed a car, and her husband had murdered a policeman. The others were accomplices. She had everything she needed.

She pulled the gown back into place.

'What's the matter?' he said, rising.

'Is that when he built the house for that woman?' she said, her voice no longer soft and tempting.

'What house? What do you mean, Heather?'

'The one in the middle of the lake. He and that girl were lovers even then, weren't they?'

'What are you talking about? What house on the lake?'

'Please don't go on like this, Josef. I have had absolutely enough of people lying to me.'

'Jesus, what's wrong?'

'Don't use that word. And nothing's wrong except that I have a revulsion to being deceived. You know of the house, of course?'

'What house?'

'I'm aware that you can portray stupidity with the ease of one who has the benefit of considerable practice, but please don't insult me by pretending to have no knowledge of something I know exists. I know there is a house, I know that half-caste creature has been living there, and I know exactly where it is.'

'Heather, I don't know what you're talking about.' He reached out to touch her arm. She slapped his hand.

'Don't you dare maul me!' She retreated to the stove.

'What on earth's happened? A minute ago you were practically undressing in front of me and now ...'

'That is a disgusting thing to say.'

'But true. Oh, for Christ's sake ...'

'Don't say that.'

'For Christ's sake, last night you wanted me to hop into bed with you and now all of a sudden you're going on as though I'm an insect.'

'Which you are.'

'What is this? Some sort of come-on? Do you like your men to play rough? Didn't I pull your clothes off when you gave me the signal? Is that what you want me to do?'

'Don't come one step closer!'

'Oh, come off it,' he said, moving towards her. 'For weeks now you've been doing everything but throwing yourself at me. Now I know you're a married woman and all that, but I know how you feel about your husband and I know how you feel about me, so there's no need to go on like that.'

'Oh, you know all that, do you? And how am I going on, as you call it?' The words were so finely honed Josef didn't feel the slash.

'Like you are. You take my shirt off ...'

'You took it off.'

'You get me to do it. You play around with my body ...'

'I was giving you massage.' She fluttered her eyelashes, impersonating modesty.

736

Josef crossed the border from desire to anger and accomplished the journey with such pace that his face reddened instantly. 'Oh, don't give me that!' he shouted. 'You were giving me a message, not a massage! And then you started rubbing your tits against me …'

'How dare you!' She reached back and found the handle of the poker.

'You were! And then you started showing them to me. Jesus Christ, in another two minutes your nightie would have been around your ankles, but then, WHAM! Something happens. You turn on me. You wind me up then switch yourself off. What the hell's happening?'

She lifted the poker. 'What's happening is that I'm telling you to go away.'

'One minute you want me, the next you don't!'

'I've never wanted you. Who would? You're just a foolish boy. A dull and rather slowwitted boy who talks too much.'

Josef was having time to think. 'You've been using me, haven't you?'

'What on earth do you mean?'

'Using me against Adam. You've been lying to me.'

'I have not lied. Adam lies. You lie. You're the one who's been doing the deceiving. About the house. About that woman. About what's been going on here.'

'Adam said you were nuts. I should have believed him.'

She smiled.

'It's Mailey,' he suddenly announced, his head angled from the impact of the revelation. 'That's what you've been fishing for. You didn't know, did you?'

'I know all I need to know about Mailey.'

'Adam didn't tell you, did he?'

'You did. Thank you.'

'You bastard!'

'How typical of you to revert to bad language when you've been outwitted.'

He took another step. She raised the poker. He retreated.

'Why?' he said.

'Because I will not be cheated.'

'Who's cheating you?'

'You are. Adam is. Everyone is.'

'Bullshit! You're nuts.'

She smiled. 'Profanity suits you. Such language is the refuge of

737

weak minds and yours is exceptional in that regard. You have resorted to such coarseness because you have been found out.'

He put his hands on his hips. 'Would you believe me if I said I haven't got a clue what you're talking about?'

'No. I knew there was a conspiracy against me. I knew you were all involved. What I didn't know until you told me a few minutes ago was just how long this gang of yours had been operating. It seems you're well practised at deception, at law breaking. I knew you were all wicked people. What I had not appreciated was the depth of your wickedness. I did not know my husband was an escaped convict or that you and that woman had ... what is the expression? ... broken them out?'

Josef laughed. 'Adam wasn't a convict. Mailey was a crook. He was going to kill the pair of them.'

'A moment ago this Mailey was going to kill all of you. Now it's just a pair. There's no point in constantly changing your story.'

'I'm not changing anything. He'd locked up Adam and Jimmy in Coober Pedy. The other business was up here with Saleem Benn.'

'Oh, so now we have another character in this amazing game. Really, you should not keep on altering your story and inventing fresh lies. You do not lie well. My husband does but he's a master at it. You're just a boy at the game.'

'Don't keep calling me a boy.'

'It's what you are. You're a gangling, gauche juvenile.'

'I'm as old as you are, you fucking stupid twit!' he shouted and when the noise had cleared from his head he was aware of another sound. The baby crying.

Heather had closed her eyes. 'You are an oaf. Typically German. Bull-headed and boring. My father always said they were crude people and you've just demonstrated the wisdom of his words.'

'I'm glad I didn't go to bed with you,' he said. 'You might have poisoned me.'

'There was no chance of me ever allowing you near me,' she snapped and waved the poker at him. 'But where you're going you'll be able to mix with people of your own class. I'm sure among such ruffians you will feel absolutely at home.'

'What do you mean, where I'm going?'

'To prison.'

Prison? His mind was still inflamed by anger and even though he tried to think clearly and analytically, the debris from his outburst clogged the filter of reason. What the hell was she talking about? Hang on, she'd said something about an investigation. 'There is no investigator coming here,' he said, louder than he would have liked. 'That was all bloody bullshit.'

Again she shut her eyes to ward off the offensive words. 'But I shall get the police. You will all go to prison.'

'What for?'

'The murder of the policeman. Escaping from custody. I know enough to have you all imprisoned for years. I shall go today.'

'Jesus, why?'

'Because of what you've been trying to do to me.'

'But we haven't been doing anything.' He was no longer shouting. He was pleading. He scratched his forehead. This was all his fault. He'd been a fool, doubted good friends, told this mad woman too much. 'Shit, what have I done?' he said.

'You've told me things I needed to know. You've ensured that you will all go to prison. Some of you may even hang. I hope that woman does, for one. And I, despite this elaborate deception of yours, will end up a very rich woman.'

'Like hell you will!'

She raised the poker.

'You'd use that, wouldn't you? You even beat your own mother.'

She lunged at him.

He seized her wrist and the poker, flying from her grip, struck his shoulder. She clawed his face with her free hand.

'You mad bitch!' he shouted and slapped her. Her eyes widened. No one had ever struck her before. She lunged for an iron on the hot plate of the stove.

'No, you don't!' He grabbed her shoulders and flung her against the wall. She hit hard. Beside her, a frying pan jangled on its hook and fell to the floor.

Her gown was torn, exposing half her body. Josef stood above her, fists clenched. The cry of the baby reached him. It was a thin, plaintive sound and its innocence was a world removed from the menace in the room.

Jesus, what am I doing? he thought and turned. He bent to pick up his shirt. His boots were near her. Ignoring her he gathered them, picked up his hat and walked to the door. He was shaking. He had come so close to punching her, and he felt sick.

'Why don't you do the only thing you're good for,' he said, 'and

739

go and stick your tit in the kid's mouth?'

She covered herself with her arms. At the door he paused to put on his shirt. He wiped his scratched cheek. 'Going to town, are you, to tell the police? Well, we'll see what Adam has to say about that.'

The sun had risen.

She got to her feet, trying to pull her torn nightgown back into place. She splashed water on her face. I've gone too far, she told herself. Said too much too soon. They'll stop me. She moved to the doorway. From there, she could see Josef striding to the shed. He disappeared in the shadows of its open front but emerged moments later and walked quickly to the left and out of sight.

She hurried to the bedroom, dressed rapidly and threw some clothes in a bag. She picked up the baby. She took her purse and the whip which she had hidden under the bed. From somewhere to the side of the house an animal was running, splashing through water. She rushed to the door. Josef was on a camel, heading away from the homestead. He was bobbing up and down on its back, looking perilously close to falling but slapping the animal to go faster. Adam must have gone. Josef was looking for him. There was no one outside.

Carrying Cassandra who was screaming with hunger and wet, Heather hurried towards the shed where the Alfa Romeo was garaged. She would drive to William Creek now. She could not stay. As she drew closer to the shed, the shadows formed shapes and she saw the half-caste woman sitting near the car. Painfully, Nellie got to her feet.

'Where's my husband?' Heather demanded.

'He's not here.'

'I can see that, you fool. Where is he?'

'He's gone to check on the creek.'

'What creek?'

'I don't know. He said he wanted to see how much water was in it after the rain.'

'And Josef's gone there too?'

'He's gone looking for him, yes. Why?'

'It's none of your business.' She walked to the other side of the car and put Cassandra on the front seat.

'Where are you going?' Nellie was leaning on the driver's door. Heather walked around the car the whip in her hand.

'I know all about you. Where you've been living. How long

740

you've been here. About killing Mailey. I know the lot, and you're going to prison. By the time I tell my story you could hang.'

'What the hell's been going on? What's Joe been saying?'

'Just get out of my way.' Heather tried to push her but Nellie seized her wrist. She was stronger. Heather pulled back and Nellie, unable to bear weight on her injured leg, fell to the ground.

Heather let the whip uncoil. 'You're the cause of all this trouble,' she said, swinging her arm back. 'You plotted all this, corrupted my husband, and wanted to get rid of me so all this could be yours.'

'Put the whip down,' Nellie said, trying to stand. 'That thing's dangerous.'

'As you'll find out. I'm going to give you a thrashing you'll never forget. Slut. Harlot.' She swung her arms, summoning all her strength for the blow.

The long stockman's whip is a cumbersome implement. To use it properly requires knack and practice. Heather had neither. She brought her hand forward, pulling the plaited handle over her shoulder. The lash trailed along the ground and flicked around her ankle. She gasped, dropped the handle and stumbled foward.

Nellie had been frozen in a defensive crouch with her arms crossed in front of her face in fearful anticipation of the blow. Seeing the whip fall, she crawled foward and grabbed its handle. She pulled hard. The lash was still wrapped around Heather's ankle and the sudden tug upended her.

The two women, on hands and knees, faced each other.

'How would you like a thrashing *you'll* never forget?' Nellie said, and drew the whip's long leather strand behind her.

Heather got to her feet first. She ran behind the car. Slowly, Nellie rose and followed her, limping heavily and trailing the whip from her right hand.

'Have you ever had a belting?' she said. 'After the things you've done to Adam it might do you some good.'

Heather stopped by a pile of loose timber. 'Don't you dare come a step closer!'

'Or what'll you do? Give me the sack?'

Nellie was no more practised at handling the whip than her adversary but at least she had seen it used and knew what should be done. She let the lash trail behind her and brought the whip through in a long and fluent motion. The whip didn't crack but it did strike its target. The end curled around Heather's legs. She screamed and tried to run. She tripped. Nellie, still gripping the handle and off balance from swinging the whip, was pulled forward. She fell, landing on her knee and crying out in pain.

Heather had landed in the timber stack. She scrambled to her feet and rose with a long length of wood in her hands. Nellie was near her, trying to rise but hampered by the stabbing pain in her freshly bloodied knee.

Heather lifted the wood and struck with it, as hard as she could. She aimed at the head but hit across the other woman's back. Nellie slumped forward, unconscious.

Jimmy could hear the starter motor grinding. He walked around the front of the shed. Heather was in the driver's seat. The baby was beside her. She jumped with surprise at seeing him and tried the starter again.

'Have you got the choke out?' he said casually.

She tried to calm herself. When she had first seen him, she assumed he would rush forward and drag her from the seat. But he was just standing there grinning.

'No,' she said, 'I don't know where it is.'

He walked to the car and leaned over the door to reach into the cabin. He pulled out a knob.

'Try it now,' he said and stood back. 'Are you nicking off?'

'I beg your pardon?'

'Are you leaving? Going away? Not coming back?'

The engine whirred into life. The car shook and then smoothed to a regular pulsing vibration.

'Why?' she said, pushing the lever into gear. 'Are you going to stop me?'

'No fear. I just hope you get through.'

'What do you mean?'

'There's been a lot of rain.'

'Well, it's stopped raining now, in case you hadn't noticed.'

'And you're off to town?'

She was not frightened of him any more. He was a harmless idiot just standing there grinning.

'I am,' she said, 'and I hope I never see any of you again.'

He stared at her, not believing his luck. He had been wondering how to get rid of her and here she was driving off.

The car jerked forward and almost stalled. 'You're in third gear,' he said, smiling broadly, and enjoyed her embarrassment. She crunched the lever into first.

'Just leave the Alfa at the station,' he said. 'I'll get it in a day or two.'

Jerking in a series of kangaroo hops, the car left the shed. Jimmy watched her take the track to William Creek. The car passed the beefwood tree and splashed through a long and shallow pool of water. He heard the driver change gear and select fourth by mistake, but the car kept going, its engine chugging until the sound was lost in the distance.

Adam and Joe will be surprised, he thought. They'd gone down to see if the creek was up. When she goes thundering past, they will get one hell of a shock. Grinning at the prospect, he turned.

He saw Nellie.

TWENTY

Heavy rain had fallen in the country around William Creek. The creek which gave the town its name, a short and easily overlooked watercourse that normally consisted of a sandy and rocky bed meandering south towards a small salt lake, was now up and roaring, chewing its banks and spreading wide across the flat country. To the north, even more rain had fallen and longer creeks like the George, the Davenport, the Douglas and the Cooinchina were all in flood. The Douglas ran through Kalinda. It passed to the south of the homestead, cutting the track to William Creek and eventually running into Halligan Bay on the western side of Lake Eyre.

Adam was at the Douglas. He had ridden to the place he had often crossed in the car. The transformation was total. What was normally a series of sandy grooves that wound along the creek bed and into the shade of the gnarled trees was now a boiling torrent which stretched more than a hundred yards to the nearest firm ground. The water surged past Adam with the speed of a cantering horse. The flood was brown and violent and booming. Dead trees, broken branches and uprooted salt bush bobbed past on their voyage from one point of desolation to another.

He rode upstream to higher ground where there was timber and a little grass for the mare. There he dismounted and marvelled at the sight. It was awe-inspiring: a sight one might see perhaps every ten or twenty years. It would not last. By tonight he reckoned the creek would be down. By tomorrow it would be reduced to a stream trickling through the deepest channel. Within three days, the only water remaining would be in ponds and then merely in the deepest, shadiest places. By the end of the summer, the creek would be as dry and powdery as ever.

But for now, the Douglas was running and spreading. The earth could drink its fill. Grass and top feed would flourish. He sat down for a while and watched the brown stain spread into the distance, and thought. No matter what he did, how much he tried or what miracles he accomplished, it would always be this way: nature would be in control, taking her own wilful path just as surely as that flood scouring its way towards the rising sun and the distant lake. Dust storms could bury him. Droughts could scorch his miserable pastures. Floods could carry away his richest soil. Or he could have unending seasons of gentle sun and generous rains. He would do his best but, ultimately, nature would decree whether he succeeded or not.

He was happy with that. He was comfortable with nature, no matter how wayward her moods. He could endure heat, cold, wind or rain, hardship and suffering, because, eventually, things changed. Nature had balance.

People did not. He could sit on a rise like this, watching a creek rage in flood and feel good, knowing that despite the power, the violence, the threat, there was good being done. Beneath all the swirling and uprooting, water was soaking into the ground, and that was life. But people raged and tore up things – important things, like friendships – and no good came of it. Deluged by greed or anger and caught in the whirlpools of jealousy or pride, they spun off at impossible tangents, did hurtful things to each other and, not knowing why they had behaved as they did, were unable to correct the damage they had caused. To others and to themselves.

Josef was approaching the crossing, looking as always, as though he was about to fall from the camel. Adam stood and waved. The camel turned towards him.

Josef was on Bozo. He ordered him down but began dismounting too soon and was pitched on to his face. Adam stood back, allowing him to rise unaided. He was still angry from the previous night and prepared himself for some fresh onslaught.

Josef got up, brushing himself with violent sweeps of his arms. To his astonishment Adam noticed that Josef was weeping. His anger vanished.

'Oh, Jesus, Joe, what's up?'

Roughly, Josef wiped his face. One cheek was scratched. He prepared to speak, gulped and turned towards the camel. Adam approached, sensed the barrier of embarrassment, and stopped.

'I've been a bloody idiot,' Josef said and wiped his face again. 'Do you know what she's going to do?'

'Who?'

'Your wife. Heather. She's going to the police.'

'What about?' Adam asked, fearing he knew the answer.

'Mailey. She knows the whole story. I told her. I didn't mean to.' He turned suddenly 'She's a cunning bitch! She was pretending she knew and getting me to say things. Oh, shit, I'm such a fool!'

'Who isn't? Specially when she's around.'

Josef tried to smile. 'She called me a boy. God, she sounded just like my father.' He attempted a laugh which stalled in his throat.

'What's she going to do?'

'I don't know. Probably go into town.'

'Well, she won't be going there for a day or two.' Adam jerked his thumb towards the creek.

'Christ!' Josef said, noticing the extent of the flood for the first time. 'Adam, I hit her.'

'What?'

'This morning. When I realized what she'd been doing I got angry and she waved a poker at me and I pushed her and she fell real hard.'

'Is she all right?'

He nodded. 'I think I gave her a hell of a scare. Did you ever hit her?'

'No.'

'She said you did.'

Adam shrugged.

'I want you to know I never slept with her.'

'That's all right.'

'No. It's not. I wanted to. I'm ashamed to say it, but I wanted to sleep with your wife.'

'So did I.'

'What do you mean?'

'Well, it wasn't my idea to sleep near the stove.'

'But she said ... oh, I see. More bull. Jesus Christ, she fed me a lot of it.'

'Tell me more about Mailey and the police. What's she going to do?'

'Get the cops. Have you arrested. Have us all arrested. She's talking about hanging. She's mad, Adam, stark raving nuts!'

'Was she serious?'

'Deadly serious. Bloody hell, here she comes!' Josef had seen the car.

The Alfa-Romeo was still a long way from the crossing. It sparkled in the early light, a black and red beetle on a panorama of shadowed sand and long, glittering pools of rainwater. The car was travelling slowly and weaving between the chain of puddles that lapped the track.

They could see Heather at the wheel. Josef groaned. 'She's going to do it. She's going for the police.'

'Well, she won't get far. There's six feet of water in the creek.'

'I'm going to stop her anyhow,' Josef said and began to run towards the track. His sudden action frightened the mare, which reared and swung towards the camel. Bozo lurched upright. Adam ran to the horse, making soothing sounds, and grabbed the reins. Then he calmed the camel. By this time Josef was halfway to the crossing. He was running wildly with his arms waving, shouting to ensure the driver noticed him.

Adam mounted the mare with the camel in tow and began to descend the rise. He was in no hurry. Heather would have to stop. Josef would do a lot of shouting. Heather would argue. He was sick of all the fighting and would let things quieten down before reaching them. He reined the mare to a halt and watched.

Josef reached the track and stood at the edge of the flooded creek. He folded his arms, spread his legs and took a deep breath. He looked formidable. He waited.

Heather stopped the car twenty yards from him.

'Get out of my way!' Adam heard her shout.

'You're not going anywhere,' Josef called out. 'The creek's in flood. You can't cross. Get out of the car.'

'I will not.'

'Then I'll drag you out.'

Adam dug his heels into the mare's flanks. He didn't want them fighting again. 'Hang on, Joe,' he called but Josef was already moving towards the car. He walked slowly, each step an ultimatum to obey his order or suffer the consequences.

Adam heard the engine beat rise to a snarl, heard Heather shout something – the words were lost in the noise – and saw the rear wheels spin as she floored the accelerator. The car seemed to leap at Josef. Surprised by the sudden move, he had time only to stop and lift his arms in a vain attempt to protect himself. The radiator hit him squarely in the body. His head and shoulders snapped forward across the bonnet. One arm grabbed a headlight stay. His right leg was bent up and clear of the ground; the other dragged beneath the car.

Still jerking from the rough start, the car accelerated towards the creek. Heather had lost control but near the water she braked hard and the engine stalled and the front wheels slid into the water. Josef was catapulted into the flood.

Adam dropped the camel's lead and galloped down the hill. He saw Heather half rise in her seat, sit down again and try to restart the motor. Still in gear, the car stuttered forward, rolling the front wheels further into the water. She pushed at the gear lever. Flustered and looking at Adam riding towards her, she tried again. The motor fired.

Josef, winded or hurt, tried to stand but couldn't straighten his body and fell back into the water. He was swept away.

Adam was close to the car now. Its wheels spun in the wet sand, then gripped. Heather had the steering wheel turned and the Alfa spun in a wild semicircle. He saw her face, white with anxiety. He saw a flurry of clothing as Cassie, on the front seat, was thrown to the floor. He saw Josef's hand and head above the brown torrent.

He galloped past the car.

He took the mare wide of the creek to dodge a clump of bushes. They leaped a fallen tree trunk, floundered in deep mud, and when they were clear and he could look back to the creek there was no sign of Josef. He could see a bush bobbing in the churning current and behind it a thick branch with one limb poking high in the air like a bent mast. On the branch was a hand. He saw the head. It rose briefly. A mouth gasped for air. A wave curled over the head.

Adam jumped while the mare was still running, hit the ground, stumbled and waded into the creek. The force was unbelievable. He tried to make for the middle of the steam but his legs were whisked from under him and he was on his back and rolling. He was not an elegant or fast swimmer but he was strong. He fought to right himself in the rush of water and with high powerful strokes tried to swim towards the middle. He was ahead of the branch but in a different stream. There were several currents in the flood. He swam through one and entered a region of swirling waters and spun and submerged and came up choking. It was chaos in that current. The water curled and dipped and reared as it plunged along the defined course of the creek, and spilled wide to tear through clumps of bushes and over gullies and past trees whose straining branches cut low waves of foaming brown. For every stroke Adam gained in his struggle to swim to the middle, he was swept ten times that distance to the side. He ran aground once and used the higher ground to leap, in a crude belly-buster of a dive, further into the current, to put him on the same course as Josef.

Six hard strokes and the branch was bearing towards him, not tumbling but staying constant with the bent limb pointing skywards. That meant, he hoped, that Josef still had hold of it.

The current whirled and carried Adam backwards. He was swept into rougher water, upended and swallowed beneath the surface. He hit something with his shoulder. He was spun upside down. He came to the surface gasping for air and swallowed water. Coughing and spluttering, he went under again. He came up flailing the water, breathed deeply and got air.

The branch was almost beside him. He seized it, saw Josef's arm and reached for where he thought the head should be. He grabbed hair. The head shook violently. With one hand holding the hair as high as he could, he thrust for the bank.

He would probably not have made it but for the current sweeping them both into a tree across whose trunk was wedged a large log. He caught the log with his free arm and they swung into a calm area behind the tree. There were stones there and he was able to stand.

It took him five minutes to establish that Josef was alive and another five to carry him on his shoulders through shallower water to the bank. His face was cut and his mouth had the taste of mud and blood. He whistled the mare and sat down, feeling too weak to stand. Josef had fallen where Adam had unloaded him from his shoulders. He was lying on his face with his head downhill. Muddy water ran from his mouth.

Adam slapped him on the back. Josef's hands, outstretched and almost touching the water, twitched. Adam slapped his back again and again.

Josef coughed.

The mare came part of the way but, frightened by the roar of water, stopped well clear of the bank. By now, Josef was trying to sit up. Adam helped him to his feet and, half dragging, half carrying him, brought him to the horse.

'Got to be sick, mate,' Josef mumbled and slumped to his knees and was sick. After a couple of minutes he stood. 'Can't ride,' he said, but allowed Adam to lift him into the saddle. 'Ribs are sore,' he said, and coughed and slumped across the horse's mane.

Adam climbed up behind him and took the mare at a slow walk with his arms on either side of his friend to stop him falling. They returned to the crossing.

The car had gone.

'How are you feeling?'

Nellie felt the bump on the back of her head. A pain like fire ran across her back and her neck was so sore it hurt to move her head. Her knee throbbed.

'Not bad,' she said.

'Like some water?' Jimmy said and offered her a can.

'Thanks.' She drank but spilled much of it. She could not stop shaking.

'What happened?'

'I'm not too sure. That mad woman, Adam's wife, tried to hit me with the whip.' She drank more water. 'Must have hit me with something else.'

He grinned. 'You were lying under a length of four by two. I'd like to have seen it.'

'Why?' She lowered herself to the ground. He squatted beside her.

'Never seen a white sheila fight a black one.'

'The wrong one lost,' she said.

He took the can and drank until it was empty.'Want some more?' he said.

'No thanks.'

'What are you doing here anyway?'

'Working. At least I was. I got the sack ... again.'

Their eyes met. Jimmy looked away.

'Why do you hate me?' she said.

'Don't hate you.'

'Yes, you do. You got me sacked by Gooly, didn't you?'

The shoulders twitched. That was the only concession he made to the accusation.

'I know you did. Why?'

'You're trouble.'

'Well, Jesus, who isn't?' She struggled to sit up again. 'Anyhow, trouble for who?'

'You know.' He got up and walked out with the water can in his hand. He came back with it full and passed it to her. 'Here, have some more.'

'I don't want any.'

'Yes, you do. It'll help you cool down,' He grinned. It was a peace offering. 'What happened to your leg? Did Adam's missus do that too?'

'No. Dingo.' She told him the story.

He squatted again. 'She reckoned you were trying to steal the kid.'

'I wasn't, but I wish I had.'

'She's gone, you know.'

Only then did Nellie realize the car was missing. 'Where to?' she asked, looking around her.

'Town. Hope she makes it.'

'What do you mean?'

'I hope she gets there and she doesn't come back. The creek might be too high for her to get through, but.'

'What'll happen then?'

'She'll come back. Did you really kill a dingo with a rock?'

She nodded and winced. Her neck hurt.

'I'd like to have seen that,' he said.

'That was one fight the right one won,' she said and returned his smile.

Jimmy scratched the earth. 'About what happened at William Creek ...' he said.

'Just don't tell me you didn't mean to do it.'

'Oh, I meant it all right. I felt crook about it afterwards though.'

'Good. So did I.'

'Look, I'm trying to say I'm sorry.'

'Can I have some water now?' He passed her the can.

'How'd you get here anyhow?'

'I'd just been sacked. Joe brought her to town. She gave me a job.'

He laughed. 'Been better if I'd said nothing.'

'You should try it sometime. It'd be a good habit to get into. Jesus, Jimmy what were you trying to do?'

'Stop people getting hurt.'

'Who?'

He let the question fade before answering. 'Adam.'

'You mean Jimmy Kettle.'

He stood and walked to the pile of wood scattered by Heather. He began stacking pieces against the wall. 'It's not right, you and Adam,' he said eventually.

'Why? Because of his wife?'

He laughed. 'No. Not any more. It just never works.'

'Because he's white and I'm not?'

'Didn't work for you, did it? You've never seen your old man. It never works, Nellie. A white bloke who shacks up with a gin ends up a drunk or pisses off and leaves her with a couple of brindle kids.'

'Like me.'

'It's true and you know it. Everyone treats them both like garbage and the bloke ends up not being able to take it and shoots through.'

'Do you reckon Adam would?'

'Are you thinking of staying? Seriously?'

'Maybe.'

'How's Adam feel about it?'

'The same.'

He turned from the stack of timber. 'You are in trouble, aren't you?'

'Yes. We'll need good friends.'

He grunted. Agreeing. Disagreeing. She couldn't tell.

'All the whites will hate you. And you know what they'll do to Adam. You'd better be good company for him because he won't have anyone else.'

'Why? Where are you going?'

He raised an eyebrow. 'Me? I guess I'll be around.'

'Well, that's someone we can talk to. Will you talk to me?'

'Don't know,' he said. 'At least I'll give you this. You'd be a mile better for him than that fair-headed devil he married.'

'Anyone would be better ...' she began and stopped. She could hear a horse approaching.

The car was bogged.

Heather had been driving east straight into the morning sun. She had come a long way, avoiding the worst pools of water and the deeper mud patches. The car had skimmed easily over the damp sand. East, the one-armed blackfellow had said. Just go in the direction of the rising sun and you'd come to the lake. She couldn't cross the flooded creek. She couldn't return to the homestead. She had to go to the other house. It was a place where she could hide. Where she could regain her composure after the simply dreadful things that had happened to her that morning. She had outwitted Adam and his gang but they would come looking for her. She would get to this house on the island in the middle of the lake, and lock herself in. She could find out what was there, gain more information to use against the others and then, when the water level in the creek had dropped, drive back into town and get the police.

But the country had become drier as she drove east, and now the car was stuck in sand. She had wasted an hour trying to extricate it. Cassandra was crying.

'Honestly, if that child cries once more,' she said to herself not silently, for she needed the comfort of her own voice in such an empty place, 'I will just leave her in the car and walk away. Maybe I should walk anyhow. The lake must be nearby. I have been driving for simply ages.'

The sand which had snared the car was beside a low hill. She walked to it and started to climb. The hillside was gravelly and she slipped many times, but even before reaching the top she saw a sight which made her heart pound with excitement. The lake. It was a blistering white strip visible beyond the next low ridge. She scrambled to the top.

Now she could see the edge of the lake. It had bands of colour. Reds, browns, greys. Some of the colours were in neat parallel rows. Others broke away in swirls. There were hillocks of sand with clumps of vegetation. Gutters of mud, as kinked as lizard's tails, ran to the edge.

She searched for an island but it was difficult to see anything clearly beyond the shoreline because the salt was so white that to stare at the distance was to be blinded by the glare. Still, she assured herself, it can't be far. I shall walk. There may be some person living out there, a caretaker perhaps. I shall get him to come back for the car.

She descended the hill, collected Cassandra and began walking to the lake.

The sand was so soft that walking was difficult. She took short steps and expended much energy. She was thirsty. There should be water at the lake. Adam had said it was a dry lake but goodness knows what that meant. It seemed an absurd contradiction in terms, like a wet desert. He was probably lying to her. There would be water there. There had to be. It was a lake. In any case, it had rained.

She rounded the last ridge and saw a pool. Putting the baby on the ground, she hurried to it and knelt to drink. The edge was rimmed with white. Reaching beyond that to where the water was clear, she scooped some in her hand and drank.

It burnt her mouth. She fell back, coughing and retching. She tried to claw the taste from her lips. It was so salty that it ate into her like an acid.

The child was crying. She stood up and wanted to scream at the baby. What are you crying about! You're not the one who's burnt or poisoned. You're not in agony. But no sound emerged.

She was giddy and sank to her knees. They had not mentioned these poisoned pools. They knew she would drink. They might have poisoned the water themselves. That was it, she thought, clutching her throat. They had poisoned the water at several places, knowing she would drink and die.

Well, she would not die. They would. They would hang. She would tell the police what they had done and the police would hang them all. For murdering Mailey, for attacking her with the whip, for poisoning the water.

A thought occurred to her. They might already be dead. Josef had fallen in the creek. Clumsy man! He had fallen; she had nothing to do with it. He had tried to attack her and then fallen in the water. Adam had jumped in after him. She had seen that before driving away. She had been frightened at the time; frightened that they would stop her and pull her from the car and hurt her, and she had only been concerned with getting away. But Josef was definitely in the water and Adam had gone in too. They might both have drowned. Was that possible? The water was flowing extremely fast. They could have drowned. If Adam was dead, if Josef was dead, then that only left that ridiculous blackfellow and the half-caste girl. She could handle them. No one would listen to them anyhow. That meant the property was hers. She could sell it. Be a rich, rich woman. Live in Sydney. Have the sort of life she was meant to lead.

Oh God, she thought, staring up at the bleached sky, was it too much to hope that Adam and Joe were dead? Please. Please. It would make things so much easier.

She felt sick. Her throat and mouth were burning. She had to have a drink. The house on the lake would have water.Lovely, cool, fresh water. She had to get there quickly.

She gathered Cassandra and shook her to stop her crying but it didn't work. The baby screamed. She put the child under one arm. She was too weak, too hurt, to carry her properly and she staggered down to the lake's edge. She needed water quickly. She walked on to the salt. Avoiding the muddy patches, she followed a path where the surface was white and covered in chain wire patterns of brilliant crystals.

Where was the house? She could not see anything clearly. The lake was a mirror, dazzling her. Eyes narrowed against the glare, she tried to hurry. The child was such a burden. The salt beneath her feet began to sway. She must be imagining it. She was about to faint, that was it. She needed water.

The salt cracked and one foot went into mud. She dragged it out. The salt was swaying and breaking. She was not imagining it, not about to faint. The lake bed was moving. She tried to run. Another foot broke through the crust. It went up to the ankle in mud that was blue-black and thick and stuck like half-dried glue. She dragged her foot clear but lost the shoe. She reached down for it. The mud felt revolting. There was a crack, like a plate breaking, and a whole patch of salt broke into squares. The other foot sank in mud.

It was impossible with Cassandra. She put the baby down and, bracing herself on her hands, dragged her feet clear. She took a step, and went down to the shin. The mud was a disgusting colour. She rubbed her hands. They were coated in slime and salt crystals, as sharp and cutting as glass fragments.

She was filthy. Her clothes were now covered in mud, her hands were stinging from small cuts and her leg was wedged in place. With all her strength she tried to drag herself clear. The more she struggled, the more she was trapped. The leg sank to the knee and then, with a plopping of mud and pulverized salt, it disappeared and she was tilted to one side with one leg deep in a hole and the other spread out at an awkward angle.

With great difficulty, she bent the other leg and tried to push down to drag herself out. The free leg broke through the salt. She struggled and wriggled and pushed and succeeded only in boring herself deeper into the mud. She was now buried up to the hips. She could not turn. It hurt to bend. She pounded the salt crust and broke it into smaller fragments. She kept pounding until she was surrounded by a moat of churned mud.

She tried to twist, to reach back for Cassandra, but the baby was beyond her fingertips.

Terrified now, she could feel herself sliding beneath the surface.

The mud was squeezing her. Her feet, were cold and numb. She tried to move them. There was no feeling down there. Just the cold. In a frenzy she thrashed her arms, driving her body deeper. Her chest hurt.

A jagged edge of salt touched her chin.

She heard someone call her name.

TWENTY-ONE

Adam looped his knee across the saddle and searched in another direction. He called again. The young camel shuffled in the sand, reacting to the movement as Adam twisted once more, looking for any sign of Heather or the baby. He let the camel walk around the deserted car.

'Heather!' he shouted.

'She's not going to answer,' Jimmy said, lounging on the saddle of Rumble, 'I don't know why you want her back anyhow. Let her go. It'd be good riddance.'

'She's got Cassie.'

'The kid'll be all right.'

'Not with her.'

Jimmy scratched his head. 'You're probably right. OK. I'll see what I can find.' He dismounted and began searching for tracks.

Adam rode towards the flat-topped hill. 'She went up here,' he called excitedly. Jimmy walked over. He examined the ground for a few minutes.

'She came down again,' Jimmy said and followed the trail back to the car. 'Then she went that way.' He pointed beyond the front of the car. 'Do you want to let her sit in the sun for a while and stew a bit? It might calm her down.'

'Not with Cassie. The kid's been through too much already,' Adam stood in the saddle and shielded his eyes against the glare. He had lost his hat in the creek. 'What I can't work out is why she came out this way. We must be almost on the lake.'

Jimmy had been leading his camel and walking with his head bent to observe the trail. He stopped suddenly. 'The lake? I bet that's it.' A grin spread across his face.

Adam, riding beside him, looked down. 'What is?'

'Oh, when I saw her last night, she was going on about Nellie. You know what she's like.'

'And what happened?'

'Well, I got a bit sick of it all. She kept on hammering me about where Nellie had been living and about this other house you were supposed to have built.' He saw some footprints and was silent while he followed them.

'And?'

'And I'd had a bellyfull of all her nonsense, so I said the house was out in the middle of the lake.' The grin grew wider. 'And she swallowed it. Adam, that sheila of yours might be educated but she's got no more brains than a wombat. I bet she's gone looking for the house.'

Adam spurred Bozo into a run.

'Oh Jesus,' Jimmy grumbled and kept walking. His camel carried a load of rope, water and cans of petrol and it was simpler to walk than bring the animal down and climb on board with all the gear. It wasn't worth hurrying, he reckoned. They could just as easily have stayed at the house for a few hours and had something to eat. Better still, wait for a day or two. The kid wouldn't go hungry but the woman might get a real fright and that would serve her right. Then Adam could pick her up and give her a belting and dump her on the train. She deserved to be given a hard time, particularly after doing what she had to Nellie and Joe. She could have killed them both. Those two were back at the homestead looking after each other, not that either of them could do much. Nellie was fussing around Joe and trying to do things for him even though she must have been in a lot of pain. Jimmy couldn't make Nellie out. Maybe he'd been wrong about her all along.

Adam, who had ridden out of sight around the next ridge, suddenly reappeared. He yelled to Jimmy and rode off again. Jimmy couldn't understand the message but there was sufficient urgency in Adam's manner to suggest he should get on the camel and find out what was happening. He guessed Adam had seen his wife and was chasing her. Might be fun. He brought the camel down and climbed into the saddle.

At first, Adam hadn't seen Cassie. He had ridden around the ridge and, seeing the lake, had stopped to search for any sign of a figure. By now the day was well advanced, and mirages played on its surface. Painstakingly he checked the lake, section by shimmering section. It took time, for it was a place where the immobile wavered and the flat and wide became narrow and tall. A headland to the north confused him because the rising heat vapours cut it into a picket fence of greys and whites and any one of its tantalizing shades could have been a human. Then from the overwhelming stillness of the lake, he heard Cassie. It was her distinctive cry. He searched for its source. There was something near the shore at the end of a line of black smudges. The lake was peppered with mounds but this was different.

He wheeled the camel, called to Jimmy, and raced for the lake. The ground became soft. He cut across a salt pool and the camel's legs sprayed flakes of white crystals. Near the shore, Bozo balked and tried to turn away. Adam smacked its rump and the camel snapped at him. He tried to calm it and to prod it into moving but the animal would not budge. It wheezed nervously.

Adam slid to the ground. He could see Cassie clearly. She was on the salt and on her back. And on her own. Surely Heather hadn't left her again? The sun was fierce. The child could be dying. He ran, not thinking, and pounded on to the salt. Only as he neared her did he clearly notice the other marks: small black islands in a broken sea of white.

His foot plunged through, striking mud, and he realized what he was doing. In a salt lake the crust was thickest towards the middle where the lake bed was at its lowest because most sediment, from which the salt was formed, settled there. At the shore line the bed was at its highest and so the salt was thin. He dragged his foot from the glutinous gypsum mud and slowed his pace, but the damage had been done. Around him the thin skin of salt jelly-wobbled and cracked into long jagged fractures.

Ahead of him, Cassie kicked her legs. He called out to her and he heard her make a noise and saw her kick again. He managed another step. The foot went deeper into the mud. Both feet were in now. He'd heard of animals bogging and drowning in mud. What was it Tiger had said? They thrashed around and only drove themselves further into the bog, which then sucked them down. The stuff was like axle grease. It had no bottom. Just an underground ocean of black ooze as deadly as quicksand.

The thing to do was not panic. He stopped moving and waited. His feet were stuck but he wasn't sinking. Slowly he leaned forward until his hands were on the salt. As gently as he could, he withdrew one foot from the mud. Resting on that knee, he extracted the other foot. He lowered himself to the surface and spread his arms and legs and waited to see what happened. Nothing. He was not breaking through, not sinking. He tried leaning on his elbows. All right. He crawled forward.

Near the baby the salt was badly broken. Just beyond was a ragged opening in the crust. From it projected slivers of salt as sharp as pieces of shattered plate glass.

Adam crawled towards the broken area and felt his elbows sink. He squirmed a retreat and tried from another angle. Again he began to slip into the mud.

Cassie was kicking and waving her arms. Stay still, he muttered. She was on top of the salt because she was light and because she was on her back. She was whimpering.

'Just stay there,' he said. 'Daddy'll be with you in minute.'

She started to howl.

'Cassie, it's all right.'

She rolled over. She could do that now. He'd played with her at nights, encouraged her to roll and told her what a clever girl she was, and now, when it was vital that she stayed on her back, she rolled on her front and faced him. Her face was red and streaked with dry tears. She pushed and immediately her hands were buried in mud. Her chin touched the black slime and she arched up screaming. Pushing more, her arms tunnelled beneath the surface.

Adam slithered to her, breaking through the salt but not caring. He plucked her from the mud and lifted her clear. The extra weight drove him down.

Jesus, I'm going to sink in this stuff, he thought, and I'm going to take my little girl with me. He remembered Jimmy and screamed his name. The answer seemed to come from a long way. With difficulty he turned to look, for his chest was in the mud. Jimmy was edging towards him, carrying the tow rope.

'Do you want a hand?' Jimmy shouted. 'I've only got one but you're welcome to it.' The teeth flashed encouragement. He stopped where the surface was still safe and cast the rope.

The first throw landed short. Adam tasted mud. He had Cassie above his head and the strained action drove his face down.

The second throw landed across his back. He twisted, hooked one arm around the rope and let Jimmy haul them clear. It was a slow, exhausting journey, for Lake Eyre yielded its victims reluctantly.

Only when he was near a spit of sand did Adam dare stand. He spat out mud and wiped his eyes.

'Crikey, mate, you're looking more like me every day,' Jimmy said, trying to joke, but his face had the pallor of intense shock.

'Heather must have left her there,' Adam said, the words rushing out to overwhelm his fear. He had seen that awful black hole. He held the baby tightly. Jimmy turned away.

'Can you see where she went?' It was a plea for a miracle.

Jimmy looked back. 'Mate,' he said, making an effort to control his voice, 'I tracked her all the way to the edge. Those are her marks in the salt. There's no track out.'

'Oh, Jesus, no, Jimmy!' Adam turned to go back.

'Where do you think you're going?'

'I've got to look!'

'She's gone, mate. You'd never find her.'

They scouted the shoreline in case there were other tracks. Adam went back out on the salt, holding the rope with Jimmy on the other end. He searched for clothing, marks on the salt, anything. He let his leg dip into the mud and probed as deep as he dared until Jimmy screamed at him to come back.

After an hour they left the shore and went to the ridge. Adam marked the spot by piling a few stones together. When he had finished he walked a long way, to a place where a low cliff cast shadows towards the shore.

Jimmy waited and closed his eyes, not wanting to intrude on his friend's misery. He heard the whirr of insects, the cry of birds and the sound of sobbing, echoing from the distant cliff.

It was a starry night. They had made a fire on a flat, sandy patch between the house and the spring and they sat around the flames late into the night. The fire was huge, an extravagant sacrifice of precious wood, but it was bright and warm and pure and the fierce light helped banish the horror of the day.

'It was my fault,' Jimmy repeated. He was nursing the dingo pups. His sheepdog slept near his feet.

'No, it wasn't,' Adam said. They were the same words he had used a dozen times before. He was hunched forward, not moving, staring into the flames.

'I made up that silly story.'

Josef moved closer to the fire and threw another dead branch into the flames. 'She wanted to believe it,' he said.

'But I knew salt lakes were dangerous. The old people in my tribe used to tell stories about them. They wouldn't go near the edge. Reckoned there were monsters living there, or some crap like that. The only monster was the mud. Like bloody quicksand. I've seen cattle die in them and yet I told her that bloody silly story and she believed me and tried to walk on the bloody stuff.'

'She wasn't rational,' Josef said, standing so close to the mesmerizing flames that he had to blink to stop his eyes being scorched.

'What's that mean?'

'She wasn't thinking clearly.'

'Neither are you. You'll get burnt.'

Josef turned away, the skin on his face tight from the heat. 'No one's fault,' he said. 'But it was a bugger of a thing to happen. Thank God the baby's safe. She all right?'

Nellie was nursing Cassie. She was sitting beside Adam, not touching him but within comforting distance. She had made food for Cassie and the baby slept on her lap. 'Hasn't stirred for two hours,' she said.

'Must like you,' Jimmy said and stroked the pups.

Still standing, but with his back to the fire, Josef said: 'I think I might go back south for a while.'

Adam looked up.

'If you can do without me, that is,' Josef said.

'How are you feeling?' Adam hadn't enquired since returning from the lake.

'Fine. It's not that. It's just that I've been thinking. It wasn't nice, the way I left my mother. And my father too, for that matter. I should go back and see them. Make friends again. You know what I mean.'

'Sure. You'll come back?'

'Christ, yes.'

Christ. Every time I hear that word, Adam thought, I'll think of her. Christ. Jesus. God. Words of love, and yet when I hear them now I'll think of someone who hated me. Or did she? God knows. I mean, who knows? I can't think about her. Not now. Not yet. Maybe later. Maybe I'll understand better at some other time.

He stared at the brightest part of the flames.

'Your parents were nice people,' Nellie was saying. 'I liked them both. And you ought to give your father a fair go, Joe. I'm sure he loves you.'

'Yeah. He's got a funny way of showing it, though.'

'A lot of people don't show the things they feel.'

'Yeah.' He coughed. 'Jesus, I can still taste the creek. What about you, Jimmy? Want to come south for a while?'

Jimmy held up the pups. 'Who'd look after these?'

'I'd look after them for you,' Nellie offered.

'Yeah?' He pulled the legs from under one and let its needle-sharp teeth bite his finger in retaliation. His eyes wandered towards Nellie and they almost said 'thanks'. He tipped the pup on its back. 'And what if I left? Who'd run this place?'

'I hadn't thought of that,' Josef said, looking earnestly at Adam. 'Will you be able to manage if I go home for a while?'

Jimmy chipped in. 'Listen, mate, with what we'll save on food by not having to feed you, I reckon we could buy another five hundred head of sheep. That's if you stay away six months.'

'I'll stay for a year and you can get another thousand.'

Jimmy concentrated on the dogs. 'No, go and see your people but don't be too long.'

'Jesus, Jimmy, you're not trying to say you're going to miss me?'

'No, I just want to see you trying to ride a camel again. Why don't you go to bed? You look so pale you could make a living renting yourself out to haunt houses.'

Josef threw a twig at Jimmy. 'I might go to bed all the same. Adam, can I come with you when you go to town?'

'Of course.' Adam intended driving to William Creek to report Heather's death. He didn't know whom to tell. There was no policeman. Maybe the stationmaster. Nothing could be done. It was just that people had to know – Heather's mother, people who knew her, people who didn't. He had no idea what he should say. 'My wife thought there was a house in the middle of the lake and tried to walk there. My wife tried to drown my friend by knocking him into a flooded creek and then drove off and we never saw her again. My wife started to whip the girl who works in the house, the girl who's going to look after the baby. My wife was mad, you see, and drowned in the mud.'

What could he say? Something simple. Something people would believe, and that wouldn't shock too much. He would think of the words tomorrow – words that would make his wife sound like a normal, loving wife who had just died a normal, rotten, horrible death.

'I'll have to go tomorrow, though,' he added. 'I think I should do that straight away but the trouble is your train doesn't go for two days.'

'That's all right. I'll have a good look around town.' He walked to Adam and ruffled his hair. 'By the way, thanks for what you did this morning.'

'Forget it.'

'Yeah, forget it,' Jimmy said. 'You needed a bath, both of you.' He stood, nursing the pups in the crook of his arm. 'I'm going to bed too. You all right now, mate?'

'I'm OK,' Adam said. 'Thanks for everything.'

'No worries. See you in the morning.'

Adam and Nellie stayed at the fire. The flames diminished and they moved closer.

'Cassie hasn't stirred,' she said. 'She must like me.'

Adam was looking at the stars. They seemed brighter now the flames had died. Orion the hunter was above them, his shining belt and sword miraculously straight as ever. He was thinking of other times. 'You'd have liked my father,' he said.

'Would I?'

'He used to tell me all about the stars. We used to sit like this with the fire going out and stare up at the sky, and talk.'

'It was good?'

'Yes.'

'Would you tell me about the stars?'

'What I can remember.'

'I'd like that. I'd like us to spend our nights out in the open, looking at the stars.'

Cassie's foot projected from her blanket. Adam stroked it. Instinctively the foot curled back. Nellie covered it.

'She doesn't look like you,' she said, studying the baby's face. 'Does she look like your father?'

'No.'

'Your mother?'

'I don't remember what my mother looked like. She parted her hair in the middle – I remember that. That's all. Silly, isn't it, how you remember little things. My father used to say she was beautiful.'

'I didn't know my father. We make a good pair.' And without pausing, she added: 'Adam, would you like me to go away?'

He looked surprised. 'No.'

'For a little while, maybe.'

'Why?'

'I thought it might be better.'

'No. I don't want you to go. I couldn't stand that.'

'There'll be problems.'

'There always are.'

'People will talk.'

'Not the people I care about.'

'It's going to be hard, Adam.'

'I'll need help,' he said, and reached for her hand.

Adam slept. He was sore and stiff and drifted uncomfortably into the familiar dream. He was following a woman in the dress he remembered from the old photograph. She had her back to him and was walking – no, floating – away from him. No matter how much he hurried, he was unable to make up ground. They walked through dark places and, although he tried to run, he could not reduce the distance between them.

As always, he could not see her clearly. She was a shape, rounded by a hint of lost memories. He became distressed. For the first time in his dreams, he stopped the pursuit. A strange thing happened. The woman reached a patch of brightness where sun streamed upon her in a shaft of intense whiteness and, very slowly, she turned. And he knew who she was. He could not distinguish features – her eyes lay behind a radiant glow and her hair was an outline of light with no colour – but he knew her. His mother had turned and was smiling and stretching out a hand and exuding love. He was a small boy again, and he smiled up at her.

'What's up?' The voice woke him. Nellie stroked his cheek, her face concerned but prepared to smile. 'Are you all right?' she whispered. She was nursing the baby, who slept with one tiny white hand clasped around Nellie's brown finger.

The fire had degenerated to a jumble of grey ash and red embers. A solitary row of flames, feeble and yellow, fluttered from the ruins of a burnt branch.

'You were talking in your sleep.' Her hand stayed against his cheek.

He rubbed his eyes. 'What was I saying?'

'Nothing I could understand. You were mumbling. You seemed happy, though.'

He gripped her hand and kissed the palm. 'I am.'

'Good,' she said. No more than that. She was saying you can tell me more if you want to, but you don't have to, and Adam smiled. He liked that. Dreams were private things. His was a child's dream, a silly fantasy. He felt good, but he didn't want to talk.

'Can I hold Cassie?'

Carefully, as though not trusting his grip, she gave him the baby. 'She's sound asleep. She's such a good girl.'

He nodded agreement and rubbed a finger tip along his daughter's chin. His skin seemed so rough and hers so delicate. 'How are we going to feed her and look after her?'

'We'll manage. One thing's for sure. She's not going to miss out on any love.'

Mesmerized by the dying fire, they sat until the flames had popped and spluttered and danced themselves to extinction, and all that remained of once thick timber was a heap of glowing cubes with red cores that winked and hissed smoke. Nellie let her head rest on his lap. She was soon asleep. Gently, Adam put Cassie down and lifted Nellie in his arms. He carried her to her bed in the shed. She stirred and examined him through half-opened eyes.

'We *will* make out,' she murmured.

'I know.'

He made sure she was sleeping before returning to the baby. Cassie was awake. He took her in his arms, surging with love for his child. She was looking intently at him. Not crying, not smiling, just staring. He adjusted the blanket around her.

'We haven't had much of a chance to talk, have we?' he said and thought he saw the suggestion of a smile. 'I love you. Do you know that? Do you know what that means?' He stroked her cheek and the stare intensified. 'Probably not, but I'm going to show you. Me and Nellie are going to show you what it's like to be loved and looked after.' Her eyes were bright, bright as the stars. 'Do you know how many stars there are?' Again he stroked her cheek. 'Thousands. And when you're a big girl, I'm going to help you count them.'

He walked around the fire, holding her to his chest and rocking her gently. The Southern Cross was high in the sky, its kite of stars spangling the soupy tail of the Milky Way. Adam walked around the fire, searching for the saucepan. Orion. It was on the other side of the heavens, upside down as always. The strands that formed the belt and the sword were so miraculously arranged, so pure in their sharp pinpricks of light, that he stood for a few moments and gazed in awe at the constellation. Then he felt Cassie kick. The first suggestion of a cry squeaked from her lips. Cradling his daughter in his arms, Adam resumed walking and began to tell her the legend of Orion the hunter.

THE SNOWBLIND MOON

John Byrne Cook

On a remote cattle ranch in a peaceful Wyoming Valley, in the hushed villages of beleaguered Indian tribes, among the government troops advancing through the bitter winter landscape, the time of the Snowblind Moon heralds the beginning of an apocalyptic clash between the Indians and the whites.

THE SNOWBLIND MOON

And caught up in the tragedy are the men and women of the West, passionately committed to peace, seemingly helpless to prevent tragedy: Chris Hardeman, former army scout haunted by his part in an Indian massacre; Lisa Putnam, young, independent owner of a ranch; Bat Putnam, legendary mountain man; Johnny Smoker, a white boy, raised by the Cheyenne; Amanda Spencer, a circus performer who falls in love with Johnny; and Sun Horse, a Sioux chieftain struggling to reconcile peace with freedom and dignity.

THE SNOWBLIND MOON

An epic, haunting novel of the beauty and tragedy of the West.

'An enormous and vital story, resoundingly told.' *Publishers Weekly*

'Anyone with a soft spot for the Old West . . . is bound to relish THE SNOWBLIND MOON.' *Observer*

Futura Publications
Fiction
ISBN 0 7088 2915 5

THE LADY

Alan Stratton

THE LADY is Gina Rossi: warm, spirited and beautiful – but her young life is blighted by tragedy. A refugee from fascist Italy, struggling to protect her young brother and sister among the teeming millions of New York in the slump, she nurtures two burning ambitions. One will make her; the other could destroy her.

THE LADY is the dream Gina shared with her father: the most fashionable restaurant in New York, her passport to wealth, fame and security. But within her burns a lust – for revenge. And that lust could lose her everything: her love, her dreams and all she holds dear.

THE LADY: a magnificent rags-to-riches saga of love, ambition and revenge, sweeping from Rome to New York, from war-torn London to the birth of Las Vegas, and starring an unforgettable heroine.

'SPLENDID' *Annabel*

Futura Publications
Fiction
ISBN 0 7088 3158 3

CHIKARA!

Robert Skimin

CHIKARA: a uniquely Japanese word meaning inner personal resources; capacity; talent; with overtures of destiny.

To Sataro Hoshi, *chikara* was the key to the restoration of his family fortunes in the alien America of 1907, land of every immigrant's dreams.

For Itoko, his beautiful, strong-willed wife, *chikara* meant her reunion with Hiroshi, her younger son, left behind in Japan to find his fortune in the Japanese army.

To Miyuki Takano, tragic 'picture' bridge exposed to every horror of the Barbary Coast, *chikara* lay only in her relationship with Hoshi.

For Sachi, Hoshi's grand-daughter, *chikara* was the strength to hold a perilous balance between her grandfather's vision and an uncertain modern world.

CHIKARA! – the compelling saga of Japanese life, of the conflict between tradition and changing values, of a family – and a nation – in conflict.

'absorbing . . . rich in understanding of the Japanese spirit' *Publishers Weekly*

Futura Publications
Fiction
ISBN 0 7088 2721 7

All Futura Books are available at your bookshop or
newsagent, or can be ordered from the following address:
Futura Books, Cash Sales Department,
P.O. Box 11, Falmouth, Cornwall TR10 9EN.

Please send cheque or postal order (no currency), and
allow 60p for postage and packing for the first book
plus 25p for the second book and 15p for each additional
book ordered up to a maximum charge of £1.90 in U.K.

B.F.P.O. customers please allow 60p for
the first book, 25p for the second book plus 15p per
copy for the next 7 books, thereafter 9p per book.

Overseas customers, including Eire, please allow £1.25
for postage and packing for the first book, 75p for the
second book and 28p for each subsequent title ordered.